MW01128147

PURE DARK

VØLUMES 1 - 3

Pure Dark Volumes 1 - 3

Written by Andrew Mackay

Edited by Nessie Braeburn

Cover design by Kveather (Iván Cornejo)

ChromeValleyBooks.com

ISBN: 9781973304487

Volumes & Chapters

Pure Dark Vol 1

Pure Dark Vol 2

PURE DARK

VOL 1

Chapter 1

Induced: The Beginning

My name is Charlie Ferrari. I'm sitting in the passenger seat of my car waiting for a friend. Her name is Oksana. She's upstairs right now talking to my dealer, trying to work out a deal to save my life. I have a fair idea of what the arrangement is going to be. I owe my dealer ten grand and I can't pay it back.

Why?

Because I'm a worthless. I went up there and tried to sort it out myself. Complex, the fat mound of whale blubber that he is, decided he didn't want the cash any longer. Once he clamped his sweaty, fat eyes on Oksana he decided he wanted her instead of the money. She's a model - tall and with a great figure. Irresistible.

Who was I to disagree with the arrangement? It's not as if Oksana hadn't slept with guys to save my useless ass in the past.

She's my guardian angel as if you hadn't already figured that out for yourself. Complex told me to go back to the car.

So, here I am in the front of the car outside a place called Delta House.

Complex gave me a syringe. In the barrel is a solution he wants me to try out. It's called *Angel of Death*, or something like that. It's an especially vicious brand of heroin. He's planning on selling it on the streets. He has a factory in the building producing it great quantities. I've rolled up my sleeve and am prodding around for a vein. Most of them are shot to hell, though.

I can see my ugly face in the wing mirror looking right at me. My green Mohawk has softened.

A few hours ago Oksana knocked me out at her fashion show. I was causing a scene due to my inebriation. She hid me behind the curtains with one of her friends who'd overdosed on cocaine.

I suspect she may be dead, now. The building caught fire and no-one knew she was there.

Why can't I find an unused vein? I'd rather not go intramuscular with this hit. I keep tapping around the underside of my forearm. Black spots. My elbow crease is yellow and black, full of bruises from my last umpteen hits.

Ugh.

Oh shit, there's that blonde woman friend of Oksana's coming back to the car.

"You really are a useless piece of crap, aren't you?" she says to me as she climbs into the back. "You're letting Oksana pay for you? You disgust me."

"I'm a n-no good loser," I yelp in desperation, sliding the belt from my jeans. Trying to protest against her assertion would have come across as misguided.

At last! A good vein has presented itself. I slip my belt around my arm and tug it back between my teeth.

Ugh.

The needle punctures into the tiny blue tube pulsing beneath my skin. I pull the plunger out, drawing blood into the syringe.

The red stuff mingles with the *Angel of Death* solution. I squint at the swirling motion of the fluids. The needle scares me, but it's a necessary scare.

Imagine that! A junkie who's deathly afraid of needles. I really am pathetic.

My thumb presses the plunger back into the vein.

Three seconds whizz by. The spaghetti junction of wires through my body fill with lava and then cool down.

The sensation is unreal. I'd ordinarily remove the needle and put it somewhere safe. This stuff is rattling through me at an intense speed. I can barely move, let alone put the needle somewhere safe.

It's no use - *Angel of Death* has kicked my ass. My body responds in a way I've never felt before.

"No, no," I bang the window to try to dilute the feeling, but it's no good.

The blonde woman behind me huffs and puffs as I pant and giggle like a rabid dog.

She gets out of the car and slams the door shut in disgust. I'm left alone in the passenger seat, hassled by a heroin angel working its way through my veins.

"Ohhhh," My eyelids weigh down. It's like every single atom in my body is having an orgasm. A warm and fuzzy feeling. I imagine this is what being born is like, but ten times more intense.

Breathing isn't an option now.

My brain feels like it's going to shut down. I feel like I'm wearing a balaclava made out of molten lava.

I look down. My mind tries to lift my right arm. It's not moving.

I try lifting it again and, this time, it works.

But my fucking arm isn't actually moving. What the *hell* is going on?.

It's stuck. The needle is still hanging out. A trickle of blood runs down my elbow.

I know, I'll wiggle it and hopefully, the needle will fall.

Yes, there it is wiggling. Why won't the needle drop? It just digs further into my arm…

I close my eyes. Maybe if I reboot my body and switch it back on, everything will work as it should.

Closed, shut. A deep breath.

A colossal "bang" comes from the bonnet of the car. It shakes me, but I don't move. I can't see it because everything is dark.

Everything is black.

I'm sure I heard the blonde woman scream "Jesus Christ!" in shock from outside of the car.

I can hear Oksana call her name. "Joy, Joy," although she pronounces it "Choy" on account of her Russian accent.

The car wobbles and then grinds to a halt.

A few hours later I can hear the car engine spring to life. I say hours, it was more like seconds…

My head hurts…

I can't move any part of my body…

I can hear everything, though…

I think I may have overdosed.

***

The car sped along the road with Oksana at the wheel. Charlie's puny body rocked around as she took a corner.

Determined, she stepped on the gas. She needed to find a hospital.

The blonde woman, Joy, was in the back of the car, holding on to the door handle for dear life.

"What happened to the other guy?" Joy asked.

"I cut his fucking *dick* off," Oksana shouted as she slammed the steering wheel to the left. The action sent Joy flying in the opposite direction.

Charlie spat up some white fluid. Specs of it spattered up the passenger side window and down his chin.

"No. No," Oksana screamed, turning to her left, "Charlie."

"What's happened?" Joy screamed, trying not to have a heart attack.

"He has overdosed."

"Oh no," Joy cried, "Not him, too."

"For fuck's sake," Oksana floored the gas pedal, shunting everyone back against their seats. The car shot past all the others on the road.

"Keep his head forward," Oksana screamed at her friend in the back seat. She'd ordered Joy to lean over Charlie and try to move him onto his side. If Charlie choked on his own vomit, he'd die. Neither girl needed this in their lives today.

"Is he breathing?"

Joy felt across his chest for any sign of life. "I don't know."

"Check him."

Joy held her ear as best she could to his chest. The car shook around as Oksana's driving became more erratic.

Charlie snored. His eyelids were open, but his eyeballs had rolled into the back of his skull.

"Well?" Oksana kept her eyes on the road, "Push down on his chest."

"Okay, okay," Joy placed her palms over his chest bone.

"Push. Push," Oksana roared as she turned a corner.

"I am," Joy screamed, "Wait. He's breathing."

Oksana blasted the horn, sending a few cars in front to swerve out of her way, "I do not want him to go into prophylactic shock."

"You mean anaphylactic shock," Joy corrected her in haste.

"Now is not a time to correct my English," Oksana roared. "Charlie, can you hear me?"

He didn't respond.

Oksana's erratic driving caused the messy flood of blood and mucous to warble out from his lips.

Joy had tried to massage Charlie's chest, but it wasn't any use. The syringe had fallen into the foot well. Every cloud and all that jazz.

Oksana entered a state of sheer anger. She thumped the steering wheel and looked over her shoulder.

"Choy?"

"What?"

"Blow into his mouth, quick."

Joy looked at the gory milkshake that was the interior of Charlie’s mouth. He was long gone, now. If it weren’t for the weak heartbeat and occasional snoring you’d have thought he’d been dead for weeks.

Charlie’s face was sickly white. His tongue lapped over his chin. This was a man not long for the world.

Poor Joy, too. She hadn’t signed up for this. She was spending the day with Oksana so she could write a book about her and the fashion industry. She hadn’t counted on having to resuscitate a heroin junkie today.

Right now, she’s preparing to do mouth to mouth for her very first time.

"Ugh, for God’s sake," Joy closed her eyes and shook her head.

"Blow into his mouth, quick."

Oksana looked back at Joy, taking her eye off the road for a long period of time. About five seconds. She was met by a curiously nervous look from her friend.

"Do not be worried, Choy. Two breathes," Oksana turned back to the road ahead, "Slow and hard."

Joy played ball. She leaned over Charlie and opened her lips. As the car shunted forward, it threw her onto him, lips-first. A rope of wet drool and white shit yanked between his mouth and hers.

Joy forced herself forward and exhaled deep into his throat.

GLUGG! GLUMPH!!

Joy threw herself back, missing a blast of vomit from Charlie’s mouth. Most of it hit the upholstery. Chunks of spew rained back down on the pair of them.

"Gahhh," Joy screamed and flew back into her seat. "For fuck’s sake."

"He's breathing!" Oksana screamed and tapped the wheel. "He's going to be okay."

"Good for him," Joy huffed, wiping her lip with her sleeve.

***

Okay, I can't feel much, but I know I'm on a stretcher or a trolley. It feels like there are wheels squealing from underneath me. My body is rocking back and forth. Not of its own accord, but because the tray I am laying on is sliding around all over the place.

The wheels underneath are squeaking

I guess you're expecting it to be all dark as I can't see anything. No, I can see. Even though my eyes are looking back into my head.

I can see a succession of electric pulses orbiting what looks like a huge mound of thick spaghetti.

Is that my *brain*?

The electric pulses fizz and pop. For every pop, the pulses multiply by five, like an angry, luminous firework.

I can hear voices of people I don't recognize. Something about taking me to ICU Three, whatever that is.

ICU? I don't see you, though. Even in times of crisis, I make jokes.

"Okay, strap the IV in, please," someone to my right yelled as the trolley stops. A deafening sound of a Velcro strap erupts around my ears. It hurts.

God damn it. It hurts so much.

I look down. I can see my feet in their trainers. A rumbling noise is dead ahead of me.

Why am I standing in front of a volcano?

Charlie, where are you?

It's beautiful. Look at it. A million foot high volcano in the distance. The tip has exploded and is shooting a fountain of lava into the air. The orange-red stuff smokes as it runs down the sides.

I look back down to see my son, Johnny, standing next to me. He's only seven years old. My pride and joy. He watches the volcano eruption with me.

Then, his hand slips into mine and we hold hands. "Daddy, why are we here?"

"I don't know, son," I whisper back as the lava reaches us. The fierce smog of ash wafts past our noses.

"Daddy, the lava is flowing around my feet."

Curious. Johnny never speaks. He has an issue. Oksana has told me what it is, but I was never attentive.

Here, in the comfort of the volcanic eruption, he's vocal.

"Please help, Daddy," he says, looking up at me. He's sinking into the lava. He grabs my arm with his other hand and tries to lift himself up from the pool of fierce heat.

"Shhh," is my only response. "Don't worry, son, it'll be fine."

"Please, help me."

The molten lava lifts a few feet from the ground and engulfs his legs. It chews through his trousers and burns the skin off his legs, before yanking him down.

I let go of his hand. His entire body, followed by his screaming mouth, drowns into the molten mixture. A flap of his scalp ignites as it rests atop the skin that's formed over the hardened fire.

His screams don't perturb me, though. I know he'll be safe.

Beep. Beep. Beep.

A mouth forms on the side of the volcano. Two lips and a set of teeth, "We've got swelling on the brain."

"Swelling on the brain?" I asked, somewhat confused.

"Yes, you're going to relapse."

"Okay."

Then, something punches me in the temple. It hurts so bad. Like someone firing a 9mm carbine shotgun right at my head at close range.

The force of the shotgun cartridge is so powerful, it forces my head to face right. A few globs of my brain hangs, suspended in mid-air, surrounded by a paused splatter of blood.

Both are stuck in mid-splat. Like an ornament or museum exhibition.

I take a step around the gore and analyze both.

A section of my frontal lobe. I can almost taste it with my fingertips. I extend my thumb and push it through a glob of suspended darkened blood. It passes over my thumbnail, painting itself past the knuckle.

"Is this me?" I wonder out loud, "Am I dead?"

Those incessant beeps are still playing all the while. Then, a huffing and puffing sound from a machine to my right.

Whufff. Puuuff. Like a bellowing sound.

"Okay, that's all we can do for now," a man's voice says. "We'll take a break and reconvene in a couple of hours."

I am left alone now with my brain suspended in mid-air. The eruption of the volcano has subsided and cooled down.

I can sleep now.

***

"Mrs Oksana Volkov?" asked a female doctor as she approached Oksana and Joy in the corridor. "My name is Dr Jennifer Long."

"*Ms* Volkov," Oksana rose to her feet and shook Dr Long's hand, "How you know my name?"

"The patient said it a couple of times while we were trying to resuscitate him. I sort of guessed it might be one of you."

"What's the prognosis?" Joy asked.

"I'll get straight to the point," Dr Long scanned her notes, "We've had to medically induce him, I'm afraid."

"What it means? Mechanical induce?" Oksana asked. She was deathly worried for Charlie. He may have overdosed once too often, now.

"It means we've had to induce a coma. He overdosed on a particularly strong narcotic. It had a massive impact on his heart and brain. They're unable to function without help."

"Oh no," Oksana sat back down. The news made her lose control of her knees. "Oh, Charlie."

"We need to wait till his body naturally expels the narcotic, and then reassess. It could take some time. I'm very sorry, Ms Volkov."

"So what happens now?" Joy asked.

"We wait," Dr Long turned to Joy, "He's in safe hands here. It's simply a matter of time. We're confident he'll come round eventually. We just don't know when that will be."

"Okay."

"I'm sorry I don't have better news," Dr Long looked down to Oksana, who had burst into tears, "It really is just a matter of waiting."

"It's okay, I'm here," Joy massaged Oksana's shoulder and consoled her as best she could.

"Thank you, Doctor."

***

How long has it been, now? It's hard to say. The intermittent voices that appear in my head have spoken all day. Something about me not making it. How later tonight they'll get a curry and a beer.

I've lost track.

I'm sitting in a white room with my sister, Rhonda. We're on plastic chairs facing each other. I can't see where the walls, ceiling and floor join up. It's all so white.

My sister looks at me like she hates me. Her eyes are bloodshot. "I should never have let you get away with it."

"Why do you keep looking at me like that?"

"Because I hate you, Charlie Ferrari."

"Why do you hate me?"

This was news to me. I hadn't done anything to her. As a matter of fact, I hadn't seen her for ten years. The last time I had anything to do with her was when I went to her funeral. My family didn't want anything to do with me after her death.

"You've wasted your life, you worthless junkie."

"No I haven't," I screamed back through my chest. My lips weren't moving, although I could hear my voice.

"Always a worthless runt since the day you were born," she screamed, "You're an animal. You *know* what you did."

"Rhonda?"

"I hate you."

"Please stop saying that."

"I hate you," Her final cry echoed around the room. Then, she vanished in the blink of an eye.

"Rhonda?"

I turn around. She's definitely gone.

A few twangs from an electric guitar pang all around me. Oksana appears in the room to the right of my periphery vision.

She's naked, walking to my left. It's seductive. Her eyes shoot at me as her long dreadlocks bounce off her back.

She's wearing stilettos. They tap and clang across the surface with each step.

"Hello, Charlie," she says, licking her lips, "The doctor asked me if you had any next of kin."

"Hey, Oksana," I say back through a hole in my neck. I grab it, wondering where it came from. "What d-did you say?"

"I told them about your sister." She stopped dead in front of me. Ten feet away. She placed her hands on her hips and licked her top lip, "You know I'm sick, don't you?"

"Y-Yes, of course, I d-do," I stutter, wondering why she's asking me the bleeding obvious. She's behaving strangely. "You kn-know I do."

"I know you love me," her voice screams into my right ear. The action pushes my head to the left.

I see Joy make her way over to the right. She's naked, too. It'll only be a matter of a few seconds before she and Oksana meet in the middle, right in front of me.

"Hello, Charlie," Joy smiles, her voice doubling over itself around the room.

She wipes her lips and flings the mucous to the floor. Joy arrives next to Oksana. She slides her arm around her back.

"What's g-going on?" I scream through my neck.

Oksana giggles and licks her lips, "Oh, *Charlie*. You are so funny." She turns to Joy and slips out her tongue.

But it's not the pink slip of flesh I expected. It was black and split at the end.

Joy looks up at Oksana and squeezes her, "This is what you want, right?" She looks into Oksana eyes as their lips meet. It's like she's in love with her.

It's weird. The apocalypse is coming. My body can't handle the trauma.

"No, no—"

I look down as I shift in my seat. My ankles fasten to the legs of the chair as I look down. My arms are bound behind my back.

The chair rumbles, shaking my internal organs. "No. No."

To my mind, if the girls kiss, my body will explode.

"Don't."

Oksana's snake-like tongue slips into Joy's mouth. She sucks it in and kisses her back with all her might.

"God, n-no," I shuffle forward, sending the legs on the chair forward.

As they kiss and slide their hands around each other's

bodies, I scream. My mouth yawns open.

My nose pushes up between my eyes and unravels over my forehead. "Gaaaahhh."

I can feel the skin on my face tear as my top row of teeth envelope my vision. My two front teeth pop out of their gums and scrape over my nose.

Oksana and Joy won't stop kissing. They're making out even harder. Oksana keeps an eye on me and my head.

The top row of my teeth pulls back over my head, taking my hair and scalp along with it.

My brain freezes over as my skull exposes itself to the room. A beam of blue light bursts out of the cracks in my skull, cause the bone to shatter.

"How do you like us now?" Joy asks in a seductive overtone. She resumes kissing her new friend.

I shuffle forward again, trying to stop their actions. As they kiss, their lips meld together. The sides of their cheeks melt into each other, forming one, giant flesh-covered head.

Oksana pulls Joy into her. Their breasts attached. The skin fuses together, engulfing one another.

"No, no. Stop."

The pain is excruciating as my skull crumbles down my chest and shoulders. My jaw is next to go as I watch the fragments of bone shatter around my feet.

The top halves of Joy and Oksana pulsate as they merge together. Oksana's knee strikes Joy between the legs. As it connects, its splashes in a gory fusion of melted skin and gloops up inside her. Joy's vagina sucks and chews away, absorbing the skin and bone.

Oksana's shin is devoured by Joy. She hulks her body forward, forcing her blonde hair to fall forward. The unrelenting scream I offer won't stop in my brain. I try to shut my eyes, but it doesn't work. An ungodly force holds my head forward, forcing me to watch the amalgam of both girls' bodies together.

Joy and Oksana are now one. The same ball of

humankind.

I ask myself what the hell is going on as the monstrosity stands before me. It's beyond hell - a complicated fusion of flesh, skin and bone.

There's no reason for it. This *thing* standing before me doesn't have a head. It resembles a human being.

Then, it topples and slams to its back on the ground.

The glistening surface allows me to see my reflection. My head is now a spinal column with a stork below a suspended brain. I have no eyes.

The ugly mesh of flesh and skin ten feet in front of me rolls onto its side.

A flash of my mother's face appears and disappears as it rises to its knees.

The sound of an electric guitar tuning up and striking a cord.

TWAAAANNNGG. KEERRACCK.

The back of the monster's head flips up. It then climbs to its knees. It's as if it's all happening in reverse.

It covers its "face" with its hands and lets out an almighty wailing noise. Like cattle squealing in tune to the kiss of a snake.

I tense all the muscles in my body, except the ones in my face. They are on the floor, but tense along with my shoulders and chest.

The monster exhales and slips its hands apart.

"Peek-a-boo," it shouts, sending me back in my chair.

TWANG!

Another electric guitar chord strikes down, thundering through my body. The monster laughs and moves its hands away from its head.

As I regain my composure in the chair, I notice that the monster has a face.

It has limbs and a full torso. It's a naked man in his forties standing in front of me.

I blink a couple of times in my mind, only to see my eyeballs roll up and down to the floor. I tilt what little remains of my head to find the man in his forties smiling back at me.

Completely naked.

He holds his hand in the shape of an air guitar.

TWAAANNNGGG!

Another electric guitar cord. Like a skewer through the fucking stomach. I feel like puking.

"HA! HA! HA!" laughs the man, taking delight in my pain, "Charlie Ferrari."

"Huh?" I look back at him. He presses his palms together and takes a bow.

"Allow me to introduce myself," he says in a dramatic drawl, like a game show host, "My name is Max."

I attempt to ask what relevance he, or any of this, has. But I don't have a mouth.

Or a neck.

Or vocal cords.

"Don't try to speak," he says, taking a few steps forward, "As you know, you're in a coma. That shit you took will be flowing through you for a long time."

I can feel the stem of my spinal column starting to weaken. This Max character holds up his right hand and presses his thumb and forefinger together.

"Welcome," he yells at the top of his lungs. He clicks his fingers, "To *Pure Dark*."

SNAP.

The floor drops away.

I fall out of the chair and hurtle into the infinite black chasm underneath me...

Chapter 2

Zoe Triptych

"Welcome to *Rylerstarr Cosmetics Incorporated*, the home of exquisite beauty. Our unique science has helped advance the industry. Permanent youth is now affordable and available. Two years ago, our greatest success helped eradicate aging skin altogether."

The woman on the TV screen seemed to smile at a visitor as she entered the building.

Her name was Yanni Angiou. She buttoned the cuff on her pristine suit sleeves. She tucked her portfolio under her right arm. The heels on her black shoes clomped across the delicate floor's surface.

The reception desk neared; a circular frontage with a giant Rylerstarr Inc. Logo.

Behind the desk was a woman with spectacles. She smiled at Yanni as she approached.

"Good afternoon, madam."

"Good afternoon," Yanni said with a smile, "I'm here for the one o'clock."

"Certainly, madam. Your name?"

"Yanni Angiou."

"Ah, yes," The receptionist scanned her screen. "Charlie Angiou."

"Uh, no?" Yanni huffed. "*Yanni* Angiou. Not Charlie."

The receptionist smiled at her as if she was insane. "Who's Charlie?"

"You just called me Charlie."

"I don't think I did," the receptionist muttered, taken aback, "If I did then I apologize."

An awkward pause. Yanni was the first to back down. She didn't want any trouble.

"Oh, I'm sorry if I appear to be a bit short." Yanni rubbed her eyes and rolled her shoulders, "I didn't get much sleep last night."

"That's perfectly fine, Ms Angiou," The receptionist smiled once again, "You're one o'clock. So, please do go straight up. She's expecting you."

"Thank you. Where am I going?"

The receptionist pointed to her left and handed Yanni a sheet of A4. "Take the elevator to floor seventeen, and it's to your right as you exit."

"Okay, thank you."

Yanni waited for the lift with several businessmen and women all dressed in suits. A man in his fifties smiled at her and licked his lips. Yanni wasn't happy with the attention and looked down at her shoes.

TING!

The elevator arrived. Three men got in behind two suited women. Yanni was last to enter.

Everyone seemed silent as the elevator closed. They faced the doors to the metal box and let the piped-in jazz music dispel the silence.

The metal box whizzed up the side of the building. It offered a magnificent view of the London skyline. *Rylerstarr Cosmetics Inc*'s headquarters was based in St Paul's. The dome loomed under Yanni's feet and shrunk.

One of the suited women turned to Yanni. "Good morning."

"Huh, good morning," Yanni replied and looked away.

TING! Floor seventeen.

The doors slid open and everyone tried to get out at the same time.

"Oh, excuse me," Yanni allowed the three men out first, "Please, after you."

The men shuffled forward and dispersed in all directions. The two women followed out after Yanni.

"Well, I hope you do well in your interview," one of them said and walked off down the right-hand corridor.

"Uh, thanks?" Yanni offered. How did the woman know she was there for an interview? Was it *that* obvious?

After all, Yanni *could* have been an employee. She didn't look any different to the other people milling around. The building had been full of well-to-do businessmen and women. What gave her away, she wondered?

As she turned right, Yanni arrived at another reception desk. The receptionist seemed very familiar.

"Oh, it's you again," Yanni smiled and placed her portfolio on the desk.

"Excuse me, madam?" The receptionist looked confused. "Again?"

"Oh, weren't you downstairs a few minutes ago?"

The receptionist screwed her face and picked up the handset on her desk phone, "No, I don't think so."

She tucked the phone under her chin and nodded at the paper in Yanni's hand, "Miss Triptych, yes."

The receptionist scanned the document.

"You're one o'clock. A Miss Yanni Angiou is waiting for you."

"It's *Mrs*, actually."

The receptionist shot Yanni a look. She hadn't appreciated the correction, "Yeah," she continued into the phone, "I dunno, thirty-five?"

Yanni took a step back. The woman behind the desk was making assumptions about her right in front of her face.

"Good body, yes. Five foot two or so."

The receptionist rose out of her seat and tried to peer behind Yanni, "Yes, very good. Okay, no problem."

She replaced the handset and smiled at Yanni, "Mrs Triptych will see you now."

"Thanks," Yanni spat, sarcastically. She swiped her portfolio from the desk and lodged it under her arm.

The door to the office had "Zoe Triptych - Head of Department" inscribed in the frosted glass. Yanni knocked on the glass three times and pushed the door open. She was careful to be gentle in case she might have interrupted something.

"Hello?"

A slurping noise came from within the room.

"Just one moment, please," came a female voice.

"Oh."

Yanni moved back and allowed the door to close.

"Okay, you can come in now."

Yanni pushed the door inward and stepped into the room. She walked to the desk and extended her hand to the woman behind it.

"Hello, I'm Yanni Angiou."

The woman swivelled around in her chair. She was in her forties and sported jet black shoulder-length hair.

She smiled and stood to her feet, revealing a silver suit. A very attractive woman.

Yanni raised her eyebrows at the woman's stunning physique and beauty.

"Hello, Mrs Angiou," the woman took Yanni's hand and shook it, "Zoe Triptych, head of department for R&D."

"Very nice to meet you."

"You too," she smiled. "please take a seat."

Zoe sat down and watched her prospective employee take her seat. Yanni set her portfolio to the desk and unclipped the metal hook. A pen slid out from underneath and between her fingers.

"My oh my," Zoe raised her eyebrows. She was very impressed already, "You *are* prepared, aren't you?"

"You don't mind if I make notes, do you?" Yanni asked.

"Not at all, no, go for it," Zoe smiled and ran her tongue across the top row of her perfect teeth.

"Thanks. It's just that I want to make sure I answer all your questions as best as I can and not leave anything out."

"I understand," Zoe clasped her hands together, "So, I guess, first thing's first."

"Okay."

"Why do you want to work for *Rylerstarr*?"

Yanni looked to the desk and cleared her throat. A picture of Zoe and what looked like her husband and son smiled back at her.

"Well, I've had experience in research and development for sixteen years now, and I feel that—"

"—*Sixteen* years?" Zoe spat. The woman sitting before her didn't look a day over thirty.

"Yes, sixteen years."

"God, you look so—" Zoe heaved, quite out of the blue. Her chest expanded a few inches and sunk back down. She nearly puked on the desk.

"Ugh. I'm sorry about that. We just had a corporate lunch and I think I may have a bit of indigestion."

"That's quite all right," Yanni smiled.

"You look *so* young. Do you really have sixteen years of experience in this departme—"

HICCUP.

Zoe widened her eyes with embarrassment. She clenched her fist and held it to her mouth.

BRRAAAPPP. A loud burp sent specs of cream up her fist, "God's sake."

She thumped her chest a couple of times and gasped. Finally, she swallowed back.

After a few seconds, she seemed to be back to normal.

Yanni didn't know how to respond - so she didn't, and

kept smiling as best she could.

"I'm sorry about that," Zoe cleared her throat. "Should never have had the fish."

"Oh, that's okay," Yanni giggled to herself, forgiving the entire strange episode, "We've all been there."

"Isn't that the truth?"

Yanni nodded at the picture. She looked toward the cityscape offered behind the large window.

"Yes, when I was pregnant with my first son, I—" Yanni's words stopped falling out of her mouth. She noticed something underneath the window, leaning against the wall.

Three white eggs the size and shape of a luggage bag.

"—Umm," Yanni tore her gaze away from the eggs and looked at Zoe, "What are those?"

"What are *what*?"

"Those *eggs*?"

Zoe squinted at Yanni. She thought she was sitting in front of a mad woman. What did she mean "what are those eggs?" - for heaven's sake, woman, they're eggs! Have you never seen an egg before?

Zoe tilted her head at the strange arrangement and smiled, "Yes, problem?"

"Are they real or ornamental?"

"No, they're real," Zoe reassured Yanni. She double-took and became very sympathetic, "God, I'm sorry, are they bothering you?"

"No, I'm—"

"—It's just that I could have them removed or covered up if they're distracting you?"

"No, that's *fine*," Yanni looked down at her portfolio, trying to shake off any embarrassment.

Zoe placed her elbows on the desk and clasped her hands together once more. She took a deep interest in Yanni's faux avoidance of any awkwardness.

"You were saying?"

"Huh?" Yanni failed to realize that she was still in an

interview.

"Your past experience?"

"Oh, yes," Yanni cleared her throat and tried to block the view of the eggs from her periphery vision, "Sixteen years with *The Klitschko Corporation*, trainee assistant for R&D, there, and then I—"

"—*You* worked for *Klitschko*?"

Yanni looked surprised, "Uh, yes? It's all in my CV."

"Your CV?"

"Yes," Yanni said, confused, "Didn't you get it?"

No, no," Zoe said, looking around her desk. She shrugged her shoulders, "Do you have a spare?"

"Uh, sure," Yanni pressed her fingertip onto the third piece of paper within her portfolio. She slid it out and pushed it toward Zoe.

"Ah, thanks."

"No problem?" Yanni became less and less happy with how the interview was going.

Zoe had a strange manner about her. What with the burping and the hiccups - and having avoided a puking session. Her behavior was *off*.

Zoe bounced her head in time to an imaginary soundtrack as she scanned the sheet of paper. Yanni noticed that she wasn't so much reading as singing along to the words. Humming to herself.

"I could always go and wait outside while you read?" Yanni tried, leaning back in her seat. She was taking a more formidable approach, now.

If she'd hired Yanni on the spot then surely this would mean that Zoe was out of her tiny little tree.

"What did you say?" Zoe looked up from the sheet.

"I said if you need some time, I could always—"

"—Oh, God. No, don't move. Sorry, this is all my fault," Zoe clenched her fist and held it to her mouth.

"Are you feeling okay?" Yanni asked, quite concerned.

Zoe lifted the paper down and revealed her face. Scores of wrinkles had formed across her cheek, under her eyes, across her forehead, and up the side of her neck.

"Oh my God," Yanni gasped and gripped the armrests on her chair.

Zoe set the paper to the desk and smiled, "Is everything all right?"

"Your, your," Yanni traced her own face with the tip of her finger, "Your face is—"

"—Oh no! It's not coming off, is it?"

"Well, y-yes?" Yanni squeezed the armrests harder.

"Damn *Lexicon* products, honestly," Zoe rubbed her fingers across one of the wrinkles, "Ugh. I'm sorry about this, Yanni."

She stood up and turned to the full-length mirror on the wall beside the frosted glass. She took the hanging cord and twisted it around, shutting the blinds.

"Whatever you do, sweetheart, never ever buy *Lexicon* concealer. They're a terrible company. Shoddy products."

"Right?" Yanni wheeled herself back.

Those damn eggs were *still* there. Yanni looked back at Zoe as she attempted to fix her face. What she was actually doing was anyone's guess. Yanni couldn't quite see from this distance. It was almost as if Zoe was taping her face back together.

"Sorry. Two more seconds."

"T-Take your time," Yanni stammered, trying to hold her anxiety back.

Zoe turned around and revealed her face.

"Whoa," Yanni jumped back in fright. Parts of her interviewer's face had crumbled off. A shiny second layer of skin on her cheeks and fore head glinted in the sunlight. Her chin had seen better days, too; red and gunky.

"You, uh, *missed* a bit," was all Yanni could offer.

Zoe held her forefinger to her face. The digit, along with its neighboring ones, had fused together.

"Oh, Jesus," Yanni yelped and kicked herself back. "Your f-fingers."

"What?" Zoe looked down at her fat, meshed hand. It dripped with gloop. "Oh, no."

Yanni took her mobile phone from out of her pocket and swiped the screen, "I'll call for an ambulance," She struggled to hold the device in her hand.

"No, no need," Zoe strode back to her chair and sat down, "Look, please don't tell anyone, but I have a bit of a skin condition."

Yanni looked up, startled, "You *don't* say."

"Yes," Zoe looked at her hand and quickly hid it under the table, "Uh, it's an advanced form of eczema. It happens when the temperature is a bit warm."

"Oh, oh-kay," Yanni lowered her phone. As ridiculous as the reason was, it wasn't *too* hard to believe, "But y-your face?"

"It's fine, really," Zoe smiled and leaned back in her chair. She grabbed at her trouser belt, "I'm sorry, do you mind if I take my suit off for a moment?"

"Uh, no?" Yanni wheeled herself forward.

"Thanks, it gets *so* hot in here, sometimes," she said, kicking her trousers away and hit a button on her desk phone.

"Ms Triptych?" came the voice of the receptionist.

"Hi, Sally. Listen, can you get Connie to turn the air conditioning on for me, please?" Zoe whispered at Yanni. "A bit hot in here, right?"

Yanni nodded back. She felt helpless. Who else would have said "no" and risk screwing up their interview?

"Are you sure you want to do that, Ms Triptych?" the voice asked.

Zoe screwed her face. Another flap of skin flaked away from her cheeks, "Yes, why wouldn't I be?"

"Well, you don't want your office to get too cold, you know."

"Look, you stupid woman," Zoe screamed and flung her trousers aside. She rose to her feet and screamed into the handset, "You turn the air conditioning on right now or I'll have you *raped*."

As she screamed at her employee, her tongue flew out of her mouth and slid across her chin.

Yanni's eyes jumped out on their storks. In any ordinary shouting-at, you'd expect a pink tongue to wag as the spittle flew in the air. Not so in Zoe's case; instead of a pink tongue, she had a split end of what looked like a warped, salivating bin bag.

Zoe shot Yanni a look. Her eyeballs stretched out into a weird sort of dome and clipped shut. She opened them again; her once-beautiful brown pupils had turned a urine-yellow.

"Just do it, bitch." She growled.

SLAM! The handset hit the phone on the desk.

Yanni took a deep breath and closed her eyes.

"I'm sorry about that," Zoe said, looking down at her from behind the desk. She was now trouser-less. Her thighs, much like her face, had become scaly. If it weren't for the hideous skin deformation, her legs would be the envy of most supermodels.

"That's, uh, okay," Yanni couldn't believe what she was seeing or hearing.

WVHRROOOOM. A rumbling sound fired through the pipework beyond the ceiling.

"Aha, that's better."

A gust of cold air plumed out of the unit in the corner of the room.

"Now," Zoe coughed, "Charlie, can you tell me of an instant where you were faced with a challenge in the workplace? Also, how did you solve it?"

"Huh?" The sound fell from her mouth.

"Are you okay?" Zoe asked. She put on a brave half-face.

Yanni closed her eyes and slapped the side of her face, trying to wake up. It was no use, this was real. "Did you just call me Charlie?"

"No?"

"My name is Yanni. Yanni Angiou." She said, becoming concerned for her own sanity.

"Duuh. I know it is," Zoe croaked. "Where did you get Charlie from?"

Yanni shook her head, "Something's not right here, Ms Triptych." She scanned the room. The three giant eggs were still resting against the wall under the window.

"I d-don't think I'm doing too well. I'm not feeling very well. Maybe I should leave," Yanni stood up and swiped her portfolio from the desk.

"What are you doing?" Zoe slipped off her suit jacket, "Is it too warm in here? We could always take the interview to *Starbucks* downstairs if you'd prefer?"

"N-No," Yanni stammered and tried to make sense of her surroundings, "I think I should go. I'm sorry to have wasted your time."

She turned around to the door and grabbed the handle. It wouldn't budge. A furious downward yank still wouldn't open the door. Yanni turned around to find Zoe smiling back at her, topless. All she was wearing was her panties.

"Uh, the door," Yanni yanked it again, demonstrating its refusal to cooperate, "It won't open."

"Won't it," Zoe rose to her feet and made her way over to Yanni. The streaking wrinkles over her skin crawled up and along her arms and wrapped around her waist, "Here, let me try."

Zoe reached the door and lifted her right hand toward it, "Oh, m-my arm."

"Your arm."

Zoe's right arm had amalgamated into the side of her stomach. The appendage dripped with yellow, phlegm-like gunk.

"Ugh, ugh," Zoe looked down and lifted her left arm, "Oh *no*. Not again."

"Jesus Christ," Yanni stepped back and watched Zoe's stomach slit open and absorb her entire left arm. It wasn't especially gory; the action resembled an animal smothering its prey.

Zoe had no arms. Just one fat torso. "Help me, Charlie. Please."

"Stop calling me Charlie." Yanni screamed, pointing at her stomach, "What the *fuck* is going on?"

Zoe looked up and took a step toward Yanni, "I d-don't know!"

CRUNCH!!

Zoe's left knee hit the floor. The bone splintered and squashed her thigh up into her waist. The hip bone began to munch away at the thigh and suck through the cavity like a ravenous cannibal.

Glub-glub-glub. The thigh conveyor-belted into her hip. It swallowed up and absorbed the flesh into her stomach.

"Help me, Charlie," Zoe screamed and fell to her back.

"Shit," Yanni screamed. The portfolio dropped to the floor, "Someone, please! Help!"

She banged on the door with both fists. Slurping and gurgling noises occurred from behind her.

"Heeeeellppsssssshhhggguuuurrrggghhhh," Zoe's voice mutated into a meld of woman and beast.

THUMP-THUMP. Yanni had no luck with the door. No-one was coming to their rescue.

She ran over to the blinds and unraveled them.

"Help, help. Ms Triptych is unwell," Yanni shouted through the glass.

A few of the men at their computer desks turned to face her and scowled. They, too, had scaly skin.

"Jesus Christ," Yanni stepped back.

RRRIIIPPPPP!

Yanni turned around, slowly. She held her breath. Zoe writhed around on the floor like a woman possessed.

"Oh my G-God," Yanni moved forward.

Zoe's face peeled apart and folded into itself, sputtering blood onto the carpet.

The eggs in the corner of the room vibrated and

bounced around. They were furious.

Zoe's cheeks puffed out into a long curvature. The scales of the skin underneath protruding through her face. Her tongue flapped out over her chin and rolled off her shoulder. A black fork shunted out from between her lips.

Her legs fused together and the skin shed away. Each stump slowly glooped across the carpet.

"Hiissssssssss," Zoe's lips rescinded up into her skull. She flopped over to her side. Her head slapped against the floor, vomiting out whatever was inside her stomach.

Slither-slither...

Zoe's body contorted and stretched out. Her eyeballs rolled off onto the floor. Her shoulders thinned out and a scaly skin burrowed its way through the exposed flesh.

"M-m-my God," Yanni screamed and jumped over whatever was left of Zoe and banged at the door once again. "Help. Someone, please."

"Hisssssssssss."

Zoe's body slithered across the carpet. Slow, and calculated. Her shoulders broke apart and entwined around her newly-formed chest. She crawled along the carpet toward the three eggs using only the pores of her skin.

Yanni looked down and stepped over Zoe's carcass. She had turned into a Cobra.

The piped monster rolled around and lifted its head a few inches into the air.

The scales on each side of its face puffed out. The black venom duct spat a glob of acid poison to the floor. The carpet sizzled away, sending a puff of smoke into the air.

"Z-Zoe?"

"Saasssshhh," Zoe screamed, keeping her head perfectly still. Two fangs hung from its mouth.

Yanni squinted and noticed that the Cobra's face looked a lot like her interviewer. Despite being a snake, it had the same facial features as Zoe. From the shape of the face and eyes, right down to where her cheekbones used to be.

"Please don't h-hurt m-me."

The Cobra bowed its head and slithered toward the three eggs. Zoe the cobra weaved her twenty-inch body in and around the three eggs as they began to crack apart.

Zoe's head lifted up and rasped its tongue at Yanni.

"Your ch-children?"

"Snaaeesshh," The Cobra punched its head forward. It yanked itself back with a frightful speed. The black tongue licked the side of the egg shell and ran its face across the smooth, shiny surface.

Yanni held her hands out and tried to calm herself down. It was clear to her that Cobra Zoe wasn't interested in killing her.

"B-But, what's going—"

Cobra Zoe swished her tail.

CLANG!

The picture of her husband and child slid off the edge of the desk. It crashed to the floor, shattering the glass frame. Cobra Zoe jutted her head in the direction of the mess.

Yanni looked over her shoulder and pointed to the picture frame, "You w-want me to b-bring it over to you?" She was beyond puzzled.

The Cobra bowed its head and turned to the three eggs.

Yanni moved to the desk and crouched down. She took the picture into her hands and looked at it.

The man was handsome enough, no older than forty-five. The child was sweet. Around ten-years-old, and with a cleft palate.

Yanni rose to her feet and turned to the cobra who, by now, had made herself comfortable around the eggs.

"Ssssss," Cobra Zoe said, nodding her head to the eggs.

Yanni stepped forward and reached Zoe and her offspring, "What now?"

Cobra Zoe daggered her head to the floor, indicating that Zoe should sit down.

As instructed, Yanni sat on the floor and crossed her legs. The Cobra tapped the shell of the closest egg.

Yanni set the picture against it and moved her fingers to her mouth. She readied herself for any perversion of science that was about to take place.

CRI-ICK-CRAACK.

The shell top shattered, sending long cracks down the sides. Cobra Zoe lifted her head back to allow some room.

"Honey?" came a man's voice from inside the egg. The shell splintered apart and broke off.

A face moved forward, covered in transparent and pale-yellow slime. He was wearing a pair of glasses. The darkness had rendered him blind. He felt around the inside of the shell, wondering what had happened.

"Honey," the husband asked, lifted his head around, unable to see anything, "is that you?"

"Hisss," Cobra Zoe chomped onto his neck, Her fangs sunk deep into the flesh.

"Bloooaarrgghhh," Her husband's head melted and slopped down his shoulders. The gunk bubbled up a storm. His heart beat so fast that it exploded. The organ pushed through his rib cage and killed him instantly.

Yanni held her hand over her mouth. She was in deep, frozen shock, "Oh m-my God!"

"Ssssssss," Cobra Zoe knocked her head against the second egg.

The top cracked apart and slid off.

The Cobra's head turned to Yanni and spat at her. It got her attention.

"Wh-what's going on?"

The Cobra tiled its head at Yanni, "Sssssssssssssson."

"S-Son?"

The egg wobbled, shooting dozens of cracked lines down the sides.

KLUTCH!

A hand moved out from the broken part of the egg. The hand of a child.

"Mommy?"

"Sssssss," The Cobra ran its left scaled up the side of his wrist. Yanni gasped in terror. The snake re-emerged from the interior of the shell. It coiled around her ten-year-old son.

"Mommy, why do I have to be a snake?" He asked, his speech hampered by his facial impediment.

"Ssssssssss," Cobra Zoe waved her head back and slipped out her two-pronged tongue.

He wiped away some of the goo from his face, "Mommy, it's cold out here. I don't feel too well."

"Hissss," Cobra Zoe bit down on her son's top lip, wrestling the skin away from the bone.

"Moogghhmmmyyy."

Cobra Zoe yanked its head back, taking with it a large chunk of her son's mouth. The boy's jawbone slid down the length of its eight-inch neck. Protrusions through the scales saw the bone digest and break apart as it slumped down the funnel.

"Ghhoommyy," Her son gasped, gushing blood out of his eyes and nose. The Cobra held its head under the fountain, proud of itself.

Yanni kicked her feet forward, trying to scramble away from the carnage. "Oh God, no. No."

The Cobra released its son and spun its head toward Yanni.

"Get away from me." She was in such a frenzy she couldn't bring herself to her knees, "Get away."

Knock-knock.

The Cobra smacked the side of its face against the shell of the third egg. It began to crack apart.

"No, no," Yanni screamed, lifting herself to her knees.

The Cobra scowled at her, causing Yanni to yelp and roll over on her side, "Please, no. No."

The third egg rattled. The shell casing bust apart and

flung ropes of thick, warm slime in all directions.

A large string of it slapped against Yanni's face. She wiped the goop from her eyes and blinked a couple of times.

A fuzzy image of a body climbed out from the busted eggshell. The image came into focus.

It was Yanni.

"What the *fuck*?" Yanni screamed and pointed at the body. Cobra Zoe turned and rasped her tongue at her.

Yanni kicked herself back along the carpet. She needed to push herself away from this gargantuan nightmare.

Cobra Zoe slithered forward, threatening to catch up to Yanni's kicking feet. She screamed for dear life, "Nooo."

SNAP! SNAP! The Cobra bit the ends of her shoe and spat them against the wall. It was toying with her intended victim.

"Get away. Get away." Yanni screamed, trying to kick Cobra Zoe in the face.

SCHTAAAMPP! Zoe caught Yanni's left foot in her mouth. Her scales bulged as she coated it in venom and broke the flesh and bone down inside her mouth.

GLOMMPFH. GLOOMMPFH.

"Yaaaooowww," Yanni screamed and grabbed the skirting board. She tried to pull herself away from her attacker.

Zoe devoured her left leg. The shin bone snapped and folded into the snake's elongated mouth. The kneecap and the its bone soon followed.

Yanni's screams died down as a torrent of dark blood gushed along the floor.

The Cobra chomped at Yanni's waist, tearing her clothes apart. The fangs of the beast sunk into her organs, tearing them apart.

Yanni closed her eyes. The back of her head slammed against the floor.

The Cobra pressed its face against the corpse's forehead. It opened its mouth and shimmied it around the whole of Yanni's head, gulping the women down its long body.

Yanni's head bulged out through the Cobra's neck and it gulped it down.

GOOMPH. GOOMPH. The Cobra swallowed her way down Yanni's neck, shoulders, chest, and waist and began to digest it.

WHUMP. The Cobra heaved and broke down the body of its victim over and over again. The protrusions through the scaly skin deadened out.

The acid worked its magic in breaking down the food.

Zoe rolled across the floor and pushed herself back over to the egg remnants.

She opened her mouth and went for her son's head.

***

"Hi, my name is Bae Beaumont. I'm here for the one o'clock," said the oriental woman to the receptionist. "This is the right floor, isn't it? Seventeen?"

"Yes, it is." Sally looked up at the woman. "Please take a seat. I'll let Ms Triptych know you're here."

"Thank you."

Bae took her seat on the three-seater couch and crossed her legs. Sally looked over at Bae and picked up the phone.

"Ms Triptych," she said. "Your one o'clock is here, now. Oh, very pretty, yes. Long, firm legs…"

Bae looked over and covered her knees with her hands.

"No, I wouldn't have thought so by the look of her," Sally held the phone between her neck and shoulder, "Excuse me? Bae?"

Bae turned to the receptionist, "Yes?"

"You haven't fucked a spastic in the past two weeks, have you?"

Confused, Bae took offence to the line of questioning, "Uh, no? Why do you ask?"

"Oh, no reason," Sally shrugged the challenge off and returned to the phone call, "Yes, she's a chink. I reckon she's perfect."

Bae folded her arms and leaned back into the couch. She was less than impressed at the company's treatment of her so far.

"Okay, Ms Triptych will see you now."

"Fine," She grabbed her bag and stood up, "This isn't right, you know."

Sally winked and licked her lips, "I know," Her tongue split down the middle, too quick for Bae to notice.

Bae stormed off toward the interview room.

Knock-knock.

"Come in."

Bae pushed the door open, ready to make a complaint, "I have to say, I'm not impressed with—"

Bae stopped dead in her tracks. She froze at what she was looking at.

"What's wrong, honey?" a voice asked in an intense high pitch rasp from behind the desk.

"Oh, Jesus Christ."

Bae's bag dropped to the floor. A tube of lipstick and a packet of mints fell out through the buckle.

"What's the matter, Bae?" the voice gurgled behind the desk.

"Mooommmmy," The boy's cries were infused with the sound of a steak sizzling, "It's too cold in heeeerrreeee..."

"It's o-okay, I'll j-just—"

Bae stepped back and grabbed the door handle to stop it from closing.

"No, it's noo-oo-ooot as bad as it looks," groaned a man, half in tears, half in agony.

"N-No," Bae trembled, "I think I n-need to g-go—"

"Please d-don't goo-ooo," the man's voice heaved in pain. The sound of agony turned into an amalgam of Yanni and Zoe's shrieks, "we want you to staaa-aa-aaay..."

"No way," Bae flung the door open and ran out of the office

She whizzed past Sally at reception, "You b-better call the p-police, or the a-ambulance or—"

SPRAAA-ASSSHHHH!!

Sally's cheeks puffed out like a pair of scales. She lashed her tongue out and threatened the woman.

Bae stepped back and covered her head, "Nooooo."

"Thaaa-aaank y-youuuu for v-visssitt-innnggg Rylerrrr-starrrr."

Sally's Cobra-like face hovered up over the counter. The mouth yawned back, revealing its fangs. She bent her head back, ready to bite Bae's head off.

"No, please. Don't."

"Yoo-oo-oouu-uuuu're beeeaaa-utiiifffuulll."

"Noooo—"

SWOOSH-SNAPP!

Chapter 3

Majesty

Lizzie's legs swung back and forth under the bench. Her knee-high white socks were dirty from the school day.

A pair of hands gripped the edge of the seat, forcing her legs into a bigger swing.

Lizzie was smart for a fourteen-year-old. She'd been asked to wait behind for her classmate after school. According to the *InstaBate* app on her phone, the time was fast approaching 4:00 pm.

She set her phone down next to her and took a look around. Nothing but a long road and looming trees. Most of the children had already gone home. It was summertime and the daylight would last.

4:05 pm. Still no sign of her friend.

Lizzie looked over her shoulder and pulled the down hem of her skirt. A cool breeze blew past her face, causing her to shudder.

Chrome Junction Academy had experienced many setbacks this academic year. The grades were falling well behind the national average. The children's parents demanded meetings with the school governors about this issue.

Another concern arose in the past few weeks.

According to the head teacher, there were sightings of strangers in recent weeks. Men approached the children as they made their way to and from school. Lately, these people had dressed as clowns and gave the kids the fright of their lives. *Maxwell Gooder's Comprehensive School* in Wiltshire reported two missing children only a month ago.

But that was Wiltshire The ass-end of nowhere. No-one seemed to care very much about that report.

This academy was in North London.

Lizzie resumed her leg-swinging in total confidence. She shouldn't be out alone now.

"Hey, you waited," came a girl's voice.

It was Lizzie's best friend - the effervescent Vicky.

Lizzie smiled as she watched her friend run up to her, "Hey," She stood to her feet and grabbed her satchel.

"Man, Mr Langham is a creepy so-and-so."

"What, from Media studies? I think he's all right," Lizzie moved toward the mini roundabout with her friend.

Vicky threw her arms through the rucksack and hoisted it over her shoulders. She walked a bit faster than Lizzie, "C'mon, let's hit the sweet shop before they close."

Something wasn't quite right. Lizzie was apprehensive. It was as if she didn't want to be with her friend.

Vicky stopped and turned around, "Well?"

"I'm coming, I'm coming," Lizzie huffed and continued forward.

"You're such a numpty, sometimes," Vicky huffed and stepped onto the road, "Always slow. Always late for everything."

"But I was on time waiting for you."

"Yeah, that was a first."

Vicky reached the long road and eyed the entrance to the school grounds a hundred feet in the distance. Lizzie caught up to her.

"Why did you get a detention?" Lizzie asked, losing her breath.

"Ah, I told Mr Langham to piss off."

Lizzie chuckled, "Wow, that was brave."

"Yeah, he's a creepy dude and deserves to piss off, you

know," Vicky spat before stopping in her tracks. She held Lizzie back and paused, "Wait, wait."

Lizzie stopped alongside her friend. Vicky held out her finger and turned around, "Can you hear that?"

"What?" Lizzie stepped back and looked around. Trees and foliage rustled in the wind.

"I swear I could hear bells or something," Vicky whispered, looking around at the tree branches.

"I didn't hear anything?"

"Nah. Maybe I'm just going mad," Vicky chuckled and continued down the road, "Can't be too careful. A lot of bad men out here."

A heavy chuckling rumbled through the trees. Both girls heard it.

Vicky stopped once again, "Okay, now *that* is freaking me out."

"Yeah, I heard it, too."

"God, as long as it isn't clowns. I *hate* clowns." Vicky began walking once again, "This road always gives me the creeps."

Lizzie and Vicky hit the main arterial road. At least it was busy with people and heaving with traffic.

The SUVs honked in the traffic build-up. The drivers were very impatient.

Vicky walked past a van. She spotted a clown dressed in a white fright wig at the wheel. He scowled at her, revealing large fangs for incisors. "Yaarrgghh."

"God," Vicky gasped and picked up the pace, "What a nut case!"

"What happened?"

"That man. Look," Vicky pointed to the clown driving the white van. She rubbed her eyes and looked at the driver once again, "Dressed as a clown. Mad man."

It wasn't a clown driving, though. A black man sat behind the steering wheel. Angry at being stuck in traffic, he flicked the ash from the end of his cigarette out of the window.

"Who, him?"

"No, but—" Vicky swallowed back her sentence, "It was a clown."

Lizzie chuckled to herself in utter disbelief, "What is it with you and clowns, Vicky?"

They continued along the road, "You know the story, I told you it."

"No you didn't—"

BEEP-BEEP! A car horn blared in front of the girls. Vicky jumped out of her skin.

"C'mon, man," the driver yelled. "what's the holdup, here?"

Vicky cleared her throat and continued walking with her friend, "My uncle gave me one as a toy on my third birthday. It was called *Babydoll.* It was there when he visited me. I hate them. Always have, always will."

Vicky looked over her shoulder and stared at the white van. She stopped walking and squinted at the driver, "I think I must be going bonkers."

"There's no clown there, you know," Lizzie offered a smile, "Come on. Let's get some sweets and get home."

BEEP-BOOP.

Vicky and Lizzie entered the convenience store. It was nothing more than a glorified newsagent. The back wall had shelf upon shelf of confectionery.

A brown cashier smiled at the girls as they walked through the first aisle.

Vicky winked at Lizzie, indicating that they were out of sight from the shopkeeper, "Okay, I'll go to the sweets. You keep Patel busy over by the tampons."

"What?"

"Oh don't *start,*" Vicky licked her lips and shuffled off to the side, "Pssst."

Lizzie looked in the direction her friend was nodding to. A shelf of sanitary products.

"Keep him busy."

"Okay, okay," Lizzie huffed and made her way to the counter. Vicky sneaked off toward the sweet shelf.

"Hello, young lady," the shopkeeper said to Lizzie, "What are you looking for?"

"Oh, uh," she looked up at the tampons and traced her finger around the shelving, "Looking for some fanny pads."

"Bottom shelf, by your knees."

"Oh. Thanks," Lizzie crouched down, making sure her skirt rode up her thighs. She looked over to the shopkeeper and giggled.

He smiled back, trying not to ogle at her legs.

The giant security mirror in the corner above his head shone down on confectionery aisle. Lizzie looked up and saw Vicky scoop a bunch of sweets from the second shelf. She slipped them in her pocket.

"Just finished school," asked the shopkeeper, snapping Lizzie out of her gaze. She turned to him and hoped he hadn't cottoned on to the thievery.

"Oh, uh, yeah."

"What year are you in?"

Lizzie bought her friend some time and reached down for her sock. She pulled it up and pretended to adjust herself, "Oh, year ten."

"Year ten?" The shopkeeper became flummoxed, "Strange, I'd have thought you were older."

"Huh?" Lizzie yanked her other sock up against her knee, making damn sure he could see her legs.

"I said it's not nice to steal sweets, little lady," he growled. "Bitch!"

A carnival tune echoed around the room. Lizzie looked up, shocked. The man had turned into a clown, puffy red hair nestling either side of a white bald patch. A giant red nose and evil, black eyes.

"HA! HA! HA!" He blurted.

Lizzie rubbed her eyes and stepped back. She crashed

into the sanitary shelf, sending most of the boxes to the floor.

"Oh, shit."

"What are you doing?" The shopkeeper tutted, reaching for a plastic bag. Lizzie looked up at him. He was no longer a clown.

What the hell was going on?

"Okay, I got' em," Vicky screamed, running out of the shop with a skirt-full of sweets, "Run."

Lizzie bolted after her friend.

They ran into the street and off up the road.

"Hey, come back," The shopkeeper ran out onto the pavement. "Thief, stop."

The girls cackled like witches as they ran off across the road and into the distance.

A few minutes later. The girls were well away from trouble. Their shoplifting escapade was a rousing success. The need to run wasn't so urgent as they made their way into a forestry.

"Wow, look," Lizzie watched as Vicky pulled out several bars of chocolates from her pockets.

"You cleaned him out."

"Yeah, man," Vicky giggled to herself, "Got some more down my socks, as well."

She pulled out ten bags of *MegaStarz* chewy bears from her knickers and offered them to Lizzie.

"No, wait," She turned around and offered Vicky her rucksack, "Open me up and put them in here."

"I should have taken the bag myself," Vicky yanked down on the zipper. She posted the bars of chocolate and bags of sweets into Lizzie's rucksack.

"Hurry up," Lizzie hushed, "Someone will see us."

The girls were deep in *Three Springs Common*, off the main pathway. Secured behind a hedge, there wasn't much chance of capture.

"I'm going as fast as I can," Vicky complained. She

took out the last two bags of *MegaStarz* and slipped them in the side pockets. She pulled the zipper up and over and tapped Lizzie on the shoulder.

"Okay, all good."

"Good?"

"Yeah."

"Let's go—" Lizzie looked forward and froze in her shoes.

A clown stood one hundred yards in front of them from between two fat trees. He was carrying three helium balloons and two red lollipops. He snarled and revealed two white fangs.

"V-Vicky," Lizzie muttered, "D-Do you see him?"

"Who?"

Vicky looked dead ahead. She could see the clown, judging by the alarmed expression on her face, "Christ, yeah. That's *him*."

"Him?"

"The clown. I can see him."

The girls stared at the clown. He reached into his breast pocket and pressed a button on his red, white and black overalls.

Carousel music played through the trees, "HA! HA! HA!"

Vicky and Lizzie jumped back and held each other's hand. The clown licked his lips and pointed at his eyeballs with two fingers. He turned his forefinger toward the girls.

Lizzie pointed at her own chest, deep in shock.

"Uh-huh," the clown muttered. He took out a small black device from his engorged trouser pocket and held it to his neck.

"I… see… you..." He said in a distorted, gravelly voice. He clicked the black device once again. "I… know... what… you… did."

"Oh, sh-shit."

The clown extended his teeth and bit into one of the helium balloons.

POP!

The girls jumped back and squealed.

"HA! HA! HA!"

The clown disappeared behind the trees in the blink of an eye.

Lizzie and Vicky blinked and turned to each other, "Let's get out of here."

Two sets of school shoes crunched through the leaves and mud.

"I'm scared, Lizzie," Vicky snapped as she quickened her pace, "I just wanna go home."

"I know, I know," Lizzie looked over her shoulder. The exit to *Three Springs Common* loomed in front of them.

"We'll get to the gate and stay to the main roads, okay?"

"Yeah, good plan," Vicky said, sliding in front of her friend.

As the girls approached the gate, the clouds seemed to darken. Vicky looked up and saw a couple of birds fly from the tree. Shafts of sunlight sifted across her face through the branches.

Vicky looked down at her shoes as she walked, "It's going to rain, you know."

The sun disappeared behind a cloud, darkening the area.

"Not much we can do about it. Let's just get home."

A couple of cars sped along the main road behind the gated exit. A distant thunderclap rolled across the bleak sky.

"Ugh, c'mon," Vicky huffed, "Hurry up."

"My bag is heavy," Lizzie quipped, careful to avoid the vast muddy patches on the ground.

Circus music accompanied the rolling thunder. It was coming from a mile away.

"Do you hear that music?" Vicky turned to Lizzie as she walked.

Another car whizzed past.

"Ignore it."

"We're gonna get soaked—"

SCREEEEECCCHHH! A giant white van slammed on its brakes right outside the gate.

The girls backed up in fright.

"Oh, shit." Vicky stepped back and slid in some mud, sending her onto her ass.

Lizzie bent over and offered her friend a hand, "C'mon, get up."

Vicky took Lizzie's hand and got to her feet. The girls turned around to find the van's side door was open.

In front of it was the clown they had seen earlier.

A mere ten feet away, the clown presented himself in crystal clarity.

The white, bald patch.

The fangs for incisors.

The bleached-out white and red face paint.

The giant red bubble for a nose.

The yellow and green overalls.

The stupid, baggy trousers, in pink and purple.

Two red lollipops.

A pair of giant clown shoes.

And a hideous hole in his throat. He held a black device to the hole under his chin. A couple of raindrops splashed the clown make-up from his face, revealing his natural white skin.

"Hello, girls," his vocal chords bellowed through the device.

Neither Lizzie nor Vicky could bring themselves to speak. They stood on the grassy verge, speechless.

The clown reached up to his breast pocket and hit a button. "Hi, my name is Majesty," a young girl's voice played from his chest, "The friendly clown! I want to be *your* friend!"

Majesty tilted his head and waited for a response.

The girls turned to each other, aghast, and then back to

the clown. He took the black box and pressed it against his throat cavity. With his free hand, he strapped it around his neck with a long strip of Velcro.

The clown now had a choker around his throat.

"Guh, guh," he cleared his throat. The action rendered his voice unnatural-sounding and threatening, "Don't be scared, girls. I'm here to help you."

KROO-BOOOM. The thunder rolled ever-closer.

"Wh-what do you w-want?" Vicky stuttered.

His gargling electronic voice bellowed through the tracheotomy box, "I want to get you home safely and out of the rain."

Lizzie tried for a smile, "No, we're fine, thanks—"

"—Don't interrupt me!" The clown stepped forward and held out his arms, "Come with me, darlings."

"No, no," Vicky yanked Lizzie back with her, "We'll walk, thanks."

"Oh, no, no, no," the clown said, stepping into their comfort zone, "Not when I have *these*!"

SCHJUNT! Two canisters flew up his sleeves and into each palm. He angled them side by side and scooshed a clear mist of water into their faces.

The girls fell back, unconscious.

"HA! HA! HA!"

***

A playful whistling sound from someone's lips came from the other end of the room.

Lizzie opened her eyes and groaned. It was still dark.

She turned her head. Nothing. Darkness.

"Mfgghhhh," came another voice close to her left ear.

Lizzie tried to speak, but her lips were sewn shut, "Mgghhh."

A clanging of metal shimmied across the room.

Lizzie kicked her feet, only to find her ankles tied to whatever she was sitting on. "Hrmph. Hrmph."

She kicked her ankles forward, enabling some success in shifting the chair forward.

"Oh no, no, no," the tracheotomy-voice insisted, "You stay where you are, young lady."

Lizzie gave up screaming and bowed her head to her chest.

"And now, ladies and gentlemen, will you please give it up for *the one, the only...*"

WHUMP! The hood flew off Lizzie's head.

"*Majesty.*"

Lizzie widened her eyes. A huge theatrical display loomed in front of her in the medium-sized room. A pair of toy curtains and a crappily-painted living room made up the backdrop.

The clown lowered behind the metal workbench, keeping up his shit-eating grin.

A hand puppet appeared from behind the work surface, right in the middle of the table. A fierce strip light illuminated the "show" from above.

The puppet turned to Lizzie. It had a huge nose and a jester's hat. The bell tinkled.

"Hello, Lizzie," the jester said.

She couldn't respond. Her muffled screams were of no use. She mumbled into the gag and kicked her chair forward.

"Awww. It looks like Lizzie doesn't like me."

Another puppet sprang up an arm's width away from the jester. A mini clown with deadened, black eyes and a toy hammer sewn to its hand.

"What do you mean she doesn't like you?" The mini-clown asked.

WHUMP. The hammer struck the metal surface. An assortment of tools rattled around the top. A vicious-looking metal hammer and a serrated-edge twelve-inch knife.

"Mffgghhh," Lizzie screamed and turned to her right. Another person was sitting a chair next to her. She had a bag secured over her head. Lizzie could tell who it was by the white knee-high socks and shoes.

It was Vicky, of course.

She kicked forward and cried under her legs.

"Lizzie?" The jester waggled its head, operated by a hand, "Does your friend like clowns?"

"Ngggg." Vicky screamed and hulked her hips in all directions. "Nggg."

"Mffgghhh."

"Aww, bugger," the jester thumped his head to the metal workbench, "She doesn't like clowns, either?"

"Maybe she likes jesters?" asked the mini clown.

"Nah, she's just a little coward. Just like her friend."

Lizzie watched the mini clown smother the jester. He grabbed it between his hands and ripped off the jester puppet, revealing a white hand.

The middle finger extended at Lizzie.

"HA! HA! HA!" Majesty's free hand tore off the mini clown. He grabbed the edge of the work bench and hoisted himself up to his feet.

PHROOOT! A sound effect occurred with the jump.

"Hello, Lizzie," Majesty laughed, making his way along the bench, "Izzie Wizzie, let's get *busy*."

He squatted in front of Lizzie and tugged the end of the tape, "I'm going to take off your gag, now. Promise you won't scream?"

Lizzie's eyes widened as she caught a glimpse of the soul behind the black eyeballs in front of her. "Mffggh," She nodded.

"Okay."

SCHWIPP-PP!

Lizzie gasped as the tape ripped away from her lips. "HA! HA! HA! It's a shame you didn't have a mustache, little one."

Majesty slapped Lizzie across the face. It forced her head toward Vicky, who still had the bag over her head.

"Well, well, well," Majesty tiptoed, playfully, over to

Vicky, "What *do* we have here?"

He tugged the back of the bag, forcing her head up toward the ceiling.

"Mfgrrrhh."

Majesty grabbed his junk between his clown pants, "Don't speak with your mouthful, sweetheart! HA! HA! HA!"

WHVOOM! Off came the bag. Lizzie blinked up at the light and kicked around in her chair.

"Ohhh, aren't you a pretty little thing?" Majesty grabbed her chin and forced her head toward Lizzie. "See, Lizzie? This one is much prettier than you, and she knows it, too."

Majesty breathed over Vicky's face, "You *are* prettier than her, aren't you?"

"Mgh, mgh," Vicky shook her head away, releasing her chin from his clutches.

He pinched the edge of the tape and pulled it down, "Okay, if I take this off, you promise you won't scream at Majesty?"

Vicky's head vibrated with fear. She blinked twice, forcing a tear to roll down her cheek.

"Okay," he giggled, "Off we go!"

SCHWIPP! The tape scraped off, enabling Vicky to scream at the top of her lungs. Her piercing, high-pitched squeal sounded like a fire alarm from hell.

"Shut up, bitch," Majesty slapped her across her face. Vicky gulped in terror. She choked back her screams.

Majesty burst out laughing and honked the horn on his nose.

BONK-BONK!

"HA! HA! HA!" He stood up straight and took a few steps back toward the darkness, "Now, now, Vicky. A little birdie told me that you despise clowns?"

"Huh?" Lizzie turned to Vicky. She knew that her friend didn't like clowns, but how did Majesty know this?

"Neeww, please, mister—"

"—That's *Majesty*, to you."

"Majesty, p-please. D-Don't hurt me—"

He stepped forward and pressed his hands against his hips, "Who said I was going to hurt *you*?"

Vicky bawled for dear life. Snot and effluence ran down her top lip, "I j-just want to g-go home…"

Majesty play-rubbed his eyes and mocked her, "Oh boo-hoo, I just wanna go home," he flung his arms back and roared in her face, "*Like a fucking coward*!"

Vicky wailed in front of Majesty's ugly face. He paused for a moment to soak up her anguish. He seemed to be feeding on it.

"Wh-what are you going to do?" Lizzie asked.

Majesty turned to Lizzie and stepped back toward the darkened corner of the room.

"I'm putting on a show for you! HA! HA! HA!" Majesty produced the two red lollipops, "But first, suck on these."

He shoved the first lollipop into Lizzie's mouth. She caught it between her lips.

"Good," Majesty eyeballed her and licked his lips, "Now suck it good and hard."

Vicky watched through her tear-strewn eyes as Lizzie sucked on the candy. Majesty turned to Vicky and bopped her on the head with the last lollipop.

"Icky Vicky, you sick little puppy, here," Majesty squeezed her chin and yanked her jaw down, "Suck on my candy, you icky little dog."

SCHLOMP!

He clamped her jaw shut and forced her to suck on the candy, "There you go."

Majesty reached up and yanked down on a cord that hung from the ceiling.

The light snapped on tor eveal a man in a chair. He, too, had his mouth taped up.

"Ladies, I'd like to introduce you to Lawrence Stone," Majesty moved around his captive and massaged his shoulders. Lawrence didn't try to scream. He knew it'd fall on deaf ears.

"Lawrence has been a bad, bad man," Majesty leaned into his ear. "Haven't you, Lawrence?"

Majesty's victim closed his eyes and nodded.

SCHLIP! Majesty untied a piece of plastic that shackled Lawrence's wrists together.

"Hold out your hand, Mr Stone," Majesty winked at the girls and chuckled to himself.

Lawrence did as instructed. His hand rose in front of the girls, "You're a naughty, naughty, naughty boy!"

Majesty slapped his hand over and over again, "You shouldn't steal from people. Do you know what we do to people who steal things?"

Vicky closed her eyes and wailed down the front of her shirt. Her lollipop fell from her mouth and hit the floor.

Lizzie gasped and looked over to the corner of the room. Her rucksack nestled against the wall, half-open.

"Shit, shit," she spat the lollipop to the floor, "The sweets!"

"What's that, my dear?" Majesty asked as he moved toward the workbench, "Did you say something?"

"Uh, uh, no," Lizzie gasped. "I didn't say anything."

"Sounded like you said something to me," Majesty yelled and swiped the knife from the worktop, "Little girls should be seen and not heard. And preferably not *seen*, either."

He yanked Lawrence's right wrist and placed the serrated edge across it, "Do you promise not to do it again?"

Lawrence looked his captor in the eye. He'd decided to go down like a man and not fight back.

Cheerful clown music piped up around the room. The chirpy accordion swung into full effect.

A glitter ball sprang to life and illuminated Majesty and his victim with shards of blue and pink lights.

"Now, watch what *we* do to thieves."

Majesty sawed through Lawrence's wrist. He closed his eyes and screamed. Torrents of blood splattered up Majesty's laughing face. "Whoa, oh, oh, we got a gusher, here!"

Majesty sliced away at the man's hand. The final strings of skin snapped apart.

He presented it in both hands to the girls, "There you are! A helping hand! HA! HA! HA!"

Vicky shuffled around in her seat, unable to contain her distress.

The hole in Lawrence's wrist puked blood and gore down the chair leg. He was in severe danger of bleeding out.

"Oopsie," Majesty said, pulling down on his clown zipper. He fed the severed arm into the slit and moved it around, "Naughty, naughty, Lawrence."

Lizzie turned to Vicky. She looked back and closed her eyes, knowing that they were next.

"Now, a little birdie tells me that you two girls have been badly behaved?" Majesty paced around in deep contemplation, "I'm going to ask you both a question, and I want an honest answer."

The girls turned to him and held their breath.

"Which one of you two stole all those sweets?"

"It was her," Vicky screamed, immediately taking the opportunity to dump her friend in the shit.

Majesty tilted his head at Lizzie and adjusted his tachometer, "Is this true, Lizzie?" His voice deepened, "Did you do it?"

"No, no," Lizzie pleaded, "It was *her*."

"Don't lie to me, Lizzie." Majesty's voice resembled a fatally wounded bear, "Because if you're lying to me, I'll have to teach you a lesson."

"Lizzie stole them," Vicky added, loudly, hoping that it'd put her in the clear, "She took it all. She threatened to hurt me if I didn't go along with it."

"You lying bitch," Lizzie screamed back.

"Let me go," Vicky pushed her knees forward, causing the chair to screech along the ground. "Let me go."

"Ah, da-da-da," Majesty moved forward and slapped Vicky across the face. Her spent tears splashed to the floor, "What did I tell you about screaming?"

"P-Please Mr Clown, let me go—"

—Majesty," he screamed in his low-pitch wail, "My name is MAJESTY you jumped-up little *cunt*!"

"*Majesty*, I'm sorry," Vicky gasped, "please, it's *her* you want, not me."

He pressed the tip of his nose against hers. A slow and calculated movement. "So. Lizzie did it, then?"

"Yes."

"You liar," Lizzie slumped back in her chair and growled. "Traitor."

"Yes," Vicky went on, "It was her."

Majesty closed his eyes and nodded. He stood up straight and looked down at Vicky, "I believe you."

"Good, good."

Lawrence pushed back in his chair and thrashed around. He was having a coronary as he held his severed wrist in his good hand. The blood flushed out down the side of his chair and ran along the ground.

"Aren't you going to help him?" Vicky squealed, crying her eyes out once again.

"Who, him?" Majesty approached the table and didn't even look back at his dead body, "I cut his hand off! He was bound to bleed to death. Why would I help him?"

"He's, he's—" Vicky gasped and turned to Lizzie, "Do something."

"What?"

"Do something," Vicky watched Majesty lift the metal hammer from the table.

"How am I going to do something, you idiot?" She looked down and tried to kick her ankles away, "I'm tied up!"

"Oh God, oh God," Vicky hushed over and over again,

"He's going to kill us. He's going to kill—"

SCHLAAMMM! The head of the hammer thumped against the table, "Silence, Vicky," Majesty yelled.

"Oh-okay—"

"—Thank you for telling me who the thief was."

"Umm, okay?" She snorted a glob of phlegm out through her nose and tried to inhale.

"Now, let's discuss Lizzie's punishment, shall we?"

"Wh-what?"

THWACKKK!

Majesty struck Lizzie's kneecap with the hammer.

"Gaaooowww," Lizzie squealed in pain. Her kneecap bone shot through the skin and spat out a phlegm of blood.

"HA! HA! HA!" Majesty stood back and admired his work, "I do love a good ol' *knees up*, don't you?"

Vicky took a deep breath and shifted back in her seat, "No, stop—"

SCHTAA-AAM.

Lizzie's second kneecap split open. The hammer smashed the bone right through the skin.

"Aggghhh," Lizzie tilted her head back and chewed her lip, desperate not to faint. "Agh, agh, agh."

Her breathing slowed down. The pain was too much. Lizzie's eyelids lowered.

Vicky looked at her poor friend. She felt sorry for her. Did she feel compassion or any sympathy for having lied? After all, if justice prevailed, it'd be *her* on the receiving end of this beating.

"You think she's had enough?" Majesty asked Vicky.

"Yes," she gasped and slowed her breathing, "She's had enough."

Majesty produced a flick knife, "Okay."

SPLICK!

The blade flicked out. He walked over to Vicky and held the sharp end to her face, "Okay. Let's do you, now."

"No," Vicky yelled, kicking her chair back, "Please."

"Oh come on. It'll be fun," Majesty smiled and licked his bottom lip. A bit of his makeup came off on his tongue, revealing his white chin, "HA! HA! HA!"

"No, no," Vicky closed her eyes as the blade swerved close to her face, "Please, don't."

A hand grabbed her knee. Nothing else occurred after that. Vicky felt Majesty's chest press against hers and an arm reach around the back of the chair.

SNIP, SNIP.

Majesty cut her wrists free. The plastic tie slapped to the ground. Vicky looked down at her legs in amazement. He snipped her ankle ties away from the chair.

He folded the blade back into the handle and slipped it into his top pocket.

"Wh-what?"

"Stand up."

Vicky pushed herself off the chair and stood up straight. She was in utter shock and confusion.

Majesty rolled his shoulders and brushed out Vicky's collar.

"Turn around."

Vicky turned around. Majesty brushed the wooden splinters from her skirt. He grabbed the back of her shoulders, spun her around and looked her dead in the eyes.

"What are you going to tell your friends and teachers at school tomorrow?"

"I, uh—" Vicky stammered before being interrupted.

"Nothing. That's what you will say," Majesty winked at her, "I'm leaving you alive because I like you, Victoria."

She bit her lip and tried not to cry.

Freedom, at last, was on the cards. Victoria had genuinely thought she was going to die.

"What will you tell your mum and dad when you get home?" he asked. "Be inventive or else I'll change my mind."

"I w-went round a friend's house," Victoria's

imagination came to her rescue, "Nothing happened, they'll n-never know."

"Good girl," Majesty pinched her cheek and wiggled her head, "Look at you, so pretty. Are you still scared of clowns?"

She shook her head, "no." Of course she was lying. She pissed herself right there in front of Majesty.

He looked down and watched the urine treacle across the hard ground.

"I'm s-sorry—"

"—Shh," he said, pressing his finger against her lips, "Don't apologise. Just go."

"O-Okay," she sniffed and nodded her head. Careful not to change his mind, she side-stepped toward the door, keeping an eye on him.

"Get out of here, Vicky."

She turned around and ran out of the door.

Vicky hit the stairs and grabbed hold of the railing. The white light at the top promised a permanent escape.

She cried hard as her legs buckled from step to step. Vicky coughed and spluttered and disappeared into the light.

Gone forever.

Back in Majesty's lair, he set the hammer down onto the workbench. "Gosh. You know it's so sad," he sighed and removed the tracheotomy device from his neck. His natural voice seeped in; higher in pitch, and feminine, "They grow up so damn fast."

He clasped the sides of his red hair in each hand and removed the fake scalp away from his head.

The bald cap flew to the floor.

He shook his natural hair out. It flew from side to side and rested against his shoulders.

"Okay, guys. Enough bullshit. The cunt's gone," Majesty said removed the make-up from his face. He pouted his lips in a pocket mirror and mopped up the remnants of white paint from his face.

Lizzie opened her eyes and reached down to her ankles. She untied them and stretched out her legs. The grey bone props dropped to the floor.

Lawrence reached over his chest and unbolted the fake arm from the left side of his body.

"You were right, sweetie," Majesty said, turning to Lizzie. "That Vicky cunt is a fucking snitch."

"Mum, was the voice box really necessary?" Lizzie picked up the black device and spoke through it. "I am Majesty! HA! HA! HA!"

"I couldn't very well have her run off thinking it was *me*, could I?" Mom said as she cleared the table, "Get your rucksack. We gotta get out of here."

Lawrence walked over and pecked mum on the cheek. "Did I do okay?"

"You did fine, sweetie," she giggled and turned to kiss him, "You know, I think that was your jerking hand I took off."

"Mom," Lizzie chuckled and cleared away the jester puppet into her rucksack. She dumped the mini clown to the workbench surface in protest. "That's gross."

"Sorry, sorry," Mom watched her daughter bend over and place the weapons into her bag. "Lizzie, honey?"

"Yeah, mum?"

"How did I do?"

Lizzie threw the bag over to her Dad. He caught it and slung it over his shoulders, "You scarred her for life."

Mum slid her arms around her daughter and walked with her toward the exit, "You really think so?"

"Yeah. She *hates* clowns."

"How did you know she'd drop you in the shit, honey?" Dad asked as he pulled the door open.

"Once a liar, always a liar," Lizzie walked through the door. Her parents followed after her, "I hope it's fucked her up for life."

"Ha, yeah," Mom giggled and slapped her daughter on

the back, "Hopefully, the little maggot will commit suicide over it."

The door shut behind them as they chuckled away at their endeavor.

The mini clown lay lifelessly on the workbench, illuminated by the light. Its eyes beamed skyward; a perpetually evil grin plastered across its face.

"Oh, shit. I forgot to switch off the light," Mom's voice came from behind the door.

It creaked open. An arm slipped through the crack in the door and flicked the switch.

"Okay, let's get the fuck out of here."

Mini Majesty the clown stared up at the light. He smiled slightly and stuck his tongue out. "Ha! Ha! Ha!"

SNAP. Darkness.

Little did the family know that Vicky would go on to kill herself the next morning.

Chelsea, Vicky's mother, found her body hanging from the bedroom door beam just after 7 am.

Chapter 4

Push

Chrome Junction Network Rail has had a reputation of late. The trains seldom run on time. When they do arrive they're often late and crammed with commuters.

You should never attempt to enter platform six between 07:00 and 08:30.

Suited businessmen and women eagerly make their way to the thin, yellow paint that lines the edge of the platform.

There's often a large crowd. It's dangerous.

A woman in a silver suit managed to sidestep against a mother pushing her buggy. Its wheels nearly careened off the platform and onto the tracks. When the train arrived, do you think that the suited woman stood back to allow the mother onto the train?

No.

The businesswoman climbed aboard and made sure she was first in the carriage. She got a seat, much to the chagrin of the horde of commuters behind her.

Selfish bitch.

The woman with the buggy got on, backwards. There was enough space on the 8:54 to Waterloo to stand with her baby in her arms in the gangway. The folded buggy wedged between her and the carriage door.

Many of the men brushed past her on their way to the

first class carriage. It was air conditioned, unlike the cattle-class carriages. The windows fogged up a treat with the breaths, farts, and burps of the passengers sitting by them.

The baby in her mother's arms looked out of the window as the train pulled away.

From the sheltered staircase that led to the platform, she spotted three boys walking onto the platform.

She waved at them.

Of course they didn't see the tiny human being waving. The baby was too small and in amongst a thousand bodies in one of eight carriages.

She saw them, though.

"Mate, you're a fucking gay man," huffed the teenager in the middle. He slung his hood over his head and walked along the platform.

"Why you calling a batty boy, man?" his friend complained. "You're the one who sucks dick."

"Fuckin' 'low it, man," said the boy in the middle as they walked over to the benches, "Sit yourself down, innit."

The boy in the middle was the tallest. His name was Nicholas. His friends called him Narc for reasons that will become clear in about two minutes' time.

Narc was of mixed parentage. Those out of tune with the politically correct crowd might have described him as "half cast."

He looked as intelligent as he sounded.

"Allow me, man. Look at all these fuckers walking around. We got 'nuff motherfuckers here right now, innit? Swear down."

"Passengers are reminded that smoking is not permitted on any platform," advised the speaker address system.

Narc reached into his pocket and pulled out a fat roll-up stuffed with tobacco and weed. He pressed the end of it with his thumb and threw it into his mouth.

"Fam, what are you doing?" asked the second boy - Tompan - who hailed from somewhere in Asia; an inch shorter than Narc but no less fierce-looking.

"Blazin'," Narc sparked the end of his joint with his lighter. The tobacco and weed-ends sizzled and spat out some smoke. He took a lungful in and passed it to Tompan, "Fam, hit it."

"Safe."

Tompan took the joint from Narc and sucked on the end. Narc looked around the platform and kept the smoke held in his lungs.

A flurry of men in suits made their way across the platform. A train was approaching. Dead ahead of them were two older women. They were out for a day at the beach.

Opposite the women on the platform was a line of people waiting for the train. The platform was still very busy with people. Men and women of all shapes, sizes and dispositions walked around in all directions.

"The train now approaching platform six is the nine-oh-two to Waterloo," the speaker announced, "Please stand back from the platform edge."

"Hey, Tampax, man," Narc nudged Tompan in the ribs. He took the joint from his fingers, "Next man's train pulling up."

"Nah, fam. That's gonna be full of suits," said the third teenager. A pasty-faced and Leukemia-riddled squirt named Lena. Okay, so she didn't *really* have Leukemia - it was the way her white skin seemed to indent in her cheeks. A rigid jawline. Her brown eyes didn't help matters much, either. It was little wonder she wore a hood.

"Narc, man. Check it out," she pointed at the people exiting the train.

A woman in a black trouser suit was first out of the carriage. Without paying much attention to anyone else, she hopped out of the train. She jogged toward the staircase that would lead her down toward the ticket gates.

She barged past a young couple who made their way to the top, "Excuse me, sorry."

"Hey, watch where you're going," came an angry reply.

Narc slung his arm around Lena and chuckled, "Man, that bitch is in a hurry, innit?" He followed up his statement by hocking up a phlegm and spitting it to the ground.

"Yeah, man—" Lena butted some white powder from a tiny container onto the top of her fist. She snorted it up in one hit, "Bitch is gonna get it."

"—No, hold up," Narc pushed his hand over Lena's mouth, "Shut up, man. We'll wait till it dies down."

Narc turned to Tompan and pushed his jaw with his fist, "Fam, you ready?"

"Yeah, 'course I'm ready."

"Okay, safe."

The train pulled away. As it gained speed, the trio stood up and walked alongside it.

"There," Narc folded his hood over the back of his head, "Bitch in the silver suit."

He trained his gaze on the dark-haired woman in a suit walking to another set of stairs. She was carrying a paper coffee cup.

Narc walked faster, "Lena, check yo' six."

Lena turned around as they marched forward, "Mate, no-one there," she turned to Tompan, "You good, bro?"

"Yeah, man," Tompan said, "I'm good."

"She's reaching the top step in five… four…"

Narc and Lena split apart as Tompan pushed between them. The woman in the silver suit paced toward the top of the stairs. She held out her hand, intending to grab the hand rail.

"She's going for the rails," Narc said, "Fuckin' run."

"Okay," Tompan sprinted forward.

"Do it, man."

Narc and Lena stepped to the side of the stairwell opening. Tompan darted after the woman. Her palm was about to clasp the top of the handrail.

Tompan grabbed his right fist in his left. He bent his arm out and launched himself between her shoulders.

WHUMP!

The cup of coffee splashed to the floor. Tompan dived to the right and watched the woman fly face-first down the endless chasm of stairs. She tumbled down the steps.

Two men jumped out of the way as her body bulldozed its way down the steps.

CRUNCH-CRACK-SNAP.

The sound of bones snapping and muscles tearing.

Finally, she rolled over the bottom step in front of a horrified crowd of onlookers.

She squealed in pain, spitting out a few bloodied teeth, "Ugh, ugghhh, h-help me."

"My God," one woman said, "She fell down the stairs."

Narc peered around the shelter and looked down, "*Fuck*. That was a good one."

"Yeah, I fucked her up good," Tompan giggled.

"Shit, she's busted her ankle. Her leg's fucked," Narc chuckled. He walked forward and rolled his shoulders, "You're definitely on the team, Tampax. That was *sick*, bruv."

"Yeah, you see her leg, all fucked up and twisted?" Lena chuckled as they walked past the refreshment stand.

"Okay, so now it's your go." Tompan said to Lena. He wiped his nose.

"Cool. Name the hit."

Tompan looked around and settled on a woman with crutches trying to make her way to the third staircase, "Her, innit?"

"What?" Lena chuckled and gasped, "She's a fuckin' spastic, blud."

"Yeah. Well easy."

Narc looked down the second stairwell. A couple of paramedics ran up to the injured woman and attended to her.

"Shit, man, keep your fuckin' hoods up. They got cameras, still."

Lena reached behind her neck and threw the hood over her head, "Okay, I'll do the retard."

"Nice, man," Tompan said, "But if you chicken out, you suck my dick, yeah?"

"I ain't chickening out, though," she spat, moving forward. Narc and Tompan walked to the west pillar and leaned against it, "Allow me, man."

"Yo, Tampax," Narc whispered whilst keeping his eye on Lena, "Y'ain't fucked her, though?"

Tompan closed his eyes and cackled.

"Nar, man," Narc grinned and punched him on the shoulder, "Fuckin' look at you!"

Tompan interrupted him, "Shut up, fam. Look."

They watched the overweight woman in crutches hobble toward the staircase.

Lena looked over her shoulder as she marched up behind her. She slipped past a few commuters who got in her way. She weaved through the sea of people making their way out.

"Fuckin' careful," Narc mouthed.

Lena winked back and faced the woman as she crept up behind her. She crossed her left arm over her chest and picked up the pace, ready to push her over.

"Push, man. *Push*," Narc muttered under his breath, eager to see the destruction his friend was about to cause.

The woman in crutches stopped and turned around. Lena slowed down and, fast-thinking, smiled at the woman.

"Hey, you all right?" Lena asked, turning on a dime.

"It's my sticks," the woman said, "I need someone to carry them for me while I hold the rail."

"Oh, okay," Lena smiled and held out her hands, "Here, let me."

The woman handed Lena her crutches, "Thanks, sweetie. What's your name?"

Quick thinking, Lena found a bullshit response. "Uh, *Charlie*."

"Aww, Charlie. That's a lovely name," the woman took hold of the stair rail, "How old are you?"

"Sixteen."

"You're very thoughtful, young lady."

Lena smiled and perched the crutches against the rail, "Thanks."

Satisfied and appreciative, the woman turned around and took the first step.

Lena turned back to Narc and Tompan. She raised her eyebrows.

"What are you doing?" Narc mouthed back at her. "Don't do it and walk way."

Lena winked and blew him a kiss.

"Yo," Lena turned to the lderly woman and screamed in her face, "Granny."

WHUMP!

Lena shunted the her between the shoulders with her elbow.

"Whugh," The woman crashed head-first against the third step. The impact punched most of her teeth out of her gums. She spat blood as the rebound of the collision forced her waist over her head. Her calves slammed against the tenth step, shattered her ankles.

"Jesus Christ."

A man ran down after her, careful to avoid tripping himself. The woman tumbled, smashing her forearm and skull against each step. Her body slid down the last few steps and rolled to the ground floor.

"Crippled bitch. How ya like me *now*?" Lena snorted a lungful of phlegm and spat down after her. She skipped away and over to Narc.

"Someone call an ambulance," yelled a male voice from the staircase tunnel.

"Did I do good?" Lena chirped, skipping alongside Narc. They made their way across the platform.

"You're fucked in the head, playin' an old bird like that, you know," Narc huffed, taking out another joint.

"Least I don't have to suck his dick now, innit?" Lena beamed at Tompan, who stopped in his tracks and turned back, "Allow it, man. You fucked up some next man's mom."

"Yeah, so what?" Lena chewed her tongue and placed her hands on her hips, "You done it, too."

"Yeah, but my one was fresh."

"Fresh, yeah?"

"Yeah—"

"—Fuckin' shut up," Narc spat and pulled out his smart phone, "We got two down, now. I'mma call Spunx and tell him we on two. Tell her that *Chrome Valley Crew* ain't gonna be fucked with, you feel me?"

"Yeah, man," Lena threw a stick of bubble gum in her mouth, "Tell Spunx we fuckin' killing it, fam."

"For real," Narc held the phone to his hear. Someone picked up. "Yo, Spunx."

"Are you faggots at Chrome Junction Station?" Spunx's Alan Rickman-esque voice came through the phone.

"We on two. We about to take it to the next level."

"Fuck you," Spunx quipped through the phone, "Pics or it didn't happen. And your Dad is dead."

"Yeah, yeah," Narc said, "I'mma send you it now, cool?"

"Whatever, arsehole."

Narc hung up and flicked his thumb across the screen. A video icon showing the first suited woman at the top of the stairs appeared. He pressed the share icon and waited for the loading bar to reach the end.

"Narc, man," Lena tugged his sleeve.

"What, what?"

She pointed into the distance. A security guard looked at the trio and made his way over to them.

"Fuckin' filth have spotted us," she said. "We gotta

ghost."

Narc and Tompan looked up. "Shit, shit. Let's bounce," Narc pushed his two friends forward.

"Hey, stop," screamed the security guard, speeding toward them. He unclipped the radio from his chest, "I need back up on platform six. We've found them."

"Fuck this. Go, go," Narc, Tompan and Lena ran toward a double set of stairs.

"They're heading for the Cobra Concourse," shouted the security guard.

"Roger that, S-2, we are en route to your location," came the response from the radio.

Narc barged Lena and Tompan out of his path and stormed toward the double staircase, "Move."

He pushed a dozen people out of his way, creating a path for his two friends, "Quick, down here."

Tompan caught up to Narc, leaving Lena a few steps behind, "Get out of the fuckin' way."

His right foot hit the top step. As he looked down, he saw a sea of commuters descending the steps in front of him.

Tompan clasped the rail, stopping himself from barging into the back of the person in front of him, "Shit."

He looked back at Narc who, in turn, looked over his shoulder. The security guard was fast approaching.

"Do it, man," Narc took out his phone. He tilted it up to portrait mode and focused on his friend.

Tompan unclenched both hands and extended his arms forward.

WHUMP!

The chest of the man in front of him flew out, knocking the back of the lady's head one step below.

The man tumbled over her and crashed into the stream of people in front of him.

"Fuck, man," Narc said, catching the entire event on camera.

Like a perverse set of dominoes, the man and the

woman barreled through a dozen other commuters. Anyone in their path down got knocked down the steps toward a dangerous death.

One girl landed teeth-first against the sixteenth step. Her face clipped the ankle of an elderly lady who fell back, shoulders-first, onto the step behind her. The back of her skull popped open and coughed out a torrent of congealed blood.

The elderly woman's arm crunched under the tread of a businessman's sole. He lost his footing and hurtled into the oncoming traffic heading up the stairs.

CRUNCH! SPLATCH!

The man's forearm broke apart, swiping the legs of a young boy. He flew into the air and inadvertently drop kicked a woman's face as she made her way up the steps.

CRAA-AATCH!

His foot smashed against her cheek, forcing her body backwards. The small of her back slammed against the penultimate step, snapping her pelvic bone in two. She tumbled over and over, screaming blue murder. She finally rolled to a stop on the ground floor in sheer agony.

Narc and Lena kicked the injured and screaming commuters out of their path. They legged it down the steps. Tompan led the way.

"Quick, man."

"Hey," screamed the security guard as he chased after them. He was more careful than the trio he was chasing not to do any more damage to the poor souls who had broken their bones.

"Get them. Get them."

The trio reached the final few steps. A crowd of passengers had formed around the litany of injured commuters. Some staggered to their knees and screamed in pain. The less fortunate remained unconscious, bleeding from their injuries.

Narc jumped from the third-to-last step and landed into the Cobra Concourse. He looked up at Tompan and

Lena making their way toward him.

"Fuckin' hurry up," Narc said, pointing ahead to the exit. A series of staircases lined the sides of the narrow gangway.

Yet more passengers made their way toward him on the left side of the tunnel.

Lena and Tompan caught up to Narc. He looked in the opposite direction. Two more security guards ran toward them. "Stop."

The pink tiles on the walls started to rumble. The vibrations were violent, caused by a passing train several feet above their heads.

"Let's ghost, man," Narc shouted. He barged past the oncoming commuters. "Get out of the way."

"Stop where you are."

The security guard from platform six jumped down and joined his two colleagues, "They're over there."

Narc grabbed Lena's wrist and hoisted her along with him. Tompan ran behind them.

The shocked commuters stepped aside to avoid the oncoming collision.

Several screams and cries echoed down the corridor. Many of the commuters had seen the carnage a few feet behind the trio.

The end of the concourse loomed in the distance, promising a way out of the station and into the streets.

"Run, man," Lena screamed, "Nearly there."

As they kept running the exit didn't seem to get any closer. Narc looked over his shoulder and saw Tompan slowing down, "Fam, hurry up."

"I'm running as fast I can."

Schloop, schloop, schloop…

With every footstep, Tompan's feet got stuck into the oatmeal-laden floor. His trainers sunk into the ground.

Narc raised his eyebrows, "*Tampon*, man. The fuck you doing?"

SCHLOMP. A final slam of the sole of his left foot

slunk into the floor. He couldn't move. It was like he had trodden in fresh, wet concrete.

"Help me, man. I can't move my leg."

The security guards caught up to him.

"Shit, shit," Narc screamed as he watched the security guards jump on him from behind.

CRACK!

Tompan's body fell forward from the sheer force of the attack. His face smashed to the floor. The top half of his body contorted over itself, leaving his left leg upright to the knee. His thigh had folded down, leaving a bloody stump buried into the ground.

"What the fuck is going on?! Narc muttered to himself as the guards fell on Tompan's body and kicked the living shit out of it.

The commuters walked right by the scene, taking very little interest.

"We gotta run, man." Lena looked down and inspected her shoes. The ground was stable. "Let's go."

She knocked Narc's arm and ran off. He followed after her. "Shit's fucked up, you know."

"It don't matter," Lena screamed as she bolted forward, "Let's get the fuck outta here, bruv."

The walls of the concourse heaved out. The inhalation funneled the stream of commuters together. Lena side-stepped through them.

The walls exhaled back to normal.

Narc caught up to her and kept running. That damn exit still wasn't getting any closer, "Fuck, man. I'm outta breath."

"Keep running."

The walls inhaled, narrowing the concourse. The left-hand side blew inward, knocking Lena into the oncoming commuters.

Exhale.

The walls bellowed out.

A white light at the end of the tunnel glimmered but

was still no closer.

A protracted and deathly gurgling sound rumbled through the concourse. An insane tearing noise followed. It was like the sound of a carving knife slicing through a slab of meat.

"What's that noise?" Lena looked up at the ceiling lights.

SPISH-SPISH-SPISH!

One by one, the concourse bulbs blew out. Fragments of glass showered down around her shoulders. Sections of the tunnel snapped into darkness.

"Narc?" Lena's voice echoed.

The commuters paused perfectly still, as did the security guard who was chasing after them.

Narc was nowhere to be seen.

Lena stood, alone. The icy breath from her tiny gasps wafted out in front of her face.

The light at the end of the tunnel flashed blue and white. Police sirens wailed in the distance.

"Narc?" Lena's voice echoed three times. She looked behind her. There were scores of statued commuters in mid-walk. "Help me."

Narc stepped back and fanned his hands out in front of his body, not wanting to go near her.

A train thundered across from above.

CRASH! CRASH! CRASH!

The violent shaking powered across the walls. The large print advertisements slipped off their hooks and smashed to the ground.

Panes of glass from the frames shattered into the air.

The left wall bulged out and began to tear apart, releasing a beautiful purple beam of neon light.

Lena inhaled and screamed. The purple hue covered her face.

She watched the inflated wall unzip itself. The strength of the beam intensified, burning at her face.

The hood flew off her head, sending strands of her hair

over her shoulders.

She kept on screaming as the flaps on the wall peeled back. The chasm moved forward and threatened to engulf her entire body.

"Noooooooo."

The flaps on the walls splayed out and crept around her body. The protruding brickwork threaded around her neck like a soft tunic and tightened.

CRUNCH.

The back of her neck snapped and folded her body in half. Her scalp buried itself between her shoulder blades. The sheer force of the neck-break forced the skin across her throat to slit open and free her head from her body.

Narc gasped in terror as he watched his friend die in agony, "*Fuuuuuck* me."

Lena's chest was next to go. Folding back over her waist, splitting her shirt open. The buttons pinged either side as her nipples met the small of her back and meshed into the skin.

CRACK-CROCK.

Lena's spine broke at the base. Her waist threaded between her legs. Above her hips, her head folded onto itself once again over her chest.

The sound of her shattering bones was louder than her grunt for help. Her entire body folded upon itself. With each shunt and crack, the bones in her body daggered out through her skin. Pangs of blood splashes against the brickwork.

The brickwork applied the finishing move; the back of Lena's head slammed between her heels. The walls heaved once again and allowed the balled-up girl to roll into its mouth.

The concourse rumbled once again and let out a sound resembling a burp. Lena's body disappeared into the pink neon.

The walls closed shut and zipped itself back up.

Narc closed his eyes and turned to face the exit, "This ain't happening, man."

He opened his eyelids and ran toward the exit. The police had got there first. They were waiting for him.

No turning back.

He'd seen two of his friends die. Risking arrest was a far better proposition than a painful death.

"Please, help me," Narc screamed as he ran toward the light.

Five policemen lined the exit, urging him to come toward them, "That's it, come over here. Nice and slow."

It was only after a few feet of running that Narc realised that the commuters had disappeared.

He picked up the pace as he ran toward the policemen at the exit. It *still* wasn't getting any closer.

"Help me," he cried, flipping down the back of his hood. The perspiration dripped from his forehead. His jacket and jeans soaked through to the bone.

Narc continued running and looked left, then right. The walls seemed to be closing in the more he ran.

"Sir, please," One of the officers yelled, holding a pair of handcuffs.

Narc ran even faster, "I'm trying, man."

The walls closed in fast as Narc ran even faster. He closed his eyes and ran as if his life depended on it.

The rumbling occurred once again. Narc kept his speed up and felt a rubbing against his shoulders. He looked down at his right shoulder as he ran to find it scraping against the wall. The friction slowed his journey down.

Narc pushed forward further.

His left shoulder scraped against the other wall. If he ran further, he'd get lodged between the walls to the point where he wouldn't be able to move at all.

He slowed his sprint down and stopped running. Sure enough, he was completely stuck between the two walls.

The white light from the exit seemed to laugh at him. The police officers giggled amongst themselves.

"Okay, sir. That'll do."

"What?" Narc screamed in terror. He pushed forward with his arms straight against his sides, "No. No. Wait for me."

"That's okay, sir," one of the officers said from the white light. His colleagues dispersed and climbed back into their vehicles, "We have everything we need. You're free to go."

Narc shook his head and heaved himself forward a few feet. The walls scraped against the sides of his face.

"What the *fuck*, man? Don't leave me h-here."

The policeman shook his head in jest and climbed into his car.

"Nuuuuuh!" Narc screamed as he pushed forward even more. The sides of his face caved in as the walls tightened.

SK-LOTCH!

The further he moved, the tighter the escape. His cheekbones punched into his face. He wedged himself even further forward.

"Gahhh," He pushed his head forward in a desperate bid to make it to the exit.

SPLATCH!

It was too much. He wedged his face so far forward that the sides of his skull shattered and pushed into his head. His left eyeball inflated out of its socket and burst.

"Wait for me. *Please*."

SCHTLUNT!

The right side of his skull burst out through the skin, dislocating his jaw. His tongue hung down across his neck.

"Gnnnwaaaiiisshh."

Narc puked down his front and threw his body forward. The walls wouldn't let his body closer to the exit, but they allowed for it to move toward its doom.

Narc's right shoulder slid out of its socket and pressed into the side of his torso. He slid the broken fingers on his left hand along the wall. His elbow snapped in two and swung down to his crotch.

"Gllisshhbbb."

Still, he kept moving forward. His tongue slapped to the floor in time for his right foot to tread on it. Then, his left foot moved in front, crunching his thighs together.

"Gnnnwaaarr."

Narc's skull crunched against itself, killing him. His body slumped, held up by the walls.

His knees hung five inches from the floor. His body twisted and broken in a complicated mush of brick, skin, flesh, and twisted bone.

A dead statue.

***

A steady beeping noise came from a life support machine.

Narc's eyelids fluttered.

"He's moving," Dr Long's voice came from the room.

The darkness let in a flood of white light. An immediate headache shot through his brain. The beeps didn't help. One beep every two seconds, like a prize fighter punching him in the head.

He looked down the length of his front.

The sheets of the bed tugged over his body. His feet had plastic slippers on them.

"We didn't think you'd come round this soon, Nicholas," Dr Long smiled.

"Wh-what?" Narc tried to rub his face, but the sheet kept his arms down. "Where am I?"

"Chrome Junction General Hospital," Dr Long smiled and looked at her clipboard. "You were out for a few days."

"Wh-what h-happened?" He hulked his body around, but couldn't do much with it. "Where's L-Lena?"

"I'm afraid Charlie didn't make it, Nicholas."

"Huh?" Narc looked up at Dr Long and tried to make a go for her but his arms were immobilized. He started to freak out. "Who's Charlie?"

"And there we were thinking your brain couldn't operate alone."

Narc shook his head and screamed, "Why can't I m-move?"

"It's for your own safety, I'm afraid," Dr Long explained. "You experienced quite the concussion. Three lacerations. You've managed to break most of the bones in your body. You're lucky to be alive."

"Huh?" Narc looked back down at his feet and wiggles his toes. "But—"

"—You have a couple of visitors, Nicholas. They'd like to talk to you."

The life support machine beeps sped up. The green line jumped about, "Wh-who?"

"You can come in now," Dr Long threw her red hair back over her shoulders and winked at Narc, "They want to ask you a few questions. I'll be back shortly."

The two policemen moved in and took a seat either side of the bed, "I'm Detective Inspector Cohen. This is my colleague DC Moriarty."

Cohen took out a notepad and pen, "How are you feeling, Nicholas?"

"Uhm," Narc looked down and shifted once again, "They're telling me I broke some bones and hurt myself."

"Yes, that's right," Moriarty offered and slapped him on the shoulder.

"Owww."

"Ha. Looks like you're in perfectly good shape to me," Cohen said at his notes.

"Yeah, not bad for a dude in a coma," DC Moriarty offered.

"Coma?"

DI Cohen coughed into his hand and clicked his pen,. "Now, tell us about you and your friends at Chrome Junction Station."

"Wh-what?"

"Please, sir. It's in your interest to let us know what you

remember."

"Ummm. We were just hanging out, minding our own business—"

"—Right, but this was a school day," Cohen interrupted, "Why weren't you at school?"

The heart beats quickened on the machine. Narc swallowed, nervously.

"Oh. We finished what we were meant to be doing," Narc struggled, trying to think of an excuse.

"Playing truant from school were you?" Moriarty thumped him on the chest and chuckled, "Decided to play *Push* at the station, right?"

"No," Narc quipped, starting to fear for his life, "We wasn't doin' that."

"Bullshit," Moriarty spat at his face, "You were playing *Push*. Barging innocent people down the stairs for your sick game."

Beep-beep-beep.

"No, no, we didn't—"

"—Moriarty, please," Cohen smiled, "let the boy explain himself. Sorry, Nicholas, you were saying?"

"We was just hanging out."

"*We*?"

"Yeah. Me and my girlfriend and my other friend."

"What are their names?"

"Lena and Tompan."

"Oh yes," Cohen flipped the paper on his notepad, "Tompan Chi and Charlie Ferrari. They were both found dead when the emergency services came."

"Who the fuck is Charlie Ferrari?" Narc spat.

"Sorry, I meant Lena Royal."

"Lena? Dead?"

"Yes," Moriarty scowled. "Your girlfriend had broken every bone in her body. Your mate snapped his leg and bled out. He didn't make it."

Narc could feel his heart thump against his ribcage.

"I should tell you that we retrieved your phone. We

found some interesting evidence," Cohen produced Narc's smart phone and showed him the screen.

He pressed play.

Scores of people tumbled down the stairwell, crashing and slamming against one another, "I take it you filmed this? It's your voice laughing on the camera."

"No, man, but—"

"—Do you know how many people's lives you ruined? For the sake of this sick game?"

"No, no, no, it wasn't me—"

"—Shut up, you feral fucking *snake*. This is *your* fault," Cohen slammed the notepad onto Narc's waist.

"Ooofggh," he screamed. The machine beeped six times per second.

Cohen stood up and looked at Moriarty, "I think we have all we need, don't you?"

"I think so," Moriarty rose out of the chair. Both officers looked down at Narc and smiled, "You just concentrate on getting better, okay?"

"Wh-what?" Narc gasped. He shifted his body around, trying to free himself.

"Okay, Doctor Long, we're done here," Cohen said as he joined his colleague at the door.

Dr Long came back in and stopped to talk to them. She whispered something to them and looked at Narc.

"No. No," He screamed, lifting his arms under the taut bed sheets. "Please, no. They're keeping me prisoner in here. Help."

The life support machine beeped faster and faster.

Dr Long smiled at the officers as they left the room. She turned around and walked over to Narc, "Seems you've been a bad boy, haven't you? Involving yourself in that silly *Push* craze?"

"No, I didn't—"

"—Look at me."

Narc looked confused. His chest vibrated and rattled from within the bed. His breathing quickened. The beeps from the machine ran quicker. It was almost flat lining.

" C-can't b-breathe—"

"—Look at me, sweetheart," she repeated and kept her eyes focused on his, "Look at me."

Narc puffed and panted. Beads of sweat formed across his brow and ran down his cheeks, "Please, doctor, h-help me."

"Look at me."

Narc looked at her dead in the eyes. Dr Long's eyeballs, cheeks and nose filled his entire field of vision.

"Look at me, Nicholas."

"Whu-whu," The longer he kept staring, the blacker and deeper her pupils became.

"Look at me."

"Nuh, nuh," Narc panted, his heart dancing a merry jig around his chest, "I think I'mma having a heart atta—"

The beeping stopped.

His breathing ground to a halt.

The life support machine. Beeeeeeeep.

"Nicholas," Dr Long lifted her index finger to her lips very slowly. "Welcome to *Pure Dark*."

SCHPLATT!!

Narc's heart exploded through the bed sheets, splattering Dr Long's face with congealed globs of blood.

She kept staring at him and began laughing.

The back of Narc's head hit the pillow. His lifeless face stared up at the ceiling. A pool of blood had splashed against it.

Dr Long sighed and tilted her head at him, "What a waste."

She gripped the edge of the bed sheet and moved it up and over his face.

Her long, red hair swung around her face as she shook her head. She grabbed a fistful of hair and yanked it up and over, tearing her scalp and the skin of her face down the back of her head.

FLUMP.

The convincing red-haired mask hit the floor beside her shoe. She walked toward the door and exited the room.

Chapter 5

Fine Dining:

La Mort Magnifique

"Welcome to *La Mort Magnifique*. Do you have a reservation?" The head waiter asked. His immaculate evening suit was imposing, confirming how high-class the establishment was.

"Yes, a table for two at eight," Zeeba extended her arm and inspected her gold wristwatch. The material of her sleeve ran up her elbow, revealing a tattoo of a cobra on her forearm. "She should be here any moment, now."

"Very good, madam," he said with a smile and turned toward the restaurant, "If you'd like to take a seat, now? We'll make sure your table is ready."

"That's great. Thank you."

Zeeba took a seat on the plush ten-seater couch and took out her mobile phone. She set her bag to the side of her left leg. Soft jazz music played through the speakers.

A text message from her sister read: "So sorry, babe. Running a bit late. Love you, P x."

The head waiter returned and clasped his hands together. He grinned and waited for Zeeba to acknowledge his presence, "Madam, your table is ready."

"Ah, very good." She stood up and grabbed her bag,

"I'll get a drink in first, perhaps."

"Excellent, madam."

The head waiter ushered Zeeba into the restaurant.

"Wow, this is very nice," Zeeba muttered under her breath. She clocked the magnificence of the restaurant. The interior decoration was unique but bizarre. A chandelier hung above the table of the vast space. A door to the kitchen loomed to the left. The velvet-covered floor produced a satisfying dig-in for each footstep. The outline of where you had stepped would puff back up and out a few seconds later.

It wasn't busy at all. There was a reason for this - the restaurant only had one table. Two chairs faced each other from the opposite ends.

"This way, madam," announced the head waiter. He bent his left arm and indicated the chair.

"Thank you," Zeeba made herself comfortable.

"Would madam care for an aperitif to begin?"

"Oh, yes," Zeeba took the wine list from his hand, "I'll have a bottle of *L'Ambrosia 1955*, please."

She closed the drinks menu and handed it back to him.

"An excellent choice, madam." He noticed that Zeeba had thrown a cigarette between her lips, "Ah, allow me."

With great expediency, he produced a lighter and struck the flint. The flame shot up and burnt the crisp tobacco at the end of her cigarette.

"Thank you," she said, taking in a lungful of smoke. Her head turned to another waiter who walked up behind his colleague and smiled.

"This is Gloria, your waiter for this evening," announced the head waiter.

"Gloria?"

"Yes," he said in his thick French accent and courtesied.

"Unusual name for a *bloke*, isn't it?" She blew out some smoke and leaned back in her chair.

The head waiter disappeared through the door to the kitchen.

Gloria handed her an iPad, "Madam. Today's menu."

"Ah, great," Zeeba took the iPad from him and perused the screen. She raised her eyebrows at Gloria, indicating that she wanted to be alone.

It took a while for him to cotton on, "Aha, très bon. I will leave you to peruse the menu, madam."

"Thank you, Gloria."

He made his way back to the kitchen as Zeeba scrolled through the lengthy menu from top to bottom.

"For God's sake," came a hurried voice from the door to the restaurant. Zeeba looked over to see her sister walk toward her in a mild hurry, "I'm so sorry I'm late, sweetie."

She reached Zeeba and pecked her on the forehead, "How are you, honey?"

"Yes, I'm fine," Zeeba held her sister's waist and nodded over at the free chair. "It's okay, take a seat. They've given me the menu."

"Okay, great."

Zeeba's sister, the beautiful Proxy, took her seat. She sported a silver suit and some exceptional bling. Two gold necklaces, a flowery brooch, and a 24-carat gold ring with a cobra engraved on it.

Proxy made herself comfortable as Gloria made his way back to the table, "Ah, the other party has arrived. Please, allow me."

He handed Proxy an iPad and waited as they scanned the menu.

Zeeba looked up and blew out a plume of smoke into his face, "Could you leave us for a moment, please?"

"Certainly, madam," He said and made his way back to the kitchen.

Zeeba flicked a nugget of ash into the ashtray. She smiled at her sister as she scanned the menu.

"God, it all looks so delicious."

"How have you been, sweetie?" Zeeba asked, crossing

her left leg over the right.

"Oh, you know, not so bad," Proxy looked up from the menu, "I heard this place is just divine."

"Yes, I've heard that, too," Zeeba smiled. "I booked this ten months ago."

"Yes, it's a shame we couldn't have met up more often," Proxy sighed and returned to the menu, "How long, now?"

"They said I had two weeks left ten months ago. I didn't think we'd ever honour the booking to be perfectly honest with you."

"Yes, well," Proxy eyed the cigarette, "It's not as if it wasn't your own fault."

"Yeah, I know," Zeeba huffed. "So, what are you thinking?"

Proxy settled on an item on the menu, "I think I'll go with the prawns from Gairloch, oyster and celeriac. How about you?"

Gloria was hiding behind the door and eavesdropping on their conversation. No sooner had Proxy suggested her dish had he made his way back to their table. He set Zeeba's glass on the table and proceeded to pour her drink with extreme efficiency.

"Prawns Gailoch. A superb choice, madam," he turned to Zeeba, "And for yourself?"

Zeeba tilted the iPad toward her chest, "Flamed mackerel, almond, beetroot. For the main, I'll have the Belt Galloway beef curtain and artichoke, thank you."

"Very good, madam."

Zeeba squinted her eyes at him, "The curtain of beef is underdone, correct?"

"Oh, yes, madam. Most certainly."

"Good," Zeeba looked at her sister. "What you having for mains, sweetie?"

Proxy traced her finger down the screen, "What do you recommend, waiter?"

"Gloria, madam."

"Gloria?" Proxy looked puzzled. "What's that? Is it chicken?"

"No, madam, it's *me*."

"Why would I want to eat *you*?"

"No, no," Gloria blinked and backtracked, "It's my name."

"Is it?"

"Yes, madam," Gloria smiled and pointed at the iPad, "I personally recommend the roasted monkfish."

"Is it good?"

"It is magnificent, madam. Garnished with courgette and lemon balm. A most satisfying delicacy."

"Okay, I'll have that, then," Proxy handed the iPad back to him, "And get us a glass of house red while you're on."

"Certainly, madam."

He walked off through the door to the kitchen. Zeeba swished a mouthful of *L'Ambrosia 1955* around her mouth and gulped it down, "Whoa, that is magnificent. Pricey, too."

"Yes, I noticed that they don't include the prices in the menu. It must be expensive."

Zeeba sniffed the rim of her glass, "How's Dad? I've not managed to see him lately."

"Oh, you know, he's doing fine," Proxy tailed off, finally clocking some of the decorations lining the wall, "What are those?"

Zeeba turned around and looked at the wall behind her.

A bank of seven-foot tall glass enclosures containing real-life mannequins looked back at them.

"Not sure. Maybe some classy French art or something?"

"Hmmm," Proxy picked up a brilliant white spoon from the table. She knocked it to the cloth on top, splintering the ivory, "The cutlery needs a bit of an overhaul."

"Yeah," Zeeba huffed. "So, has Dad mentioned me when you've spoken to him?"

"Why do you ask?"

"No reason. Just curious."

"Look, Zeeba, I thought all *that* was behind the two of you?"

Gloria made his way over to the table with the entrees and Proxy's bottle of house red. Zeeba leaned forward and hushed at her sister, "I don't think his molesting me is ever behind—"

"—Here you are, madam," Gloria announced. He set the glass down and poured the wine, "Cobra Rouge, with a delicate touch of elderberry. I am quite sure you will love it."

"Thank you."

"Your starter, madam," He slid the plate of mackerel, almond and beetroot in front of Zeeba. She smiled and picked up her fork.

The finger-shaped mackerel was pristine. The garnish surrounding it completed the perfect presentation.

"And your prawns Gairloch, madam," Gloria slid a plate full of fish in front of Proxy. The curled, pink flesh sizzled on the plate.

"Thank you."

"My pleasure," he smiled and moved back to the kitchen.

Zeeba licked her lips at her food. She held up her glass and offered a toast, "Here's to a fine dinner with the world's best sibling."

Proxy smiled and clinked her glass against her sister's. "Amen to that."

They both took a mouthful of their drink and swallowed. "Ahh," The swishing liquid coated their gums, palate, and teeth. A final gulp sealed the deal.

Zeeba shook her head, "Whoa, that's fantastic."

"Mmm," Proxy cleared her throat and squinted at the bottle of Cobra Rouge, "Tastes a bit like zinc, but it's got a fruity finish."

"Shall I start?" Zeeba enquired, pressing her middle and forefinger together.

"Please."

Zeeba slid her two fingers into her mouth as Proxy smiled and watched, "Further, further…"

"Gike Gis?" Zeeba pushed her fingertips to her esophagus and into her neck.

"Yeah, that's it. That's it," Proxy moaned as she speared a prawn with her fork.

CLUCK. Zeeba gasped and forced her fingers even further down her neck.

"Nearly got it, honey."

GLARK. Zeeba hulked her chest forward. Her throat buckled even louder. The muscles in her neck contorted and forced her eyeballs to bulge out of their sockets.

Proxy clapped her hands together with giddy excitement, "There you go, you got it."

BLLOOOAAARRRGGGHHHHH!

A thick stream of beige puke splattered up Zeeba's plate of mackerel. A couple of them bounced off the plate.

She rammed her fingers down her throat even further; forcing her fist into her mouth. Her lips wrapped around the fleshy ball.

"One more?" Proxy threw a prawn into her mouth and chewed away to the tune of her sister's emetic behavior, "Go for it."

Zeeba's throat muscles contorted once again. She threw her fist out of her mouth.

BLOOOOOOARRRRR, SPLAAAT-TCH!

Another elongated fountain of puke blasted most of the contents from Zeeba's plate. She sat back in her chair and heaved, wiping her lips.

"Good job, sweetie," Proxy winked at her and took another sip of her house red.

Zeeba leaned forward and adjusted her collar. She picked up her fork, stabbed a puke-covered mackerel piece and flung it into her mouth.

"Mmmm," she chewed, "This is wonderful."

"I'm pleased you like it, madam," Gloria had returned. He looked at the vomit-covered starter and turned to Proxy, "Madam?"

"Yeah, garcon. This is lush," she said with a mouthful of prawn, "How's it cooked?"

"Aha. Chef's masterpiece. Each prawn digests through an infant's stomach. It is then refrigerated for twenty-four hours before serving."

"Mmm, it's delicious."

"May I refill your glass?"

"Sure," Proxy held it up for him, "Go for it."

Gloria picked up the bottle of Cobra Rouge and knocked the bottle neck against the edge of the table. The top broke off, revealing an array of tiny glass daggers, "Your wrist, madam?"

"Oh, yes. I'm sorry," Proxy apologized and offered him her wrist. He took it in his hand, turned the underside toward the ceiling, and stabbed her with the sharp crack of the bottle.

A splat of blood puked up against his shirt. Gloria scored a long wound up from her wrist to the crease of her elbow. The deep cut bled profusely down the length of her arm.

"My, you're wonderful at this," Proxy said, astounded.

"Thank you, Madam," Gloria smiled, admiring his work, "Always *up the lane* and never *across the road*. It's where everyone goes wrong."

He held her wrist over the glass and gave her a vicious Chinese burn. The steady flow of blood from her wrist poured into the glass.

Proxy smiled at him, "Do you serve *Baby Champagne* here, Gloria?"

"Ah, no," he apologized. "I'm afraid it is very elitist and almost impossible to get. May I ask, madam, if you have ever tried the second red?"

"The second red?"

"Yes," Gloria said, squeezing her forearm and filling the glass to the top with her own brand of claret.

"Perhaps with your main meal?"

"Sure, I'm game."

"Very good," Gloria offered Proxy her glass of "new house red."

She held the rim of the glass to her nose and sniffed, "Mmm, good body."

"Well, quite."

She took a sip. The blood smeared over her top lip, "Yes, that's very good."

"Would madam like a bandage for the wound?"

"God, no," Proxy protested, admiring her long forearm slit. She held it up for Zeeba and smiled, "It's wonderful."

"Enjoy your entrees," he moved back to the kitchen with the broken bottle in his hand.

Zeeba scooped up the bilious gore from her plate with the side of her hand. The underside of her little finger collected up the sludgy contents of her stomach. She released her tongue and slurped her fist. The last batch of vomit-soaked sludge sunk into her mouth.

"Mmm, delicious," Zeeba swallowed and patted her mouth with a napkin.

Proxy necked the contents of her wine glass in one go. She slammed it to the table and burped. Tiny fragments of blood sprayed in Zeeba's direction.

"Hmmm. Tastes a bit like zinc."

"How are the prawns Gairloch, Proxy?"

"Yeah, they're okay," she prodded one of them around with her finger, "They're not the same as *you*, though."

Zeeba stood to her feet and placed her palm at the edge of the table, somewhat put-out, "You want me to help?"

Proxy deliberated Zeeba's offer as she looked at her half-eaten starter, "Umm. Okay, yes."

Zeeba nodded and made her way around the table. She

cupped her sister's head in her hands and smiled down at her.

"Let's get you fed."

Proxy looked up and smiled. The congealed blood from her wrist blotched right across her otherwise pristine teeth.

"Open up, sweetie," Zeeba introducing two fingers into her wide-open mouth.

Proxy's jaw yawned open. She eyeballed her sister, expectantly.

"Tongue out."

Proxy slid the tip of her tongue down to her chin, her mouth opened as wide as possible.

"I don't know how much I have left. This is all going to get regurgitated, I'm sure."

Zeeba jiggled two fingers down the back of her throat.

BLLOAARRGGHHH!

Zeeba projectile vomited the contents of her stomach into her sister's open mouth and down her neck. Proxy kept her eyes open. Chunks of twice-recycled mackerel seeped into her eyes and face. Most of it shot down her throat. She didn't even flinch.

Zeeba clamped her sister's mouth shut, "Swallow, honey, swallow."

GLOMPFH! Proxy swallowed it down.

SMACK! Zeeba's hand struck her little sister as a reward, forcing her to swallow the last of the puke.

"Good girl," Zeeba smiled and returned to her seat.

Proxy blinked hard and munched on her sister's freshly-delivered puke, "My God, that was filling," She let out a humongous burp. Flecks of spew and spittle flew across the table.

Zeeba returned to her seat and started another cigarette, "If you see Dad, tell him I've hired someone."

"Oh yeah?" Proxy mopped her face. She held the gaping wound from her arm and topped up her glass with blood, "You finally hired someone?"

"Yes, I did," She blew out some smoke and clutched at her waist, "Cost me a fortune, so he'd better do a quick and clean job of it."

"Who did you hire?"

Gloria returned and made for the empty dish, "I trust everything is to your satisfaction, ladies?"

"Everything but the interruption," Zeeba snarled at him.

"Ah, yes. Of course," Gloria said, picking up the plates and refilling Proxy's glass, "Your main courses will be here momentarily."

Proxy wolf-whistled at Gloria as he walked back to the kitchen, "Oi, Gloria!"

He turned around, balancing the plates in his left arm, "Yes, madam?"

"Show me your cock."

"I beg madam's pardon?"

"I said show me your cock."

Gloria squinted his eyes and made out like he'd misheard her request. Ever the polite servant for the two sisters, "My cock?"

"Cock au-fuckin' van, mate."

"Very well."

He reached into his zipper and wrestled around. Finally, he took out his penis. All twenty-five inches of it unraveled like a hosepipe and slapped to the floor.

Proxy's eyes widened. She held her freshly-slit forearm over her mouth in surprise. Zeeba was less interested and took a puff from her cigarette.

"My God, that's so small."

"I know, madam."

"Gloria, do me a favour?" Proxy asked, fluttering her eyelashes.

"Madam?"

"I ordered the Monkfish, didn't I?"

"Roasted Monkfish, yes?"

"Can you *cum* on it for me, please?"

"Certainly, madam," Gloria ravelled his lengthy, soft penis onto itself. He tucked it back into his zipper. "Would madam prefer heterosexual or homosexual porn for the ejaculate?"

"Is there a difference?"

"Well, yes, madam. If I masturbate to homosexual porn, the texture of the ejaculate is thicker. A softer finish and extra layer of skin."

"Can you do me a bestiality porn load?"

"Certainly."

"Magic," Proxy turned to her sister, who blew out her cigarette smoke and wrestled something around her ankles.

Gloria walked back into the kitchen.

"Going for the international condiments today, then?"

"Beast porn cum is more filling," Proxy licked her lips as Zeeba leaned back into her chair, "I hope it's some African guy with an otter. Or maybe a rabbit."

"I don't know why you have to show us up in polite society, asking for come like that. You could have started small with midget loads," Zeeba held her pantie lining out through her thumb.

"Oh, you've started already?"

"Yes. I figure it's that time of the month. May as well make the most of it."

"Haven't the drugs stopped all that?"

"No, the lesions are getting worse," Zeeba spat, "They're all over my body, now."

The kitchen doors burst open, catching the girls' attention. Gloria pushed a huge silver trolley toward them.

"Your mains, ladies."

"Magic," Proxy beamed and rubbed her hands together. The blood from her wound fountained down to her elbow and over the edge of the table.

Two giant, covered silver dishes lay atop the trolley. He opened the lid of the left one. A huge slab of sizzling, blackened meat fumed atop the plate. He turned to Proxy and smiled.

"Your Roasted Monkfish, madam," He lifted the plate up and set it in front of her, "And for garnish?"

"Oh, that's okay," Zeeba stood to her feet and hitched up her skirt. She showed off her spotless, fleshy vagina, "We've brought our own."

"Very good, madam," Gloria moved the lid from the second silver dish, "And your Belted Galloway beef."

"Yeah," Zeeba perched her left foot on the table. Her vagina lips splayed out as her legs right-angled over the table, "Can you pass me the funnel, please?"

"Very good, madam," Gloria placed Zeeba's beef between her cutlery. He reached underneath the trolley and produced a ten-foot tube with a wide funnel mouth at the end, "At your service."

"Very nice, Gloria," Zeeba slid two fingers into her vagina and yanked out a blood-covered mouse. Its tail flapped around, sending specs of period detritus up her face, "Could you?"

"Certainly, madam. A wise choice," Gloria took the dead mouse and broke its neck. He poured the blood from its neck into Proxy's glass.

Zeeba placed the rim out the plastic funnel around her vagina lips. She took a deep breath and tightened her stomach muscles. Proxy took the other, small end of the funnel and aimed it over her roasted monkfish.

"Hang on, hang on," Zeeba squeezed in pain, "Almost got it."

BLOICK!

A slew of embryotic fluid and blood flushed down the tube and blurted out over Proxy's meal. The track marks from the funnel cut around Zeeba's groin as she fucked her hips forward. A final thrust farted out the gunky remains of her uterus. The gelatinous red sludge slopped its way down the plastic tube, "Oh my, I think we had one, there!"

Gloria smiled and held out his hand to Proxy, "Would you like me to carve?"

"Yes, please," Proxy marveled at her sister's dead embryo. It simmered between her monkfish and courgettes. The squelching of coagulated blood seeped through her fingers. She slurped the smelly jelly from her thumb, "How long ago was this cooked?"

"Just now," Gloria revealed, taking out an enormous carving knife. He stepped forward and clutched her thigh, "I'm sorry, madam. Could I ask you to lift your leg, please?"

"Sure," Proxy said with a mouthful of miscarriage-soaked fish.

Zeeba cut into her beef, which busted out like battered bathroom pipe, "You unloaded on the wrong dish, waiter," She stabbed the inch-wide piece of meat with her fork and held it up to her nose, "Yeah, this definitely smells like cum."

"I'm most sorry, madam," Gloria yanked Proxy's panties down past her knees. "I think chef may have got the garnish the wrong way around. I will fix it presently."

Zeeba threw the beef into her mouth and chewed. She watched Gloria toss her sister's lace panties aside and aligned the sharp end of the knife across her thigh.

"Be gentle," Proxy flirted and bit her finger.

Gloria sawed through the skin and flesh. Red and yellow liquid flew everywhere as he macheted through to the bone.

"Ooooh."

Proxy slung her thigh over his shoulder and continued to saw. He burrowed through the bone, snapping it in two and sliced away at the remaining veins and flesh. "Nearly there, madam."

Proxy moaned and threaded her fingers across her vagina, pulling her lips apart, "Oh, Gloria. You're so good at this."

"Thank you, madam," he pinged the last thread of skin apart and took her leg in his hands, "There, we've managed to—"

SPRRRIIISSHH!

A lengthy blast of urine hit him in the face. Proxy and Zeeba cackled as she kept on pissing.

Gloria stood up and flicked away the orangey-brown droplets of urine, "Very good, madam."

"Hey, garcon," Zeeba said with a mouthful of beef, "This actually doesn't taste too bad."

"Now, give me my fucking cum," Proxy winked and went for his zipper.

He stood back and covered himself with his hands, "No, please, allow me."

He took an iPad from out from the trolley and laid it on top the dining table, "Please, you may continue."

Proxy slid a finger into herself and watched Gloria swipe the screen.

Neither of the girls could see the screen but could hear everything that came from the speakers.

"Fucking shut up, you little cunt," screamed a man's voice. Gloria unzipped and pulled out his gargantuan penis. He slapped it across the width of the table. The tip of his cock hung over the far end and faced the carpet.

Zeeba reached down and picked up her sister's severed leg.

"Enjoy, sis," Proxy smiled.

"You fucking cat *fuck*," shouted a deep male voice from the iPad, "Take it all."

Gloria took the first ten inches of his enormous slab of penis and began to masturbate himself.

"When are you next due to see Dad, sweetie?" Zeeba asked as she sank her teeth into the flesh of her sister's ex-thigh.

"Oh, he's set up his new business," Proxy revealed. She took a long slurp from the gory slab of fish at the end of her fork, "So he's busy with that, right now."

"I guess that'll make his shareholders happy—"

"—You feline fucking twat!" screamed the man's voice from the iPad.

MYAH! MYAH! MYAH!!! The unwieldy screech of someone buggering a cat came from the iPad.

"—Yeah, he recently got it onto the stock exchange, so he's coining it in."

The relentless soundtrack of cat-rape wouldn't stop. The first thirteen inches of Gloria's penis rumbled and stiffened. He doubled over himself and tried to masturbate the softer, further parts.

"Raaoooww," the cat screamed in agony. The breathless panting of the heavy man in the video screamed back, "Take this dick, you fluffy motherfuck—"

"—So, it's a shame you've hired someone to *take care* of him," Proxy lifted her only foot and placed her sole on the tabletop. She used her hands at the edge to balance herself, "He's doing very well, you know."

"Well, I could always stop the hit." Zeeba licked off some semen-drizzle from one of her sea greens, "If it means his business is making more money. We are the beneficiaries, after—"

MIIAAAOOOOOWWWW! Glup, glup, glup.

"Shut up," the man followed by a punch to the cat's stomach. It snarled as the thudding of the love-making continued.

"—Yes," Proxy continued, pinching her clitoris between her thumb and forefinger nails. She pulled the string of flesh away from the mouth of her vagina. As she yanked it out to full capacity, she fired a splat of diarrhea down the back of her thigh, "Give it until October and it should—"

SPROIINNGGG! Gloria's twenty-five-inch cock sprang into the air, lifting with the contents of the table with it. The cutlery flew off the table, taking the ashtray with it, spilling the ash onto the girl's food. The glass of wine splashed to the carpet. The tip of his penis grazed across the ceiling.

"Stand back," Gloria stepped back and aimed his huge cock slit at Zeeba's plate.

"Fuck's sake. About time," she complained, leaning back into her chair.

The man in the video growled his last and came. "Take this you funky feline prick. Arrgghhh."

Gloria yanked the foreskin back on his elongated penis.

SCCHHHPLLAATTTTCCHHH!!

A rope of thick white cream globbed out over Zeeba's plate, coating it in a rich, creamy white Bernaise sauce.

Zeeba lifted Gloria's thick baguette cock with her right hand. Her left hand slid the plate out from underneath. She opened her mouth and tipped the entire meal down her neck.

Guzzle-guzzle-guzzle. A streak of white cream splattered across her cheeks.

Gloria grabbed the cleaver and sawed at the base of his penis. The knife edge chomped through his flesh and veins. Blood and semen flew in all directions.

"Aagghh."

Proxy sat herself down. She'd cut off the bleeding from her leg wound by tying her clit in a double knot around the chasm of flesh.

The muscles inside Gloria's penis-beast contracted and simmered down. The flesh hose slinked off the edge of the table, taking the iPad with it.

Everyone took a deep breath.

Gloria tucked himself back into his trousers and pressed his palms together.

"Will there be anything else?"

"No. Thank you," Zeeba burped a thick, chewy batch of semen into her napkin.

"Very well," Gloria took out two steak knives in each hand, "In that case, I'll fetch the bill for you."

"Thanks, Gloria," Long gloops of cat semen saliva roped from Proxy's bottom lip. She placed the side of her cheek on the table and closed her eyes.

"Thank you for dining at *La Mort Magnifique*."

He pinched the sharp end of one steak knife and

hurled it at Proxy.

STCHUNT!! The knife slammed into the side of her head, blowing her brains out across the table cloth.

"And, madam?"

Zeeba looked over and smiled, "Yes?"

He flung the last knife at her with all his might.

THWUMP-SCHPLATT! The knife shunted between Zeeba's eyes, killing her instantly.

FLUMP. Zeeba's head hit the tabletop.

Two dead sisters, covered in puke, piss, blood, period effluence, semen, and shit.

Gloria hit a button on the iPad.

A giant circle formed around the table. The sisters' bodies slumped in their chairs. The girls were dead.

The hole opened up to reveal an endless chasm, below. The dinner table and chairs suspended by metallic poles.

The seats vibrated and flung back, tossing the girls' corpses into the pit.

The hole closed back up.

***

"Welcome to *La Mort Magnifique*, do you have a reservation?" the head waiter asked.

A young, rich couple smiled back at him.

"Yes. A table for two at nine," said the smartly-dressed man.

"Very good, sir," the head waiter turned toward the restaurant, "If you'd like to take a seat, we'll make sure your table is ready."

"Thank you," the man said, giddy with anticipation. He smiled at his female companion.

The young couple sat at the lone dining table that Zeeba and Proxy had frequented not ten minutes before.

They sat facing each other in the middle of the restaurant in deep conversation.

"I've heard it takes months to get a booking here," the woman said. "Apparently the raw Dexter beef is out of this world!"

"Yes, it's very difficult to get a table," the man said.

The doors to the kitchen burst open. Gloria pushed a giant silver trolley toward them, "Your mains, madam. Sir."

He removed the lid of the first plate.

"Beef, pumpkin and kohlrabi."

"Yes, thank you."

Gloria placed the piping hot dish in front of her and turned back to the second dish, "And for you, sir…"

The lid came off, revealing what looked like a bloodied steak, "Medium rare, with turnip and chamomile?"

"Very good, thank you," The man leaned back and invited Gloria to place his meal in front of him.

"Will sir or madam be requiring anything else?"

"Not for the moment, no," the woman said, looking at her glass of wine, "Although, I could use a refill."

"Certainly, madam." Gloria turned around and made his way back to the kitchen.

The man turned to his companion and smiled, "This looks delicious."

He scraped away some of the sauce and raised his eyebrows, "What's this?" he asked, puzzled, as the woman took a mouthful of her meal.

The sharp end of the knife scraped the garnish off the skin, revealing a inking of a cobra. "Huh? This steak has a tattoo."

CLUNK. The woman stopped chewing her mouthful of beef. She reached into mouth, "Ngg, what's this?"

She picked out an especially tough bit of meat, only to discover that it wasn't animal flesh. It was a 24-carat gold ring with an engraving of a cobra, "Oh my!"

"They really do spoil you here, don't they?" She set it down to the side of her plate and continued eating her meal.

"I guess that's why they've never had a bad review?"

The man asked and took a sip of his red wine. He winced and finally swallowed. "Whoo."

"Is everything okay, honey?"

"Yeurgh," he gasped and set the glass on the table, "This wine tastes of zinc.".'

Chapter 6

Assault on Mesi Orji

The purple lipstick twisted out of the holder. It stood proud and unused. The tip tilted to the side and hit a dark wrinkle on a lip.

The stick ran along the random bumps on the slight curvature and reached the corner of a mouth.

Along the top lip it ran - to the right and back to the left. The lips closed together and puckered out.

Mesi looked at herself in the mirror. Dressed in jeans and a white blouse, she looked the part for tonight's adventure.

A silver balloon tied to the mirror bounced around. The draught came in through the bedroom window.

"Happy 18th Birthday!" was scrawled across it in bubbly red writing.

Pleased with her application, she hitched up her waist and inspected her behind.

She wasn't a tall girl. Standing at a mere five feet and two inches she wondered if she'd get into *Panzer Tank* without getting carded. It was one of London's premiere nightclubs and the place for her birthday celebrations.

Today was Mesi's first day as an adult.

She knew she wasn't the prettiest girl in town. Hell, she was likely not the most attractive girls on the suburban street she lived on. She didn't care, though.

Mesi smiled at herself and buffed up her not

inconsiderable cleavage.

Thud-thud-thud.

Mesi clomped her way down the stairs and reached the front landing. The jacket flew off the coat rail and slung around her shoulders.

Jelani, her father, perched himself against the living room door. A huge African gentleman standing six fet and eight inches. His muscles pressed through his shirt. Mesi meant the world to him, being his only daughter.

His pride and joy.

Jelani smiled and wiped his face, "Mesi, you know, I want you back by midnight. No later, you hear me?"

"Yes, father."

"Text me when you're leaving. If the cabs are all taken up, or you can't get an *Uber*, let me know and I'll pick you up."

"Okay, I will."

Mesi turned to the full-length mirror by the door and brushed her hair back.

A vision of beauty smiled back at her.

"No messing around tonight, okay? It is not safe out there."

"I know, Father," she said to herself in the mirror. Her unmistakable accent hailed from the African continent, as did her father's.

Mesi appreciated her father's concern but was more preoccupied with how she looked. She took out her phone and looked at the screen. "Please do not worry."

"Okay, well. Have fun."

"Love you," she pecked her father on the cheek.

He smiled and hugged her, "Love you, too."

Mesi typed a text message on her phone in the back of the cab, "We're here."

The cab rolled up outside a semi-detached house a few roads down from where Mesi lived. A white teenage girl ran up the driveway and climbed into the cab.

"Hey Mel," Mesi smiled and leaned over to hug her.

"Sorry I took so long," Mel snapped. She waved the driver to continue the journey, "Couldn't decide whether to go with the *The Brand* or *Cutprice Cobra* jeans."

Mesi looked down at Mel's tight-fitting jeans. She squinted and giggled, "Well, it looks like you are displaying a bit more than intended."

Mel looked down and kicked her legs open. She frowned and shook her head.

"Oh, man. You should've seen me when I was sitting down."

Mel was right - her jeans were tight. They advertised a part of Mel's anatomy that was better left unseen.

"Hey, you know, it is fine," Mesi chuckled, "Just cross your legs if we end up sitting down."

"Cross my legs?" Mel joked and folded her arms, "If I sneeze I'll get cut in three."

The *Panzer Tank* night club, North London. 9:10 pm.

The exterior of the rectangular building was heaving with people. A long line snaked up the side leading to two burly bouncers. They checked the entrants' tickets as they filtered in through the pink walkway.

Mesi and Mel stood in the line and filtered forward. A young man in a Ralph Lauren shirt made eyes at Mel.

"Hey, he's checking me out," Mel whispered to Mesi, "Look at him. He's got some front, right?"

Mel smiled back at the man and watched him nudge his friend in the ribs. His friend sported a cobra tattoo on the side of his neck. He pointed at Mel and winked.

"He is very attractive," Mesi offered.

It was typical that Mel caught all the attention. She was a stunning blonde. Leggy and slender. Mesi felt a bit left out. Not too many guys her age were checking her out.

The bouncers undressed the girls in their minds.

Panzer Tank had lost Levi Oxide, its primary owner, in

an assassination attempt. Earlier in the year two women attacked him in the VIP rooms. As a result, security on weekend evenings was particularly tight.

"Okay, you can go through," one of the bouncers winked at Mel. She giggled and waited for Mesi as the other bouncer checked her out.

"Hang on, darling. How old are you?"

"I'm eighteen," Mesi smiled and held out her hands, "Today's my birthday."

The bouncer wasn't convinced.

"No, really. She is," Mel offered, coming to her friend's defense, "It's her birthday today."

"Hmmm," The bouncer looked at Mesi's shoulders and then at her legs, "Okay. But next time I'll need to see identification."

"Okay, thank you."

Mel took Mesi's hand and walked her through the pink entrance.

"Happy birthday, by the way," the bouncer said after the pair.

"Thanks."

The club itself was loud. Its atmosphere was borderline toxic. The dance floor might have sent an epileptic into a foaming pit of despair.

Booths lined either side of the dance floor.

Mesi looked up and saw several windows overlooking the dance floor. "I've heard about the Lizard's Tongue, The VIP area."

"It's not for us, sweetie," Mel made her way to the bar, "Only hookers and slags go up there. Let's get a drink."

The girls managed to barge their way forward. The men far outnumbered the girls in this establishment. Many of them hung on the side rails watching the girls twerk themselves into early onset arthritis on the dance floor.

Mel handed Mesi her drink, "Happy birthday, sweetie."

"Thanks," she clinked her glass of champagne against

her friend's and took a gulp.

Twenty minutes later, the girls were dancing away in front of the elevated DJ deck.

"I hear it's a certain girlie's birthday today," said the DJ, changing the track to a hip hop beat, "Give it up one time to Mesi Orji."

"Woohoo," the dancers clapped and cheered.

Mesi felt completely nude in the spotlight as everyone sang happy birthday to her. Scores of eyeballs looked in her direction and chuckled.

The champagne was getting to her head.

She stepped backwards and into the path of a man. He nearly spilt his drink.

"Oh, my. I am so sorry," Mesi apologised at the Ralph Lauren shirt staring back at her. The pectorals behind the fabric twitched before her very eyes. She adverted her gaze upward and clocked a very handsome young man staring down at her, "Ah, no problem."

"I'm so, so sorry," she reached forward and tried to mop the stain away.

He grabbed her wrist and chuckled, "No, that's fine," The young man turned to Mel and smiled, "Gonna introduce me to your friend?"

Mesi turned around and gasped. Mel was smitten by this young man, "Oh, uh, yes. This is my friend, Mel."

"Hello, Me,!" he shouted over the music.

"Hey there," Mel took his hand. She winked at Mesi and yanked him toward her. It was love at first sight.

Mesi couldn't have been happier for her friend finding someone she liked. She watched Mel and her new partner dance together. The moves were suggestive.

Mesi turned around and spotted the young man's friend. A lanky white guy and not anywhere as good-looking as his friend. That damn cobra tattoo was still visible on his neck.

He smiled and shook Mesi's hand, "Hi, I'm Blake."

"I'm Mesi."

Blake chuckled and nodded over at his buddy dancing with Mel, "Seems they're gonna be occupied for the rest of the night, right?"

Mesi looked over and wiped her brow, "Yes, I think so."

Blake ran his hand over Mesi's shoulder. The action took her aback, but it didn't feel sexually suggestive or imposing. She giggled in her drunken stupor and looked up at him.

She burped, spitting some saliva down her front, "Oh, oh, my goodness."

"Whoa," Blake shouted over the music. He ran his hands across her chest, scooping up some of the spit, "Now I can see why they call you Messy."

"No, no," she said, running her hand over his wrist. His finger passed over her nipple.

She shuddered and swallowed, "Look, I'm not sure if—"

"—Nah, it's okay, Mesi," Blake wiped the drool off on his shirt and slung his arms around her neck, "Are you okay? How much have you had to drink?"

"I think, uh," Mesi thought aloud as she tried to keep her balance, "About one bottle of ch-champag—"

A squishy feeling licked over her lipstick as she closed her eyes. She fell forward, her breasts greeted by what felt like a washboard.

The music was intense. Each beat of the track stabbed her through the ear and flirted with her brain. The fleshy snake-like object ran across her teeth.

The only way to stop the intrusion was to push it back with her tongue. She did so, but caved in and massaged the fleshy intruder with her tongue.

Mesi and Blake kissed with tongues. She could feel finger tips trace around her waist, hitching up her blouse.

She wriggled her hips in time to the music and fell into her new man.

Mesi moved her lips away from his. She stared her new dance partner in the eyes.

Blake smiled and nodded over at his friend. Mel and her charming young dance partner were also kissing and feeling each other up.

He turned back to Mesi and smiled. She tried to suppress her need to belch.

The room began to spin around.

At first, she thought it was an optical effect to heighten the intensity of the music.

She knew in her heart of hearts that she was drunk.

Blake's tongue slid between her lips once again. She covered it with her own and pressed her mouth into his.

She could feel the rumbling of an engine under her thighs as she tongued-kissed her new friend.

Blake and Mesi were in the back of a cab, headed somewhere. She didn't know the destination.

Five fingers burrowed their way into her jeans and through the lining of her knickers. She thrust her hips forward and encouraged the fingers to probe around her thighs.

"Mmmm-mmmm," she moaned into his mouth and grabbed the sides of his face. She kissed harder, hoping it would force the fingers down further.

Blake licked her face and ran the fingers of his free hand through her jet black hair.

"You like this, sweetie?"

"Yes, yes," Mesi shuddered and kissed his neck.

Blake looked down and pushed his hand further into her jeans, "You like my fingering you like this, you little clown monkey?" He looked back up and shunted his hand downward.

"Muh, muh," she gasped and closed her eyes not having heard his racist remark.

"You ever fucked a white guy before?"

"No," she gasped, "Never. I've never had sex…"

Blake giggled and shot her a look, "Can you feel my finger pressing against your black pussy?"

"Yea-huh," she moaned. "Oh my…"

"Uh-huh, yeah," he grunted, evilly. He bit his bottom lip and scrunched his nose, indicating that his actions could get far more violent.

He thrust his knuckle into her, "you like it when I wiggle around like that?"

"Mmmm."

"You make my dick so fucking hard."

"Mmhmmm," She closed her eyes and clutched his sides as hard as she could.

SLAM!

The door to Blake's bedroom smashed against the dresser. He yanked her by the hand and threw her onto his bed.

Blake threw off his shirt and climbed out of his jeans, "Come here, you dirty little monkey."

Confused, she had ended up in a stranger's bedroom. This wasn't part of the plan at all. How did she get here? She knew that alcohol made you lose your inhibitions.

This moment of temporary insanity caused her to reassess her actions. She wasn't in full control of herself. Every angry remark from Blake had gone unnoticed.

She stepped over to Blake and noticed his abs, "Oh, m-my," She couldn't help herself. Her hands pressed over them, admiring every inch of his white skin.

"You're so b-beautiful, B-Blake," Mesi grew transfixed and tried to keep her balance. She looked down at his underwear and bit her lip. Blake was concealing something the size of a python between his legs.

"We gotta get the clothes off you so I can see your tits and fat ass," Blake whispered. He lifted her blouse over her head. She unbuckled her jeans and stepped out of the crumpled heap.

This was serious, now.

Mesi had some serious thinking to do and only had about five seconds to make up her mind.

She stood before Blake in her bra and panties.

"*Fuuuck me.* Look at them titties and that ass, man," Blake whispered. He enjoyed every heartbeat through her chest, "Come here, my beautiful little porch monkey."

She obeyed and took a step forward.

"Turn around and lift your arms."

She did as instructed and hulked her elbows into the air. Her bra unclipped and fell down her front. Her buttocks flicked up and down as the lining of her panties ran down her legs.

A hot breath enveloped her right shoulder, followed by a wet sensation, "Mmmmm."

Fingers ran around her stomach from her back and reached up, taking each of her breasts in their palm.

She closed her eyes and fell back-first into his chest.

"Turn around," instructed the voice from behind her.

She did so and looked up at her new lover. She shuddered, feeling unwell and very cold. The cobra tattoo on his neck hissed at her.

"I'm sorry, Blake," she reached up to the cobra and petted its head, "I don't feel very well."

"What?" Blake snapped.

The cobra went to bite her finger, but she pulled it away before it sank its fangs into her flesh.

"Actually, no. I think I should go—"

"—You ain't going anywhere," Blake screamed and took a fistful of her hair, "You're staying here. You understand me, you dirty little slave?"

"No, no," She reached behind her head for his hand, "Please, d-don't."

"Are you staying?" Blake wrenched her head back by her hair. He licked his lips at her convulsing jugular.

"No, p-please d-don't—"

"—Fuckin' bitch," He slapped her across the face and dragged her by the back of her head toward the bed,

"Come and lie down with Uncle Tom, you fucked-up little turd."

He flung Mesi to her back. Her feet slapped against the pillow. Her head hung over the bottom edge of the bed.

"No, no. Stop," She begged and attempted to climb away. Her efforts were futile. Blake pressed his palm down on her neck as it hung off the edge of the bed.

She blinked and gasped. Her view of his bedroom was upside down. She tried to lift her head, but his palm kept her face pressed down.

"You ever breathed dick before?" Blake shouted and grabbed his penis.

"No. No. Mffgg," A hand crawled over her mouth and clasped shut. Blake's manhood hung before her eyes.

"Shut up," he stepped his legs out and lowered his waist to her nose, "I'm gonna let go of your lips and you vacuum this dick like a good little slave."

"Mmmffggghh," She bellowed into his palm. "No, no, don't."

Her bottom lip peeled up, followed by two fingers sliding into her inner cheek. She closed her eyes and thrashed around but her legs were nowhere near her assailant.

"Naaaa—"

Her muffled cries dampened. A long, thick fleshy tube slid across her tongue. The thick end of his penis jammed against her throat.

Blake grabbed her head and lowered himself into her mouth, "Time to suck cock, you dirty little cunt."

Mesi lifted her arms and slapped against his waist. Her efforts were futile.

She was suffocating. The fleshy tube stiffened in her windpipe and hardened out across her tongue and teeth.

"Don't fucking bite now, little doggy, or I'll fuck you up," Blake whispered, pushing forward even further, "Ahhh, yeah, that's it. You got it, baby, you got it."

Mesi felt two balls of skin press against her eyelids. She

whelped and gurgled, trying to breathe. No air could get in.

Or escape.

Blake slapped her across the face and slid himself out. The long flesh-pipe coated in saliva.

Fleck of spittle rasped around her mouth as she held her neck and gasped for air. The muscles in her throat contracted and bulged.

Finally, she opened her eyes to see an upside-down Blake check her out. He walked out of view.

"You take dick like a proper slave, you know," Blake's voice came from her feet.

"N-No," she writhed around and heaved.

Two sweaty palms clamped over her ankles. She tried to kick back, but the sheer weight held them down to the mattress cover.

"Shut the fuck up."

She lifted her head up. Blake climbed in between her legs. He walked forward on his knees and held his stiff manhood in his hand, "I said shut the fuck up, you whore."

Mesi felt her thighs punch apart. His knees pressed against the inside of hers.

"No, no."

A set of fingers sneaked under the small of her back and lifted her waist a few inches into the air, "P-Please, d-don't."

"Fuck, that's some *sweet* black pussy," Blake made a spitting noise. A slap of saliva hit her vagina.

Mesi had no choice but to lay there and accept what was happening. Every kick of her legs met a pin-down from an arm far stronger than hers.

"Happy birthday, sweetheart," Blake giggled. The drink was getting to him.

A dome-shaped ball pushed through between her legs and inside her. Mesi gasped in pain.

She gripped the duvet as tight as she could, trying to block out the agony.

"No, no, no."

The dome moved inside her uterus and burrowed its way inside her. She felt her vagina trying to strangle it. The pain was beyond excruciating.

Mesi let out a prolonged scream. Blake's palm slammed against her lips, deadening her cry.

He brought her waist up to his hips and pushed forward, settling inside her, "Be fucking quiet."

He pushed forward. Mesi closed her eyes and squeezed her muscles back, trying to fend off of the fleshy intrusion.

"Uh, uh," Blake panted, keeping his hand clasped over her mouth, "Fucking scream into my hand. Scream."

"Mmmffh," Mesi puffed and wheezed through her nostrils, "Mmfffh," Her breathing slowed and her chest sunk into her delicate frame. She allowed it to continue.

The pain had abated but she let the assault continue. She was in no position to fight back.

"Uh, come on," Blake grunted and hulked his hips forward, "So tight, so tight. That's it. Yeah."

Blake moaned and slid halfway out of Mesi's vagina. He gripped the bottom half of his penis and started to masturbate himself.

"Just lie there, just lie there," he gasped, "Fucking just lie there."

Mesi lay still. She relaxed every muscle in her entire body. Her spine relaxed in his hands.

Blake grunted and slid the top of his penis along the groove of her vagina. He pressed his thumb down on the head of his manhood and plunge back into her once again.

"Ah, ah," Blake whispered and shook the sweat from his head, "Are you ready for Pure Dark, baby?"

Mesi looked up at him, tears streaming from her eye ducts along her face, "Wh-what?!"

"That's it, yeah, look at me," Blake forced himself into her, "Look at me. Are you ready for Pure Dark?"

She stared him out and let out a tiny yelp. Her hips buckled. Blake rammed forward and kept himself held deep inside her.

"Yeah," He thrust his hips in as the back of Mesi's head hit the mattress, "*Fuuuuuuuuck.*"

A hot, warm rope of slime fired into her uterus. The pain was beyond anything she'd ever experienced.

"I love you so much. Oohh," Blake yelled and ground himself deep into her, releasing his foaming liquid. "You fucking black bitch. Take this *dark*, man. Take it *pure*."

Mesi felt her knees hit the mattress as he climbed off her. He ran the side of his thumb over the end of his penis and sniffed at it.

"Mmm."

He put the fleshy digit into his mouth and sucked off the slime.

A pair of jeans slapped against her face, waking her up out of her assault.

"Get the fuck out of my house," Blake's muffled voice came from over the jean legs. She looked over to see him looking down with his penis in his hand. He slipped his foreskin over the head of his penis and wiped his thumb over the slit.

He spotted her gasping at him, "The fuck you looking at?"

Mesi staggered around, picking up her discarded clothes. Shaken, afraid and cold.

She staggered toward the front gate with her shoes in her hand. She had managed to put her jeans back on. Her torn blouse ends straggled her sides.

She burst into tears as she pushed the gate open. Losing her balance, her knees hit the floor.

She rolled onto her side and pushed herself over.

Her mobile phone rang from within her jeans pocket. She took it out and stood to her feet.

Dad was calling.

She coughed out loud a couple of times and cleared her throat. Mesi made a convincing go at not sounding traumatized.

"Dad."

"Mesi, it's one thirty in the morning," Dad's voice came through the phone, "Where are you?"

"Oh, uh, I'm sorry," she staggered forward trying to find out where she was, "I am running a bit late."

"You want me to pick you up?"

"No, no, it is fine."

"Is Mel there with you?"

"Yes," she lied, clocking the white picket gate that led to the house she'd left. "She's with me now, I'm very safe."

Jelani didn't sound too pleased, "Come home now."

"Yes."

Mesi cut the call off and swiped the screen. A cab company's number. She hit dial and spotted a street sign: *Sears Road.*

"Yes, c-can I have a cab, please," Mesi asked and chewed back her tears, "Yes, I'm a-at Sears Road."

***

The weekend had been one of silence.

Mesi and her father had gone to visit her mother, Jelani's ex-wife. During that dinner, Mesi had offered nothing apart from the obligatory salutations.

Mesi hadn't been in contact with Mel, either. She'd received fifteen texts over the course of the weekend and hadn't responded to any of them.

Jelani had remarked a couple of times that his daughter wasn't her usual self. It was true - she wasn't. She'd about managed to say "hello" to her father in the morning.

Mesi's excuse was that she had partied hard and was trying to recover. She was very tired, according to her bullshit.

It was now Sunday night. Forty-eight hours after her assault. It took this long for her to begin to process what had happened to her.

She sat on her bed with her arms wrapped around her ankles and sobbed.

The quiet, gentle cries kept within the walls of her bedroom.

She didn't dare close her eyes. If she closed them, an image of a cobra would snap at her. The pain she had felt inside her body would come flooding back.

As it was approaching the dead cold of winter, the nights had gotten shorter. The night sky didn't help matters much. It was getting to her. She thought she could fight off the inevitable trauma. After all, this is what sex was like.

Wasn't it?

She stood to her feet and looked in her full-length mirror. Staring back at her was a monster. The clothes torn from her body lay in the corner. One day she'd get around to torching them in the back garden. She had to identify a time when her father wasn't home to do it.

After she burned her clothes she'd throw herself onto the bonfire and kill herself. That was the plan, anyway.

A glint from a piece of metal ran across her eyes. The small scissors on her dresser.

She picked them up and cut a few strands of hair from her fringe. The blades snipped across her hairline.

The mirror revealed a pudgy girl looking back in her direction. Her body was fine but, somehow, in the mirror it looked like a blancmange.

The face of the person staring back at her was beyond ugly, too.

"I hate you," she yelled and snapped the scissors in her fingers, "I fucking hate you."

She held the sharp prong up and pushed the loop of the metal object through her finger. Mesi was now carrying a dagger in her right hand.

She turned the underside of her left arm up to the ceiling. The tip of the scissor pressed into her wrist.

Mesi looked at the image in the mirror and scowled,

"You deserved to die."

The prick punctured through the skin, releasing a blob of blood. She ran it back down to her elbow crease.

The door burst open, causing Mesi to drop the scissor to the floor. Her wrist and the underside of her forearm were bleeding, but it wasn't fatal.

"What is this noise?" Jelani ran into the room, "I heard screaming, what is—?"

Mesi wailed at the naked image in the mirror.

"My God," Jelani gasped, walking over to his naked, bleeding daughter. He grabbed her left arm and held the wound up to his face, "What on Earth are you doing?"

"I want to d-die," she wailed, yanking her arm away from his clutches. "Leave me alone."

"What the hell is going on?" He grabbed her by the shoulders. The demon that had gotten into his daughter needed removing. "Where are your clothes?"

"I'm nothing but a whore," she spat, snot and tears flying everywhere, "Let go of me."

"Mesi, calm down and tell me what's happening," Jelani clutching her shoulders and tried to shake some sense into the woman standing before him.

She calmed down and looked at her arm. A trickle of blood hit the white carpet. The woman in the mirror looked back. A suggestive smile streaked across its face.

"C-Can you s-see that, Dad?" Mesi said, beginning to calm down, "She's looking at me. She thinks I'm a whore."

"What?" Jelani looked at the mirror. The reflection wasn't doing any such thing, "Who?"

She pointed at herself in the mirror, "Her."

Jelani shook his head and took her to the edge of her bed. He sat down with his daughter and cradled her in his arms, "I knew something wasn't right."

"It's okay, Dad," she sniffed. "I had a nightmare."

Jelani couldn't contain his anger any longer. He held up her cut arm and pushed it into her face, "You call this a nightmare?"

She looked at her father and squealed through her closed lips, "He raped me."

"What?" Jelani released her hand, "Who raped you?"

"Some guy called Blake," she sniffed, pressing the palm of her side onto her thigh, "H-He raped me."

Of course, it was all becoming very clear to her father. This revelation explained her weird behavior this weekend. It explained what was occurring right now.

"You were raped?" he asked.

She nodded her head, starting to cry again.

"Who did this?" Jelani could have exploded. But all he wanted was a name, "Tell me who did this."

"His name is Charlie."

"Charlie?

"No," Mesi corrected herself, "No, not Charlie. Blake."

"Blake. Are you sure?" Jelani stood to his feet and tilted the mirror toward the window. At least Mesi didn't have to look at herself from the bed, "Where does he live?"

"I c-can't r-r-emember—"

"—do not lie to me, Mesi Orji," her father snapped, "You tell me where he lives."

"Sears Road."

"Which number?" Jelani asked.

"I don't know," Mesi sobbed. "Please Dad, don't do anythi—"

"—What does the house look like?"

"Dad, please, don't do—"

"—Do not interrupt me again," Jelani screamed and picked up the mini scissor from the floor, "Tell me."

"It w-was a white p-picket gate."

"What does he look like?"

"Wh-what?"

Jelani took a deep breath and roared, "I said what does he look like?"

"He's white."

"You made love to a white boy?"

"Yes."

"Tell me who I'm looking for or so help me God I will tear this place apart."

"He has a Cobra tattoo on his neck," Mesi scrunched the duvet in her hands. She moved it across her breasts, hoping her father wouldn't attack her, "He's tall, and has a tattoo."

"Tattoo, Cobra," Jelani muttered. He stormed out of the bedroom and hit the stairs.

"Dad, no."

Jelani recited the details over and over and under his breath as he bounded down the stairs, "Cobra, tattoo, white gate."

He marched into the kitchen and yanked open a drawer full of cutlery. He poked around, pushing the silverware from left to right, "Motherfucker, you're going to pay."

He settled on a twelve-inch serrated edge knife.

SLAM. He pushed the drawer shut with his knee and made for the front door.

Mesi ran down the stairs, holding the duvet across her body, "Dad, please, don't!"

"Sears Road, white gate," he repeated and threw the front door open.

"Dad, please. Don't."

The door crashed shut behind him as he stormed over to his car.

***

Jelani drove along the street. He kept an eye out for the street signs. The sat nav on his phone displayed a pink streak across the roads. The device advertised that he was a mere five minutes away from Sears Road.

The knife rattled on the passenger seat as he turned the next corner.

Jelani was a man possessed, much like his daughter. Whereas she had been catatonic, Jelani was incandescent with unfiltered rage.

"Motherfucker," He slammed the steering wheel. A glimpse of his own reflection sneered back from the windscreen, "You raped my daughter. I will take your fucking dick."

"Turn right on Grand Street in one hundred yards," advised the female sat nav app.

"Damn straight," he muttered to himself, "Get me to this fucker. Now." He thumped the steering wheel once again and wiped the sweat from his cheek. Jelani had worked himself up into an unfiltered bout of anger, "Get me there."

"Okay, okay," exclaimed the female automated voice, "I will get you there. The rapist lives on Sears Road."

"I know he does."

"He deserves to have his penis removed," the sat nav suggested. "You could call the police—"

"—Ain't calling no police, for fuck's sake," Jelani screamed at the sat nav, "They don't do nothing, anyway. I'll take care of this cunt on my own."

Sears Road.

No sign of life. Parked cars lined the pavement as Jelani drove down it looking for a white picket gate.

"There must be fifty houses down here," he whispered to himself, keeping an eye out for a white picket gate.

"You have arrived," the sat nav advised. "Please exit the car carefully."

A young couple walked alongside the car. Jelani drove at a steady seven miles per hour, scanning left and right.

The man looked over and made eye contact with Jelani. He honked the horn and rolled to a stop.

"Hey, you," Jelani said to the couple, "I'm looking for a white gate. I don't know the number."

"Oh, you want one-one-eight. Four doors down, on the right," the woman said.

"Thanks."

Jelani allowed the couple to walk on. He applied the

handbrake, switched off the engine and opened the car door.

He stepped out. A fat hand reached for the knife handle and took it from the seat.

SLAM! The passenger side door shut.

Knock-knock.

A young man opened the door. Loud dance music wafted out into the night sky as the occupier sized up his guest.

Jelani stood, heaving, with the knife in his right hand.

The young man looked at the blade and back at Jelani, "What?"

"Are you Blake?"

"Huh?"

"Don't fuck with me," Jelani spat and took a step forward, "Are you Blake?"

"No, man, you've got the wrong—"

"—Where Blake at?"

"Who are you?" The young man folded his arms and tried his best to conceal his anxiety.

"Never mind who I am. Where Blake at?"

"He's not here."

"So I've got the right house, then." Jelani stepped forward and held the serrated edge up at the kid, "One more time, where Blake at?"

The young man unfolded his arms and held his hands out, "He's n-not here."

"Bullshit, I'mma ask you one more fucking time." Jelani grabbed the back of the young man's head. The knife blade slid under his chin, "You sure he ain't here?"

"Yeah, man. H-He's here."

"Good."

SCHTAAMM! Jelani head butted the young man on the nose. The cartilage busted out through his nostrils, vomiting blood down the front of his shirt.

"Motherfucker, move," Jelani threw the man against

the wall. He slumped down, gasping and bleeding through his fingers.

"Blake?" Jelani roared as he stormed through the landing and into the living room, "Where you at?"

Two guys and a girl were taking turns on a bong in the middle of the living room floor. They looked up Jelani and nearly shit themselves with fright.

"Who are you?"

"Which one of you is Blake?"

One of the boys clocked the knife in Jelani's hand, "Nah, m-man. He's upstairs."

"Upstairs?"

A thundering of footsteps descended the staircase.

Jelani looked around but couldn't see. They were around the corner on the landing. He turned around and held the knife up at the trio.

"Oh shit," came a voice from the landing, "Tony, man, are you okay?"

"Some g-guy nutted me."

Jelani turned back to the trio, "Which room is he in?

"Who are you?" asked the petrified girl as she coughed out some smoke, "What do you want with Bla—"

"—Which fucking room is he in?!"

"First on the left."

Creak-creak. A noise came from the door to the living room. Jelani turned over his shoulder and noticed a nose protruding from behind the wall.

The head it belonged to was eavesdropping on the interrogation.

"First on the left, yeah?"

"Yeah, man," said one of the boys. He nodded at the door frame.

Blake's face emerged from around the corner. His eyes made contact with Jelani.

"Who are you?" Blake asked, anxiously.

"Are you Blake?" Jelani turned the knife toward him. They stood ten feet apart from each other. Blake gripped the living room door handle. He was cautious not to set this giant stranger off.

"Yeah, man."

Jelani took a deep breath and scowled at his intended victim.

"Who are you?"

"Motherfucker," Jelani launched himself forward. Blake slammed the living room door right into his path and ran off.

SCHLAMM! Jelani kicked the door open and made for the landing. Blake hightailed it up the stairs.

Tony, the man Jelani had head butted, cupped his nose and tried to stand to his feet.

"Fucking prick," Jelani kicked him across the jaw. The back of his head slammed against the coat stand.

Jelani gripped the railing and barreled up the stairs after Blake.

SCHWUMP!

The first door on the left slammed shut, "Hey, man," Blake's voice punched through the closed door. "I didn't do nuffin'."

Jelani reached the top floor landing and slammed the door with his fist, "Open the door."

"No," Blake pleaded, "You'll kill me!"

"Open the fucking door," Jelani clutched the door handle and yanked it down. It rattled in his palm.

Locked.

He took a step back and exhaled. A puff of smoke escaped his nostrils. His collar, neck and head turned red like an angry bull.

"Open the door, you fucking rapist."

"No, no," Blake's voice trembled from behind the door, "Please, don't!"

"I'mma count to three," Jelani cross his chest with his right arm, "One…"

The trio of pot smokers gathered around the bottom of the stairs. They blinked up at the commotion.

"Nawww, man," Blakes cried through the door, "Can't we talk about this?"

"Two..."

"Oh shit," the stoned girl said from the bottom of the stairs, "Blake's so fucked."

"*Three.*"

"No, don't."

Jelani roared and ran toward the door, extending his elbow.

CRAAA-SMASSSHH!

The sheer weight of the beast outgunned the pathetic door. It blew apart and hit the back wall.

Blake stepped back and tripped over his bed. The very bed he had raped Jelani's daughter on.

He stomped forward and held the knife up to Blake, "You raped my daughter."

Blake kicked back, pushing himself back up against the headboard, "No-no-no, man, no—"

Jelani savoured his moment of revenge. He kept the serrated edge pointed at his victim. There was nowhere to run.

"You raped my baby girl," Jelani growled, his eyeballs turning rage-red, "You took her innocence. Now, I'm going to take something from you."

"No, man, please," Blake cried, "Please."

Jelani looked his prey up and down. Blake was dressed only in a pair of briefs and shoes. A naked young woman was cowering behind the dresser, panting with great anxiety.

"Lady?" Jelani asked. "Get out of here."

"O-Okay," she rose to her feet and covered her bare breasts. "Blake, call me, okay?"

"Y-Yeah, sure," he said after her as she ran out of the room and down the stairs.

Jelani exhaled and swung the knife back in Blake's direction. "Take off your underwear."

"Wh-wha—?"

"—Remove your underwear, rapist," Jelani screamed.

"Okay, o-okay," Blake held out his hands, trying to calm his attacker down. If he acted as instructed it might just save his life.

Blake kicked his briefs away and scrambled back against the headboard. Jelani moved forward and looked between Blake's legs.

"This you, is it?" Jelani's knees hit the edge of the bed. Blake's toes curled around beside his knees.

"This m-me, wh-what?"

Jelani placed his left knee on the bed and climbed forward. Blake bent his knees and pushed himself back.

Jelani held the sharp end of the knife at Blake's well-endowed penis, "You used this on my daughter."

"I didn't rape her," he begged, kicking his feet and trying not to cry like a sissy in front of his house mates. "It was consensual."

"Nah, motherfucker. You're a lying rapist cunt," Jelani shot him a grin of pure evil. He walked his knees up the bed, "If it was consensual, then this would be, too. I'm going to remove your penis for what you did. Maybe then you will learn."

Jelani slid his palm underneath Blake's manhood and lifted it a few inches in the air. He tightened his grip and pulled it toward his waist.

The elongated skin and flesh roped away from Blake's groin. The base of his penis was taut.

"Nah, nah," Blake screamed, "P-Please, don't."

Jelani placed the side of the blade against his groin and ran the sharp teeth atop the base of his shaft.

A long, smooth, metallic grate tore the skin and sliced through the flesh. The penis ripped away from the base and peeled off into Jelani's hand in three swift slices.

Blake clutched his cheeks and screamed for dear life. The blood-letting was intense. Red stuff careened across Jelani's knees, soaking the mattress to the bone.

Jelani held up the severed penis in his left palm and

pointed the blade at Blake's face with his right.

"We're even, now."

"Gaagghh," Blake looked down. He cried at the gushing pipework of blood and gore sloshing down his thighs. "Gwwuuurrr."

Jelani climbed off the bed and walked out of the bedroom.

The three stoners - and Blake's naked girlfriend - stepped out of the man's path. One of them puked to the floor when they saw what was in Jelani's left hand.

"Oh m-my God," the stoned fainted into her friend's arms.

Jelani scanned each of their faces.

The soundtrack of Blake's deathly screams underscored the intensity of the horror.

Jelani held out Blake's penis in his hand, "If any of you say shit about me, you're next."

No-one would be telling on this giant of a man anytime soon. They nodded their heads in agreement and stepped out of his way.

"I know where y'all live."

Jelani walked out of the house.

Back home, Mesi had finally fallen asleep. More than sixty hours of having been awake had taken its toll.

The bedroom door unbolted and opened. The tiniest sound was enough to wake her from her slumber.

"Sweetie," Jelani whispered, "Wake up."

Mesi lifted her elbows to her chest and looked at the door. "Uh, who's that?"

"It's Dad," said the silhouette. "Close your eyes, I'mma turn on the lights."

Mesi closed her eyes as the lights snapped on.

"I got something for you," Jelani whispered.

She opened her eyes. Her jaw hit the top of her chest. She tried to scream, but paralysis set in when she saw what was in her father's hand.

"I got him, baby," Jelani whispered and moved to the dresser. He stopped and placed the dismembered penis on the dresser, "I got him."

"Nuh, nuh," Mesi shook her head and kicked her feet forward. The tip of Blake's penis hung back at her, "Nuh, nuh—"

"—Goodnight, honey."

Jelani stepped into the landing, closing the door to the bedroom behind him.

A job well done. A dish served cold.

"No-no-no," Mesi hopped to her feet and backed up against the mirror, "No, Dad. You d-didn't…"

Her breathing quickened. The room began to spin around and around like a carnival carousel.

She crossed her arms in front of her chest and grabbed her shoulders. Her breathing turned to hyperventilation as she ducked her head.

"Nuuh, nuhhh, nuuuhhhhh."

She took a deep breath and crouched to her knees. Her arms flew forward.

Blake's severed penis took center stage on her chest of drawers.

"Nooooooo."

The walls of the house rumbled as her lungs emitted the longest wail of utter despair.

Chapter 7

Hazmat

Friday Night, 7:30 pm. *Chrome Junction Arena*. A popular place to see your favourite act or band.

The town's train station was a few hundred yards from the arena and the *Kaleidoscope Shopping Centre*. Two sheltered concourses will lead you to one or the other.

The place was heaving on a warm Friday evening. People of all shapes and sizes made their way to the arena. Some had been drinking if you'd studied how they were walking.

There were more men than women tonight. Hardly surprising considering who was headlining that night at the Arena.

The train pulled up at platform six. A flurry of passengers exited the carriage, followed by a man who stood out. He was dressed in a yellow plastic suit, mask and black gloves. You'd have thought his costume might have caused some consternation.

They thought he was on his way to a fancy dress party. It was none of their business what the man was up to. He kept himself to himself on the carriage, holding on to the roof railing as the carriage rocked to a stop.

A typical British reaction. Look the other way, avoid eye contact. Let others take the embarrassment.

A group of five men were the first to leave the carriage. Hazmat got off right after them and made his way to the Cobra Concourse.

It led to the arena.

The five men were carrying some beers; getting tanked up before the gig. Hazmat didn't pay them any heed as he kept walking. The alcohol got the better of one of the young lads.

"Oi, mate," he slurred his words, "Nice yellow suit."

Hazmat ignored them.

"Oi, Hazmat suit," screamed the young lad's friend.

Still, he continued looking forward and chose to ignore them.

"Fuckin' weirdo," The young lad's friend found the yellow-covered man a bit creepy. His friends taunted the man in the yellow suit for "*being gay*".

The congregation area outside the arena itself was heaving with young adults. Hazmat approached them, heading for the sets of doors. A few heads turned to watch.

A man ran his fingers through his green Mohawk, bemused at the sight. A Hazmat suit is usually used when a virus or airborne disease is around. Tonight, though, the air was clear. The temperature on the wrong side of comfortable.

A giant banner encased in glass advertised tonight's main attraction.

Rectal Prolapse

The "Feed Me, I'm Hungry" Tour

The dates promised three gigs at the arena this weekend starting tonight. The poster advertised four members of the band. They looked like Hitler youth; angry, fists in the air, like they were about to go nuts.

Oh, the irony.

Hazmat scanned the poster. The purple Perspex covering his face reflected the hundreds of people at the entrance.

The waiting horde thought he was a part of the act and hadn't found the stage entrance around the back.

It seemed plausible.

Hazmat pushed through the doors and through the reception area. The box office sat to his left.

A bouncer approached him and held out his hand. "Excuse me, mate."

"I'm with the band," Hazmat said. His voice funneling through the internal breathing apparatus.

He held out his ID in his gloved hand.

"Oh, right?" asked the bouncer, "Why didn't you use the stage B door?"

"I didn't know."

"Okay," the bouncer said, satisfied. He looked over his shoulder and nodded at his colleagues, "Just through the side door there, and that'll take you through to the green room."

"I know."

"Cool, cool," the bouncer stepped aside and let him past. It was to be one of the biggest mistakes of his life.

Hazmat knew where he was going, though. He marched straight toward the stage B door and pushed his way through.

A long, dank corridor lay behind the door.

Hazmat found himself walking down it. A series of technical doors flew by as he paced along the walkway.

The distant sound of musical instruments tuning up barreled through the walls.

"One, two," a male voice boomed, "One, two, testing. Testing."

Hazmat looked up at the ceiling. Two thick, plastic

veins ran along the near-side corner. Two foot wide each. The gurgling air shot through the pipes as Hazmat continued down the corridor.

He walked past a door with "Band" written on it. The door was ajar.

"Yeah, cool," came a voice from within the room. "So, set list A through B. We start with *Dark's Palsy* and then onto *The Wank Room*."

"Cool," came the reply, but up the tempo on *Palsy*, yeah? Get the fuckers proper jumping an' that."

The conversation dissipated as Hazmat walked further along the corridor. He held out his right gloved hand and yanked the lip up over his wrist with the other.

Finally, the door he knew he needed. Security. Next to it was the disposal room.

Hazmat took out a pair of pliers and gripped the handle. He pushed the door open and looked inside.

SNAP. The light came on.

The room was frosty and cold. A giant plastic container about four foot high stood in the corner of the room. A plume of white mist surrounded the beast.

Hazmat pulled the door shut and stood still in the middle of the corridor.

He folded his arms.

"Ladies and Gentlemen," the speaker system said from behind the walls, "The band will be on in ten minutes. Please ensure you keep your ticket with you at all times."

The corridor rumbled like a sore throat as a stampede of footsteps ran from left to right. The audience were making their way into the arena proper.

The dampened hubbub grew louder.

"Shit, man," someone's voice said, "There's four thousand of the fuckers here tonight."

"Yeah," coughed a female voice, "Biggest night of the tour, sweetie."

Three people made their way from the far end of the corridor. They were the band members.

The first was the aptly-named Tool, the lead singer. He sported a leather jacket, shades and a nasty scar down his right cheek.

The second was a lady named Utero. It wasn't her real name of course, but it suited her embryonic look. Her eyes were bloodshot. It was difficult to tell if the special effect was genuine or not.

She sported a padlock through her nose. Her body was muscular. The type that might play the electric guitar. She provided the backing vocals, judging by her sixty-cigarettes-a-day voice.

The third man, Choke, had a green Mohawk. The fans loved it. A belt "choked" his neck. It was tight - you could tell because the leather pinched at the skin on his Adam's Apple.

The three of them walked right past Hazmat without a care in the world.

"C'mon, Pest," Tool said, bopping Hazmat on the shoulder, "Get your sticks. We're on in five."

Hazmat didn't react. He kept calm, arms folded, and stared dead ahead.

"Pest, man?" Choke said, punching him on the shoulder, "Let's go, you fuckin' nonce!"

Utero giggled to herself and stepped backwards, flipping Hazmat the middle finger, "You know what, fuck you, Pest. Drummers are fucking gay, anyway."

She spun around and made for the green room. "C'mon you pair of pedos. Let's go out and kill "em."

"You okay, Pest, man?" Tool asked, as Choke pushed past and joined Utero.

Hazmat nodded.

His chest bulged out and then back in. It perturbed Tool, somewhat. He stood there looking at who he thought was his drummer. There was no fathoming why the man was behaving so strangely.

There was a simple explanation, of course. Pest, the band's drummer, named because of his inclusion on the sex offender's register, wasn't the one in the yellow suit.

"You toked a bit too much, mate?"

"Tool, man, fuckin' hurry up," Choke shouted down the corridor, "Let's strap in, we're gonna be late."

Tool turned back to Hazmat. His own face shone back at him through the purple visor.

"See you on stage, yeah?"

No response.

Tool winked at Hazmat and then backed off down the corridor.

***

So, what happened to the drummer?

The band rocked up to the *Chrome Junction Hightower*. A four-star hotel just off the M25. Tool and Utero weren't an item, but a month ago, in the first week of the tour, they ended up fucking.

A lot. At least four times a day.

They decided that the band didn't need four luxury suites for their hotel visits.

So, one room was for Tool and Utero. Another for Choke, and a final suite for Pest, their drummer.

Choke decided to get some sleep. He'd stayed awake after last night's gig and jerked himself dry watching a particularly gruesome type of porn on the *DogPounder* website.

Tool and Utero got down to business on the four poster bed. How do we know this? Because Hazmat was waiting for Pest in his room next door to theirs.

When Pest walked in, Hazmat was in the single chair by the television set. He was waiting for the big, burly black guy he'd seen on YouTube. *Rectal Prolapse* might have been a neo-fascist and homophobic death metal band. When it came to skin color it was blind.

"Who are you? What are you doing in my room, man?" Pest looked put-out by the intruder.

Hazmat stood to his feet and didn't say a word.

Pest threatened to clump him, "Get the fuck outta my room, you prick."

Hazmat took out a pair of metal pliers and pointed the thick ends at Pest's face.

Snip-snip.

Pest laughed. A pair of pliers? What the hell could a man do with those? He sure as hell couldn't take down a three hundred pound drumming machine.

Pest clenched his fist and went to throw it at Hazmat's face. But he missed and ended up punching the TV. It smashed to pieces around his wrist.

The sound created a somewhat perverse sound effect for Utero's repeated cries of "fuck me harder, daddy!" coming from the other side of the wall.

Hazmat stepped aside and kept the pliers held up at Pest. He was about to throw another punch.

"Wanker. I'll take you the *fuck* down."

Pest threw another punch. Hazmat ducked and slipped to the right. The man's fist smashed into the wall.

He was stuck and in a great deal of pain.

"Motherfucker."

Hazmat wasted no time. He withdrew a syringe from a hardened case stored within his utility belt.

Off came the cap.

SQUITT. Flick-flick. All the air bubbles removed as Hazmat pinged the side of the barrel.

JAB.

The sharp end punctured Pest's buttock, through his jeans. The entire solution sank from the barrel and into Pest's bloodstream.

Hazmat wrenched the Velcro away from his own helmet and reapplied it.

Pest's fist was still stuck in the wall. He choked and spluttered as the solution coursed through his veins.

Eventually, the virus branched out into his organs. First his lungs, then his heart.

"Gaaaahhhhh."

Pest's eyes bulged out of their sockets and released a frothy white liquid. His tongue lapped out from his mouth and melted down his chin.

Hazmat slapped his palm onto Pest's forehead, expecting it to make a "thudding" noise.

Not this time.

Instead, it made a sort of "splat" sound. A squelching whine, followed by a blood-orange fusion of skin and flesh streaking across his face.

Smoke rose up from Pest's shoulders as his body began to liquefy. He tried to hit Hazmat with his free hand, but when he moved his shoulder it dislocated all on its own. The arm shunted to the ground.

His fingers ran white and yellow, dripping to the floor like sloppy, loose paint.

Hazmat kept his grip on Pest's head. He reached up with the pliers and clinched the ends around his front tooth.

POP.

A squirt of blood. More like a drop of tap water in an ocean.

Hazmat's grasp on Pest's head was so tight it crunched his skull inward. It wasn't that he was strong. Far from it. It was that Pest's entire skeleton, including his skull, had softened to the degree that it couldn't hold its contents in any longer.

A bit like squeezing jello in your hand.

Pest's neck roped downward, acting as a pathetic gummy bridge between his head and torso.

The majority of Pest's body splattered against the floor. His head remained in his killer's grip.

And then - the final squeeze. Pest's head exploded like a pumpkin. Fragments of blancmange-like phlegm in all directions.

That's how Pest died.

A little while later, Hazmat (pretending to be Pest) explained to the rest of the band that he wanted to wear the yellow contamination suit. He said it would give the final three gigs a certain toxic vibe. It was an aura they strove for.

Hazmat chose the right time and place to tell his “new” band members. During the night when all three were off their tits on mescaline.

They never mentioned it again. The band members had a gossamer-thin recollection of the conversation. Like true Brits, no member of the band wanted to be the one who’d forgotten about it. Looking like a tit-end was out of the question for them.

So, everyone “got on with it.”

Hazmat knew that this would be the case. At this point, no-one even knew Pest was missing.

If anyone wanted to find him then they’d have to steam clean room 118’s carpet.

***

"Wankers and motherfuckers," growled an extremely angry voice through the arena, "give your fucking souls to the devil. He plays with your kids. He fucks with your family. He pounds the ass so hard, the hole looks like a rosebud… this is *Rectal Prolapse*."

The four thousand-strong crowd went ape shit mental. They cheered and roared as the band members head-banged their way onto the stage.

Tool reached the microphone and screamed into it, shaking the sweat from his brow, "You ugly cunts ready to fuck shit up?!"

The crowd cheered and whooped.

"Introducing, the girl who gave you fucking AIDS. She’s in your head, she’s *in*, she’s *Utero*!"

"U-ter-oh. U-ter-oh," the crowd chanted, holding up their thumb and little fingers.

Utero pushed Tool to his ass and took the microphone. She slung her devil guitar around her waist and pushed her thumb down the front of her belt-like skirt.

"Ya wanna piece of this, do ya?"

The crowd roared once again as she peeled down the front of her skirt. A tattoo of a cartoon devil child with its legs open shone from between her thighs.

"Yeah. Fuck this," Utero dropped the mic and struck a chord. The crowd went feral, pushing and shoving each other as the music started.

"Did you know?" Tool screamed into the microphone.

"No?" the audience shouted back, expectantly.

"We snuck a spastic into a sperm bank. This is *Dark's Palsy*."

The crowd went wild as the track kicked in. Choke jumped onto the drums and banged them as best he could.

The audience screamed as they saw what they knew to be the bass player take to the leather skins. He did a good job of filling in for the missing Pest.

Tool roared incomprehensibly into the microphone. Utero rubbed the strings of her electric guitar over her bare nipples.

Backstage, Hazmat wandered into the security office. Three guards lay dead against the wall. Each was missing their teeth and bleeding from the gums. Parts of their skulls had subsided, their faces melting down their jackets.

An evidence bag full of teeth hung beside Hazmat's trousers as he carried them out of the room. A pool of blood had collected at the bottom. The bag resembled a perverse goldfish prize from a fairground.

Hazmat closed the security door shut. The muffled music from the concert shot down the walls. The wailing and cheering underscored the intensity of the performance.

It didn't faze Hazmat as he arrived at the disposal room. He pushed the door open and walked in.

The vast, frosty container loomed in the middle of the room. Hazmat placed the bag of teeth on a desk in the corner of the room and looked up at the ceiling.

The two thick pipes that were running along the corridor terminated in this room.

He held out his hands and pushed the container along the floor. It was heavy, but not heavy enough to withstand Hazmat's continued application of pressure.

SCCRRRAAAAAPPPEE!

The container knocked against the wall. The ventilation unit hung on the wall a few feet above the lid.

Hazmat reached around his waist and flicked a switch. A green light came on the back of his head.

His oxygen unit was now in service.

The breathing deepened and loudened. Conserving oxygen was of paramount importance.

Hazmat threw both arms forward and inspected his suit for signs of tearing. There weren't any to be found. His hands grasped the sides of the container. His thumbs flicked the latches on each side.

Off came the lid.

Out came a smooth, smoky residue from within the container. Hazmat looked inside. Nothing in there but a delicate black gas.

He threw the lid to the floor and walked back to the desk, all the while keeping an eye on the gas. The air unit sucked in the black moisture through its grills and into the two foot thick pipes.

Hazmat picked up the see-through bag of teeth and made his way to the door. The gas drifted up toward the ventilation unit with frightening speed. He looked over at the two pipes and traced their journey into the corridor.

SLAM.

The door shut behind him as he walked along the corridor. He never tore his purple-hued gaze away from the pipes snaking along the ceiling.

The music pummeled the walls from the stage. The

further Hazmat traveled down the corridor the louder the performance came.

The audience's screams were almost deafening.

The door to the stage was right at the end of the corridor. Hazmat reached it and pushed through.

Behind the blackened curtain on the stage, Hazmat could see the band. He'd timed it right on the money. The song came to a crashing halt, leaving the crowd to shit themselves and start fights.

"Yeah, muthafuckers," Tool wailed into the microphone. Choke kicked one of the drums over and head butted the cymbals as a finishing move.

Utero held up her left breast and sunk her teeth into her nipple. Blood smeared over her lips, "You bunch of fucking disgusting wank-fucks," She spat a gob of blood into the crowd.

The mosh pit at the front of the stage went berserk. Dancers fought over who got some of the detritus flying in their direction.

"Well fuck my arsehole with a pneumatic drill!" Tool yelled, looking behind him. Hazmat was making his way to the stage, "Pest!"

The crowd looked up, "Pest. Pest. Pest," They chanted over and over again.

"Where the fuck have you been, you dumb coon?" Choke spat, and barged his way past Hazmat. "Get on the skins, you cunt."

Hazmat watched Choke walk over to the bass guitar stand and remove the instrument.

"Well?" Choke screamed, "Sit the fuck down, dickhead."

"Okay," Tool screamed into the microphone. Utero started plucking the strings on her electric guitar, "You know where I wanna go on my holiday?"

"Where?!" screamed the audience.

"I wanna go to a place where I can fuck the person I

love most in the fucking world. *Me.*"

The next track fired to life as Utero smashed the shit out of her guitar.

"Get on the fuckin' skin you fat fuck," Choke screamed, running back to the drum kit, "Fuck's sake!"

Hazmat held out his bag of teeth above his head. The crowd scrambled toward the stage, but couldn't climb up because it was too high.

"What the fuck are you doing?" Tool mouthed to whom he thought was Pest.

He didn't get a response.

Instead, Hazmat tipped the bag over the crowd. The tiny, blood-caked bones flew over the mosh pit. Several members of the audience careened into the crowd in front, slamming them to the ground. Feet and hands trampled over them to collect their little white souvenirs.

The scrunched up bag was the last thing to hit the ground.

"What the fuck?" Tool muttered before realizing the first verse was due. He turned to the microphone and grunted into it.

Hazmat jumped down from the stage. He walked along the gangway that separated the mosh pit from the first section of the audience.

The head bangers swung their hair around like a lasso. Others violently jammed their heads back and forth.

Hazmat crossed the first concourse and headed for the gangway that led to the back of the arena.

A thousand hands and palms pushed and shoved him. They all wanted a taste of their favourite drummer. Several topless women were sitting on their shoulders of their male friends.

The Wank Room track kicked off. A few male participants took out their penises and swung them around. Another man spun the woman on his shoulders upside down. He slammed her face against his penis and buried his face between her upturned legs.

The atmosphere was absolutely electric. A frenzied spectacle of hell and the apocalypse entwined together.

"You fucking wankers," Utero screamed into her microphone as she slid to her knees. Her miniskirt tore open. Both her thighs widened. She leaned back on her left elbow and propelled her waist into the air.

With her other hand, she planted the strings against her vagina. The twangs and of the strings erupted almost as loud as the audience's roars of approval.

Hazmat turned around and walked backwards. He looked up at the ceiling of the arena. The pipes ran along the corners and mouthed open in four separate sections.

SPLAT.

A dead fly landed in Hazmat's gloved palm. It wriggled around in pain and then melted down the creases of the fabric.

Hazmat wiped his hands together and stepped back, taking out his pliers. He snipped them together as he watched Utero rub her guitar between her thighs.

"You ready for this, ya cunts?" she shouted and pushed the guitar to the floor. A torrent of white fluid ejaculate sprayed out from her vagina and covered those in the mosh pit.

Utero orgasmed over and over again, hulking her hips forward. Ten thick ropes of squirt flung into the air and latched over the crowd.

Tool screamed into the microphone. The lyrics being sung were damn-near incomprehensible.

"Chrome Junction Arena," he strained his larynx as he yelled, "This is *the* ultimate wank room!"

He unzipped himself and took out his penis. The end swung back and forth between his knees as he continued to growl into the microphone.

Hazmat slowed his breathing.

The crowd kept fighting and screaming, but the noise began to subside. Hazmat looked to his left and saw a row of teenagers drop to their knees. They dragged their fingernails across their faces in pain, tearing off the skin.

To his left, fifty concert goers projectile vomited into the air. The spew splashed down onto the crowd, creating an antagonistic sizzling of body parts.

The music wouldn't relent.

The gasps and cries of the back row dying on their feet were drowned out by the chanting and crying from the audience.

The splotches of vomit sizzled and burned into the scalps of ten more head bangers. As they thrashed around, their swinging hair chucking more vomit into the faces of others.

The pipes along the ceiling coughed out more black gas into the arena.

SPLATT-TT!

A woman sitting on her boyfriend's shoulders gasped in agony. The skin on her legs bubbled and frothed, sweeping away down to the flesh. The meat on the bone slunk off and melted down her boyfriend's waist.

He hadn't noticed - it wouldn't last for long.

The boyfriend's jeans burst apart as the liquid soaked through and chewed at his body.

He fell knees-first to the floor, flinging his girlfriend forward and into the crowd. Her body convulsed and exploded as the gas drifted over the commotion. Sections of her head splattered along the floor. The remains of her face hit the ankles and shins of her immediate neighbors.

"Help me," screamed a bald girl from the middle of the left-hand section. She looked down to see the flesh on her arms burning up a storm.

The liquefied flesh ran down her forearm as a man stepped back and snapped her joints.

"Oh, sh-shiiit," The man gasped as he watched the woman melt before his eyes.

Her backbone putrefied through her shirt, folding the top half of her body onto her knees. The complicated fusion of limbs crumpled to the floor. The messy blend of guts and gore ran around the shoes of the others, heading toward the stage.

Hazmat stepped forward and admired his work. The virus piping in through the air vents was working.

To his right, the woman being held upside by her boyfriend continued to gag on his penis.

Glug-glug-glug. Choke.

Her eyeballs sucked into her skull, pushing the contents of her head out through her mouth.

BLOOOOAARRRGGHHHH! A wave of puke shot out through the sides of her mouth.

The rest of the insides of her head jetted out of her nostrils, sending a blast of nitrous toxic puke between her boyfriend's thighs.

He screamed between her legs. The screaming turned to a coagulated retch of puke as he vomited his guts into her vagina opening.

SCHTA-AAMM!

The throw-up motion caused an involuntary knee-spasm. He crunched his girlfriend in the face with her knee, taking her head clean off.

It rolled to the floor and made its way down to the stage. The severed end of the penis hung out of her mouth. The fat end stuck out of the cavity in her neck, forcing her severed head to roll to the right.

WHUMP!

A head-thrashing audience member kicked the woman's head by accident. It flew into the air, causing the fleshy head-ball to spray toxic puke and slime all over the front row.

The audience's screams died down which only exacerbated the music and noise from the stage. The entire middle section of the auditorium was on its knees, gasping and choking.

Several sets of palms pressed against the floor as they tried to suck in some air. The harder they breathed, the more likely they were to lose their lungs.

Another man scratched down his chest. His fingers caught in his rib cage. The man to his left smeared the last remnants of his eyeballs across his cheek. He lost his footing and fell against his neighbour.

The ribs popped out, releasing a fountain of putrefied heart, lungs and intestines. The gory mixture collected around his knees and funneled toward the stage.

"Have you cunts had enough yet?" Utero screamed. She stopped strumming her guitar and looked at the audience, "Jesus Christ!"

Tool kept on roaring into the microphone. He was unable to hear his guitarist.

Utero looked back at Choke on the drums. What remained of his body had slumped over the main kit. His wrists, and the majority of his forearms melted toward the floor like hot candle wax.

He lifted his head and looked at Utero. "Help m-meee."

"*Fuuuck* me," she gasped.

Half of his head was missing. The left side of his face bubbled-up and glooped onto the drum kit.

"Schhhlleeeelllppp meeeeheeee."

CRASH.

Choke fell forward over the drum kit. He thrashed what little of his body remained around in intense excruciation, "Gshllaaawwww."

Utero watched Choke bubble away into a patch of watery flesh and gore. All that remained were his boots.

Tool screamed the last words of the track as it came to an end.

The cries of murder and death blasted him in the face. He turned to Utero, "The fuck's going on?"

"I dunno?"

They looked back to the mosh pit. Every punch and kick resulted in a caving-in of someone's face, or the removal of a limb.

The pit no longer resembled an amphitheater of rage. Now, it looked like a death arena of bodily splatter.

SPATCH-CH! SPLATT!

A disgorged arm splatted to the ground. A head missing its jaw landed teeth-first to the ground, splitting the skull open. Knees and wrists mushed apart as bodies hit the ground.

A furious bubbling pool of human remains festered within the mosh pit. The liquid meshed together and rose toward the stage.

Hazmat stood at the back of the arena with the pliers in his hand. He snipped them together, facing the stage.

The different sections had gone silent. The gas had killed all four thousand members of the audience, reducing them to a messy, liquid human soup of all sorts of horrifying colors.

"Tool," Hazmat screamed from under his hood.

"Pest?"

Hazmat shook his head slowly.

"Who are you?"

Hazmat squatted to his knees and grabbed the side railing of the middle section. He gripped a latch on the metal with his pliers.

SPRUNG!

The middle audience section vibrated as Hazmat wrenched down on a jack by the latch.

He pushed it down over and over again. The section elevated. The action forced the pool of melted skin, shit, puke, blood and gore to slide through the mosh pit and up to the lip of the stage.

"What the…"

Hazmat turned around and did the same to the right section. The plier prongs squeezed over the latch.

SPRUNG!

He pushed the jack down, elevating the railings. The ocean of ex-humans sludged down toward the pit.

"Feed me, Hazmat," Tool roared and removed his cap.

He threw it at Utero.

"Honey, wh-what are you d-doing?"

Tool smiled and pinched her cheek, "We're gonna have a little dinner."

As the sections of the arena elevated, Tool dropped to his knees and held out his arms.

He took a deep breath and exhaled. His chest expanded, busting out the buttons of his shirt.

His jacket tore off as his arms and torso expanded.

Tool's head inflated, stretching out the skin from his face. The interior red skull ballooned through and snarled.

"T-Tool?" Utero gasped in shock, "What's happening? You're s-scaring me!"

Tool's giant red devil face shot over to Utero, "Shut up, *bitch*," A plume of smoke dusted out of his nostrils.

Hazmat chuckled and folded his arms. He watched the giant pool of human remains flood against the stage.

"Feed me," Tool snarled in a demonic voice, "Feed me."

Tool's body enlarged. He was now ten foot. His arms as big as two men's thighs. His body covered in red scars.

One jet black horn protruding through his forehead.

"Honey, wh-what's g-going on?"

Tool let out a loud growl. He pressed his palms to the edge of the stage. He lowered his giant chin between his fingers. His buttocks started to rupture and shed its skin.

"Ugggggghhh," he grunted.

WHUMP!

A twelve-foot tail burst out from his spine and slapped against the floor.

"Get in," he bellowed.

"What?" Utero fanned her hands in front of her, scared.

Tool's voice grazed across his lungs as he snarled, "I said get in," He looked like an angry, otherworldly bull at the front of the stage. His tail flapped around as he grew impatient.

"I ain't getting in there, you stupid cunt!" she protested. Inside, she was shaking to the core.

"Yes you are, woman."

SCHWIPPP!

Tool's tail smashed against the floor and cowboy whipped her across the back.

"Yarrrghhh!"

SPLOSH!

She splashed into the cavernous milk shake of human gore. Her arms thrashed around trying to keep her afloat. She gasped for air. "I'm drowning! Help me!"

Tool laughed monstrously as he watched his girlfriend thrash her arms around, trying to stay afloat.

"I will *drink* you," Tool snorted, fixing his double dilated black pupils at her as she drowned.

Her body broke apart in the sea of human filth. Her arm drifted away from her body as she splashed to the surface. Her nose and chin slid away from her face.

One of her lungs came through her lips as the rest of her face faded away into the ocean of red, yellow and orange.

The demonic beast that used to be Tool sighed. Two tongues slid out of his mouth and coated his lips.

A puff of smoke shot out of his nose as he replaced his chin at the edge of the stage. He yawned as wide as he could.

Hazmat tore off the railings from the middle audience section. with his pliers.

The ocean of ex-human sludge slid toward the stage and into the beast's mouth.

He let it flow over his extended tongue and slosh around inside his mouth.

TCH-LOAK!

The beast's esophagus panged opened, allowing the sea of human remains down its throat.

CHOMP, CHOMP, MUNCH!

Hazmat watched the beast swallow the liquid down. He

moved to the central section of the auditorium. The prongs of the pliers grasped the metal bolt and released the railings.

The edge of the section sprang up and sent the gore and shit down towards the stage. The beast turned its head to the left and drank down the infusion of melted skin, flesh and blood. Items of clothing swam down with it.

CHOMP, CHOMP, GULP!

The beast chugged down the meal.

BRRAAAPPP!

Hazmat nearly blew back on his feet as the waft of stomach-air ventilated past him. "Happy now?"

The beast rolled the side of its face on the stage. The black horn knocked against the surface as it curled up into the fetal position.

"Sleep."

Hazmat clicked his fingers.

KA-BRAAA-BOOOOOOOM!

The Beast exploded into a thousand gloopy pieces. Strings of black blood and shit launched into the air, splashing against the walls.

All that remained was its skeleton. The ivory shell cindered away from the aftermath of its detonation.

Hazmat looked at the four doors dotted evenly around the arena. They unbolted one by one.

As Hazmat made his way through the auditorium, a gang of security guards ran past him.

"What's going on in there?!" asked one of them.

His colleague barged past Hazmat and reached for the door. "Dunno. Suspected suicide bomber or something."

NEEE-NAAAWW!

Police and ambulance sirens wailed in the distance. Two police cars slammed on their brakes in front of the center.

No civilians around. It was spooky.

Hazmat kept on walking as police officers and

paramedics ran past him with the security guards. They reached the doors to the arena stage and saw the carnage.

"Oh, Jesus Christ," came a terrified voice from the arena, "What the fuck happened here!?"

Hazmat walked down the Cobra Concourse that led to *Chrome Junction Railway*.

An empty bench presented itself before the ticket barrier.

Hazmat took a seat and placed his hands on his knees. A trio of teenagers in hoodies walked past him. Their leader, the tallest of the three, looked over as he walked past.

The hooded teen threatened him, "The fuck you looking at?"

The girl yanked her friend on the arm, "Narc, man. Leave him alone. He didn't do nuffin' to you."

"Fuckin' wanker," Narc spat at Hazmat's feet and marched on toward the station.

Hazmat exhaled and shook his head.

He reached up and unfastened the Velcro from his neck. His palms hit the sides of his visor.

Off came the mask.

It was Tool. But he wasn't a youngster. This was a much older Tool, in his sixties.

He reached down and unfastened the straps around his waist. He stepped out of his yellow suit, down to his underwear and gloves.

A train thundered past in the distance as he lay across the bench on his side. He slid off the gloves and slid them under his head as a makeshift pillow. He shifted into the foetal position and made himself comfortable.

His eyelids closed and before long he was fast asleep.

He probably looked like a homeless man to anyone who walked past.

Chapter 8

In Utero

The receptionist smiled at her guest, "Welcome to *Uterox Industries*, how can I help you?"

"Yes, I'm here to see Maxwell Dark?" Rhonda said, placing her bag on the counter. "I think he's expecting me."

"Ah, right, you're the reporter?"

"Rhonda Ferrari, yes."

"Excellent, one moment."

The receptionist typed the visitor's name into the computer. "Our machines are a bit sluggish today, so apologies in advance."

"Oh, that's no problem."

Rhonda scanned the reception area.

Uterox Industries didn't mess around when it came to conveying its importance in the world. The building stood several stories high, looming proudly on the horizon amongst all the other well-known skyscrapers in London. You could see it as you traveled in on the open parts of the underground.

The reception area was full of men in suits making their way to the swipe gates. The doors whooshed out and in as staff members entered and exited. They weren't hurried in any way. These people were professionals. You could tell by the way they moved.

In this day and age, it was something of a marvel that they weren't distracted by their mobile phones.

Part of the reception wall had a screen built into it. The footage showed animated sperms swimming along a pink canal. One of the sperms edged forward, beating the others, and arrived at an animated egg.

The Uterox logo spun around in the bottom right-hand corner.

"Ms Ferrari?"

She turned around to the receptionist, "Yes?"

"Mr Dark is on his way down."

"Oh, good."

The receptionist smiled and turned to the next person waiting in line. The young lady was in a wheelchair and wearing a white gown. Her husband held the handles on her wheelchair.

"Yes, can I help you?"

"Mr and Mrs Weller."

"Aha, one moment," the receptionist scanned her computer. Rhonda was fascinated by the efficiency of the organization. She took out her iPad wrote on the screen with her stylus.

"Yes, just through here, please."

"Thank you."

The easy access gate swung open. Two men in white lab coats hopped over and took the wheelchair handles from the husband, "Thank you, sir. Hello Mrs Weller, how are you today?"

"Oh, I'm fine," she giggled, clearly very anxious, "A bit nervous."

"Not a problem," one of the lab technicians said, "You'll be absolutely fine."

His colleague looked up at the husband and shook his hands, "We'll take it from here. Thanks very much."

"Okay, that's great." He shook the white coat's hand and turned to his wife. She looked up at him with a tear in her eye.

"Now, you just concentrate on relaxing," the husband said. "I'll come and get you once they call."

"Okay."

He kissed her on the forehead and smiled.

"Thank you, Mr Weller," the technician said, "She's in safe hands. Okay, let's get her into prep."

"Bye, sweetie."

They wheeled her off down an infinite white corridor.

The gates swung back at Mr Weller's knees. He waved goodbye and turned around to see Rhonda had been watching.

"Hi."

"Hi. Do you mind if I ask you a question?"

"Uh, no?" he took out a handkerchief and wiped his eyes.

Rhonda poised her right hand over the screen, "Can you tell me why you chose to use *Uterox* today?"

"Oh, it was a no-brainer," Mr Weller sniffed, "They have a reputation for—"

"—Mrs Ferrari," came an overconfident voice amongst a set of footsteps. Rhonda turned around to see a man in a jet black suit walking toward her and adjusting his collar.

He held out his hand and interrupted Rhonda's interview, "I'm Maxwell Dark, CEO at *Uterox*."

"Oh, hello," Rhonda shook his hand and completely ignored Mr Weller.

"So glad you could make it," Max ushered her along to the swipe gates, "We were rather worried you were going to be late."

"Oh God, no, I'd never be late. I consider it a discourtesy to others."

Mr Weller held out his hands in a huff. He'd been completely negated, "I thought you were asking me questions?"

Rhonda looked over her shoulders as she walked away with Max, "I'm sorry, maybe another time."

Mr Weller shrugged his shoulders and headed for the entrance, "Rude woman."

"So, I take it you've done your homework?" Max giggled as he held his lanyard to the swipe gate. The Perspex panels slid out and allowed them through.

Rhonda followed and walked with him to the elevators, "Yes, of course."

"Oh, good. It's just that we had a journalist from some book series who had booked an appointment. Joy something-or-other. She never showed up."

"That's a shame."

"Yes."

Max and Rhonda waited for the lift with a few other suited men and women.

"So, how many staff do you employ here?"

Max looked around at the golden enclave. The digital numbers above the elevator entrance wound down.

"We have one thousand at the moment. One hundred admin. Around three hundred technicians. The others are an assortment of development, head-hunters and project specialists."

"Wow, that's very impressive," Rhonda made a note on her iPad.

Max and Rhonda exited the elevator on the fifteenth floor. A white corridor led them to a set of metallic double doors.

"Okay, this is where all the magic happens!" Max beamed as he strode in front of her. Rhonda clocked the artwork on each wall. Pictures of embryos, ultrasounds, and various stages of pregnancy adorned the walls.

Max held his lanyard up to gate. It beeped. The doors slid into the wall, allowing them into the next room.

"After you," Max smiled.

"Thank you," Rhonda moved through the doors.

She took a few steps into the next room. It wasn't a room so much as a vast, circular lab.

"Wow."

She flipped her iPad over and held the back camera out at the giant cylindrical desk in the middle of the room. A dozen masked technicians were busy on computer terminals.

Others were making notes on the glass surface with their styluses. Two of them looked up and noticed that they were being photographed.

SNAP. SNAP.

Rhonda took her photos and twisted the iPad into her palm, "Sorry, Mr Dark. You don't mind, do you?"

Max smiled and rubbed her shoulder, "Please, call me Max. And, no, I don't mind."

The two technicians turned back to their work. They seemed put-out at having their picture taken.

"So, what is this place?"

"The control center," Max moved forward, "This giant hub here is named Utero. She handles all the day-to-day stuff. She can process over ten exabytes of information in less than a sixth of a second. Utero, hello?"

"Good afternoon, Mr Dark." Utero said in her sultry voice. It sounded like something of a come-on.

"How are you today, my love?"

"I'm very well, thank you. This afternoon's results are most impressive."

"Let's not get into that just yet, Utero," Max smiled at Rhonda, "I wanted to show you off to a friend of mine."

"Very well, Mr Dark. May I continue with my work, now?"

A faint sound of a warbled heartbeat came from the grills in the ceiling.

"Yes, Utero. Thank you. Have a productive day," Max said at the ceiling.

"She seems nice," Rhonda joked.

"Yes, Utero is one of the more agreeable employees we have. Unlike some of the others I won't name."

He winked at Rhonda and nodded his head toward a pair of technicians. They looked grumpy as they slaved away at their machines.

"So, you're probably wondering what's going on, here?" Max smiled at Rhonda and reached for a plastic cup on the desk.

"Yes, please, show and tell me everything."

"With pleasure," he sniffed the contents of the cup. He turned to a technician and snapped his fingers, "You."

"Yes?"

"How many minutes has this extract been sitting in here?"

"The placenta?" the technician asked and looked up at a set of digital numbers, "Only three minutes. Extracted from the Error Room."

"Good," Max turned to Rhonda and offered her the cup, "Here, drink this."

"What?" Rhonda took the cup and ran the rim a few inches from her nose, "What is it?"

"Just drink it."

Rhonda shrugged her shoulders and gulped the contents down. She flapped her tongue over her chin.

"Yagggh," she licked her lips and slurped the solution down, "It's delicious. Tastes a bit like zinc."

"Good, isn't it?"

Rhonda held the cup out and inspected the inside, "What is it?"

"I'll show you," The first giant glass door to the left of the entrance slid open, "Follow me."

Max ushered Rhonda into the first room. Trimester One. Classical music played from two ceiling speakers.

"Ahh. I love a bit of Strauss," Max said as he walked with Rhonda up to six rows of twenty beds. All but one of them contained a pregnant woman curled up into the fetal position; naked as the day they were born.

Their necks and right wrists had an IV tube that ran across the floor and up the right-hand wall. The ends of the tubes plugged into a giant display.

The screen displayed one hundred and twenty square images of the women. Each had a white number in the corner. 001, 002, 003… all the way up to 117.

The pregnant women were all sleeping. Some of them snored in tune to the constant beeping sounds.

"Welcome to Trimester One."

"Jesus Christ," Rhonda gasped, overcome by the clinical yet orderly nature of the set-up. It was akin to a quarter sized football stadium.

The final three beds were empty.

"There's three missing?"

"Yes. Unfortunately, they didn't make it past the first six weeks."

"Six weeks?"

"Yes, it's all part of the speed-up service we provide. The first trimester at Uterox lasts just six weeks," he said, making his way to the control panel at the front of the room. He flicked a switch, "The idea is to speed up the process by up to fifty per cent."

The machine ground to a halt. The sleeping women stopped their breathing.

"The preliminary stage of the embryo's life cycle produces amniotic fluid. Look at the second tube from the womb."

Max lifted a woman's thigh as she slept.

Rhonda held her fist over her mouth. She could scarcely believe what she saw.

A tube stitched into the first woman's groin produced a clear fluid. It sucked down and shot toward the large unit at the back wall.

"We siphon off the amniotic fluid. It collects in the unit along with the others."

"But why?"

"So we can create our subsidiary product," Max tried to not to laugh, "I believe you sampled some in the control center."

"Jesus Christ," Rhonda spat to the floor in disgust. "You mean to tell me that *that* was amniotic fluid?"

"Yes. Well, not *just* amniotic fluid," Max explained. "It's fermented, first. Then treated with the usual stuff you find in champagne."

"*Baby Champagne*?"

"That's right. So now you know how it's made and why it's so expensive."

"I feel sick."

"I wouldn't worry about it, Mrs Ferrari," Max said. "Soon you won't care what happens to you."

Rhonda squinted her eyes at the revelation, "What do you mean?"

"Well, I—"

Three women in wheelchairs came through the opposite door. They were being pushed along by technicians.

"Aha, they're here. Load them in."

"Yes, Mr Dark."

The three technicians helped the women up. Max rubbed his hands and licked his lips.

"See how they're hooking them up to the IV?"

"Yes," Rhonda looked on as the technicians sliced into their necks, stomachs and wrists with a scalpel.

One of the girls winced, "Oww."

Rhonda turned to the woman who had complained. "I know her. I met her downstairs at reception."

"Oh yeah?" Max seemed very interested. "That's great."

"Yes, I think her name is Weller."

Mrs Weller turned to Rhonda as her technician buried the end of the tube into her groin. He took out a soldering iron and singed the skin around the lip of the tube.

"Hey, how do you know my name?" she asked Rhonda then turned to her technician, "Owww, that hurts."

"Sorry, Mrs Weller."

"Be careful with that."

Rhonda moved over to Mrs Weller, "We met at reception. Or, rather, I saw you and your husband at reception.

"Oh, right," Mrs Weller hushed, starting to feel woozy, "Good for you."

Rhonda looked at Max, "Mr Dark, do you mind if I ask Mrs Weller a couple of questions?"

"No, of course not. But you'll have to be quick," Max nodded at Mrs Weller's head, "She's about to *go dark*."

"Okay." Rhonda moved the stylus over her screen, "Can you tell me why you chose Uterox Industries for your prenatal care?"

"My h-husband and I c-could afford… to do it…" Her eyelids ran down the surface of her eyeballs, "Wh-who are y-you?"

"And can you tell me the benefits of using this service?"

"I shaarr… sharrrsshh," Mrs Weller's speech began to slur, "fassshh… laar…."

She started to snore and bunched her arms against her chest. She rolled over to her side and raised her knees to her stomach.

"Oh dear," Max giggled. "Looks like Mrs Weller has gone sleepy-bye."

The tube protruding from her neck filled with liquid and buffered down the side of her bed. Her snoring grew violent as the tube slurped the fluid from her throat.

"What's happening here?" Rhonda asked.

"Oh, a simple transfusion," Max explained. "In order for the first trimester to quicken all the bodily fluids are replaced by *Utoxin* from the generator. She's technically in incubation until it's over. The fluids produced from the embryo are siphoned off and stored in the lab for processing."

"Okay?" Rhonda couldn't believe what she was hearing, "Where does that go?"

"Well, it's shipped off for profit. Restaurants the world over are of the mind that *Baby Champagne* is the product of tomorrow."

"Isn't this dangerous?"

"No, we experience maybe one in two hundred errors," Max said as he stroked Mrs Weller's face.

"Errors?"

A woman in the second-to-last row began to convulse. Her unconscious body shifted around in the bed. The tubes swayed around and slapped against the floor. A dark, red liquid sloshed through them and piped toward the generator unit.

"Shit, shit. Error in seventy-one," Max clicked his fingers at a technician.

The lab guy in the white suit and mask ran over to her bed. The woman's waist and chest bulked into the air. The back of her head smashed against her pillow like a woman possessed.

He grabbed at the woman's groin tube with both hands. "She's *erroring*."

"Stop her," Max yelled, "Unplug it. Now."

"I'm trying," the lab guy screamed. He placed his knee against her waist and yanked back on the blood-filled tube. A tiny embryo wedged into the plastic tube.

Its black eyes looked up at the technician.

"Pull it out," Max screamed, keeping an eye on the monitor. The text "071" turned red and blinked.

"It's entered the tube," screamed the technician, tugging at the plastic neck.

"Just get it out," Max screamed back and turned to Rhonda, "Sorry about this."

"I, uh—"

POP!

The lab guy wrenched the tube from the woman's groin. The first half of the embryo lodged into the tube's opening.

"Oh *dear.*"

The tiny ball of flesh tore in half like two ends of chewed gum being torn apart. Its split waist slopped out through the bloody chasm in her groin.

The woman opened her eyeballs and blinked. She felt around her waist and looked down in shock.

"Oh my God. My God. My baby."

"Terminate it, now," Max screamed.

The woman thrashed around in pain and screamed.

Rhonda took a step back as she saw the tube snake around and fly out of the technician's hand, "Oh m-my God…"

Another technician, with his hand buried under his yellow coat, ran over to the commotion, "Calm down! Everything's going to be all right—"

SCHPLATTT!

The lip of the tube splatted to the ground, pulverizing the embryo's elongated forehead.

"You bastards," the woman screamed and plugged the gushing hole in her groin with her thumbs, "Where am I?"

She looked around to see Max, Rhonda and two technicians staring back at her.

The woman burst out crying, fearing for her life, "Where am I? What did you do to my baby?"

Max nodded over to the yellow-coated technician. "Okay, do it."

The technician removed a tiny pistol from under his jacket. The woman didn't see him do it. He stepped around her and buried the barrel of the gun in the back of her head.

The lab guy took out a small plastic bag and yanked it down around her head.

She gagged and thrashed around, trying to breathe.

BANG-SCHPLATT!

Her head exploded. The interior of the bag turned red. The woman's body slumped back into the technician's arms.

"Get the body out of here," Max huffed and turned to Rhonda, "Like I say, very exceptional circumstances."

The technician kicked the casters on the bed and wheeled her out from the row of beds.

The lab guy scooped up the woman's remains and carried the wreckage over to the machine. The plastic front yawned open and took the messy gore from his arms.

"So, that's the first room."

"My God, you're murderers," Rhonda said, placing her iPad to the desk. She stepped forward and watched Mrs Weller's tube fill with red and clear fluid. The generator sucked the liquid through tubes.

"Not really," Max pressed his hands together in deep thought, "We're just providing a service that people want. Speed and efficiency. People are busy and they value their time. They don't want to spend it being pregnant."

Rhonda was having second thoughts about venturing any further into her story. She looked around the control center and marveled at its simplicity.

She'd been a journalist for a few years now and thought she had seen it all.

"Utero," Max looked up at the console.

"Yes, Mr Dark?"

"Outlay and execute. Marker Tee-one, oh-seven-one."

"Understood, Mr Dark," Utero's reassuring voice bounded across the giant circular room, "Tee-one, oh-seven-one. The *error* has been dealt with."

"Thank you," Max turned to Rhonda. He watched her trying to get over the trauma of what she had seen, "It's okay, you know."

"What's okay?"

We're experts. We know what we're doing. Trust me."

"I'm feeling a bit woozy, actually." Rhonda cleared her throat and winced.

"It's a typical reaction to what you've seen. You get used to it."

Rhonda sniffed and swallowed back a tear, "I don't think I'll ever get over what I've just witnessed."

"Would you like to continue?" Max tried to smile and sympathize. All Rhonda needed was a few moments to regroup and continue, "There's Trimester Two to see next."

"Give me a minute." Rhonda closed her eyes and placed her palms on the console.

"Hey, don't touch my work surface," a technician yelled and batted her arms away.

"Don't talk to Rhonda like that, you jumped-up little shit," Max yelled at the technician, threatening to punch him, "You want me to smack the life out of your face?"

The technician backed away, very scared, "No, Mr Dark."

"Well get back to work," Max huffed. "Leave her the fuck alone."

Rhonda shook her head and fluttered her eyes.

She slipped her jacket off, "God it's warm in here. Do you mind if I just—"

"—No, not at all. Make yourself comfortable."

Rhonda placed her suit jacket over the back of a stool at the console desk. She was now in her blouse. Sweat marks ran under her armpits.

She pulled at her collar. A waft of warm body air ran up her face.

Max smiled and rubbed his hands, "Feeling better?"

"Yes, a bit," Rhonda licked her lips, "Actually, could I have another cup of Baby Champagne, please?"

"Sure," Max smiled and grabbed a cup from the console. He sniffed at it and closed his eyes, "Mmmm."

Rhonda grabbed it from his hands and tipped the entire contents down her neck.

"Whoa, easy tiger."

Rhonda slurped the last few drops like a woman possessed. The transparent liquid ran either side of her cheek. She gasped and licked her lips.

"Very more-ish, isn't it?"

"Uh-huh," Rhonda said, wiping her mouth, "I could go for another few glasses."

"All in good time. Let's take a look at the second room, Trimester Two," Max skipped over to the room, "I think you'll *love* it."

Strauss's *Blue Danube* appeared over the speakers as they walked to the second door in the complex.

"Here we go," Max swiped his ID card. The doors opened.

Rhonda ran a knuckle over her eyelids in a futile attempt to gouge out the sleep and beads of sweat.

When she opened her eyes, she had to blink a few times to process what she saw.

"Here we are. Trimester two."

Max danced to *The Blue Danube* music as he moved in. He swung his arms in the air like an orchestra conductor, "Our pride and joy."

"Whoa," Rhonda's face fell.

A giant grid of white metallic tables. Ten by ten. Each with a naked pregnant woman on her hands and knees. This time, though, the bulges were very easy to spot.

They were heavily pregnant.

The sides of their faces were chained to the surface of their table. Their arms bent out at the elbow with their palms flat on the metal.

The women's chests pressed against the surface of their trolley. Their backsides pushed into the air by a black plinth grating into their pelvic bone. Their stomachs bulged over the end.

Their bent knees splayed out, held by a fat pin wedged into their thighs. A chain around both ankles completed the look.

Very uncomfortable, and very compromising.

"Most survive the first room. Once that period is over, they enter Trimester Two."

"Jesus Christ," Rhonda held her hand over her mouth and burped.

Max giggled, "Well, that wasn't very lady-like!"

"I'm sorry," she hastened and cleared her throat, "Why are the women positioned like this?"

"Good question. This is week seven through thirteen. The final period. The subjects are in this position because at the very end, they give birth. It must happen in the position they're in now."

Max and Rhonda walked in amongst the grid of pregnant and unconscious women. Their asses were in the air. Each woman's splayed thighs exposed their genitals, leaving less than nothing to the imagination.

"Why do they have to be in this position?"

"The first series of tests we did ended up stillborn or, even worse, the subject of Nuchal cord death."

"What's that?"

"It's when the baby comes out with the umbilical cord around their neck. Like a noose. As they come out, they get strangled and die on delivery."

Rhonda tripped back over her feet. Her shoulders banged against one of the beds.

The woman on it rocked back and forth, undisturbed.

"My God, the smell. It's unb-bearable," Rhonda sniffed and drooled from the mouth.

"Yes, it takes some getting used to."

"I d-don't feel very w-well."

"Yeah, I know," Max chuckled and pushed her to the ground, "That's because of the *Baby Champagne* you drank a few minutes ago."

The room began to spin. A thousand thighs, feet, vaginas, assholes, and toes whizzed around her head.

"Whoa," Rhonda dropped her iPad to the floor, "I c-can't st-stop it sp-pinnin-gg—"

"—Shhh," Max crouched down over her and clasped his hands together. As he spoke, his voice echoed wider and wider, "Just relax and sleep, Mrs Ferrari."

"B-But I—" she tried to reach out to Max, but failed. Her arms were too heavy. The room span around, faster and faster.

Max stroked her face and tugged at her trouser leg. "It'll all become clear soon."

"Wha-wha," she said, her eyelids shutting tight, "Whuuu—"

Her voice ground to a halt and everything went pitch dark.

***

Whvum-whvum-whvum.

The warbling effect from an ultrasound echoed around the darkness.

"Can you feel hear that sound? Those tiny little beats?" Rhonda spoke in a soft and calming intonation, "It's the sound of my baby's tiny heartbeat. Listen to it."

Whvum-whvum-whvum.

"Isn't it magnificent? I've been here for two months, now. *Uterox Industries* is looking after *us*..."

"Did you make it through the first trimester?" asked an angelic male voice.

"Yes, I did."

"How was it?"

"It was wonderful," Rhonda's voice doubled-over itself, "There was a moment where we thought he might not get through."

"*He*?" asked the male voice, "So you know it's a boy?"

"I do *now*," she giggled. The laughter tripled and then quadrupled.

Rhonda opened her eyes.

She was on her elbows and knees - patient zero forty-four, among the hundreds of others. The left cheek on her face lay on the cloth that covered her trolley.

Her ass stood out, carried by the weight of the plinth underneath.

"Doesn't it hurt?"

"Does what hurt?"

A technician walked among the grid of pregnant women on all fours. He took some notes on a clipboard.

"Face down, ass up. Being in that position twenty-four hours a day with no break?"

"No, not at all," Rhonda's gentle voice fluttered around the room, "I'm a work of art. Look at me."

"How did you get there?"

"It was perfect," Rhonda's speech slowed down even more, "I visited them for an interview and they convinced me to take part."

"How could you take part if you weren't already pregnant?"

"They put a baby inside of me."

Mr Dark watched one of his masked lab technicians apply lube to a five-inch thick tube. It jutted out of Rhonda's out-turned vagina.

The technician slipped two fingers inside her and splayed his fingers.

The tube slipped in with great ease. Rhonda's vagina sucked the tube in a few inches and settled.

Max looked at the tube and followed its path back to a different generator. The machine lit up and flashed a pair of green lights.

A thick, white liquid shot down her tube. It took about a minute for the solution to travel from the machine, across the floor, and up the bed and into her body.

Her hips bucked up and down as her lower half drank the flowing contents inside.

Max held her groin down. The technician grabbed the neck of tube with his gloved hand. The white fluid continued to pour in.

Before long, Rhonda's belly was full to the brim. A trickle of gloop spat out from around the end of the tube.

Max nodded at the technician. He took out the plastic end and wiped it with his glove. Another tube replaced the one that had been extracted from between her thighs.

"Okay, we're good," Max looked at the screen of inserts, "Patient forty-one. Insemination successful."

Max traced the tip of his finger up Rhonda's lifeless body. From her hips, up past her belly button, through to her chest and neck.

A hole in her throat had another tube coming out of it. Like the hundreds of sleeping women around her.

"Go to sleep, my beautiful woman," Max leaned over her and pecked her on the cheek, "Take care of your baby."

For forty-two days and nights, Rhonda's womb incubated her baby without budging an inch.

Over the course of those days and nights, two women suffered a terrible episode.

They were taken to the Error Room.

One woman's body retaliated against the treatment. She had a heart attack and died while her baby was in utero.

The second woman, Mrs Weller, woke up during the incubation process and freaked out.

The shock killed the fetus.

She had the option of aborting the child or carrying through to the end of the second trimester. If she chose the latter, she'd have produced a stillborn. The company had offered her an undisclosed sum for the second option.

We never found out which route she chose.

Rhonda slept like a baby. During the sixth week, she put her thumb in her mouth and sucked on it. The skin under her knuckle had wrinkled over time.

She had no idea of the little activity she had performed.

"So what happens at the end of the second trimester?" asked the male voice.

"That's the beauty of the whole thing, Charlie," Rhonda's voice warbled around the still women, "There *is* no third trimester."

"No?"

"No, brother," she said. "Look at me. Peaceful in the lab. I can feel you kick against me. You're ready, now, honey."

A smile streaked across Rhonda's face. The technician smiled back and turned to the screen.

A red light flashed in the middle of the screen. Patient forty-one was about ready to drop.

"Eighty-eight days I've had you inside me, now, Charlie," Rhonda's voice sparkled even though her mouth didn't move. It was as though she were thinking aloud.

Of course, no-one else could hear her words but her and her baby.

***

My fantasy will make people think I am strange. Let me explain…

I imagine I am in my sister's womb. Yet to be born. She's on all fours on a table surrounded by one hundred men. They're all naked and priapic. She's off her head on drugs. Mescaline, probably. Maybe some barbiturates. Something that keeps her happy and in fairyland. It also maintains a perpetual state of arousal.

She's naked on the table and ready to accommodate the men. They're jacked up on Viagra, or some other, more potent, narcotic that produces virility.

As the electric pulses whiz down my feeding cord, my forehead protrudes and my brain forms.

The first man climbs behind her and slips his penis into her fat cunt.

His penis moves in and passes by me as I play with myself.

The slit on the man's cock head opens up. It blasts several jets of thick semen over me. Then, it rests.

Eventually, the organ slides away and is replaced by another.

This new appendage does the same thing.

All the while, I am growing at an exponential rate within my sister's amniotic sack. The plain and simple thrill of claustrophobia. It enables a ridiculous acceleration of my heart rate.

You could hear it through an ultrasound if you waved the Doppler over my sister's belly at the right time.

I imagine the course of this experience to last several hours. Man after man violating my sister and me, her unborn child. My only regret is that I am not on the outside looking in, seeing the pleasure on her face.

The intensity builds up, enticing her and me. She swallows a load of ejaculate from another man. Her stomach digests it and separates the waste from the nutrition.

The nutrients pass through my umbilical cord to feed me and keep me alive.

More and more semen from the different shoot up her fallopian tubes, filling the uterus. There's a slim possibility that I might drown.

But I don't care.

The clincher comes when there are ten men left to unload the contents of their testicles inside her.

One penis enters her carrying another with it. Like a double barrel shotgun. Then a third and fourth, like a bunch of flower stems wrapped in zip ties.

How the men position themselves to enact a quadruple penetration, I don't know.

All I care about is that it happens.

I fantasize about a twin being formed next to me. He, or she, climbs inside one of the penises and impregnates the man. Don't ask me how. All I know is that I am left alone to face the music.

And what sweet, considered music it is.

The men have to ejaculate at the same time, though. If one of them came early, he'd risk losing his stiffness and slinking back, being carried by the others.

It would be very painful.

The one-hundredth man climbs over my sister and "finishes" inside her. The twist in the fantasy is that it is not a man, but a woman. She is wearing a device.

The device punches me against the back of her womb over and over again. Because it cannot "come" in the traditional sense, it means I would forever suffer the torture of being pulverised over and over again.

The punishment never stops.

All this occurs in my final formation from embryo to fetus. My fingers have formed. I can see, though not very much. I can hear everything that is being said.

"Fuck me harder, sweetheart," Rhonda's voice emanates from within the pink illuminated walls of light.

The plastic, turgid device smashes into my face repeatedly. Fingernails and lanugo forms on my digits and head. I take great pleasure in the pain; nearly as much pleasure as I have knowing that my sister is taking care of me.

When the time comes, I will grab hold of my umbilical cord and masturbate it so it stiffens. If it is hard, then it cannot slack and twist around my neck as I swim toward the daylight.

I scrunch my knees to my chest and throw my body forward, effectively diving toward freedom. Swashing my arms out in a breaststroke style, I push down the cervix.

The walls cling to me, refusing to let me go. It can't stand to exist without me. Still, I push forward, hoping not to get stuck.

It would be horrible to get stuck like that.

Finally, I am out of the vagina in a whoosh of light, covered in my sister's Wharton jelly and birthing detritus.

My name is Charlie Ferrari. I am reborn.

***

"Look at her. So peaceful."

Max looked up at the screen in the central control center. The machines and devices bleeped and whirred.

Several masked lab technicians watched her stillness on the screen.

"Any moment now, sir."

"Yes, I know," Max said and knocked the circular table with his knuckles.

"Yes, Mr Dark?" Utero's voice beamed from above, "What can I help you with?"

"Oh, uh, nothing."

The swishing sound from an opening door occurred behind him.

"I thought you wanted me to do something? You knocked my console."

"No, Utero, it's all fine—"

"—Mr Dark, sir," hurried one of the technicians who ran out from the third door. "We have a problem in the Error Room."

"What problem, Jamie?"

"Please, just come."

Max and Jamie ran over to the third metal door. It was adjacent to the Trimester Two room. The Utero console in the middle of the control centre stood in between both doors.

They stepped inside the Error Room. The doors slid shut behind them.

"Holy shit, what happened here?" Max gasped, looking around the interior of the room.

"I don't know, they just started… *dancing*?"

"Dancing?"

Max looked on at a handful of upright corpses lining the back wall. Six pregnant female corpses - five white, one black - stood still and snarled at Max and Jamie. Rigor mortis had set in. Their eye sockets were empty, black caverns.

The stench was putrid.

"Yes, they've stopped dancing now, though, as you can see."

"What the fuck?" Max yelled, "Do you mean to tell me they're *still alive*?"

The walls around the Error Room rumbled, heaving in and out. The lights fizzled off and snapped back to life in an instant.

Max crouched and held his hands over his head, "What the fuck is happening to my lab?" Utero?"

Jamie slipped on a yellow plastic jacket and held a couple of ballpoint pens up at the six women.

"Yes, Mr Dark," Utero's plain female voice piped in through the room, "How can I be of use?

"Why have I got six *errors* staring at me?"

"One moment, please," Utero advised. A few beeps ran in succession, "I cannot ascertain with one hundred per cent accuracy why this has happened."

"Well shut them down, then!"

"Mr Dark," Utero said without a shred of emotion, "I am unable to shut down organic life. It is beyond my capability."

"Well, *fuck*," Max shouted, "Maybe I'll shut them off once and for all."

He stormed over to the first and raised his fist, "Right, you're fucking dead. So stay fucking dead."

As he threw his punch, the first woman sucked in some air and screamed a wave of death at him. He flew back onto his ass and tumbled over toward the door.

"Silence," she gurgled and coughed up the tip of an unidentified organ. The five other corpses turned to face her. She sported a pregnant belly which she held in her palms.

"Shit," Jamie helped Max to his feet, "They never removed the fetus."

Max threw Jamie's hand away in anger. "Get off of me, you fucking nonce. What do you mean they never removed it?"

BEEEEP-BEEEEP-BEEEEP!

The internal alarm systems sounded off. The room's light snapped off. The bulbs of the emergency strip lighting flashed. An alarm sounded off.

"Warning. Code red in the Error Room," Utero's voice advised. "Please exit and quarantine. I repeat, code red in the Error Room."

"Quick, let's get out of here."

The six corpses' stomachs started to rumble. They lashed their tongues out and fell to their knees.

"Shit, let's go," Max swiped his ID card down across the box by the handle. The door slid open.

Jamie and Max ran out into the middle of the hub, "Get that fucking door closed!"

SHWISSH-TCHUD. The door sliced into the wall and locked itself.

"I wanna know how the fuck that happened," Max screamed and clapped his hands together.

He spun around to the technicians and Jamie, "We've got over three hundred women incubating in T1 and T2. If you fuck this up I swear to fucking Christ I'll drop you back outside that decoy house where I found you. Let the lynch mob take you down, you sick fuck."

"Okay, okay," Jamie protested.

The technicians stared back, blinking. They didn't have a suitable response. After all, no single person was responsible for what had happened in the Error Room.

Baby cries came from within the room, followed by a splitting and sloshing sound.

Max looked toward the error room, "What the fuck is going—"

WHUMP. WHUMP. WHUMP

The door to the Error Room thumped from within. Cries of several babies came from within.

"Shit, everyone clear the area."

The technicians dropped their tools and slid their masks down to their necks. They ran over to the main entrance.

"Get out of here. Go," Max swiped a scalpel from the control desk and held it out in front of him, "Utero?"

"Yes, Mr Dark? How can I help—"

"—What the fuck is going on in the Error Room?"

"The women have given birth, Mr Dark. They'd like to speak—"

"—*Given birth*? But they're fucking *dead*."

"I'm sorry, Mr Dark."

"This isn't possible."

He ran over to the central control unit. Jamie walked with him, "What are you doing, sir?"

"Shutting Utero down."

Max lifted a plastic case on the control panel and slammed down on the red button.

BZZZZZ-OWWW.

The humming from the control unit ground to a deafening silence.

"Sir?"

"What?"

BANG-BANG-BANG! The door pushed outward. Snarling and growling sounds came from behind the black Perspex glass.

"I think they want to get out," Jamie said.

THUD, THUD, SMASSSSHHHH!

The door to the Error Room flew open. Max and Jamie stepped back behind the control unit.

"Who's there?"

The grunting noises stopped.

"Oh m-my God," screamed one of the women from inside the Error Room.

She stepped out and examined her naked, fluid-coated body.

Max squinted at her and lowered the scalpel, "Are you o-okay?"

"What h-happened?" Strands of her hair clung to her sweaty face. She shivered and examined her arms and hands, "Where am I?"

"Miss, how did you get in there?" Max asked, somewhat relieved. "Tell me your patient identification number."

She looked up and brushed her hair to one side. It was Zeeba, who we last saw dining with her sister at *La Mort Magnifique*.

"What number? I don't have a number," She screamed and ran toward the console, "Who are you?!"

"You don't remember?"

"No, I don't—" she stopped in her tracks and picked up a scalpel from the console, "You tell me what the fuck is going on! Where are my clothes? Why am I covered in gunk—"

"—I'd like to know, as well," came a deep, male voice from behind her. He stepped into the control room and looked at his arms and legs, "What happened to me?"

"Sir?" Max asked the man as Jamie looked on, astonished, "What happened to the women in that room? What's your name?"

The man looked up and wiped some clear fluid from his face, "My name is Jelani Orji. I don't know what's happening."

He looked down and covered his modesty with his hands.

Zeeba stepped back and kept the scalpel held out in front of her, "Stay away, you black bastard. You hear me? Everyone stay back."

"I don't know how I got here. Where's my daughter? Is she safe?" Jelani screamed and clenched his face, "What's going on?"

Max and Jamie turned back to the door. A man in a yellow hazmat suit walked through and surveyed the control room.

"Hey, you," Max shouted, "Get back to work and clear that mess up."

Hazmat took out a pair of pliers and snapped them together. The breathing through his purple visor was intense.

A slithering noise was next to come. It made everyone jump back in shock.

"What the fuck is *that*?" Jelani screamed. "A snake? I hate snakes."

He tried to trample on it with his bare feet. The scales on the side of its head puffed out. Its tongue rasped at Jelani.

"Don't fucking touch it, man," Jamie said, "That's a King Cobra. It's poisonous."

Everyone screamed and jumped onto the control desk. They tried to get away from the six-foot beast slithering its way around the central control room.

HIISSSSSSSSSSSS... SNAP.

"Shit. Get your feet off the floor, now," Max hopped over to the entrance. He grabbed his lanyard and tore it from his neck.

From out of nowhere, he started chuckling in pure insanity, "Oh, Majesty? Are you there?"

Clown music rumbled from within the error room. Toodle-ooo, toodle-oo, de-dum-de-dum.

"HA! HA! HA!"

A huge clown foot stomped to the ground from inside the Error Room, "Hello, boys and girls! It's your favorite entertainer!"

STOMP!

Everyone's gaze went from the shoes, up the legs and past Majesty's patchwork costume.

"My name is Majesty. HA! HA! HA!" he chuckled and hit a button on his lapel.

A jet of acid shot out and landed on the ground, fizzing away.

"Ladies and Gentlemen," Max took a bow and yanked the handle of the entrance door down, "You made it!"

Jelani, Zeeba, Majesty, Hazmat and the cobra turned to Max. They wanted answers.

"I believe there is one more?" Max shouted at the door. "It's okay, *fam*. You can come out now!"

A hooded man wearing trainers and jeans sauntered out of the error room. It was Narc.

Hazmat recognized him from the train station.

Narc stood in front of the door and rolled the flint on his lighter.

"Okay, you're all here."

Jelani turned to Max and clenched his fist, "Tell us what the fuck is going on. Who are all these people, man?"

"Yeah," Zeeba shielded her breasts from Narc's salacious gaze, "Why us? Why are we here?"

"Ah, yes, it's quite simple," Max nodded down at the cobra, "Narc, watch your ankles, *bruv*."

SNASSHH!!

The Cobra went for Narc's ankle, but he stepped away in the nick of time. He climbed onto the console and sparked up a joint. "Fuckin' 'low that faggot-ass snake, man."

"—As I was saying, it really is quite simple," Max chuckled, "The six of you are here because you don't exist."

The door to Trimester Two slid open.

"Don't exist?" Narc coughed up a phlegm and spat it to the ground, "What kinda gay shit are you talkin', bruv?"

"What do you mean we don't exist?" Zeeba choked and held her neck, trying not to be sick.

"Jamie," Max rubbed his hands together in sheer delight, "Can you wheel Rhonda out so our imaginary friends can take a look, please?"

"Yes, of course." Jamie ran off through the door. The others turned to Max as he kept the entrance open with his foot.

Jelani took a deep breath and crossed his arms. "Well?"

"All six of you are the figment of someone else's imagination."

Narc chuckled and knocked the console with his knuckles, "Nah, this gotta be some next man's fucked up dream or something."

The paint on Majesty's face turned from happy to sad. A small, blue painted tear rolled down her cheek, "Awww, but that's not fair. I want to be a *real* clown."

"Well, you're not, Majesty," Max tried to sympathize with him, "I'm sorry."

"Who's imagination are we a figment *of*, then?" asked Jelani.

"Some fucked-up heroin junkie," Max said. "In an induced coma."

Jelani shook his head and shot Max a dirty look, "This is bullshit."

"Don't take my word for it! Go and see for yourself," Max smiled. "She's pregnant with him as we speak."

"Him?" Zeeba screamed. "I'm a masturbation fantasy of some *bloke*?!"

"Yes," Max retorted. "Ah, here's Jamie, now."

Jamie wheeled Rhonda's bed into the main control room. The tubes remained slack and fed themselves back through the room.

"I should mention that my assistant, Jamie, isn't one of you. He works for me. Paying his dues for trying to molest a little girl."

Jelani and Narc watch Jamie wheel Rhonda into the room, "You fucking sick cunt."

Max reached Jamie and held the scalpel to his face, "Take off your pants."

"Wh-what?"

"Take them off."

Jamie did as instructed. He stepped out of his trousers and threw them to the side.

Max turned the handle to him, "Take the scalpel."

"Oh, dear God. No," Zeeba closed her eyes and looked away.

Jamie took the scalpel in his right hand. Max stood back and looked down at his Jamie's penis.

"Cut it off."

"Wh-what?!"

Narc and Jelani watched on, smiling to themselves.

"Cut off your dick."

Jamie reached down and lifted up his soft penis. He placed the blade at the base and pressed down.

"HA! HA! HA!" Majesty laughed and honked the horn on his nose, "Look at the pedo *curing* himself."

The blade ran across the flesh in his dick. Max licked his lips and screwed his face, "That's it, that's it, right across. Take the fucker off and hand it to me."

The severed penis fell into Jamie's hand. A jet of blood flew out from the hole where his penis used to be. Jamie burst out crying and handed his penis to Max.

"I'm s-sorry."

"Shut up."

Max took the appendage in his hands and showed it around, "See, ladies and gentlemen? The power of Pure Dark? A place where anything can happen," he beamed and turned to Jamie. "You think it's okay to fuck little girls, Jamie?"

"N-No, p-please," Jamie begged, "I said I was sorry."

"Fuck you," Max launched forward and grabbed the back of Jamie's hair. He yanked his head back and shoved the severed penis into his mouth.

"Jelani? Would you do the honors, please?"

"Sure," he bounded over to Jamie hoofed him in the nuts, forcing the man to bend over in pain.

"Gmmmppffhhh."

Max walked toward the door to the control center, "Ladies and gentlemen, there's his mother."

Rhonda was still on all fours - face down, ass up, legs apart, revealing her anatomy to anyone who chose to look.

Which was *everyone*.

"Meet Rhonda Ferrari."

"The fuck's this bitch?" Narc eyed her between the legs.

The cobra shifted its body around the leg of the bed and climbed up. It waved its venomous split-tongue, "Zzzzzzzzzzoooeeeeeeeeeeeee..."

"Ah, da-da-da," Max shouted at the Cobra to get down, "Not yet, Zoe. Not now."

The Cobra unfurled itself and hit the floor.

"Rhonda's about to drop any moment now," Max pointed at her stomach. "You're all a figment of her baby's imagination."

"What the fuck?" Jelani didn't buy a single a word, "This is *horse shit.*"

"I don't care if you believe me or not. It's true," Max chuckled and tucked his lanyard into his top pocket.

"So, what do we do now?" Majesty scowled at Max and the others.

"Last figment left alive wins," Max stepped back and held the door ajar, "But I'd be careful not to hurt Rhonda or her baby. Could be bad news."

The six of them stared at Max. He chuckled to himself and took a deep breath.

"Welcome," Max bellowed, evilly, his face turned red and his eyeballs bulged out of his sockets, "To *Pure Dark.*"

SLAMM! The door shut and locked itself.

"Hey, hey," Jelani screamed and ran after Max. He reached the door only to find it was locked, "Let us out!"

"You heard the man," Narc reached into his jacket pocket and took out a flick knife, "Which one of y'all wanna get cut first?"

HISSSSSSSSS.

The cobra slithered around the floor and stuck its split-ended tongue out at the other five.

"We have to do something about that fucking snake," Jelani stepped back and held the scalpel blade at it, "If we don't, it'll win before we've had a chance to discuss what we're gonna do."

"Cool, fam," Narc jumped to his feet and approached the snake. He raised his left foot.

"No," the cobra squealed, "I'm not a snake. I'm a woman."

"The fuck?" Narc threatened to stomp on her.

Zeeba, Majesty and Hazmat stepped back.

"I'm trapped in here."

Narc stepped back, also. The woman's voice coming from the mouth of the cobra seemed very genuine.

Zeeba backed into Hazmat's arms, "Don't let the snake bite me," Hazmat inhaled as Majesty looked over at the pair.

"You sure you want to do that, girlie-girl?"

Narc crouched down to his knees, "Yo, lady. How do we get you out of that snake?"

The Cobra kept her head up at Narc's face. Dead still.

"Be careful, man,' Jelani squeezed the scalpel, "No sudden movements."

Narc moved his face to the utterly still cobra. Her face suspended in mid-air, waiting for a conversation, "I'm trapped in here and I can't get out."

The tip of Narc's nose moved forward as he tried to look into her eyes, "So, how do we get you out—?"

HISSS-SCHWAPPP!

Her tongue lashed out and cut across his top lip. A blob of venom followed and landed on it, sizzling into his skin.

"Motherfucker," Narc stomped down on the cobra's neck. She screamed and wiggled her head around.

SCHPLATTT! The cobra's head exploded. Blood and snake skin splattered in all directions.

Narc fell back and clutched at his bubbling wound, trying to get the hoodie off of his head, "Gaaaahhh. Help me."

"I guess that's one down, now," Jelani looked at the smoke billowing from Narc's hood. The others didn't feel obliged to step in and save him, either, "Now which one of you cunts wants to die first?"

"What?" Zeeba began to heave, "No, don't kill us."

"You heard the guy. It's last man standing. And I ain't going down for no-one."

Jelani booted the end of Rhonda's bed. It flew across the room and smashed head-first against Jamie's on the floor. The impact knocked him out cold. The hole between his legs pumped out the rest of his blood.

The severed penis fell out from between his lips. Jamie was dead.

Jelani held the scalpel up at Hazmat, "How about you?"

Hazmat held out his hands. The pliers snipped together in his right. In his left gloved hand sat a small glass container.

"How about *you*?" Zeeba shrieked and pushed Hazmat away, "Fucking bastard."

She pushed her clenched fist into her mouth and swallowed down her forearm to the elbow.

GWULP-GWULP! Her chest heaved and pulsed.

"Oh my God," Majesty looked from Jelani to Zeeba, "That's messed up!"

BWWOOAAARRRGHHHH!

A thick jet of puke blasted from her mouth, covering the floor in spew. Majesty slipped on it and crashed to his ass.

Hazmat stepped over the taut tubing that ran across the floor from Rhonda's body.

Snip-snip-snip. The metal ends of the pliers tapped together.

"Yeah, you want some now, you cunt?" Jelani roared and launched himself at Hazmat.

SMACK-THWUMP.

Jelani smashed Hazmat in the face three times in a row. He stumbled back against the wall and kicked himself forward.

THWACKK!

Hazmat stabbed Jelani in the side of the mouth with his pliers, puncturing through the cheek. He clamped the pliers shut around his tongue and wrestled him by the head.

Majesty looked over to Zeeba, "You wanna?"

"Fuck yeah, motherfucker."

"HA! HA! HA!" Majesty reached into his ridiculously large trousers and took out a hand saw. He yanked on the cord and fired up the blade.

WHIZZZZZZ!

"Come get some, you fuckin' slut!"

Zeeba backed up and jiggled two fingers down her neck.

GLUMPFH, GLUMPFH—BLLOAARRGGHHHH!

A torrent of vomit jetted out of her mouth, blastingMajesty up against the central console. Bubbles of spew shot in all directions. The jet dripped down her chin.

"Don't fucking come anywhere near me, you clown cunt."

Zeeba jumped into the air and kicked Majesty across the face, sending his fake red nose against the wall. "Come here, you wannabe sack of paedo spunk."

Zeeba slid across her own vomit and grabbed a tuft of Majesty's fake hair.

He screamed in pain as the chainsaw nicked him across the leg.

"Ohhhhh, blood," Zeeba smashed the back of his head against the floor, "I fucking *love* blood."

Two more fingers down the throat.

BLLOOOARRRGGGHHHH!!

An angry blast of orange vomit thundered into majesty's screaming mouth. He lifted the chainsaw up as he gagged and wretched.

BZZZZ-SPRIINNCCCHHH!

The teeth of the furious blade rode up between Zeeba's thighs and chewed away.

Zeeba's entire body jiggled as Majesty launched the angry blade up between her legs. He spat out a wedge of her puke and watched her waist split apart.

The saw chewed its way through her spine and up through her liver. The squelchy organ slipped through the crater between her legs.

"Oh, ho, ho, that *stinks,*" Majesty chuckled and hit a button on his jacket, "Looks like children are off the cards now, huh, *bitch*?"

Carnival music began to play as the saw ate its way through her intestines and stomach. Blood and mucous shot out from her nose and mouth.

"HA! HA! HA!" Majesty's face fell angry as he continued sawing Zeeba in two up her middle, "*Bitch.*"

Hazmat threw another punch at Jelani but missed. He stormed forward and hit the central control panel chest-first.

Jelani grabbed him by his shoulders and head-butted the back of his skull.

"Ommfpph," Hazmat tuned to his side, keeping the glass container away from the impact.

"No, d-don't," Hazmat pleaded and shook the container, "If this breaks, we'll all die."

"What the fuck is that?"

"It's like Ebola. It'll fuck you up."

"Fucking put it somewhere else, then," Jelani offered him his hand, "Give me that."

"No."

"I don't give a fuck about me," Jelani wailed. "So it looks like we're all gonna die."

He bashed the container out of Hazmat's hand. The glass shattered across the floor and released a black mist.

Hazmat kicked himself back, "You fucking stupid prick. You just let me win."

He climbed to his feet and watched Majesty finish Zeeba off. The saw curved out of her throat, releasing the flesh. Her entire naked body slipped into two halves - split up the vagina through to the top of her head.

Majesty climbed to his feet and held the chainsaw at Jelani and Hazmat.

"HA! HA! HA!" the clown chuckled and waved the chainsaw above his head, "Which one of you two ugly goat fuckers is next?"

VROOM-VROOOOOOOMMM!

The petrol from the attached canister coughed out the back as Majesty revved the engine, "Want some candy, cunts?"

"It's too late," Hazmat's muffled voice came through the visor, "I've won."

"Huh?" Majesty followed Hazmat's gloved finger down to the black smoke rising into the air, "What's that?"

"The reason I'm going to win. I'm guessing you have about thirty seconds."

"Motherfucker," Jelani socked Hazmat in the side of the face and caught him by the arm.

A giant tear sliced through the suit. Hazmat looked down and gasped, "Oh no. Oh shit, what did you do that for?"

"Suit's no good to you if it has a split, right?"

"Fuck you," Hazmat kicked Jelani between the legs.

Majesty looked up from the black mist and sniffed. His nose began to bleed.

"Yaarrrrrggghhhh!" Majesty ran toward Jelani with the chainsaw in front of him, "Fucking meet the saw, child!"

The end of the chainsaw shunted into Jelani's crying face. Hazmat didn't know whether to help Majesty or take him down while he was busy.

Jelani's head yawned open, releasing a jet of white and red gore. He reached up to the whirring blade and tried to push it away. Instead, it took most of his fingers off.

Hazmat stepped back and allowed Majesty to continue murdering his victim.

"HA! HA! HA!" Majesty screamed as the fire burned his eyes, "How'd you like me *now* you black fuck?!

WHUUURRR-SCHLOMP-CHOMP!!

The saw buried itself down into Jelani's neck. His entire body looked like an ejaculating Pez dispenser. Blood and throat meat splattered up the wall and across the floor.

Jelani choked and glugged his last. His body below the neck slumped in a messy heap to the floor.

His neck and head remained pinned to the wall by the blade. Majesty sawed right through the wall and into the electrical circuits, frying the corpse.

SCH-BIZZZZZ! Majesty dropped the chainsaw to the floor and began to cough. As he stepped back, his heel skirted over Jelani's bust-open cranium.

"Wooopsie Daisy," Majesty gasped and regained his composure. He turned around to find Hazmat was missing.

The black mist was now floating halfway up the room. Majesty turned around to see Rhonda's hips pulsate and buckle. Her body's actions made the trolley she was on jiggle back and forth.

Majesty coughed and choked as the black mist drifted into his airways, "Brroooo," he spluttered and wiped his eyes.

He made it to Trimester Two and saw Hazmat standing amongst the hundreds of women on beds on all fours.

"Close the door," he said. "It might be too late, but if less gets in, the better chance we have of surviving."

Majesty tilted his chin to his neck. He looked back at Hazmat and shot him an evil grin, "You mean *this* door?"

Hazmat threw his hand up. "No, Don't—!"

SWIISSHHH!

He swung the door to Trimester Two back and forth as viciously as possible. The motion caused the black mist to waft from the control center and push its way into the room.

"No. Don't do that. Are you fucking crazy?" Hazmat stormed through the grid of pregnant women.

"Yes," Majesty slammed the door shut, locking Hazmat in with the incubating women, "I'm out of my tiny, little mind. HA! HA! HA!"

Majesty stepped back and dry heaved. The canister had emptied. Looking through the window to Trimester Two, he saw Hazmat drop to his knees.

The pregnant women started to erupt. The belly of one melted, sending a long, pulsating rope of slime down to the bed.

Three women's vaginas engorged and released the gelatinous contents of their wombs down their legs.

An accumulation of gore from the women slapped to the ground all around Hazmat.

He banged on the window of the door, choking and screaming. "Help. Help. Let me out."

The black mist had crept into Majesty's airwaves already. He spat some blood against the window as he watched from the other side of the door. He scooped the blood splat away and saw a pregnant woman's stomach explode all over the trolley. The impact tore the flesh of her thighs. Her corpse slumped to the ground in a disgusting concoction of gore.

Hazmat removed his visor and slammed it to the floor. His face sizzled and melted down his neck and chest. He caught his mushy upper palate in his hands and pressed it back into his skull.

"Why, w-why?"

Majesty pretended to rub his eyes with his hands and mock-mouthed, "Boohoo."

Rhonda's thighs shunted wider on the trolley.

Majesty took a step forward and buckled under his own weight.

SCHLUMP!

His right knee hit the floor first, followed by his left.

"Oh, oh," he gasped, saliva running down his chin. The white paint squelched away, revealing the skin on his face, "You're h-having a b-baby."

Rhonda bucked her hips. Majesty turned onto his ass and leaned against the wall, trying not to breathe.

"I c-can't b-breathe," He closed his eyelids. They squished and glued to his cheek. When he tried to open them, they tore off and slid down his face.

Trimester Two was filling with the embryonic and gory human remains of the melting women. The sludge filled the room like a swimming pool. The inside of the window bleached out yellow, white and red.

Blood trickled from Majesty's nose. He held his fingers to his nostrils and sniffed.

"Hmmm. Smells funny. Like zinc."

The tip of his nose melted down his fingers and down his wrist. Majesty's right hand bubbled and was the next to go.

"Oh f-fuck… f-f-fuuu… f-f-lllaarrccch."

Rhonda's out-turned vagina bust apart. The sheer force of a cream-coloured ball punched through from within.

It was the last thing Majesty would ever see. His corneas liquefied down his face, taking his softened cheekbones down his neck.

"Gaaaooowwwww," he gasped as his face caved in and swallowed down into his neck, "Naooowww."

Majesty's torso slumped to the ground in a puddle of its own effluence.

Rhonda launched her hips up.

The head of her newborn push through between her lips. A green Mohawk fanned out over its bald scalp.

Two tiny fingers slipped out from inside Rhonda's vagina. The baby hulked itself through the opening. Its chest, followed by its waist. It shrieked blue murder. Until finally…

SPLATTCCHH.

It landed back-first onto the table in a puddle of its own jelly and excrement.

Shivering cold and crying.

The baby extended its arms toward the ceiling, trying to fend off the abrasive strip lights.

It kicked its feet up and out, toward the ceiling.

"Waaaahhhhh," The baby cried for the first time and opened its tiny eyes.

Then, the screaming stopped. The baby lay under his mother, breathing slowly. The white gloop from his face drooled down his cheek and hit the trolley.

"I think he's coming round," a female voice yelled, "Quick, get a doctor!"

"No. Let's wait," came another voice.

The baby rolled over and onto its side. His mother's splattered thighs acted as a makeshift tent a few inches above.

The baby curled up into the foetal position. A few sparks of electricity ran through its body.

He held out his thumb and placed it in his mouth, closing his eyes shut. The green hairs on his hair crept out further along the trolley's surface.

"No," Dr Long's voice drifted around the room, "I'm afraid Charlie's not quite with us yet. His body is still expelling the last of the narcotics he took. We don't know how long he'll be under. It could be some time."

Baby Charlie closed his eyes and fell asleep.

"Okay, doctor," said the friendly female voice, "We'll wait as long as we have to."

PURE DARK VOL. 2

Chapter 1

Charlie's Still Under

"Charlie?" Dr Long's calming voice entered the darkness, "You have a visitor."

She flicked her flowing read hair behind her shoulders and looked down at the hospital bed. Breathing apparatus sprawled around Charlie's face. The sound of assisted mechanical breathing underscored the beeps from the life support machine.

Charlie Ferrari looked peaceful. Asleep.

The doctors put him into an induced coma three days ago. The weekend had flown right by.

A woman entered the room carrying a bunch of flowers and a bag. Dr Long looked up at her and smiled, "We'll have to make it a quick one, Mrs. Ferrari. If that's okay?"

"Yes, of course."

Rhonda stepped over to the desk and set the flowers down on it. She took a chair at Charlie's bedside and placed the bag on her lap.

"Well, I'll leave you two to it," Dr Long smiled at Rhonda and left the room.

Rhonda examined Charlie's face. His Mohawk had subsided away from her on the right part of his scalp. A long piece of gauze ran around the left side of his head, tucked under his chin.

"Charlie, can you hear me?"

No response. The beeping continued. The mechanism kept his organs alive.

Rhonda looked at her shoes. She wondered if she should reveal the sad news she'd brought. It didn't matter. Charlie was unconscious.

"Charlie, listen," Rhonda swallowed hard and looked away. Her eyes focused on a poster on the wall for sanitary products available on the hospital foyer.

A tear ran down her cheek.

"Oksana committed suicide."

Charlie didn't respond. A slight skip on the heart monitor was the only acknowledgment she got.

"I know you know that I didn't much like her," Rhonda continued and tried to keep her composure, "But she didn't deserve that."

She reached into the bag and rummaged around, "I brought you some flowers. They're on the counter."

Rhonda pulled out a black and white toy cat. She put it on the desk and reached into the bag again.

"That blond woman who was with her, Joy *somebody*, the one who resuscitated before you arrived. She saved your life. But we can't find her."

Rhonda pulled out a plastic baby doll and set it beside the fluffy toy cat, "Johnny's on his way over. Mum's picking him up after school. He lost his favourite toy. That big panda thing. So I got him these."

Rhonda folded the bag and tucked it under her arm. Charlie's closed eyelids fluttered. She didn't notice - she was too busy staring at the door.

"I'll say the gifts are from you," Rhonda stood to her feet and bent over his face, "I'm sorry, Charlie."

She pecked him on the forehead, softly.

Dr Long pushed the door open and stood against it, "Everything okay?"

"Get better soon, brother," Rhonda whispered to his face. She turned around and patted down her suit, "Yes, everything's fine."

"Jolly good." Dr Long walked over to Charlie's life support machine and made a note on her pad.

"Doctor?"

"Yes, Mrs. Ferrari?"

"How long is Charlie going to be under?"

"Hard to say," Dr Long returned to her notes, "The swelling on his brain hasn't helped, I'm afraid. As I was telling your sister-in-law when she brought him in, we're waiting for the opiates to leave his system."

"What's the bandage on his head for?"

Dr Long made a note of the machine's diagnostics. "Charlie's experiencing intracranial pressure."

"What's that?

"ICU. Swelling on the brain," Dr Long said. "We're waiting on the MRI results. Prepping him for surgery as a precaution."

Rhonda looked down at the floor, "Okay. Can you please call me if there's any update."

"Yes, of course," Dr Long smiled and spotted the flowers and toys, "Those are nice."

"Yes," Rhonda made for the door, "Hopefully I'll hear from you soon?"

"Yes, of course."

Dr Long waited for Rhonda to leave the room. She heard Rhonda's footsteps pass down the corridor, further and further away. She put the notepad on Charlie's waist and detached the tube from his wrist.

"Charlie?"

Click-click. She snapped her fingers over his face, "Can you hear me?"

Click-click.

No response. Dr Long smiled and leaned into his ear. "Everything's going to be okay."

She removed the plastic bag from the clip and placed it on the bed, "Okay, you can come in now."

A hideously obese black man with dreadlocks wheeled himself into the room. His name was Complex - the dealer

Charlie owed money to. His legs and head were bandaged. The wheels on the chair buckled under his sheer weight.

"He's all yours."

Complex licked his lips and reached under his seat. He took out a plastic IV bag. It was full of a creamy substance, "Motherfucker gon' pay for tryna kill a brudda."

"Very well," Dr Long took the new bag from his palm, "We'll get him plugged in."

Dr Long turned around and hooked the bag over the metal clip. Complex wheeled up to Charlie. He watched on as Dr Long threaded the tube back into his arm.

They both smiled at each other.

Complex leaned into Charlie's ear, "Ya man, Charlie. My nigga," he grunted. "Ya ganna be livin' offa dis shit, ya'kna. Mah doctor girlie girl wit de orange hair gonna be feedin' ya, man."

Dr Long blushed and held her fingers across her face, "Oh, stop it."

He chuckled and thumped Charlie's stomach. The beeps quickened, but Charlie was still unconscious. The billowing from the pumps sped up.

"Ya feel me, man?" Complex threatened, knowing that Charlie would somehow react, "*Angel O'Deth*, bruh. Be runnin' troo dem veins for 'nuff time."

"Okay, that's enough," Dr Long quipped. "We better get out of here before someone gets spooked."

Charlie licked his lips and smiled. A gold tooth glistened from the sunlight pouring through the window, "Dat ass of Charlie Ferrari belongs ta me, nah. Feel dem opiates run troo ya body and fuckin' choke on dem, blud."

Dr Long sauntered around the bed and grabbed the back of Complex's wheelchair.

"Get me atta here, Doctor," Complex said. "Me hate 'ospitals, ya knaa."

She wheeled him to the door. He took over and pushed his wheels into the corridor.

Dr Long walked back to the bed. She took a final

glance at the IV full of heroin that would keep Charlie in her domain for a very, very long time.

She smiled and loomed over Charlie's face, blocking the light from the ceiling.

"Charlie?"

No response. His body ingested the new heroin solution from the IV, "Who's a cute little boy?"

Charlie lay fast asleep, his organs feeding on the drip. She pressed her fingertip on his nose and play-acted all cutesy.

"Yes, you are," she giggled, playfully, "You're my cute little boy."

***

"What are you? Yes, that's right," Rhonda's voice was playful. Her finger moved from Charlie's little nose and stroked his cheek, "Such a cute little baby boy, aren't you?"

A smile streaked across newborn baby Charlie's face. He kicked his spindly little legs around and gurgled, trying to catch the giant finger.

"Mommy loves you?" the voice beamed. "Mommy loves you."

"Haha," Baby Charlie laughed, enjoying the ticklish prodding.

The silhouette from a woman blocked the lamp from the ceiling, "Awww, you're such a beautiful little baby."

Baby Charlie felt two snake-like forearms slithering around his back. He looked left - white bars, like a picket fence. He looked right - the same again.

Baby Charlie floated into the air. A giant chest wearing a blouse flew up and screamed toward him.

Rhonda pulled him to her bosom and hugged him tightly. She rocked him from side to side and buried her cheek onto of his head, taking in his newborn baby smell, "I love you so much, Charlie."

He gurgled and nuzzled into his mother's chest.

"Honey?" came a man's voice from the kitchen. "Has he gone to sleep, yet?"

"Ah, no," Rhonda hollered back and carried Charlie with her to the kitchen, "I'm trying to get him to doze off."

"Aha, there's my little boy," the man turned around and made silly faces at baby Charlie, "Who's my favorite little prince?"

Baby Charlie laughed back at his Dad and went for his fingers.

"Aww, you're so sweet," Dad pecked Charlie on the forehead. He turned to Rhonda and kissed her on the cheek, "Dinner's nearly ready."

Dad moved to the kitchen counter and picked up a knife. He sliced through the vegetables.

Charlie diverted his attention to a ten-inch line of sugar on the chopping board. He held out his hand and giggled with approval.

"Ohh, what's that, sweetie?" Rhonda asked and carried him toward the kitchen counter. "You like the white thing, do you?"

Charlie giggled again, trying to reach line of white powder. He found it hilarious.

So, too, did his mother and father.

"Aww, he'll be a chef one of these days," Dad beamed.

Charlie's eyes widened at the granules as they glistened in the light.

DING-DONG. The front door bell chimed.

"I'll get it," Dad chirped and walked out of the kitchen, leaving Rhonda cradling little Charlie by the kitchen counter.

Dad opened the door. A man with silver hair and a pristine dark suit and gloves stood with his back toward him.

"Hello?"

The man turned around and smiled, "Mr. Ferrari?"

"Yes, who are you?"

"Maxwell Dark." He took a bow and held out his hands, "At your service."

"Who are you—?"

Two of Max's men burst through the door. One of them, Max's burly bodyguard, grabbed Dad by the chin and wrenched his arm behind his back. The gloved palm slipped over his mouth.

Max stepped into the landing and kicked the door shut with his heel, "Oooh, I do love family get-togethers, don't you?"

SLAM!

"Mffggghhh," Dad screamed into the bodyguard's hand. The second man unhooked a TEC DC9 semi-automatic from his shoulder and aimed it down the corridor, "All clear."

Max faced Dad and smiled, "Where's the kid?"

"Mfgghhh."

Max looked up at his bodyguard and frowned, "How's he meant to tell us if you're covering his mouth?"

"Sorry, Mr. Dark." He released his grip on the firearm as Dad puffed and panted, choking for air.

"I'm so sorry about that, Mr. Ferrari. I'll ask again," he took Dad's chin into his gloved hand, "Where's the fucking child?"

"In the k-kitchen—"

"In the kitchen, in the kitchen," Max threw Dad's chin aside and turned around. He hopped, skipped and jumped his way through the landing, "In *de* kitchen… dum-de-diddly-dum."

Rhonda looked up at the kitchen door and froze. "What the hell?" She clutched Charlie to her chest and stepped behind the table.

Charlie began to cry.

"No, shh," Rhonda pressed her finger against his mouth. Charlie wasn't having any of it. He shook his head and cried hard.

"Charlie, no," Rhonda whispered. "Shh."

"Ohh, Mrs. Ferrari?" Max sung from the landing. His voice grew louder as the footsteps came closer, "I have something for you."

"Oh, shit." Rhonda stepped back to the patio door.

Max's head tilted into the kitchen. "Hello, Rhonda."

"Wh-what are you doing h-here?"

"It's me," Max jumped into the room and held out his arms, "Maxwell Dark, *Uterox Industries*."

The bodyguard pushed Dad into the room and kept his mouth covered with his hand.

"Mffgghhhh."

The armed man held the DC9 at Dad's head and smiled.

"Wh-what are you d-doing?"

Max chuckled and pointed at baby Charlie, "We want the baby. How about a trade?"

"What?"

"Mfggghhh!" Dad screamed into the glove.

Max thumped the kitchen table. The vegetables flew into the air, "For fuck's sake, we want that… *thing* you're holding in your arms."

"You're not taking him."

"He's not well," Max chuckled.

"You're not taking my baby."

"I beg to fucking differ, *Rhonda*."

The armed man pushed the barrel of his semi-automatic into her husband's head.

"Yeah, look. You give us the kid and we won't shoot your husband. A perfectly fair deal, right?"

Dad closed his eyes and bawled into the bodyguard's glove.

Max turned to Rhonda, "Well? How about it?"

Rhonda took a deep breath and held Charlie closer than she'd ever held him before.

"Why do you want him?"

"*Fuck you*, that's why," Max offered. He'd prepared that retort for days, it seemed.

"You said he's not well?" Rhonda stepped back.

"We, uh, need to run some tests on him."

"No, no, no," Rhonda tried not to cry. "He's three days old. He's healthy and happy. There's nothing wrong with him."

Max snapped his fingers. The masked gunman jammed the barrel of the gun further into Dad's temple. "Yeah, except he'll be fatherless in about two seconds if you don't hand him over."

"No."

"No?" Max shook his head and held his hand to his ear, "I'm sorry. Did you say *no* to me?"

"That's r-right," Rhonda stammered, sick to her stomach. She rubbed her hip against the patio door handle.

"You're sick. Everyone at Uterox is sick—"

"—Now, now, Rhonda—"

"—I've heard the fucking stories about you. About that palsy thing, and you're fucking sick."

Max made quotation marks with his fingers, "*I'm* fucking sick?" Do you want me to tell your husband who Charlie's *real* father is?"

Rhonda froze dead still. Her pupils dilated. She was in deep trouble, "Y-You wouldn't."

"Mr. Ferrari," Max turned to Dad and sneered, "Did you know you're not Charlie's father?"

"Hunnghh?" Dad belted into the gloved hand.

Rhonda held out her palm. "No. Don't tell—"

"—That's right," Max explained in a delirious manner, "Her *brother* is the child's father!

Rhonda burst out crying, "Fuck you. You bastard. You're not taking my baby."

Max sighed and rubbed his hands together, "You sure?" He turned to the masked gunman.

"Yes, I'm quite sure," Rhonda made eyes at her husband. "It's okay, honey, we're insured. We signed the indemnity before they incubated me. There's no way they're going to hurt—"

BLAMMMM!

The right-hand side of Dad's skull blasted against a family photo hanging on the wall. His body crashed to the oven, neck-first and slumped to the ground.

"Now look what you made me do," Max play-sighed and nodded at the armed man, "Get the fucking kid."

"No," Rhonda kicked the patio window with her foot. She ran through the glass with Charlie crying in her arms.

"Fucking get her," Max shouted after the gunman as he ran around the table.

BLAM! BLAM! BLAM!

Rhonda ran across the patio and around the garden table. Slabs of wood burst apart from the gunfire. She made her way to the back gate.

The gunman and bodyguard chased after her. Max ran after them.

SCHLAAAAMMM! A boot kicked the back gate against the railings, causing it to break off its hinges. A startled black and white cat jumped away and squealed.

Rhonda darted through it in bare feet and headed down the alleyway.

"Help me. Help me."

"She's heading for Sears Road," Max's voice screamed from behind the gate.

Rhonda's feet splashed through a puddle. Her feet avoided two discarded syringes left at the side. She looked up and clutched the crying Charlie against her chest as she ran.

Two little girls playing in a puddle looked up and screamed. Rhonda hurtled toward them.

"Help me. They're trying to take my baby."

The girls climbed to their feet. The brunette child grabbed her baby doll from the ground and ran alongside her friend, "What's going on?"

"Run. Don't look back, just run," Rhonda screamed over her shoulder, "Go home, now!

The gunman ran into the alleyway and fired off a round of bullets. THRAAA-TAT-A-TAT!

The bullets whizzed past Rhonda, missing her. The two girls climbed up a metal railing into one of the gardens.

"Get out of here, now."

"Okay, okay," cried one of them, her dress catching on a sharp piece of metal.

THRAA-TAT-A-TAT-A-TAT!

The gunman reloaded, "Motherfuckers." He ran through the same puddle Rhonda had splashed through seconds ago. He slotted a new clip into the gun and flicked the catch back.

The gunman fired half a clip up the alleyway.

Rhonda sprinted for her life toward the busy main road a few feet away.

SCHPLATCH!

A bullet hit her in the hip. "Ofgghh," She continued to run toward the main road. If she could make it, she'd have the pick of the alleyways to lose her assailants.

"What the fuck are you doing?" Max screamed after his gunman, "How fucking hard is to shoot a fucking woman carrying a baby, you fucking retard?"

"I'm trying," He took aim again and fire another round. The two girls jumped down into the garden and hid behind the metal fence.

The gunman, Max and his bodyguard ran past them.

The black and white cat followed. "Miiaaooowww."

The gunman turned around instinctively and unloaded the last half of his clip at the cat, "Fuck."

THRAA-A-TAT-A-SPLATCH-HH!

Several bullets tore through the cat. Its bloodied carcass smashed against the metal railing. The girls squealed in terror.

Max exhaled and looked at the gunman, "Are you quite finished?"

"Sorry, Mr. Dark," he said, releasing the clip and replacing it with another.

"Go."

Rhonda reached the busy road. She looked left; a long stretch of pavement. Not a wise decision.

To her right, the pavement came to an end. There was only one way forward.

The busy road.

WHIZZZ-SWOOOSH-NEEAAAWW

The cars flew past at seventy miles-per-hour from both directions, "Charlie. Hold tight, sweetie."

She looked over her shoulder. The gunman raised his DC9, seemingly in slow motion.

She turned around to the road, equally as slow.

"Nooooo," She stepped into the road.

SWISH-SWARSH! A passing car clipped some of the fabric of her jeans. She stepped forward and dashed across the four lanes.

"Fucking get her," Max screamed. "Now."

The gunman aimed down his sight as her body disappeared into the traffic, "I gotcha. I gotcha."

THRAA-AAA-AATT!

The driver of a speeding red car's head exploded. The interior splattered red gore along the upholstery. The car smashed head-first into an oncoming blue VW, sending its driver through the windscreen.

FLING! The blue VW tumbled into the air and crashed down onto the empty road.

A speeding car raced turned the wreckage. The driver slammed on the brakes. The wheels slid across the road.

Rhonda turned around. The carnage of several cars slamming into the backs of others was deafening.

She looked ahead. One more lane until freedom. She looked down at her bleeding hip and kissed Charlie on the head.

"Charlie. Hold tight."

She ran into the last lane. The right side of her body buckled under its weight, sending her to her knees. She looked to her right. A number plate screamed toward her - “TR4X”

NEEEAAWWWW-SPLATTCHHH!

The license plate slammed into Rhonda, killing her instantly. Charlie flew out of her hands and into the air.

Max arrived at the road and stepped back. He almost fell on his ass as he saw Charlie flying several feet into the air.

"Jesus fucking Christ," Max looked up and over as Charlie reach the summit and careen back down to the ground.

"Fuck, no," Max screamed. "He’s going to splatter all over the road. Get him."

The gunman ran into the wreckage, keeping an eye on the baby making its descent from fifty feet up in the air.

He held out his hands.

NEAAWWW-SPLATTCCHH!

The gunman’s body turned to red mist as a truck barreled into his side.

BEEEEEEEEEEEP!

The truck skidded to a halt as Max held his hands behind his head in despair, "Nooo. *Fuck*."

Charlie’s body plummeted to the ground.

WHUMP.

He landed in the middle of a bush. The soft leaves broke his fall and gently rebounded.

"Gagaaa," Charlie said, kicking his arms and feet into the air.

Max picked up the DC9 and held it up at the drivers who were still alive in their cars.

The horns stopped blaring.

"Get the fuck out of here," Max fired a round into the air. The drivers opened their doors. Some of the passengers darted from the other sides of the cars.

"Move. Now," He reached into his collar and flicked a

switch, "Sears Road."

Max turned to the bush and emptied the semi-automatic's clip. He reached the bush and held out his hands, "Come to Daddy."

Charlie wasn't there.

"What the *fuck*?"

Max's bodyguard ran up behind him, "You got him?"

"No, I don't fucking *got* him," Max punched him in the chest in an apoplectic rage, "You fucking retard. Does it look like I have a baby with Dark's Palsy in my hands?"

"Sorry, Mr. Dark."

Max ran his palm over his forehead, "Where the fuck did he get to?" He looked into the distance and saw a woman cradling a blanket in her arms. She turned back and held her shaking finger to her lips.

"Shhhh."

Max squinted. The woman wore a V-shaped bodice. Her face wasted away, the skin wrinkled to the bone.

"Over there," Max screamed. "That woman—"

The old lady forefinger erupted in white sparks. She drew a six-foot line from her head to her feet. The air opened up, releasing a blast of pure white light.

Charlie screamed in her arms.

"What's she doing?" Max whispered to himself.

A rumbling noise shot across the road. Long chasms and cracks erupted across the ground, shattering the concrete.

The car alarms went off.

"What the fuck's happening now?" Max grabbed his bodyguard for balance. The road and surrounding environs earthquaked violently.

The sky darkened as the eruptions became more fierce.

A baby's gurgling and laughter whizzed around the scene as the cars rolled into each other.

A proper earthquake.

The woman stepped into the white light with baby Charlie. The hole zipped up behind her.

"Max Dark," roared a demonic, angry voice from in the sky. Max looked at his bodyguard and then up at the sky.

The sun fizzed away as a black circle peeled across it. A long shadow cast over the road, darkening the environment.

The clouds warbled and turned into a tofu-like series of fleshy tubes. Pangs of electrical sparks ran through the soft tunnels.

ZIP! ZAP!

Max held out his arms and screamed toward the heavens, "What the fuck is happening around here?"

The streetlights snapped on due to the falling darkness. The clouds drifted apart.

A mad blast of wind blew Max back a few steps. The lapels on his collar shook.

"Charlie?"

A baby-shaped cloud appeared in the sky among the sparkling cerebral cortex. The kid gurgled and chuckled.

"Hello, Max."

"What are you d-doing?" Max shouted over the noisy wind and rumbling.

The cortex dissipated and broke apart. The baby's voice deepened and slowed to a near-halt.

"Welcome… to *Pure Dark*!"

Max fell to his knees and ran his hands through his hair, "Noooo."

The streetlight bulbs burst one after another.

Max's cry echoed into the night sky…

Chapter 2

Babydoll

"Zack," his mother shouted from the top of the stairs, "Get your shoes on, we'll be late."

"Okay, mommy," Zack was sitting on the floor watching his favorite TV show *Star Jelly*. He'd managed to get his shirt on. He'd also managed to spill a tiny bit of orange juice down the front of it.

"Oh, look," whispered the narration on the TV screen. "There are two burglars coming in to help themselves to the house. But here's Star Jelly to the rescue."

A starfish made of colorful gelatin sprang on to the screen. Its pointed edges made up its arms and legs. A giant grin streaked across his friendly face. Star Jelly hit the floor and couldn't move.

"Oh no, what's wrong Star Jelly?" asked the narrator as the burglars made their way up the staircase, "You don't have any bones, do you, Jelly Anderson? You can't move."

Star Jelly shook his head and let out a tear, "No, I cannot stand upright. I have no bones."

The sound of footsteps bounded down the stairs. The coat stand knocked against the wall from the landing. Mom was inches away.

Zack stood up and pointed the remote control at the TV. He pressed a button and shut the TV off.

"Zack?" Mom's voice came from the landing, "Have you got your shoes on, yet?"

"Yes, mommy," Zack grabbed his trousers and stepped into them. He clipped the buckle across his waist and grabbed his school shoes.

Mom came into the room and caught him red handed. She placed her hands on her hips and sighed, "I thought you said you were ready?"

"I am, I am," he slipped his feet into his shoes. He looked down his front and tried to keep the stain away from his mother.

"Right," Mom huffed and walked toward the kitchen. "Have you got all your stuff?"

"Come on, Babydoll," Zack grabbed his doll. It dangled next to his thighs as he walked to the front door.

Babydoll was Zack's "brother." Of course, he wasn't his brother at all - it was just a silly old doll.

Zack once had an older brother named Michael. He thought about him a lot during car rides. He never really knew his brother, though. He went missing two years ago when his younger brother was still in diapers.

Zack sat in the back seat of the car as mom drove to the nursery. He was fascinated by the trees, hedges and random semi-detached houses that whizzed past.

He turned to Babydoll, who was sitting in the passenger seat next to him. Zack made sure his brother was safe by fastening the safety belt around him.

"It's okay, Babydoll," Zack said, "mommy is a good driver."

They reached a red light. Babydoll had rocked around the back seat as Zack's mother took many sharp corners. It ended up leaning against the door handle and staring at Zack.

He chuckled to himself and tightened his own safety belt. "You're so small. If we have a crash you might slip through the belt."

The doll stared at Zack with its perpetual smile. The diaper had slipped off due to the slip and slide across the seat.

"Okay, Zack," Mom said from the front of the car, "If anyone asks, what will you tell them?"

"That I fell over," Zack repeated as if rehearsed. "And it hurt and you rescued me and it was okay."

"Yes, good," Mom sniffed, "And you don't tell anyone what really happened, right?"

"I don't know what really happened," Zack said. "I just know that it hurt."

"Okay, okay," Mom reached for her ringing mobile phone as she applied the gas.

Zack turned to Babydoll and rolled up his sleeve. A black and purple bruise ran up the underside of his forearm.

Babydoll seemed to focus on the bruising.

"I had an accident last night, Babydoll," Zack revealed. "While I was sleeping I fell out of bed."

"—Yeah, Dad. It's me," Mom said into the phone as she steered the car, "Has he been in touch?"

Babydoll's eyes drifted down and then back up. The water within the plastic was heavy enough to at least feature some lifelike movement.

"No," Mom screamed, "You keep that no-good prick away from the house."

Zack looked at his knees, "I didn't do anything wrong, Babydoll."

The doll fell to its side and stared at Zack. He turned to the toy and smiled, "But you'll look after me, right?"

Babydoll didn't reply - he wasn't a sentient human being.

"Okay, settle down," Mrs. Pershar said to the children as they sat on the carpet in the middle of the room. Their brown-skinned and frightening-looking old teacher pressed her palms together.

"Today we're going to play a game," she made eyes at little Zack holding his doll, "It's called *My Best Friend* and it will be fun."

The children giggled and shifted around on the carpet.

"Hush, now, children," Mrs. Pershar said. "Just raise your hand and tell us about your best friend."

A hand shot into the air immediately. It belonged to Mia, an adorable blond girl sitting a few kids away from Zack.

"Me, me," Mia lost her breath as she yelled.

Mrs. Pershar sighed and ignored the other hands in the air, "Okay, Mia, tell us about your best friend."

"Well, miss," Mia rose to her feet, "My best friend is Zack."

This was news to everyone - including Zack.

"Really, Mia?"

"Yes, miss," Mia beamed and turned to Zack, "He is really funny and cute and one day we might get married."

"Eewwwwww," screamed the rest of the children from the carpet.

"Okay, so Zack is your best friend because he's funny?" Mrs. Pershar asked.

Mia nodded rapidly. Her shoulder-length locks flew up and down her shoulders.

"Miss," Zack said. "Can I go next?"

"Yes, you may as well."

Zack stood to his feet and held Babydoll in his arms. He smiled at Mia and then turned to his teacher, "My best friend is Babydoll."

Many of the children chuckled. None of them had a mascot. Only Zack.

"Shut up," he protested. "It's not funny. Miss, they're teasing me."

"Pipe down, children," Mrs. Pershar yelled over Zack's classmates as they suppressed their giggles, "Okay, why is your toy your best friend?"

A couple of chuckles came from the other side of the

carpet.

"Because he's my brother. He went away when he was a real boy and he came back as a toy and he looks after me."

"That's very nice, Zackary," Mrs. Pershar said. "Would you like to—"

"—That doll is creepy," screamed another boy with green hair.

"Charlie," Mrs. Pershar snapped. "That wasn't a nice thing to say. Apologize to Zack."

"Sorry, miss," Charlie bowed his head, apologetically.

"Not to me," she huffed. "To Zack."

Charlie looked up at Zack. He had a point, though - Babydoll was *really* not attractive in any sense.

"Sorry."

Zack looked down and toyed with the idea of being upset. He thought against it and sat back on the carpet, "It's okay."

Nap time. What a busy morning the children had gone through!

First was the debate on what made parents annoying. That was fun.

After that, a bit of a play in the sand pit and a trek around the nursery grounds. It was enough to knacker anyone out.

Nap time wasn't so much for the kids as it was for the staff. Mrs. Pershar had fallen asleep at her desk. Most of the kids were out cold on the carpet.

Zack wasn't one of them. Neither was little Charlie. They'd ended up reconciling their argument during the morning. They ended up together on the carpet. In the space of a few minutes they'd gone from mortal enemies to best friends forever.

Zack placed Babydoll against the desk at the end of the carpet. He looked peaceful there, sitting upright with his hands on his lap.

"Hey," Charlie whispered, trying not to wake up anyone up, "What happened to your brother?"

Zack shifted on the carpet and laid his head on the folded blanket, "We don't know."

"Did he, like, run away?"

"No," Zack drifted off, "One day he was here, and the next day."

Charlie waited intently for the rest of the sentence. Zack had fallen asleep.

The boy bopped his head on the cushion and looked over at Mrs. Pershar's desk. She was still asleep, as were the others.

"Ugh," Charlie muttered. He covered his eyes and rubbed his face. Resigned to the fact that he wasn't going to fall asleep, he started counting the paint numbers on the wall.

One, two, three…

"Pssst," came a child's voice from the end of the carpet.

Charlie looked over. There was no-one there at all. Only Babydoll. Charlie closed his eyes and exhaled.

It was only a matter of time before he was asleep.

"Pssst."

That voice again. Charlie opened his eyes and looked to his right. No-one was there.

"Who said that?"

Babydoll lifted his head and smiled at Charlie as he lay on his side, "It's me."

"What?"

"It's me," Babydoll said in a very recognizable child's voice, "It's Zack."

"Zack?"

"Yes," Babydoll shifted himself to his hands and knees and crawled over toward his new friend, "Shh, don't say anything. You'll wake everyone up."

"But, but—"

"—Shhh," Babydoll arrived at Charlie's head and rolled

over onto his bum, "I have a secret."

"What is it?"

A little girl shifted and murmured, threatening to wake up. She was right by Charlie's feet.

"I know what you did," Babydoll said. "You've been bad."

"No I haven't?" Charlie rubbed his eyes, "What did I do?"

"You haven't done it yet," Zack's voice came from the doll's lips, "But you did a very bad thing."

"Zack?" Charlie became anxious, "Wh-what are you doing in the doll?"

"It happens when I'm asleep," Babydoll nodded over to the sleeping Zack beside him, "Go on. Wake me up and see what happens."

Charlie looked over at Zack fast asleep on the cushion. He turned back to Babydoll, puzzled, "If I wake him what will happen?"

"I'm stuck in here with him," Babydoll whispered. His movements were lifelike, "I need you to help me get him out."

"Who?"

"Charlie Ferrari!" Mrs. Pershar shouted from her desk, "Who are you talking to?"

"Oh, uh," Charlie turned to the doll which lay across his right arm, "No one, miss."

"It sounded like you were having a conversation to me," Mrs. Pershar said. "Were you talking to Zack?"

Charlie bowed his head and frowned, "Sort of, miss."

"Zack, why were you talking to Charlie?"

Zack opened his eyes and yawned. He had no idea what was going on, "What, miss?"

"The two of you were talking," Mrs. Pershar huffed. The children on the carpet began to wake up due to the commotion, "See? You've woken everyone up."

Zack looked at Charlie. Babydoll was still lying in his arms.

"Hey, give me that," He snatched the doll from Charlie and hugged it, "It's mine."

"But," Charlie shook his head. He didn't know what to think. He looked at Zack a bit differently, now.

"Okay, boys and girls, nap time is over. Up you get."

The children obliged and sat up, wiping their eyes. Mia smiled at Zack. He didn't return the sentiment.

Mrs. Pershar ushered the children along the playground, toward the pick-up area. Happy that the day was over, they filed out in pairs.

Charlie, Zack, and Babydoll were last in the line. Charlie couldn't help but stare at the doll. It stared right back at him as it hung beside Zack's left leg.

"How did you get inside it?" Charlie whispered.

"Huh?"

"You said when you're sleeping you go inside."

Zack shot Charlie a look of crazy, "What are you talking about?"

"You told me you go inside the doll."

"No I didn't."

"Did too."

"Did not," Zack insisted. He genuinely thought his friend was going insane, "When did I say that?"

"When you were asleep."

"That's rubbish—"

"—Okay, children. Wait against the wall, please."

The children obliged their teacher and perched their behinds on the wall.

Mrs. Pershar turned to the mothers and fathers. They made their way to the playground from the car park.

Charlie swung his legs as Zack tried to look away from Mia. She waved at her potential husband. Zack could see it in the corner of his eye. Instead of looking, he clutched Babydoll to his chest and bowed his head.

"That's one weird doll," Charlie said.

"Leave him alone. He didn't do anything to you."

"He said I did a bad thing," Charlie revealed. "But I haven't done it yet."

"Yeah, you did a bad thing," Zack got annoyed at the accusation and lies Charlie had told him.

Zack's mother arrived and offered her son her hand, "Come on, Zack, let's go."

He took it and stood to his feet. mom marched him past the children. Zack looked troubled as he held the doll in his arms.

"Bye, Zack," Mia beamed as he walked past her.

"Yeah, bye."

Two Years Ago

"Happy birthday," Mom and Dad cheered. "Make a wish, sweetie."

Zack closed his eyes and thought for a few seconds.

He blew out the candles on his birthday cake. It took a few attempts but he nailed the third candle on a twelfth try.

mom took out a knife and cut into the cake.

Dad clapped, as did Michael, his older brother, "Happy birthday, Zack, look what I got you."

Michael took his hand from behind his back. In his palm was a folded piece of paper in the shape of a duck, "Quack, quack."

"Wow, a duck," Zack snatched it from Michael's hand and played with it, "This is the best present ever."

The front doorbell chimed. mom dropped the knife and wiped her hands on her apron, "I'll get it."

She walked out of the dining room. Dad turned to Zack and smiled. "So, what did you wish for, sweetie?"

Zack looked up and smiled. "I wished for a—"

"—Oh my God!" Mom yelled from the bottom landing, "Petey. Are you okay?"

"No, no I'm not," a man's voice echoed from the landing. "It's over, it's all over."

"What the hell?" Dad ran to the landing. Zack and Michael turned to each other and giggled. They hopped off their chairs and ran to the landing.

Petey was an ungainly man. His stomach hung over his belt as he sobbed into their mother's arms. The man was inconsolable, "I'm so sorry, Petey."

He removed his tear-strewn face from mother's apron, "She said this was it. It's over."

mom and Dad turned to their boys. Their father was keen to get them away from the turmoil on display.

"Ugh, Zack, Michael, could you go to the front room—"

"—Oh no, no," Petey tried for a smile and chewed back his tears, "It's okay. Happy b-birthday, Zack."

Zack didn't know how to respond. All he wanted was three things: A: make Uncle Petey smile again, B: to discover what the large gift in his hands was, and C: find out why he had a black eye. The object was covered in birthday wrapping paper.

"That's okay uncle Pete," Zack quipped. "Please don't be sad."

Petey laughed through his tears and calmed down.

"Where's auntie Nancy?"

Mom and Dad winced and looked away, hoping their son wouldn't ask that question. It was obvious things hadn't gone well between him and his wife.

"Oh, she's sick," Petey held out the four-foot gift. "So she said to say sorry. But we got you this."

"Oh, *wow*," Zack snatched it from his hands and ran into the front room. "Thanks, Uncle Petey."

mom and Dad turned to Petey and smiled.

"You know us well enough, Pete, man," Dad said. "You could have called and come over another day."

"Are you kidding? Miss Zack's birthday because of that psychotic woman? No way," Petey calmed down and wiped his nose, "I'm not letting that bitch spoil his big day."

"Well, if you're sure?"

"Yes," Petey patted Dad on the shoulder, "Do you mind if I stay a few days? I've nowhere else to go."

"That's fine," Mom said, eying her husband for approval, "Right, honey?"

"Uh, sure," Dad said. "But you'll have to bunk in with the boys, we only have the two rooms—"

"—Oh, wow," Zack's elated voice shot around the house, threatening to crack the windows apart, "A doll."

"A doll?" Mom leaned into the front room. "You do know Zack's a boy, right?"

"Yes, I know," Petey said. "But I made it myself. It'll last a long while."

Dad chuckled and threw his arm around his wife, "Well, he seems over the moon."

Indeed, Zack *was* over the moon. As was Michael. They fought over who got to hold it first in amongst the torn gift wrapping, "Hey, give me it."

"Boys!" Dad shouted. "Michael. Let Zack play with it first. It's his present."

"But Dad—"

"—No buts. Let Zack play with it first."

It had been a long, warm evening. Zack and Michael had erected a play tent in the corner of the front room and invited the doll to a pretend dinner.

Dad, Mom, and Petey talked the evening away over a few beers. Mom didn't drink, though, so endless cups of tea was the order of the day.

And frequent trips to the bathroom.

It was bedtime for the boys. mom tucked them in. Michael took the top bunk and Zack had the bottom. He was yet to brave the wooden stairs that took him to the bed above.

"Night, Michael," Mom pecked him on the cheek and moved down to Zack.

Being top bunk suited Michael, though, being the older

brother. He was the king of the room, "Night, mommy."

She pulled up the duvet up to Zack's - and the doll's - neck, "Happy birthday, poppet."

Zack's attention was on the inflatable mattress in the corner of the room. A can of deodorant and a toothbrush he didn't recognize sat on the dresser.

"Mom, what's that for?"

"Oh. Uncle Petey's staying with us for a few days."

"Why?"

"Because Auntie Nancy is a bit sick," mom explained. "So, uh, he needs somewhere to stay so he doesn't get ill."

"Okay."

Mom smiled at the toy and patted its head, "So, what's our new friend's name?"

"*Babydoll.*"

Mom looked at her son. She made a value judgment. He was still so very young, though. She smiled and squinted at the toy. It was perfect. "Hmm. Babydoll. I like that."

"It's a stupid *girl's* name," came Michael's voice from the top bunk.

"Shut up," Zack turned onto his side and squeezed the toy in his arms.

Mom smiled and kissed Zack on the cheek. She ran her thumb over her son's brow and smiled at his cuteness, "Night, sweetie—"

"—And Babydoll, too, mommy."

"Oh, yes," Mom leaned in and kissed Babydoll on the forehead, "Night, night, Babydoll."

She stood to her feet and flattened out the sheet on the inflatable mattress, "Okay, Uncle Petey knows you'll be asleep, so he'll try not to wake you up later when he goes to bed, okay?"

"Okay."

"Do you want the light on or off?" Mom asked.

"Off," Michael said.

"But—"

"—Okay, off it is." She switched the light off and exited the bedroom, "I'll leave the door open a bit, okay?"

"Okay, mommy."

A shaft of light from the upstairs landing beamed in through the crack in the door.

"Night, Michael," Zack clutched his new doll in his arms. He didn't get much of a response. Instead, he got a snoring sound from the top bunk. The excitement of the day had taken its toll.

Zack closed his eyes and shifted under the sheets. A perfect silence. It wasn't too long before he, like his brother, drifted off to the land of nod.

"Pssst," A voice came from nearby.

Zack remained asleep and turned onto his side.

"Pssst."

The second sound jolted Zack from his slumber. His eyes opened on the inflatable mattress in the corner of the room. Petey hadn't gone to bed, yet. He must have been asleep for all of five minutes.

Babydoll sat idly in the middle of the mattress. He pressed his palms into the puffy material, "Hey, it's me."

Zack nodded.

Babydoll pressed his plastic forefinger to his mouth, "Shhh, it's okay. Come here." He patted a space on the inflatable mattress next to him.

Zack crawled out of his bed and tiptoed over to the mattress. He sat next to the doll and crossed his legs.

"What are you doing?"

"I wanna show you something," Babydoll whispered. "But you have to promise you won't tell anyone."

"I promise."

Babydoll held out his hand and rolled his three plastic fingers around to his palm. Then, he waved his clenched hand over to his nose, "See?"

Zack nodded and smiled.

"I can make it move all by myself."

"Wow."

Babydoll pressed his fingers against Zack's bottom lip, "Do you like that?"

"Umm," Zack blinked and looked down his nose, "It's funny—"

"—Shhh, just let me."

Babydoll stood to his feet. His size meant that he was chest-high to the cross-legged Zack. He slid his tiny plastic hand into Zack's mouth.

"Don't do anything," Babydoll whispered. "Just let me put my hand in."

"What if someone sees us?"

"No, they won't," Babydoll slipped his baseball-sized hand in Zack's mouth and felt around.

"Teeth… tongue… what's at the back?" Babydoll asked. "Ooooh, a tunnel."

"Gwuurrgghh," Zack tried to speak.

Babydoll slid his entire arm into Zack's mouth and grabbed his ear with his free hand, "Shhh, let me in."

He slid his other arm into Zack's mouth and hoisted himself up to his nose, "Can I go inside?"

Zack blinked and nodded. Anything for his friend.

Babydoll winked and pushed his head between the top and bottom rows of teeth. He perched his foot against Zack's neck and kicked his torso and waist in between his lips.

Zack turned to the door. Babydoll's body half-hung out of his mouth. The shaft of light hit his face as he turned to see his brother sleeping on the top bunk.

"We don't want to wake your brother," Babydoll whispered from within Zack's mouth.

Finally, Babydoll launched his legs and feet into Zack's mouth and pushed himself down his throat.

"Zack?"

"Mffghh?"

"Wake up."

"Mfgghh?"

"Wake up, sweetie."

Zack jumped up in his bed and gasped. He rubbed his hands over his eyes and looked at the inflatable mattress.

It had been slept in, but Petey wasn't there.

He looked down next to him. Babydoll had disappeared.

Zack yawned and extended his jaw a few times, "Mom."

No response. Zack jumped from out of his bed and looked up at at the top bunk. "Michael?"

Michael had gone, too.

It was early in the morning. There were noises coming from the kitchen.

Zack ran as fast as he could down the stairs to see mom, Dad and Michael at the breakfast table. She poured a glass of orange juice for her brother as the others munched on their toast.

No sign of Babydoll.

"Mommy!"

"Hey Zack," She sat down to her cereal and coffee, "Come on. Sit down and have your breakfast."

Michael spat out a mouthful of cereal into his bowl, "Ugh."

"Michael."

He rubbed his stomach and winced, "Mom, I don't feel very well."

"Are you okay?" Zack asked, all chirpy.

Petey dropped his spoon and looked at Michael, "What's wrong?"

"I feel sick."

mom stood up and helped Michael off his chair, "Come on, let's get you some medicine."

They walked toward the kitchen counter. She opened the cabinet door and rummaged around.

"Where's Babydoll?" Zack complained. "I can't find him."

"Did he go to bed with you?" Dad asked and took a sip from his coffee.

"Yes, but he wasn't there when I woke up."

Petey looked at Zack and took a bite from his toast. His right eye lowered, suspiciously, "Are you sure you took him up with you?"

"Yes."

"He must be around here somewhere."

Mom found some stomach medicine from the kitchen cupboard. She unscrewed the cap and poured some of the contents into it.

"Is it your tummy?"

Michael nodded and stretched, "I feel like I need to go to the toilet."

"Okay, drink this. It'll help your stomach."

The phone on the wall began to ring. Michael took the cap of medicine and sniffed at it, "But it smells."

"Just drink it, sweetie."

Mom picked up the phone and tucked it under her chin, "Hey, Nancy. What's up?"

Michael necked the medicine in one go and gasped, "Ugh, that's horrible."

"Really?" Mom sounded surprised. "No, he spent the night with us."

"Finished," Michael slammed the lid on the kitchen counter.

"Okay, give it a few minutes and see how you feel," Mom nodded at the dining table. Michael walked off as she returned to her call, "What do you mean he just left?"

Michael took his seat at the dining table and helped himself to a tall glass of orange juice. Petey smiled and stirred his coffee with a spoon, "Feeling better, champ?"

"A bit," Michael held the glass to his lips.

Mom walked back into the dining room in a state of confusion.

"Everything okay, honey?" Dad asked.

Mom had a puzzled expression on her face. She looked at Petey.

"What's up, sis?"

"Everything okay?" Dad asked once again.

"Yes," Mom pressed her palms against the table, "Pete, what happened last night?"

"What do you mean?"

"I had a call from Nancy. She's wondering where you are. You just disappeared."

"Oh."

Zack looked at Michael. They giggled, knowing that their mother wasn't happy with their uncle.

"Whatever she says happened, she's lying, sis," Petey insisted.

"No bust up? No argument?" Mother asked.

"She's very modest," Petey took a sip of his coffee, "She's always downplaying everything. And besides, how could I miss young Zack's birthday?"

Mom looked at Dad. He didn't know how to respond.

"Pete, that's—"

Mom tripped over an object on the floor. She bent down and picked it up. It was Babydoll.

"What's this doing on the floor?" Mom fumed.

"Babydoll," Zack hopped off the chair and grabbed it from her arms. "I knew you were here."

He gave it a great big hug and examined its face. The right eye was damaged. The eyelid wandered up and down as the pupil drifted around.

"Mom, you hurt him."

"I barely touched it," Mom huffed and turned to her brother, "Pete, are you saying Nancy is lying about last night? That you guys *didn't* have a fight?"

"Honey," Dad interrupted, nodding at their boys, "this isn't really the time or the place."

"No, I want to know what happened. Pete?"

Pete looked up and frowned, "No."

"No?"

"I just, you know, wanted a bit of time away from her."

"And you thought I wasn't going to find out?" Mom looked angry, yet solemn. She sighed and folded her arms.

"I'm sorry, sis," Petey said. "But I couldn't tell her. I just needed a bit of time away. Spend time with my real family."

He smiled at Zack as he played with the doll.

"I hope you don't mind."

Mom scratched her face and grabbed a tea towel from the dining room, "No. It's fine."

A Year Later

"Bastard," Mom screamed into her husband's arms.

Blue flashing lights peeled around the front landing mirror. Two policemen carried a man toward one of their units.

"Shhh, honey. Calm down. Please."

"Shut your mouth, you fucking prick." She cried out loud and threaten to punch him, "You fucking bastard."

"Honey, *please*," Dad held out his arms, trying to fend off the attack. "Please don't."

A black woman in a suit left them to it and eyed the staircase.

Zack watched from the top step as his mom went crazy with rage. She was attacking his Dad. He clutched Babydoll tight to his chest. He couldn't process what he was seeing.

His brother had been missing for a week. The turmoil the family had endured was incomprehensible. The incident happened right after Zack's fifth birthday.

He didn't understand what was going on. Until an hour or so ago, when the very mean-looking men and women were in the house, mom and Dad were inconsolable. Now that those men and women had left, and taken Uncle Petey away, his parents were furious.

The black woman held out her hand at Zack. "Son, my name is Clara. Can you come with me please?"

Zack nodded and climbed down the steps.

A match struck the side of a matchbox.

WHVOOOM.

The head ignited and bubbled up a storm. The fingers holding the wooden edge tossed it onto a small bonfire.

Mom and Dad watched as the collection of objects; clothes, toys and Babydoll, went up in flames.

"Noooo," Zack burst through the kitchen doors and ran into the back garden, "Not Babydoll."

"Zack, *please*," Mom sniffed, wiping the tears from her eyes. Dad looked at his son and frowned.

"Sorry, son," Dad hushed. "It's for the best."

"I want Michael to come back," Zack said to his father. Dad looked away and tried not to cry. He held his wife as she bawled into his arms.

"Why did the police take Uncle Pete away?" Zack said.

"Because he did a bad thing," Dad said, unable to offer much else, "He was bad."

"A whole fucking year," Mom roared through her tears into Dad's arms. She pushed herself away and gasped into her hands, "H-How did we not *see* it?"

She fell to her knees and watched the flames tear into the memory of her eldest son, "How could we have not known?"

Zack watched Babydoll's face melt and bubble into the photos and clothes belonging to his brother.

"I miss Michael. When is he coming back?"

Dad looked down at his shoes as the flames licked higher. Could he honestly tell his son that his brother wouldn't be coming back? That his body was found in *Three Springs Common* five days after he went missing?

"I want to die," Mom spat as the floods of tears drenched her cheeks, "Someone, please. *Kill me*."

"Stop saying that," Dad barked from out of nowhere,

"We're all fucking affected by this. He was *my* fucking son, too. And the cunt who did it was *your* fucking brother."

Zack looked at his Dad, then mother, as they exchanged their tirades.

"He was no brother of mine," Mom looked down and cried hard into her hands.

Zack's first sleep since Michael's body was discovered and Uncle Pete had been taken away.

He lay on his bed and stared at the underside of the top bunk.

"Michael?"

No response.

"Michael? Are you up there?"

The bed didn't move. It was empty. Zack closed his eyes and took a deep breath.

"One day you'll come back. You're just hiding."

"Boo."

Zack opened his eyes and yelped. Michael peered over the side of the top bunk and chuckled, "Hey, Zack."

"Michael."

"Yeah. It's me."

Michael seemed chirpy but his face looked weird. A bloody scar running across his forehead. Grazes and specks of blood lined the sides of his face. He spat a couple of teeth on the floor.

Plonk-plonk.

Zack looked up and watched his brother wipe the blood away from his mouth.

Michael ruffled his yellow hair. A dozen leaves spat out and wafted down to the ground like a feather.

"What happened to your face—"

"—Zack, it's okay. I won't ever leave you," Michael hushed and moved out of Zack's eye line, "Look, I got something for you."

"What, what?" Zack smiled and clapped his hands together.

Babydoll's face appeared in place of Michael's. It looked down and smiled.

"Peek-a-boo," Babydoll smiled. It's left eye wandered around, "It's *me*. Michael."

"Huh?"

Babydoll flipped his body over the edge and made for the wooden stairs at the side of the bunk bed. He began to climb down.

"It's okay, Zack," Babydoll jumped to the bottom bunk. He crawled up Zack's leg and front and sat on his chest. Zack smiled and stroked its face, "You'll look after me, won't you?"

"Always and forever, Michael."

"But you can't call me *Michael*," Babydoll said. "You have to call me Babydoll, like you usually do. Or it might upset Mom."

Babydoll smiled and rolled over onto his side. He snuggled up next to Zack and hugged him.

"I love you, Zack."

"I love you, *Babydoll*."

Presently

Zack sat in the back of the car as mom drove. He had his seatbelt fastened. He leaned over to the window and breathed on the glass.

SKWOOT. SKWOOT.

His traced his finger around the condensation and drew a picture of a smiley face.

"You been hanging out with that Charlie kid today?" Mom asked.

Zack smiled and clapped his hands together, "He's my best friend."

"He's got weird hair," Mom kept an eye on her child in the rear view mirror, "I don't want you to play with him, okay?"

"Why?"

"I don't know, sweetie," Mom said. "Bad things happen when he's involved, so please don't invite him home. Okay?"

"Awww, why?"

Mom slammed the steering wheel, "Just do as I say. Okay?"

What Zack didn't know was that Charlie's father had a bit of a past. Some of the parents knew it. It was supposed to be a secret. Charlie attended seven different schools due to the rumors about his father.

He was in his early thirties. According to the rumor, he spent most of his life in and out of jail for drug offenses.

Two years ago to the day, Charlie was taken into care. His father had injected an especially potent form of heroin. He overdosed pretty badly and was rushed to a hospital. The doctors couldn't do very much for him.

Charlie's father slipped into a coma. His mother had died from a drug overdose six months earlier. The gossip didn't extend to what became of Charlie's father. No-one gave much of a shit about him.

They did care about Charlie and child service's involvement. He was found a foster family in Shotterlay, Manchester. A freak accident at the hospital killed one of his two foster parents.

He was found another family down south.

Charlie settled down with his new family in *Chrome Valley*. A small suburb of *Chrome Junction* in northwest London.

Zack would become a neighbor of his.

The gossip surrounding Charlie was especially vile. Everyone hoped it wouldn't turn out to be true. Legend had it that his biological mother spent most of her pregnancy out of her mind on dope. It would account for Charlie's unusual behavior.

The listless paranoia.

The erratic and sudden bouts of violence.

The attention deficiency which they had no name for.

The parents at the nursery hoped that Charlie wouldn't grow up in his father's footsteps. Or his mother's, for that matter. Anyone associated with Charlie would meet with scorn. He was a social pariah.

It wasn't anyone's fault, it was simply the way Britain worked in the present 1980s.

Mom shut the car door and got out of the car, "C'mon, sweetie, I have a surprise for you."

"Okay, let me get Babydoll first," Zack unfastened his safety belt.

Mom shook her head and huffed, "Okay, whatever."

Zack reached over and grabbed Babydoll. He clutched it tight against his chest and got out of the car.

mom put the key in the lock and turned it. She pushed the door open and stood aside to allow her son through the door.

He walked with his left arm around across his chest, as if he was carrying something. But there was nothing in his arm.

"One day, Zack," Mom whispered. "You'll get over that damn doll."

Zack walked into the front room and plonked Babydoll onto the floor. mom watched him and ran her hand along the door frame. She was never able to get over her son's reaction to what had happened.

Zack bent down and lifted his hands down to the floor. He patted the air, stroking the face of the doll that wasn't actually there.

"Okay, Babydoll. You sit there," Zack brushed the doll's chest down, "Be a good boy, okay?"

Babydoll looked up. His right, wonky eye floating around, "Of course, I'll behave—"

"—Behave, Zack," He finished his sentence in as confident a voice as he could muster, "You're my brother and I love you…"

Mom bit her lip and covered her mouth as her son

talked to thin air. Zack looked at his mother and smiled.

"What's wrong, mommy?"

"N-Nothing, sweetheart," she lied through her fingers and tried to suppress her anguish, "I, uh, I got you a present."

She made for the dining room table and reached for a three-foot rectangular box.

"Why don't you open it?" She said, staring at the empty patch of carpet where Zack had "put" Babydoll.

"Oh, mommy. A present."

Zack tore away at the gift wrapping and threw it to the floor. He lifted it to the ground and analyzed it.

A *Cabbage Friend* doll smiled back at him through the packaging.

Zack wasn't happy, "What's this?"

"It's a *Cabbage Friend* doll," mom smiled and cleared her throat. She hoped Zack would be on board with adopting it as his new friend, "A real one you can play with and—"

"—I don't like it," Zack screamed and held the sides of his head in his hands. His response was baffling and very violent, "Get it away from me. I don't want a new friend."

He kicked the *Cabbage Friend* box over onto its side. "I hate it. I hate it."

The troll-like face smiled up at him from behind the Perspex sheet. Mom bit her fist in horror at her son's sudden outburst.

"Babydoll is my friend," he spun around and picked the imaginary doll into his arms.

"Tell her, Babydoll," Zack said to his empty arms.

Babydoll looked up at him with his wonky eye and smiled, "Okay, I'll tell her."

"No, no, Zack. Please—"

"—You can't get rid of me," Babydoll yelled with an intense rage from Zack's arms, "He's my fri—"

"—end," Zack continued in his gravelly voice, "And he's never going to leave me."

Mom stepped toward Zack and held out her arms.

Tears streamed down her cheeks as she reached the end of her tether, "But, Zack, there's nothing there—"

"—Silence," Zack snarled in his made-up voice and scrunched his face. He held his arm against his chest, "Don't come any closer. Stay away from us."

"Yes," Zack said in his regular voice, "You tell her, Babydoll."

"But, sw-sweetie—"

"—Mommy, why don't you like Babydoll?"

"I do, sweetie," she sniffed and slumped to her knees, "But he died in a fire a year ago. He's not there, look."

She reached forward and tugged on her son's arm. Sure enough, it was empty. Zack didn't believe her and yanked his arm away.

"That's why I got you a new friend—"

"—I don't need a new friend," Zack screamed into her face, "Let go of Babydoll."

Mom pulled his arm away. She met a furious resistance, "Zack, sweetie—

"—No! Don't touch Babydoll."

"Please. Come to me, sweetie."

"Get off me."

"Please, Zack. *Please.*"

Zack lifted his arm and smacked his mother across the face, "Shut up, bitch," He passed Babydoll into his right arm and cradled it.

Mom held her face in complete shock. "B-But—"

"—You can't take me away from Zack after all he's lost."

"Wh-what?" Mom gasped and clenched her fist.

"*You* killed Michael," Zack said in Babydoll's gruff voice, "You let Uncle Pete kill him."

SMACK!

Mom slapped Zack across the face. He crashed arm-fist into the *Cabbage Friend* packaging, unconscious from his mom's vicious right palm.

"Oh my G-God," she rose to her feet and stammered

into her hands. The damage done to his arm was particularly gruesome, "What h-have I d-done?!"

The *Cabbage Friend* box tipped over onto its side.

mom burst out crying and stepped back. She looked at her son and completely lost her shit. "No, no. I'm s-sorry, Zack, I'm—"

A scuffling sound came from behind the lip of the dining room table. mom lowered her hands and pressed her palms to the surface.

She peered over to see Babydoll look up at her from the floor. His wonky eye waved around.

"Tut, tut," Babydoll walked over to the unconscious Zack. He fell to his knees and brushed past his hair, "Why did you do that?"

mom blinked over and over again, trying to understand what she saw. Babydoll, well and truly alive, attending to her injured son.

"I d-didn't mean to."

"You hit him," Babydoll turned around and scowled at her. "You hit my special friend."

Mom jumped in fright as Babydoll shimmied up the dining room table leg and climbed onto the surface.

"My, m-my—"

"—God?" Babydoll surmised and chuckled. "No, not quite. But I *am* very much alive and real. And you, sister, are fucked."

"Wh-what are you t-talking about—"

Babydoll raised his hand to his jaw and squeezed his chin. "Hmmmm…"

TCHA-KLOMP.

His jaw came off in his hand. He dropped the plastic bit to the table. A partial row of teeth and flesh were visible.

"You shouldn't have told anyone about me, sister," Babydoll reached behind his head. He peeled the end of his plastic scalp over the top of his head, revealing a pulsating brain nestling inside its opened skull.

"Don't you think your boy has been through enough without having to assault him?"

"Jesus Christ," Mom's hands shook. She didn't know what to do or where to look.

"I come alive when your boy is asleep, sister."

"Sister?" mom gasped.

"Yes," Babydoll said as cracks shot down his front and limbs. The shell casing split apart and slapped to the top of the table, "You're my sister."

"Pete?"

Babydoll was no longer plastic. He was a two-foot human being covered in skin and gore. His throat was missing. The wonky right eye still hovered every which way, "Hello, sister."

"B-But?"

"—Oh, it's quite simple," Babydoll Petey explained. "I did a bit of research while I was inside—"

"—You killed yourself?"

"Yes, I did." He pointed to his neck. "Zack never got over the trauma."

"What are you talking about?"

Babydoll Petey bent down and snapped off a jagged edge from what used to be his plastic arm, "I didn't mean for it to happen. How could I have known?"

"Known what?" Mom acclimatised herself to the fact that she was talking to a two-foot mound of flesh and gore. She picked up a piece of plastic casing and examined it.

Babydoll Petey held the shard of plastic in his right hand. "You know, what *you* say I did to him. If I was guilty, which I wasn't, then maybe this wouldn't be happening. All that unnecessary trauma you caused him."

"You *did* do it. You sick *fuck*."

"Hey," Babydoll Petey barked, holding the jagged piece of sharp plastic to her face, "I was innocent. I didn't touch either of them and I *wasn't* responsible for Michael."

"Bullshit," she screamed and grabbed him around the

waist. His body squelched in her grip. "You fucking listen to me—"

"—No. You listen to me," Babydoll Petey roared into her face. "You accused me. They believed it."

"Your DNA was all over the place," Mom screamed back. "Both with Michael *and* with Zack. A whole fucking year—"

SCHWWIIIIPP!

Babydoll Petey cut her throat with one swish of the plastic. He held himself forward with his free hand and stabbed her again in the neck.

"I didn't. I didn't. I didn't."

Stab-stab-stab.

He daggered her ten times in the neck, repeating himself over and over again, "You lying fucking bitch."

Baby Petey threw the plastic dagger over his shoulder. It hit the floor behind him.

mom reached for her bleeding neck with both hands. Babydoll Petey climbed from her clutches and wiped the spurts of blood from his body.

"So what if I did touch, them, anyway?" he tried not to laugh as he watched his sister's blood fountained out of her neck, "He was too young to know what was happening, anyway. So what if he goes a bit *doolally* and thinks he's a doll when he's asleep. Big deal!"

Fountains of blood shot out of mom's neck and splashed along the dining table.

"But it's the principle, isn't it? You took my life, now I take yours."

"Zhhhhhh," Mom gasped, holding her hand out to her unconscious son. "Zhhhaaaa—aaccckk."

"What are you doing?" Babydoll Petey asked and squinted at her.

She thumped the table causing the blood from her neck to splatter up the walls, "Zhhaaa-aaacccccckksssshhhh!" She grabbed a piece of his discarded plastic leg and lifted her hand into the air.

"Oh no," Babydoll Petey spat. "Don't you fucking *dare*!"

"Zhaaa-aack," she squealed, her voice bubbling through her severed throat.

Babydoll Petey turned around in anger to the unconscious Zack, "No, stay asleep."

Zack's eyelids fluttered. He was close to waking up.

Babydoll Petey fell to his knees in agony, "Noo."

"Zhhaa-aaahhh—"

Babydoll Petey started bleeding from the eyes and gums. He held his fleshy hands to his face. "No, no."

Mom flung the plastic leg piece at her son. It bopped him on the head, waking him from his slumber.

"Whaa—"

"—Zhhaa-aaa-aack," mom cried, the torrent of blood blasted through her fingers.

Zack rubbed his eyes and stood to his feet. He froze and watched his mom bleed.

"Noooo," Babydoll Petey cried.

Zack looked down and gasped. A two-foot man was vomiting blood onto the dining room table.

"Uncle Petey?"

"Yes, y-yes," he gasped and looked up at his nephew, "P-Please, help me."

"Why did you hurt my Mommy?"

"I didn't, I didn't," Babydoll Petey started to melt. First, his arms turned to mush. His body and legs were next to go, "I c-can't."

Zack slapped his own face, waking himself up.

The last of the monstrosity sizzled and bubbled into a pool of its own liquefied flesh and skin.

Zack looked over to his mother. Her lifeless body hung against the back of her chair.

"Mommy?"

No response.

Babydoll's remains dripped off the edge of the table. Some of it hit Zack's shoe.

He looked down and saw a bloodied piece of plastic. What was once Babydoll's leg was now a string of orange and yellow goo.

The front door opened from the landing.

"Hey guys, I'm home."

Zack rose to his feet with the bloodied piece of plastic in his hand. He stepped back and tried to figure out what was going on.

Mom lay dead on the dining room chair. His best friend, Babydoll, slid off the table and hit the floor.

Zack was holding the weapon that had killed his mother.

"Helloooo?" Dad chirped, "Anyone home?"

Zack turned around to face the front room door. His Dad walked in and smiled at him.

"Hey, son," he said and made the mistake of looking over Zack's shoulder, "Where's your mom— *oh, holy shit.*"

Zack held up the bloodied plastic dagger and shuddered. Dumbfounded, Dad looked back at him and widened his eyes, demanding an explanation.

The boy just stared at his Dad.

"B-Babydoll did it."

Chapter 3

Klitschko

Max Klitschko has done very well for himself. At the tender age of twenty-five, he's become one of the most successful businessmen in the UK. His company, *Klitschko*, is the world's leading manufacturer of feminine hygiene products and employs over twelve thousand staff in five countries.

The man himself is always well-dressed. Very well spoken, contrary to his modest upbringing in the east end of London. His parents were factory workers who emigrated to the UK from Africa when he was a little boy. Tonight, he's showing off his elitism, dressed in a sparkling three-piece suit.

We join Max and his girlfriend having dinner. Tonight, they have chosen London's most prestigious Japanese restaurant - *TempuraMental!*

The place isn't exactly heaving on this warm Wednesday evening. It's past 10 pm and most of the punters are now at the bar and onto the drinks to wash down their meals.

Soft jazz music playing in the dining area softens the mood.

Two large plates of tempura are set at his table. He thanks the waiter and digs in. Piping hot pieces of battered-coated vegetables break apart in their fingers. They're about to dip into little dishes of chili sauce.

Despite Max's elitist appearance, he fits in well with the other guests. His girlfriend, Chloe, is a spectacle. Max is head over heels in love. You can tell as much from the look in his eyes. Chloe sits opposite him guzzling down her third flute of champagne. He looks at her lips as the lipstick smudges around the rim of the flute.

Three years Max's junior, Chloe is a ridiculously attractive woman. Voluptuous lips. Long brunette hair that runs down to her shoulders.

She's the center of attention this evening.

"Mmm," Chloe swallowed and wiped her bottom lip, "This is fantastic."

"I told you this was good, yeah?" Max tore off the end of his piece of tempura and sucked it between his lips, "Been ages since I was last here."

Chloe turned around and looked at the other punters. "It's so nice to finally eat somewhere *normal* for a change, you know," she dipped a piece of tempura into the bowl and analyzed it.

Max smiled as he shoveled the rest of his vegetable in his mouth. Chloe smirked at his chewing. He looked *so* cute.

"What?" he asked with a mouthful of food.

"Oh, nothing," she winked back and giggled, "You're just adorable with the gap in your front teeth, that's all. I love it."

She threw a straw between her lips and sucked down on her lemonade.

"I can't believe you never had Japanese food, before," Max wiped his mouth with a napkin. He looked over at the waiter by the bar and nodded.

Chloe put her drink down and half-burped. "Oop, 'scuse me."

"Too much?"

She looked down and made for another piece of fried vegetable, "God, no. I *love* it."

A Japanese waiter arrived at the table and smiled at the pair, "I hope the food is to your liking?"

"Yes, it's great," Max winked at the waiter and nodded over to the bar, "It's *wonderful*, actually."

The waiter wondered what Max was playing at. He acted like he had a facial tick. He cottoned-on and remembered what this was all about.

"Oh, yes. Very good, sir."

Chloe watched the waiter hop over to the bar. She turned to Max and raised her eyebrows, impressed with the service, "They're very attentive."

"Yes, some things never change."

Chloe scrunched her nose and acted all cute, "Aww."

Max chuckled to himself and looked at his wristwatch. He bit into another piece of vegetable.

The waiter came back with another plate of tempura, "Sir, your *third* dish."

"Ah, fantastic," Max held his hand over the middle of the table, "Please, just there. Thanks."

"Very good, sir," the waiter winked at him and set the plate down. It contained *one* piece of tempura with a light dusting of chili around it.

Chloe looked down at it, "Eh? Only one piece?"

"Yes, babydoll."

"Shouldn't there be more?"

"No, this is a special one," Max offered her the piece of tempura, "Take it and break it apart."

"You what?"

A small crowd of staff had gathered behind her. They held in their giggles and nudged one another in the ribs. Something was about to happen.

"Open it, babydoll," Max repeated, losing his patience.

"Oh, okay."

Chloe took the piece in both hands, "Ouch, it's hot." She dropped it on the plate and blew on it, "Do I have to hold it?"

She grabbed a knife and held the blade over the tempura. Max gasped, as did the staff members watching.

"No, babydoll, don't."

"How else am I supposed to break it, lover?"

"Just *be careful.*"

"Okay," She dropped the knife and licked her thumb and forefinger. She took both ends and pulled apart.

The steam rose from within the batter. A "clink" noise hit the plate as Max slid down to one knee on the floor.

"What are you doing, lover?"

Max nodded at the plate. The staff peered in from behind to see what was on it. A diamond ring dislodged from inside the broken halves, surrounded by a cough of steam.

"There, babydoll," Max said, taking her left hand in his.

"Oh, *Max*," Chloe gasped and held her right hand to her face. "You, you… *oh my God.*"

She picked up the ring. The lights from the restaurant bulbs bounced off the ring and illuminated her face, "Oh, it's *wonderful.*"

The waiters tilted their heads to the side and smirked.

"Will you marry me, Chloe Volkov?"

"Yes," she gasped. The ring slid down her fourth finger, "Of course I'll marry you."

Max and Chloe embraced at the table. They stood up and kissed to an uproarious wave of approval from the staff and punters.

"Congratulations, Mr. Klitschko," the head waiter beamed over the cheering and hollering.

"Thanks."

The car ride home was eventful. Both Max and Chloe were mildly drunk. The driver kept one eye on them in the rear view mirror and the other on the road.

The pair groped each other like the apocalypse was due. A hand down his trousers. His hand around her back.

Tongues flapping at mouths.

A vigorous embrace.

"I love you Max Klitschko," Chloe panted into his mouth. She took his wrist and shoved it down the front of her jeans, "Touch me there."

Max licked his lips and slid his hand into her panties, "Mmm. The future Mrs. Klitschko. What *have* you got down here for me, I wonder?"

"Ohh. You'll find out, lover," she gasped and kissed him again.

Max caught the driver's eye in the mirror. He sniggered and returned to his fiancée.

The driver winked back and chuckled to himself. He turned up the radio and rolled up the glass compartment.

Marvin Gaye's *Let's Get it on* boomed through the speakers in the back of the car. The music only made the pair fornicate harder.

Chloe panted into Max's neck as he nuzzled at her chest. "Oh, Max!"

"Oh, *Chloe*," Max kissed his way up her neck, over her chin and back onto her mouth. "This car can't get us home quick enough."

SLAM! The door to Max's luxurious Mayfair apartment banged against the wall as the pair walked in. He hit the light switch. Soft jazz music began to play as the lights blinked on.

The living room was spectacular. The ten foot high windows offered a fantastic view of London all lit up against the night sky.

Three giant white sofas surrounded a lengthy glass coffee table. A true centerpiece for the apartment. The middle of the room sunk in by a step. A pool table, an extensive dining counter, and a in-built kitchen completed the look.

The apartment, given its modernity and size, must have set Max back at least five million pounds. A wonderful view of London's skyline lit up the night sky.

Chloe led him by the hand to the largest of the three sofas, "Come with me, you sexy motherfucker."

Max didn't protest. He kicked off his shoes and walked with her. She spun around gripping his hands and pulled him to her chest.

"The future Mrs. Klitschko?"

"The future Mrs. Klitschko," Max stared at her beautiful brown eyes.

Before he knew it, they were on the sofa. They made out like their lives depended on it. She lay back and placed her head on the plush armrest.

"Mmmm," she tore off her shirt and flung it to the floor. Her heaving breasts seem to bulge out as she took a deep breath. She grabbed Max's ears and rammed his head between her boobs, "You like it when I do that?"

"Mfgghh," Max flipped his head to the side and ran his tongue along her left breast. He kissed his way down to her stomach as she bucked her hips into the air.

Off came the jeans.

And then the panties.

Max unfastened his belt and slipped off his trousers. He was now topless; down to his white briefs and socks.

He looked up at his fiancée as his lips kissed down her body. She looked back at him and hiccupped.

"Ooops," she chuckled, holding her fist to her lips.

Max chuckled, "Too much to drink?"

"Too much food, I think," Chloe shot him a look and pushed his forehead, "Now you get down there for your dessert, you bad boy."

"Oh," He looked down between her opened legs, "Dessert."

"Mmhhmmmm," she groaned and ran her palms down her front, "Yes, sweetie. You go *down*."

Max rolled his shoulders and lowered his head onto her thighs. She swung her right leg over the backrest and pushed her thighs apart.

Max and Chloe started dating two years ago. They agreed that they would wait until marriage before consummating the relationship.

It was a formidable gesture on both their parts. Some of their friends even knew about it. In this day and age of playing around, two souls agreeing to abstinence was a rare find. Max and Chloe respected each other. There was no need for a prenuptial agreement in his view. The relationship wasn't based on sex and Chloe had stood by him since the day they fell in love.

Sexual congress would only take place once marriage was a certainty.

It was never discussed when the consummation of the marriage would take place, though. Max had always thought it'd be on the night of their wedding.

Tonight's meal and alcohol intake begged to differ.

Max was about to discover his intended in a whole new light. Chloe was about to discover how sexually charged her husband-to-be actually was. A year of pent-up sexual frustration was about to unleash itself.

It was a mistake neither could have seen coming.

Max pressed the side of his face against her inner thigh and closed his eyes. He wanted the occasion to be special. Her feminine scent wafted across and up into his nostrils.

"Mmmm," he moaned and looked up at her. His tongue had beaten his brain to the exploration of his fiancée's most intimate area.

"Do it, lover," Chloe closed her eyes and ran her fingers through his hair. She moaned with delight, "Do it. Lick me."

"Yes, babydoll."

He extended his tongue and pulled apart her vagina. A cute strip of pubic hair ran up to the top of her groin. She'd kept herself in immaculate condition.

Max buried his face in and caught a glimpse of his

bride-to-be's pink flesh. A finger slipped in and held her open. The tip of his tongue nestled into her vagina's opening.

She quivered and grabbed his ears, "Oh yes. *Yes*."

"Mmm," Max pushed her apart and placed his chin underneath her vagina and slipped his tongue right in.

She reached down and pulled her vagina lips opening up and out. For Max, the sight was magnificent; like a flower in bloom.

Another undiscovered area of his lover's anatomy he'd still not seen. He was about to get very, very intimate with it.

He jabbed his tongue in and circled it around.

"Oh m-my God," Chloe gasped, hitching her lips out even further and exposing her clitoris.

Max's nose rubbed against it. An accident. Chloe shivered and moaned once again, "Lick it, lick it."

He placed his fingers over hers and pushed back against the skin. Her clitoris protruded from inside its fleshy hood, begging for some love.

Max extended his tongue and swiped left and right, up and down. The beady end of the clit wagged in the same direction. His chin got wet from the intense application of tongue on flesh.

"Oh, *fuck yes*," She clutched his ears and ground her hips against his face.

"Glumsfhh,' Max tried to moan with her, his face buried deep between her thighs.

"Glomfpphh," he blurted, his tongue, top lip and nose nestled right into her.

Max stopped speaking out of the blue, "Gah, Schitt."

Chloe looked down the length of her body. All she could see was the hair on his head, "What's up, lover?"

"Gny'm schtucck."

"Huh?"

She looked down and pushed his head away. The agony was intense. "Gaaooww, *shit*," She pushed him back between her legs, "What the fuck?"

"Gasssh, ischttuck."

Max couldn't move his head. He lifted his arms and prodded around her thighs. His mouth was stuck to her vagina.

Even though neither of them could see it, Chloe's clitoris had slid between Max's two front teeth. The gap was thinner than the gland itself.

Her clitoris jammed up against his gum. Every time he pulled his head up, it took the clitoris with it, rather than sliding down the gap.

He was stuck. Communicating what had happened wasn't on the cards. He sounded like a boy with learning difficulties and a speech impediment.

"Glowwshhhh-mob," he groaned, pressing against her thighs.

"What are you talking about?" He pushed his forehead back and yelped, "Oww."

"Istcchh, clitsch."

"What?" Chloe screamed with worry. "What's going on down there?"

"Iscchklisschh," Max's chin caught most of the drool, "Gummff."

"Hold still, lover," Chloe placed her hands on the sides of his head, "I'll try moving back."

"Ungkay."

She squeezed his head and hitched her hips back. His face went forward with her vagina.

"Aaaagggghhh, *fuck*," she screamed and cried as her clit pulled away from its hood, "Jesus Christ."

She loosened her body and took a few deep breaths, "Is my clit jammed between your teeth?"

She felt Max's head nod against her pubic bone, "Gnesh."

"Fuck. What do we do?"

"Ahd'nah," he offered into her vagina, "Ischtuhck—"

"—Fuck's sake. Don't move your head," Chloe threw

her hips forward and exhaled, "Please don't move. Oh, God."

She rolled her head and looked to her left. The kitchen loomed in front of her. She turned down to Max, "Won't it move?"

"Gnaah," he slobbered through his saliva, "Ah fing ah'm schtugg."

"Don't move," she cried. "Please."

"Unggkay."

"Shit," she gasped and quickened her breathing, "What do we do?"

"Gownk gnow."

"Okay, okay," she tried to calm down. "Look, just lift your mouth up a *little* bit and see if it slides down through the gap."

"Unggkay—"

"—But do it *slow*, okay?"

"Yuungg," He pressed his two front teeth against her urethra opening. Careful to avoid any pain, he slid his two ivories upward. Chloe's clitoris went up with it. She winced and squeezed his shoulders.

She closed her eyes and expected the worst, "Is it coming down?"

"Gunnow," he slid his nose up to her pubic area, "Ung Gown't—"

"—*Fuck-k*. It hurts so bad," Chloe screamed and thumped him on the scalp, "Ah, Christ. Get back down."

Max obliged. He moved his face down between her thighs. His two front teeth jammed against the crook where her clit should have been.

"Ohhhhh, *shit*." Chloe tilted her head back and placed her palms over her face, "What are we gonna do?"

"Gleessshh," Max shifted his head which caused her to cry again, "Oh God, stop d-doing that. Don't m-move."

"Unggkay."

She looked over to the kitchen again, "Have we got any ice?"

"Uh fing schow."

"Yes?"

"Gnessh."

"Okay. You'll have to take me with you, then."

Max's head jostled around in protest. "Wha—"

"—fuck, stop moving!" she moaned, "oh Christ, I think I'm going to come. Stop moving, sweetie. You need to keep your head, your teeth, exactly where it is."

She squinted at the refrigerator. "Carry me. I think we can get the ice from the freezer. Cool my clit down. You'll have to lift me."

"Gni Ghunt—"

"—you're gonna have to, lover," Chloe moaned. "Careful!"

"Unggkay."

Max slid his upright arms underneath her body and grabbed her shoulders.

"Careful!"

Max tensed the muscles in his arms and lifted her a few inches into the air. He kept his face buried up against her vagina.

It looked rather silly.

Max sitting on the couch in his briefs, holding his fiancée up in his arms with her thighs wrapped around his head. If anyone should enter the room it'd look like they'd taken up wrestling and were practising unusual moves.

"Unnggggg," he cried under her weight, "Heavy."

"Okay," Chloe reached down and held his shoulders for balance, "Stand up. Slowly."

"Unggkay."

He rose to his feet and kept her held upright around his face.

"Don't drop me."

"I ghan't schee."

"It's okay, I can see for you," Chloe barked over her shoulder, "I'll guide you."

He took a few steps forward. The only thing he could

see was a strip of pubic hair and a shaft of light across her belly.

"Wait, wait," Chloe looked at the top of his head.

"Whuu?"

"I'm going backwards. You're going to have to turn around and walk backwards so I can see where we're going."

"Wog bugwuscchh?"

"Yes, yes," Chloe tapped him on the head, "Turn around."

"Unnggay."

He turned around to face the bedroom. The action made it look like Chloe was riding a bucking bronco.

"Okay, good. Good," Chloe shouted and raised her finger toward the kitchen, "Step forward. Mind the coffee table."

"Ungggkay."

Max stepped back and made for the kitchen.

"Hold me still!"

"Eygn Tryin'"

"Okay, keep going," Chloe's body bounced on his shoulders as he kept her upright and moved backwards.

BANG!

His shin slammed the coffee table. "Owww," He screamed, shifting his head sideways. Her clit yanked out between his teeth.

"Ohhhh," she gasped, her eyes rolling into the back of her skull. Her stomach began to rumble "Holy Mary mother of God, *my poor clit.*"

"Gloweey?"

"Yea-huh?" she moaned as his face returned to her vagina, "Fuck. I am going to cum *so fucking hard* if you move your head again."

"Gnesh, whug—"

"—Nearly there," Chloe gasped and bit her bottom lip. She kept one hand on his shoulder and reached out to the refrigerator with the other, "Just a couple more steps."

"Gnwoaah?"

"I said we're nearly there. Move forward a bit," she extended her fingertips and reached for the freezer door handle. As she did, her stomach growled again, "Oh God, mind my guts."

"Gnwot?"

"I think I'm going to—"

SPLATCH!

A violent torrent of shit burst down Max's chest. He moved forward and lowered his body.

"Sorry, honey," she winced at the sight and smell of her own bubbling fecal matter, "That Japanese food went right through me."

"Isscchh ungkay," he sobbed as he tried to keep her upright around his face.

"Got it," she grabbed the handle and flung the door open. A waft of icy cold air drifted past the pair.

"Hold on, hold on!" she yelled as she yanked the drawers open. A spaghetti meal for one and a loaf of bread was all that was there.

"Is that *it*?" Chloe cried. "Where's the ice?"

"Nguuhh," Max buckled to his knees. She went down with him with her legs wrapped around his face, "I ghaaaann't."

"Shit."

Max couldn't hold her for much longer. He fell to his knees and held her vagina tight against his face.

"Ghun't ghuarryneemoore."

"No," Chloe screamed and hit the deck with him. He leaned forward and lowered her back-first to the cold kitchen floor.

"Ugghhhh,' he cried with his face buried between her legs. The quick motion of her body hitting the floor pulled at her clitoris once again.

"Fuck. Fuck," she growled. "Stop moving your… your… oh, oh…"

She moaned out loud and grabbed her hair, "Fuck me."

"Agghh," Max cried.

SCOOOOSHHHHH!

She orgasmed and squirted a torrent of come down his throat. "Awww baby," she moaned and bucked her hips into his face, "Yesss, yess."

GLUMPH! GLUMPH!

His neck muscles contorted. Her cum shot out through his nose and splashed around her legs.

"*Fuuuck, yes*," she moaned and ground her hips against his face. She damn near chewed off her bottom lip and ground her waist into his face.

"Groowwllscchh," Max dry heaved. His throat gagged and his stomach grumbled.

"Oh, oh, baby," Chloe whispered. "I'm sorry, I didn't mean—"

BLLOOOARRRGGHHHH!

Max projectile vomited into her splayed-out cunt. Her uterus filled up, causing the spew to splash back into his face.

"Grraagghhh," He screamed and moved his head, once again taking her clit with it.

"Agh, fuck. *Fuck*," she slapped the back of his head and wrenched his face back between her legs, "Stop fucking moving, you prick."

"I ghan't."

He exhaled and relaxed his body. His face buried between her legs and his body nipples-first on the floor in a puddle of his puke and her come and shit.

"Broooooogh."

Chloe closed her eyes and wiped her face. She started laughing at their ridiculousness of their predicament.

Max bawled between her legs. The poor guy was knackered. Chloe wasn't exactly the lightest - or smallest - girl in the world. His arms were killing him and his shoulders ached to the point of nausea.

"Hey," Chloe yelled down to him. "Do you have any

pliers here?"

Max sniffed and tried to look up. He forgot that he had her clit lodged between his two front teeth. The fleshy dongle pulled three inches out of its enclosure.

"Yaaooowwww. *Fuck*," she screamed and bopped him on top of his head with her fist, "Stoppit."

"Gnuuuh," he placed his palms on the floor and tried to raise his body. He was careful to keep his face positioned between her thighs, "Why?"

"It's no good. You're going to have to remove a tooth."

"Whugh?" Max dribbled down his chin in horror, "Nuurrghh way."

"It's either that or the hospital, lover," she quipped.

Max couldn't believe the predicament he was in. What a dilemma. Either extract a tooth which would free his fiancée's balled gland from his mouth. Or go to the hospital looking like *this*.

"Ghoschpituurrrll."

"Okay, it's probably for the best," Chloe reachedover her breasts and grabbing his shoulders, "Lift me again and go to the couch. We'll call your driver."

"Nhuuug," Max blurted into her vagina, "Schloo tchired."

"Too tired?" Chloe bent her elbows back and leaned against the floor, "I can push you there?"

"Unggkay."

She pressed the soles of her feet on the floor and pushed her hips forward a few inches. Max's face and body crawled back.

"Push," Chloe hulked herself forward, pushing Max back with her vagina, "Keep going."

Schooch… schooch… schooch.

His palms and knees - and her buttocks and elbows - squeaked across the linoleum floor as she pushed forward, "Mind your ankles."

"Ugghhh," Max groaned between her legs.

Schooch… schooch… schooch…

"Nearly there," Chloe yelled.

BOMP!

Max's ass hit the side of the couch. Chloe dug her elbows into the floor and pushed her shoulders up.

"Your phone is on the couch, just behind you."

Max reached his left hand into the air and felt around the couch, "Hunnggh?"

"Yes, left a bit, left a bit."

His fingers guess-worked around. The tip of his middle finger hit the phone. "Goschit," Max murmured and clasped the handset. He waved it above his head.

"You can't talk," Chloe said. "Gimme the phone."

Unable to see what he was doing, his tossing of the phone was pure guesswork. He threw it into the air and hoped for the best.

It landed between her breasts.

Chloe grabbed it and hit a number on the screen. She held the phone to her ear as Max drooled between her legs.

"Hey. Is that Charlie?"

"Yes?" came a voice from the phone.

"Ah, yeah. It's me, Chloe." She thought of the best possible way to explain what it was she needed, "Can you meet us outside the Mayfair Apartments, please?"

"Certainly. Would you like me to come now?"

Max squealed to himself. He cursed his embarrassing predicament.

"Yes, please, Charlie. We'll be down in a minute. We need to go to the hospital."

"Oh my," Charlie said. "Is Mr. Klitschko okay?"

"Oh, we're both fine," Chloe looked down at Max. "It's a bit *sensitive*."

"I'll be there in ten minutes."

"Thanks."

The phone slid out of her hand and hit the floor, "Max, honey?"

"Whuh."

"Charlie's meeting us downstairs in ten minutes. He'll take us to the hospital."

"Ughh," Max slumped to the floor and spread out his arms, "Fuggin' hell."

"I know," Chloe sighed. "What else can we do?"

"Ughmpfh," Max balled up his body and pressed his knees against the floor.

"It's okay, honey," she reassured him. "It's after midnight. No-one's going to see us."

"Uggghhh," Max slid his arms under her buttocks and up the length of her back.

"Lift me up, carefully. We'll go straight to the lift."

Two minutes later, Max had managed to pick Chloe up with her thighs wrapped around his ears. Saliva, semen, shit and specks of blood smeared across her legs and Max's chest.

The pair looked like they were at a rock concert. Like a girl sitting on her boyfriend's shoulders, but in messy, painful reverse.

Max had to be careful as Chloe's waist blocked his view. She kept her head turned over her shoulder and opened the door.

"Okay, into the landing."

The door shut behind Max as he stepped along the landing. Chloe held out her left arm for balance.

The elevator door was a few feet away. "Okay, nearly there. Steady."

Max kept moving forward, one foot in front of the other.

Chloe's shoulder blades hit the wall. She reached over and pressed the "down" button on the panel.

"Max, honey. Just keep me resting against the wall. Take a bit of the weight off till the lift arrives."

"Uggnnhhh," Max took a few, slow breaths. He waved the heaviness out from his arms.

TING!

The elevator arrived and the doors opened.

"Okay, it's here," Chloe whispered. "Let's go."

She gripped the side of the opened elevator door and pulled herself in, taking Max's face with her.

The door slid shut.

"Okay, we made it."

She looked to the panel. They'd entered the lift on the twelfth floor. It started to descend.

As Chloe analyzed the buttons on the panel she noticed a man in a jacket standing with a cigar between his fingers. He squinted at her and looked at Max's hair between her legs.

From the man's angle, it looked like Chloe's body twisted around and contorted. Her feet were facing the wrong way.

"Evening," Chloe smiled as if nothing was out of the ordinary.

The man shot Max a disapproving look, "Hey, fella. What you got that lump of plastic sewn to your face for?"

"Ungh?"

"You keep that nasty shit in your own apartment, mate," the man turned to the elevator door, "Don't bring dolls out into the open. That's sick."

"Hey," Chloe protested. "I am not a dumb piece of plastic."

The man ignored her and placed the cigar between his lips.

TING!

The doors open and the man exited.

"Okay, he's gone," Chloe turned over her shoulder, "Let's go!"

"Unggkay," he sighed and tightened his grip around her waist.

Max moved out of the elevator with Chloe wrapped around him. He paced, carefully, toward the double doors that led out onto the street.

"Mr. Klitschko, sir," Charlie the driver pushed the entrance door, "Oh my, what's that smell?"

"Open the door," Chloe screamed.

"Did you shit yourself, sir?" Charlie eyed the brown sludge running down his chest and waist.

"Openfgghh."

"Oh, certainly, sir," Charlie reached up and grabbed at Chloe's waist, "What's going on?"

"What does it look like?" she huffed, leaning into his arms, "My clit got stuck between his teeth."

Charlie looked her in the eyes. "Really?"

"Yes, really," she panted. "Don't move me. Open the back door."

Charlie left Max holding her around his face. He opened the back passenger door, "Okay, what now?"

"I think you'll have to lay me in first, and Max can follow."

"Okay," Charlie stepped back and allowed Max to traipse toward the car door. "Careful, Mr. Klitschko."

"Charlie," Chloe said as they reached the door, "Don't tell anyone about this—"

SCHWOOOP!

Charlie's foot hit the curb. His heel jabbed to the road, causing him to lose his footing.

"Agghhhhh," Chloe screamed as she fell back-first into Charlie's arms.

"Got you."

Max hit the floor, ten feet away from her thighs.

He rolled over and held his face. "Agghhh," he roared in pain across the pavement.

Chloe looked down between her legs and shrieked for dear life. A geyser of blood fountained out from her vagina. It coughed and puked red stuff onto the pavement.

Charlie gasped and dropped to the ground, "Oh, shit."

Max rolled onto his side and gasped at the torrent of blood gushing out from where her clitoris should have been.

"Oh no. Oh *no*," Chloe held her fingers over the gaping hole.

Max blinked and double-took. He pressed his fingers against his teeth. A thirteen-inch piece of torn-out clitoral flesh hung between the gap.

It forked out under his nose.

"Uggghhh," Max pulled on it. It stretched out like a piece of gum and finally snapped in two.

The first half held between in his fingers. The remaining piece fell onto his tongue. He spat it out and climbed to his feet.

Charlie looked aghast at Max. "Sir?"

"Yeah?" Max spat some blood to the floor.

"I think… I think I'm going to *faint* now, sir," Charlie stammered and crumpled to the ground in an unconscious heap.

Chloe's cries turned to squeals. She tried to plug the gushing fountain of blood between her legs.

"Babydoll," Max clambered to his knees in front of her, "It's okay, we'll get you to a hospital."

"You tore my clit out," she cried at the top of her lungs, "I hate you!"

PSCHHT! SQUEEEEEEEEEEEEEE…

Flecks of blood spat up Max's face. The hair on his head flew back.

He held his hands up over his eyes and tried to block out the intense air flow.

Chloe opened her thighs and kicked herself back against the unconscious Charlie.

"Help. Help. What's happening to me?" she wailed as her vagina expelled air at a furious rate. She pressed her belly down, enabling the air to escape even quicker.

"Oh, sh-shit," Max kicked himself back against the car, "What the *fuck*?"

Chloe's belly deflated the more he pressed down on it. Her thighs lost air - the skin sunk in.

"M-Max, h-help me," she screamed and held out her

hand for help.

Max watched her arm deflate and wrinkle up like a balloon losing air. Her chest sucked in after her waist, rendering her thin and empty.

SQUEEEEEEEE!

"Max, baaaaybbiieeeeeeeee," Her skull punctured and let out a gust of air. Her forehead sucked in and folded over her eyes and nose.

Max screamed in horror as his fiancée's body slumped to the ground. Her head rolled over her neck and chest, cramming into her stomach.

The last fart of air escaped her body as the skin collapsed in a heap over her deflated legs.

"Oh, shit," Max rose to his feet and pointed at his deflated bride-to-be. "Charlie."

The driver blinked. The plastic blow-up doll entered his field of vision. It shocked him awake. He scrambled back on his heels, "Jesus Christ."

"What happened to my intended? Look at her."

Charlie rose to his feet and brushed himself down. A fist bopped on his shoulder. A passer-by chuckled with his pal as they walked past Chloe, "Nice sex doll you got there, mate."

His friend chuckled as they walked off.

"Sir, I think you damaged her valve," Charlie walked over to the airless, plastic doll and turned the face up toward him. A crude face with brown eyes and a wide, red mouth stared back at him.

Chloe was scarily lifelike.

Charlie lifted its waist and stood back up. The deflated doll stretched across his arms. He pulled the valve from between its legs. It had torn.

"Ah yes, sir," Charlie smiled. "A bit rough with it tonight, were we?"

"But, but," Max couldn't believe what he was seeing - his driver carrying a deflated sex doll.

"It c-can't *be.*"

"I’m afraid so, sir."

"Oh my God," Max gasped. He leaned out of the back passenger seat with genuine perturbation, "All this time?"

"All this time, sir. The staff at the restaurant obliged because, well, it was you."

Charlie lay “Chloe” across Max’s lap.

"We didn’t want to say anything because, well, we thought you knew. And it was none of our business, anyway—"

"—Why didn’t you tell me?"

Charlie sighed, "I’m sorry, sir."

A tear rolled down Max’s cheek. He sniffed and mourned the death of his bride. Charlie tried for a smile.

"It’s okay, sir. We can dump this one and get you another. Would you like that?"

Max cleared his throat and nodded in agreement, "Yes, I’d like that."

"Very good, sir," Charlie closed the back passenger door. Max put on his seatbelt as Charlie sat into the driver’s seat.

He started the engine.

"I hear they’re doing very young dolls now. Very lifelike so I’ve heard. They ship from Asia. Designed to allay a pervert’s desire to act upon their urges."

Max threw the deflated doll to the empty seat. "Okay, let’s try one."

"Very good, sir."

The car bolted off down the road.

Chapter 4

Spunx

Little Mia Hellman sat in the passenger seat of the car. Jean, her mother, was driving. She'd collected her daughter from nursery school a few minutes ago.

Mia looked a lot like her young mother. Petite and adorable. Beautiful shoulder-length blond hair ran to her shoulders.

They were beating the traffic on account of her school day ending before the juniors did.

Mia sat in the front passenger seat flicking through the radio channels. She arrived at a news channel.

"Clear skies for the rest of the day and the evening in the south. A reminder that tonight to keep an eye out for that passing comet coming our way—"

"—Mommy?"

"Yes, poppet?"

"What's a comet?"

Mum giggled and smiled at her daughter, "It's like a big rock that flies through space."

"Why does it fly in space?"

"I don't know," Jean turned her attention to the road, "There are lots of rocks in space."

Mia turned up the volume on the radio. A woman gave her thoughts on tonight's event, "Yes, the comet, or

Homophagea K-Twelve, to use its proper name, is due to pass a few thousand miles away from the Earth."

"Is this a frequent occurrence?" asked the radio DJ.

"It happens once every one hundred and fifty years. It'll look like random shooting stars—"

"—One hundred and fifty years," Mia's jaw dropped at the revelation, "Wow, that's long."

Jean tried not to smirk at her little girl's amazement.

"Mommy, mommy, can we stay up and watch the shooting stars?"

She thought about her response. It was a Friday. The family wouldn't have to be up early in the morning, "Okay, why not? Should be fun."

"Yay," Mia giggled and looked through the windshield. A supermarket loomed in the distance, "Are we going to the shops?"

"Yes, poppet. We need to pick up some food for Sphinx and get some tea in."

Jean pulled into a mother and child parking space outside *The Y* supermarket. An advert for *Church City* cheese hung in the window by the sliding door entrance, *"Five blocks for a pound!"*

"Okay, poppet. Let's go."

Inside *The Y*, little Mia tried to push the trolley down the pet food aisle. She looked up from the handle bars and saw shelves and shelves of dog food to her right.

To her left, shelves of cat food.

Jean picked up a slab of *Ultra Species* cat food tins. She showed them to Mia, "Hmm, tuna and squid. Unusual. You think Sphinx will go for it?"

"Yea, Sphinx likes fish."

"She likes chicken as well."

Mia nodded her head from side to side in her cute little way. She scrunched her nose and arrived at a conclusion, "Nah, let's try the fish."

Jean inhaled and examined her daughter's face. She was

growing up so damn fast. A regular little adult.

"Hmm, okay, your call."

CLANG!

Five tins of *Ultra Species* Tuna & Squid hit the trolley.

"Right," Jean examined her slip of paper, "Need some cheddar for the macaroni and Dad wants some, uh—"

"—Wants what, mummy?"

The paper had *"rubbers"* written on it. The explanation wasn't worth having in *The Y*, and certainly not in front of the other shoppers.

"Oh, uh, nothing," Jean lied. "Just thinking aloud."

The cheese aisle.

Mia pushed the trolley along. The entire metal grid was full to the brim. She pulled the trolley to a halt and admired the length of the refrigerated shelves, "Wow."

A packet of biscuits wobbled over the edge of the metal.

"Oops," Mia ran over and caught it before it fell and hit the ground. "Got it."

Jean took five slabs of *Church City* from the shelf.

"They're on special offer. Dad can have some with his toast. Should be plenty."

"Mrs. Pershar says that if you eat cheese when it goes dark that you get nightmares," Mia offered. "Is she lying?"

"That's a bit of an old wives tale, poppet," Jean grabbed the handles on the trolley, "C'mon, let's pay for all this and go home.

4:30pm. The car rolled into the *Three Springs* estate. The playground loomed in the bright sun several yards away. A few kids played on the slide. Another child climbed up a busted chain that used to be a swing.

Jean looked at the playground, lost in her own world. The play area was the "dodgy" part of *Three Springs.*

It's where the dreaded "social housing" was.

The main road separated the council estate from the

much nicer suburban area. Both ends were visible to each other.

Jean was happy that she and her husband, John, had managed to avoid the west side of *Three Springs*. They had recently moved to *Chrome Valley*. Thanks to John's parents they managed to top up their savings. Their mortgage meant that they could afford a semi-detached house on the east side.

Jean looked away from the playground. After all, Mia, their only child, could play on the plastic swing in the back garden. Used needles weren't likely to litter the back patio, at any rate.

WHUMP!

Jean closed the boot shut. She carried three bags of groceries in both hands. Mia, a mere five years old and no taller than three-foot five, struggled with her grocery bag.

"C'mon, sweetie," Jean placed one of the grocery bags on her bent knee. She reached into her pocket and took out the door key, "Let's get these all put away."

"Afternoon, Mrs. Hellman," came a voice from next door. Jean looked over and saw Bill pruning his flowers. His big belly bulged over his thighs, "Nice day for it, isn't it?"

"Yes, Bill," she unlocked the door and pushed it forward. "Ugh, can't he see I'm carrying heavy bags?" she muttered.

Bill hopped over his flowers, "I say, Mrs. Hellman. About your cat."

"Sphinx? Ugh, what's she done now?"

"I'm afraid she's been doing her business on my lawn, again."

"Oh, uh, I'm sorry about that," Jean struggled with her bags and made damn sure Bill knew it, "I'll, uh, sort it out when—"

"—And, I'm afraid to report, she's taken to *cleaning* herself on the side of my house after she's done."

"Cleaning herself?"

"Yes, she wipes her bottom on my brickwork," Bill pointed at a brown streak splattered on a brick on the side of his house, "See?"

"Oh, right. Look, Bill, we're a bit busy right now. I'll get John to have a word with her."

Bill scrunched his face, "A word with the *cat*?"

"It was a joke," Jean slid the key into the lock.

"Oh."

"Yeah, I'm a bit busy right now. We'll take care of it, though."

"If you wouldn't mind," Bill smiled and looked down at her daughter, "Hello, Mia."

"Hello."

He winked at Mia and walked back to his garden.

Jean stepped into the house. Mia followed after, struggling to keep the bags up.

"Sphinx," Mia beamed as she made her way through the landing. Her little black and white tabby cat snaked around her feet, getting in her way, "No, Sphinx."

"Miaaooww."

"Mia, poppet, can you shut the door before Bill sees Sphinx."

"Okay," Mia kicked her leg back and booted the door shut.

"Sphinx, move," Jean booted Sphinx's behind away with her foot, "Go somewhere else, we've got bags."

Sphinx fell onto her side and purred. She watched as Mia's feet disappeared around the corner into the kitchen.

She extended her claws and gave them a good licking. "Miaooww."

"In a minute, Sphinx," Mia's voice came from the kitchen.

The sound of items hitting the kitchen counter rattled through the landing. Sphinx rolled up onto her legs and headed toward the kitchen.

Plod-plod-plod. Sphinx trundled along the landing, careful not to get in the way.

She saw two legs in white shin-high socks in front of her.

An opportunity for a cuddle!

Sphinx tilted her head and moved forward. She ran the side of her face along Mia's left leg.

"Wha—!" Mia stepped back and kicked Sphinx by accident.

A slab of *Church City* hit the floor, startling Sphinx.

"Miaaoow," The cat backed up and hissed at the cheese.

"Oh, you silly sausage," Mia giggled and picked up to the cheese, "This isn't for you, you silly billy."

She stroked Sphinx's face. In the cat's eyes, all was forgiven. A perfect opportunity to extend the claws and dig them into the carpet on the landing.

"Sphinx. *No*," Jean shouted. "Bad pussycat."

The cat looked up at the human, wide-eyed. She couldn't believe she'd been told off.

When the humans weren't at home, they never told her off for running her claws through the carpet. The fact that they never saw her doing it was neither here nor there. Claws needed doing.

So, Sphinx tried again.

"Dah," Jean's quip startled Sphinx once again, "What did I *just* say?"

A stand-off between mother and cat occurred. Who'd break first?

Well, it certainly wasn't mum. Sphinx looked down at the floor and turned around. She'd shown Jean her asshole but meant nothing by it.

"Muuuh," Sphinx apologized.

"You'll get fed in a minute," Jean said as she continued to unpack the bags, "Give me a minute."

Sphinx smiled and purred again.

6:45 pm. Dinner time.

Mia, her dad, John, and Jean ate at the dining table. Sphinx had given up on the Tuna & Squid delicacy in the bowl on the floor. She flapped her tongue around her chin and sniffed back at the gooey gunk the humans had decided was dinner.

"Muuuh," Sphinx walked around in a circle. She tried to fool herself that the dinner might change in the interim.

No such luck.

"So, Mia, honey," Daddy said with a mouthful of macaroni cheese, "How did you get on at nursery today?"

"We had a fun time," Mia beamed. "Mrs. Pershar asked us to talk about our best friends."

"Oh yes, poppet?" Jean wiped her mouth with a napkin, "So, who's your best friend?"

"Zack. Me and him are going—"

"—He and I, poppet," Jean corrected her.

"Zack and you?"

"No," Jean waved her hands out, "Not me and him, it's him *and I*."

Mia looked at her mother. She thought she'd gone bonkers. "He and I," she repeated, slowly, as if she'd missed something.

Dad giggled, "It's okay, sweetie. What are you and Zack doing?"

"We're going to get married."

Jean nearly choked on her food. She looked at her husband and mouthed at him, "That's the freaky kid."

"Oh." John looked down and nodded, "Yeah, the one with the uncle who got put away."

"Not in front of Mia, dear."

"Sorry."

Sphinx rubbed herself against Mia's leg. Her coarse tongue hit her left shin. She wanted fed.

Mia looked down and picked up a piece of pasta between her fingers, "Yes, and then we had a nap."

"That's nice sweetie."

Mia looked for a diversion. She saw the jug of water on the table, "Mommy, can I have some water?"

"Yes, poppet," Jean took the jug and poured some water into a glass. Mia watched her mom and waited. John and Jean turned to each other.

Bingo. Mia dropped the cheese-coated pasta between her legs. Sphinx hit the floor and scrambled to eat it. She was ravenous.

"I don't like Charlie, though."

Dad took a sip of water, "Uh-huh. Who's Charlie?"

"He's weird. His daddy is a bad man. Everyone talks about him."

"Bad man?"

"Yes, he did bad things," Mia explained as she dropped a second piece of pasta between her legs, "No-one likes him."

"Mia," Jean blurted and stared at her hand, "Why is there cheese all over your fingers?"

Busted. Mia thought on the spot. She looked at her fingers and wiggled them, "Oh, I prefer to eat with my fingers."

She dipped her thumb and forefinger into the rich, creamy sauce. It was disgusting.

"I think you should use the spoon, sweetie," Dad said.

Sphinx looked up and frowned. She wasn't getting any more pasta. Since there were no food opportunities left, she walked off with her tail between her legs towards the hall. She had a spot on the floor above a hot pipe with her name on it.

RING! RING!

Sphinx jumped ten feet into the air, "Miaaooww."

The phone in the landing was very loud. "Oh, I'll get it," Dad's voice came from the dining room.

Sphinx watched as John made his way to the hall. He was behaving suspiciously. She'd seen humans answer the phone many times before. John had a hurried rush to his demeanor. He looked somewhat thankful.

John picked up the phone and looked down to Sphinx.

"Hello?" he whispered. "Mike, what did I tell you? You can't call me at home, you know."

John turned around and held his hand over the mouthpiece, "No, Mike. Calm down. You can't call here. My wife is home. She'll get spooked."

Sphinx squinted and tilted her head. What was daddy human up to? Why was he behaving so strangely? So evasive and anxious?

"Yes, I know, I know," John turned to Sphinx. "Yes, she thinks it's a business trip. Just you and me, all weekend."

Sphinx growled in the pit of her stomach. She'd not grasped the concept of infidelity. She was a cat, after all, and had slept with most of the males on the estate in the three years she'd lived in *Chrome Valley*.

"Yes, you and me," John peered behind the door to the front room. "Bottle of *Baby Champagne*, candles. That hot Jacuzzi you like. Yes, it's going to be great. Look, I gotta go now, we're having dinner."

Sphinx got up to her feet and walked off toward the kitchen.

John turned around and tried to finish the call. "Okay, love you too. Yes, bye," he kissed the receiver and hung up.

"Who was that, honey?" Jean asked as John sat back at the table.

"Oh, just a work colleague," he lied. "Making sure the hotel reservation was done for the business trip."

The cat flap rattled from the kitchen.

John looked at Mia and smiled, "You okay, honey?"

"Yes, Daddy."

He bit his bottom lip and returned to his food. Jean looked at her husband. Even she knew something was a bit *off*.

"Are you all right?"

"Yeah, I'm fine."

Bop-bop. Something hit John's ankle. He yelped and looked down at his foot, "What the hell is—?

Sphinx looked up at her Daddy human with a dead rat between her teeth.

WHUMP.

She dropped it beside John's foot. John stared at the cat. Sphinx stared up at him and squinted as if to say *"here you go, philanderer."*

At least, that's how John read the message.

She turned around, showed him her asshole and marched off out of the dining room.

Jean leaned over and saw the dead rat by John's foot. She gasped and held her chest, "Oh, for goodness sake."

She stood up and walked out of the dining room, "It's an infestation out there."

9:20 pm. The back garden.

John sat on the brick wall with Mia on his lap. The stars were out. They looked up at the beautiful, clear night sky.

"How big is the comet, daddy?"

"It's hard to say, honey," John hugged her tight, "Oh look, there."

A streak of light lit up across the stars. Mia's face lit up at the sight, "Wow, is that one?"

"Yes, sweetie, look," John pointed at the white light. Two shooting stars zipped across the sky, "There's another."

Mia's jaw dropped in awe at the brilliant show. "Wow," she held her forefinger up to the stars and tried to catch a streak of light.

"Pretty good, huh?"

"Yes, Daddy," Mia gasped with amazement, "It's pretty."

"Just like you, honey," John smiled and kissed her on the head. He squeezed her tight, absorbing her into his arms.

Sphinx came out and stood next to them as an array of stars shot across the sky, "Miaaoow."

Mia looked at the cat, "Sphinx, look," she picked her up and placed her on her lap.

"Maaah," Sphinx whined, not knowing which of the stars to look at.

"Pretty, isn't it?" Mia whispered.

The stars stopped shooting. Mia waited patiently for more to appear. The show was finished.

"Okay, honey," John removed Mia from his lap and stood to his feet, "Time for bed now. It's already very late."

"Aww."

"Come on, no arguing. Put Sphinx down."

"Okay."

Mia planted Sphinx paws-first on the ground. John stepped back as he watched the sky, "You know, that really was somethi—"

SPLATT!

John buckled slightly and looked down. Mia watched her father lift his left shoe and inspect the sole.

She squealed at the sight. Her father had trodden on a rat. The flesh and blood roped from the squelchy ex-carcass all the way up to the sole of his shoe.

"Oh, *bollocks*."

"Dad," Mia gasped and covered her mouth. "That's gross."

"Damn it," John slipped his shoe off and turned around, "C'mon, let's get in."

He hopped across the patio floor with Mia in tow, leaving Sphinx all on her own by the brick wall.

John closed the kitchen door behind him, "Okay, get to bed honey," his voice came from behind the glass.

Sphinx walked over to the squashed slab of dead rat. She wiggled her nose around the corpse. Her head jutted back as a fly circled around it.

She tried to swat the fly with her paw. It was no use - the fly was far too fast.

"Miaoow."

Swish-swoosh. Sphinx *could not* catch that damn fly. A burst of light flashed above her head in the night sky. Sphinx looked up and blinked.

SPITCH!

Sphinx's tilted her head, following a small piece of light headed straight for her. She stepped back along the patio and watch the light snap out, revealing a small chunk of sizzling rock.

It fell from the sky, headed straight for the ceramic frog. It had a stone dish in front of it filled with water.

Shweeeeoooooo… *splish.*

The piece of rock hit the water in the dish. It sizzled and smoked as it floated to the bottom a few inches below.

Sphinx turned left and then right. No-one had seen what she'd just witnessed.

She was curious.

She carefully paced over to the frog dish and perched her front paws on the brick wall. Her wet nose sniffed around the bubbling water.

Then, the real experiment came. Sphinx extended her tongue and lapped away at the water.

Lap-lap-lap.

It wasn't long before she decided it tasted nice. She was thirsty, after all.

Sphinx gulped down the water and removed herself from the wall.

The rat stared at her.

Sphinx widened her eyes and growled. Her tail bushed out, ready for an attack.

The rat turned around and mourned its squashed friend.

Sphinx's right paw slowly moved forward. Then her left. She sunk into her haunches and prepared to strike.

The live rat nibbled around its dead friend. "Squeak," it

jumped up and looked back at Sphinx.

Sphinx stood perfectly still and watched the rat turned to its friend once again.

She threw all her weight down to her hind swished her tail, "Grrrr."

The rat scurried around to the other side of the squelchy, bloodied mess.

POUNCE!

"Roowwaarrr," Sphinx squealed as she tussled with the rat. Her fur messed up with the blood on the floor as she clawed at the rodent.

The rodent fought back and ran between her legs.

Sphinx flipped over onto her paws, "Miaoow. *Grrrr.*"

She made for the rat again, but it pounced and sunk its teeth into her hind leg.

"Roowwaaarrr," Sphinx rolled over, bleeding from the bite. She flipped onto her paws again and watched the rat scurry off into the bushes.

Wrutch, wrutch.

Her body wobbled slightly. She opened her mouth and vomited her tuna dinner onto the dead rat, "Muuuuhhh."

Sphinx licked her paw. She turned around, slowly, and growled at the kitchen door.

***

3:15 am. The bedroom door opened. John felt around in the darkness on the landing dressed only in his night gown.

He gripped the stair rail and placed his foot on the top step.

"Raaoowww," A scurrying of footsteps flew down the stairs.

John shook his head and inhaled, "Ugh, Sphinx."

The sound of cat's paws scurried toward the kitchen as John made his way down the stairs.

Moments later, he switched on the kitchen light and

rubbed his eyes. The refrigerator door was open. The cold air wafted through the kitchen.

"What the hell?"

John took hold of the door handle and looked inside. "Christ, I'm starving." He rummaged around. Tins of cola, bottles of ketchup and ready-made meals. Some fruit in plastic containers. The shelves were sparse.

There was a large gap where the cheddar should have been.

"Huh?" John muttered. He pushed the fruit away and looked for the yellow stuff, "Where is it? Christ, she only bought it yesterday?"

John huffed and took a glass bottle of milk from the shelf.

He pushed the door shut to reveal Sphinx looking at him from the floor. Discarded *Church City* wrappers lay all around her. Sphinx had eaten every last ounce of the cheese.

She licked her paw and froze, looking at John.

BRAAAAPPPPP! She let out a nasty-smelling burp and stood up on her hind legs.

"Jesus *shit*."

The bottle of milk smashed beside his shoes, sending fragments of glass across the floor.

"Hello, John," Sphinx said in a strangely masculine voice. It sounded a bit like Alan Rickman at his most sarcastic, "Midnight snack, is it?"

"But, b-but—"

"—What's the matter, John?" Sphinx shook the milk from her face, "Never seen a talking pussy before?"

John blinked and rubbed his face with an intense vigor. He closed his eyes and took in a lungful of air, "No, no, this is just a dream."

He exhaled and paused. Then, he opened his eyes. Sphinx was still there, watching him.

"See, I told you," John giggled, nervously, "It's just a drea—"

"—Why don't you *gay off?*" Sphinx threatened.

John gasped, "S-Sphinx? You c-can talk?!"

"Open the door."

John's jaw hit his chest. He gripped the door handle and yanked it open. Sphinx hopped onto the counter opposite and held her paw out at the fridge, "I ate all the cheddar."

"Wh-what?"

"I need more cheese."

John couldn't believe what he was witnessing, "Wh-what?"

"Cheddar, you *fuck*," Sphinx fumed and extended a claw from her paw, "You want me to unblock out your ears, prick?"

"But… I-I c-can't—"

"—You fucking will, John," Sphinx threatened and indicated the cheese wrappers, "See if you don't get me some *fucking* cheddar within the next five minutes, I'm going to stab you in the *fucking* knee."

The sharp claw glinted in the moonlight.

John was ready to beg, "Sphinx, p-please—"

"—My name's not Sphinx, you cunt!"

"N-no?"

"No. My name is *Spunx*."

"Spunx?"

"Yessss."

"B-But… the store is closed, *Spunx,*" John stammered, afraid for his life, "How a-am I supposed to get you some cheese—"

"—Okay, that's enough. Lie on the floor, cunt."

Spunx hopped down to the ground and nudged his shin with her head, "Don't fuck me about, faggot. Get on the fucking floor."

"Okay, okay," John fell to his knees and leaned back, "Please d-don't hurt me."

"You fucking shit-stabber. I know what you've been up to."

"Wh-what?"

"Lie down."

"Okay."

John laid himself out on the floor. Spunx licked the rim of her mouth and clutched his night gown with her sharp claws.

"I know what you've done, John. Cheating on your wife, you prick."

She removed the flap of his gown to the floor and licked her lips at the sight of his naked body.

"What?"

"Shut up. I heard you on the phone. What's her name, Mike?"

"Mike is a man."

"That's disgusting, faggot. I bet you join wank clubs, too, like a pair of *homosexualists*."

"God," John closed his eyes and chuckled to himself, "This is a bad dream."

"I'm afraid not, you big gay," Spunx growled in her frightening, male voice. She hopped onto his waist and looked around, "Now, let's see. Aha."

She walked over to his groin and looked down between his legs.

"Oh *my*, John. I didn't know you were so *well endowed*. I bet Mike likes that, doesn't he? The little gay man."

SCHTING!

The claw sprung out from her paw like a flick knife. She reached into the air and threatened to stab him in the penis.

"Noooo," John squirmed and writhed around.

"No cheese, no cock," Spunx explained. "Do you understand me, John?"

"Spunx, no."

SCHTAAAAM! Spunx stabbed John in the shaft with her claw, "Haha!"

"Arrggghhhhh…" John screamed his last.

***

7:45 am. Mia rubbed her eyes as she left her bedroom.

She reached the stairs and grasped the handrail. The door to her mum and dad's room was shut.

As she made her descent, she could hear shuffling and rustling coming from the kitchen, "Hunh? What's that noise?"

She jumped to the bottom landing and turned around. A giant swimming pool of what looked like mayonnaise and ketchup watered around the kitchen floor. The majority of it had caked into the landing carpet.

Sphinx, or Spunx as she preferred to be called, sat upright in the sink. She blinked at Mia as she made her way to the kitchen.

Mia gasped at the gore-flooded the kitchen. Her Dad's gown floated gently atop the sea of carnage.

"Hello, Mia."

"Oh my God," Mia stuttered and approached the kitchen, "What happened here?"

She looked around the gory puddle of liquefied organs, blood, and dark mustard-colored shit. A severed penis floated against the cupboard. The stench was incredible.

"Hold on a second," Mia put two and two together, "Did you just say *hello*?"

"Yes. Where's the fucking cheese?"

"Cheese?"

"The fucking cheddar," she snapped. "Where is it, you little cum bubble?"

Spunx hopped out of the sink and jumped into the ocean of Mia's father's remains.

She rubbed the side of her face against the severed penis.

"See this?" Spunx joked in her Rickman-esque drawl, "This is your father's cock."

"Wh-what?"

"There," Spunx pointed at the severed penis, "That'll

be you if you don't get me my fucking *cheddar*."

"Aghhh," Mia let out a prolonged squeal on the spot.

"What in cunt's name are you doing? Shut up. Stop screaming."

Mia turned around and ran up the stairs. "Mommy. Mommy."

Spunx chased after her, "For fuck's sake. Come back here, you little bull-dyke!"

She reached the top of the stairs in tears, "Mommy."

THUD-THUD-THUD!

Mia rapped her knuckles on the door, "Mommy, let me in."

Spunx skidded to the bottom of the stairs. She'd trodden John's remains all over the carpet.

Jean opened the door, sleepy-eyed, "What is it, poppet?"

Mia gasped and looked down to her feet. Spunx crept up the stairs and smiled at Jean, "Get downstairs you pair of lesbians."

"*Jesus fucking Christ*," Jean squealed and slammed the door shut on Spunx and Mia.

Spunx tilted her head to the aghast and frozen Mia, "The fuck are you looking at, labia-face?"

The door opened again, this time a few inches. "Uh, Mia?" Jean whispered.

"Yes, m-mommy?"

"Can you c-come in here, please?"

"I d-don't know. If you open the door Sphinx will get in."

"Kick her down the stairs," Jean whispered.

Spunx couldn't hear the conversation. Fed up, she held a claw at Mia's shin as she hit the top step, "Right, that's enough faggotry, dickheads. Open this door or I'll kill the kid."

"No, don't hurt her," Jean shouted at Spunx.

"Open the *cunting* door."

Jean shot Mia a look, "*Now*," she mouthed, surreptitiously. Mia looked down and smiled at Spunx.

"Okay, I'm opening the door now, Sphinx."

"My name is Spunx, you *prick*," the cat yelled. "Open the fucking door—"

BOOT!

Mia kicked Spunx in the chest, sending her hurtling down the stairs. "Fucking cunts. Gay fucking pricks."

Bop-bop-bop... Spunx rolled head-over-arse to the bottom step. She twisted around and jumped to her feet.

"Okay, now."

Spunx placed the extended claw between her teeth. She clamped down on it and tore it off. She took an intake of air.

PTCHOOO!

She spat the torn claw from her mouth right at Mia.

The little girl dived into the room as Jean slammed the door shut.

The claw knifed into the plant pot on the table by the door.

"Fuckin' *cunts*," Spunx yelled.

The petals of the flower started to wither and smoke. The stem melted down into the soil, bubbling up a brown storm.

Spunx ran up the stairs.

WHUMP!

Jean pushed the door shut. She and Mia were safe, for now.

"Okay," Jean gasped and took Mia by the shoulders, "Poppet, tell me what's going on?"

"It's Sphinx," Mia cried. "She's acting weird and *talking*!"

"I can see that," Jean turned around to see John wasn't in bed. "Where's Dad?"

"I don't know."

"What do you mean you don't know?" Jean shouted

into Mia's face.

"H-He's in the kitchen."

Jean shook her daughter by the shoulders, "In the kitchen?!

"Well, most of him, anyway."

Bomp-bomp.

A tiny paw hit the other side of the door. An interruptive clearing of a throat, followed by Alan Rickman's voice, "Excuse me."

Jean and Mia turned to the door and held each other.

BOP-BOP-BOP. The paw hit the door three times.

"Excuse me," Spunx repeated, calmly, from the other side of the door, "Let me in, please."

Jean turned to Mia in haste, "Are you sure Dad's not downstairs?"

"No," Mia shrieked, scared for her life, "But the kitchen is all messy. Sphinx tried to give me Dad's cock."

"What?"

"I don't even know what a cock is."

Jean shook her daughter, "What happened in the kitchen?"

"It's full of mayonnaise and ketchup and stinks really horrible."

"What mayonnaise and ketchup?" Jean inspected Mia's night gown. She scooped a bit of red stuff from it and held it to her nose.

"Listen, *faggots*," Spunx said from behind the door, "If you don't let me in I'm going to start murdering cunts."

Jean winced at her fingers, "This is *blood*, poppet. How did it get there?"

"The kitchen is full of ketchup. It splashed on me."

BANG-BANG-BANG!

"Miaaaooowwwwwwww," Spunx screeched from behind the door and cleared her throat, "Let me in, you pair of rug munchers."

BANG-BANG-BANG!

"Okay, okay," Jean held Mia back and approached the

door. "Sphinx?"

"Ugh," Spunx huffed. "Fuck's sake, why does everyone keep calling me that gay name? My name is Spunx, you fuck."

"Ah, uh," Jean winced and tried again, "umm, *Spunx*?"

"The very same," came the response.

"Look, I d-don't know what's g-going on," Jean swallowed. "But I have a very scared child in here and we don't want any trouble."

"That's okay, cunts," Spunx reassured Jean. "Just open the door and take me to the cheddar."

Jean turned to Mia, "Cheddar?"

Mia shrugged her shoulders. Jean thought about this unusual request for a second and then turned to the door.

"You mean… if we give you *cheese*, you'll stop threatening us?"

"Yes, for fuck's sake, yes."

Jean paused again. She squinted at the door, "You promise you won't hurt us?"

Spunx knocked her head against the door over and over again. "Yes, yes, yes, for fuck's sake. Hurry up."

"Okay," Jean turned to Mia, "Look, poppet. Whatever that thing is, it isn't Sphinx, okay?"

Mia nodded. A couple of tears rolled off her cheek. "I want Sphinx back."

"I know, poppet," Jean hugged Mia and looked her in the eyes, "Let's just give it what it wants and call the police."

"Can't we call them now?

"No fucking pigs, faggots," Spunx advised from behind the door, "Just take me to the fucking cheese."

"Yes, all right. We know," Jean shouted at the door turned to Mia, "Clothes on. We'll take it to *The Y* and try and get help."

Spunx stood by the front door with her arms folded. She watched Mia come down the stairs, fully dressed,

"Nice and slow, Mia. That's it."

Mia kept her gaze on Spunx as she reached the last step.

"Get your fucking shoes on, you sloppy bag of cum."

"I am. I am," Mia sat on the bottom step and slipped her trainers onto her feet.

Jean came down the stairs, also fully clothed. She couldn't believe what was happening.

"Where the fuck have you been, lesbian?"

"Getting changed," Jean said. "I can't go to the store in just my gown?"

"Why not, faggot?" Spunx enquired as she moved up to Mia. She extended her paw and produced another claw. It jabbed against her knee, "Hurry the fuck up, cunt."

"I am, I am," Mia stepped into her sneakers, "Okay, I'm done. See?"

"Good. Stand up."

Spunx held Mia hostage, burying her claw into Mia's leg, "You know what happens when you get fucking stabbed, don't you?"

Jean looked at the melted flower in the pot at the top of the landing. She turned back and nodded, "Yes."

"Good," Spunx said. "Now get in your fag-mobile and take mt to the yellow stuff."

BEEP-BOOP. The car unlocked.

Jean walked to the driver's side and opened it. Spunx held her child hostage with a claw pressed against the skin of her knee. They moved to the back passenger side of the car.

"Good morning, Mrs. Hellman," came a voice from across the front garden. It was Bill, in a white hat and sunglasses, watering his flowers.

"Ugh, shit," Jean muttered. She turned to him and smiled, full of the joys of spring. "Hi, Bill."

"Shit," Spunx muttered under her nasty breath, "Not that fucking fat, annoying mound of whale cum, again."

"Nice day for a spot of gardening, right?" Bill chuckled as he looked over his shoulders.

"Oh, Jesus Christ," Jean closed her eyes and muttered under her breath, "Not now, Bill. Not now."

Jean got into the driver's side and pulled the door shut.

"Oh, moody today, huh? Hey, Mia," Bill finally clocked onto the cat hugging her left leg, "Out shopping, are we?"

Spunx looked up and dug her claw into Mia's shin, "Don't tell him."

Mia looked up at Bill, shaken. She smiled and brushed her blonde hair over her shoulders. Her response sounded like a vague cry for help.

"We're just going to the store."

"Oh, jolly good," Bill peered in further and saw Spunx's claw pressed against her knee. "Is Sphinx okay? She seems a bit clingy, what?"

"Tell him to mind his own fucking business."

Mia swallowed and moved her lips, "Mind your own fucking business, Bill."

"No, cunt," Spunx grunted. "Don't *literally* say that to him. Fuck's sake."

"I *beg* your pardon, Mia?" Bill turned around and placed his hands on his hips, offended, "You shouldn't be using language like that, young madam."

"I'm s-sorry, Bill."

"I say, Jean," Bill tossed his hose onto the lawn, "Did you hear what your daughter just said to me a moment ago?"

Jean held her head in her hands and exhaled, "Aww, bollocks."

"Jean. I say," Bill hastened, jogging over to their car, "Did you know that your daughter just told me to fuck—"

"—Okay, enough of this faggotry," Spunx removed her claw from Mia's knee and hopped over to the lawn, "Yo, *William*."

He stopped in his tracks and spun around on the spot. His eyes widened in utter shock. A talking cat, tearing out a claw from her paw with her teeth.

"My G-God!" Bill stuttered and clutched his chest, "S-Sphinx?"

"Neither," Spunx placed the extracted claw between her teeth.

"What in God's name?"

Spunx fired the bullet-like cuticle at Bill.

PTCHOOO-THWACK!

The claw darted into Bill's chest.

"Fuck you and your father. Ha, ha," Spunx jumped into the back seat and waved her claws at Mia, "Get in, you dumb cunt."

"Gaaahhh. Gaaahhhhhaaaaaa," Bill spat a mouthful of blood down his shirt. He fell to his knees and clutched his chest.

"C'mon, bitch," Spunx nudged Mia toward the car, "Let's get out of here before Bill fucking melts all over the damn place."

"No, no," Mia cried and stepped into the car.

"Drive. Or you're a dead pair of gays."

Mia climbed into the car in utter turmoil and tears. Spunx pulled the door shut and crept over the back of the driver's seat. She breathed on Jean's neck. The sharp end of one of Spunx's claws prodded at Jean's neck.

"Start the car, bull dyke. No sudden movements," Spunx instructed in her manly voice, "Drive nice. I'm not in my cage and I fucking hate cars. I don't want you getting ideas and flinging me all over the place."

"Okay, okay."

"Good."

Spunx hopped back alongside Mia, "Put your fucking seatbelt on, faggot."

Mia clipped her belt around her chest. She cried into her hands.

The car pulled out of the driveway and rolled past Bill. His legs had melted into the grass. The top half of his body was putrefying and bleeding out like an ice cream in direct sunlight. He held out his arms for help as he gargled his organs from his soft head.

Spunx laughed hard through the window as the car drove past. She hit the electric button on the car window. It slid down

"Hey, Bill," Spunx tore another claw from her paw and clenched it between her teeth.

"Groooowwllscchhhh," Bill's lungs liquefied out of his mouth and into the air, only to be yanked back by his arteries. Bill turned around and took his last ever breath.

"I wipe my asshole on your house at night, cunt."

PTCHOOO!

The claw fired through the air and bulleted into his forehead. It was enough to take his head clean off.

His body exploded. A shower of soft guts, skin, bone and flesh rained down onto the lawn.

"Ha-haa," Spunx rolled up the window and sat back into the seat, "*Prick*."

Ten minutes later.

Mia had stopped crying. Jean was driving, hoping above hope, that Spunx wouldn't stab her or her daughter.

Her claw was close to piercing Mia's skin and killing her.

"The fuck you crying for?" Spunx asked Mia.

"You killed my Dad and Bill. I hate you."

Spunx licked her mouth and looked at the passing scenery, "Yeah, so what?"

"That wasn't nice."

"This is ridiculous," Jean slammed the steering wheel. "Sphinx, what—"

"—I told you. My name is Spunx," she threatened and jabbed the tip of her claw into Mia's knee, "Call me Sphinx one more time and see what happens."

"Mummy, don't."

"Okay, *Spunx*. Chris,!" Jean stepped on the gas, "What happened to you? What's going on?"

"I don't have to tell you fuck all," Spunx said. "But seeing as you asked and I'm going to kill you if I don't get my cheese, I'll tell you."

Mia turned to Spunx. She tried to move her exposed knee away from the claw, but it was no use. Spunx kept it held against her leg.

"I am from *Homophagea K-Twelve*. From a galaxy named GN-Z11."

"What?"

"I come from a place that despises homosexualists."

Mia thought aloud. "What's a *homosensualist*?"

"*Homosexualist*, you dumb fuck," Spunx turned to Mia and scowled. "We hate faggots."

"I don't get it," Jean titlted the rear view mirror down to glean a better angle on her murderous cat, "Why cheese?"

"I got bitten by one of your fucking vermin. Now I'm technically half cat, half fucking rat, thanks to you."

Mia had an epiphany, "Mummy, the comet!"

"Yes, poppet," Jean applied more gas and turned a sharp corner, "I think I know what's happening—"

"—John was cheating on you, Jean," Spunx rolled to the side as the car bent around into the next road, "I heard everything."

"What?"

"John was one of those *gaymen*, apparently," Spunx chuckled. "Arranging to have sex with *men* behind your back. Does the name Mike ring a fucking bell?"

"Mike?" Jean looked over her shoulder as the car drifted into the opposite lane, "He was cheating on me with fucking *Mike*?"

"*Yeeeess*—" Spunx spotted an oncoming truck, "Fuck's sake, woman. Look where you're fucking going."

NEEEEAAAAWWWWW!

Jean spun the wheel and avoided the oncoming vehicle. Everyone, including Spunx, took a deep breath. They thanked their lucky stars they were still alive.

"That bastard," Jean hit the wheel again, "Bastard."

"Mummy, who's Mike—"

"—I *had* your Dad," Spunx interrupted and turned to Mia, "He was quite happy fucking around with *Miiiike. I t*ried to make a *man* out of him. Offered to have sexual intercourse with the gay, but would he agree? Nooooo. He turned down Spunx's sexual advances. So I stabbed him in the cock."

Mia burst into tears, "My Daddy."

"You little fluffy *bitch*!" Jean muttered under her breath and looked in the rear view mirror. She shot the cat a look of sheer anger, "You're an abomination."

"Abdomin— what?" Spunx spat. "What kind of shit-stabber's language is that?"

Mia cried again and slapped her knees, "I want my Daddy back."

"Sweetie?!" Jean snapped. "Are you wearing your seatbelt?"

"Of course she's wearing her fucking seatbelt," Spunx screamed.

"Good." Jean pushed the gearstick into fifth. *The Y* supermarket loomed in the distance.

"Fucking rug-muncher," Spunx lifted her right leg and licked her asshole.

Jean bit her bottom lip and looked one final time into rear view mirror. Spunx stared her right back, "Let's see how a half rat, half cat little bastard survives a head-on collision."

"What the fuck are you talking about—"

"—Poppet, hold tight," Jean shouted.

"What?!"

"What?" Spunx asked.

The car sped up, heading for the trolley park at the side of *The Y*.

BEEEEEEEEEEEP! Jean slammed the horn. "Move, move," A dozen punters ran screaming out of the bulldozing path of the car.

"No," Spunx shrieked and clawed the back of the seat, "You fucking cun—"

KRAA-SMAAASSSSSSHHHHHH!

It all happened in slow motion.

The front of the car smashed into the engine, shattering the windscreen. Jean and Mia's bodies flung forward, protected and held back by their seat belts. They rocked forward and up, legs swinging, and back to their seats, covered in glass.

Like crash test dummies.

The impact launched Spunx through the fragments of the shattered windscreen.

She hit the ground a few feet away from the wreckage.

Jean reached down and checked her chest and stomach. She was dazed but otherwise uninjured. She unfastened her seatbelt and turned to Mia behind her, "Poppet, are you okay?"

"Yes, mommy," Mia felt a slight cut on her forehead.

"No time to stick around," Jean grabbed her daughter's hand, "Quick, let's get to security. Go!"

Spunx rolled over in front of *The Y*. A crowd had formed around her as she blinked up at the sun.

"Gahhhh."

She jumped to her hind legs and stood up, threatening the shoppers with her sharp claws.

SWISH-SWASH!

She bit off the sharp end of her claw and kept it between her teeth, "Get away from me, *cunts*. You want some of this?"

"*Shiiiit*," the shoppers screamed and backed away in amazement. Jean and Mia ran toward the crowd outside the entrance.

"It's dangerous," Jean shouted and yanked Mia along with her, "Get away from it. *It'll kill you*."

Spunx bit off five more claws from her paw. She had a line of them in her teeth.

"Fuck all your dads."

RAT-A-TAT-A-TAT-A-TAT

Spunx machine-gunned a round of venomous claw-ends at the shoppers as they ran away. A few of them got hit in the back and fell over.

Two overweight female shoppers received sharp claws to the thighs. They stumbled and crashed to the ground.

The fallen victims started to smoke and scream. "Gaaahhh. Help meeeee."

"Fat cunts."

"Spunx," Jean stopped in her tracks. A couple of security guards came running out with batons. "Stop. Just *stop.*"

Spunx scrunched her nose up at Jean as the shoppers melted into the concrete, "Fuck all your dads."

She turned around and stopped still, gawping the storefront. An advert for *Church City* cheese. *'Five blocks for a pound!"*

"Ohh," Spunx gasped at the banner, "Cheese."

"Madam," the security guard pointed at the crashed car, "What's this rat doing?"

"Get away from it," Jean hushed. "It's here for the cheese."

Spunx sprinted into the entrance. The security guards ran over to the car.

"Shit," Jean and Mia ran into *The Y.*

"Move it, faggots," Spunx screamed as she hopped down the feminine hygiene aisle. The shoppers stepped out of her way. "Fucking cunts."

"Jesus Christ."

Jean and Mia hit the feminine hygiene aisle and ran toward the end, "Where did it go?"

"Down there, to the right," yelled a punter, who pointed at the third aisle, "Towards dairy."

"Thanks."

Spunx slid across the squeaky floor and turned into

aisle three. At the very back wall was the dairy produce. Milk and Cheese.

"Aha," Spunx licked her lips and picked up her sprint. A fat, elderly woman with a full trolley blocked the path. "Move, you thick cunt."

The woman looked down at the angry rat-like cat barreling towards her, "Oh my."

Spunx launched into the air and clenched her fist.

THWOCK!

She planted a sharp right-hook across the fat woman's face, knocking her out, "*Cunts.*"

Spunx landed to the floor with grace and magnificence. Standing before her was heaven. Shelves and shelves of sparkling, chilled cheese as far as the eye could see.

"Yes."

She walked over to the elongated fridge and hopped up to the second shelf. She burrowed her way down the first few slabs of *Church City*.

Nom-nom-nom.

The shredded wrappers flew in the air as she chomped her way through the first section of the second shelf. Spunx never looked up. She couldn't care less about anyone - or anything else; she was in dairy Nirvana.

Jean and Mia screeched to a halt a few feet away. A crowd gathered behind them.

"My God," Jean gasped at her cat munching its way through the cheese section, "Look at that."

Mia leaned in and whispered to her mother, "Is she going to eat *all* of that cheese?"

"I don't know, poppet."

Around fifty punters and staff members crowded around the end of each aisle. They whispered in hushed tones as Spunx gnawed her way through her twelfth packet of cheddar.

Nom-nom-nom. Another discarded wrapped flew up into the air. It landed with the others on the floor.

A security guard came running over to Jean with his

radio in his hand, "What's going on?"

"Shh. *Look*."

Spunx chewed over and over again and shook her head, completely unaware of the audience she had attracted.

The security guard double-took and squinted at the abomination on the shelf. "Is that a *cat*?"

"Yes," Jean whispered. "It's eating the cheddar."

"But, but, that's *ridiculous*," he squinted and tilted his head, "Is that a green Mohawk on it?"

"Yeah. It's a long story."

BRRAAPPPPPP

Spunx finished another block of smoky style cheddar and started on the mini *Babybels*, "Ugh, how d'you get this gay red plastic off of it?"

"Oh for fuck's sake, we gotta stop it," Jean held the security guard back.

"No. Don't go near it."

"Why not, it's just a rodent?"

"It's deadly," Mia said and watched her cat chew through the red plastic, mistaking it for cheese.

"Ugh," Spunx spat the soft red mush out from her mouth. "This is useless."

She moved into the Camembert.

"Right, that does it," the security guard said, "She's onto the expensive stuff!"

"She'll be onto the Brie and Goat's Cheese next," offered another punter who watched on.

Before long, Spunx consumed the entire second shelf of fermented curd.

A man moved out from behind the security guard, "Okay, who's in charge here? Are you security detail, sir?"

"Yes, I am. Who are you?"

"Chief Grundy," he said, producing his identification, "We received a call that a crime is taking place. Do you know where the—"

Grundy looked to the refrigerator shelf, "Oh *dear*."

"Yeah, it's that thing," the security guard said.

"Is that a *cat*?"

"Yes, but it's dangerous," Mia said. "Don't go near it."

Spunx let out a long, warbled burp and rolled onto her back. Her stomach had inflated to three times its normal size.

The fur slipped off her body, revealing a fine white undercoat.

Around twenty armed officers arrive behind Grundy, "Sir?"

"Okay, keep your voices down," Grundy said as he turned to his men, "Look, you're gonna find this hard to believe but—"

The armed officers looked at Spunx nursing her fat, cheese-stuffed belly. She hopped to her feet and started on the blue cheese and Roquefort.

"A cat?"

"Yes," Grundy turned to watch her, "She seems quite happy there. We'll let her do her thing, and then move in and get her."

"Don't do that," Mia whispered. "Her claws are deadly. If you get stabbed you'll get melted."

"Did you hear that, lads?" Grundy asked. "Keep your sights on it, but no sudden movements. And don't fire until I say."

"Affirmative, sir," confirmed an armed officer. He held up his rifle and aimed down the sight, "Just give me the order."

Spunx rolled over and kicked away the Brie wrapping. It landed in the refrigerator grill. Her calves shed its skin, revealing spindly little legs.

"What's happening to her?"

"I don't know."

SQUEAK! SQUEAK!

The crowd held their breath as Spunx's body shriveled. Her face melted onto the shelf. She was turning into a rat.

It scurried across the shelf and nibbled on the cheese remnants.

"Don't fire," Grundy whispered. "You'll destroy the shelves."

Mia stepped forward and held out her hand. "Sphinx?"

"No, little girl," Grundy said. "Don't do that."

"Poppet, no."

The rat turned around and showed Mia its two front teeth, "Squeak."

"It's me," she said, approaching the rat with caution, "It's Mia."

The rat perched itself on the edge of the shelf and burped. Its belly continued to inflate.

"It's okay," Mia turned over her shoulder and whispered to the others, "Her claws have dropped off. Look."

She pointed to the discarded coat and claws on the shelving unit.

"Sphinx?"

The rat tilted its head and looked at Mia, "Squeak."

"It's okay, you can trust me," Mia said. "I just want to help you down."

The rat turned its head to the cheese and squeaked as if posing a question.

"Yes, we'll take all the cheese with us." She arrived at the edge of the shelf and cupped both her hands together, "Let's go home, Sphinx."

SQUEAK!

The rat scurried into Mia's hands. Everyone held their breath as she retrieved the rat from the shelf and turned around.

"I think she's unwell," Mia said as she stared at the rat, "It's okay, Sphinx. I'm going to put you down, now."

"Little girl."

"Her name is Mia," Jean barked.

"Mia," Grundy ordered, as the armed officers moved in, "Put the rat down. We'll collect it up. Someone, get a plastic bag from the tills."

"They're ten pence, sir."

"Fuck's sake," Grundy yelled at the officer and handed him a ten pence piece, "There. Just go and get a bloody bag, nitwit."

Mia crouched down to her knees with the rat in her hand. It looked up at her. Its belly had inflated so badly that it wouldn't be able to run.

"I'm going to put you down, now," Mia whispered to it. "The nice men will take you."

"Squeak."

She released the rat to the ground and stood up straight. The rat stood by her side and squeaked at the crowd.

"Oh, Spunx?" Mia said, raising her left foot. The rat looked up and squeaked at her.

"This is for my Dad."

SPLAAATTCHHHH!!!

Mia stomped onto the rat and ground her foot into its body, "Die, you filthy rat. Die."

"Mia," Jean screamed and ran forward, "What are you doing?"

She jumped up and down, splattering the rat's intestines, skeleton and face along the floor. It was very dead.

"She killed my daddy."

Everyone turned away and dry heaved A couple vomited onto the floor.

Grundy winced as one of his armed officers moved in with a plastic bag.

"Okay, I have the bag. Oh my goodness me," he scooped the gory cocktail against the side of his hand. He flicked the mess into the bag.

Mia burst out crying. A day's worth of trauma, agony and emotion ran down her cheeks.

"It's okay, poppet," Jean said as the crowd dispersed. "Let's go home."

"Okay, guys, thank you," Grundy tried his best to not

throw up, "It's all over. Move on, please, nothing to see here."

Jean held Mia's hand. She cried at the splatter as the officer cleared it up.

"Let's go."

"I don't want another cat," she cried and walked with her mother toward the supermarket entrance.

"I know, sweetie," Jean tried to console Mia. "They're more trouble than they're worth."

Mia hugged her mother's side as they approached the sliding doors. The punters continued their shopping. The armed police filtered out through the aisles like a virus.

The speaker system came to life around the store.

"Good morning, and thank you for shopping at *The Y*, Chrome Valley. This is a staff announcement. Clean up on aisle three, please. Clean up on aisle three. Thank you."

Chapter 5

Dark's Palsy

"Okay, we're in."

SHUNT. The metal door unlocked.

The gloved hand pulled the ID card away from the gate and slipped it into a trouser pocket, "Let's go."

The man moved through the door and waved two other people in. A woman wearing a pig mask and what looked like a juvenile boy crept through the door.

"Shh, keep behind me," The man tiptoed along the metallic corridor that seemed to run into infinity. A long fluorescent strip light fizzed above him as he moved forward.

The man also had a rubber pig mask over his head. In his right hand was a baton. He paced forward as the woman behind him grabbed his rucksack, stopping him from moving.

"Psst," she whispered. "Look. Over there."

"Shit."

A security guard sat on a plastic chair at the far end of the corridor. He was reading a newspaper and hadn't seen the trio.

The young boy started to squirm and throw his hands around, "Mommy, I can't—"

"Shh, sweetie. Not now," she covered his face with her hand and held him close to her waist.

"Mfgghh."

"*Quiet.*"

She jiggled his head in her hands, indicating that he should stop screaming.

The man stepped forward and reached a door to the left. The large lettering on the Perspex glass read "CryoBank."

"It's here, it's here," he whispered back, waving them in. He pushed the handle and opened the door.

A waft of icy cold air drifted into the corridor. He looked over at the security guard to see he'd fallen asleep. He snored as his chin hit his chest. The newspaper wilted in his hands.

"Okay," the man said. "Get in."

He moved through the door. The woman and the boy followed.

CLOMP. The door shut. The man looked dead ahead of him, "This is it. The jackpot."

"Wow," The woman marveled at the scene. Ten frosted shelves carrying around eighty glass containers of white gloop. The cold air drifted around them as the man placed his bag on the floor.

He removed his mask and stuffed it under his arm as he rummaged through the bag. This was Deacon, the mastermind of the plan they were about to enact. A good-looking guy, too.

The woman slipped off her pig mask and clamped her rucksack between her knees. Her name was Amanda, Deacon's better half. With unmistakable long, blond hair and red lips, she stood out like a sore thumb. Amanda and Deacon were in their early thirties and very determined to act.

She turned to the boy as she unzipped the bag, "Joey, honey. Just wait there. Mommy and Daddy won't be long.

Joey remained as still as he could under the pig mask. His arms jiggled around, out of his control. From under the rubber mask, his mouth and facial features make some very strange sounds.

Deacon took out a pint-sized glass tube and passed it to Amanda, "Here, take care of Joey. I'll do the rest."

"Okay," Amanda took the glass jar and turned to Joey, "See this?"

Joey nodded and continued to murmur under the mask.

"Good, we're going to go over into the corner while Daddy takes care of business, okay?"

"Wh-whut iz Dhuddy dooin'?"

"Doesn't matter," she took the boy's hand in hers, "Come with me."

Joey grabbed Amanda's hand and walked with her to the corner of the chamber.

Deacon grabbed a soft, plastic rolled-up sheet. He flung it into the air and unraveled it like a bin bag.

Whoosh!

The bag rolled out like a deflated balloon. He tore the glued ends apart and made a mouth at the end of the sheet.

"Okay. Nearly there," he barked at Amanda, who looked over and smiled.

"Good," She turned back to Joey and unbuckled his belt. "Okay. Pants down, honey."

"Wh-wh, wh-y?" he stammered.

"Because I said so," Amanda took off his trousers and looked at his underwear, "Boxers, too."

"It's ca-ca-ca—"

"—Cold?"

"Yuh-yuh-yuh—"

"Don't worry, it's fine. I'll warm you up." Amanda yanked his boxer shorts around his ankles.

She handed Joey the glass jar, "Here, hold this. Don't drop it."

"Uh-k, uh-k, uh-kaaay.'

He took the jar as Amanda took his penis into her palm. She began to beat him off, "Feel nice, sweetie?"

unload."

"Good, make sure you catch it all," Deacon yelled from across the room. He poured four fifths of each container into the giant see-through plastic slab, "Bring it here when you're ready."

"Okay."

Joey moaned from behind the pig mask.

Amanda turned around to see Joey had ejaculated into the jar in her hand. She looked up at him and winked, "Finished, sweetie?"

"Ooof," he buckled one last time. A final glob of semen dropped into the jar.

She patted him on the back and kissed the pig masks' forehead, "Good boy. You've done so well."

"Nuh, nuh," was about all Joey could manage.

Amanda spanked his buttock and rose to her feet.

"He done, yet?" Deacon moved onto the twentieth bottle of semen. The contents slimed from the lip of the jar and into the plastic bag. He was careful to leave at least a sixth of the original specimen in each jar before moving on to the next.

"Yeah, got it."

Amanda walked over to Deacon and took a quick whiff from the jar in her hand.

"Ugh, whoo," she winced in disapproval. "Very potent. A sort of zinc-ish aroma to it."

"Yeah, well, it's *special* cum, isn't it?" Deacon explained, nodding at the jars he had emptied. "Unlike this gourmet shit *The Spunk Bunker* feels the need to use. Gimme the jar."

Amanda giggled and handed him the jar. He took the lid and siphoned off a glob of semen against the rim. He slipped a tiny teardrop of Joey's cum into the first jar.

Then the second.

Then the third.

"He's produced quite a lot. Not bad for the tenth week."

Amanda stepped back. She looked at the two frosted rows containing countless vials of semen, "Well, it's all over tonight."

She held up her right hand and massaged her arm, "Every week for two months."

Deacon thought about the assessment and looked at Joey, "Yeah. Lucky bastard."

Amanda turned to Joey and called him over, "Sweetie, come over here."

Joey hopped over in his pig mask. He walked like he had some kind of muscular dystrophy, "Mommy, me dizzy."

"Shh," Amanda whispered. "Help Daddy put the jars back on the shelf."

"Are you kidding?" Deacon huffed as he moved on to the thirtieth vial of semen, "He'll shake and drop them."

A loud rumbling came from outside. It coughed and spluttered, shaking the jars of cum on the shelves.

"What's that noise?" Amanda whispered. "Sounded like a truck."

"Oh, *shit*," Deacon gasped and wiped the sticky fluids from his fingers on his jacket. "They're not supposed to take the specimens until tomorrow."

Amanda looked at her watch - ten past midnight, "Um, it *is* tomorrow, babe."

"Fuck it," Deacon slammed the last jar on the shelf and crouched down to the cum-filled plastic bag, "Damn it. We gotta get out of here."

He caught sight of his son's naked bottom half.

"For fuck's sake. Can we get his pants back on at least?"

"Yes, yes," Amanda hopped over to Joey's boxers and trousers and collected them. She ran back over to Joey.

"Moohhhm?" Joey asked.

"Shh, sweetie?" she slid to her knees and opened his boxers shorts, "Quick, put your pants back on.

THUD, THUD.

Deacon and Amanda turned to the door. Joey stepped into his underwear.

"Shit, someone's at the door."

"Bugger it," came the voice from behind the metal entrance, "I don't have the key on me."

WHUMP, WHUMP.

Joey made his way over to the final shelf. He played with a couple of the jars.

The man behind the door shoved again to ensure it was definitely locked, "Steve, can you get the key, please."

Deacon and Amanda turned to each other.

"Is there another way out?" she asked.

"No. It's just that one door."

"In a cryogenic fridge? One door? Bollocks, there must be more than one."

She turned around to Joey to find him scooping a finger's worth of come from one of the jars. A string of sloppy white effluence roped to the floor.

"Joey, sweetie," Amanda hollered. "Don't touch the jars."

"Whaaar, moohmy?" he turned around and stepped back, protesting his innocence, "Ahh n-never did n-nuffin—"

His back heel slipped in the puddle of semen. He stumbled back and crashed against the shelf. The *Uterox* placard dislodged and swung above his head.

"Mooommyy."

"Oh, shit," Amanda gasped as her son fell back-first against the twelve-foot-high shelf.

"No."

CRAAASSSSHHHHHH!

Dozens of vials of semen hit the floor, crashing all around Joey. He looked up and saw the shelf topple over him.

"Awwwnaaahhh."

SLAMMM-SMASSSHHH!

Joey remained standing as the shelving units fell either

side of him like a perverse Buster Keaton stunt. The jars and vials of semen exploded against the floor. A mini tidal wave of white spunk splattered up the floor.

"Mhooommiiieeeee."

"Shhh," Amanda and Deacon looked behind the shivering Joey. A back door loomed behind him now that the shelf was on its side.

"You okay, son?" Deacon asked.

The pig's mask nodded over and over again.

SHUNT.

A key entered the front door. Deacon glanced at it and bent down to zip the plastic bag up, "Right, let's get out of here."

"Okay," Amanda ran up to her son and made for the door, "Watch your step, sweetie. There's retard cum all over the floor."

"Uhhhhhh."

Amanda grabbed his hand and pushed the lever across the back door. She turned to Deacon and watched him hulk the six-foot cellophane bag of cum in his arms. It warbled across his forearms like a weighty water balloon.

"I'm coming, I'm coming."

BEEP! BEEEP! BEEEEEP!

The alarm fired off around the building, "Alert, alert! CryoBank One. Illicit entry."

"Quick, run," Amanda held the door open for Deacon. He slipped across the cum-soaked floor but managed to keep on his feet.

"Let's go."

She pushed Joey through the door. Deacon ran after him.

Amanda dived through the door. She slid herself behind the wall as the main entrance door unbolted and swung in.

The trio found themselves in a gated exterior causeway lit up by the moon and a sole flood lamp.

"The car," Deacon scanned the barb wire fence, "There's no way out. We're gonna have to jump the railings."

Amanda quickened her breath and peered round the back door. She looked inside the chamber.

A security guard and two van drivers wearing *Uterox* overalls made their way in.

Nothing was amiss except for the broken shelf scattered over the floor in an ocean of sperm.

"Shit. One of the shelves has fallen."

"Pssst," Deacon whispered at Amanda, "Over here."

She turned to see Deacon carrying the huge sack of cum. Joey stood next to his father in his pig mask. The condensation from his breath weaved out of the nostrils and eye slits.

"Come on. We got what we came for," he made for the railings, "Let's go."

Amanda looked up at the ten-foot railings. Circular razors lined the sharp metal ends. It was either make a break for it or, worse, get caught.

She closed her eyes and controlled her breathing.

Ten years Ago

A young Amanda sat on a hospital trolley bed. An IV ran from her arm into a drip. The screen beside her displayed a series of numbers.

Deacon walked into the room, "Sweetie?"

"Yes, babe?" she smiled, expecting some exciting news, "Where is he?"

"Time to meet your son."

A nurse brought in a newborn baby wrapped in a blanket. The *Uterox* logo was pinned to both the baby's blanket and the nurse's scrubs. Amanda's face lit up.

"Here you go, mommy."

The baby opened its eyes and adjusted his pupils to the light.

"Waaaaaahh," he cried as the nurse placed him into his mother's arms.

"Congratulations, Mrs. Triptych," said the nurse.

Deacon leaned into to smell his son and caught an impressive sight between its kicking legs, "It's a boy, *for sure.*"

Amanda looked down and smiled at her son. She couldn't contain her emotion, "Ohh, look at you, you cuddly little thing. Mummy loves you, doesn't she?"

A tear rolled down her cheek. Deacon started to well up.

The nurse smiled and backed out of the room, "I'll leave you guys to it, then."

"Thank you, nurse."

Amanda looked into her baby's beautiful brown eyes. She took a deep breath and whispered to him, "Mommy carried you for eighty-eight days and nights, here."

"You want to call Zoe to come and meet her new nephew?"

"No, it's okay," Amanda whispered. "She's probably busy, anyway."

Deacon smiled, "So, have we settled on a name?"

"I kinda like *Joey*," Amanda inspected his fingers and toes.

"I thought we were going with Charles?"

"No," Amanda cupped his tiny foot into her palm, "I've kind of gone off that name. I like Joey. Look at his little toes. Toey! Toey-Joey!"

Deacon chuckled to himself, "Yeah, he kinda looks like a *Joey.*"

***

The following day. Amanda had yet to be formally discharged. She and Deacon sat in a meeting with Maxwell Dark, the CEO of *Uterox Industries*. He stood up from behind his desk and perched himself on the side of it. Such was his rather eccentric and flamboyant nature.

Amanda looked shocked. She processed the news and looked up at Max.

"Dark's Palsy?"

"I'm afraid so," Max sighed and cracked his knuckles on his right fist. He blew the dead skin away, "Of course, we're more than willing to remunerate you for your trouble."

Deacon slammed his fist against the arm rest on his chair, "*Payment*? For what you did to our baby?"

"Mr. Triptych, I can assure you that this anomaly wasn't our fault."

Deacon stood up and grabbed Max's collar. He was inches away from head-butting the man, "Something is *wrong* with your fucking procedure here, motherfucker. You're going to have to do a fuck of a lot better than *anomaly*."

"Mr. Triptych," Max pleaded. "It wasn't our f-fault. The process is hereditary. A random, unaccounted gene caught in the system."

"I'll *unaccount* your fucking head off your shoulders if you don't give me some fucking answers."

Max hit a button his desk, "Okay, I'll show you."

The desk came alive and displayed a cross-section diagram of a brain on the glass surface.

Amanda crept between the two men and held her belly, "Sweetie?"

"Fine," Deacon huffed and released Max's shirt from his grip.

"Very good," Max turned around and adjusted himself. How very dare Deacon for accosting him, of all people!

"Dark's Palsy," Max traced his finger along the diagram of a brain, "A neurological abnormality in the dark area of the brain."

"What are the symptoms?"

"Your son is healthy. However, he will experience a loss of control for some of his senses. Some muscular dystrophy. The good news is that his condition will not deteriorate."

Deacon cried into his hands. He felt helpless, "So, he's a fucking *spastic*?"

"I wouldn't use such a vulgar term, Mr. Triptych," Max switched off the screen and returned to his seat, "As I say, we are more than happy to compensate you for your experience with us. We'd rather leave our customers happy with good will. Of course, we'd insist an embargo on what has been discussed in this room."

"What sort of compensation are we talking about?" Amanda asked, seriously intending to talk money.

Deacon turned to her and didn't recognize the woman he'd married. How could she ask such a thing? How could she be so apathetic to the idea that they now had a son living with Dark's Palsy?

"What? You're not seriously thinking of accepting a pay-off, are you?"

Amanda turned to Deacon and gave him a look, "Let's hear Mr. Dark out."

She raised her eyebrows as if to suggest the pay-off might be worth entertaining. *Uterox* was a large conglomerate, after all.

Deacon wiped his nose and coughed. He turned to Max and cleared his throat, "Well?"

"I think one hundred and twenty-five thousand pounds is more than reasonable?"

Amanda felt like launching out of her seat. She squeezed her husband's hand over the arm rest.

Deacon didn't feel the same way, "Are you fucking *joking*?"

"No, Mr. Triptych. I'm not."

He rose to his feet and slammed his fist against the table, "One hundred and twenty-five for a retarded kid? You're taking the *fucking piss*!"

"I don't think we are at all, sir. It's a most generous offer."

"*My* child is going to grow up an invalid," Deacon huffed.

Max frowned and nearly took offense, "Now, sir, that language is uncalled for—"

"—Sweetie, let's just take the money—"

"—No, Amanda," Deacon flung her arm from his wrist and turned back to Max, "Our boy is going to grow up disadvantaged. He's going to need constant care throughout his life. For *fuck's* sake."

"Now, now, sir—"

"—You fucking *shut up*. Just shut up," Deacon huffed, smoke billowing through his nostrils, "See you and your company? You're fucking sick. Speeding up the birthing process to make a cheap buck. Don't think I haven't noticed that little *side* business you've got going on with that drink you make—"

"—Baby Champagne—"

"—I don't give a fuck what your demon juice is called, you *prick*." Deacon pushed himself from the desk. He gripped Amanda's hand and pulled her to her feet.

Deacon opened the door to the office. He held his index finger at Max and scowled, "Keep your blood money, you vampire."

"Please, Mr. Triptych—"

"—No. You hear me? No," Deacon kicked the door open, "You haven't heard the last of this. Of *us*."

Deacon marched Amanda out of the office and slammed the door shut behind them.

Earlier this morning…

Max Dark made his way out of the *Uterox* building. His bodyguard ushered him down the steps. A horde of media and reporters took photos and attempted to ask him questions.

He made his way to the stretch limo waiting for him at the side of the curb. "No questions, thank you!"

A reporter ran up to him as he tried to descend the steps, "Mr. Dark. How do you respond to the abnormal rise of defective births owing to your company?"

"No comment, thank you," Max smiled politely for the camera. His bodyguard reached the door to the back of the limo and opened it.

"Get me the fuck out of here, *fuckwit*," he said through clenched teeth. To the surrounding press it looked like he was smiling.

"Yes, Mr. Dark."

Max continued down the stairs with a woman in a silver suit next to him. She shoved a microphone into his face, "Donna Doubleday, *Sense Nation News*—"

"—Fuck off," Max whispered and kept his smile up.

"Will *Uterox* be addressing the Freedom of Information Act findings? A forty percent mortality rate for the women in your care at the company?"

"No," Max offered. "Excuse me."

"How about claims that so-called *Dark's Palsy* is now rife in your business's output?"

Max reached the limo door and slipped into the back seat, "I have no comment at this time, thank you."

Donna stared at Max as he strapped his seatbelt on,. "Over seventy-five percent born with *Dark's*, Mr. Dark?"

WHUMP.

The bodyguard slammed the door and jumped into the front. The press chased after the car as it shot off into the distance.

A few minutes ago…

Just outside of the CryoBank, Deacon lifted the six-foot sack of semen across his arms. The weight of the bag began to take its toll. He looked around to see more cars pull up into the car park a few railings to the left.

A black limousine screeched to a halt.

"Amanda. Come on," he whispered.

She opened her eyes and peered back into the room, "Hold on a second."

Deacon looked down at Joey. The pig mask looked up at him.

"For fuck's sake. You're still wearing that bloody mask."

He gripped the flapping rubber neck and pulled the mask off Joey's face.

Amanda concentrated her gaze on two technicians. They took an inventory of the remaining jars of cum.

"Vials one through three-hundred and eight B are clear," he said, making a note.

The door to the CryoBank opened. A man stepped in and made way for another. Mr. Maxwell Dark.

Amanda raised her eyes and held her hand over her mouth.

"What the hell?" Deacon's shocked voice came from the metal railing. Something strange had happened to Joey. "Is this some kind of sick joke? Amanda?"

She turned to look at Deacon and Joey. She squinted at her son's head, "Huh?"

Deacon pointed to his scalp, "What's this? Did you do this to him?" Joey had a green Mohawk running over his bald head.

"No. I don't know, it wasn't there when we set off."

"Whatever, let's go!" Deacon struggled with the sack of semen in his hands, "We gotta dump this good stuff."

"Hold on!" Amanda peeked through the door. Max flew into a tirade.

"Bring me security detail right now."

"Yes, Mr. Dark."

Max slammed his gloves to the counter and looked over at Amanda, but didn't spot her. She froze still as he turned to his bodyguard, "Tell the technicians to get the specimens out and loaded into Utero."

"Yes, Mr. Dark."

A technician returned with the security guard. The

same man who'd been reading the newspaper in the corridor. He looked very scared. Max turned to him and rubbed his hands together.

"Okay. You're security detail for tonight's shift, right?"

"Yes, Mr. Dark."

"Right," Max pointed to the last shelf scattered on the floor, "Can you tell me what happened here, you useless cunt?"

The security guard stammered for an answer. "I, uh—"

"—I, uh, uh, nuuurrrr," Max's couldn't contain his fury any longer. He played out a spazzing mocking fit of the security guard, enacting a faux-palsy fit, "I'm just a fuckin' *thecurity* guard, I dunno what ahhmmm doooooin'."

"No, sir, i-it's just that—"

"—You're a fucking *retard*, that's it, isn't it?" Max grabbed the back of the security guard's shirt and marched him over to the fallen shelf, "Say it."

"I-I'm a f-fucking retard, Mr. Dark."

"Correct," Max pushed the man to his knees, the force of which sent his spectacles flying into the puddle of semen.

Max crouched down beside him and grabbed the back of his hair.

"Oh, Christ. *No*," Amanda muttered.

"Fucking drink it, you prick," Max roared into the guard's face, "Seeing as you take pride in your work."

The bodyguard and the other technicians looked away in disgust. Max took out a Glock 17 from his belt and buried it against the Guard's temple.

"B-But, Mr. Dark, s-sir—"

"—Shut the fuck up," Max pressed the gun's hammer back, "You guzzle down every last drop."

The security guard blinked and held out his tongue. He lowered his chin to the ground, trying to please Max. The tip of his tongue skirted across the thin layer of white skin that had formed atop the puddle of semen.

"That's it, you fucking clown," Max chuckled. "Get a

gooood slurp going on."

GLUMPH.

The guard swallowed a mouthful of it and dry-heaved. Ropes of it slapped down his chin.

Max giggled and pushed against the man's head with the gun, "How does it taste?"

"Uh, uh—" the security guard stuck his tongue out and gasped. He tried to make out that he liked it to save his own life, "It's, uh, nice."

"That's *Uterox* sperm, dickhead," Max whispered into his ear, "It's the finest fucking *nut* on planet Earth."

"Y-Yes, Mr. Dar—"

"—And *you* let it go to waste." Max yelled and pulled the trigger, "*Cunt*—"

BANG!

The guard's head exploded. A fountain of brain, skull and half-digested cum splattered against the penultimate shelf.

SPLOTT!

The guard's corpse splashed face-first into the puddle of semen. Globules of the white stuff jumped in the air.

Max stood up and pulled down on his suit. He turned to his bodyguard and the technicians, "Find the motherfuckers who broke in. Find them, *now*."

Amanda pushed herself from the wall and ran up to Deacon, "Fuck. They're here."

"Who are here?" Deacon balanced the giant bag of cum in his arms.

"Him, him," Amanda took one end of the bag, "We need to get out of here."

"I know that," Deacon yelled. "I've been saying it for the past two minutes. The only way is up and over the razor wire fence. Be careful with the bag."

"Okay, I—" Amanda stopped and looked at Joey. That damn green Mohawk made an appearance once again, "What the fuck?"

"Mohhmmiieee?" he looked up and blinked.

Joey's face was contorted and twisted. The jawbone protruded from his face. His right eye sunk lower than the left and inverted. An indication of the physical abnormality that was Dark's Palsy.

"Yes, sweetie?"

He felt around his Mohawk, "Whhuuhh dooo ah hev green hayre?"

"Uh, I don't know," Amanda pushed him to the railings, "we'll figure it out later, sweetie. But now we have to climb the fence and run away."

"Why?"

"Stop asking questions, Charlie," Deacon said, gripping the railings and climbing upward. "Just get ready to climb."

"Who's Charlie?" Amanda said.

Deacon stopped half way up the railing, clutching his end of the bag. "Huh?"

"You called Joey *Charlie.*"

"No I didn't?" Deacon huffed. "Did I?"

Max screamed from within the CryoBank, "I want those Nazi maggots found and castrated right fucking now."

"Fuck it, let's go."

Deacon reached the top of the railing and placed his hands through the coiled razor wire. He nestled his thighs over the top. The blades sliced at his skin, "Ahh, shit. Pass me the bag. Quick."

Amanda threw her end of the bag up to her husband. "Be careful."

"I am," Deacon caught the majority of the bag and waited for Amanda.

She looked up to Joey, "Okay, sweetie, climb up. Be careful. I'll be right behind you."

"Ahhh kay, mommy," Joey made his way up the metal fence.

"Good boy. Go to daddy."

She pushed him by the buttocks. He reached his dad at

the top, "Be careful of the sharp silver bits, okay?"

Joey looked down and saw his mother clasp the railing, intending to climb, "Whay are we dooing thees, Muuhmmiiee?"

Amanda looked at her son's good eye, "Because we're taking revenge on the bad people."

"Okay."

Amanda looked back and saw the commotion near the back door, "Shit, they're coming."

She turned around and placed her foot on the railing. It juggled back and forth. The rustling from the frame was loud.

"Hey," a voice yelled, "Stop right there."

WHOOOSH!

A huge spotlight illuminated Deacon and Joey atop the fence with the huge bag of cum. Amanda's back lit up. She looked over her shoulder and squinted at the light.

"You, woman. On your knees with your hands behind your head," the voice demanded. A click of a gun barrel came from within the brilliant white light.

She jumped to the ground and held up her hands, "Who's there?"

The man lowered the light, revealing himself - and his Glock 17.

She stepped back into the railing, causing it to rock back and forth.

"Moohmmieee," Joey screamed. He looked down to see the two random razors gnawing at his skin, "Eeet huuuurts."

"Be quiet, sweetie," Amanda hushed. "Mommy's busy."

"You two, up there," the man addressed Joey and Deacon. "Stay where you are. I want that ejaculate in pristine condition. We'll get a ladder."

The man stepped out from the floodlight. It was Max, happy that he'd caught the intruders.

"Oh m-my God," Amanda gasped.

"You're all in a lot of trouble," Max said, surrounded

by a flurry of technicians and suited men with weapons.

Seconds later, an army of thirty officials aimed their machine guns at Amanda.

Max waggled his finger at her, "You. Come here."

Amanda looked up at Deacon. He tried to smile. But they were caught. It was over.

She took one step forward and stopped dead still, "Mr. Dark?"

"Eh?" he said, confused. "How do you know my name?"

"I know everything about you, Mr. Dark."

"Amanda?" Deacon whispered from above, "What are you doing?"

She ignored him and continued, "I know about Uterox. I know everything."

"Who are you?" Max asked before turning to the others, "Who is this bitch?"

Everyone shrugged and muttered, "I dunno."

"I'm Amanda Triptych, Mr. Dark."

Max swallowed and lowered his gun. He couldn't believe what he was hearing, "Amanda *fucking* Triptych."

"Yes, you remember my son?" She pointed at Joey atop the railing, who waved back as politely as possible, "He's ten years old now."

Max looked at Joey and nearly threw up, "Jesus *shit*. That's *one* fucking ugly retard."

"Dark's Palsy," Amanda screamed. "A neurological abnormality in the dark area—"

"—of the brain," Max finished her sentence, "Yes."

"One hundred and twenty-five thousand pounds for our silence?"

"I remember." He pointed the gun toward her, "You should have taken the money."

"Never."

"So you thought tainting my product would be a good way to get revenge and harm my business?"

Amanda took a lungful of air and closed her eyes. She

paused for a few seconds and turned into an apoplectic fit of rage.

"Right at the fucking *source*, motherfucker," Amanda roared and jumped back against the fence with her full weight.

"Open fire," Max ordered.

RAT-A-TAT-A-TAT-A-TAT-A-TAT-A-TATT-TT

The officials opened fire on Amanda. Her entire body weight punched against the metal railings.

The bullets tore through her chest; fifteen across the torso, and another twenty across her waist. The blood spat in all directions as the ammunition shredded her corpse to nothing.

BANG-BANG-BANG! The officials wouldn't stop shooting.

Amanda's forehead bust open. Her top lip shattered from a bullet hit, pinging what little remained of her head against her shoulders.

"Maaahhhmmiieeeee," Joey cried as the force her body against the fence tilted it backwards.

Deacon lost his grip and toppled over the side.

RIPPPPPP-PP!

The bag of cum fell onto the razor wire, tearing lines into the plastic. A huge slew of semen bled through the slit like squeezed toothpaste out of a tube. The white stuff puked down the railings, seeping over and into Amanda's bullet-shredded body.

"My semen," Max shouted. "Fucking get them."

Deacon's leg's slipped. He threw his hands up and grabbing a fistful of razor wire in his each palm.

"Gah, *Fuck*."

Joey reached out and lost his footing, swinging to his mother's side of the fence, "Daddy."

"Ch-Charlie, son," Deacon gasped. "Run."

"Whaarrr, Duuhhdy?"

"I said run—"

SPLAAATCH!

Joey screamed in terror as a bullet shattered Deacon's upper palate and blasted through his brain.

Deacon's dead body hung against the railing, pinned by the razors through his wrists, forearm, chest and what little remained of his neck.

The frothing blood from his neck cavity ran down the railings. The red gore meshed with the stinking cum remnants.

"Daddy," Joey cried. "No."

"Get that fucking spastic down here, now," Max ordered the men. They marched forward and kept their rifles pointed at Joey.

He looked down and grabbed the sodden plastic semen sack in his palm, "Yeeeewww killed muuuuh duhhdy," he screamed in his monstrous, garbled voice.

"Son, get down," ordered an official with a machine gun.

"Naawww."

Max made his way over to the railing. He growled and punched at it over and over again, "Get the fuck down, you mongoloid *shit*."

THUWMP! THUWMP!

The railing lilted back and forth. Joey held tight as the razor wire chewed through his arms, "It huuuurts, it huuuurts."

THWACK!

Max kicked the railing over and over again, "Get down, then, you daft cunt.'

"Naawwww."

Joey clung tighter to the razor wire. The splats of cum and blood flicked left and right as the fence flew back and forth.

"Right."

Max gave up and held out his hands. He was *seriously* fucked off, "Okay, champ. What in the name of mummy's cunt do you want?"

Max kept his hands held out to suggest Joey had won,

"Hmmm?"

An official turned to Max, "Shall we just put a bullet in it, sir?"

"No."

"We can put it out of its, and our, misery, Mr. Dark?"

"He's one of ours," Max screamed and pointed at Joey, "Look at him. He's a complicated little fucker. Several of a kind."

The official turned around and examined the kid's crying face, "Ugh, that's messed up."

Max took an outrageously dramatic step forward. He stomped his feet to the ground and punched the air in a furious rage, "What will it take to get your spastic behind down here?"

Joey looked down the length of the railing. One side revealed his dead father. The other, what remained of his mother's shredded body soaked in semen.

He blinked a couple of times and thought about what it might take to get him down.

The officials - and Max - waited for what seemed like an eternity.

A tear rolled down the child's hideously deformed cheek.

The droplet of water fell through the air in slow motion. It traveled through the bullet hole in his mother's chest and splashed against her breast bone, sliding over the bullet.

Joey looked up and took a deep breath, "Ahhh wurrnnaa gow howmmee."

Max raised his eyebrows. He wrenched his shoulders back as if he'd been a stupid joke, "Go home? Really? Is that all?"

Joey nodded.

"Well, fuck my arse with a broken glass and call me Sheila, Charlie," Max chuckled, "Why didn't you say that in the first place, you nasty little bucket of diarrhea?"

Joey blinked at Max, innocently, not knowing how to

respond.

Max clapped his hands together and waved the officials forward, "You heard the boy. Let's get him back *home*."

The armed men moved forward and helped Joey down from the railings. One of them turned to Max as he reached his bodyguard, "Are you sure about this, Mr. Dark?"

Max nodded rapidly and slapped his bodyguard on the back, "Yes, yes, yes, yes, yes, yes. Just do it."

His bodyguard leaned into his shoulder, "What are you doing, sir?"

"Why, I'm taking little Charlie, here, back to his *home*."

The officials managed to lift Joey away from the razors with a minimum of fuss. Two of razors slipped out from his forearm. A light bleeding trickled to his elbow as one of armed men set the boy to his feet.

"Charlie?" Max crouched to his knees to face the boy.

"Muhhh nemm is Jowwiiie."

"Come here, you hindered little cat-fucker," Max tapped his knees. "So, you wanna go home?"

Joey nodded and arrived in front of his captor.

Max smiled and held out his hand, "Hi. I'm Max."

Joey shook his hand. Rather, he took Max's little finger in his hand and shook it, "Ah'm Jowwiiee."

"No, you're Charlie."

"Ah'm not."

"Are, too."

"Naaww," the kid salivated and wiped his lip. "Ah'm Jowiiee."

"Okay, fuck it. You're *Joey*, whatever," Max giggled and obliged the kid. "Very pleased to meet you. Let's get you home."

Max rose to his feet and kept hold of Joey's hand. They walked back to the CryoBank.

Joey looked up at Max, "Whurrawee goiing, misstah?"

"We're going home, Char— uh, *Joey*." Max corrected himself, "Your new home."

"Uhhhkaay."

Max and Charlie stepped into the CryoBank as officials swept Amanda's remains - and the contents of the bag of cum - away from the fence.

"Can we get someone to hose this shit down, please?" one of them said.

Max looked down and squeezed Joey's hand as they walked into the frosty plume of gas at the door to the CryoBank.

"Joey?"

"Yeath?"

"Welcome to Pure Dark."

Chapter 6

Die in a Fire

The *Freeway Five* estate was the bane of *Chrome Junction*. The structure was the last of the seventies social housing projects in North West London. Five twenty-floor high rise *apartment blocks*, as the residents insisted they were known as. Calling them apartments (and not *flats*) made the awful blot on the landscape sound luxurious.

The five ghastly buildings sat right in front of the M25 motorway. The road ran along behind the buildings, a third of the way up. It was as if someone had drawn a line through them.

Freeway Five had something of a reputation. People who had to walk past the monstrosity were glad they didn't live there. A rumor had gone around *Chrome Junction* that a brothel had been set up somewhere in the third building. It was an area known for its drug misuse.

The gossip-mongering may have been true. Inexpensive hookers frequented the buildings most nights. It was unclear to the residents whether they lived there or were seeing clients. Their visits were that frequent.

The social cleansing effort in this borough had begun in earnest a few years ago. A new luxury apartment block was erected across the road. Some residents took a keen interest in purchasing a property in the building. It had a gym on the second floor and a twenty-four-hour concierge service.

The prices for the average apartment in the luxury block was punitive. No-one could afford it. Situated a couple of miles from *Chrome Junction Station*, it boasted excellent transport links.

Unlike *Freeway Five*, the new luxury flats were mostly uninhabited. All the units were bought-out. You'd see the odd person arrive in their car and stay the night. Clearly a case of the wealthy buying up property and waiting for their investment to pay dividends in a few years.

Some of the residents on the *Freeway Five* estate had complained that the new building blocked their sunlight. This started another rumour; their own homes may be torn down to make way for the rich.

The housing association held a meeting with the residents to get their feedback. "Fuck you" was the overwhelming response.

Two years ago, the residents on the council estate received some news. The five buildings were to be renovated, including the fitting of a new frontage. The interiors were to be strengthened to protect against the elements. The residents couldn't believe their luck. It was never going to increase the value of their residences.

It seemed that there was light at the end of the tunnel for *Freeway Five*.

Who on Earth would bother renovating these buildings if the council was going to tear it down?

Of course, no-one would. The residents of *Freeway Five* slept soundly knowing that their childhood homes were safe.

7:30 pm. The sun disappeared behind the fifth building.

Nursery school teacher Nisa Pershar was one such resident on the estate. In her late fifties, she and her husband, Ali, and their two children, Imran and Abby, lived on the twelfth floor of *Freeway One*. When friends came to visit, which wasn't often, they'd get confused about which of the five buildings was which. It wasn't hard to figure out.

One, two, three, four, five…

If you could count to five, then you'd know which building to go to.

Nisa had lived in *Freeway One* all her life. She was born there. When her parents passed away, they left her the keys to apartment 118.

***

Nisa stepped off the bus with two bags of groceries. She walked past the playground out front. A few children were playing on the busted swings. Not so much two chains and a plastic seat as a hanging metal noose with which to hang around on.

"Hello Mrs. Pershar," said one of the boys as he whizzed down the slide. Nisa smiled back at the boy.

"Young Aaron. You're out late tonight. Does your mother know you're down here?"

"Yes, Mrs. Pershar," he said and climbed to his feet. He turned around and pointed to a window on the fifth floor, "She's watching us from the window, look."

Nisa looked up and saw a woman smoking a cigarette from an open window, "Oh yes, there she is. Hello."

The woman sucked on her cigarette and flung it out of the window. She moved away and spluttered.

The cigarette hit the ground; the hot ash burned into the already dried-out grass.

Nisa tutted to herself and made her way to the building, "Okay, Aaron, you take care. Don't be out here too late."

He ran up the steps of the slide and had another go, "I won't, I promise."

As Nisa made her way from the pudgy ground, she kicked away a used syringe. "Ugh, *honestly*."

She adjusted her neck scarf. Tonight was an especially

warm evening for this time of year. The majority of the windows up the front of the building were wide open. Of course, there was no air conditioning in any of the buildings. Battered old fans tried to cool the air and reduce the humidity in most apartments.

It was going to be a close night. Nisa knew she couldn't sleep in this ridiculous heat.

She held her fob to the plate by the door and let herself in. A dank gangway led to the one elevator the building had. Opposite the dug-out area was the sole staircase that ran up to the twentieth floor.

Graffiti and puddles of liquid lined both the walls. It seemed that a new daubing had appeared in black writing. *"Pakis Out!"*

Nisa shook her head and muttered to herself. The elevator doors opened and she got in.

At the very last moment, a man in a leather jacket wedged himself in between the doors.

He made it into the metal box, "Jeez. Nearly took my damn arm off."

He brushed himself down and hit the button for the twelfth floor. Then, he noticed Nisa struggling with her shopping bags. "Oh, hello, Mrs. Pershar."

"Good evening, Richard."

"Can I help you with your bags?" Richard asked and offered her his arm.

"Oh, uh, yes. Thanks," she passed him the heaviest of the four grocery bags she was holding.

"Whoa. Heavy," Richard giggled.

The lift made its way up the shaft. The shafts of light illuminated their bodies from toe to forehead.

"How was your day, Richard?" Nisa asked.

"Ah, you know," he chuckled. "Just moving in some white goods to Mr. Peterson on the fourth floor."

"A big and strong man like you shouldn't have a problem with that."

"Tell me about it. Everyone's asking me to carry out odd jobs."

Nisa looked at Richard's hand carrying the bag, "Yes, I suppose so."

They smiled at each other and counted the lights crawling up the numbers on the panel.

Nine… ten…

"Well, nearly there," Richard rocked back and forth on his heels. "Got much planned for this evening?"

"Ah, not really. Just going to relax and—"

TING! The twelfth floor.

"—Maybe get an early night."

"Great idea," Richard stepped against the metal wall, "After you."

"Thank you."

Richard walked Nisa to her front door. He set the bag on the floor and looked over his shoulder, "Well, better get back to it."

"Yes, thank you, Richard." Nisa threw her key into the lock and turned it, "Most kind of you to help me."

"Oh, don't mention it," he smiled. "Have a good evening."

She pushed her front door inward, "Yes, you too."

Nisa watched Richard walk to apartment 117. She couldn't quite see his front door from her own. He had to walk ten steps to the end of the landing, turn left, past the stairs and elevators, and make a right to reach his own apartment.

Nisa walked into the hallway and pulled the door shut, "I'm home. Don't everyone get up at once," she joked under her breath.

She moved into the kitchen and set the bags on the counter, "Can someone help me unpack, please?"

Out came the carton of milk. The bag of apples and vegetables for tonight's dinner.

She walked out of the kitchen and saw her husband fast

asleep on the couch in front of the television, "Ali, honey?"

"Hunh?" Ali shifted in his seat and woke up, "What?"

"It's me, *silly*."

"Oh."

"I'm unpacking. Can you set the table?" Nisa returned to the kitchen, "I want to get dinner over with and get an early night."

"Yes, pet," Ali stood to his feet. He reached for his crutches and slung his arms through them, "Abby, Imran. Mum is home."

Imran played *Combat Shock*, a first-person shooting game, in his bedroom. He shouted into his headset and yelled at the other gamers.

"Smoke grenade through the door."

His military character kicked open a door to a wooden hut. He tossed a small bomb into the room. The enemies ducked as he fired at them. The bomb popped apart and fizzed, releasing a cloud of smoke.

"Okay, get in. Get in," Imran aimed down his sights and shot two bad guys. His friend, on the other end of the headset, came in from the opposite door and took down the remaining enemies.

"Got "em."

"Imran," Ali said from behind the door, "Come through for your dinner, innit."

"In a minute," he said moving his avatar away from an exploding grenade.

BOOM! *"Wasted."*

Imran's character died, "Aww, shit. Look, man, I gotta go."

"Safe," his friend said. "See you later, yeah?"

"Yeah, safe, man."

Imran quit the game and ran out of his room. He knocked on the door next to his. "Abby, man, dinner's nearly ready."

"Yeah," she said from inside her room, "Hold on."

Imran headed toward the front room.

Abby lay on her bed and ran her fingers through her hair. She pressed the cordless phone against her ear and continued her conversation, "Nah, just my stupid brother."

She sat up straight and peeled the curtain away from the window. It was night-time. The luxury apartment block lit up the night sky as cars whizzed by on the main road, below.

"I dunno, you know," she said into her phone. "I might have to rain check tonight. Yeah, I know it's Friday, but I've got a bit of a headache. I'd rather rest up. Maybe go out tomorrow."

She twisted her body over the bed and planted her bare feet on the ground.

"No. I do *not* fancy him," she giggled. "Fuck off! Yeah, he's fit, but maybe tomorrow."

Thud-thud.

"Abby, dinner," Her father's voice came from behind the door.

"Yeah, I'm coming," she yelled back and returned to her call, "Ha, very funny. I might say that to him too, one day. Look, I gotta go. Dad's calling me to dinner."

8:00 pm. Nisa dished out everyone's dinner around the table. Ali poured himself some water.

"Okay, you can start."

RIIIINNNNGGGGG! The alarm on the oven buzzed from the kitchen. Nisa moved away.

"So," Ali tucked into his meal, "What you guys got planned for the weekend?"

"Not much," Imran nodded at Abby. "I heard Baji's got a date, though, innit?"

"I do *not*," Abby protested and dropped her fork to the table. She whacked Imran around the back of the head. "Liar."

Imran and Ali giggled, "Oh, it's okay, honey."

"She bloody *does* have a date," Imran added.

"I don't believe this," Abby yelped in disbelief. "Mum, tell him."

Nisa returned with some steamed vegetables in her cloth-wrapped hands, "What is going on here?"

"Imran is embarrassing me, mum."

"What's he saying, now?" Nisa placed the steamed vegetables on the table and wiped her hands, "Is it about your date tomorrow?"

"What?" Abby fumed at the unwanted gang attack, "I do *not* have a date."

Nisa giggled, "Not what I heard."

"Yeah, his name's Daryl or something, from sixth form," Imran said as he poked at his food with a fork.

Nisa turned to Abby as she took her seat, "You're dating a white boy, now?"

"Ugh, *no*," Abby threw a tantrum and stood out of her chair in defiance, "You guys suck. I'm not even hungry, anyway."

She stormed off. The other three tried not to laugh. A few squirms of suppress hilarity came from their mouths.

"You think it's funny?" Abby yelled from the landing. The coat stand rattled as she removed her jacket, "Allow me, man. I'm going to see Samantha."

"You're not going to finish your dinner?"

"No."

The front door slammed shut. The flap on the letterbox clanged a second later. Abby was going out into the warm Friday night well and truly pissed.

"Maybe she'll find a job while she's out," Ali giggled to himself.

"Yeah," Imran smirked, "A *blowjob*, probably."

Nisa gasped and dropped her cutlery to the table, "Imran Ali Pershar."

"What?" he said with a mouthful of chicken.

"Do not talk about your sister like that, you know,"

Nisa picked up her knife and fork.

Ali turned to his wife and stroked her back, "How was your day, sweetie?"

"Ugh," she rolled her eyes. "Stressful, as usual. Fridays, you know what they're like."

"Kids all jacked up on *Menace* energy drinks and ready for the weekend?"

"Tell me about it," Nisa thought out loud. "I have one kid in the class who's a bit peculiar."

"Aren't they all like that? Little tykes running around," Imran reached for the salt, "Nothing but little fart and puke machines?"

"No, not this one. His name is Charlie. Only been with us for a week. Apparently, he's from a troubled family."

"What kind of trouble?" Ali asked. "Or can't you talk about it?"

"No, it was just something that happened during nap time. He started talking to Zack, another weird kid. They kept looking at the cupboard and talking to someone that wasn't there."

"An imaginary friend?" Ali proposed.

"No," Nisa poked around at the vegetables on her plate. She dropped her fork and pressed her head against her fist, "It was just *odd.* That Charlie boy gives me the creeps."

"Yeah, I know what you mean," Imran finished his meal. "There's this guy on *Combat Shock*. Calls himself *Mr. Dark*. Keeps saying that he's going to put a curse on me. He sounds like a ten-year-old."

"You need to stop playing that stupid video game and get yourself a part time job, young man," Ali shot Imran a look. He meant every word of what he'd said.

"Yeah, yeah."

Nisa opened her eyes and stared at the peas on her plate. The conversation between her son and husband dulled as the small green pods began to vibrate.

"Huh?" Nisa muttered, before realizing that the peas

were rearranging themselves into letters.

The first twenty peas formed a straight line - the letter *D*.

"What's going on?" Nisa nudged her husband, "Look, look."

"What is it?" Ali looked at her plate.

The next dozen pods rolled around and lined up next to the first letter. They formed a straight line - the letter *I*.

"Can't you see it?" Nisa quipped. "Look."

"They're peas, sweetie. What's wrong?"

"Imran, can you see—"

The remaining fifteen peas rolled around and formed another line, with three prongs - the letter *E*.

Nisa blinked. Imran looked at her plate and shrugged his shoulders, "So?"

"Die…" Nisa squealed at the top of their lungs, "Oh my God."

"Mom?"

WHVOOM!

Imran's head burst into flames.

"No, no," Nisa held her husband back and stumbled back over her chair. Imran rose to his feet. The roaring flames on his head shot into the air and set the ceiling lampshade set ablaze.

"Mum? What's happening?"

"Imran, Imran."

Nisa pushed herself forward and grabbed the jug of water from the table, "Shit."

SPLOOSHHH!!!

She threw the contents of jug over Imran's head. The fire fizzled out as Imran fell to the floor screaming with his head in his hands. Ali turned to her and clicked his fingers.

"Nisa, are you okay?"

"Agh," she screamed and opened her eyes. Her cheek moved from her fist, taking her out of her temporary slumber, "What, what?!"

In her other hand was the empty jug of water. She looked up at her son. Imran's face and chest were soaked. She may have been dreaming, but she'd thrown water over her son.

"Is this revenge for what I said about Abby?" Imran huffed and slung the water from his hands, "Are you sleep-watering now, or something?"

"I'm, I'm s-sorry, son," Nisa muttered, wondering what strange force possessed her to attack her son in this manner.

"I'm gonna get a towel," Imran stood up and wrung his soaked t-shirt onto his palm, "Can I dry off and go back to my room?"

"Yes," Nisa feared for her sanity. She released the jug and looked down at her plate.

The peas didn't say "die" at all. They were scattered around her plate, and a bit wet.

"Honey, why don't you go and lie down?" Ali smiled at her.

Nisa nodded and cleared her throat, "Yes, okay. Bit of a headache, I think. Are you okay clearing up?" She got up and kissed her husband on the cheek.

"Yes, leave it with me. You go and rest."

***

Imran had been playing *Combat Shock* for at least three hours. His sister had run off to be with her friends for the evening. He could hear his father snoring in the front room.

As for Mum, who knows. She'd been quiet all evening. Maybe she was reading a book or had gone to bed early.

Imran looked at his wall clock for a brief moment before returning to his game. His character crept up on a bad guy with a large army knife.

"Okay. I'm gonna take out this tango, you know."

He pressed a button down on the controller and poised

himself, ready to attack a bad guy from behind.

"Cool, fam," came the other player through the headset, "Do it."

THWACK!

Imran's character stabbed down onto the bad guy's neck. Blood squirted from the wound.

"STEALTH KILL!"

"Yes. Got the batty man, man."

Imran looked up at the window and dropped the controller, "Yo, cover my six, I need to open the window. It's bare warm in here."

"Cool, fam. I got you."

Imran pulled the curtain aside and unlatched the lock on the window frame. He pushed the window open and wiped his eyes. Three straight hours of gaming had taken its toll.

He sniffed and heard some commotion coming from outside. It sounded like a few people complaining and crying, "What the fuck?"

Imran placed his hands on the sill and leaned out of the window. A crowd of around fifty adults and children had gathered eleven floors below. They looked up and spotted Imran peering down from out of his window.

"There's someone else," one of them screamed. "Up there. Look."

"Huh?" Imran looked back into his room. Nothing seemed out of the ordinary. He turned back to the crowd and yelled at them.

"What's going on?"

"Quick. Get outta there," A man in his gown carrying a small boy in his arms shouted up at Imran, "The building's on fire."

"What?" Imran was sure he had misheard the man. He set his child to the ground and held out palms either side of his mouth. "The building is on fire. Look."

Imran sniffed again. An unmistakable scent of burnt bricks and plastic wafted up his nostrils.

He leaned out and looked down the fiery exterior wall, "Oh, *shit*."

The flames licked up, producing an intense heat. People screamed from the windows underneath his. A woman leaned out from her fourteenth-floor window and looked down at Imran, "The building's on fire."

"I know, I know," Imran gasped. "Shit. What do we do?"

"The fire's tearing the building up," The woman wafted away the smoke from her face, "We've been told to stay in our flats and wait to be rescue—"

THUD-THUD-THUD.

A violent banging came from the front door. Imran spun around and dashed out of his bedroom.

THUD-THUD-THUD.

"Mrs. Pershar," a man's voice hastened from behind the door, "Open the door."

"I'm coming," Imran reached the door and slid the chain from the lock. As he opened the door, a plume of dark grey smog coughed into the landing. Imran waved his hand through the specks of black dust hanging in the air.

Richard ran in and pushed the door shut, "Everyone get up. We need to get out of here."

"Okay."

"Where's your mom and dad?"

"I dunno," Imran followed Richard to the front room, "I think Mom's in bed."

"And your sister?"

"She's out."

"Thank God. Right, we need to wake your mom, *now*," Richard banged on the front room door, "Mr. Pershar? Wake up, this is urgent."

Imran ran along the hall and barged his way into his parent's room. "Mom. Mom." He reached the bed and rocked her shoulders. "Mom, wake up."

"Ughh, what is it, Imran?" She opened her eyes and groaned.

He removed her gown from the hook on the bedroom door, "We have to get out of here, *now*."

He threw the gown into her arms.

"Leave you stuff here."

"What? Why?"

Imran could've just come out with the news. Before the information slipped through his lips, he took a second to evaluate the panic it might cause, "We think the building has caught fire."

"You *think*?"

Nisa climbed out of bed and held her gown against her bare chest. She reached the window and pulled the curtain open.

The crowd gathered outside had doubled in size. The orange blaze reflected off the window pane, "My God."

"Yeah," Imran pointed at the door. "Richard's here, he's getting Dad. We have to go, *now*."

"Oh my God. The building."

"I know, I know."

Nisa ran into the landing and slipped on her gown, "Ali, Ali," She reached the front room to see Richard helping her husband into his crutches.

"Richar.!"

"Nisa," Richard spat, "We gotta move. Now."

Ali struggled forward with his crutches, "Ugh, it's no use."

"Mate, abandon the crutches," Richard held him across the shoulders, "I'll take you."

"Okay. Thanks."

"Imran, go and run some towels under the tap."

"Okay." Imran ran toward the bathroom as his mother turned to the front door. A plume of smoke drifted in under the door, "Oh my God, what do we do?"

"We're supposed to stay in our apartments. The fire brigade is on their way, and they'll come and get us."

"Look," Nisa pointed to the door. The smoke continued to cough itself through the gap.

SPRRRIIISSSSSHHHH! Water blasting out from the kitchen sink.

Richard's eyes widened at the smog flooding in under the front door, "I don't believe this. The doors are meant to be fire retardant. They're meant to keep the smoke *out*. Imran?"

"Yeah, yeah," Imran yelled from the kitchen, "I'm on it, man."

"Get those towels *now*," Richard turned to Ali and looked him up and down, "How much do you weigh, Ali?"

"I dunno."

Richard looked him up and down. He can't have weighed very much, "Roughly?"

"About ten stone?"

"Right, you're coming with me," he took Ali's hand and looked at the door, "Anytime you're ready with those towels, Imran."

"I know, I know. Just got one more," Imran panted from the kitchen.

Nisa pushed the window open. The flames from the building were furious. They licked higher and higher. The heat was intense. She had to yank the window back.

She held her fist at her mouth and bit down, "My God, it's raging. The fire brigade will never get here on time."

Richard looked at her and held his breath. His facial expression indicated that there was a plan B.

Nisa realised what that might entail. "Ohhh, no. No, no—"

"—yes, Nisa," Richard nodded, unsure of his own proposal, "If we stay here we *will* die. If we run, we have a chance."

"Down twelve flights of stairs?!"

Imran bounded into the front room with three soaking wet towels, "Okay, I got the towels."

"Right," Richard ordered. "Give one to your mother, one to me and keep the last one for yourself."

Imran threw the soggy towel at Nisa. She caught it and

opened it up. The water drops splashed against the floor.

"Wrap it around your nose and mouth. Quickly."

Richard pushed the wet towel in Ali's hand. He lifted his half to his face. Richard did the same.

Imran wrapped the soggy towel around his head; nose and mouth. Nisa watched him and tried to do the same. It slipped through her fingers.

"Oh, mom," Imran's muffled voice pushed through his wet towel, "Quick, here."

He slid in behind her and tied the towel shut around her face, "Okay?"

She nodded.

Imran moved to the front door. Nisa followed him, with Richard and Imran close behind her.

Richard slipped a finger into his towel so he could speak, "Right, hold your breath. Conserve your oxygen."

"How long do you think it'll take to get down to the ground?" Imran asked.

"Dunno, dunno," Richard closed his eyes and inhaled. He wafted the smoke away from his shin, "What do you think?"

"Could be five minutes, maybe more."

Nisa started to freak out, "Oh God, oh God—"

"—Mom. Calm down, man, yeah?" Imran took her by the shoulders, "Keep your breathing steady."

A tear rolled down her cheek. She grabbed his waist and pulled him close. Her wet towel dampened his shirt.

"Okay?"

Nisa nodded and closed her eyes.

"Okay, I'mma open the door. If the smoke is too bad, close your eyes. Imran, take your mother's hand. Whatever happens, do *not* let go. Okay?"

"Yes," Imran slid his right hand into her left. He grabbed the front door handle with his right, "We good?"

"Yeah, I've got Ali," Richard tried his best to keep everyone's optimism up, "Good luck, everyone."

"Let's do it."

WHUMP! The door slammed against the outside wall. Imran sprinted through it.

A colossal ghost of smoke wafted into their apartment. Nisa clutched her son's hand as they made their way down the corridor.

"Go, go," Richard screamed ahead of them.

Imran waved the smoke away. The light at the top of the staircase blinked and sputtered.

"Quick, down here. Hold the rail."

Nisa and Imran grabbed the handrail and ran down the bank of stairs. Richard and Ali hobbled along behind them. They kept their ends of the damp towel against their mouth and nostrils, "Keep going."

Imran reached the ninth floor.

BOOM.

The apartment doors shook either side of them. The walls cracked and splintered. "Shit," Imran tightened his grip on his mother's hand and descended the next bank of stairs.

"Son, son," Nisa gasped and removed her towel. "Please, son. Slow down—"

"—No time. Put the towel back on your face."

Nisa's pace threatened to slow to a grave halt, "I c-can't, I can't—"

"—Mum," Imran looked up the staircase. Richard had hoisted Ali over his back, "I'm okay, keep going."

"Okay."

Imran hit the stairs and ventured into the haze of smoke. His foot connected with something on the landing. He tripped and nearly fell onto his behind, "What the hell?"

"What?" Nisa asked.

He kicked whatever it was with his heel. It rolled over onto its side, "Oh, shit. Mom, lift your leg and step over whatever it is."

Nisa raised her left leg and launched herself over.

KRAAA-SMASSSHHH!!

Imran ducked and looked around. A deafening blast of exploding concrete shattered around them, "Oh, God."

He threw his hand forward and pulled his mother to the top of the next flight of stairs.

Nisa yelped as she followed down with her son.

Richard struggled with Ali on his back. They, too, met with the unknown object on the floor. It produced a deathly gargling sound, "Ali, keep the towel on your face."

"I am," he spluttered. "I am."

The eighth floor. Total and utter darkness.

"Help, help!" a male voice came from around Imran's knees. He felt a hand clutch at his jeans, "Huullghh."

Imran shifted the hand with his shin. He felt around for the hand rail and grabbed it.

Nisa's hand loosened its grip. The pure darkness overwhelmed her. "I c-can't b-breathe," she gasped into her towel.

Imran pulled the towel an inch away from his mouth, "Hold… your… breath."

They hit the next set of stairs. The sound of the inferno was so loud they could barely hear themselves think. The squeak of the handrail was no longer audible.

They may as well have been buried alive.

Imran didn't know what floor they had arrived on. He'd lost count. Was it the fourth floor? He had hoped it was the third.

He removed the towel and felt the wall, moving along it. "Richard?" he screamed and immediately replaced the towel over his face.

No response.

Imran closed his eyes. He squeezed his mother's hand and pulled her forward.

BWOOOOM. SCREEEE!

A large squealing pierced above his head. He couldn't see anything.

WHUMP.

A heavy, flat object crashed inches in front of his face to the floor. He stepped back and onto his mother's foot.

Nisa squealed into her sodden towel for dear life. Imran squeezed her hand twice, indicating that he was sorry.

A gurgling noise came from the floor. The sound of a child wheezing and choking. Imran bent over and felt around. His fingers hit a nose, and then a forehead.

"Hey," his muffled voice came from within the wet towel, "Are you okay?"

"Uh, uh," child's voice came from under their knees.

"It's okay, I got you," Imran grabbed the child's hand and passed it to his mother's, "Mum, take him and keep moving."

The walls rumbled, followed by an almighty crashing sound. Even though they couldn't see a damn thing, they knew they were sweating. As they moved, the squelching in their shoes threatened to trip them up.

"Over here, over here," a man screamed from below, "Get them to the ground, now."

"Huh?" Imran lost his bearings. He felt around and lifted the towel from his face, "Up here. We're up here."

How far down the voices were was anyone's guess. Imran's breathing was restricted.

The smoke seeped through the towel and entered his lungs.

He paced forward and banged against the wall. Finally, he found the stair rail and pulled his mother up to him.

A shaft of orange light glistened against the end of the metal rail on the next floor down.

CREEAAKK!

An intense heat accompanied the beam and ghastly rumbling noise.

Imran opened his eyes and soon regretted it. The smoke glazed over his pupils.

He placed the sole of his trainer on the top step.

First step…

Second step…

Third…

A blockade knocked against the tip of his shoe. He let go of his mother's hand and flew down to the next floor, elbows-first. "Gahhh," He scrambled for his dropped towel and plastered it back on his face.

To his left, the door to an apartment had blown apart. The smoke drifted through the hallway and out through a shattered window. The apartment was roaring with fire.

The heat from the inferno smothered the landing. He reached up with his right hand. "Mom?"

"Imran," Nisa held out her hand.

SLAP. Their palms hit together. They grabbed each other's hands. They'd found one another.

"Get up," Imran climbed to his feet and yanked his mother toward him. The object he had tripped on was a dead body.

Nisa recognized the boy. It was Adrian, whom she'd met earlier in the evening in the playground. His eyes stared back at her. His tongue hanging over his chin.

"Oh no," Nisa gasped as she wafted the smoke from her face. She held all four fingers and thumb up at Imran, "Five."

Imran nodded and grabbed the stair rail and made his way down, yanking his mother behind him.

A crowd of hundreds had gathered a few feet away from *Freeway One*.

Most of them were in tears at what they witnessed.

The building was ablaze. The roaring inferno climbed and battered its way up each side of the building.

"Oh nooo," screamed a woman with her young child in her arms, "Look. They're trying to get out."

She pointed to a man screaming from the eighteenth floor, "Help."

Dozens of residents leaned out of their windows,

screaming for their lives.

The fire truck had extended its gantry, carrying two firemen in its metal enclosure. They aimed the hose at the building and fired a prolonged jet of water at it.

They may as well have been using a Super Soaker for all the good it was doing.

"As you can see, here, a building ablaze," a reporter said to her cameraman, "Families still trapped inside with no-one coming to rescue them."

Five firefighters exited the building and removed their breathing apparatus. A handful of residents ran out with them, coughing and crying.

A car pulled up at the side of the road, along with dozens of others. Abby hopped out of the back seat and tore across the playground. She ran through the congregation of civilians watching the inferno erupt against the perfect night sky.

"Mum. Dad," she ran right into the arms of a police officer.

"Excuse me, miss. You can't go in there."

"My family is in there," she screamed at the top of her voice.

"Miss, please. It's not safe."

"They're on the twelfth floor," Abby looked up and saw the helpless residents in on the higher floors screaming for their lives, "Oh my God. Oh my God, they're trapped. Help them."

"We're doing all we can—"

Abby threw the officer to one side and ran deep into the crowd, "Mom? Dad? Imran?" She looked at all the faces lit up by the inferno. One face, then another - none of which were recognizable.

Imran and Nisa felt their way along the walls of the third floor. The little boy's grip in her other hand softened. It got heavier.

As Imran tried to pull his mother with him, she slowed

down. She was dragging a dead weight behind her.

The heels of the shoes scraped along the floor.

"He's h-heavy," Nisa placed the towel back against her mouth.

"Let go, mom."

"Nuuuh."

SMASSSHHHH!

A giant slab of *something* hit the ground outside. From the screeching of the material to the sound of the crash, Imran knew they only had a couple of flights left to go.

He toed around for the top step with the tip of his shoe and planted his weight onto it. Nisa followed with him, dragging the body along with her in her grasp.

Imran knocked her on the shoulder and reached for her other hand. He prized her fingers away from the hand of the person she was holding.

He turned around and grabbed the hand rail and made his way down.

"Sir?" a voice came from within the darkness, "We got another one."

Imran clutched the man's blazer. A coarse fabric. He felt up the person's chest and reached a plastic tubing.

He thumped on the man's shoulders. The sound of breathing apparatus shot past his face. Nisa's grip in her son's hand wilted.

"Sir, come with me!" The man shone his torch at the final set of stairs. Imran threw his arm around his mother's shoulders and helped her down the stairs.

"Nearly there, let's go!" shouted the invisible man.

Nisa's shoulders rode down Imran's side as he descended the final set of stairs, "Nuh, nuh," He stopped and reached down. She'd fallen over.

"Sir, no," the man's plastic helmet knocked hit Imran's shoulder. "We need to get you out of here."

The stranger yanked him back by the shirt and held him by the shoulders.

Imran screamed, "Muuuuuhhhhhh."

"That's it, we're here."

Blue flashing lights licked up the sides of the ground floor landing, dampened down by the billowing smoke.

Imran was losing oxygen. The doors crept forward slowly. The light from outside illuminated the fire fighter's yellow helmet.

The walls groaned long and low as another firefighter held the door open.

"Go, go."

The firefighter pushed Imran out through the doors and onto the grass verge. He whipped the towel away from his face and fell to his knees.

"Gaaaaahhh," He took in a lungful of air and gasped.

"Okay, sir. Stay there. We'll get a medic over to you."

Imran fell onto his side. His eyelids fluttered. The roar of the fire thundered from above. He rolled onto his back and quickened his breathing.

Freeway One looked down on him. The building roasted in the dry night sky.

"No, no," he gasped as a shooting star whizzed behind the inferno.

"Imran," Abby barged past a horde of onlookers and slid to her knees, "Thank God. You're out."

He grabbed her sister's arms and pulled himself to his knees. He pointed at the inferno and choked before he could speak, "M-Mom. D-Dad."

Abby stared at him and tried to process the news. She left a pause, hoping Imran would finish the sentence with good news.

He didn't.

"Imran?" Abby teared up and held her hand to her mouth.

He ducked his head and burst into tears. He shook his head and screamed at the grass.

"N-No, no," Abby couldn't believe what Imran *wasn't* saying. "They're out. They *must* be here somewhere."

Imran slumped over his knees and cried onto his lap.

Two paramedics ran over to Imran and crouched down next to him. One of them covered him with a silver foil blanket.

"Sir, we need to get you looked at. Can we get you over to the tent, please?"

Imran wiped his face and rose to his feet. The medics ushered him toward the emergency tent a few feet away.

Abby watched on. She turned to the entrance and sat down on the grass. No-one came out.

"I'm sorry," Imran wailed over his shoulder. "I tried."

She looked up at the barbecuing building. Bits of it exploded and broke apart, hurtling detritus to the ground a few hundred yards away from her.

The terror from the crowd looking up at the destruction was beyond comprehension.

Chapter 7

The Wank Room

Mark stared out of the passenger window, lost in his thoughts.

A row of shops flew past. His reflection stared back at him. His hands were shaking on his lap. Threading his fingers together didn't allay the jitters.

His left knee bopped up and down.

Josh, who was driving, noticed that his friend was anxious, "You okay?"

"Yeah," Mark muttered. "just a bit… *you know*."

Josh giggled to himself, "You're not *nervous*, are you?"

"Well, it's my first time."

"Everyone had a first time, mate. It's nothing to worry about—"

"—I can't believe I let you talk me into doing this."

Josh applied the brakes and pulled up to the side of the road. A family walked past and shot them a strange look.

"Look, you don't have to go through with it."

"No, no," Mark quipped. "I'll, uh, I'll do it."

"No, you're gonna have to do better than that," Josh shot his friend a serious look, "You don't convince me."

Mark finally looked at Josh. His face was a picture - framed around the face of a man confronted with a dilemma.

"Well?"

Mark exhaled and nodded, "No, it's cool. I'll be fine."

"You sure?"

"Yes."

Josh pushed the gear stick into first and joined the road. "Look, it's not technically *cheating*. Lisa will never know. They're very discreet."

"Yeah, yeah, I know," Mark whispered and looked through the window again.

"And you know what?"

"What?"

"Even if she *did* find out, I don't think she'd much care, anyway." Josh stepped on the gas, "It's not like you're actually touching anyone, or vice versa."

"I know," Mark smiled. "Besides, you're here. It'd be much worse if I was on my own."

"Exactly."

"I dunno how you managed to go through with it on your own the first time."

"Nah, the first time you think your heart's gonna explode 'coz it's all so new," Josh giggled. "After that first time, though, you kinda get addicted. Seriously, it's nothing to worry about at all. Just try to enjoy it."

"Yes," Mark nodded and wiped his nose. "You're right. Thanks."

Josh pulled up on a suburban street in *Chrome Valley*. It was the only road left in the borough that didn't have yellow lines along the pavement. The sun was going down and a chill in the air indicated a cool night to come.

"Okay, we're here," Josh clutched his gym bag and closed the driver door.

"Is this it?" Mark took out his bag and pushed the passenger door shut with his knee. Nothing but semi-detached houses for yards and yards.

"I thought it was an industrial complex? Like a warehouse or something?"

"Ah, yeah," Josh beamed and rummaged around inside his bag and took out two black balaclavas, "It is but no-one ever parks there. Can't afford to be seen near the building. Here, catch."

Josh tossed one of them to Mark. He caught it and opened it out.

"It's just around the corner. Put it on."

"Okay," Mark slipped on his balaclava, as did Josh.

"Almost there."

"Right, right."

Josh picked up the pace and hulked the gym bag over his back, "Would you please calm down?"

"No, I'm cool. I'm cool. Honestly."

"Right," Josh said as they turned a corner and headed for an industrial estate. A red Ferrari was parked on the side of the road.

"Nice car," Mark muttered to himself.

Josh nodded and turned to his friend, "How long have you been saving?"

"Huh?"

Josh sighed at his friend's incompetence, "When was the last time you nutted?"

"Oh, uh, I dunno," Mark caught up to Josh. "Three days ago, I think?"

"Cool. That's a good amount."

The *Book Loads* library was a few feet away from the pair. Mark squinted at the placard above the door, "A library?"

"Yeah," Josh laughed, "What, do you think they're going to advertise *The Wank Room* in big, bold letters for all to see?"

"I suppose not."

"No one ever uses libraries anymore. They're like Kryptonite. No-one goes near them. It's a perfect ruse," Josh reached the door and pushed forward, "After you, my *friend*."

"Oh, thanks."

Mark walked into the library. It was empty. No-one around.

The place resembled a library, though. Shelves and shelves of battered old books and a worn-out carpet.

The librarian behind the counter adjusted her spectacles and smiled at the two men, "Hello, welcome to *Book Loads*."

Josh made his way over to the counter and took out his membership card. A plastic credit card-sized picture of his face with his full name and ID number.

"Josh Golding."

"Splendid," the librarian examined the card. "Is this your guest?"

"Yes, this is, uh, *Charlie*."

"Charlie?" Mark mouthed to Josh in bewilderment.

Josh pulled him aside as the receptionist busied herself with her computer, "You're not a member. So why use your real name."

"Ah," Mark smiled and turned to the counter, "Yeah, good idea."

The librarian pushed a form and a pen across the counter and looked at Mark, "Can you please read the rules and sign at the bottom."

"Yes," Mark took the pen from her and perused the rules.

"There you go, Mr. Golding," the librarian smiled and handed Josh his card, "Will you be wearing green, red, or black this evening?"

"Green, please—"

The white door on the back wall opened. A naked man with a huge erection came walking through.

A cacophony of moaning and groaning came from behind the door as it slammed shut.

Then, silence. The door did a magnificent job of reducing the commotion away from the library.

The naked man wore a red balaclava and rubbed his hands together. He had a tattoo of a fairy on his right forearm.

The librarian clocked him immediately. "Ah. Mr. Johnson. Are you finished?"

"Yes, I am," Mr. Johnson removed his red balaclava and slapped it on the table, "That was great, thanks."

"Excellent," She looked down at the man's penis. A couple of blobs of semen puked around his ruffled foreskin, "Please don't drip on my floor."

"Oh, I'm sorry," he looked down and slid his thumb over the tip, "It's never easy, is it?"

Mark watched the librarian retrieve a locker key from under the desk, "There you go. That's locker 451."

"Cheers," Mr. Johnson winked at Mark and made his way to a black door to the right of the desk.

Mark shook his head and signed the sheet of paper. He handed it to the librarian.

"Thank you," she scanned his signature, "It's nothing personal, you understand. We just need to have a formal declaration that you're clean."

"I understand."

"Okay, as you're a guest of Mr. Golding, you'll both be sharing a locker," She passed Josh the locker key.

"Thank you," Josh took the key and made for the black door. He turned to Mark as he went through, "I'll wait for you in here. The librarian will explain the rules."

"Uh, okay?"

Josh opened the black door and swung the gym bag off his shoulders. It closed behind him, leaving Mark to turn to the librarian.

"Have you used *The Wank Room* before, Mr…?"

"Oh, uh," Mark scrambled for a bull shit surname. The first thing that popped into his head was the make of the red car outside, "Ferrari. Charlie Ferrari."

"Okay."

"This is my first time."

"Yes, I know,," she chuckled and took out three balaclavas from under the desk.

"What? How can you tell?"

"Well, you're nervous," she smirked and fanned the masks out side by side on the counter, "It's perfectly understandable. Everyone had their first time, once."

"Yes, okay, I'll admit I'm a bit—"

"—Yeah. So, here are the rules. Ready?"

"Okay."

"You choose which color mask you'll be wearing," she said, holding up the red balaclava, "Red means that you do *not* want to be approached. But anyone with a red mask may approach anyone they wish, as long as it's not another red."

"Right."

"Good," she put the red one down and picked up the green balaclava, "Now, green means you are happy for others to approach you. It's not a license to start touching someone else. But you're entitled to strike up a dialog. If both parties agree, then you may do whatever you wish. For reference, your friend Mr. Golding has selected green for this evening."

"Uh, okay?" Mark swallowed. "So, if I wear a green one, can I approach a red one?"

She sighed, "Haven't you been listening? No-one may approach someone wearing red."

Mark thought for a second. The penny dropped, "Right, yes. I've got you."

"Good," she put the green balaclava down and picked up the black one. It had black leather head straps and a padlock covering the mouth. A small key dangled from the hole.

"Finally, the black mask. I don't expect you to go for this one as you're new here."

"What does black mean?"

"Anything goes, really," she explained. "You're still not to approach the reds. You can, of course, approach the greens, as per the rules. Blacks can, and often do, approach other blacks. Those who go with black usually take whatever they're doing to *The Fuck Room* which is through the silver door in the main *Wank Room*. Use the padlock if you'd rather not speak, indulge in oral stimulation or ingest anything. Otherwise, it's up to you."

"Okay."

"So, which color would you like?"

Mark pushed the black one aside, "I'll think I'll play safe and go with red for now."

"A wise choice," she pushed the red balaclava into his chest, "If you change your mind, just come and see me. You can switch any time you wish."

"Thanks."

"Of course, it goes without saying, if you recognize anyone, you've signed to the fact that you will keep everything that happens to yourself."

"Yes, of course."

"We're quite keen on discretion," she said as Mark moved to the changing room, "Have a wonderful evening."

"Thanks."

The locker room was vast and empty, except for Josh and Mark, who were now down to their underwear. The locker door hung open with both their gym bags stuffed in it.

Mark looked around the changing room, "Not busy tonight, then?"

"Nah, we're a bit late," Josh lifted his leg and slipping off his briefs, "Everyone will have started by now."

Mark cleared his throat. He couldn't help but look at what his friend was packing.

"Jesus Christ. *Josh*."

"What?" Josh stuffed his underwear into the gym bag and twiddled with the locker key.

"You're so *big*."

Mark wasn't lying. Josh was certainly gifted in the reproductive organ department. A clear eight inches at the very least.

"I didn't know you were circumcised?"

Josh shot Mark a look and placed his hands on his hips, "I'm Jewish."

"Oh, yes. That's right, I forgot."

Josh looked down at his anxious friend's boxer shorts, "Well? You gonna take 'em off, or what?"

Mark looked down and thought about the question - and his feelings of inadequacy, "Uh, okay."

"Yes," Josh chuckled as he watched Mark step out of his underwear, "It tends to help."

Mark stood back up. He was very shy.

"Nice. Very nice," Josh blinked at Mark's penis, "Good weight. Not as long as I thought it'd be but totally workable."

"Yeah, well I'm not Jewish so I have to start somewhere, don't I?"

Mark stuffed his boxers into the gym bag and pushed the locker shut. Josh inserted the key and bolted the locker shut.

"Okay, you ready?" Josh peeled his green mask over his head.

Mark did the same with his red balaclava, "Yeah, I think—"

"—Look, mate," Josh held Mark's shoulders and gave him a reassuring look. They both looked like they were about to commit a nude heist. The tips of both men's penises almost touched.

"What?"

"Don't be nervous. Try and enjoy yourself. You won't get anywhere if you're all pent up and shitting it."

"Okay, okay," Mark exhaled and nodded.

"Good."

Josh and Mark walked into the library and approached the counter. The librarian pinched her spectacles as she ogled the *thing* swinging between Josh's knees, "Oh *my*, Mr.

Golding."

"Here's our locker key, thanks."

She took them from his hand and licked her lips.

"Everything okay?"

She cleared her throat and finally looked up at Josh's eyes behind the green mask, "Yes, look, if it doesn't work out in there, come back and see me. I'll make sure you're catered for."

"Ha, very funny."

Josh turned around and walked to the white door that lead to the *Wank Room*. Mark caught up to him.

Only eight seconds to go until the moment of truth. Mark felt his heart pounding away. The blood rushed through his veins.

His face heated up - although, that might have had something to do with the red cotton cloth over his head.

Mark stopped and placed his palm on Josh's chest, stopping them from reaching the door.

"Actually, no."

Josh turned around and huffed, "What is it now?"

"No, no," Mark muttered to himself, "I can't go through with this."

"What the *fuck*, Mark?"

The librarian hollered at the pair, "Is everything okay?"

Josh turned to her and held out his hand, "No, we're all good, thanks."

"I, um—"

"—Mark?"

"Yes?"

"Don't show me up," Josh grabbed the white door's handle and yanked down, "Get the fuck in there and take a seat."

"Oh, I don't—"

"—Just shut up and go in."

He yanked the door open and pushed Mark into the room by the shoulders.

WHUMP. The door closed behind them. Josh stepped

beside Mark. They both looked around.

"Pretty cool, huh?" Josh beamed.

Mark gasped and blinked, "My God."

They were standing in a giant triangular room of pure white walls and a ceramic floor.

Three walls had an inbuilt knee-high bench along them. Room for about forty or so people. Each bench was populated with men in red masks. The rest wore green and three wore black.

The ground ever-so-slightly tilted down from the wall. The elevated skirting boards enabled any spent ejaculate to race toward the middle of the room.

The middle of the room contained a black, five-foot tall monolith.

"That's where you go to finish, if you like," Josh pointed at it, "Oh, look. There goes one, now."

A lanky man in a red mask paced up the monolith and masturbated himself against it.

"Ugh, mmm, yeah. *Fuuuck*."

He yanked down the skin of his penis back over the head. Two ropes of cum jetted out from the slit and splashed against the monolith. The white effluence slithered down the sides and sunk into a grill on the ground.

The lanky man gasped and ran his thumb over the tip of his penis and flung the last globs of spunk against the monolith.

"Nice, very nice," Josh giggled as he watched the man walk past them, "You know, all the spunk is collected up and shipped off to a sperm bank."

"A sperm bank?" Mark gasped. "But that's—"

"—Pretty cool, right?" Josh slid his palm under his balls. "Getting paid to empty your nut sacks. Making bank while filling theirs."

The lanky man approached Josh, "You all right? You all right?" he patted him on the back as he made his way to the white door.

"Yeah, that was *hot*, mate."

"Cheers," The lanky man left the room.

Mark looked up at the three conclave walls that bent into a pyramid at the ceiling. The screen on the left showed hardcore porn. Two men and a woman.

The screen to the right showed a man getting fisted by another. A ball gag rammed in his mouth as the guy's asshole clamped around the other's fist.

"Shut the fuck up," yelled the man on the screen as the other cried in pain. He jammed his fist in further and twisted it around the man's guts, "Fuckin' take it."

Moaning and squirming came from behind Mark's head. He turned around to the third wall.

"Oh my God," Mark stepped back. His right heel slid across a wet substance and caught his balance. He pointed up at the third screen, "What's that?"

Josh giggled and shook his head. He looked at the adjacent wall and winked at the thirty or so men sitting on the bench. They masturbated to the images on the third screen.

"Don't worry about it, mate," Josh patted Mark on the back, "All dark web material. Nothing you've seen before, I guarantee it. Just sit somewhere where you can't see it if you don't like it."

Mark dry heaved and stepped back, pointing at the screen, "B-But that's fucking *wrong*!"

"Some guys like it," Josh whispered in Mark's ear, "Don't ruin it for them, okay?"

The ghastly sounds drifted from the third screen. Mark turned around and make a conscious effort never, ever, to look back.

He scanned the row of men in front of him masturbating themselves to the first screen. They grunted and groaned.

Some of them stretched their legs directly in front. Others perched the sole of their feet on the bench. Their testicles hung over the edge of the bench as they masturbated.

"Go and sit down," Josh said. "Just relax."

A pudgy man with a green mask made his way over to Josh. He held out his hand.

"Hi," he clenched his erect three-inch penis in his other hand, "I'm Gerald. You're hot. You wanna come to the bench with me?"

"Josh," he shook the man's hand and looked him up and down, "Sorry, man, I—"

"—Yeah, I get it. I'm too fat, right?" the man huffed, clearly rejected a few times already this evening.

"No, it's not that," Josh lied and massaged Mark's shoulder, "It's just I'm with my friend today."

"I understand," the pudgy man frowned and made for a free spot on the bench.

Mark sat on the bench facing the first screen. He was conscious that the third screen was above his head. As long as he didn't look up and catch a glimpse of the atrocity being displayed he'd be fine.

The row of men opposite him loved every second of the action on the third screen. Some tried to masturbate to both the second and third and were largely successful.

Josh sat next to Mark and nudged him in the ribs, "Hey. Look at those two lovebirds."

His finger arrived at two green masks masturbating each other, "How long do you think they'll last?"

"I dunno?" Mark blinked and ran his palms over his lap.

"I bet you the guy on the left goes down first."

"Ugh," Mark said. "I'm straight. I don't want to see this—"

"—Aha, bingo."

The fat guy on the left pushed open his skinny friend's thighs and dropped his head between his legs. He extended his tongue and slipped the skinny's guy dick into his mouth and bobbed up and down.

The skinny guy hooked his elbows under his knees and bent them back to the sides of his chest.

"Yeah, yeah," the skinny guy slapped the back of his new friend's head, "Down to the balls, you fat little doggy."

Mark felt a twitch between his legs. Josh looked down, "Oi, oi. What's happening down there?"

Mark stared at the fat man performing fellatio on his neighbor. He took a hold of his penis and ran his thumb up and down it, "That's wild, man."

Mark opened his legs and took himself into his palm.

"There, you got it," Josh smiled.

A tall man with a green mask obstructed Mark and Josh's view of the blow job occurring on the other side of the room.

"Hey."

Josh looked up at the green masked man. "Hey."

He took the man's hand and rose to his feet, "You're fit. Nice ass, mate."

"Thanks. You too."

"You wanna wank together?" asked the man.

Josh looked down at Mark. He'd grown hard in his hands and appeared to be relatively happy watching the blow job.

"You cool, mate?"

"Yeah," Mark looked up to the screen with the woman on it. The two men with her were engaged in a sixty-nine. She slapped their asses as they guzzled on each other's member.

"Cool."

Josh and his new, tall friend moved off to a space on the bench to the right.

"First time here?" Mark's neighbor asked out of the blue. He wore a red balaclava and weighed about two hundred and fifty pounds. His arms were heavy and his demeanor suggested he may be at least twenty years Mark's senior.

"Oh, uh, yeah," Mark muttered. "I thought you weren't allowed to approach red masks?"

"I'm not approaching you," he chuckled and fumbled his fingers along his lumpy penis. "Just making conversation, that's all."

"Oh," Mark looked between the man's legs. "Yeah, fair enough. You, uh, come here a lot?"

The man burst out laughing, "Haha, very funny. *Come*. I love it. Yeah, been here since they first open two years ago."

"Oh, cool. How often do you co— uh, *attend*?"

"Couple of times a week," the man slid his palm under his balls and fingered around his asshole, "The wife won't fuck or suck anymore. So I come here and release."

"You're not afraid she'll find out?"

"It's not cheating, is it?" the man pinched the base of his cock and retracted his foreskin. He slapped the head against his palm, "She thinks I'm working late at the office. I haven't done anything wrong, anyway."

"I guess."

The man looked down and licked his lips at Mark's legs, "Nice cock, by the way. *No homo*, obviously."

"Thanks," Mark said, trying to be polite. The next thing out of his mouth was an utter white lie. "You too. *Obviously*."

Mark turned his head to Josh with his new "friend". They sat side by side, their legs interlocked, beating each other off to the second screen.

"You ever been wanked off by another guy?"

Mark double-took and looked to his neighbor, "Huh?"

"You ever felt the warmth of another man's hand?"

"Oh, no," Mark whispered and watched three random men ejaculate onto the floor, "No, I'm not *that* way."

"Wow. Check out the loads on that guy," the man whispered as they watched a tiny man aim his penis to the floor. He squirted several ropes of semen up the floor and ground his buttocks against his middle knuckle.

"*Fuuuck*," Mark gasped and leaned back against the wall. He pulled on his balaclava with his right hand and stared at the tiny man as he slapped his withered penis against the bench.

"Mother nature's pick-me-up," the man next to Mark giggled, "I'm Geoff, by the way."

"Oh, hi," Mark said. "I'm, uh, *Charlie*."

"Hi, Charlie," he smiled at Mark and shook his hand. First contact had been established.

Mark felt three fingers slide under his penis. He looked down to see Geoff and taken his penis into his palm.

Mark didn't stop him, "Oh."

"Yeah," Geoff gripped Mark's erect penis and pulled the foreskin back over the head of his penis.

"Oh, m-man."

"It's nice, isn't it?" Geoff whispered.

Mark was overcome by a tingling sensation. He closed his eyes and snorted. "Yes, it's nice."

"Yeah," Geoff began to masturbate him. "No homo, Charlie. It's just a hand, right?"

"Right." Mark exhaled and nodded, trying to convince himself this was all okay.

He opened his eyes to see two men finish each other off at the monolith. He leaned the back of his head against the wall and averted his gaze the first screen.

The woman rode the giant of a man up against a brick wall. He squeezed her tits and pushed her face against the wall, fucking her with the force of a traction engine.

Mark closed his eyes and licked his lips, "Mmmm, don't stop."

"It's okay, sweetie," came a female voice as he kept his eyes shut, "Just enjoy it."

"I love your touch," Mark gasped. "You're so beautiful."

"I know, honey," the female voice grew louder, "You're beautiful too, Charlie. You know I love you, right?"

"Rhonda?" Mark's voice fell from his lips and tumbled across the room.

"Yes, sweetie," Rhonda's voice affirmed, gently. "My baby boy…"

"Mmmmm."

Mark opened his eyes and watched the first screen. Rhonda had taken the place of the woman being fucked against the wall. The guy wouldn't stop smashing her. Her hair mussed over her sweaty face. She turned to Mark and moaned.

"Charlie, *Charlie*," she panted. "He's fucking me so hard. Look."

Mark's voice floated from his lips, "I know, Rhonda. I can see him."

"Help me, sweetie."

"I c-can't, I'm stuck in the room."

"Ugh, ugh, ugh."

Mark blinked and looked to his lap. The weight of his head forced the padlock to rattle under his bottom lip. Geoff still had his penis in his hand. Mark reached down and removed his neighbor's hand from his penis

"Hey. What's wrong?"

"I'm sorry, Geoff," Mark rose to his feet, "I can't."

Geoff took offense and frowned, "Was it something I did?"

"No, no," Mark smiled. "You did great."

"But you're fair game."

"What?"

THWUMP!

A giant hand landed on Mark's shoulder, "You, fuck-bitch," came a gruff voice from behind his head. He felt a slap across his buttocks.

The man spun Mark around on the spot. A man in a black leather mask stared right back at him like a possessed bull. His pupils were blood red.

"Black mask, huh? Very brave," the man grabbed Mark's erection and tightened his grip, "How much you packing here, faggot?"

"Uhmmmm," Mark quivered in his bare feet, "I d-don't think—"

"—Answer me, you cunt."

"Uh, maybe f-five inches?" Mark's heart stopped beating, "But y-you're not supposed to approach me."

The black masked man tilted his head. The light from the ceiling bounced over his freshly-shaved scalp. He lifted his knuckle and stroked the padlock over Mark's mask.

"Then why are you wearing black?"

The man grabbed his shoulders and pushed Mark toward a silver door in the corner of the room.

"I'm not wearing black."

"Get the fuck in there, you lump of fuck-meat."

He smacked Mark's buttocks and booted him through the opened silver door.

The others stopped touching themselves as they watched the door swing back to its metal hinges.

SLAMM! The silver door shut behind the man in the black mask.

Mark picked himself from the floor and held out his hands.

"Wait, *stop*," Mark pleaded with the man storming toward him. "I'm wearing red—"

Mark blinked and looked around the room. Triangular, much like the *Wank Room*, but made of mirrors. Including the floor.

Mirrors everywhere.

Mark caught his reflection. He wore a black mask with a padlock - not a red one. He stared at one of several thousand concertina Marks looking back at him.

"Oh, n-no," Mark felt around his mask. An unmistakable touch of leather, "Oh, *no*."

"Oh *yes*, my pretty little fuck pig." The man rode up to Mark and blew him a kiss, "Call me Caesar."

"M-M-Mar— uh, Ch-Charlie."

"Charlie, huh?" Caesar ran his giant fist of Mark's soft, brown hair. He kissed him on the forehead, "What kind of gay-shit name is that, anyway?"

"I d-don't kn-know—"

"Oh, I d-don't kn-know!" Caesar grabbed Mark's wrist and placed his hand on his penis, "Squeeze my fucking meat."

"Wh-what?!"

"I said squeeze my rape-meat, you dumb AIDS Monkey."

Mark looked down. Caesar's sheer weight and size put Josh's to shame.

He felt Caesar's hand tap the side of his face, snapping him out of his mire, "Hey. You poz or neg?"

"What d-does that mean?"

"You *positive* or *negative*?"

"Oh, uh, I think I'm negative."

"Hehe," Caesar winked at him and hollered at the far end of the dwelling, "Yo, guys! Look what I found out in the *Wank Room*."

Mark shuddered and looked behind him. A giant metal workbench loomed in the middle of the pyramid. Nine huge men wearing black masks looked up from the table.

Five of them worked on one green-masked man. His ankles were tied behind his head, making him look like a balled-up chicken.

They clapped and cheered. "Whoa. Nice one, Caesar, mate."

Four men knelt on another table and masturbating over two guys fucking doggy style.

One of the men in the green mask gasped for air and screamed for his life, "Enough, enough! I can't take it anymore—"

"—shut the *fuck* up," shouted a black masked man, plowing into him at the edge of the table. He looked up at his masturbating masked friend, "Get his fucking ankles."

"You got it."

The masturbating man let go of his penis. It waved around as he gripped the green masked man's ankles and wrenched them back by his ears.

The guy doing the fucking grabbed the green masked man by the thighs and launched his full weight down on him.

"Grrraaaaaooowwwww," the man on his back screamed.

"Shit, man," shouted the man holding his ankles, "I think his man-cunt is about to fall out."

"Fucking shut up," the man standing at the edge of the table pumped in and out with such alacrity that his victim's asshole's opened up and coughed blood down his thighs.

"*Fuck*," the rapist said, "Is this one *ripe*?"

Caesar scowled at Mark and folded his muscled arms. His giant penis swung in front of their victim's face, "Ripe, virginal, and *negative*."

The man pulled his penis out of his victim's anus, "Not for much longer. Welcome to the club, my little, raw *pig*."

SCCCHHHPLLAAAAARRTTTTT!!!

A torrent of bloody shit and guts blasted out of the green-masked man's anus and splattered up the floor.

Caesar cleared his throat and spat to the floor, "Ugh, you fucking sick *fuck*! You gave him *the bug*, man."

The man in the green mask puked up, splashing the masturbating man in the face with spew.

"Ugh," the man punched Mark in the face. He pulled his foreskin over the head of his cock and aimed it at Mark's mouth, "You think it's funny to puke in my face, you cunt?"

He masturbated himself and shot a jet of semen into the man's eyes, "Naawwwwuuurrrggghhhh."

"Come here you sick little pig."

Mark froze in terror as the man in the black mask punched his fist into his victim's anus.

"Gaaaaahhhhhhh," the man in the black mask clenched his fist and slid it out, taking with it the end of his victim's large intestine.

More guts and blood exploded down the green-masked man's thighs. His body went limp. The muscles in his asshole flowered out like a rosebud and coughed the last of his guts to the floor.

Caesar jumped up and down and clapped his hands, "Nice one, Brutus."

The man who'd administered the ruthless punishment paced toward Caesar. He looked him up and down and scraped the gore from his fist, "Who's this little cunt, Caesar?"

"This is our new friend, *Charlie*," he bopped him on the shoulder, "Charlie, say hello to Brutus."

"H-Hello."

"We gonna have some fun with this kitten," Caesar chuckled and turned to his black masked colleagues, "Ain't that right, boys?"

They turned around from their fucking and masturbating and roared, "*Fuck yeah*."

Brutus grabbed Caesar's junk in his hand and planted a sloppy, French kiss him on the neck, "Fuck, mate. You're so hot."

"Mmmm," Caesar stood his legs apart and allowed Brutus to nuzzle him, "You get me so fucking boned, man."

Mark burst into tears, helpless.

"Oh, don't cry, little one," Brutus mocked as he stroked the young man's cheek with his knuckle.

Caesar looked down at him as Brutus played with his dick, "The fuck you crying for?"

"I just w-want to go home."

"Eh?" Brutus wrapped his manly arms around Caesar and chuckled, "What are you, some kind of faggot?"

"No, no," Mark bawled. "There's been a terrible mistake."

"Oh no, no," Caesar planted a kiss on Brutus's lips, "No mistake at all. Ain't that right, Brutus?"

"No," Brutus turned around to his black-masked colleagues and pointed at the body in the green mask. "Yo. Can we get some bitch in here and clear that fucking shit off the floor? It's stinkin' the fuckin' place up, man."

"Yeah, I'll go get the librarian."

"Cool," Brutus turned to Mark and snuggled up to Caesar's shoulder, desperately in love, "Your first time here, Charlie?"

Mark slid his thumb under his mask and wiped away a tear, "Yes."

"Very brave to wear black the first time, I have to say," Caesar grunted and shoved Mark to the table. He went flying forward and turned around. Brutus and Caesar cackled as Mark landed against the metal table.

He caught his own reflection in one of the thousand mirrors staring back at him.

Brutus and Caesar walked arm in arm toward Mark. He kicked himself back against the wall.

"No, no," Mark bawled and held his hand out. "Please, don't."

The two men chuckled like cock-hungry witches. Brutus moved forward and knelt beside Mark.

"P-Please."

Brutus grabbed Mark's chin and yanked his mouth open, "Mmm, pretty little mouth. How's its gag reflex?"

"Dunno, we haven't throat-fucked it," Caesar snarled. "Not *yet*, anyway."

"Yeah, man," Brutus peered into their victim's and saw a tongue, gums and teeth, and a long, dark tunnel with an esophagus hanging in its way, "Charlie. You're gonna love this one."

"Mmmmm," Caesar hitched up his penis.

Brutus grabbed Mark's hair and lifted him to his knees, "Naaaaawwwwww."

"Shut up."

"Maybe he needs a bit of encouragement?" Caesar nodded at Brutus as he slapped his semi-erect cock around

Mark's face.

CLICK.

The sound of a hammer being wrenched back. Mark opened his eyes and saw Brutus holding a Glock 17, "I think this'll do."

"Nice one."

Brutus held the gun to Mark's temple. "Now, today you're gonna learn all about *breathing* cock. We don't do blow jobs, here. We do *breathe jobs*. In your fuckin' lung. Get your throat muscles used to the shape of cock."

"Yeah," Caesar hung the tip of his member against Mark's quivering bottom lip, "Feed you oxygen through my piss pipe."

"Do it," Brutus roared, burying the nozzle of the gun into Mark's temple.

Mark opened his mouth and allowed the retracted penis head onto his tongue. He clamped his shaking mouth around the crown. Careful not to vomit, he walked his lips up the length of Caesar's shaft.

"Good boy, good boy," Brutus moved to the dead man in the green mask and grabbed the protruding colon organ in his hand. He yanked on it, retrieving a length of large intestine.

"Oh, fuck me. This stinks,"

Yank, yank, yank. The intestine unraveled in his hands and coughed shit and blood around Brutus's thighs.

Caesar closed his eyes and inhaled, "Awww, yes. Fuck," he grabbed Mark's head in both hands and slowly fucked his head.

Mark was in hell. The soft flesh in his mouth felt like it was expanding. His airwaves tightened. Snot and saliva burst through his nostrils, "Glummpphh."

Caesar laughed and rammed his hips forward, "What's that, Charlie?"

"Glummphh."

"I think he's saying he loves sucking your dick, man," Brutus walked over to the pair, carrying the dead body's intestines in his hands. "Aint' that right, Charlie?"

A deathly cry came from the top of the table as another masked man finished inside another, "Fucking shut up."

THWACK!

Mark kept his eyes closed. A thick cloth-like substance grew inside his neck. The only way to breathe was through his messy nostrils.

Brutus wrapped the intestinal tract around Mark's throat and tucked it underneath itself, tightening the grip.

Mark was effectively shackled to the intestines that hung out of the corpse's anus from twenty feet away.

Caesar tapped the back of Mark's head as he thrust his hips forward, "Don't you go running away, now. I'll be starting on your left lung soon."

"Okay, good. Keep his throat going, Caesar, honey," Brutus whispered and tightened the intestinal tract, "He's gonna pass out, so don't thrust too hard, okay?"

"Yeah, man."

Mark opened his tear-strewn eyes and up at Caesar. He didn't look back down. He kept his hands behind his head and thrusting his hips forward. Mark's head moved back with every pump.

Mark sucked oxygen in through his nostrils. He clenched his fists.

"Yeah, yeah," Brutus cheered Caesar on. He lowered the gun. In the corner of Mark's eye, he could see the weapon in the palm of Brutus's hand.

"Gnnnnnrrr," Mark grunted. "Gnnnrrrrr."

"Oh, look. He's loving it."

CHOMP! Mark bit down on Caesar's with all his might.

"Gaaahhhhhhh."

CHOMP, CHEW. Mark's teeth closed together as he pulled his head away. Spurts of thick, black blood and pre-cum burst through his lips and nose as he tore Caesar's penis away from his waist.

"Gnnnnng."

Blue veins, lumps of flesh and a burst semen pipe splattered up Mark's face as he moved his head back.

THWACK! Mark knocked the gun out of Brutus's hand, "Fuck."

Mark picked up the gun and scrambled to the other side of the room.

THWOMP!

The dead body hit the floor, having been wrenched off the edge of the table by its intestinal tract. Mark felt around his neck and loosened the fleshy tubing.

Tug, tug. The congealed knots of guts wouldn't break apart.

PTCHOO! Mark spat the half-chewed dick to the floor and slid the dead man's slimy tract between his teeth.

Brutus looked up and held his head in his hands, "Jesus Christ."

"Nnngggg," Mark's teeth chewed through the shit-smeared gristle, tearing the fleshy valve tract apart.

SNAP! The intestine spat partially-digested bloodied shit into Mark's mouth as it slapped to the floor. He spat the fluid out, stepped back to the wall and caught his breath.

Caesar dropped to his knees and bled out, screaming bloody murder.

"Stay back," Mark screamed. Blood and shit-laden spittle flew from his mouth as he kept the gun pointed at Brutus.

"You chewed his cock off, man," Brutus cried, indicating his friend bleeding on the floor.

"Awww, fuck," Caesar gasped, "Help me. Please, *help*."

"We'll call him an ambulance," Mark wiped the gunk away from his mouth with his wrist, "But first, I'm calling the police."

"No, don't do that."

The other men in the room stopped what they were doing. They held their hands in the air. Mark looked at the corpse of the green masked man on the worktop. He swung the gun back at Brutus.

"We don't know each other, so I'm going to leave."

"Okay, that's fair," Brutus said over the death cries of the freshly-castrated Caesar.

Caesar fell to his side and reached for his mask, "I think I'm gonna bleed out. It hurts so bad. Take my mask off, I can't breathe. I'm s-suffocating."

"Shut up," Mark swung the gun at Brutus, "Get his mask."

"Okay," Brutus helped Caesar remove his mask. He flung it to the table top and helped the bleeding man to his knees.

Mark swung the gun at the others, "Don't fucking move."

"Uh, uh," Caesar looked down between his knees. A one-inch stump of flesh gushed blood along the mirrored floor. The red stream collected into the grill at the base of the workbench. His knees were awash in his own blood.

Mark pointed the gun at Caesar and stepped over the discarded intestinal tract. He reached the silver door in the wall.

"Are you okay?"

"My cock," Caesar cried at Mark. His face contorted like an angry devil as he looked between his legs and saw the carnage, "Aww, *you cunt.*"

Mark froze solid.

His heart stopped.

He didn't realize it at the time, but he lowered the gun.

He couldn't fucking believe what he was seeing. The castrated man wailing before him was someone he *fucking knew!*

Mark gasped and shuddered, "Dad?"

Caesar kept his head down. That one word - "Dad." He looked up, slowly and took a pause, "Mark?"

"Oh, no," Brutus muttered. "Oh no, no, no—"

"—What the fuck are you doing here?" Mark screamed and pointed the gun at Caesar's face.

"Son? What am I doing here?" Caesar screamed, "What the *fuck* are *you* doing here?"

"Ugh, ugh," Mark dry heaved and doubled-over himself. "Oh, f-fu—"

BLOOOARRRRGGHHHH!

Mark vomited the contents of his stomach on floor and staggered back, slipping over his lunch. The puke pushed away and slimed around the discarded intestinal tract.

Caesar held out his hand, "Son, look—"

"—Stay the fuck away from me," Mark belched and doubled-over himself. "Oh God, this can't be happen—"

BLOOOARRGGGHHH!

Mark projectile-vomited into the air. He held the gun back at his father, "You sick fuck."

"Aww," his father winced and tried to shake away the trauma, "No, no."

Mark squealed in terror and pushed through the silver door, leaving the crashed world of his life behind him.

Mark stumbled into the *Wank Room* caked in every conceivable bodily fluid known to man.

The men gasped and as they clocked the gun in Mark's hand. A man finished ejaculating on the monolith, "Ugghhh."

Mark pushed the man out of the way. Josh threw his partner's hand from between his legs and stood up.

"Mark?"

"Ugh," Mark rolled over and pushed himself to his feet. White, sticky gunk coated his hand from the floor. He kept the gun aimed at the fuck room door.

"Why are y-you wearing a *black* mask, man?" Josh screamed.

"Everyone get out of here," Mark pointed the gun at the men. "Now."

All the naked men jumped to their feet and made for the exit door.

Josh hopped over to Mark, "What's going on?"

Mark removed his red balaclava and flung it on top of the cum-coated monolith, "This place is *hell on Earth.*"

"What do you mean?"

The silver door flung open, revealing the mirrored walls of the fuck room. Brutus stepped forward with his hands outstretched.

"Charlie?" Brutus tried, not wanting his friend's son to lose his shit, "He's gone, Charlie."

"What do you mean he's gone?"

"He bled out. He's dead."

Josh threw up his hands, "Who bled out? Why have you got a gun?"

Mark lowered the gun and slunk to his knees. He was catatonic; staring at his knees, he realized his life was over.

Josh looked down, "Mark, man?!"

Brutus walked through the door and kept his distance, "I'm sorry, mate. I didn't know."

Mark shifted his body, trying to jolt himself awake. Perhaps this was all a bad dream.

"Charlie?" came a female voice from the first screen, "Charlie, look at me."

Mark looked up and saw Rhonda on the screen. She knelt on all fours on a metal tray. Her labia melted and bubbled down her thighs, utterly busted apart, "Daddy says it was *your* fault."

"It wasn't my fault," Mark squeezed the gun and shouted at the screen, "How was I to know?"

"How was *he* to know? Rhonda winked and wiggled her hips.

"Huh?" Brutus and Josh watched Mark talk to himself like a madman. They looked up at the screen fizzing with white noise.

"You're right, sister," Mark looked down at his knees, "Neither of us could have known."

"Did you have fun in the *Wank Room*, sweetie?" Rhonda asked. "Was it more fun than the time you impregnated me?"

A tear rolled down Mark's cheek. He lifted the gun up to his temple.

"Charlie, no. Don't do that," Brutus stepped forward and went for the gun.

Josh went for the gun, "Mark, no—"

BANG-SCHPLATTTTT!

The bullet tore through his brain and out of the adjacent temple, taking the majority of his cranium with it.

Sodden clumps of bloodied gray matter splashed against the monolith. The splats of flesh pushed the dripping cum down the side of the monolith.

Josh stepped back and watched his friend fall back-first against the semen-soaked floor.

Brutus panted and turned to Josh. He didn't get a look back, though. Josh just tried to process the suicide as the blood and cum ran through his toes and past his heels.

A giant pool of blood bleached out from under Mark's corpse. It turned a prawn-colored pink as it met with the ejaculate-soaked floor.

Chapter 8

For the Masses

The *Waddling Gate* estate was vast. Three hundred acres of land with two lakes and fields as far as the eye could see.

The graveled path that snaked to the mansion was half a mile long.

Waddling Gate Mansion was a sprawling three-tiered Jacobean work of art. It boasted - among other things - ten bedrooms, two kitchens, a pantry, a smoking room, three porches (one uncovered), two libraries and an exterior chapel.

The proletariat used this building every Sunday afternoon. The vicar, Mr. Helmsworth, held a dual role as the parish minister, and as the estate's cleaner every other Thursday.

Pity poor Dowager Fairfax.

An elegant and refined lady of society. At a mere fifty-two years of age, her husband was murdered at sea. For the past year she has been in a state of perpetual mourning. She'd spent most of the first half of the year indoors lamenting the life she used to have.

Her late husband, Maximilian Fairfax, was the country's leading importer of sugar. For months at a time, he and his ship traveled back and forth to Brazil.

Rhonda met her husband at Portsmouth harbor when she was just seventeen. He was twenty years her senior. They fell in love immediately. Maximilian was certain that he'd found the perfect woman. Her large bosom and not-unimpressive posterior meant that marriage was an inevitability.

That was thirty-five years ago, shortly after Queen Victoria took the throne.

Maximilian Fairfax, the devilish rogue of the seas, was a fitting match for the impressionable teenager. Grapevine rumors among the upper echelons of society concerning the couple were rife. The speculation was that Lord Fairfax was a father to many illegitimate children born out of wedlock. "A downright philanderer" was a particularly worrisome headline printed about him in *The Waddling Herald*. This was seven days before he passed away.

Lady Fairfax had elected to sever all ties to her family.

The last telegraph she had received was from her brother. He had suggested that the United States was "embarking on a dangerous faction of civility", whatever that meant. A matter of months, not years. Spending four months aboard a ship was simply out of the question. Returning to the land of the free was a dangerous proposition. It would have been an unnecessary relinquishment of her entitlement. An ill-advised footstep into the middle of a war zone.

The years had not been kind to Dowager Fairfax. Her increased dependency on illicit substances and a more than generous relationship with alcohol meant that she was slowly losing the plot.

In this case, quite literally.

Waddling Gate was hemorrhaging money. As executor and beneficiary to his will, she received his sugar export company and its revenue. Alas, she did not know how to run it. No-one had put themselves forward for the job as it was deemed too dangerous.

Little of this mattered, though, as we shall see. Dowager Fairfax kept a terrible secret from her peers. A secret that Maximilian had taken to his grave. The burden gnawed away at Lady Fairfax's conscience.

This evening is the one year anniversary of Lord Fairfax's death. The Dowager called upon a number of society's egalitarians and most revered figures to celebrate his memory. It is a ruse. Her agenda is to reveal a most unsavory fact about her family before society's gossip-mongers beat her to it…

***

Clippity-cloppity-clop. The horses neighed as they pulled their carriage forward.

"I fear we may be in for a spot of rain this evening."

Vanna Blackwood peered through her carriage window as it rocked from side to side up the gravel path.

Her husband, Bennett, only half-acknowledged her displeasure. He was deeply involved with his newspaper.

"I beg your pardon, dearest?"

Vanna turned to him and sighed, "Must you always bury yourself in that darned newspaper, Bennett?"

She took it from his clutches and tossed it through the latch.

"What in Egad?"

"Heavens, dear. You are the most terrible bore, sometimes," Vanna crossed her arms and pinched her bodice, "Can you try to be agreeable this evening? We are guests, after all."

"Very well, my dear."

The horse-drawn carriage pulled up outside the *Waddling Gate Mansion.*

"Here we are, m'lady," said the carriage boy as he opened the carriage door for his passengers, "Waddling Gate Estate. The residence of her Ladyship Fairfax."

"Much obliged," Vanna took his hand and stepped out, hitching her petticoat against her knees. She looked at the front of the mansion and raised her eyebrows, "Oh my. What a magnificence."

"Quite, dear," Bennett said, closing his side of the

carriage. He turned to the gate and noticed a woman standing on the porch. She wore a large, turquoise hat.

"My lady," he beamed as he approached her. Vanna caught up to him and slipped her wrist through her husband's arm.

"Lord Blackwood," Rhonda clutched the rim of her hat and offered Vanna a smile, "Lady Blackwood. How marvelous it is to see you again."

"Yes."

"Please, do come inside."

Rhonda led the couple into the front hall. Large oil paintings of various men and women lined both walls. The echoes of her fine brogues against the varnished floor underscored the silence.

"I hear we are in for a treat," Vanna giggled to herself. "We are most honored to be patrons of your soirée this evening."

"I am obliged," Rhonda sighed. "Be that as it may, this evening is one I would rather not be a part of."

"I quite understand," Vanna sympathized, "T'would have been more fitting to have coalesced under different auspices."

"Indeed so." Rhonda clutched her chest. "For I have a most enervating announcement to impart after the entrée."

"Who's this chap?" Bennett looked up at a painting and threw a cigarillo between his lips. He took out a box of matches and patted it against his palm, "I presume you do not mind my indulgence?"

"I would rather you refrained from smoking in the hall, Lord Blackwood."

"Very well," he pocketed the cigarillo and pointed at the portrait of what looked like a perverse jester, "A striking vision, Dowager Fairfax. A relative, perchance?"

"Not is all as it seems, Lord Blackwood," Rhonda clutched at her petticoat and continued walking, "It is a portrait of a late magician. One of supreme and majestic rule."

"I must confess, I had not heard that your estate entertained such wizardry."

"A heathen if ever there was," Rhonda huffed. "Majesty, alas, is no more. I despised his peculiar ways."

"Then why adorn your beautiful abode with such a hideous beast, in your view?"

"Alas, Maximilian was *desirous* of him," Rhonda sighed and ascending the first of five steps toward the dining room, "He had feelings for the monstrosity and desired a constant reminder, much to my dismay."

"My word," Bennett protested. The news of his esteemed peer's homosexual tendencies was difficult to swallow. "Did your husband not love you, Lady Fairfax?"

Rhonda stopped walking and turned around to Vanna on the bottom step, "How dare you entertain such an abhorrent view, Lady Blackwood! I'll have you know that my husband loved me *very* much, as did I, he."

Vanna looked down and clasped her hands together, "A thousand apologies, Lady Fairfax."

"*Dowager* Fairfax," Rhonda spat. "You presumptuous hussy."

"Now, now," Bennett broke the girls apart, "I fear there has been a most unfortunate crossing of paths, here. Dowager Fairfax, I can assure you my wife meant you no ill with her remark. Is that not correct, dear?"

"Yes, husband. That is *not* correct."

Rhonda huffed and scrunched her face, "Did you issue a writ and summon them to court, Lady Blackwood?"

"Whom?"

"Your finishing school?" Rhonda issued Vanna with a sarcastic grin and turned toward the dining room.

Vanna huffed and followed her husband and host up the steps.

The dining room. A dwelling of glamour, velvet and an enormous amount of space.

A circular dining table made from fine mahogany took center stage in the middle of the room.

"My Lords, Ladies and Gentlemen," Rhonda ushered Vanna and Bennett into the room. "May I introduce you to Lord Blackwood and his lady wife, Vanna Blackwood."

The men and women sitting around the table halted their conversations and looked at them.

"Good evening," one of the guests said.

"Please. Make yourselves comfortable at the table," Rhonda made her way to the head of the table and took her seat. An effortless and gracious movement.

Vanna and her husband sat on the two chairs their host had indicated. Bennett looked above Rhonda's head to see a giant painting of a silver-haired man in a suit.

"The late Lord Fairfax, my lady?" Bennett asked. Rhonda looked up and crossed her heart. Up, down, left and right.

"May the Lord have mercy on his soul, yes."

A man in his seventies looked at Bennett from across the table. His right cheek held a monocle in his eye above his yellow mustache, "I say, very good to meet you."

"Charmed."

The monocled man stood up and offered Bennett his hand, "Gray Levenson-Fox."

"How do you do?" Bennett smiled.

"And my lady wife," Gray continued. "The venerable, but not wholly disagreeable, Bernadine Levenson-Fox."

"How do you do."

"How do you do."

Bernadine bowed her head and took Bennett's hand in hers, "Charmed."

"I say," Bennett copped an eyeful of Bernadine's bountiful cleavage, "Gray, sir. I must congratulate you on your wife's ample bosom."

"Why, thank you, Lord Blackwood."

Bernadine giggled coquettishly and returned to her seat.

Rhonda stood up and tapped the side of her glass with

her dessert spoon, "May I have your attention please?"

Everyone turned to Rhonda with respect. Two servants moved in with empty glasses. They set one down in front of each attendee and proceeded to pour some wine into them.

Rhonda cleared her throat, "As you know, I have summoned you here today for good reason. I wish to dispel the grapevine rumblings you may have gleaned regarding my late husband's estate. It is, therefore, my utmost privilege and honor to welcome Mr. and Mrs. Hellman. Mathis, and his wife Madeleine."

She pointed to a strikingly gorgeous blond woman in her late teens. A shifty looking gentleman next to her smiled at the guests, "Good evening."

"Perhaps, Mathis, you'd care to elucidate our guests regarding your involvement this evening?"

"With all pleasure, Lady Fairfax," Mathis rose to his feet, "My wife and I are most honored to have been invited. I'm the feature editor from *The Waddling Herald*."

Bennet smiled, "A magnificent periodical."

The others nodded their head and muttered among themselves.

"I am of course cognizant that my involvement may be perceived to be somewhat intrusive. However, I can assure you that I am here to pay tribute to the late Lord Fairfax. It is my intention to do right by the facts revealed to me during the course of the evening. Thank you."

Madeleine smiled as he returned to his seat.

"I say, Mathis, my good man?" Gray turned to him and squinted, "Are you *quite certain* you are not here on a sensationalist agenda?"

"Verily, my good man," Mathis swished the wine in his glass around the edges, "I am not desirous of sensation. Should Lady Fairfax elect to impart any facts that may be deemed so, then rest assured I shall do my utmost to ensure my reportage is fair and balanced."

"Don't sell me a dog, Mathis," Gray heaved. "I shan't

stand for it."

"Upon my good standing it is not in my remit to tell a tall tale to our readership."

"Very well," Gray wasn't very convinced at what he'd heard.

"Much obliged, Mathis," Rhonda watched the servants move in with plates of food, "Now, the starters. Prawns Gairloch."

"My. This does look exquisite," Bennett licked his lips and ran his palms over his bulging stomach.

"Dear, *please*," Vanna whispered into his ear, "Do *try* not to fiddle with your parts during the entrée."

"It is only my belly, dearest."

The servants moved away. Another man, to Bennett's left, looked down and poked around the plate with his fork, "Mackrel and almond? A nice touch."

"Heavens," Rhonda stood up and held her palm at the man. "In my absence of mind, I did fail to introduce one of London's most distinguished Rotarians. Lord Alfred Townshend, by the grace of God. Forgive me, Lord Townshend."

"What? Oh, please, don't apologize." He looked up and waved his hands at her. Everyone looked at him as he smiled back, "Please, I am rather insignificant. Merely a friend of the late Lord Fairfax—"

"—Not at all," Rhonda decried his modesty, "You are one of the most influential men of our times."

"Whatever you are led to believe, Lady Fairfax," he shoveled some prawns into his mouth and winced at the temperature, "My word. They *are* thoroughly cooked, are they not?"

Rhonda took some mackerel in her mouth, "Mmm."

Mathis and Madeleine tucked into their prawn starters. They whispered something to each other and looked at Bennett and his wife.

Vanna kept one eye on her husband as he slurped the food from his fork. It was loud.

CLOMP!

A thump underneath the table rattled the crockery. Bennett looked down and rubbed his knees.

"Please, dear," Vanna whispered, "Don't slurp your meal."

"Apologies."

One half hour later, the guests and their host had polished off their starters. They awaited their main course. Many glasses of wine had been consumed with gay abandon. The effect of the alcohol kicked in.

"Pardon my intrusion, Mr. Hellman," Gray adjusted his monocle at Mathis, "May I ask, was it you who reported on the comet that will be passing later this evening?"

"Indeed it was, yes. A most invigorating feature and a very popular piece."

"Oh, yes," Bennett felt the effects of the alcohol and burped into his fist, "*Homosexualist Twelve* or something?"

He felt Vanna nudge him in the ribs, "Not in polite society, dear."

"*Homophagea K-Twelve*," Mathis corrected Bennett. "Passes our orbit once every one hundred and fifty years or so."

Rhonda smiled, "I hear it will be quite the spectacle and light up the night sky."

"That is the refrain so I am led to believe," Mathis rubbed his palm across Madeleine's knee. She chuckled and gasped. Everyone turned to her and wondered what she was playing at.

"Pardon me," she burst out laughing and snorted like a pig.

"Do excuse my beloved wife," Mathis apologized, "She is not accustomed to the fermented beverage."

"She is barely out of her cradle," Bennett suggested, eyeing her cleavage.

Alfred winked at Madeleine, "A jammiest bit of jam I ever did see."

"Dowager Fairfax?" Gray asked, patiently.

"Lord Leveson-Fox?"

He held up his glass of wine and shook it around, "This is a most fine number. Pray, what is the title of this delicious beverage?"

"Apologies, Lord Leveson-Fox. I am not in receipt of its name at this time," Rhonda said. "I shall endeavor to interrogate Waterstone, my butler."

Gray swigged some of the wine and gulped it down. He held the rim of the glass to his nostrils, "Tastes somewhat like champagne. Smells a bit like an… *infant*. Most bizarre."

Rhonda smiled and turned to Alfred.

"And what of this evening's main feast?" Alfred chuckled in his half-drunken stupor, "Pray, what magnificence might we expect from such a wonderful engagement?"

"Ah, all in good time." Rhonda looked to her knees and retrieved a handkerchief from her sleeve, "Pardon me, I must leave for a moment."

Rhonda rose to her feet and wobbled. She gripped the table of balance.

Gray took another sip from his wine, "Not at all. Please do take your time."

Rhonda staggered into the water closet and poured a bucket of water into the basin. She splashed it against her face and looked in a small mirror on the shelf.

"Rhonda, you can do this. Stop stalling and tell them," the reflection said.

She blinked and traced her finger around the mirror, "B-But what if th-they are d-desirous of proof?"

"They'll believe you," her reflection insisted. "You simply need to produce a pair of lady glans and stand your ground."

Rhonda slipped the glove off from her right hand and extended two fingers.

"Now, expunge those nasty nutrients."

"Uh-kay."

Rhonda threw her fist into her throat and wriggled her fingers around.

"That's correct. Quite, quite deep. Allow your throat to close around your digits."

"Gumph."

"And, any moment now—"

BLOOOOAAARRRGGGHHHHHH! Rhonda yanked her fist from her throat and upchucked a blast of vomit against the wall. Pieces of mackerel and prawn-ends hit the wooden slats and raced towards the floor.

The dinner guests chatted amongst themselves. Vanna inspected Grey's monocle and tried it on.

"Ha. Richly comic," she laughed, much to the chagrin of Bernadine, who'd yet to offer anything to the merriment. She huffed and turned to her husband.

"Gray, *really*."

“"T'was only in jest, dearest," he slurred and pinched her thigh, "Please lighten your spirits."

"I'm sorry," slurred Vanna. Bennett chuckled as the monocle slipped from her cheek, "I hope I didn't cause you embarrassment."

Rhonda held her petticoat up as she walked past Mathis talking to Alfred.

"So, d-do y-you think—"

"—Think what?" Mathis burped.

"That this *thing*. This, perversion of sexuality, homosexuality—" Alfred tried to get the words out.

"—Yes?" Mathis blinked and tried to keep his composure, "What of it?"

"Is it like a virus?" Alfred asked with all seriousness, "Are you of the mind that such an ailment can be cured?"

"Oh, a cure is most inevitable, I think," Mathis held his glass to his lips and winked at his young wife.

"Make a stuffed bird laugh," Alfred snorted in disbelief as he kept an eye on Madeleine's cleavage, "Imagine. One man entering another's posterior when there's so much talent on offer. Truly, a perplexing proposition to a man."

"Well, quite," Mathis nodded and agreed.

"My Lords, Ladies and Gentlemen," Rhonda held out her hands. She'd been building up to this speech for an entire year, "I have an announcement to impart on you all."

Everyone stopped chatting and turned to Rhonda.

Raindrops hit the windows that overlooked the stables. Gray looked out of the window and saw two horses neighed from the stable.

Rhonda picked up her half-consumed glass of wine and held it up. "My late husband, God rest his beautiful soul. Gone, but by no measure forgotten."

"Hear, hear," Bennett held up his glass. The others followed suit and joined in the toast.

They all took a sip of their wine and swished it around their mouths. "Ahhhhh."

Clink-clink-clink.

The bottoms of the glasses randomly hit the clothed tabletop.

"Mathis, my liege?" Rhonda turned to him and smiled.

"Yes, my lady?"

"You may wish to make use of your quill and paper at this time."

"Oh," Mathis leaned to the side of his chair and reached for his satchel, "Naturally. Please, do continue."

He took out a quill and filled the fine China well with a packet of ink.

Rhonda pressed her palms together, "Presently, I ask you, my esteemed guests, to join me in offering thanks."

Everyone apart from Mathis pressed their palms together.

"Lord, we thank you for this day. Our daily bread. The feast upon which we are about to embark. And this, the anniversary of my late husband's death, we ask of you to comfort his soul. Bestow upon him your infallible love and eternal forgiveness. Amen."

Everyone inhaled and repeated after Rhonda, "Amen."

"F-Forgiveness?" Bennett hiccupped and poured himself another glass of wine.

"Indeed, Lord Blackwood," Rhonda smiled. "Forgiveness."

He topped up Vanna's glass and looked to the end of the table. Rhonda became upset, "Then you have some information you deem we should be in receipt of?"

"I do indeed, Lord Blackwood."

"Very well, then?"

Rhonda closed her eyes and held her hands by her sides. She opened her eyelids to find everyone awaiting her revelation.

"As you know, our estate has benefited from our primary source of income from the sugar trade. For years, my husband slaved like a nigger to establish and cultivate our enterprise."

Everyone nodded.

"Alas, it is with great dispirit that I must reveal the truth. Fairfax Industries does not, and never has, exported sugar from the South American continent."

"Egad," Alfred slammed the table and demanded an explanation, "What illogical ramblings of a mad woman must we tolerate? By God, woman, explain yourself."

"I am indebted to you, Lord Townshend," Rhonda began choked. "You must lend me your ear first so that others may not molest the truth I am about to impart."

"By Jove, woman, this had better be satisfactory," Alfred leaned back in his chair and folded his arms, "Well?"

"My husband did, in fact, export products to our British Isles. Not sugar canes, alas, but *opium*."

"Opium?" Mathis dipped his quill into the well and scrambled to record as much detail as possible on his paper.

"As in r-religion?" Bennett burped and looked over his

shoulder, "To wit, the esteemed pop-up vicarage that adorns the grounds of your estate?"

Rhonda smiled and blinked, "Lord Blackwood, was it not Marx who opined that religion was the opium of the masses?"

"I rather believe it was," Mathis shot Alfred a look of evil. The old man wasn't impressed.

"No favor, naturally, to us," Rhonda explained. "From Mesopotamia to Afghanistan, my husband and his niggers did export the finest opium that the world has ever seen. Doctors and surgeons across our fair isles demanded the substance in such high volume. We became millionaires over the course of an evening."

"My Lady," Alfred shook his head. "You and your husband. Nothing more than degenerate drug peddlers."

"Yes, Lord Townshend. I am afraid it is the truth. For shame."

"Verily, Lady, I am of the mind to challenge the veracity of such a claim," Alfred stood to his feet and threw his hands out. "I am most reluctant to take the word of a harlot who seeks to besmirch the name of her good husband."

"Lord Townshend, I beg your ear for just a few moments more to establish that my revelation is based in fact. Please, return to your chair."

"In hardship and protest," Alfred sat back into his chair. "Whatever next? You'll be saying this wine is made from infants or some such nonsense."

Rhonda snapped her fingers behind her head, "Waterstone?"

Her butler moved in with a team of servants. A silver tray balanced in his hand carrying six hypodermic needles. Each barrel featured two gold-coated rings under the plunger.

They glowed a soft, purple hue.

"Esteemed guests, allow me the courtesy of demonstration." Rhonda nodded at the five servants and her butler, "Waterstone, would you?"

"Certainly, ma'am."

Waterstone took a syringe and flicked the needle. The contents of the barrel resembled floating, creamy sand.

The five servants each took a needle and made their way to the table.

"It is one thing to speak of the wrong doing that my family had undertaken," Rhonda watched a servant take their place beside each of her guests, "It is quite another to prove that my claim is true."

Waterstone rolled up Alfred's sleeve.

"What in God's name are you doing?"

"Hold still, Lord Townshend," Waterstone struggled to keep Alfred's arm still.

He shot Rhonda a nasty look, "By God, woman. Have you run mad?"

The needle entered Alfred's arm. Waterstone sucked out a half-barrel of blood. It mixed in with the solution.

"Opium?" Alfred looked to Rhonda.

"Yes, Lord Townshend."

The solution plunged into his arm. Waterstone pinched the needle and slid it out of the old man's arm.

Rhonda watched on as Bennett and Vanna Blackwood, Gray and Bernadine Leveson-Fox and Mathis and Madeleine Hellman, each received their injections.

Mathis rolled his eyes as the solution introduced itself into his veins, "Woah, Dowager Fairfax," he slurred, "It is heavenly. You are an angel."

"No, Mathis," Rhonda beamed, "Angel *of Death*."

"Oh… oh… dee…" Bennett slowed his speech, "Oh-dee…"

"Over," Vanna whispered to herself, losing her ability to remains upright, "D-Dose."

FLUMP. Vanna's head hit the table.

FLUMP, FLUMP, FLUMP.

Alfred's eyes rolled into the back of his head as it fell cheek-first to the cloth. Followed by Bennett, and then

Gray.

Bernadine inspected the bleeding prick in her arm. She prodding it with her sheathed finger. A speck of blood bleached around the fabric. "Dowager Fairfax?"

"Lady Leveson-Fox?"

"Is this what they call *heroin*?"

Rhonda smiled. She held her forefinger to her lips, "Yes. Shhh."

FLUMP. Bernadette's head hit the table, causing the chrome cutlery to jiggle around.

Last to go was the gorgeous Madeleine. She chuckled and felt around her shoulders. She appeared to be experiencing an orgasm.

Rhonda clenched her fists and pushed them against the table. She waited for the ditsy blond tart to drop with an intense patience.

"Mmmm, Dowager Fairfax," Madeleine moaned and tilted her head. Her hands slipped under the table, "Your husband may not have dealt with sugar. But his opium does make my pussy tingle. Oooop."

Rhonda scowled at her and clicked her fingers, "You are meant to be under."

"Oh."

FLUMP. Madeleine's head hit the table.

Rhonda brushed her hands and watched as the servants followed Waterstone out of the room.

"Good work, gentlemen."

"You're welcome, ma'am," Waterstone winked and made his way through the door with the metal tray in his hand.

Rhonda surveyed her unconscious guests and licked her lips.

***

The flames from the candles on the wall blew around. The guests had spent a few minutes unconscious, face-first on the table.

Dowager Fairfax sat in her chair holding her blanket in her arms. Alfred's eyelids pulsed. He reached his hands to the tabletop, nearly spilling his half-drunk glass of wine.

"Oooof," he blinked and shook his head, "What happened?"

"Good evening, Lord Townshend."

A clap of thunder lit up the room. Torrential rain splashed against the windows.

Madeleine and Mathis opened their eyes. Their field of vision contained sparkling silver cutlery.

"Wh-what on Earth?"

"Baby?" Madeleine gasped, feeling her nostrils. A blob of blood trickled down her middle finger, "What's g-going on?"

"You fell asleep," Rhonda rocked back and forth in her chair, "A consequence of the wine."

"The wine?" Madeleine picked up her glass and sniffed the rim, "Smells like zinc."

"Mmm, I know," Rhonda turned to Gray and Bernadine. They lifted their heads very, very slowly and looked at their host.

Not a word was said.

Bernadine inspected the underside of her forearm. A pinprick stared back at her, "Where a-are w-we?"

"It's okay," Rhonda whispered. "We had a bit of a nap. Perfectly normal."

"I remember," Bernadine blinked, "We were drinking the wine, and then your servants came in and—"

She looked down and hid her wrist under the table.

"It's okay," Rhonda nodded as a smile streaked across her face.

Bennett and Vanna were the last to wake from their slumber. Vanna's nose had bled much like Madeleine's. She wiped her top lip and saw the blood smeared across her fingertips.

"Vanna, dear?" Bennett turned to her, "Your nose is

bleeding."

"It's okay," she sniffed away the embarrassment, "Must be the temperature."

"Now that you're all awake," Rhonda chimed in and looked at her guests, "I feel I should tell you something important."

Everyone held their gaze at their host.

Alfred lost his patience and thumped the table, causing the cutlery and glasses to wobble, "What is it, woman?"

"Dinner is served."

Rhonda clicked her fingers above her head. The door to the dining hall opened.

Waterstone rolled a metal trolley along the ground. The casters squeaked and rattled as he pushed it along the wooden floor.

Faint beeps came from the legs of the trolley. The beep rate was constant, around every other second.

A giant, covered metal tray sat in the middle. Rhonda smiled at Waterstone as he parked the trolley.

"What is it?" Mathis asked as everyone watched Waterstone lift the plate into his hands.

"Curtains of Belt Galloway. Beef, and artichoke."

Waterstone set the plate in the middle of the table, "Et voilà," He lifted the lid and stood back.

A waft of smoke obstructed the view for a few seconds.

One of Rhonda's servants sprinted into the room and joined Waterstone, "My Lords, Ladies and Gentlemen."

The smoke dissipated, revealing a newborn baby lying asleep in the middle of the tray. It had been fried to within an inch of its life.

"Oh m-my God," Bennett rubbed his eyes and took a second glance at the dinner.

A generous garnish of lettuce and chopped vegetables surrounded the baby.

"Bon Appetite," Rhonda smiled. "Lord Blackwood, do you prefer the breast or leg?"

"Uh, uh," Bennett stuttered. "I'm good, thank you—"

"—No," Rhonda hit the table, "I repeat. Breast or leg? Or perhaps you prefer the rump?"

"No, d-don't make me—"

"—Waterstone, Rhonda scowled. "Serve the gentlemen."

"Pleasure," he said.

Waterstone reached over and grabbed the baby's right leg in his hand. He placed his free hand on its waist and yanked the leg out sideways.

CRATTCHHH!

The baby's hipbone shot out, dislocating its thigh from the waist. The baby woke up and cried in sheer agony.

"Be quiet," Rhonda thumped the table. "Silence, I say."

Waterstone dropped the leg onto Bennett's plate and scraped some garnish to the side, "My Lord."

"Uh, thank you." Bennett looked at the sizzling leg on his plate. Black blood coughed from the cavity.

Waterstone broke off the other leg and dropped it to Vanna's plate as the infant cried in pain.

"My Lady."

Vanna looked up and held a napkin to her mouth, "Thank y-you," she stuttered in utter terror.

"You may begin," Rhonda said.

Bennett picked up his knife and fork and sliced into the thigh flesh. He speared it with his fork and held it to his lips.

"*Eat it*," Rhonda threatened him.

Bennett slipped the piece of flesh into his mouth and chewed. His face contorted as he munched on it for a few seconds.

Finally, he swallowed. Everyone at the table watched on in sheer repulsion.

"How is it, Lord Blackwood?" Mathis asked.

Bennett licked his lips. His face went from disgust to elation, "It's delicious."

"For you, sir?" Waterstone offered Alfred. He looked

at the legless, crying baby and pointed between its legs.

"Ah, a wise choice."

Rhonda chuckled to herself as Waterstone pinched the baby's penis between his fingernails.

SNIP!

Its appendage lifted away a swift movement of the blade. Waterstone set it to one side on Alfred's place and held the baby's chest down.

"Waaaaaaaaahhh."

"Shhhh, little one," Waterstone hushed as he placed the serrated knife edge over its abdomen, "Go to sleeeeeeeeeeeeeep."

He ran the jagged blade across its abdomen. The metal gnawed through the flesh with each slicing action and grated against the bone.

"Make a wish," Rhonda smiled, as Waterstone snapped the baby's abdomen away from its chest.

He dropped it next to the baby's freshly severed penis, "Lord Townshend."

"Thank you."

Alfred picked up the penis and threw it in his mouth. "Mmm, chewy," he swayed in his chair in danger of falling asleep again.

CLATCH-BREAK-SNAP.

The baby's cries turned to rasping, blood-curdling death cries. Waterstone cracked its breastbone out and scraped the flesh from within onto a pair of plates.

Mathis and Madeleine held out their hands.

CRUTCH-SNAP!

Off came the arms as a side dish. They resembled fried drumsticks. Waterstone dropped the two halves of breast and one arm on each of their plates.

The room rumbled as the thunder snapped in the sky. The rain lashed against the window, threatening to snuff out the candles.

"Lord and Lady Leveson-Fox?" Rhonda asked.

They turned to Rhonda, "Yes?"

"I'm afraid that leaves you with the head."

They turned to watch Waterstone who the baby's skull in his hands like a crab. He wiggled the brain and detritus from the shell. A final scoop with two fingers ensured the frontal lobe made it to the plate.

"Thank you," Grey pushed the side of his finger against the baby's brains. He shoveled it into his mouth and looked at the guest opposite him.

Alfred chewed and hit something alien. "Hmm," he reached into his mouth and pinched the foreign object.

A sleeve-shaped string of skin peeled from between his teeth - the baby's foreskin, "Ugh," he flung it on the plate.

Rhonda rose to her feet and watched her guests feast on their meal. She looked at the plate.

Beef Galloway was being served to the guests, not a baby. The infant feast they *thought* they were eating was in their own minds.

"How are the beef curtains, everyone?"

"Mmmm," Bennett dug into his meal with enthusiasm, "Exquisite."

Rhonda took a sip of her wine, "I thought you may enjoy it."

The oil painting of her late husband loomed over the table. Its eyes faced the room dead center which meant that no matter where you were in the room, they'd always follow you.

Rhonda held her glass up to the picture, "*Infant champagne*, my dear husband."

She knocked back the rest of her wine and smiled at the painting. Her sleeve ran across her wine-soaked lips.

"That was divine," Alfred smiled and mopped his lips with a napkin. "The liver and pancreas were an inspired touch."

"I am overjoyed that you like it," Rhonda giggled and turned to face her guests, "Can I have your attention please?"

Everyone turned to Rhonda, "While you are fully aware

of your actions, I would like to inform you that, because of recent events, I have no choice but to abandon the Fairfax family name."

A blast of thunder rattled the walls once again, followed by a crashing sound of electricity.

One candle blew out completely. The rest survived. Alfred looked up at Rhonda and toasted her success with his glass. His attention was drawn to the painting. Something was happening to it.

"Er, Dowager Fairfax?"

Rhonda ignored Alfred and continued, "My late husband and I cannot afford to be remembered as societal pariahs and so we will be changing the family name by deed poll."

"Lady Fairfax," Alfred gasped, gripping the sides of his seat. He threw one hand up at the painting. "Look."

"What will you change it to?" asked Mathis, who took his quill in his hand.

"Ferrari."

Alfred stomped his finger to the ground, "*Lady Fairfax.*"

Rhonda ignored him once again, "That's F-E-R-R-A-R-I."

"Hmm," Mathis wrote down the new name, "Most unusual."

Alfred jumped to his fee,. "What in God's name is happening to the picture?"

Madeleine winced at Alfred, and then followed his finger to the oil painting, "Oh, *my word.*"

Rhonda continued to ignore them and kept her focus on Mathis, "It's a nice name, isn't it? Ferrari?"

"Yes, it—" Mathis looked at the oil painting, "—oh Jesus Christ in Heaven."

Gray and Bernadine saw it, too. They were utterly shocked, "Umm, Lady Fairfax? I wonder, do you—"

Bernadine screamed at the top of her lungs. Gray turned around and grabbed her by the shoulders, "Don't scream, you'll make it worse."

SMASH!

Her screams shattered the window behind her. A vicious draught blew into the room.

Rhonda chuckled and stepped back to the oil painting. She held out her arms and fell against it.

The paints that made up her husband's portrait liquefied and ran down the canvas. A mushy concoction of blues, reds, yellows and whites. As Rhonda leaned against it, the paint slapped down her shoulders and over her face.

Like a little girl playing in a waterfall.

"Ugh," Rhonda's voice sunk to a low, male growl, "Raagghh."

Her head crashed back into the painting, splashing oil over the floor and walls.

"Grrooaggh."

Everyone jumped back. Bennett grabbed a dessert spoon as a weapon. Rhonda's physique contorted and morphed into a complicated ball of flesh. The yellows, reds, whites, and blues streaked over the ball and twisted together.

It began to take shape.

Two shoulders.

A pair of knees.

A thunder clap, followed by a grunt and growl from the frenzied gory mush standing before the guests.

A pair of arms darted either side of the *thing*. A pair of legs hit the floor.

A grown, naked man lay in a puddle of blood, mucous and human remains.

PLOP-PLOP.

Two droplets of paint hit his exposed shoulder. Rhonda had turned into a man.

Bennett leaned in, "Okay, -I th-think it's t-time for us to go—"

The man's eyes snapped open, "Silence." In a split second, he was on his feet. A supernatural oddity. His eyes glowed bright blue. He pointed a finger at the group.

The man inhaled. His voice sounded like that of a warped lion. "There's a comet headed for Earth."

A pang of electricity fizzed around his body.

"I beg your pardon?" Alfred asked.

"There's a comet headed for us," the man coughed, lowering his voice. His entire body buzzed and fizzled, briefly becoming transparent, "There's a comet coming and you must follow me."

"But why? Madeleine asked. "Are we going to die?"

The naked man wretched and doubled-over himself, "Ugh, ugh," he screamed in an ungodly voice.

"Are you okay, Mr…?"

"Bwuck, bwuck," the man gasped and choked.

"Mr. Bwuck-Bwuck?" Alfred lost his patience threw his hands into the air, "Okay, I think I've seen quite enough.'

"You ain't seen *nothing* yet, mate," the naked man clutching his knees, "Welcome to… t-to…"

He coughed and spluttered again. On the verge of throwing up. His entire body blinked on and off, sending electric shock waves up his torso.

"W-Welcome t-to, P-Pure, D-Dar—"

BZZZZZZZ. His body blinked off and on, temporarily disabling the use of his legs.

BLOOOARRRRGGGHHHHH!

He threw his hands out and puked into his arms. Flecks of spittle and bile hit his forearms.

BLOICK!

The head of a baby shunted out of his mouth. He thumped his stomach and wretched again.

BWUCK-KK!

"Oh my word!" screamed Vanna, fainting into Bennett's arms. Half of a crying baby punched out from his throat. It cried and wailed.

"What on Earth are you doing?" Gray tried not to scream himself stupid.

The man leaned back and threw himself forward as if

trying to whip the baby from his body.

BLOAARR-THWAAAP!

The newborn flew out of his mouth and right into his hands. The fleshy little beats of tears cried in pain and waggled its limbs.

The man grunted and looked down at it, "My child." He ran his hand over the baby's scalp.

Fine green bristles fanned out from under the man's fingers as it ran over the baby's scalp.

"What's g-going on?"

A sparkling white light fizzed in mid-air three feet above the dining table. Everyone's face lit up as it streaked downward like a sparkler. A waft of purple light emanated from the tear as it hit the table.

The sound of a life-support machine beeped from within the tear in the air.

The naked man threw the baby into the split above the table, "I found you, my boy. Now, return home."

SCHLOMP!

The tear in above the table gulped the baby in and swallowed. The fizzing light zipped up to the top and sealed itself.

The life support machine stopped beeping.

"Charlie?" came a female's voice from the ceiling, "You're back. Welcome home, sweetheart."

Bennett looked up and huffed, "Who said that?"

Everyone looked up. Madeleine clutched Mathis's arm, worried, "Something strange is happening here, dear."

"I know," he picked up his paper and looked at the writing on it.

The word *"DIE"* had been scribbled in green ink across the length of it.

"Huh?"

Everyone turned to the naked man and jumped in fright. He wasn't naked.

It was Max Dark, dressed in his suit, and with a shit-eating grin sprawled across his face.

"Ladies and genitals," he laughed and clicked his fingers, "Allow me to introduce myself."

"Wh-who are you?" Gray held Bernadine back, protecting her from harm.

"I'm glad you asked," Max hopped, skipped and jumped to the other side of the table, "Let me explain. My name is Maxwell Dark. This is kinda… my *gig*, if you like."

"Gig?" Alfred asked with confusion, "Why are you talking like that? What is a gig?"

"Oh, you mean a *jig*?" Bernadine offered, pleased that she'd corrected him.

"No, no, wait," Max held out his hands, "No, I meant *gig*. Kind of like a, uh, what do you call it?"

"A party?" Vanna scratched her nose. Several whiskers shot out from the sides of her nostrils, "Huh?" Her fingernails fell off as sharp claws pushed through the tip of her fingers.

"Perhaps a slow, melodic dance?" Alfred asked, realizing his voice was muffled. He pressed his finger to his mouth. A padlock. Leather straps around his head.

"No, not a *dance*," Max shook his head, deeply irritated.

"Something you wear on your head?" Bernadine offered, holding out her hand. She blinked and looked twice. The skin on her body turned dark brown.

WHVOOM.

Her palm caught fire. She threw it behind her back and hoped no-one saw her smoking hand.

"Nah, that's a wig. Not a gig," Max thought aloud, "What's that thing where you get married?"

"A church?" Madeleine offered, followed by a prolonged squeal from between her legs.

"Ugh, did you just *queef*?" Mathis asked.

The skin on Madeleine's face hardened. "I most certainly… did not," her voice squeezed into a jet of air. Her eyeballs sunk into their sockets.

"Madeleine, dear?"

"Screeee," her skin glistened in the candlelight. Her lips

puffed out and turned to plastic.

"No, not a church," Max rubbed his face. "Like, you know when you arrange to get married?"

Gray and Bennett climbed onto the dining table, "I think it's time to go baby-byes, now."

The two men hugged one another. Bennet planted his lips on Grey's and kissed him. Their cheeks and jaws melded together. Their suits flaked away from their skin. A coagulated slush of plastic formed around their naked bodies.

"*Eengagement.* Yes, that's it. An engagement," Max shook his head and chuckled to himself. He turned around and placed his hands on his hips. An empty painting of where Maximilian Fairfax had once stood loomed back over him.

"Yes, it's my gig," Max started.

"Miaaaooww. Fuck you," screeched Spunx.

"What the fuck?" groaned Caesar's voice from over behind Max.

"Baaaabydoooolll," the wheezing of a plastic blow-up doll followed.

Max took a deep breath and spun around to face his creatures, "Yes. It's my *engagement.*"

He squinted at Mathis, who had turned into a blond woman. She stood before him in a t-shirt and jeans but still retained Mathis's undeniable facial features.

"Mathis?"

"My name is Amanda," Mathis recited in a demoniacal woman's voice, "I tossed off my retarded son and tainted an entire sperm bank."

"Oh," Max chuckled. "You did, did you?"

Spunx trundled around Amanda's legs and snarled at Mathis, "Fuck you, cunt."

"Now, now, Spunx," Max placed his hands on his hips, "You keep those vicious claws away from me, you hear?"

Nisa stepped forward and presented the group with her burning hand, "I died in a fire."

"I know," Max said with solemnity, "I'm sorry Mrs. Pershar,"

"Did my s-son survive?"

"Yes, he did."

CRAAA-SMASSSSSSHHHH!!!

Caesar kicked a chair onto its side. "Where's that little cunt who cut off my cock?" He pulled on his leather head traps and punched his fists together.

"Ah, Mr. Caesar," Max clapped his hands together. "Everyone, this is Caesar. He force-fucked his cock down his own son's throat."

"It wasn't my fault!" Caesar yelled. Something caught his attention in the corner of his eye.

A toy doll lay perfectly still on top of the table.

"Ugh, that's just creepy."

"Okay, guys, let me explain," Max jumped onto the dining table. He kicked the cutlery and plates away, "There's a perfectly good reason why you're all here."

"There is?" Amanda said.

"Yes."

"Well?" Nisa asked, frightened for her life, "What is it?"

"All of you are figments of someone else's imagination."

Everyone blinked. Spunx licked her claws and spat some saliva to the floor, "Cunt."

Max chuckled, "No, you little shithouse, it's true."

"Fuck you, you faggot," She held up her claws to her face, "You wanna get a fuckin' stabbed in the knee?"

"No, no, look. Watch this," Max extended his forefinger and lifted it above his head. A white light appeared and sparkled.

Max drew a white line down the middle of the table as if he was unzipping a pair of trousers.

He pressed his palms together and slid them through the slit. Pulling the tear apart like a pair of curtains, everyone could see Charlie Ferrari in his hospital bed.

BEEP. BEEP. BEEP. The life support machine wailed

from behind the curtain in the slit.

"See him?"

"Yeah," Caesar said. "I see him. Who is he?"

"His name is Charlie Ferrari. You're all in his head."

Chloe, the plastic blow-up doll, turned to Max. Her cheeks inflated and wheezed, "Head?"

"Yeah."

"How?" Nisa asked.

"In the twenty-first century this place won't be the *Waddling Gate Estate*. It'll be *Chrome Junction General hospital.* What you're seeing there is the future. Right where you're standing now."

Max zipped the time portal slit up with his blazing fingertip.

WHUMP! It sealed shut.

"I'm *so* sorry about this but we tried to avert this disaster."

Spunx licked her paw, "You what?"

"Unfortunately, his mother ran off before we could get him back for testing. We lost him. His mother died in a car accident a few minutes ago. We've got him back where he belongs, now."

"This is pure insanity," Mathis-as-Amanda blurted.

"Ah, no," Max corrected Caesar. "Actually, it's *Pure Dark.*"

"Pure Dark?"

"Welcome," Max extended his sleeve and looked at the figments in front of him, "As you know, there's a comet headed for the planet and you're all going to die."

Nisa panicked as her palms spat out angry flames, "What? We're going to—"

"—Die, yes. Well, I *say* a comet. It's actually all a load of bollocks," Max explained. "Charlie thinks the swelling that's developed on his brain is a comet. It's not. It's actually a *tumor.*"

Spunx was baffled, "The comet's a tumor?"

"Who's Charlie?" Amanda asked, puzzled.

"The heroin junkie who has you all as his imaginary friends. *Duh*?" Max giggled and shook his head.

"What do we do now?" Caesar asked, taking a step toward Max.

"Hey. Hold up, big boy," Max hopped off the table and backed up underneath the hanging, empty picture frame, "It's perfectly simple."

"Tell us," Amanda squealed.

"Last figment standing wins," Max jumped onto the wall and dipped his toe in the painting. He looked over his shoulder. "Oh. Be, uh, careful with that Babydoll *thing* on the table. It's a bit... *peculiar*."

"What?" Caesar asked.

"Welcome to Pure Dark. See ya."

Max jumped head-first into the picture frame. His skull broke apart and turned to paint, forming a rendition of his face on the canvas.

The rest of his body - from his shoulders and arms, down through his torso, waist and legs - splattered into a perfectly-formed oil painting of himself.

Max was no more.

The painting was all that was left. Exactly as it had been when everyone entered the room an hour or so ago.

Caesar turned to Nisa, Chloe, Spunx, and Amanda Triptych.

They all, in turn, looked at Babydoll lying in the middle of the table. Its wonky eye lilted at them.

Caesar grabbed a syringe from the table. It still had a quarter-barrel of purple blood-infused opium left in it. "Okay, so, it's a fight to the death."

Nisa spotted Caesar's gaping wound between his legs, "I've already died once, Mr. Caesar. I don't want to die again. It seems you've been emasculated."

"You shut the fuck up, bitch," Caesar roared.

"Hey, faggots. Wait, wait," Spunx hopped onto the table top and walked around Babydoll. She pressed the side of her face against its body.

ZIPPP!

Electric sparks burst out between Babydoll and Spunx, singing her fur, "Gaaooww, motherfucker."

She stabbed Babydoll in the face with her claws, "Cunt," A piece of plastic broke away from the mouth, revealing the flesh surrounding the left side of its jaw.

"Huuuuuuuuhhhhh," Babydoll breathed.

"Baaaabbydolll."

Spunx jumped back and screeched, "What the in the name of gay shit is that shit?!"

"That guy said not to touch it, or disturb it," Amanda looked out of the window and saw a fireball erupt in the sky, "Look."

Everyone turned to the window.

"The comet," Amanda gasped. "It's heading straight for us."

Caesar launched himself over the table and grabbed Chloe's plastic blow-up head, "Anyone mind if I do this bitch, first?"

"It's just a blow-up doll," Amanda shrugged her shoulders and surreptitiously swiped a used syringe from the tabletop, "Go for it."

Caesar jabbed Chloe's face with the syringe. The needle bounced off the inflated plastic.

JAB-SQUEAK. JAB-SQUEAK!

"The fucker won't burst."

"For AIDS's sake, *faggot*," Spunx chewed off one of her claws and held it between her teeth. "Lemme try. Move."

Caesar held Chloe up by her shoulders. Spunx inhaled and aimed her claw at the plastic doll.

PTCHOO-BOINNGGG!

The claw bounced off the plastic, hit the adjacent wall and stabbed into Babydoll's forehead. The shell of its face cracked and fell apart, revealing ghostly-white bone.

"Motherfucking *homosexualists*," Spunx squealed and ran over to Amanda, "Quick. Pick me up."

She lifted Spunx under the arms and held her to the Chloe's face.

"Hello, cunt." Spunx took a swipe at the blow-up doll's face

SCHWIPP! SCHWAAPP!

Her claws couldn't penetrate the plastic nor burst the doll. Chloe turned her head and opened her mouth.

Spunx growled at the doll, her predatory feline instincts overcame her, "Put me down."

"No, pop the bitch open," Amanda yelled.

"Unhand me at once."

Amanda dropped Spunx to the floor.

"Miaaaooowwww," Spunx turned around and stabbed Amanda in the knee, "*Fuck you.*"

"Gahhhhh," Amanda stepped back as the skin on her leg liquefied and bubbled. "You fucking stabbed me."

"Yes."

Caesar looked down and shouted at Spunx,"You venomous little shit."

WHACK!

He kicked Spunx into the air. She crashed back first against the wall.

Nisa backed up and watched Amanda's right leg melt up the floor, "Oh my G-God."

WHVOOOM! Nisa's hand caught fire. She wafted it away from her face.

Chloe held out her inflatable plastic hands and tried to scoop Spunx from the floor. The fluffy little rodent darted away and swiped at her, "Get away from me, you plastic lesbian."

PTCHOO-PTCHOO

Two more claws fired Chloe's way - both bounced off her plastic. She marched toward Caesar and, with a lifeless expression on her crudely-formed face, wrapped her hands around Caesar's neck.

She squeezed as hard as she could.

"Amanda," Nisa cried, crouching beside her, "You're melting."

"H-Help m-meee," she squealed as her waist meshed into the floor. She kept the top half of her body held up by her hands. Her guts and intestines roped from her severed torso.

Nisa frowned and held her upturned palm to her face. "Close your eyes, sweetheart."

Amanda shut her eyelids, "Do it."

WHOOOOOOOSSHHH

Nisa blew a vicious wave of fire over Amanda's putrefying body, killing her instantly.

WHVOOOM! The table caught fire. The skirting board and curtains set ablaze.

"Shit," Caesar jumped back, "The dining room's on fire!"

Nisa turned her face and fiery palm toward Chloe, "Hey, rubber woman."

Chloe turned around. A painted "gasp" formed over her fake face.

WHOOOOSH!

Nisa blew the fire into Chloe's face and body. She didn't catch fire. The flames only exacerbated the fire creeping up the wall.

Caesar and Spunx ran out of the dining room, toward the hall, "The place is going up."

Chloe and Nisa turned to one another.

"Let's take this outside," Nisa gasped. Chloe bowed her head and made for the exit.

"Before you go," Nisa approached Chloe, who turned around with a confused expression on its face.

"Just one thing," she blew the fire out in her palm and reached between Chloe's plastic, inflatable legs.

Chloe raised an eyebrow.

"Enjoy your flight," Nisa winked as she yanked on the valve between Chloe's legs.

SQUEEEEEEEEEEEEEE-POP!

A prolonged gust of air shot out from her open valve. Her body flew into the air like a rocketing balloon and whizzed out through the shattered window.

Nisa turned to the table top and saw Babydoll's broken, fleshy face lying still, "I guess you lost."

Babydoll didn't respond. Its glistening flesh from the partly shattered skull dripped to the table cloth.

Nisa dashed out of the room.

CRASSHHHHHHH!

The left section of the mansion crumbled down around itself. Nisa raced as fast as she could along the grand hall. The flames licked across both walls, shattering the glass of the oil paintings.

"Help. Help."

The entrance door didn't get any closer. Nisa ran faster. The walls of the hallway closed in and burst into flames.

"Help me. Heeeeelllppp."

BANG-CRACK-SMASSSHH!!!

The walls inhaled and pressed against Nisa's arms as she ran. The pictures on the wall laughed at her as the heat melted her skin away.

Still, she continued to run but the door didn't get any closer.

Nisa could see Spunx and Caesar push the door open, "Caesar. Wait for me."

He turned around and pushed the door open. "Why the fuck should I? I'm about to win."

Nisa's legs spun around and around as she tried to reach the door, "Wait."

CRUNCH-SPATCHH!

Her knee bone burst out through the skin, followed by her shins and heels. She wedged herself forward, breaking her forearms.

CRACK! CRICK!

Her skull punctured inward, squeezing out her eyeballs. All she had left was her fingers. She squeezed them together and detonated herself.

KA-BOOOOM!

Caesar dived through the door as the hallway puked out a massive fireball of dead Nisa.

Caesar tumbled along the gravel driveway. Two horses neighed and yelped and ran off into the fields.

Spunx landed to her feet and swished her claws at the horses as they ran off. "Yeah, that's right you equine faggots. Fuck off."

ROOOOOOOOOAAAAAAAARRRRRRRR"

Spunx turned around and looked up at the beautiful night sky. She raised her eyebrows. Her jaw dropped at the visual spectacle.

"My God," she squeaked to herself, "Look at it. *It's beautiful.*"

The gigantic comet rumbled toward the Earth several hundred thousand miles away in the night sky.

It was headed straight for *Waddling Gate*.

"Caesar, you homo," Spunx pointed her claw at the orange fireball lighting up the sky, "Look at that fucking thing.

Caesar turned around and held his palm over his eyes. "Holy shit. You're right. It's wonderful."

"I'm coming home, *Homophagea K-Twelve*," Spunx muttered under her fishy breath, "Spunx is coming home."

Caesar turned around and looked at Spunx, confused, "Coming home?"

"Yes, I was meant to go home, you cunt," she held a claw up at the comet and turned to Caesar, "But now home is coming to *me*."

"Fuck that," Caesar held the syringe at Spunx, "I'm gonna turn you into fluffy ukulele picks, you miserable little bag of shit."

SWISH!"

Caesar took a swipe at Spunx with the syringe. He kept himself bent and hopped after her. She jumped back onto her hind legs and tore off a claw between her teeth, "I wouldn't do that if I were you, you gay rope of jizz."

"No?" Caesar swiped at her again, "Why not?"

"Because if you get one of my fuckin' claws in you, you're dead."

PTCHOOO!

Caesar dived onto his side. The claw shot past him and jutted into a tree trunk.

"Shit, shit, shit," Spunx chased her tail in anger and tried to kill it, "Fucking gay turds."

Caesar looked at the tree trunk. The bark liquefied and glooped down the trunk, sizzling into the grass, "Jesus Christ."

"See, fag?" Spunx did a merry little dance and courtesied. She flicked a claw from her paw and approached Caesar as he sat on the ground, "Now, come here for a murdering."

Caesar hung his head and accepted his fate, "Please, make it quick."

"Oh, don't worry, faggot," Spunx tried not to cackle, "Anywhere I stab you will result in instant fucking death."

She held up her claw and prepared to swipe at Caesar, "Nighty-night. You gay, bald fuck."

SCHPLATTTTTT!!!

Spunx exploded. First her lungs through her coat, then her head, sending her brains into the sky. Her torso and waist blasted apart, covering the ground in acid.

Caesar rolled back and got a few drops of her venom on his arm. The spots sizzled and chewed through his skin. He dragged it through the wet grass and brushed the acid from his arm.

"Jesus Christ."

He looked to the flaming mansion to see a tiny, plastic Babydoll crawling from out of the fiery door.

"Oh f-fuck me," Caesar climbed to his feet and held the syringe at the toy. It crawled down the steps and along the gravel.

KA-SMASSSSHHH!

The fire gnawed through the hinges of the mansion door, sending it crashing down a few inches behind Babydoll.

"Babydoll?"

"Dad-da..."

Caesar kept the syringe held toward it, "What did you do to Spunx?"

"Cat explodey," Babydoll giggled and pressed its plastic finger against its temple. Its voice sounded pre-recorded. All that was missing was the pull-string.

Caesar closed his eyes and screamed. The furious eruption from the comet pierced through his ears.

"Daddy," Babydoll recited, its wonky eye wavering as it crawled along the gravel.

"Gaahh, no. No."

Caesar fell to his knees, the syringe in his right fist, "Nuh, nuh, my h-head."

Babydoll arrived eight feet away from Caesar. He held his head in his hands and let out a blood-curdling scream.

"No, no," He wailed in severe pain, "It's in my h-head."

Babydoll rolled onto its back. The comet thundered through the sky. It was only a matter of a few minutes before it hit the Earth.

Babydoll lifted its arms and reached for the comet. It giggled.

"N-Nooo," Caesar fell to his front and scrambled toward Babydoll with his hands. He kept the syringe held in his right hand as he pulled forward, "Y-You're not going to w-win."

Babydoll gargled and kicked its feet into the air. The comet hurtled to toward the Earth.

KA-BOOOOOOOOOOMMMM

The mansion exploded. The brickwork shattered, sending bits of the structure crashing onto itself. The fire chewed through the roof and pulverised the windows.

"Yaarrgghh," Caesar screamed at the top of his lungs as he reached Babydoll. He lifted the syringe into the air and daggered between the doll's eyes.

"Bwwaarrgghh," Babydoll's eyes popped out of their enclosures.

PLUNGE!

Caesar jammed his thumb on the plunger, filling its face with opium, "Take it! Take it all you freaky fuck—"

KA-SPLAA-AA-ATTCCHH!

Caesar's head exploded like a smashed cantaloupe. His limbs sizzled into the gravel. Babydoll gurgled and kicked his feet with excitement.

The comet was seconds away from impact.

Babydoll's body rumbled and shuddered. The plastic fell away from its face, revealing a set of whiskers and leather straps across its face and over its head.

"Oh, no. Doctor Long, get in here," screamed a man's voice from the comet, "His brain is hemorrhaging. He's going into shock."

Babydoll was now dexterous enough to bend its limbs and torso. It rolled to its side as it vibrated and curled up into the fetal position.

The comet's deafening rumble grew so loud it all became silent.

A set of beeps raced faster and faster, quickening their pace. The comet grew larger and larger in the sky, illuminating Babydoll. The fleshy ball focused its eyes on the blinding white light.

Babydoll smiled and closed his eyes. The sky swelled and ruptured. Several tubes of brain matter seeped out from between the twinkling stars.

The night sky now resembled the interior of a vast cranium. The fleshy tubes pulsated and shot electric sparks around the sky. Like little shooting stars.

"What is it, nurse?" Dr Long's voice hastened, "Show me."

The beeps quickened. The electric sparks rattled through the brain-laden sky.

Only five seconds from the comet's impact.

"Quick, move to the operating theater," Dr Long's voice shattered around the sky, "ICU Three, now."

"Neurology team on standby."

"Sweetie? It's okay," a maternal voice came from the comet as it roared toward Babydoll, "Charlie? If you can hear me, we're right with you, okay? No need to be afraid."

BOOM.

The comet struck the planet's surface.

Babydoll's body bleached out into a glorious white light. Everything was white. Not a sound.

Nothing but a beautiful, zen-like serenity.

PURE DARK
VOL.3

Chapter 1

The Church of Charlie Ferrari

Dr. Jennifer Long walked into the hospital waiting room. Rhonda Ferrari sat in the corner with a nervous expression on her face. She watched Charlie's son, Johnny, play with the stuffed cat on the corner table.

The little boy didn't speak much. He had a condition which meant speech was all but non-existent. Only in cases of complete silence would he let out a scream.

The radio in the waiting room was playing, allaying any anxiety on Johnny's behalf.

"Welcome back ladies and gentlemen. I'm Sebastian Sibald, and this is *The Solitude Hour*, a chance for you to keep calm and reflect on what's going on in your life—"

Dr. Long turned off the radio and clutched her clipboard to her chest. She noticed Johnny playing with his toy by the table.

"Oh, this must be Johnny?"

"Yes, that's right," Rhonda said, deep in contemplation. She was on the verge of bursting into tears.

Dr. Long walked over to Johnny and crouched beside him, "Hey, Johnny."

He didn't say anything. The stuffed black and white cat was far more entertaining to him.

"You're here to see your Daddy?"

Johnny nodded and bopped the cat up and down on the table. He pushed one of its paws to its mouth and pressed down on its head. His fingers pinched the fur and aimed the cat's face to Dr. Long.

He mocked a spitting noise, "Ptchoo."

She looked confused as he picked up a snow globe from the table.

"Oh, that's pretty," Dr. Long took it from his hand, "Is this for your daddy?"

Johnny didn't confirm who the recipient was. Instead, he became fascinated with her stethoscope.

"Oh, this?" She looked down and picked the end up.

Johnny nodded and held out his hand. She pinched the diaphragm and handed it to him. He smiled and breathed on it.

"Here," Dr. Long removed the ear tips from around her neck. She pushed them into his ears, "Say something."

Johnny blinked at her, not sure what to do.

Dr. Long pointed at the diaphragm, "Speak into the circle thing with the bell."

Johnny took a deep breath, his voice ready to scream, "Hello—"

He tore the ear tips from his head and screamed. His voice was so loud through the device he could barely stand it.

"That's enough," Rhonda yelled at the pair. She rose to her feet in defiance, "Dr. Long?"

"Yes, I'm sorry," she took the stethoscope from Johnny, replaced it around her neck and walked over to Rhonda.

"Johnny, you know you shouldn't play with adult things."

He looked down with an apologetic look on his face. Dr. Long took pity on him and turned to Rhonda, "I'm sorry, it was my fault."

"Just tell me how my brother is doing."

"He's with the neurosurgeons right now."

"You call me up to tell me you need to see me, and all you can say is that he's with the surgeons?"

"It's a bit more complicated than that," Dr. Long said. "Look, can we talk outside, away from Johnny?"

"Right." Rhonda wasn't happy, but she stepped out into the corridor with her.

Dr. Long closed the door shut and perused her clipboard, "Mrs. Ferrari, I'm afraid there's no easy way to say this—"

"—I've been waiting here for half an hour, so please get to the point."

"Okay, it's the least I can do—"

"—Why isn't he resting up?"

Dr. Long frowned and looked down the corridor. She saw a surgeon a few feet away walking toward them.

"His MRI scan revealed a swelling."

"Yes, I remember you saying."

"A tumor. In the back of his brain, near the cerebellum."

"Ah, Doctor," a big man with a beard said. He looked as if he'd performed surgery a zillion times in his career, "The patient?"

"Yes, Mr. Mulberry," Dr. Long said. "Theater one one seven."

"Thank you," he nodded at Dr. Long and made his way down the corridor, toward the operating theater.

Rhonda looked confused, "A tumor?"

"Yes, we've been prepping him since I called you. They are going to remove it now."

"Oh, Jesus," Rhonda lowered herself to the corridor bench and placed her hands on her lap, "Is he going to be okay?"

"We're going to do our best," Dr. Long took a seat next to Rhonda and tried for a smile, "If you'd like to wait, then that's fine. But it could be an hour or two."

"He's still not out of his coma," Rhonda cried.

"I know," Dr. Long's pocket buzzed. She reached into her coat and took out a pager, "I'm needed in the theater."

She stood up and looked down at the poor woman crying into her hands, "I'll send someone down with a cup of water. I'll be back soon, okay?"

"O-Okay."

"Great," Dr. Long sprinted toward the operating theater.

Theater 117

Mr. Mulberry, the lead neurosurgeon, snapped his gloves on his hands. A face mask adorned his nose and mouth.

His colleague, Thatch, rolled a trolley with various cutting tools laid across the top.

The room was immaculate and white. Several diagnostic machines whirred around and emitted a low hum.

"A pretty straightforward procedure," Thatch peered at Dr. Long and sized her up, "Ah, you're here."

"Yes, sorry. I was held up talking to the patient's next of kin."

"Paperwork, please," Mulberry noticed an unusual object resting on Charlie's body. A snow globe, with a small crucifix inside surrounded by snow.

"Can we remove this, please?"

"Certainly," Dr. Long took the object from Charlie and passed her clipboard to Thatch. He took a look and then scanned the screen above the patient's head.

"Seems straightforward enough," Thatch handed the clipboard back to Dr. Long.

The comatose Charlie Ferrari lay face down on the bed. Two metal rods held his head still.

A tall metal rod clamped to a trolley loomed over him. Several bulbs shone down onto the back of his bald head.

In a curious vision of emancipation, his Mohawk had been completely sheared off. It took its place on a tray near the wash basin in the corner of the room.

A red line streaked across the back of his scalp.

Mulberry placed the fingers on his left hand around it and produced a cutting device with his right.

"Making the incision now."

He scored along the line, tearing open the skin. Dr. Long turned away, "Am I needed any longer?"

"No," Thatch moved over to Mulberry, "That is all. Thank you, Doctor."

"Very well."

Dr. Long stepped into the corridor and closed her eyes. She took a deep breath. A moment of solace in an otherwise emotionally eventful day. Not least because she had to attend a funeral this afternoon.

"Jennifer?"

She opened her eyes and nearly shit herself, taken by surprise by her boss, Dr. Langham, "Oh, David. You frightened me."

"Are you okay?"

"Yes, yes, I'm fine."

"I wanted to talk to you about Mr. Ferrari."

"What about him?" Dr. Long caught Rhonda looking over at her from the bench a few feet away.

"A week since he was admitted. His blood work is still reporting a significant quantity of opiates."

Dr. Long swallowed hard. She knew why this was but couldn't tell her boss the truth. "I know, it's puzzling."

Dr. Langham shook his head and tried for a professional stab at humor, "Anyone would think someone was tampering with his IV or something. Haha."

It took her a few seconds longer than it should have to realize it was a joke, "Oh. Haha, yes."

She looked away and widened her eyes, relieved she'd not been caught.

"Refresh all the instruments you're using, please," Dr. Langham said. "I'll do the tool audit myself."

"Yes, sir," Dr. Long said. "Oh, I just wanted to remind you."

"Yes?"

"I'm clocking off at one, today."

"Yes, I know," Dr. Langham said. "I remember."

"Thanks."

***

"Any plans for your impending week off, Gideon?" Mulberry asked as he sliced through Charlie's skull with the surgical saw.

"Ah, the wife wants to go to Fallopia for the week," Thatch said.

SCHAAWWW-CRUUNNNKKK!

Mulberry removed a ten-inch rectangular section of the skull away. A thin layer of cranial slime roped out from the cavity. He placed the removed section of skull onto the metal tray.

"I hear Fallopia is very nice this time of year."

"Really?" Thatch looked up at the monitor on the wall. It displayed a close-up of the section removed from Charlie's skull, "Yeah, well she won't have it. They'll be serving lobster thermidor and Gairloch prawns there. That's all she cares about. Food, glorious food."

"Ugh, that's disgusting," Mulberry spat. "Big, red mutant creatures, those lobsters."

"Not a fan, then?"

Charlie's eyeballs fluttered ever-so-slightly. He remained completely unconscious.

"Gosh, no," Mulberry sliced away at the transparent sack that covered the exposed part of the patient's brain, "Okay, going in now. Camera please, angle-in on one-one-eight."

Thatch angled the camera to the side of Charlie's cavity, "So, I say, you're not a fan, Morton?"

Mulberry pinched at the sack and wrapped it over the rectangular hole. "A fan of what?"

"Lobster."

"Dear God, no. An ugly proposition. Ugly red creatures to a man."

Thatch sniggered and took a peek at the screen, "Aha. There's the little fella," He pointed to a spongy white blob in amongst Charlie's gray matter.

"Yep, should probably come at it from the side," Mulberry scooped the jellied object with the end of a blade. He looked into Charlie's head, "Right next to the cerebellum, Mr. Ferrari. You don't mess around, do you?"

Thatch giggled, "With that amount of junk going through his system, I'd be surprised if he can hear you."

"Hello?" Mulberry shouted into the hole to little reaction, "Nah, he can't hear us. Needle, please."

"Yep," Thatch picked up the cutting device and passed it to Mulberry, "Okay, Mr. Ferrari. Stay perfectly still, now."

Thatch contained his smirk. Mulberry nearly lost it laughing at his colleague's joke. They both remained professional and chewed back their hilarity.

"Right," Mulberry leaned into the hole in Charlie's head as he sawed around the tumor, "Let's clear this brain of yours."

***

The sharp end of a chrome-plated knife.

A coarse patch of skin.

The blade lowered to the pink fibers among the fine hairs growing from the surface.

It sliced through the skin, causing it to bleed on either side of the sharp edge.

The knife traveled further and further along the skin. The layers split apart and bled as the blade cut through it.

Charlie Ferrari sat on a chair, completely naked. His right foot perched on top of the dining table in front of him.

A low hum moved around the pure, white room.

Charlie had no hair. No green Mohawk.

He didn't know how he got here. The only items on the perfect white table in front of him were a knife and fork. The latter remained untouched.

A jug of water and an empty glass sat behind the empty plate on the table.

Charlie stopped slicing through his shin when he saw a silver-haired man in a suit walk into his field of vision. He stood behind the table and smiled, "Good morning, Charlie."

Confused, he looked up at the suited man, "Who are you?"

"Oh, do forgive my absence of manners," the suited man placed his palms on the table top and leaned in, "My name is Max Dark."

"Who?" Charlie returned to slicing through his right shin. The blood ran up the underside of his calf and dripped to the floor. Max looked down and tutted.

"Can I ask what you're doing, Charlie?"

"I'm hungry," he said as he attempted to control his right eye's involuntary spasms, "I'm, I'm going to have something to eat. It's been a week."

"Yes, you must be ravenous," Max stood up straight and rubbed his hands, "What's wrong with your eye?"

The right side of Charlie's face spasmed. He tried to mute the muscular convulsion by squeezing his cheek, "Nothing, nothing."

"I didn't know you had a facial tic, Charlie?"

"I d-don't," Charlie clamped both hands to his head and wrestled against the contortions. The evil humming noise from the other side of the walls grew louder.

"Listen to me," Max said.

Charlie released his head from his hands. He pinched the bloodied knife handle between his thumb and forefinger, "Who are you?"

"A week ago, you used, didn't you? You picked it up

from your supplier and he told you to shoot up in the car. Do you remember that?"

"Sort of," Charlie sliced away at his shin. It didn't seem to faze him in the slightest. No pain, no trauma.

Lots of blood, though.

Max clapped his hands together in anger. It caught Charlie's attention. Long enough for him to stop burrowing through his right leg, anyway.

"Sort of? What do you mean *sort of*? You either remember or you don't?"

"Look!" Charlie yelled, impatiently, "Can't you see I'm trying to have dinner, here?

"Damn it, Charlie. Answer my question. What else do you remember?"

Charlie blinked and thought over his answer. He kept the blade held at his foot, "I injected the shit. It felt great. Felt like my organs fused together. Felt like death—"

"—Did you know Oksana killed herself the day after you overdosed?"

"What?" Charlie kicked the table toward Max a few inches, "What the fuck?"

"That's not the fun part, Charlie."

"What the *fuck* happened to Oksana, fuck stick?"

"She shot herself in the head. She was found by her mother the morning after."

"What happened to my son? Where is he?" Charlie jumped to his feet. He'd failed to remember he'd sawed through the flesh of his right shin.

"Gaahhh."

He buckled and hit the floor, ass-first. Max laughed at his misfortune, "Oh, Charlie, Charlie…"

"What the fuck?" He scrambled to his feet and prepared himself to hit Max.

"You gonna hit me?"

"Tell me what happened to my son," Charlie clenched his fist and exhaled, "You fucking prick."

"Charlie, sit back down. I need to tell you something."

"Fuck you."

Charlie lunged toward Max and threw a vicious punch at his face. Max didn't seem perturbed about this action *at all.*

Charlie's fist flew through Max's face like a swinging bulldozer flying through a cloud of smoke.

He fell forward and turned around to Max. He was unscathed and, more to the point, completely untouched.

"It's no use, mate. You can't touch me. Sit down."

Charlie took another swing. Max didn't even flinch. The fist whooshed through his face like it wasn't even there.

Max grabbed his hips and acted put-out, "Happy now?"

Charlie looked around at the white room. Fear set in straight away.

He sat in the chair, "What's going on? I've been in this room for what feels like years."

"Are you ready to listen, now?"

"Yes. Tell me what's going on."

Max folded his arms and took a deep breath, "After your overdose, you fell into a coma."

"A coma?

"Yes," Max revealed. "You're still in it."

"I'm *still in it?*"

"Yeah, they induced you," Max chuckled with near embarrassment, "Man, that Angel O'Deth stuff really does kick some serious arse, you know."

Charlie held up his arm and looked at the track marks, "Jesus Christ."

"I'll come to *that* in a moment," Max said. "Rhonda is in the waiting room with Johnny, now."

"Rhonda's there?"

"Yes."

"I can't believe it."

"Charlie, my friend, you won't *believe* the shit I've had to put up with since they induced you."

"What are you talking about?" Charlie asked. He was in

no fit state to comprehend what was going on. Even if he was, there was little he could do about it.

"What I'm about to reveal to you is going to sound strange. Actually, it'll sound bonkers, but I'm afraid it's the truth."

"I can take it," Charlie said as the right side of his face twitched again, "Ugh, my head hurts."

"Ignore it. They're removing the tumor from your brain."

"Tumor?" Charlie stuttered and grabbed his right cheek with his fingers, "Mwaaarrghhhsshhhh."

"It'll hurt for a while, but I know you can hear me. So let me speak," Max stepped forward and pressed his forefinger to his head, "I am a figment of your imagination."

"Gnnneerrgghhh," Charlie squealed as he pushed both his cheeks up and down his face. "Gwaarrrrr."

"I don't exist. Purely a result of your imagination. I'm stuck in your head along with all these inexplicable creatures and people and, uh, fucked up *stuff* your brain is inventing."

"Whaaarrrrrrrsshhh," Charlie's mouth widened released a flood of thick saliva. Much of it gushed down his bare chest. He pressed his hands into his face and yanked the skin around, trying to normalize himself.

Max continued, "You *need* to wake the fuck up, Charlie. We need you to wake up. If you don't, we're all fucked. Sooner or later your mind will create a situation or *thing* that's going to take us down. We've all held out as long as we can, but time is running out."

Charlie ran his fingernails from the top of his scalp down under his chin. The skin burst apart, spitting out blood. "Whhhhaaaaaaaa."

"Charlie, please, wake up. That pretty ginger doctor of yours is working with your dealer. They're keeping the heroin running through your veins. You'll be in a coma until they're stopped. None of us in here can stop them.

I'm stuck in your head permanently."

Charlie slipped his fingers through the tears in his skin and screamed blue murder. The front of his face peeled down over his bloodied head and collected into his palms.

Max grinned, "I think I know how I can get you to wake up. I have to suppress the urge for you to remain under. I have that under control. You'll know it when you feel it. It'll feel like a million red-hot irons puncturing your body. And a final blow to the brain. Can you hear me? This is important."

Charlie clawed away at the flesh stuck to his skull. Before long, the ivory-white bone pushed through. The skull nodded and tilted its head.

"Parts of reality are starting to manifest into your head. I just need a sign. Send me a message. I'll find it and I'll use it to give you the signal. That's your cue to wake up."

Charlie stopped screaming. His bloodied skull stared back at Max and sized him up.

"You'll give me the sign?" Charlie's skull asked in its deep voice, "Like red-hot irons puncturing my brain?"

"Yes, hundreds of red-hot irons. When you feel that sensation, I want you to scream as loud as you can and kick and punch everything in sight. It's our best shot."

Charlie lowered his skull and sighed. The rest of the blood in his eye sockets poured onto the floor, "Glllawwwwww."

"In the meantime, if you could try *not* to think or imagine anything nasty or troublesome, then that'd be great."

"Ahhhmmmm," Charlie produced a deathly-growl as he stared at his knees.

"I'll leave you to your meal," Max winked at Charlie and tapped the table top with his knuckle. "See you soon, Charlie."

"Blllueergggghhh."

He looked up. Max had gone.

Charlie slammed the heel of his right foot against the table edge and placed the knife into the cavity. He yelled as he sawed through the bone.

CLATCH!

His right foot came off in his hand. He placed the bloodied foot onto the plate.

Charlie hoisted himself onto the table. The blood from the end of his leg puked across the white floor and up the legs of the table.

He picked up his foot and moved the toes between his teeth.

CHOMP. CHOMP

He munched away on his foot and spat the bones to the floor. He released the stump from his hands and grabbed his right, footless leg and bent it over his left.

The blade of the knife began to cut through his thigh. Through the skin and into the flesh. Globs of blood ran down each side and splashed to the table top.

He reached into the cut with both hands and tore the flesh out between his fingers.

MUNCH, MUNCH.

His skull chewed on the thigh flesh. As he chewed, he snapped his thigh bone from his groin and threw the slaps of skin and ivory to the floor.

Charlie swallowed and wiped what should have been his lip. Instead, he smeared blood and bile above his row of exposed teeth.

Charlie shuffled backward with his buttocks and leaned back on his left elbow. He looked down the length of his body.

One leg missing.

Charlie sat up straight and pinched the foreskin on the end of his penis. He lifted it up, stretching the skin out a few inches. The bulbous head punctured through the skin.

He sawed through the base of his member with the knife, a clean cut. His penis came off in his hands, which moved to his mouth.

CHOMP, CHOMP.

The taste of fortnight-old ejaculate hindered an otherwise pleasurable feast. It wasn't long before he was able to swallow.

Next up, his stomach. Charlie lay down on his back for this one.

His left hand grabbed around his belly as his right hand circled the blade of the knife above his belly button.

That damn umbilical cord was still attached, like a messy string of black electrical tape. Where it came from was anyone's guess.

The blade cut through the skin and deepened into the flesh as it travelled along.

He reached into his body with his left hand and felt around. Something squishy and oblong.

Charlie grabbed it in his hand and lifted it from his body. His stomach, with the duodenum piping back through the cut. He yanked on it and it pulled his esophagus back, causing him to choke.

The blade did its work and cut through the fleshy pipe, severing the stomach.

It wasn't to be consumed, though. Where else would the food go? Charlie set it beside his hip and slipped both hands into the cavity.

Reaching up, he grabbed two soft, heaving balloons in both hands. Closing his eyes, he screamed as he yanked and detached them from their home.

Two beautiful coats of sloppy red meat stared back at them as he hung them above his head.

The lungs.

MUNCH, MUNCH.

The left lung was bigger. Tender, cooked to perfection. In the real world, it would have been raw. Inside Charlie, it was a delicacy and slipped with ease down his throat. The tender flesh melted on his tongue.

The second lung was blacker than the first. Char-grilled, noticeably from years of smoking, gave the jacket of flesh a distinct barbecue flavor.

MUNCH, CHEW.

Pangs of blood spat from the skull that gorged down on the fillet steak that once provided his body with air. He swallowed it down and let out a burp.

Charlie wiped his palms on his sides. The skin took away most of the human remains that had collected over the grooves of his hands and fingers.

Back into the stomach slit, he took hold of his ribcage in both hands and pushed them through his chest. The skin tore apart, coming out of his body in much the way mayonnaise would through an air vent's grill in a wall.

The rib cage was of little use to Charlie. But it did make for an exquisite protection device for his severed stomach to his left.

He felt something beating through his spine, against the table top.

Charlie clutched the ball of flesh and held it in his hand. His heart.

His jaw yawned open and took it in. The exposed front teeth clamped down on the aortic valve. The chewing action tore the left and right ventricle apart like a chicken wing.

It made the organ easier to consume.

Right ventricle, then the left.

Charlie rolled to his right as he swallowed the last remnants of the jellied organ. The food ran its way through his neck and down the diaphragm, finally wedging itself into the stomach that lay next to him.

Charlie would have closed his eyes if he possessed eyelids. Or eyes, for that matter.

Instead, he lay the back of his skull against the table top and stared at the ceiling.

There was no ceiling.

White light, the same as the walls and the ground.

He lifted the knife up to his neck and sliced away. The sharp blade ran further and further down as he cut from left to right.

Only the cervical vertebrae kept his skull attached to the rest of his devoured body. He placed his fingers, one above, the other, and…

SNAP.

The spine broke in two, releasing his body from his skull. The weight of his right leg caused the human tarpaulin of consumed organs, flesh and skin to slip off the table.

The complicated arrangement of remains slapped to the floor, splashing into the pool of blood.

Charlie's jaw hit the table top. There was no moving to be done.

Permanently facing the bright white light of the infinite ceiling was his only future.

"Charlie Ferrari," a whisper whirled around the room as if singing a lullaby. "Our Lord and savior. Deliver us from Pure Dark."

Charlie's skull lay perfectly still on the table.

The arrangement of his skull and what remained of his body had the appearance of being crucified.

His arms were stretched out. His hands hung over either side of the table, bloodied.

His chest and torso draped over the table, letting out blood onto the chair.

The right leg lay across the wet, red floor at a right angle to the rest of his body slouching a few inches above.

"Rest now, dear Charlie. For we have faith in you."

Chapter 2

Stun of a Gun

Welcome to *Waddling Gate Cemetery*. Home to over ten thousand lost souls buried in this three-acre plot. If you didn't opt for cremation then taking your place in the soil at this hallowed ground is costly.

The cemetery was built five hundred years ago. Until a recent lighting strike, it even had a chapel. A fine place to pay your respects.

Today, the late Morton Mulberry is being lowered into the ground. His family demanded a private service, which was understandable.

Morton was something of a public figure. A true industrial pioneer. His company, which, to this day, continues to thrive, manufactures chrome cutlery.

His wife of fifty-eight years, Ruby Mulberry (nee Triptych) stood by his side during numerous scandals. The family's history was full of them.

None of their four children worked. They didn't have to. In fact, today's send-off was the first time the entire family had been together for almost a decade.

"And so, in the sight of our lord and savior, Charlie Ferrari, we commit his body down to the ground. Ashes to ashes, dust to dust." The priest turned to Ruby, who hid her face from view. Her black veil obscured her distress.

Her twin daughters, Vesta and Tammy, cried for their father.

Ruby crouched to her knees and opened her hand. A chrome-plated spoon sat in her palm. Her husband had given it to her on their first courtship almost six decades ago.

The spoon dropped to the coffin's surface. "Sleep well, my sweet."

Caspian, the handsome, assumed patriarch of the family - in title only - stood by the grave and paid his respects. It was he who had made the funeral arrangements. He'd traveled from Paris and was the first on the scene when Morton passed away.

He glanced at his wristwatch. The disrespectful action confirmed what the rest of the family already knew about him. Caspian was duty-bound to attend but rarely saw eye to eye with his father. Having to attend the funeral was a chore.

This caused great consternation between him and his half-brother, Christian. The young man was twenty years his junior.

Christian was the youngest of the four siblings. An undergraduate at Oxford, he'd go far in the field of embryonic research. He'd always known that Ruby wasn't his real mother.

Morton had been confronted by his wife about the affair. That was seventeen years ago. The family, on the whole, had dark features. Christian was fair-haired and simply looked different.

Everyone in the family knew that Christian wasn't a genuine Mulberry.

The Red Shell hotel was a short walk from the cemetery. It wasn't worth taking the cars for a thirty-second drive. Besides, the walk was refreshing this early in the afternoon.

"Mom?" Tammy asked her mother, "Are you going to be all right tonight if Vesta and I go back to the house?"

"I'll be fine," Ruby hitched her dress as she walked along the grass, "But you'll stay for the next hour or so, won't you? Gideon Thatch is due to meet us there."

"Yes, we'll stay," Vesta said. "Is he here on official business?"

"I think so. He'll tell us what we need to know."

Christian walked with Caspian. The priest joined them and tried for a smile, "You know, boys, your father was a great man. He'll be sorely missed."

"We know," the brothers replied in unison.

Caspian wiped his cheek as the trio reached the gated entrance. A tall metal railing carried a *"Danger, electrified fence!"* sign.

"I didn't realize the gate was primed?" Christian looked shocked.

"Oh yes," the priest said. "Please, don't touch it. It'll give you a nasty shock."

He opened the large metal gate for the brothers to walk through.

"Thanks," Caspian made his way toward the road.

"You're very welcome."

"I have to ask. Why do you need to electrify the gate?"

The priest closed the gate shut, "Well, we've been having trouble with theft and all sorts, lately."

Christian felt spooked by the revelation, "Are people stealing bodies?"

"Sometimes. Mostly it's just nitwits gate-crashing and having fun with the headstones."

Ruby and her daughters approached the gate. The priest kept it open for them.

Vesta looked to the trees and noticed a woman, dressed in black and with long red hair and red lips, looking back at her.

"Who's that?"

Ruby stopped and looked toward the trees, "Who's *what?*"

Vesta pointed at the trees and looked at her sister, "Her. That woman over there."

"I don't see anyone there," Tammy quipped and resumed walking.

Vesta looked back at the trees. The flame-haired woman had gone, "Ugh, I must be seeing things."

"Looks like it's going to rain, soon," the priest smiled at the women as they made their way through the gate, "Let's get to the hotel before it buckets down."

***

The Red Shell hotel and restaurant. Quite why Caspian booked such a large reception room was any of the family's guess. Due to the size and grand nature of the place, it might have been more befitting for a larger group of mourners.

"Caspian's just showing off," Vesta whispered to her sister. She helped herself to a sausage roll and looked up at him from the food counter, "Typical. He doesn't visit us for ten years and when Dad dies, he's all over us."

"Right," Tammy downed her first flute of champagne, "But this is him, though. He paid for the service and all of this."

"I know," Vesta sobbed, "It's just that he could have shown his face more often."

"Hey, hey," Tammy put her flute down and gave her sister a hug, "We're here now."

"I miss Dad, Tammy. That's all."

"I know you do. We all do."

Ruby sat alone with a plate of finger food on her lap. She looked catatonic, staring into nothingness a few inches from her face. Deep in contemplation.

Caspian took a seat next to her and massaged her

shoulder, "Hey, mom. Are you okay?"

She didn't respond. A single tear rolled down her cheek. Ruby was a widow, now, and the procession allowed the reality to sink in.

She'd never see her husband, ever again.

To her, an afterlife wasn't a possibility. The family was religious, once upon a time. In today's world the kids had been brought up by their father to be inquisitive. It worked well for their careers and lives.

It worked less well for the staunch reverence of religion, and so it was swept under the carpet.

"Mom?" Caspian tried again.

Ruby couldn't speak. Instead, she cleared her throat and tried for some cheese on a cocktail stick.

She chewed on her food, lost in her own thoughts.

Christian sat alone, playing with his mobile phone. This teenager hadn't been brought up like his elder siblings. If there were a hint of slowing down or boredom, he'd immediately revert to his phone for company.

Caspian wasn't too happy about this, "Oi, mate."

"What?" Christian looked up.

"C'mon, man. It's Dad's funeral. Have a bit of respect, yeah?"

"What do you mean respect?" Christian snapped. "Like you?"

"What's that meant to mean?"

"You know what it means," Christian blurted back with a venomous amount of snark.

Caspian stood up and removed his hand from his mother's shoulder, "No. I don't know what it means. Tell me."

A woman stood in the doorway and watched the brothers about to argue. Tammy and Vesta spotted her immediately. The strange guest's appearance failed to stop the show between the boys.

"Christian?" Caspian asked, preparing himself for a fight.

Christian stood up and prodded his half-brother on the chest, "You're just after Dad's money. You know it. I know it. We all know it. It's the only reason you're here."

"Ahem." Vesta gave a polite cough and broke up the fight. She turned to the figure in the doorway. The woman from the graveyard.

Flame-haired, red-lipped. Beautiful.

"Can we help you?" Tammy asked the woman.

She smiled and removed her black veil. A white collar protruded from her jacket.

"I'm sorry to bother you all," she smiled and looked at Christian, "Could I come in? I was a friend of your father."

The family members turned to each other. No-one disapproved.

Caspian turned to her and pulled his suit down, stretching out the creases. This new woman could only lighten up the room if nothing else.

"Sure, why not? Help yourself to some champagne."

"Oh," the woman beamed at the food table. "Is that the placenta stuff?"

Christian smiled and flirted with her, "Yes, it is. Only the very best for our family."

"Look at her. The prissy little bitch," Vesta whispered to her sister.

"Really," Tammy checked the new woman out as she sauntered to the food table.

She picked out a flute and poured some champagne into it. Christian ogled her as she necked the champagne in one go.

"Whoa," she wiped her lips. "Just what I needed after the day I've had."

Caspian smiled and felt his heart flutter, "Good?"

The woman swallowed and wiped her mouth with a napkin, "It's wonderful. Tastes a bit like zinc, actually."

"Yeah, that's what we said."

"Sorry to be rude," Vesta piped up. "But, who are you?"

"Oh, I'm sorry," the stranger brushed her red hair back and rolled her shoulders, "I was a friend of your father's—"

"—Yeah, you said that already," Tammy snapped. "What are you doing here?"

"I wanted to pay my respects."

"The public service is the day after tomorrow, actually," Caspian revealed.

"Oh, I know. I'm sorry, it's just that Morton was a very dear friend of mine," she said and turned to Christian, "My name is Jennifer Long. I'm a doctor."

"Why are you looking at me like that?" Christian asked her. He felt spooked that this stranger in her thirties was taking an interest in him.

"I'm sorry, Christian, I know—"

"—How do you know my name?" he asked, getting angry. "How do you know my Dad?"

"Umm, excuse me?" came a voice from behind Jennifer. Everyone looked at the doorway, "Is this the Mulberry service?"

A balding man in his fifties smiled at everyone in the room. He squeezed the cardboard box in his hand, "Gideon Thatch. Mr. Mulberry's solicitor."

"Yes," Ruby rose to her feet and walked over to him, "Hello, Gideon."

"Ah, Mrs. Mulberry," Gideon made his way over to the writing desk, "Can I say how very sorry I am to learn of your husband's passing."

"It's okay, I'm over it now," Ruby lied. She wasn't over her late husband's death. It had been a week. She felt the need to show face in front of her family, "Can we get this over with, quickly?"

Gideon unlocked the briefcase that rest atop the cardboard box, "Certainly. This won't take a moment."

Ruby turned to her children - and Dr. Long - and pointed to the random chairs surrounding the table.

"Pull up a chair. Mr. Thatch is about to tell us of your

father's intentions."

"Yes, that's correct," Gideon took his seat at the desk and opened the large cardboard box. He took out six smaller boxes and laid them out side by side on the desk.

A lone sheet of paper sat beside them. He picked it up and smiled at the six people in front of him.

"Well?" Caspian folded his arms, eager to get the proceedings underway, "What's the story?"

Gideon took a deep breath, "As executor to the will, I am duty bound to relay to you the details of Morton Mulberry's wishes, in the event of his death."

Everyone's ears pricked up. Jennifer slid her chair next to Christian's and sat beside him. He looked away as she attempted to smile at him.

Ruby closed her eyes and expected a degree of comfort. She was sure to take care of her family after the will was read.

"Being of sound mind and body, I, Morton Mulberry, do bequeath my estate, fortune, and belongings to—"

Gideon left a pause. Everyone thought he was reading to himself. They had yet to learn that he had read the document many times over. The contents needed re-examining.

"—whomever is left *standing*."

"Eh?" Caspian asked on behalf of his family's bewilderment.

Gideon put the paper down and picked up the small boxes. He approached the family with them.

"Left standing?" Ruby was the most surprised of the bunch, "What are you talking about?"

Gideon passed one of the boxes to Caspian. It had his name written on the side in big, black marker.

"What's this?"

"Please, open it. But do not touch the contents."

Gideon proceeded to pass Ruby, Christian, Vesta, Tammy and Jennifer, their own boxes. They tore off the tape and pulled open the flaps.

Gideon returned to his seat and picked up the sheet of paper, "A message from Morton himself to be read at the execution of the will reads as follows."

Caspian's eyes widened as he looked inside the box. Vesta gasped. Tammy squealed. Ruby couldn't believe what she was seeing. Christian and Jennifer inspected each other's boxes.

They contained the same item.

"I am of the belief that my family has wished me ill-health for a while. They have not fully executed their duties in my time of ill health. Rest assured, this has not gone unnoticed."

"I don't believe this," Vesta cried.

Ruby closed her eyes and rested the box on her lap, "What is this?"

Gideon continued and tried to avoid any questions, "The fortune and estate are in my name. You presumed you'd all get a fair share of my estate. You presumed incorrectly. A general disregard toward me during my final months from each and every one of you, including my beloved wife, will now finally reap what it had always sowed."

"I don't get it?" Christian turned to Jennifer, "Why did you get one? You're not even family."

She turned away and listened to the reading.

"It is my prerogative that my true feelings come to light this day, the day of my funeral. I resent the fact that I have created a family that is intolerant of society. Apathetic toward charity. Certainly, ill-at-ease with respect, honour and due diligence where I was concerned. Therefore, whomever has been dutiful enough to attend is to be given a tool."

Gideon looked up from the paper, "That's those boxes I gave you."

Caspian reached into the box and pulled out the device. A small, black gun with two metal prongs.

"A stun gun?"

Vesta, Tammy, Ruby, Christian, and Jennifer each took out theirs.

"The challenge is to take place at the cemetery. The last person left standing will be in receipt of everything."

Vesta inspected her stun gun, "*Charlie Ferrari*," she exclaimed.

"Don't blaspheme, Vesta," Ruby snapped. "This is obviously some kind of sick joke—"

"—Note that this is *not* a joke," Gideon continued reading from the paper, "The last person left standing will inherit the estate and over one million pounds in hard currency."

The cogs in Caspian's imagination spun a million miles a minute, "A *million*?"

"They will get everything," Gideon finished reading.

Everyone turned to look at everyone else. This was some challenge.

Gideon put the sheet down and pressed his hands together, "It's unusual, I know. But does that all make sense?"

"He wants us to zap each other until one of us is left standing?"

"Yes," Gideon smiled and pointed at the document, "I'm merely the adjudicator. If you shock me, you are disqualified. As per the rules."

No-one could quite articulate how they felt.

Gideon rose to his feet, "Okay. Shall we go to the cemetery?"

***

Tammy, Vesta, Caspian, Christian, Jennifer - and a very upset Ruby - followed Gideon into the cemetery. Each carried their stun gun with them.

Somehow, the clouds seem to have darkened since they were inside *The Red Shell* hotel.

"Looks like rain," Gideon yelled as he turned and

walked backward. "We'd better get this over and done with, soon."

"Shut up!" Tammy squealed, feeling the chill in the air. "This is insanity!"

Gideon sympathized with her, "I must admit, I found it rather strange, myself."

"Where are we going?" Caspian held his stun gun in front of him. He felt he needed the practice.

"Your father's grave."

The group reached the tombstone of Morton Mulberry. *Hell Hath No Fury* was etched on the marble front.

"Okay, here we are," Gideon smiled and buttoned up his jacket, "Now, each of your guns is primed to half a million volts."

"Half a million?" Ruby said, unhappy with having to hold the weapon in her hand, "But that's—"

"—Excessive, I know," Gideon took Ruby's stun gun and showed it to the others, "It's not the voltage that will cause the damage, it's the amperage. Enough here to melt an elephant, so be careful. Ruby, could you demonstrate for me, please?"

She wiped a tear from her eye and took the gun from his hand, "Okay?"

"You get one shot. Reloading takes a few seconds, which means you'll be vulnerable during that time. So, shoot wisely. In your boxes, you have five refills, or cartridges, as they're known. The release button at the back opens the slot for the cartridge."

Ruby took a cartridge from her pocket and slotted it into the gun.

"Very good. There are two probes at the front, connected to wires. Whatever you do, do *not* touch them until they're spent."

Gideon took a few steps back and held out his arms, "Mrs. Mulberry, point the gun at me, please."

Everyone watched Ruby aim the gun at Gideon. They

attempted to replicate what they saw her doing.

"Now, safety catch off. Don't shoot yet."

Ruby flicked the catch with her thumb, "Now what?"

"When you zap me, the challenge will begin. If the probes make contact with my clothes or skin, it'll stun me. I'll probably fall to the ground. It's likely, also, that I'll experience acute pain and paralysis."

Christian slotted a cartridge into his stun gun, "How long will the person be out for?"

"At least five or ten minutes. If you're hit, my advice is to lay down and stay down," Gideon turned to Ruby, "Okay, Mrs. Mulberry, when you're ready. As soon as I'm hit, the challenge begins."

Jennifer stepped back toward a gravestone as Ruby took aim at Gideon.

Tammy and Vesta parted ways.

"In your own time, Mrs. Mulberry," Gideon held his arms out and braced himself for impact.

PTCHOO-SPATTCCHHH-ZZZZ

The probe flew out of the gun and jutted into Gideon's chest.

"Grreeuuurrgghh."

He stood on the spot, jiggling around as the volts flew into his body. Finally, an orange spark exploded, sending him to the dirt, completely unconscious.

"Ferrari on a bike," Ruby gasped flipped the safety catch up the side of her gun, "This gun really kicks ass."

She turned around and pointed the gun. Everyone had run off.

"Fuck, fuck, aww," Gideon groaned in pain on the floor.

A couple of raindrops hit Ruby's forehead. She paced forward and reached into her pocket for a second cartridge, "Where are you? Where did you all go?"

"Sorry, mom," Tammy shouted from behind any one of the dozens of gravestones.

"Tammy?"

SHUNT. Ruby slotted in her second cartridge and flipped the safety catch down, "Tammy, honey? It's okay, you can come out. I won't shoot you."

A terrified squealing came from behind a gravestone a few feet away, "You p-promise?"

"Sure, sweetie," Ruby scowled and squeezed the handle on her gun. She had every intention of shooting every last motherfucker in the graveyard, "Come out, honey."

"O-Okay."

"Come out with your hands up," Ruby offered.

Tammy rose from behind one of the many gravestones. She held her stun gun in the air, offering a surrender, "Mom, we don't *have* to do this, do we?"

Ruby turned her stun gun to Tammy, "Drop the gun, honey."

"Okay, okay," Tammy threw her stun gun to the ground, "I've dropped it."

"Good girl."

SPAAA-AA-AATTCCHH-ZZZZ!

A set of wires pierced into the side of her head, frying the skin on her face. She stumbled behind a gravestone a few feet away.

"Fuckin' cook, you little bitch," Caspian's voice echoed through the graveyard.

"Holy shit," Ruby lowered her gun and ran off to a nearby tree.

The volts passed through Tammy's head, causing her jowls and cheekbones to shake and rumble.

ZWWWIIIPPP-PPP.

Tammy's eyeballs exploded out from their sockets, her beautiful blond hair set ablaze.

CLUTCH. The wires slacked down the side of her face. Her burnt skin smoldered and crackled.

"*Fuck me*," Caspian hushed and replaced his cartridge. He watched his sister's body slam to the grass. Her arms burst into flames, "Sorry, sis."

Caspian jumped out from behind his headstone, "Okay,

you cunts. Come out, come out, wherever you are."

He waved the gun around at the headstones. There was no-one around.

Vesta had found an empty six-foot grave a few yards away from Caspian. She kept her shoulders pressed back against the wall and prepared to jump out.

Her breathing quickened as fast as her heart pumped. She closed her eyes and held her gun in both hands, "Fuck, fuck, fuck."

Caspian looked north and south, turning his body, ready for someone to jump out, "Mom? Vesta? Christian? Where are you?"

Silence.

Droplets of rain hit Caspian's shirt, "Come out, fuck heads. I need the money. We all know Dad loved me the most. I'm the eldest brother."

"Fuck you, you liar," Christian's voice swirled around the graveyard.

Caspian looked up and around, "Christian? Is that you?"

"Yeah, man."

"Look," Caspian raised his voice, "It's you and me, brother. We can split the money."

"Yeah?" Christian yelled. "I can see you, you know."

The same couldn't be said for Caspian. He was a sitting duck and threatened everyone out in the open. His bravado wasn't going down very well with the rest of the family.

Christian hid behind one of twenty gravestones near the church. He knocked his head on it and closed his eyes, "Fuck's sake, man, what are you doing?"

He gripped the gun tight in both hands.

"Christian, you little fuckin' half-faggot. Join me. We'll take care of the girls together."

"No," Christian cried. "If I do, you'll zap me."

Caspian held his gun up, "I promise I won't."

Christian rose to his feet from behind the gravestone. He clutched his stun gun and aimed it at his brother, "You promise?"

"Yes, of course—"

Christian's eyes grew. He spotted someone behind him, "Caspian, look out."

PTCHOOO-STCHUUTTT!

Two electric probes flew from behind Caspian and jabbed into the dirt by his feet.

"Shit, shit, shit."

He turned around to see Vesta fiddling with her gun, "Bollocks."

"Vesta?" Caspian swung his gun at her, "Was that *you*?"

"Uh, no?" she lied as she attempted to replace her cartridge, "It was, uh—"

"—You lying *cunt*," he screamed and aimed his stun gun at her.

"No," she begged. "Please don't—"

PTCHOO-SPAA-ATTCHH-ZZZZ!

Caspian shot her in the breasts. She dropped her gun as her body convulsed on the spot.

ZWIP-ZWIP-ZWIP!

The hair on her head singed away as the current bolted through her.

"Fucking shoot *me*?" Caspian yelled and kept the trigger held back, ensuring his sister received more than maximum pain, "You little dyke."

Ruby peered from behind the trunk of the tree. She held her mouth to stop from screaming as her daughter fried away at the end of her eldest son's stun gun.

Vesta staggered back. Her blouse burst open and released a waft of black smoke, "Shhyaarrrgghhh."

Her breasts exploded around the prongs as they throttled her body with electricity. The stun gun dropped from her sizzling, blackened hands.

She screamed so loud that her mouth widened up and fried around her head.

Vesta fell to her knees, carrying with it a waft of burnt skin and flesh.

SLUMP.

She fell face-first to the floor.

"My baby," Ruby looked down at her shaking hands and flicked the safety catch off, "That fucking bastard."

GLUMPH, GLUMPH.

The ground around Vesta rumbled and began to breathe.

"What the fuck is happening now?" Caspian stepped back and watched the ground smother his sister's body.

GLUMPH, GLUMPH. The grass and dirt swamped over her sides and slid across her back.

GLUMP.

It wasn't long before her body disappeared into the ground, wholesale.

BRAAAAPPP!

The ground seemed to burp. A plume of smoke escaped through the slit that Vesta had sunk through.

"Fucking put the gun down," Christian stepped away from the gravestone and concentrated his aim at Caspian's face.

He turned around and threw his stun gun to the floor, "Brother?"

"*Half-brother*, motherfucker," Christian spat. "You shot Tammy and Vesta."

He looked at Tammy's body on the floor. It had disappeared. The ground had swallowed her, too.

"Shit. What the *fuck* is happening, here?" Christian screamed.

"Brother, it's over."

The drops of rain turn to a light shower. The stench of burned human remains was overwhelming.

Christian preyed on his brother's remorse and scrambled for his gun. He swiped it from the floor and aimed it at his head.

"Put the gun down," Caspian screamed. "It wasn't my fault. I was just doing as I was told."

A stand-off occurred between the two brothers. Both kept their guns aimed at each other.

"Put the gun down," Caspian screamed once again. "I mean it."

"No. You put yours down."

KA-SPLAAATTCCH-CHHH!

Caspian's eyeballs burst open, releasing a torrent of grey matter and blood.

"Nug, nug, nug," His tongue waggled as his body juddered on the spot. A pair of probes connected with the back of his head.

The wires ran across the ground and connected to the end of Ruby's stun gun.

"Mom?" Christian yelled. "You shot Caspian."

"Yes. I did," Ruby detached the wires from the probe and made her way over to her youngest, "Didn't you hear that vile shit he came out with earlier?"

"Yes."

Caspian dropped to his knees. His head burst into flames, "Grroooooooo," His smoked-out voice belched bloody murder. The rest of his body caught fire in the pouring rain.

Ruby palmed a new cartridge into her gun with terrific expediency, "The rain isn't helping matters, much."

GLUMPH, GLUMPH.

The ground thundered around Christian's body. It resembled a mini-earthquake where Ruby and Christian stood.

Ruby took her son's arm, "Get back."

They stepped back towards the church. The muddied ground crept its way over Caspian's inferno of a corpse.

"M-Mum. I d-don't understand," Christian burst out crying. "Wh-what's going on?"

"I don't know, honey."

The dirt swallowed Caspian's body into itself and settled down to normal.

"Why h-has Dad done th-this?"

"I have no idea, sweetie," she noticing her son had his gun aimed at her, "Honey. You're not going to shoot me, are you?"

"I d-don't know," Poor Christian had no idea how to react. He'd seen his three siblings cook alive and then sink into the ground, "I don't know what to do."

His mother took pity on him. She knew it was all over for her.

"It's okay, honey," Ruby said. She took Christian's gun and placed it at her forehead, "You can shoot me if you want."

"I don't *want* to shoot you."

"Listen, honey," she smiled and lowered her gun, "Daddy loved you. He knew you weren't out to screw him over, unlike your siblings. Or me."

"What do you mean, *you*?"

"I was unfaithful. I knew he resented me for it."

"What?"

Gideon groaned and opened his eyes a few yards away on the grass. He could barely move as the rain showered down all over him, "Oh G-God, h-help me. I'm *p-paralyzed*."

Ruby burst into tears, "Even though you're not my own flesh and blood, I know you're a good person. You deserve everything. Not me. Not some washed-up old hag."

"I never knew my mother."

"Not until now, sweetie," came Jennifer's voice from behind Christian's head, "Put the gun down."

"Huh?"

He turned around to see Jennifer holding her stun gun at his head.

"Don't you fucking touch my boy, you ginger *cunt*," Ruby screamed.

"He's *not* your boy," Jennifer roared and looked at Christian dead in the eyes, "He's *mine*."

"Yours?" Ruby gasped. "You were—"

"—I'm his mother."

Christian double-took. He refused to believe what he was hearing, "What are you talking about?"

"I had an affair with Morton nineteen years ago. I gave you up. Your mother never knew. I gave you your name before I left. There was no way I could keep you, I was a child myself at the time."

"Mom?" Christian demanded confirmation. "Is this true?"

"I've never met the woman," Ruby roared back, "It was *you*?"

"Yes," Jennifer giggled. "Now, Christian, my son. Shoot this *strange* woman in the face."

"I c-can't shoot my mum in the—"

"—She's not your mother," Jennifer pointed her gun at his face, "*I am*. Now shoot this fucking woman."

Christian looked Ruby in the face. The rain beat down on all three of them, soaking them to the bone. A chill ran down his back as a lifetime of nurture by the woman raced through his mind.

He closed his eyes and squeezed the trigger.

PTCHOO-ZAPPPP. SPAAA-AA-ATTCHH!

The water fizzed as the prongs stabbed into Ruby's forehead, instantly setting her skull and skin on fire, "Whaarrggghhhh."

Jennifer patted her son on the back and grinned at him, "Well done, honey."

Ruby stepped back and threw her right hand into the air and fired her stun gun at Jennifer.

Quick-thinking, she grabbed her son and threw him in front of her.

The prongs speared into his neck, sparking and bursting out. The blue sparks ran along the wire and pulverized his internal organs.

His chest burst open and coughed out a plume of reddened smoke. The lungs and heart were next to push through his chest.

Christian's head burst into flames as the prongs delivered over half a million volts into his body.

Jennifer hadn't accounted for her touching her son. The volts ran into both her hands via his shoulder.

She coughed up a torrent of blackened blood. The skin on her forehead broke apart and bled.

As she stepped away to try to save herself, her melted fingers roped out from her hands. Her stun gun hit the ground.

She fell to her knees and examined her melted flesh, "Graaawwww," Jennifer's long red hair flaked away as she fell sideways. Her head slammed against the wet grass, knocking one of her eyeballs out of its frying socket.

Her vision dissipated. The ground shifted up and consumed Christian and his mother.

GLUMPH, GLUMPH…

It swallowed over and over again until there was nothing left of either of them.

Jennifer continued to watch through her one liquefying eyeball. Her body rolled around as the ground enveloped her.

A tight feeling of restriction.

"Nwwaahh. Nwooooh," she screamed. A near-deaf and muffled cry for help through her bleeding and thoroughly-destroyed eardrums.

She saw the blades of grass lift into the air in among the piercing ringing sound of acute pain.

Jennifer screamed her last as the grass overwhelmed her.

Everything went black.

***

Gideon spluttered for dear life and rolled onto his side,

"Gah, gah, gah."

He placed his hands on the grass and pushed himself onto his knees.

"Ugh, ugh," he coughed as the rain pounded against his face.

The gray clouds lit up and thundered all around him as the downpour grew ever-more vicious.

He looked up at the sky and laughed at the cloud, holding out his hands, "Haha."

BOOM, RUMBLE.

The black clouds erupted and lit up with lightning. Gideon looked down, the rain falling from his face. He snatched his briefcase and staggered up to his feet, "I suppose this means I win?"

A pang of lightning smashed down and hit the church, blowing out its windows.

A giant shadow fell across the vast graveyard.

Gideon looked up into the pouring rain and licked his lips. The ground erupted, sending blades of grass waving left and right.

The central section of the graveyard bellowed out and up, into the shape of a stomach.

An evil, low-pitched whine ran around the stormy clouds, "Gideon."

"Is, is th-that you? M-Morton?!"

"Gideon," the clouds roared once again.

"Master, it is you," he said in complete awe, "Did I win?"

The entire three-acre area beveled around and inflated.

"Gideon."

He looked up and shouted, "Mr. Mulberry, sir? Is that you?"

He stepped back toward the flaming church and allowed the ground to inflate. It seemed to be the shape of the arm, the way the grass had moved around.

Beside it, a one-hundred-foot ground-inspired torso. In the far distance, a pair of legs and feet

"Mr. Mulberry, sir?" Gideon grew anxious. He clutched his briefcase to his chest and ran toward the gated entrance. He left whatever was growing in the cemetery to do its thing.

Chapter 3

Sebastian Sibald's Suicide Hour

"On air, on digital, on your phone, on point, this is *The Wank Bank* with Annie Banks on *Virile FM*."

A thunderclap accompanied by violins rattled around the radio studio.

Annie Banks pushed the cans over her head and saw the "on air" sign spring to life. She pursed her pouting lips and leaned into the microphone. It looked like she might kiss it.

"Well, my hour is nearly up," she said in a soft tone, "It's been enlightening to hear your issues on this wet and cold Saturday night."

She looked up to see a man in his fifties enter the room. The giant metal door shut behind him.

Annie nodded at the man and grabbed the microphone, "Just time for one more caller. Alan in Chrome Valley, you're on."

"Hello?" Alan's voice flew around the room from the speakers, "Am I on air?"

"Yes, you're on *The Wank Bank* with Annie Banks. What's your issue, Alan, my love?"

The man who had entered the room made a funny face at Annie. He hung his coat on the stand and took a seat opposite her at the console.

"Well," Alan's voice quivered, "My wife and I have been married for twenty years and our sex life has taken a turn for the worse."

"I'm sorry to hear that, Alan," Annie attempted to avoid the playful-but-silent smirks from the man opposite her. She hit a switch on the console as Alan bled his heart over the airwaves.

"Would you stop doing that?" she mouthed, "Yes, Alan. Continue."

"Well, recently I've been getting some attention from—"

The man threw his feet up on the console He held placed his hands behind his silver-hair, leaned back, and smirked at Annie.

"—You've been getting attention from elsewhere, have you?" Annie butted in.

"Yes," Alan continued. "And I don't know whether I should take her up on the offer."

"Well, I wouldn't advise *that*."

"Why not?"

The man at the console winked and made the *wanker* sign at her, "Yeah, why shouldn't he?"

Annie stood up and gripped the microphone, "Because playing around behind your spouse's back isn't something you should do. She will *know*. It's quite simple, really. Alan, you need to talk to your wife and let her know how you feel."

The silver-haired man at the console buried his head in his hands in disapproval.

"But we've talked, Annie. It's no use. I'm at my wit's end."

"Alan, let me ask you something," Annie clocked the time display on the wall. "We've thirty seconds left, just answer me one question."

"Okay?"

"Do you still love her?"

A brief pause flew through the room. The silver-haired

man leaned forward onto the console and raised his eyebrows.

"Alan?"

"Yes?"

"Do you?"

"Yes, I do."

"Then you'll talk to her," Annie adjusted the height on her microphone and hit a button, "Thank you for your call, Alan. Okay, that's all we have time for tonight on *The Wank Bank*."

A piece of jolly music played over her speech.

"Stay tuned for the top of the hour. After the news, it's Sebastian Sibald's Suicide Hour, only on Virile FM. Until tomorrow, this is Annie Banks saying *keep it sturdy*."

Annie hit another button on the console. A news jingle fired up, followed by a man's voice introducing the segment. She unhooked the cans from her head and slammed them to the desk.

Annie cleared away her papers from the desk, "Do you always have to do that, Seb?"

The silver-haired man jumped to his feet in protest and made his way to Annie.

"Do what?"

"Be a prick," Annie huffed and stepped away from the console driver seat, "Every night you come in and make silly faces and try to put me off."

"Oh, lighten up," Seb took the main seat and wheeled himself toward the console.

"That's rich coming from you and your show."

"Hey, it's all in the name of entertainment," He looked up at a glass partition to find his producer behind it. He held up two fingers at Seb, indicating how many minutes he had left till he was live.

"Wait till the news is on next time, *at least*," Annie scowled as she grabbed her coat and made for the door.

"Yeah, yeah," Seb winked at her. "Got anything interesting on tonight?"

"Not calling your stupid show would be my first priority."

"Good call."

"No. *No call*," Annie shut the door behind her. Seb looked over at his producer, Gary, who fiddled with the computer and adjusting his own headset.

This inspired Seb to sling the cans over his head, "Gary, man, who have we got lined up?"

"Don't you want it to be a surprise?"

"No surprises, mate. Not after the night I'm having," Seb chuckled and looked at the caller monitor. A list of names crawled up the screen along with the issues they wanted to discuss.

Tabitha - Stress
Tammy - Needs a prompt (NAP)
Darren - Undecided

"That's thirty seconds, Seb," Gary said from the control box.

"What? We've only got one NAP?" Seb shot Gary a look, "We usually have hundreds lined up by now."

"Hey, don't shoot the messenger. What do you expect for a Saturday night, anyway?"

"I expect a bit more fucking action than this."

"I'm sure they'll come in," Gary looked over his screen and giggled, "Twenty seconds."

"Right, fine," Seb ran his hands through his air and blinked at his screen.

An angelic jingle began to play. A reassuring male voice crept over the music.

"Feeling low? Need some help in making that crucial decision? Good news! It's ten o'clock, so that must mean you've come to the right place. Welcome to *The Suicide Hour* with your merchant of death, Sebastian Sibald."

Seb rolled his chair forward and placed his face in front of the hanging microphone. The jingle stopped and the

"On Air" sign snapped on.

"I've had some very interesting news this evening, boys and girls. Apparently, something I said on last night's show angered some of our sponsors. Recently, I have been the subject of a vindictive and personal attack by the media. They've called my show crass, incendiary, and an affront to base human decency."

Seb pressed his hands together and looked down at a note on the table.

"*Should Suicide Hour be allowed to continue?* Is that the rather loaded question that seems to have the media in a frenzy right now? I put it to you, my adoring listeners, that I should be allowed to continue. To provide an invaluable service."

Seb stood up and held the microphone wire as he walked toward the glass window. He smiled at Gary and nodded at the first name on the list.

"Put simply, if people didn't want my show, then no one would tune in. My career would be over in a heartbeat. But this isn't the case, is it? You *love* me and my show, and we'll prove it right now by taking our first caller."

Seb snapped his finger and rolled his neck.

"Tabitha, from Ealing, you're on *Suicide Hour*. How can I help you, peach?"

A sniffing and crying came through the radio speakers, "S-Sebastian?"

"Yeah, that's me."

"I d-don't know what to d-do."

"Well, why not tell me what's up?"

"I d-don't know where to start," Tabitha struggled to speak. She was so upset.

"Well, start anywhere."

Tabitha thought for a moment. The suspense was painful, "And a lot worse when I'm alone."

"Huh?"

"I'm sorry," Tabitha squealed. "I don't know what I've

done wrong. I'm useless."

"Whoa, whoa, Tabitha," Seb hopped over to his console, "What makes you think you're useless? Tell me."

"Nobody likes me. I don't have any friends."

"Well, that may be true, but it's not what I asked."

"No?"

"No. Tell me why you think you're useless?"

Tabitha's sniffing allayed, revealing a sound of running water from her end of the call.

"Is that water?" Seb asked. "Tabitha, where are you?"

"I'm in the bath. I've got this razor and the water is nice and warm."

"Sounds lovely, pumpkin."

"Oh. It is, it is."

"What are you going to do with the razor?" Seb winked at Gary.

"Ohh, you know, I was thinking I'd run it up my wrists and slowly fade away."

"Okay, do you need my help?"

"Tell me I'm worthless, Sebastian," Tabitha's voice slowed down.

"Yeah, you're useless, all right," Seb confirmed into his microphone as seriously as he could, "You're right, you have no friends. Nobody gives a damn about you."

"Tell me why I have no friends, Sebastian," Tabitha began to cry and squeal.

Seb closed his eyes and took a deep breath.

"Because you have no personality? Everyone talks about you behind your back?"

"That's right."

"Life's not worth living," Seb continued. "And for what, anyway? For more months and years to feel miserable?"

"Yes."

"Make sure you run the blade long-ways up and down your wrist, not across."

"Oh no," Tabitha squealed, "I did it sideways."

"You idiot," Seb's demeanour flipped on a dime. "Always *up the lane*, never *across the street*."

"I'm s-such a m-mess," Tabitha spluttered, "The b-blood looks so b-beautiful in the water."

"Bleed, bury your arms in the warm water."

"Okay, o-okay."

A gentle splashing sound came through Seb's cans, "Are those your arms I can hear? Tabitha?"

"Yes?"

"Stay with me as long as you can, pumpkin."

"Uhh."

"I want my voice to be the last thing you hear. Close your eyes for me."

Tabitha didn't respond. A tiny metallic clanging noise echoed through the studio.

"That must be the razor hitting the floor. Tabitha, can you hear me?"

No response.

Gary looked over from behind the glass partition. He smiled and waved his fingers across his neck indicating that the call had been cut.

"Another satisfied customer," Seb punched the air and adjusted his collar. He scanned his monitor and traced the screen with his finger, "Who's next? Let's go with a bloke this time. Darren from Crawley, you're on *Suicide Hour*."

"Hello, Sebastian?" A loud rumbling shot through the speakers.

"Yes Darren, it's Sebastian Sibald and you're on *Suicide Hour*. This connection is terrible. Are you outside?"

"Yes, I'm sorry. It's very windy up here."

"Try to cover the phone. What would you like to say?"

"God, I'm in so much shit—"

"—Whoa, hold up, Darren. You can't swear on the air."

"Can't I?"

"No, and of course we apologize for any listeners for the language."

"I'm sorry—"

"That's perfectly okay, we understand you're a bit on edge."

The caller smirked, "*At* the edge, more like."

"So, why did you call?"

A brief pause floated around the room.

It was commonplace for the callers to *The Suicide Hour* to be despondent or in deep contemplation. They were often considering extreme actions.

Seb and Gary usually made faces at one another to fill in the gaps.

Dead air was something that couldn't happen. *Virile FM*, much like other stations, couldn't afford people to tune in and hear nothing.

To combat this, Gary played a countdown jingle, which was what happened with Darren's call.

A cheerful glockenspiel countdown jingle designed to dispel the silence. Also, it further mocked the caller and encouraged them to speak.

"I'm so badly in debt, and my family doesn't have a clue."

"Chaaaarlie," Seb's face lit up as he feigned incredulity, "I love it when you freaks call in. Let me guess, was it a payday loan?"

"No, not really."

Seb chuckled, "Okay, you're a secret gambler? Blown your kid's university fees or something?"

"It's not funny," Darren swallowed hard. "And stop playing that music."

"I'll stop playing the silly music when you speak, my friend. Now tell us, how did you get into debt?"

"I borrowed my way out of it. Went to an unlicensed outfit."

"Oh no. Not those sharks that charge five hundred percent?"

Darren sniffed and cleared his throat, "Something like

that."

"I don't get it, why didn't you call the finance show?"

"I can't call those guys, they won't be any help."

"So you think taking the easy way out is the *only* way out?"

"You don't get it, do you?" Darren shouted. "They're coming to kill me anyway."

"How much do you owe, Darren?"

"Three-quarters of a million pounds."

"*Ferrari* almighty."

"I'm standing on the roof of my apartment block, Sebastian. There's people down the bottom looking at me. I just need someone to convince me to do it."

"You're about to jump?"

"Yes. This is it, it's just a matter of time before my wife finds out we've lost the house. My children will have to be taken out of private schooling."

"Look, Darren, no one goes up to the top of their block of flats and—"

"—Apartment block."

"—Okay, okay, *apartment block*, and threatens to jump. They usually go through with it."

"I didn't know that," Darren sniffed against the wind. "But I'm very serious."

"I can hear that, Darren," Seb sympathized. "I hear you. Nearly one million listeners tonight hear you, as well."

"Sebastian, please."

Seb looked at Gary and shrugged his shoulders, "Look, Darren, if you walk away from this without jumping, how is that going to look?"

"I dunno, like I'm a coward or something?"

"Exactly right. You turn around after this spectacle and chicken out, you'll be the laughing stock of Crawley. Your wife and kids won't be able to live it down."

Darren started to bawl from the other end of the call, "I'm such a loser."

"That's right, Darren," Seb whispered. "You are. But

you can go out with a bang, mate. You can jump. You can show them you meant business. That no one could get you."

"Yes, yes," Darren stopped bawling and took an unusually confident approach, "Yeah. I can show them that they could never beat me."

"Exactly," Seb said with utter conviction.

A bizarre, unified silence fell around the radio studio. Gary looked through the glass partition in anticipation.

"So *jump*, Darren. Do it."

"Yeah?" Darren chuckled, indicating he'd lost the will to live, "They're screaming down there. Man, it'd be such a horrible thing for them to witness."

"Yeah, of course. Look at them down there hoping you won't jump. You wanna know a secret?"

"What?"

"They'd never admit it, but they *want* you to jump. Do you know why?"

"Why?"

"Because it'll give them something to talk about. We love the gore, Darren. We love the bloody mess. You'll be at peace. Your splattered remains will be the last message you send. For them? It'll be a message they never forget."

Seb winked at Gary at the control room. He stuck up his thumb and turned back to the microphone.

"Hey, you know what's the coolest thing, Darren? I'm going to tell you. How nice would it feel to be the one who got away?"

No response from Darren. A thousand distant screams of terror hurtled through the windy line.

"Darren?" Seb asked.

No response.

"He's gone, mate," Gary's voice piped in through the studio. "You did it. It worked."

Seb blinked his eyes and stood to his feet. It took a few seconds for him to process his success.

"It never fails to amaze me just *how* easy you guys are,"

Seb wiped his eyes and hit a button on the console. A jingle came to life and underscored his last sentence.

"Feeling down in the dumps? Need that last little nudge over the cliff? Call me, Sebastian Sibald, right now on *Suicide Hour*. I'll put a spring in your step. We'll be back after these words."

"Suicide is on the increase. Ten years ago, two percent of males ages between eighteen and thirty-five took the easy way out. Today, that number is seven percent. Females have experienced a similar rise. Endless years of austerity have finally taken their toll. Actions speak louder than words. There is no hope. No way out. *Except one.* If you're thinking of cutting the talk and walking the walk, call the *Suicide Hour* right now - and see if *cashing in your chips* is right for you."

10:30 pm. The radio station wasn't busy now. The graveyard shift would be starting soon.

Seb made his way to the kitchen and poured himself a cup of tea.

Gary walked in with another man, "Ah, here he is."

Seb offered the man his hand, "Hi, I'm Sebastian Sibald."

"I know who you are." The man moved to the side and set his briefcase down on the kitchen counter. He unclipped the lid and flipped it open, "My name is Gregory Black."

"Nice to meet you."

"Yeah, this is some show you have, here," Gregory took out a plastic wallet and handed it to Seb, "The station's most listened-to show. One million listeners, according to last month's report."

Seb looked at the papers. The word "syndication' was the first thing he noticed. His face lit up as he sifted through the sheets.

"Syndication?"

"It's sort of ironic," Gregory said with a smile. "That your show is the most popular, yet your remit is to reduce your listeners by one. Every phone call you get."

"Twenty years ago, this idea would have been laughed at."

"You're not kidding."

"And anyway," Seb picked up his cup of tea and blew the rim, "I don't kill them, though. I just provide some friendly encouragement."

"Well, for every listener who goes through with it, another hundred tune in to listen. *Suicide Hour* is like the tuberculosis of the airwaves. Like Hydra."

"A profitable Hydra."

"Yes," Gregory explained and shot Gary a look, "We want to take the show into syndication. If we appeal to the right kind of advertiser, this will make us all very rich indeed. We've already had several huge pharmaceutical companies bidding for air time. They're suggesting ten times the asking price during your show."

Gary stepped forward and looked at the file in Seb's hand, "You're taking us national?"

"That's right. All we need is for you and Seb to continue what you're doing. And do it well."

Seb winked at Gary, "What do you think?"

"I think we won't compromise on quality. We keep the show as it is."

"I understand your concerns as the producer, Gary," Gregory said. "I can assure you that we won't touch the format. On the contrary, we want you to continue as you are, but more forcefully."

Gary saw his opportunity to butt in, "Can I have a word with Seb, please?"

"By all means."

A concerned Gary stood outside the kitchen with an excited Seb, "Look, mate, I've seen this before."

Seb took a sip of his tea, "Seen what?"

"We sign the contract, and then our asses belong to them. They start dictating what we can and can't do. I have a feeling they're trying to cover themselves."

"Bullshit. Didn't you see the clause in the contract? They want us to continue doing what we're doing."

"We need to seriously read the small print before we do anything rash," Gary urged. "Didn't you hear what he said? Money fucking talks. Once they own us, they'll pander to the advertisers and have us recommending stuff ending in "tex' and "in." Before you know it we're just another popular *spokescunt* for Big Pharma."

Seb screwed his face. His friend and colleague had evidently gone insane, "Wanna know what I think?"

Gary knew Seb's question was loaded, "What?"

"I'm going to go back in there and telling him we're on," Seb barged past Gary and back into the kitchen.

Gary stepped after him, "Seb, man. Wait."

Seb reached the kitchen, already having made up his mind, "Okay, we've had a chat and we want to sign—"

Gregory was gone. As was his suitcase, and the contract.

"Huh?"

"Have you lost your fucking mind, mate? Gary suddenly noticed they were alone in the room, "Where is he?"

"He's gone."

"Probably just as well," Gary spat. "Gives us time to *think* about this. Now, get back in the chair, the commercials are about to close."

Seb turned around and made his way out of the kitchen. Gary caught up to him.

"The quality of the commercials is about to skyrocket, mate. Don't fuck this up."

"I just want you to be careful. We're lucky we haven't had a lawsuit, yet."

"Look, if they don't want to take part, then they don't call in."

Seb pushed his way into the radio room and sat in the driver's chair. "Load me up with some NAPS, please."

Gary sat behind his console in the next room. He flicked a switch on his microphone, "Twenty seconds, Seb."

"Good, good," Seb scanned his screen. A new list of callers waited to be put through, "Who have we here?"

An introductory jingle played after the commercials, "Feel like you can't take responsibility for your own life? Well, why not *take* it? Consider the easy way out with *Sebastian Sibald's Suicide Hour*, weeknights from ten."

The "On Air' bulb lit up.

Seb's lips hovered over the microphone head, "My producer and I just had a visit from the conglomerate that owns *Virile FM*. He's watching us closely to see if the service we provide can be taken into syndication. I see a lot of you lined up waiting for me to take your call. Don't disappoint me."

Seb hit a button on the console.

"Simon, you're on *Suicide Hour*. How can I help you?"

A gruff and threatening voice came through Seb's cans, "Who do you think you are?"

"Say that again?"

"I asked you who do you think you are?"

"I'm Sebastian Sibald," he said, playing a trumpet fanfare sound effect, "And who the hell do you think you are?"

"Think you're funny?" Simon asked. "Let's see how funny you are with your head smashed into your monitor, you sick fu—"

Seb swallowed his perturbation and hit a switch, "Next caller. Who's this?"

"My name is Mary," came the coquettish voice from the other end of the line.

"Hello Mary. What do you want to talk about?" Seb threw his hands out at Gary. He mouthed his displeasure at him, "The fuck is going on?"

"Sebastian. I lost my son around a month ago—"

"—I'm sorry to hear that, Mary," Seb returned to the call, "What happened?"

"He was only fifteen. I came home late one night to find he'd been stabbed."

"Well that sucks, doesn't it?" Seb's flippant demeanor indicated he didn't give much of a shit. He scrolled through the list of callers and then looked up at Gary behind the glass wall.

Gregory watched on with his arms folded and a shit-eating grin on his face. Two of his colleagues stood with him, chatting amongst themselves.

They seemed serious.

Seb turned to the screen and acted as professionally as possible, "Did they find the guy that did it?"

"He'd been dead for about an hour before I came home. The police got involved, but they never caught the person who did it. There's a good reason why they never caught him."

"Oh, really?" Seb quipped and shot Gregory a wink, "Why's that?"

"Because he wasn't murdered. He took his own life."

"That's very interesting, Mary. Do you know why? Did he leave a note?"

"He didn't have to," Mary's tone turned to anger, "Your radio station was playing in his room. He was listening to your show."

"You know we don't take calls from listeners under the age of eighteen, Mary."

Gregory and his colleagues looked down at their shoes, somewhat unimpressed.

Seb frowned and grabbed the microphone.

She thought her response over very carefully, "I know that. But it doesn't stop them from *listening* to your show—"

"—I can't stop *anyone* from listening to the show, Mary.

No more than I can stop them from doing something they want to do."

"You have a powerful and persuasive way about you, Sebastian. Your actions killed my son. I hold you responsible."

"Now wait a bloody moment, Mary," Seb rose to his feet and flipped his middle finger at Gary, "Just because he caught my show, doesn't mean I'm—"

"—No," Mary screamed over his sentence. "You listen to *me*, dickhead. Do you know how much turmoil and grief you've caused me and my family?"

"Hey. I don't need talking-down to by the likes of you."

"Oh, I think you do, my friend. I ask again. Are you aware of the damage you've caused me and my family?"

Seb squeezed his eyelids shut and tried to suppress his anger, "*I don't care.*"

"You don't care," Mary repeated and then took a deep breath, "That's the whole point. My husband left me. I lost my job. I can't sleep anymore—"

A soft "click' occurred from her end of the line, "And I've got this gun."

Gregory gasped. His two colleagues looked just as astonished.

"Mary," Seb looked at Gregory, hoping he could rescue the situation, "You've got a gun?"

"Glock seventeen, nine millimeter. My husband is in the army."

"Mary, are you trying to tell me that you're going to shoot yourself?"

"No shit, Sherlock."

The line went quiet. Gary looked at Seb and waved his hand across his neck, "Cut the call off."

Seb looked back at Gregory and his colleagues. They didn't move. Our host remembered that he was paid to do a job. So, did he exactly that.

"Mary?"

"Y-Yes?" she began to cry.

"Where's the gun right now? How are you holding it?"

"Against my temple. All I need to do is squeeze the trigger."

"No. Wait," Seb spat into the microphone, "Don't do that. Put the barrel under your chin, instead."

Mary bawled down the line, "What?"

"Not the temple, only idiots do that. Put the barrel under your chin, behind the jawbone."

"Okay."

"Tuck it right under, Mary."

Mary cleared her throat and put on a brave voice, "Okay, I'm doing it."

"Is the barrel facing straight up?"

"Yes."

"Right, that's no good. Tilt it back a bit, so the bullet goes right through the middle of your skull. You don't want it to go through your face. It won't work as well, and it might not kill you."

Seb watched Gregory and his two colleagues barge their way into Gary's control room and began arguing. Seb couldn't hear what they were saying because of the thick Perspex glass.

"Okay, I've done it."

"You've done it? It's tilted backward?" Seb asked and kept one eye on Gary and Gregory.

"Y-Yes," Mary cocked the gun.

"You're good to go, Mary," Seb chuckled. "Do it. Pull the trigger, you worthless piece of—"

BANG-SCHPLATT!

The gunshot from Mary's end of the line thundered through Seb's cans. The volume was loud enough for him to throw them to the console.

The power to the room blinked on and off, causing everything to go dark.

A ringing sensation flew through his head. He held his palms to his ears and screamed.

"Agggghhh."

BZZZ. BZZZ.

Seb opened his eyes and looked at the control room. It was pitch dark. An emergency light silhouetted Gregory and his two colleagues. They scrambled around the room in haste.

The door to the control room was locked. Gregory yanked down on the handle but the door wouldn't budge.

The lights flickered back to life. The main console whirred to life.

"What the fuck?"

The control room's lights snapped back on. Seb gasped as he saw Gary sprawled across his console. A gaping bullet wound fountained blood across the desk.

The entrance wound was under his chin. He'd shot himself in exactly the same way Mary had done seconds before.

"Gary?" Seb ran over to the glass partition and banged against the surface.

His corpse rolled onto the floor, spilling gray matter around the desk.

Gregory screamed something at Seb through the window. It was inaudible. His two colleagues backed away from Gary's corpse screaming for their lives.

Seb looked at the console and ran over to collect his cans, "Hello? Can you hear me?"

The list of callers on the screen had grown into the thousands.

"Hi, uh, this is *Sebastian Sibald's Suicide Hour.* I apologize for the technical, uh, difficulties. We'll be right back after this message."

He hit a button on the console. A commercial began to play.

Seb pointed at Gary's headset and nodded at Gregory to put them on his head, "Do it, do it."

As instructed and stepped over Gary's corpse. He angled the mouthpiece to his lips, "Sebastian? What the fuck is going?"

"I don't know."

"Well, you better fix it. Whatever it is."

"Umm, umm," Sebastian clutched his cans and ran to the radio room door. He yanked the handle down but it wouldn't open.

"Oh shit," Seb stepped backward arse-first onto his console. He turned around and screamed at what he saw.

"What the fuck is going on?"

A woman's corpse lay across one of the seats. Half her face missing from a gunshot wound.

"Huh?"

To her left, in the adjacent seat, a man's flattened corpse sprawled and dripped gore over the seat and armrests.

"What the fuck is that?" Gregory's voice came through Seb's cans.

"I don't know," Seb ran around the console and saw a young woman drenched in water in the opposite seat.

The letters T-A-B-I-T-H-A had been cut into her forehead. Her bare arms were cut from her elbow crease to her wrist.

Her lifeless face stared back at Seb.

"*Ch-Charlie Ferrari* on a bike," he couldn't process what he was seeing. "I c-can't even."

Seb saw a piece of rope hanging above the console and his chair, "What's going on?"

"—So, if you need a *final* solution," the radio jingle boomed around the room, "Waste no more time. Call Sebastian Sibald now and make sure you meet your maker today."

"On air, on digital, on your phone, on point, this is *The Suicide Hour* with Sebastian Sibald. Only on *Virile FM*."

Seb sat into his chair along with his three dead in-studio guests and pulled the microphone to his face.

"Something very weird is happening on tonight's

show," he whispered into the microphone, "I'm not quite sure how to tell you this, but—"

Seb looked at Gregory, those hands pressed against the glass. He hoped that the host had a solution for what was going on. His two colleagues were terrified, holding one another at the desk.

"—Meh. I don't think you'd believe me if I told you," He said and turned to the screen to find a list of callers.

Tabitha - (vengeance)
Darren - (vengeance)
Mary - (second coming?)
Max - (final solution)

The three corpses stared at Seb. Mary's dead body shuffled in its seat. Seb thought he was seeing things. He rubbed his eyes and looked at her again.

She was lifeless.

Seb hit the button on his console, "Next caller, you're on."

"—Fucking wanker gone once and for all," a man's voice finished his sentence on the end of the line. He'd been talking to someone else, "Oh, I think I'm on. Hello?"

"Hello, caller, you're on Suicide Hour?"

"Oh, I *am* on," The man seemed to be in high spirits. "Hi, Sebastian. My name is Max."

Seb's manner was different now. He knew something wasn't right, "Yes, I can see that. What do you want?"

"Long time listener, first-time caller," Max giggled, "Seb, have you ever considered practicing what you preach?"

"I'm sorry?"

BZZZ-ZAPP!

The monitor snapped off by itself. The studio lights fizzed off and back on in an instant.

"I said have you ever considered practicing what you preach?"

"I don't know what you mean—"

"—Don't play dumb with me, *fuckbrain.* Here, let me show you something."

SPRRIIISSHHHH.

Five sprinklers in the control room sprang to life. Water sprayed Gregory and his colleagues. They looked down at their feet and gasped in terror.

One of his colleagues banged on the glass window, "Help. Help."

"What's going on here, for fuck's sake?" Seb screamed.

"Oh, I'm sorry. Let me explain," Max chuckled. "My name is Max Dark. I need you to do something for me."

"What, what?"

The water in the control room splashed against the walls and window. It was filling up fast.

"It's very simple, really. Look up the ceiling. Can you see anything unusual?"

Seb looked up to see the noose hanging directly above his head from the ceiling, "Yes, there's a rope."

"Bingo."

"What's this got to do with—"

"—Don't interrupt me, dickhead," Max barked. "This is *my* test, okay?"

"Okay?" Seb was about to lose his mind.

"I reckon your new ass-kissing bosses have about two minutes till they fucking drown in there. But it can be stopped."

"Yes, yes, okay. Make it stop."

"Oh, no," Max chuckled down the line, "It's not *me* who can make it stop. It's *you*, pretty boy."

"Okay, whatever you say. How do I stop it?"

"Hang yourself."

"What?" Seb looked up at the rope to find it lowering toward his face.

"It's an easy choice, Sebastian," Max threatened. "Look, I don't mean to come across as a prick, but I'm stuck in here with you. I need you to hang yourself so I can get out of this fucking junkie's coma."

"What?" Seb cried out loud as the end of the noose hit his nose, "What are you talking about?"

"Just fucking hang yourself, you selfish turd. Save your friends."

The control room turned into a water coffin. Gregory and his colleagues pushed Gary's corpse away as they swam around.

"If you don't do it, Sebastian, I'll switch everything back on again and cook the bastards. But if you hang yourself, they live. The choice is yours, mate."

A tear rolled down Seb's cheek. He screamed and clutched the rope. His eyes fixed on Gregory's face. A burst of bubbles flew out of his nose.

His two colleagues had drowned. Their bodies floated around in the water.

BANG! BANG! BANG!

Gregory thumped the glass partition.

"Do it, Seb. Take the noose and pull it over your head."

Seb did as instructed. The noose rested around his shoulders. The rope pulled away from the ceiling, causing the loop to tighten around his neck.

"Good boy, good boy," Max chuckled through Seb's cans. "Just let it happen."

The noose tightened around Seb's neck, causing his face to turn red. The rope moved up, lifting him out of his chair by his neck.

He clutched at the noose, trying to pull it away.

"Don't fight it, Sebastian."

Seb tried to fight it. He gripped the rope and kicked his feet. By now, he was ten feet in the air. It was only a matter of moments until his neck would break.

"Welcome to Pure Dark."

"Gahhhhhh," Seb looked down amid Max's laughter to find Tabitha looking up at him with her bleeding wrists. She clapped her hands together in merriment, cheering on Seb's suicide.

Darren's splattered body writhed around its seat and fell against the console.

"Seems you've not made very many friends lately, Sebastian," Max's voice was uneven and angry.

Finally, Mary's corpse rolled to its side The bleeding head look up, spilling blood from its gunshot wound, "Die."

"Guurrggghhh," Seb kicked around for the final time.

CRACK!

Sebastian's neck snapped in half, killing him instantly. His corpse hung from the noose, toes facing the floor.

The water from the control room drained away. Gregory swam to the surface and gasped for air.

"Well done, guys," Max's voice came through the speakers. "You did *great*."

Tabitha stood to her feet and looked at her cut wrists, "Charlie *fucking* Ferrari. What happened to me?"

Darren blinked and felt around his flattened, gory body with his mangled hands. "Oh, God."

Mary's body sat up straight in her chair. Her head dangled down her back, "Oh," She grabbed her cheeks and lifted it onto her shoulders.

She blinked away the slew of blood that ran from her exit wound down to her eyes, "Wh-what happened?"

"He happened," Max laughed as the rope jiggled up and down, "I'm just sorry I didn't get to the fucker earlier."

The door to the radio room opened. Annie Banks walked in with a cup of tea.

"Oh no, not again," she huffed and made her way to Seb's swinging corpse, "Sebastian?"

"What the fuck are you doing here, bitch?" Max's voice boomed around the radio room. She ignored it and approached Seb.

The three animated corpses watched her knock against the console, "Sebastian."

A jingle played out the show, "Tune in again at the same time tomorrow, when Sebastian Sibald will be on hand to ensure you're at peace with life's problems. Only on Virile FM."

"Sebastian," Annie screamed.

"Huh?" Seb opened his eyes and sat up in his chair. He blinked and looked at Annie, "What happened?"

She frowned and took the cans from his head. Gary ran into the room in a fit of rage, "You fucking idiot."

"What, what?"

"You fell asleep again, dickhead," Gary grabbed his shoulders and threw him across the room, "Great timing, prick. On the day the bosses come in."

"But, but," Seb looked confused. He pointed at the control room - an empty chair with Gregory standing next to it. He didn't look too happy as he made his way out of the room.

"Go and get some coffee. Wake the fuck up."

Seb was *sure* he was dead. He rubbed his face and tried to figure out what was going on, "Yeah, okay. I think I need to get some fresh air or something."

"You want me to come with you?" Annie asked. "You look a bit shaken?"

Seb seemed perfectly fine but inside he was terrified, "I'll be okay."

Chapter 4

Damage Limitation

"That's him, man," Brian pointed out suited man crossing the road.

His friend, Leo, peered through the windshield of their car. The wipers went up and down, smearing the raindrops away from their view.

The car sat on a typical suburban street in *Chrome Valley*. It was two minutes to midnight and no one was around.

"Don't do that," Leo patted Brian's hand in retaliation, "You wanna draw attention to ourselves or something?"

"Nah, I can't see the dude when the window's all wet."

The man in the suit hadn't seen the car spying on him. Leo moved forward and squinted, "You sure that's him?"

"Yeah, man," Brian opened the driver's side and stepped out, "C'mon, let's do it."

He reached into his black jacket and retrieved a crowbar. Leo got out of the passenger side and closed the door. He pulled a red balaclava over his head which inadvertently made him stand out.

He threw his hood on and walked up to Leo, "Man, you wearing red?" he asked with incredulity.

"I ain't got no hood. This is all I could find."

"Fuck's sake. Couldn't you get a bright yellow jacket as

well?"

"Shut up. Are we gonna get our man, or what?"

Brian watched the man in the suit reach his front door. He waited for someone to answer as the porch light snapped on.

"Let's do it."

Brian held the crowbar in both hands as he jogged with Leo to the front gate.

The man they were following lived in a semi-detached house. It was past midnight, now. The street lights in this part of London usually worked.

Tonight, only half of them seemed to be working. The effect created many opportunities to hide in the shadows.

Lately, in this area of London, repairs for roads and various street paraphernalia were non-existent. To an extent, this was the fault of the man they were following.

He wasn't any common-or-garden suburbanite.

"Hey, you," Brian shouted from within his tightened hood. The man turned around to see who'd spoken but was instead greeted by a crowbar.

"Who, me?"

"Yeah, you," Brian approached the man and threatened him with the tool, "You're Seth Hester, right?"

"Yes, I am," Seth tried his best to avoid revealing his terror. He adjusted his tie and pushed his spectacles up the bridge of his nose, "Who are you?"

"Your worst nightmare, motherfucker," Leo butted in. "Come with us."

A silhouette of a woman approaching the door from within the house bled across the frosted glass.

"My wife is about to open the door. What do you want?"

"*Fuck it*," Brian pushed Leo around the corner of the porch, out of sight. He turned to Seth and held his finger to his lips.

"When she opens pretend you forgot something and

tell her you have to go."

"W-Why?"

"Just fucking do—"

The door opened. Brian and Leo slipped behind the brick porch, out of view.

"Hey, sweetie," the woman said, happy to see Seth.

"Hey, poppet," Seth acted happy and then pretended to forget something. He patted his jacket pocket and sighed, "Oh, no, I forgot my phone at the office."

"What? Really?"

"Yeah," Seth bullshitted. "I'm sorry, I'll get a cab and pick it up. I'll be right back."

"Can't you just leave the phone at the office?" She moved onto the porch and slid her arms around his waist. "I'm sure your constituents won't mind if they can't reach you for a few hours."

The two villains kept their backs to the wall. Brian moved forward and saw Seth's wife's back. He had a perfect view of her buttocks and legs underneath her negligee.

"*Charlie Ferrari*. Check that out."

Seth knew that he couldn't back out of his wife's offer.

"Please, honey. Just come inside."

Seth and Brian made eye contact, "Do it," Brian mouthed to him in haste.

"Fuck, bruv, she's hot," Leo whispered a bit too loudly.

Brian tucked himself around the corner and planted his palm over Leo's mouth, "Shut the fuck up, dickhead. Are you trying to get us caught?"

"What was that noise?" Seth's wife turned around, wondering where the hushed arguing was coming from, "Did you hear that?"

Seth shrugged his shoulders. He had heard the noise but decided to pretend he hadn't, "What noise?"

"Voices. They came from round the corner."

Seth's wife peered around the porch. No one was there. Brian and Leo had left.

"Hello? Is anyone there?" She clutched at her chest as the cold, night air got under her skin.

"Sweetie, there's no-one there." Seth looked around in the hope that his two assailants had abandoned their mission.

"No, there was definitely someone—" she trailed off and turned back to her husband, "*Ferrari almighty.*"

Leo had his arm around Seth, threatening to break his neck. He looked at his wife from under the red balaclava. His warm breath floated through the fabric.

"Shut it, *bitch.*"

Tap, tap.

She spun around to see Brian standing next to her, "Oh shit."

"All right, darling," Brian smiled under his hood. "You not gonna invite us in?"

"Let's go, fuckheads," Leo kicked Seth forward and into the house.

"Get inside. Now," Brian yanked Seth's wife by her negligee and shoved her through the front door.

SLAM! Leo kicked the front door shut and took a flick knife out from his jeans pocket. He held the blade at Seth's neck.

"What do you w-want?"

He kicked Seth up the landing and pushed him into the front room, "Get in there."

His wife began to cry and beg for her life, "Please, tell m-me what's going on?"

Brian tucked the crowbar into his jacket pocket and grabbed her by the back of the hair, "We don't want you. It's your husband we want."

"What?"

Brian slapped her across the face. Strands of her hair flew across her face and stuck to her tear-strewn cheeks.

He looked up at a painting on the wall. The image depicted a newborn baby with a green sliver of hair over its scalp. It rested in the fetal position inside the barrel of a syringe.

"Are you guys religious?"

She sniffed and held back her tears, "Yes, w-we're good, religious people."

"Then act like it," Brian kicked her forward onto the floor in the front room. She avoided butting her head on the side of the coffee table, "Do unto others, as your Lord Charlie Ferrari says."

Leo looked down at his wife and scanned her body, "Fuck, Seth. Your wife is hot."

Sure enough, she'd appeal to most heterosexual men. She was a clear ten years younger than her husband who, by now, had his hands raised and was fearing for his life.

"What's your name?" Brian asked.

"Abigail."

"Ah, yeah. Abigail Hester," Brian nodded at Leo. "She's always on the telly, man. Wife of a famous politician like Seth, here."

"What do you want from us?" she screamed.

"Stop screaming," Brian took out the crowbar from his jacket, "I didn't think I'd have to use this but you're testing my fucking patience."

"Please," Seth interrupted. "If it's money you want, you can have whatever is in the house."

"No!" Brian took offense and screamed, "We don't want your fucking money, councilor."

"Then wh-what do you want?"

Leo looked at Brian for a response and then looked down at his shoes. Brian took a deep breath.

"Fuck. Fuck," He booted the side of the coffee table, knocking over a snow globe with a crucifix in it to the floor, "This wasn't supposed to happen."

"Brian, man, let's just take him—"

"—Did you use my *real fucking name*, numb skull?"

"Oh. Sorry."

"Idiots. I'm working with fucking idiots."

Seth's wife looked up at Brian and tried to assuage his temper, "Look, B-Brian, we didn't see anything."

CRAA-AA-AACK!

Brian kicked her in the face as hard as he could in the face, instantly knocking her out.

"Don't call me by my real name. Fuck. *Fuck*."

He paced around and took out his mobile phone. His thumb ran across the screen and arrived a telephoto-lens picture of Seth. He showed it to his victim, "See that?"

Seth nodded, "Y-Yes."

"All we had to do was bundle you into the car and take you back to base. But your fucking wife had to get involved, didn't she?"

Seth quaked in his boots, "P-Please, don't do anything drastic."

"Drastic?" Brian pocketed his phone and pointed at his unconscious wife, who was bled all over the carpet, "Your cunt of a wife knows you're a target. She knows my fucking name, thanks to this imbecile."

Brian bopped Leo on the back of the head.

"I swear, neither of us will tell anyone," Seth kept his hands open. It appeared as if his suggestion might work, "Whatever you have in mind, you don't need to do it. If you walk away, then none of this will ever have happened."

"Fuck," Brian booted the coffee table again in anger. He clutched his knees and took a few deep breaths.

His temperament freaked Leo out, "Hey, man. What we gonna do?"

Brian looked up and tilted his head, "We'll have to do it here. We can't take him away."

"N-No, d-don't—"

"—You shut your fucking mouth," Brian yelled. "Fuck it. We'll do it here."

"But, Bri— *mate*, we were told to take him back to the warehouse."

"I don't give a shit," Brian took out his phone and pushed it into Leo's chest, "You wanna call that number and tell the guy we have his wife as well? We're fucking dead."

"Nah, man," Leo pushed the phone away. Seth watched the exchange and grew ever more terrified.

"Thought not," Brian slipped the phone into his pocket and waved the crowbar at Seth, "We do it here. Once it's done, we take it back to the warehouse and it'll be like nothing went wrong."

"Come on, fuckhead," Brian pushed Seth by his shoulders toward the couch.

Leo followed, "Sorry about your wife, man. It wasn't our fault."

"Sit down," Brian ordered.

"Okay, okay. Whatever you say."

"You can lower your hands now. This isn't a robbery."

Seth lowered his hands and bit his lip. He was in serious fucking shit.

Brian turned from the coffee table and looked at Seth, "I can see you have a chair. Have you got any rope?"

"Wh-what?"

"Rope," Brian screamed and kicked his unconscious wife in the stomach, "Like what you hang yourself with? Rope, you fucking cretin."

"Y-Yes, it's in the utility room, third drawer on the right."

Brian lifted his head at Leo, "Go and get it."

"Yeah," Leo ran out of the front room.

Brian turned back to Seth and slammed the crowbar end into his free palm. "Is there anyone else in the house?"

"Uh, uh, oh, Charlie—"

"—I'll take that as a fucking *yes*, then," Brian looked over his shoulder, "Fam, there's other fuckers in the house."

"Okay."

"You got that rope, yet?"

"Not yet. Still looking for it."

Abigail rolled over on the carpet and groaned, half-unconscious.

Brian licked his lips and turned back to Seth, "Who else is in the house?"

"Daddy?" A young boy's voice came from the front door. Brian turned around to see a six-year-old boy in *Star Jelly* pajamas looking back at him.

Brian kept staring at him from within his closed hood. His chest heaved out and in as he took a couple of deep breaths.

Seth tried for a smile, "Mark, go back to your room."

"Where's mommy?" His son asked, before spotting her groaning on the carpet, "Mummy?"

"No, Mark don't—"

He ran into the room and up to his mum. Brian stepped into his path and grabbed him under the arms, "Ah, da-da-da, Mark, no you don't."

"P-Please, don't hurt him," Seth begged.

"I want my mommy," Mark screamed and writhed around in Brian's clutches. "Let go of me."

"Listen, Mark. This is just a bad dream, okay?"

"No," the boy screamed and wriggled free from Brian's clutches, "My mommy is hurt."

He ran to the front room door and was met by Leo, carrying a fistful of rope, "Whoa. Hey, kid."

Leo bent down and covered Mark's mouth just as he let out an ear-piercing squeal.

"Mmfggghhh."

Leo struggled with the boy and looked up at Brian, "Where did this little shit come from?"

"Upstairs. Where do you think?"

"What do we do with him?"

Seth stood up from the couch and held out his hands, "Please, don't hurt him."

Brian let out a cry for help and exhaled, "Ugghh. I don't fucking believe this. First his fucking tart, and now his fucking kid."

"Mffghhh."

Mark kicked from within Leo's clutches and screamed into his palm, "Bruv, man, he's a fierce little cunt. We can't let him go, you know."

"Knock the little shit out," Brian spat in bewilderment, "Just knock the little fucker out."

Leo spun little Mark around and grabbed a fistful of his hair.

"Mfgghh."

"Now, uh, Mark? Listen to me, okay? No fuckin' screaming, yeah? You'll annoy the neighbors."

"Mffgghhh."

Leo grabbed Mark around the legs, trying to stop him from kicking.

"I said knock him out, not touch him up," Brian blurted out in pure rage.

"Sorry about this, munchkin," Leo yanked the boy's head back and raised his fist.

Seth stepped forward and yelled, "No."

SMACK!

Leo punched the boy in the face, sending him crashing to unconsciousness a few feet away from his mother.

"My baby," she cried and tried to crawl across the carpet toward her child.

Brian grabbed Seth by his collar and marched him over to the dining area. He screamed at Leo as he moved past the unconscious boy, "I can't fucking believe this. Can you take care of her, please?"

"M-My b-baby," she cried as she attempted to reach for her son.

Leo yelled back and slung the rope over his shoulders, "What do you want me to do?"

"I dunno, fam," Brian pushed Seth down onto a dining chair and set the crowbar onto the dining table, "Take care of her."

"Okay, okay."

Seth looked up at Brian from his chair, "Wh-what are you g-going to do?"

"Shut up," Brian turned to Leo to find him tearing the front of Abigail's negligee. Her breasts fell into his palms.

"What the fuck are you doing?"

"I'm making her play ball, what does it look like?"

"Throw me the fucking rope."

Leo grabbed the end of the rope and bunched it into his hand. He flung it across the room.

Brian caught it and turned to his victim on the chair, "Hands behind your back."

Seth did as instructed, "Please, whatever you've been told to do, you don't have to do it."

"I said shut up," Brian threatened and tied his victim's hands behind the chair.

"Oww."

"Tight enough for you?" Brian spat and patted him on the back of the head.

"You've been put up to this, haven't you?"

"Shut up."

"Who told you to do this?"

"Say another word and I'll kick your son's head off," Brian spotted a box of Kleenex on the dining room table. His fingers dug into the opening and removed a wedge of tissues.

"No, please."

Brian shoved them into Seth's mouth as a makeshift gag.

"There, all good," Brian turned to Leo once again. His friend squeezed Abigail's breasts in his hands, enjoying himself a bit *too* much.

"Mmm, very nice," Leo smiled at her from inside the balaclava, "Mr. Hester, you're a very lucky man."

"Would you knock it off," Brian yelled and picked up the crowbar, "We have a job to do."

Leo stood up and made for the dining room. Brian blocked his way.

"The woman?"

"Oh, yeah," Leo apologized and turned around, "I

forgot."

He looked down at the topless Abigail crying for her life, "Please, d-don't hurt—"

THWACK!

Leo took a free kick right into her breastbone, "Shut up."

She spat out a string of blood and let out a deathly rasp, "Ghhuuurrrr."

"Fucking knock her out," Brian thumped the dining room table, "Do it."

SMACK!

Leo kicked her across the face, knocking her out. Three of her teeth hit the skirting board and tinkled to a halt on the ground beside her passed-out son.

Leo rubbed his hands and rolled his shoulders. He made his way over to the dining room table, "How was that?"

"Good enough," Brian took his phone out of his pocket and hit speed dial.

Leo looked at their tied-up victim and saw what looked like his teeth melting down his chin, "Is his mouth okay?"

"Nah, it's fine. It's just tissue paper."

"Why?"

"To stop the cunt from screaming. What do you think?"

"Oh," Leo said. "Nice."

Someone answered Brian's call. "Hello?"

"It's me. We have the target.

"Excellent," the voice came through the speakerphone, "So the goods survived the transit?"

"Uh, yeah. *About that,*" Brian switched off the speaker and held the device to his ear, "We, uh, didn't actually get the item *in* transit."

Seth's ears pricked up. These guys were not after his money or possessions. This was a targeted attack, as he'd suspected since he'd clapped eyes on the pair.

"What the fuck are you looking at?" Leo threatened

Seth, who turned away.

Brian stepped back and took the call as privately as possible, "But, look, we had an unexpected event," he said and then stopped talking. The man on the other end of the phone launched into an inaudible tirade.

"Yes, I understand," he placed the phone back to his ear, "We'll get it done."

Brian took a moment to inhale. He pocketed the phone and walked over to the table.

"We still on?" Leo asked.

Brian looked at Seth, "My oh my, you *have* been a naughty boy, haven't you?"

"Mgghhh," Seth screamed through the soggy tissue. The soggy tissue remnants wisped down his chin. He spat the gluey substance down his front, "What the fuck is going on?"

Brian picked up the crowbar and shot Seth an evil look.

"Who was that on the phone?" Seth yelled and shunted himself forward in the chair, "Who put you up to this?"

"Once we're done with you, you'll completely forget what happened. So there's no point in telling you. You'll only forget."

"What?" Seth screamed for his life, "What are you going to d-do to me!?"

Two Days Ago…

Brian came out of his bedroom dressed in a gown. Without the hood over his head, he was a handsome twenty-something.

To have afforded to buy a house in *Chrome Valley* was a remarkable achievement at such a young age. He was a black man in a predominantly white British and European neighborhood. This fact meant that some of his neighbors were jealous of his success.

How Brian got the money to secure such an investment was anyone's guess. He worked during the day but never seemed to wear a suit.

Brian was always the first awake in the house. It was seven-thirty in the morning.

The plan, as it usually was on a Monday, was to beat his girlfriend to the kitchen. He'd make himself some coffee and start breakfast for his son, Jeremiah.

Every weekday morning, without fail, the toaster was set and fresh cups of orange juice were ready on the kitchen table. The mail was usually on the floor under the letterbox.

Today, it came slightly later than usual.

The toaster spat out its contents just as the letterbox swung to a close.

Brian collected up the various pieces of mail. The usual envelopes were there. One could always tell what the mail might be by the address.

A leaflet for an upcoming vote showed a white man smiling with glistening teeth. The man's name was Humphrey Ingham.

Re-elect me this Thursday as Mayor of *Chrome Valley*.
My five key principles are:
1: Strengthen the borough's economy.
2: Improve neighborhood watch.
3: Clean up our streets.
4: Rescind Proposition 118 and replace with a more suitable alternative.

Brian tucked the leaflet under the pile of mail. As he did so, a brown jiffy bag with his name written on it stared back at him.

This *was* unusual.

He wasn't expecting anything larger than letter sized mail. No goods were ordered from the internet in a while.

The mail hit the kitchen table just as his young son, entered the kitchen.

"Hello, Daddy," he said and took his seat at the table.

He poured a glass of orange juice and grabbed a piece of toast.

His father was in a world of his own. The jiffy bag was open. He looked over at his son and double-took, "Oh, hi."

"Are you okay, Daddy?"

"Yes, yes, I'm fine," he lied and returned to the sheet of paper in his hands.

The first of four sheets of paper had a message scrawled on it.

I know what you did.

The second sheet of paper showed an inset of a man taken on a telephoto lens. It was Seth going about his daily business. To the right of the picture were his home address, physical stats, and known movements on a weekday.

Brian looked up at his son and smiled. Deep down inside, he was dreading the last two sheets of paper.

His son smiled back and guzzled down the orange juice, "Where's mom?" his son asked, buttering his slice of toast.

Brian scanned the third sheet of paper. A photograph of his wife, beautiful and with long, dark hair, showed her accompanying her son to the school gate.

Brian looked up to find his wife had entered the kitchen. A spitting image, of course, of the one in his hand. He parked the papers to one side.

"Morning, sweetie," she yawned, helping herself to a glass of orange juice.

"Hey."

She looked at her husband. Something wasn't right, "Everything okay?"

"Uh, yeah," Brian collected up the papers and made his way to the stairs, "Sorry, can you guys finish up? I need to check my phone. Important business *stuff*."

"Okay, sweetie," she giggled half-awake and rubbed her son's hair.

An hour later, Brian was in the front seat of his car scanning the papers once again. He was perturbed with the person on the other end of the phone.

"Whoever this is, they've got my fucking family."

"What?" said the voice on the other end of the line, "You mean they've been following you?"

"Fam, man, they know everything about me," Brian looked at the last sheet of paper. A picture of Leo, along with a physical profile, glared back at him, "Me, you, this Seth dude. Everything."

"The fuck?"

"Yeah, look," Brian returned to the second sheet, "It says we gotta meet some next man at half ten in his office. We can't *not* go, you know."

"Ten-thirty?"

"Yeah, I'mma pick you up right now. Be ready."

Brian threw the sheets of paper to the passenger seat and started the engine.

10:30 am

Brian pulled up into an industrial estate. He'd picked up Leo ten minutes ago.

"I thought we was gonna hit the post office today, man?" Leo asked.

Brian wasn't interested. He was too concerned with following the directions on his sat nav, "It said take a right at the cemetery. Unit ninety-two. *Penelope's Father.*"

"Let me see them papers, man," Leo grabbed them from the dashboard. His face fell when he saw that his friend wasn't lying about their impromptu meeting.

"Fuck me," Leo pointed at the sheet of paper, "That's your girl, man."

"I know."

"Oh, fuck, and look," Leo swapped the papers around, "That's me! Who is this guy?"

"I dunno," Brian blurted as he slowed the car down, "Look out for unit ninety-two, bruv."

"B-Man, this guy is serious. He knows everything about us. Hey, wait up. Who's this Seth guy?"

"I don't know."

"One clean-shaved silver fox, he is."

Brian's eyes widened in the reflection of the windshield. A man in a suit with gray hair stood outside the double door with his arms folded.

Above him was a giant banner reading *Penelope's Father*. A picture of a half-dressed teenager holding a vibrator completed the company's image.

"This must be it, man." Leo looked up as Brian stopped the car in a car parking space.

The man outside smiled and held out his hands.

Brian turned to Leo and took the papers from him, "You cool, fam?"

"Yeah, man. I'm sweet."

"Okay," Brian turned a spry eye toward the man waiting for them, "We go in, hear him out, and play it bone chilled. You hear me?"

"Yeah, man. 'Course."

"Let's go."

Brian clutched the papers under his arm. They both hopped out of the car and approached the suited man.

The stranger's white teeth glistened in the morning sun, "Hi, chaps. Glad you could make it."

"Who are you?"

"Allow me to introduce myself," he said as he danced on the spot. He threw out his hand for them to shake, "I'm Max Dark."

***

Penelope's Father was much larger inside than the exterior had promised. A giant factory consisting mainly of automated processing.

Conveyor belts rolled along to an automated robotic arm. The mechanical robot attached a bulbous-shaped lid to the end of each item.

The window in Max Dark's office offered the view of the factory and its dozens of masked workmen.

It was difficult to tell exactly what the company made. The angle Brian and Leo had as they took their seats made it difficult to see the production line.

"What is it you make here?" Brian hoped to turn the meeting into some kind of business proposition. He knew in his heart of hearts that he and Leo were in for a blackmailing.

To Brian's mind, if they were able to show some business acumen then maybe their host might want to go into business with them.

Max took his seat behind his Oakwood desk and placed his feet on the table, "I wouldn't worry too much about all that shit behind me. It's just a front, really."

"Are those *dildos*?" Leo raised his eyebrows.

"Why, yes. They are," Max threw his hands behind his head and made himself comfortable, "Are you an expert on personal sexual satisfaction?"

"No."

"Thought not," Max slipped his feet from the table. As fidgety as ever, he clasped his hands together, perched his elbows on the desk and threw Brian a dirty look, "So, you got my message, then?"

"Yeah, man," Brian threw the sheets of paper onto the desk, "Tell us what the fuck is going on."

"Okay." Max rolled his shoulders and cleared his throat, "I'll try to put this as simply as I can. You might not like what you're about to hear, but just listen."

"Whatever."

"Have you heard of something called Proposition 118?"

"No."

"It doesn't matter. You don't need to know what it is. What you *do* need to know is that it is a piece of legislation. Our beloved government is proposing to vote it in the day after tomorrow. If the vote goes through, you, your friend here, your family, and everyone you know will be set free. No more misery."

"The fuck are you talking about?"

Max slipped out the second sheet of paper. A picture of Seth's face smiled back up at them, "This guy, you know who he is?"

"Yeah, well, no," Brian stumbled. "I know who he is because of this bit of paper."

"Philistines. You don't watch the news?"

"Nah, man."

"Amazing." Max blinked and held up the paper, "This piece of shit, Seth Hester, is the brainchild of Proposition 118. He's the one who wants to put it through and get it approved."

"What's this got to do with us?" Brian asked.

"You're going to kidnap him so we can prepare him for the fight against the mayor of *Chrome Valley*."

"Prepare him?"

"Yeah," Max smiled. "You have his coordinates. The day after tomorrow, you and your friend are going to kidnap him and bring him back to this location. And then we're going to cause him some blunt force trauma so that he can take part in the vote."

Brian sat back in his seat and folded his arm. He wasn't very happy, "You want us to kidnap a politician and bring him back here for a beating?"

"Correct."

"What if we say no?"

"Ah, I thought you might say that," Max sifted through the papers and held up the picture of his wife and son, "It'll either happen to Seth Hester. Or, your wife and child."

Brian launched out of his seat and scrambled over the table, "Motherfucker."

Leo got up and held him back, "B-Man, man, don't."

Max kicked himself back. The wheels on his chair rolled toward the glass, carrying him to the window, "Haha. I knew you'd go for it."

He stood up and looked through the glass pain. Brian thumped the desk in anger, "Let go of me."

Max kept his back toward the pair.

"Listen to me, you pair of faggots," Max's demeanour turned on a dime - from jovial to demonic in a heartbeat, "If you don't do as I say, Proposition 118 won't go through and we'll all be stuck in this fucking coma."

"Fuck you."

Max turned around and stared into Brian's eyes, "You don't seem to understand, do you?"

"Understand what, you fucking prick?"

Max frowned looked down at his shoes, "I've been trapped in here for a nearly a week. There's no way out."

"What the fuck are you talking about, bruv?" Brian threw Leo's hands from his shoulders. He demanded answers.

Flames erupted from Max's ears, nose, and mouth. Brian and Leo jumped back, startled.

"I'm stuck inside this fucking *junkie's* heroin coma. I'm trapped inside his head. I can't get out," Max kicked his desk. It split right across the middle and fell apart, "Until that prick wakes up, I'm stuck here. We're *all* stuck here."

"You're out of your fucking mind, man," Brian yelled back.

"No," Max pointed to his own temple with his forefinger, "Not *my* mind. Charlie's mind."

"Fuck you, I ain't religious. I don't believe in any of that bullshit."

"It's true. We're all stuck here, Brian," Max calmed down and wiped his lips with his knuckle, "I'm sorry."

He walked over to a cupboard and opened the door,

"Do what I ask. Get Seth Hester here so we can stop Proposition 118."

Max reached into his desk and grabbed a crowbar. He threw it to Brian.

"What's this?"

"Why, it looks like a motherfucking *crowbar*," Max huffed and reached into the cupboard again. He took out a small digital readout, "Here, Leo. Catch."

Leo caught the digital readout, "The fuck's this?"

"You're going to smack Seth around the head as many times as it takes to get the readout to level out at 1.18."

"What?"

"It's simple. You tie the cunt up and you whack him around the head. Every time you do, the readout will climb. When it hits 1.18 you'll stop. Don't go above that number."

Brian picked up the crowbar and inspected it, "Let's say I just fucking whack *you* now and walk away. Problem solved?"

"I wouldn't do that if I were you."

"Yeah, man?" Brian seethed. "And why is that?"

"Because if anything happens to me, my men have been instructed to visit your house. And my men are a little bit *rapey* and *murdery*."

"Don't you touch my family."

"I will touch your family," Max barked and folded his arms, "In fact, here's what'll happen. My bodyguard, Jace, will use your son's dead body as a condom to ass rape your fucking wife. How does that sound?"

"*Motherfucker.*"

Max held out his arms and offered Brian a free hit, "Hit me, big boy. My big, black nigger. Take a swipe at me and see what happens."

It was all Brian could do not to straight-up attack his blackmailer.

Max chuckled to himself, "You're all the same, you fucking coons. Pent-up anger with nowhere to release it.

My advice is this. Save your frustration and take it out on Seth."

Brian took a deep breath and concentrated his vengeful gaze on Max, "When this is done, I'mma find you, motherfucker. I am gonna kill you."

"That's the spirit! Seth won't know what hit him," Max clapped his hands together and jumped up and down with delight.

Brian snarled at Max, "I meant *you*, you prick."

"Oh."

Presently...

Seth screamed, tied to the dining room chair. Abigail and Mark lay unconscious in the front room, bleeding from their faces.

Leo turned to Brian and saw that he'd lifted the crowbar.

"Wait, let me take the thing out," Leo screamed from under his red balaclava. He took out the digital readout and squeezed it.

Brian took a step toward Seth and grabbed his chin, "You ready to have your mind blown, big boy?"

"No, d-don't," Seth writhed in his shackles and turned his face away.

"Look at me," Brian yelled. "Look at me, you *fuck*."

"Nuuhh," Seth's face turned from the force of Brian's fingers.

"Before we start I want to know something."

"Wh-what?"

"What's Proposition 118?"

Seth raised his eyebrows, "Is th-that what this is a-about?"

"Tell me what it is."

"If I tell you will you release me?"

Brian thought about this request. He didn't have it in himself to batter the poor man *and* lie to him into the bargain, "No."

"Then fuck you," Seth spat in Brian's face, "I'm not telling you anything. I'd rather get beaten.'

A disappointed Brian exhaled and lifted the crowbar to the man's face, "You heard the man."

"Batter up," Leo gasped as he watched the end of the crowbar reach the ceiling.

Brian squeezed his grip and swung down.

TCHLAMP!!

The end of the bar smashed Seth's temple. The force of the blow dislodged his right eye from its socket and shattered the cheekbone.

A shard of ivory jutted out from his cheek.

"Oh, fuck," Leo dry-heaved. "A home run."

It wasn't so much the sight that disturbed him as the gargling noise coming from Seth's mouth.

Brian unfastened his hood. The room had become very warm since they'd arrived, "Fuck, man. Look at him."

"Schllessshhhh," Seth wavered in and out of consciousness. The pain was incredible.

Blood and saliva ran from his lips down to his shoulder, "Ah-schless, a schleeggh."

"Shut the fuck up," Brian yelled and turned to Leo, "Put the fucking measuring *thing* on him."

"Okay, okay."

Leo placed the metal plate on the side of Seth's face. The readout showed a reading of 0.315.

"How much does it have to be, again?" Leo asked.

Brian swiped the digital readout away from Seth's face, "One point one eight."

"We have to hit him again?" Leo stuttered, afraid of what another blow might do to the poor man.

"Yeah, fam. We go again."

Seth murmured down his shoulder and lifted his bleeding head. His bloodshot right eye pulsated in its gore-laden socket, "Ashesshh, yew'll."

Brian lifted the crowbar, "Stand back, man."

"Argghhsshh, flaahh."

SHWA-TCHOMMPP-PP

The end of the crowbar connected with his cheekbone. The blunt end pulverized his skull and pushed his teeth through his lips.

Glumph. Glumph. Seth's face tilted back as he swallowed down a set of teeth. He began to choke and spit some of them out, followed by a spurt of blood.

"Oh for *fuck's* sake, man!" Leo stepped forward and held his nose, "That's fucking sick."

"Put the damn thing on him again," Brian pointed to what little of Seth' face remained and tried not to puke.

His right eye bungee-jumped down his cheek, hanging from its stork. He blew out some more teeth.

"Ugh, fuck. It's meant to go against his temple," Leo analysed the man's face. He held up the digital readout and couldn't fathom where to place it, "I dunno where, man."

"Put it somewhere else, then, numb nuts."

Leo moved forward and held Seth's chin in his hand, "Sorry about this, mate."

Seth's head cradled Leo's chest like a baby. The slurping sounds from his damaged nasal passage were unbearable, "K-Kill, m-me."

"Nah, man," Leo whispered to him as he pressed the readout to his scalp, "We can't."

"What does it say?" Brian prepared to strike again.

Leo looked at the readout, "Zero point nine one seven."

"Aww shit," Brian spat and clutched the crowbar as tight as he could, "We're gonna have to go again."

"Fuck, B-Man. Look at him, he ain't going nowhere."

"We gotta do it again."

Seth's deathly gargling started to get under Brian's skin.

Leo had an epiphany - albeit a pathetic one. He pointed at Seth's face and then at his hair.

"Knock him out, on *top* of his head. That should do it."

"Oh, fuck this."

Brian lifted the crowbar above his own head with both hands, "Like, right down on top?"

"Yeah, bruv. Like a boiled egg kinda thing."

"Daddy," screamed Mark from behind them. "What are you doing to my Daddy?"

Seth angled his battered and broken face down to his son, “Schuuuun.”

"Fuck, man. Get that fucking kid out of here."

"Daddy," Markscreamed and ran over to his blood-soaked, half-conscious father slumped in the chair.

Leo ran after him and picked him up, "Oh, no you don’t. Come here."

"I want my Daddy," Leo lifted Mark into his arms and covered his eyes with his gloved hand, "No, this isn’t for you, kid."

"For fuck’s sake," Brian yelled. "Do something about the fucking kid."

Leo turned from Brian to Seth, "We can’t knock him out *again*."

"No, no," Mark tried to wriggle free from Leo’s clutches, "Let me go."

The boy bit down on Leo’s hand.

"Gaaahhhh," Leo released the kid from his grip. He landed on the floor and looked up at Brian, who was ready to administer yet another blow to his father’s head.

"What are you doing to my Daddy? You hurt him."

"Fuck off, you little cunt," Brian shooed the kid away with his feet. "Leo, man, get this little shit away from me."

"He bit me."

"Bite him back, then."

Leo launched over at Mark and grabbed him by the shoulders. He sunk his teeth into the kid’s neck.

“Gaaaoooow,” Mark screamed as a rope of blood flew out of his neck and splashed against’ Leo’s teeth.

"What in the name of *cunt* do you think you’re doing?" Brian asked with the crowbar held over his head.

Leo looked up and spat out a glob of blood from

between his teeth, "You said bite him back."

"You fuckin' *spastic*," Brian lost his temper and kicked Mark in the head, knocking him out cold, "There. See how easy that was?"

Leo got up to his feet and wiped his mouth, "Sorry, man."

"What do you think you are? A fucking vampire? Let's get this shit done and get out of here."

"Right, do it."

Brian squeezed the crowbar and roared.

SCHTAA-AAAMMM.

The crowbar smashed down onto Seth's scalp, causing the skull to crack open. A part of his brain shot out through the thinnest of slits above his left eyebrow.

"Whoa, *fuuuck*," Brian stepped back and dropped the crowbar on Mark's little stomach.

"*Daaayyummm*, boo," Leo gasped and hopped over to Seth. His brain was like jelly, threatening to spill out of the cavernous hole.

Seth's remaining eye fluttered in its socket. His breathing grew fierce and watery.

Leo placed the digital device on Seth's neck, "That's it, One point one one eight."

"Thank fuck for that."

A loud applause came from the door to the front room.

"Well done, chaps," came a familiar voice from behind the pair.

Leo and Brian turned around. They weren't expecting company.

Least of all Max Dark, his bodyguard and a couple of armed security detail. The latter pointed their machine guns and scoured the rest of the house.

"Check every single nook and cranny. Make sure the house is empty."

Max stepped over the unconscious Abigail and approached the pair. He looked at Seth and smiled.

"One point one one eight?

"Yeah, man," Leo showed Max the digital readout.

"Excellent," Max turned around to inspect the front room. He noticed the unconscious Abigail bleeding on the floor, "Jace, my good man, can you scoop that thing off the floor and take it to Uterox, please?"

"Yes, Mr. Dark."

"Have one of the boys help you with it."

"Okay," Jace bent over, grabbed her ankles and pulled her corpse across the carpet. A streak of blood followed behind.

Max turned around and cracked his knuckles, "I do love it when a plan comes together. Now, how's our friend doing?"

He walked over to Seth and slapped the side of his face. The gelatinous brain wobbled around in its skull like a bowl of fresh jello.

"Wh-what did we just d-do?" Leo asked.

Max took out a scalpel and sliced off a sliver of Seth's exposed frontal lobe, "What you've just done, my good man, is prepare our friend, here, for his engagement tomorrow."

"Engagement?"

"Have you heard of Dark's Palsy?" Max turned to Leo, believing that he might have heard the news stories of late.

He hadn't, of course. Leo and Brian weren't ones to consume news media.

"Uh, no?"

Max turned to Seth and tried to shut his dangling jaw, "Never mind. I wouldn't worry too much about the physical trauma. We'll get our friend patched up and right as rain in no time."

"Are we in the clear? Brian asked Max.

"Oh, yes. You've done well, boys."

An armed guard came running up to Seth. He almost slipped on blood patch left on the carpet from Abigail's beating.

"Mr. Dark. Sir?"

"Ah, yes," Max turned to the guard. He squinted at the helmet, unable to establish who was underneath it, "Which one are you?"

"K-Twelve, sir."

"Ah, right, Mr. K-Twelve," Max pointed at Seth's badly disfigured face, "Get K-Eleven and however many Ks you have at your disposal, and have our friend here removed. Take him back to base and have him prepped."

"Yes, Mr. Dark," he said. "Oh, and the kid?"

Max looked down at Mark's body. He crouched over it and held two fingers against his neck, "Hmm. He didn't survive. No pulse."

"Shall we dispose of it, sir?"

"Yes, when company arrives, have them scrape it off the floor and extract whatever you need from it. It's still young. We might be able to siphon bits of it."

"Yes, Mr. Dark." The guard moved in and went for Seth's face.

"If all else fails, just flog it on the *Blind Web* to the highest bidder. Preferably someone local, to save on shipping."

"Certainly, sir."

"Oh, and be careful with Mr. Hester, okay? We need him in one piece for tomorrow. Physically, at least."

A couple of armed guards with helmets came in to assist with the removal of Seth from the chair.

Max pulled Brian and Leo to one side as the guards lifted the gargling Seth away.

"A slight change of plans, but we got there in the end."

Brian was about to lose his shit, "Yeah, whatever. You tell us what the fuck just happened?"

Max chuckled and slipped on a pair of black gloves, "Ha. I do love your sense of humor."

"I ain't fuckin' around, you prick," Brian threatened.

"Ooooh, touchy," Max smiled and placed his hands on his hips. He took a step forward and upped the theatrics,

"Okay, seeing as you've asked."

"Well?"

"He should be perfectly matched with his opponent. What you boys have done is caused just enough brain trauma as to render Mr. Hester with Dark's Palsy."

"Dark's Palsy?"

"Yes," Max explained as he walked over to Seth's stereo system, "In effect, a dribbling, fucking retard."

Brian folded his arms and tried to process the information. Max, on the other hand, fiddled with the buttons on the music system. It irritated both Brian and Leo. Was he taking this whole situation seriously enough?

"Wait up. You had us hit him around the head just enough to make him a retard?"

"Indeed I did, yes."

"But *why*?" Leo interrupted.

Max took out two identical business cards and handed one to each to Brian and Leo.

"Tomorrow, the results are in. I'll meet you there with a truck of boiling water before we kick off."

Hollowpoint Inc.
254-255 Langham Park
Chrome Valley
Midnight.
By invitation only.

"What's this?" Brian read the contents of the card.

"An address," Leo offered.

Confused, they both looked up at Max for an answer.

He'd vanished.

So, too, had the guards.

And Mark's body.

And his mother's.

And Seth's.

All that remained was a splattered dining table and a nasty streak of blood on the carpet.

Brian and Leo turned to each other, "We'd better get out of here."

Chapter 5

Lobster Politics (Part One)

My beloved Astrid,

I am afraid I know no other way to tell you this, so I have chosen to write you a letter. I hope you will understand why I've done this. I trust it finds you in good stead.

I have rehearsed what I need to tell you verbally so many times in the mirror. Frankly, it comes across as ridiculous. I can't bear to verbalize it.

Something strange is happening to me.

It explains my absence since the weekend. My colleagues and I have been so busy with the Proposition 118 white paper, lately. You've barely noticed my coming home in the small hours of the morning. I am quite sure, however, that you've noticed my departure from the house before you wake up each morning.

By night, I am Humphrey Ingham, the husband you know and love.

Until a few days ago, this was true.

There's simply no other way to tell you this. When nightfall occurs, I turn into a lobster. This is not a metaphor, incidentally. My skin sheds like that of a snake, and my skeleton squeezes until I am on all fours. My hands turn to claws.

I grow antennae, which enables my senses.

I remain this way until dawn the following morning.

Of course, I completely understand how this must read, Astrid. When I am a lobster, I possess all the traits that one would reasonably expect. I am more or less permanently on a quest for food. Mainly fish and other small prey, but I am deathly afraid that my appetite for human flesh might cause you harm.

I have chosen to leave home until I can figure out what is going on.

Please do not try to find me.

Yours,
Humphrey x

Astrid, whose days of having to pay bus fare were almost at an end, held the letter in her hands. She felt the need to scan the message again to make sure she wasn't dreaming.

She wasn't.

Her initial reaction was one of hilarity. It took the woman a good three minutes to stop laughing at this supposed "joke" Humphrey had left for her.

After all, thirty years of marriage and two teenage sons will do that to you.

Humphrey was a well-respected member of the community. He was the mayor of Chrome Valley. It was a job he relished. Of course, one of the most powerful attributes a mayor could have is that of humour and persuasion.

The letter Astrid held in her hands were neither of those things. After a hearty chuckle, she set the letter to the kitchen counter and began to cry.

She tried calling his mobile phone but he wouldn't answer. This was fairly typical behavior, though. Humphrey was a busy man and rarely answered his phone.

Astrid paced around the front landing running a series of solutions through her mind.

First, was Humphrey having an affair? Touchy ground, this idea. He'd slept with his secretary once before. Astrid forgave him and tried to forget all about it.

Second, and perhaps most crushing of all prospects, had Humphrey simply had enough? Was he no longer in love with her?

There was a third, and fourth, and fifth - and tenth - thing that went through her mind. She couldn't entertain them all. One of them persistently gnawed away at her thoughts.

Perhaps Humphrey had lost his mind?

Astrid faced with an invidious decision. Should she tell her two teenage sons, Ralf and William, that Dad had run mad? That he'd fallen out of the crazy tree and hit every branch on the way down?

What harm could it do?

Perhaps they'd find it funny as well?

It needed sorting out, though, whatever this silly nonsense was.

Which is why Astrid picked up the phone and called one of Humphrey's closest allies in government.

Seth Hester, MP for Chrome Valley West and creator of Proposition 118. A bill that was set to change the psychological landscape of his constituents' reality forever.

"What do you mean he's left you a note?" Seth asked through the phone. He was perplexed. You could tell it in his voice.

Astrid twiddled the phone wire between her fingers, "I came downstairs this morning and found it. It's bizarre. I mean, Humphrey has a peculiar sense of humor, but this is taking the piss. Even for him."

"Why? What did it say?"

Astrid held the note in her free hand and tried not to look at the sixth, offending paragraph. "Ugh, this is just silly."

The line went quiet. The commotion of Seth's environment waved through the phone. Hustle and bustle. It sounded busy, like a gathering of people chatting and laughing.

"Sorry, Astrid," Seth whispered, "I'm being harassed. What did you say it said?"

Astrid sniffed and chewed back her tears. "He's claiming he's a lobster."

"I beg your pardon?!"

"That's what it says!" Astrid yelled through her tears.

Seth laughed. "Ah, that's typical of him. He's just messing you around, Astrid. Honestly."

"He even underlined the fact that it isn't a metaphor."

"Yeah, that sounds like something he'd do," Seth tried to come across as affable, but it was no use. He clocked Astrid's turmoil and launched into sympathy mode, "Look, Astrid, whatever's going on, I'm sure I and the rest of the benches would have seen it by now. Nothing is amiss."

"I h-hope so," Astrid bawled. "I just hope he's not seriously ill or something."

"Humphrey? Ill? I doubt it."

The House of Commons, Westminster

Seth looked at his wristwatch and then back up at the speaker of the house. He held his mobile phone to his face. Everyone was waiting for him to finish his call.

All six hundred-odd members of parliament.

"Look, Astrid, if I see him I'll get him to call you."

"Thanks, Seth," Astrid's voice seemed to calm down.

The speaker of the house raised his eyebrows and nodded at Seth on the front bench.

"The Right Honorable Seth Hester, MP."

The members of parliament whooped and cheered as Seth took the mantle at the front. He placed a sheet of paper down in front of him.

"Mr. Speaker, if it would please the house, I'd like to reiterate the importance of Proposition 118."

A chorus of disapproval weaved through the opposite benches.

Sets of eyeballs blinked back at Seth. He noticed a suited man on the back bench taking notes on his iPad. His stood out on account of the green Mohawk; most unusual for such an elitist and professional setting.

Seth blinked and looked back at his notes, "Proposition 118. Set out by the recommendations of Dr. Jennifer Long and other parties state the following. For each weekday, one of the brain's senses will be disabled for that twenty-four hour period."

Half of the opposition shuffled and booed amongst themselves.

"Order," the speaker of the house screamed, "Order. Please, the right honorable gentleman has a right to be heard. Mr. Hester, continue."

"Much obliged, Mr. Speaker. Namely, the first weekday, Monday, a mandatory loss of sight."

More boos and echoes of upset.

"Tuesday," Seth continued. "A twenty-four hour disabling of the sense of hearing. Wednesday, the loss of all sense of touch—"

"—Yeah, yeah," mocked an elderly politician from the opposition bench.

Seth ignored the comment and continued.

"Thursday, the pausing of the sense of smell. And, finally, Friday, the sensation of taste is to be halted. The findings of the report recommend that Proposition 118 will seek to disarm psychological and religious terrorism. For too long now, these acts have disadvantaged members of my constituency. Indeed, the population at large. The vote will take place at midnight, tonight. My colleagues and I wish that the bill is passed so we may refine the content ahead of Royal Assent."

Seth sat back onto the bench to a wave of hilarity and incredulity.

"Order," the speaker of the house screamed at the top of his lungs. The noise was deafening, "I said motherfucking order."

The men and women in the room wouldn't shut up. The speaker of the house had no alternative but to reach into the side of his chair and produced an AK-47.

He pulled back the chamber and cocked the firearm. It got everyone's attention.

"Shut the fuck up or I'll massacre every motherfucker in this place."

Everyone on the opposition bench threw their hands into the air. One lady with red-rimmed glasses who'd been verbally abrasive looked extremely scared.

The speaker swung the machine gun toward her, "You want some, bitch?"

"N-No."

Right," the speaker growled and lowered his gun, "Shut the fuck up, then."

Outside

Seth and his colleague, the Right Hon. Algernon Williamson MP, made their way out of the building.

A flurry of around two hundred protesters with banners and signs, chanted over and over again.

"One One Eight is One-One-Hate.
"Losing a sense makes no sense."

"Oh, shite," Seth whispered to his colleague. He had to walk through the protesters to get to his chauffeur-driven sedan at the side of the road, "It's them again."

"Just ignore them. Remember, say nothing and get in the car. That's what I do."

"Yes, I know."

Seth adjusted his collar and put on a brave face as he moved through the crowd.

"Oi. Hester," screamed a man with a green Mohawk. He looked identical to the MP who sported the same haircut inside, "Why are you trying to fuck us up and take away our senses?"

"Look, this is neither the time nor the place—"

"—Don't say anything," Algernon whispered, ushering him toward the car, "Don't do it."

The protester didn't like Seth's answer. He punched him on the arm, "Traitor. This is a violation of our civil fuckin' liberties, man."

All the protesters shrieked in agreement with their spokesperson. The man with the green Mohawk looked up to a pink-haired lady with scaly skin standing on top of a car.

She took out a megaphone and pointed at Seth, "Traitor. Traitor. Mr. Hester, sir, When are you going to answer your critics and tell us why you want this law passed?"

"No to Proposition 118," chanted the furious mob.

"Okay, okay," Seth approached the car with his arms outstretched, "Give me the megaphone."

"What are you doing?" Algernon yelled at Seth as he took the megaphone from the pink-haired lady. He placed it in front of his face.

"Listen. Listen."

The crowd went quiet. Algernon looked at the protester with the green Mohawk. At the north end of Parliament Square, a crowd of media and TV reporters swarmed closer to the action.

"Listen," Seth started. "Proposition 118 is being put forward for the benefit of the many, not just the few."

"How exactly is disabling our senses meant to benefit

us?" asked the pink-haired lady.

"I can't go into it, here," Seth offered to a very unhappy crowd. "We're trying to combat the terrorist threat that's been threatening our very existence."

"Bullshit."

SMASH!

An empty beer bottle crashed around Seth's feet, "This has nothing to do with it."

Seth grew angry as the protesters grew impatient.

"How many of you lost a friend or loved one during the attack on Chrome Junction Arena?"

The question got everyone's attention. Four thousand people were melted into a gory sludge. The protesters began to pay attention.

"Oh, so now we've gone quiet, have we? I'll ask another question. How many of you have turned into a snake?"

The crowd looked down, apologetically.

"Or been tortured by a clown? Or visited a restaurant and been killed? How about dying in a fire, or been viciously gang-buggered in a library?"

Seth's diatribe shut everyone up. He seethed with rage, "You do know that each and every one of you is just a figment of some junkie's imagination, right?"

A midget in the crowd stepped forward. He pointed at Seth in sheer anger, "Fuck you. I'm an atheist, I don't believe in Charlie fucking Ferrari."

"You think I'm talking about religion?" Seth asked through the megaphone, "This isn't religion."

"I don't have faith," the midget yelled insistently, "I only have the facts. We only have the facts. You're a crackpot."

The crowd piped up again. None of the hundreds of attendees were evidently religious at all.

"This is not up for debate," Seth screamed through the megaphone. "You, me, and everyone we know and love do not exist. We are not real. Until we become enlightened we need a consensus. We must defy the deity keeping us prisoner by beating him at his own game."

"The Lord Almighty, Charlie Ferrari?" the pink-haired lady spat, "You really are a crackpot."

"I know church and state are meant to be separate. I understand that. But unless we all act now, we're doomed. If this legislation doesn't pass then we're all consigned to a life of whatever He and his mind will dream up."

The crowd was against the idea. Some of them walked away in disgust. Others stood around, shaking their heads.

At the very least, they had managed to get a politician to speak honestly. A genuine rarity.

Algernon shuffled up to Seth and helped him down from the car, "You're not making many friends today, you know."

"I know," Seth jumped to the floor and handed the megaphone back to the lady, "Thanks for hearing me out at least."

She chewed her gum and winked at him, "That's your career fucked, pal."

"The bill's going to vote tonight," Seth said to her. "Do you think you can change their minds? I wouldn't be doing this if I didn't think—"

"—I doubt that, Mr. Hester," she climbed down to the ground, "You can't violate our rights like this."

She resumed chanting along with the other protesters.

Seth and Algernon reached their sedan and climbed in the back.

"Are you okay, Seth?" Algernon asked, concerned for his colleague.

"Yeah, I'm fine," He looked out of the window as the car pulled off onto the road, "It's about to get dark. I need to get back to Abigail and Mark after the surgery."

"I think it'd be best if you keep your mouth shut until the vote," Algernon huffed.

"Maybe you're right."

Algernon offered a sympathetic smile, "I'm sure the ayes will have it."

Mr Humphrey Ingham

Humphrey Ingham was an ungainly man. His belly hung over the belt of his pristine trousers.

A triple chin hung under his jowls. A monocle sat in his right eye.

He held himself up against the kitchen counter in his office. The kettle rumbled and coughed up a cloud of steam. Humphrey kept watching, trying to stare whatever fear he had inside him right in the face.

Rumble, rumble, click.

The water boiled and began to simmer. Humphrey gripped the counter and let out a sigh of relief.

"Dad."

Humphrey turned around to find his teenage son, Ralf, looking at him, "You still obsessed with that bloody kettle, Dad?"

"Yes, son," Humphrey said, turning back to the kettle and muttering to himself, "I can't help myself."

"It won't do you any good, you know," Ralf tried his best to tuck his father's two-sizes-too-small shirt over his bulbous stomach, "We gotta get you in the car park before sundown."

"I know," Humphrey warbled his way over to a chair and made himself comfortable. He held up his hands and inspected his varicose veins.

The years hadn't been kind to the mayor of Chrome Valley. He was pushing seventy and didn't look a day under ninety.

Humphrey caught his breath and placed his unfathomably large backside onto the chair.

"Oooph. That hit the spot."

The legs on the chair seemed to cry for help as they splayed out.

Ralf looked at his father and folded his arms, "Hmm."

"What?"

"If you want to keep your suit fresh you'd better disrobe now."

"Very well," Humphrey stood up and arched his back in discomfort.

"Mom said you left her a letter?"

"Indeed I did, yes."

"Real smooth," Ralf struggled to contain his sarcasm, "Would have been better if you'd just left it alone."

Humphrey said, slipping off his jacket and unbuttoning his cuff links, "I couldn't exactly tell her to her face, could I?"

Ralf threw his father a towel. It landed across his bare, blotchy shoulder, "True, but really? A fucking letter?"

"What else was I to do?"

"It's only for another day, Dad. You could've just kidded-on that you were busy."

"What if this stupidity never stops?" Humphrey kicked off his trousers and threw them onto the table.

Ralf nodded at his father's legs, "Underwear, Dad."

Humphrey held out his hands in defiance, "Ugh, do I have to?"

"Yes. Unless you want Mom to wonder where all your underwear has got to? You're not exactly The Incredible Hulk."

Humphrey yanked down his briefs to his ankles. His belly obscured any immodesty that might have otherwise hung on display.

"... maybe the Incredible Sulk," Ralf muttered to himself as his father stood up straight. Parts of Humphrey's anatomy hung in full view.

An image no son should have seen, "Oh, for Ferrari's sake, Dad."

"Hey," Humphrey spat. "Don't blaspheme. That's not on, son."

"Sorry Dad," Ralf tried not to look at it, "Just use the

towel, okay? Cover it up."

Humphrey hung the towel out and wafted it in the air, "You take the Lord's name in vain again and I'll give you a bare bottom spanking—"

"—Oh, shit," gasped a voice from behind them. William, Ralf's younger brother, had arrived earlier than anticipated, "Dad, what are you doing?"

"Your brother insists that I disrobe here before we go to training."

William thought about this idea for a moment and agreed, "Yeah, good idea, bro. Mom will start to wonder where his clothes have got to."

"Yeah," Ralf smirked. "That's what I said a few minutes ago."

William smiled and rubbed his hands together, "Right, it's nearly sundown. Shall we get ready?"

"Let's do it," Ralf and William turned to their father; a blob of ancient, grotesque human being with his little willy and large waist covered by a towel.

Ralf looked up from behind the steering wheel. A few spots of rain hit the windshield.

"Gonna be a wet night, tonight," he said to himself and looked over his shoulder. Humphrey was in the back seat fiddling with his seatbelt.

William looked over from the passenger seat, "The sun's nearly down, Dad. Are you ready for tonight?"

"As ready as I'll ever be," Humphrey coughed.

"Now, you remember the moves we practiced last night?"

"Yes—"

BLOITCH!

Humphrey's forehead cracked apart. Two sharp antennae stabbed into the air above his temples, "Oh my," he said, feeling them with his fingers.

"Shit," William thumped Ralf on the shoulder, "Hurry up. He's turning."

"I'm going as fast as I can," Ralf hit the gas, weaving in and out of the traffic up ahead, "Tell him to keep his seatbelt on."

"How can this be?" Humphrey whined, "The sun hasn't gone down yet—"

CRACK!

As he felt his antennae, his fingers broke apart like some tissue paper.

His eyeballs pushed out from their sockets. Six holes cracked apart around his forehead.

"Grraaaaawwwwww."

"Dad," William screamed, "Ralf, he's turning."

"I know," his brother glanced at the rear view mirror, "I can fucking see that, can't I?"

A giant claw snapped through the bone in his hand, pushing away the flesh. William unfastened his seatbelt and gripped the back of his seat.

"Dad. Dad?"

"Whaaaarrrrr—" as Humphrey spoke, the lower half of his skull dropped to his lap.

He began to convulse. The movements were sudden and violent.

"Dad."

Humphrey's nipples scraped away in his cutter claw, releasing the flesh down to his lungs, "Splarrsshhhh."

Humphrey gobbed up a mountain of mucus and bile over William's face.

"Gah."

Ralf slammed the horn and drove past the traffic on the hard shoulder, "Fuckin' get out of the way."

"Shit, shit, shit," William wiped the sick from his face with his sleeve.

"What's going on?"

"Look," William angled the rear-view mirror for his brother. Ralf got a good look at their father's in-car transformation.

"Oh, holy fuck," Ralf saw his father's ribcage jimmy

through into his claws. William looked down into the foot well. He saw a nasty swimming pool of gore and human remains pooled around his father's red flippers.

"Grasshh."

"Dad!"

The seatbelt kept his father pinned to his seat. The towel whipped off as his head rolled onto the seat. A shiny red abdomen punctured through his waist, producing a slimy lobster head and thorax.

SCHWOLP! SNAP! SNAP!

Humphrey's skin - and whatever else of him that resembled a human being - had fully shed over the car's upholstery.

In the back of their car was a giant eight-foot lobster. Six, deadly-looking eyes and sharp fangs to match. Each antenna scraped along the upholstery on the ceiling of the car.

SNAP!

Two giant claws the size of a human leg swiped at William.

"Get the fuck away from me, man."

The lobster snipped with its cutter claw and thrust forward with its crusher.

SNAP! SNAP!

"Ralf," William screamed and pressed his back against the dashboard, trying to kick the beast away from him, "That's it. He's gone full lobster."

SWISH!

The mutant lobster's purple tongue flapped around and nearly hit the side of William's face.

"We're here," Ralf turned the car into the car park complex and switched on the headlamps.

The sky thundered and rattled as they zoomed into the underground entrance.

7:30 pm. The underground car park was empty. A vast space for around fifty cars. It presented ample opportunity to conduct nefarious dealings with relative discretion.

William got out of the car in one piece. It was a relief.

Ralf was less happy, though. He knew escorting their father in the car wasn't the best idea.

He applied the handbrake. The two back passenger windows shattered on account of the beast's enormous size.

"The car's a fucking write-off, you know," Ralf walked toward the control gate, "Make sure Dad stays put. I'm going to switch on the lights and get the stuff."

"Okay, be quick, though," William voice echoed around the vehicular cement graveyard, "We need to be at Hollowpoint for the vote at ten."

"I fucking know that," Ralf shouted. "Just keep an eye on the bastard."

William turned to the car.

He leaned against a pillar and took out a cigarette, "Dad, you're one ugly cunt. You do know that, right?"

William flicked his lighter and lit his cigarette. The bright orange flame caught the lobster's attention in the back seat.

The beast's abdomen heaved in and out as it stared at its child. It was as if he was sizing his son up. Making a mental note of how best to attack.

Then, the lights in the car park sprang to life. Flicker, buzz, pop. It took a full thirty seconds for the bulbs to warm up.

THUD! THUD! THUD!

It spooked the monster in the back of the car. William took a long, deep drag on his cigarette and paced toward the car.

THUD. THUD.

The lobster was not happy. William flicked the ash from his cigarette onto the shattered glass around his shoes.

"Uncomfortable in there, is it?"

THUD. THUD.

"All in good time, Dad," William finished his cigarette,

"We can't have you turn against us."

SQUEAK, SQUEAK.

William turned around to see Ralf wheeling a trolley from the control gate. He wore a yellow high viz jacket and slung another one toward his brother.

"Put it on."

"Okay," William threw his arms through the jacket sleeves, "You got the thing?"

"Yep," Ralf reached into the trolley and produced two giant padded gloves, "Those are for him. Don't ask me how where I got them."

William took them and nearly buckled under their weight, "Charlie Ferrari, man. These are heavy."

"Yeah, and we have the temperance device, too," Ralf took out a giant cattle prod and hooked it over his left shoulder, "Remember what happened last night?"

"How could I forget," William chuckled. "Is it loaded?"

"Five hundred thousand volts should do the trick," Ralf approached the car with extreme caution and tapped the back door with the business end of the cattle prod.

"You okay, Dad?"

The lobster blinked its eyes and turned to Ralf. It was still very, very angry.

"Dad? We're gonna let you out, now. But if you misbehave, or try to eat us again, you'll get the prod. Do you understand?"

The lobster shuffled in the back seat. The red creature was far too big for the car. Its head tucked down toward its third leg, seeming to state that it knew pain when it felt it.

"Okay," Ralf took the door handle and opened the door, "Out, now. Very slowly."

The lobster put its full weight on its right side. Both claws gripped the door.

SCHRRIIIIPP!

As it moved out of the car, the fabric of the seat tore across. Its strong, sharp legs had got caught.

"Awww, shit," William stood back with Ralf.

The lobster's flippers were the last out of the car as the huge bundle of meat hit the concrete ground.

"I j-just can't," Ralf was in awe of the creature that lay before him. His eyes widened as the lobster stretched its body, legs, and claws out to their fullest.

"Shit," William gasped. "You think he's grown since last night?"

"He must be eight feet tall," Ralf pointed the cattle prod at the monster. "Stay back."

ZWIPP-PP!

Ralf pulled the trigger. A tiny blue current thundered between the metal prongs.

The monster backed up and cowed. It made Ralf smile. Not with amusement but more in relief.

"Good boy," he turned to William, "Bro, in the trolley. There's some fish."

"Okay."

Ralf turned back to the lobster and held the cattle prod at it. He tiled his head and examined the beast.

"At least eight foot. Those claws will crush a fucking watermelon."

"Here, Dad," William shouted from the trolley. He flung a slab of fish at the lobster, "Catch."

The piece of salmon hurtled through the air.

SWIP-SPATCH!

The crusher claw snapped onto it, squelching the fish's soft body.

The other half slapped to the floor. The lobster bent its head down and began to feast.

Ralf squinted as he watched his father dine on his pre-training meal, "You know, it does kind of look like Dad. A bit."

"Yeah," William hulked the giant padded gloves over to the car, "There's a certain resemblance."

BRRAAAAPPPP. SNAP. SNAP.

The fish didn't survive very long. Dad had wolfed it

down in less than six seconds.

William held up the padded gloves and smiled at the beast. It looked back at him and took a couple of steps forward, sizing him up.

"Ready, Dad?"

The lobster clamped its claws together and seemed to nod with approval.

Fifteen minutes later. William and Ralf were in the thick of training with their father, the lobster.

William clutched the practice pads on with his fists. Ralf took temperance duty with the cattle prod.

"Okay, Dad," William held up the pads at the angry beast, "Punch, counter punch. One-two, let's do it."

The lobster moved forward with a specially-made gown on its back. The name *Homarus No* crossed from left to right in bubbly glitter writing.

SWISH-BOP!

William threw the pad forward, only for the crusher claw to connect with it.

"Fuck, yes. That's it. Again."

SWISH! BOP!

The pad flew forward and missed the beast, but got smashed by the crusher claw once again.

"Oww. Fuck," William stepped back and waved his right hand, "He's got a helluva punch on him."

"Yeah, man. That Seth guy doesn't stand a fucking chance tonight."

"C'mon Dad, stay light on your feet," William bounced back toward him. "Southpaw."

The lobster scurried right and flicked its cutter claw toward his son.

William stepped back in time for the crusher claw to come flying at him. He parried the impact with the padded glove.

BOOM!

"Shit," William's arm flew back, almost dislocating

from its socket. "Okay, one more. One-two, knock it."

The lobster held up its claw and rattled forward. Left claw, followed by an almighty crack from the right.

BOOM!

William parried the hit once again. A small tear opened across the plastic padding.

SNIP, SNIP, SNIP.

The lobster's sharp cutter claw had nipped the pad. He beckoned his son over with his left claw.

"Oh. You want some more, do you?"

"Dad," Ralf shouted, "Keep it light."

William yelled and ran toward the beast.

Up, smack, hit.

Down low, swipe, miss.

Mid-body, pad in place, thump.

Up, thump, thump.

"Triple combo, Dad."

Cutter claw introduction to William's left pad, followed by a vicious double-blow to the right.

"Woohoo," William roared and walked away from the lobster. He took a seat on a metal stool by the trolley, "Yeah, all right."

Ralf approached the lobster as it perched its abdomen on the bonnet of the car. He chucked the towel into its right claw.

"Dad, listen. You gotta keep the spastic bouncing around, okay? Wear him down."

The lobster nodded its head and ran its eyes across the towel.

"Seth doesn't have your range energy, Dad," Ralf explained as he scanned his wristwatch, "His only hope is to wear you down."

The lobster threw the towel onto the ground and slipped across the floor.

SWISH! SWISH, SWIPE!

Dad threw a few practice punches as Ralf turned to his brother.

"Time?"

"That's thirty seconds," William sprang to his feet and rolled his shoulders. He danced back and forth, this time wearing a pair of regular boxing gloves, "Tonight's fight is ours, man. Is he ready?"

"I think so," Ralf turned to his father, "Dad? You ready?"

SWISH, SWISH!

"Okay, spar round," Ralf clutched the cattle prod firmly in his right hand. He raised his free palm in the air, "Go."

William hopped to his right and threw his Dad a clean punch, which smacked him across the face, "C'mon, Dad. Keep your guard up."

The lobster shook itself and held up its gloved claws. It threw a left punch, connecting with William's waist, sending him onto his ass.

"Nice one, Dad," Ralf chuckled. "Get up, bro, forty more seconds."

"I am, I am," William got up and produced a vicious uppercut under his Dad's head.

The lobster tumbled back and hit the front of the car, setting off the alarm.

"Shit."

WHEEE-WHAAAAWW-WHEEE-WHAAAW!

"Fuck, man. Turn the car alarm off—"

THWUMP.

The lobster returned the uppercut to his son's jaw, lifting him into the air.

"Got it," Ralf dived into the car and stopped the alarm, "Bro, what are you doing over there?"

William had landed in the trolley and was rolling back toward the control gate.

"Fuck's sake, get off that thing."

He climbed over the side and landed on his feet. He batted his boxing gloves together, determined to knock his father out for good.

"C'mon, you ugly, red motherfucker."

He stepped forward and kept his guard up. The lobster remained bouncing on the spot, waiting for his son to approach.

Ralf stepped to the side and whispered into his father's ear, "Dad. Rabbit punch."

The lobster turned to its son and tilted its head. Ralf winked back and smiled, "Throw the left, he'll duck. Slip left, and crack him in the back of the neck."

The lobster nodded and scurried forward, light on its feet.

William approached and threw a few cautionary punches. He was starting to tire, "C'mon, big boy. Come get some."

The lobster swiped with the left claw. Predictably, William ducked and dived to the right.

The lobster scurried to the left, held up its gloved left claw and—

SMACK!

A clean rabbit punch to the back of its son's neck.

BLLOOARRRGGGHHHHH!!!

William projectile-vomited a slew of blood and bile into the air. The giant puddle splashed to the ground ten feet away.

William tumbled to the ground and screamed, "Illegal move. Illegal move, man. Fuck."

Ralf turned to his father and grabbed his left gloved claw, "That's a helluva knockout."

William held the back of his neck and dry heaved. He rose to his knees and puked to the floor once again.

"You okay, bruv?" Ralf asked, half-concerned.

"Y-You c-can't do that, man," he yelled and spat some red saliva from his mouth, "You could've done some p-permanent damage."

"Fuck that. The Hester geezer's going down in the fourth—"

"—No," William barked, wobbling around on his feet, "No. If Dad throws an illegal punch, the vote is fucked."

"Oh, fuck that," Ralf pointed at his father, "Who's gonna disagree with this thing?"

"Ralf, man," William rolled his shoulders and slipped off his gloves, "We can't fuck this up. If they think we've trained Dad to throw an illegal move we'll get disqualified. Proposition 118 will pass automatically."

"But if he rabbit punches the spastic, we'll win."

"No. We can't take the risk," William looked at his father and sighed, "Don't you know how parliamentary politics works? We're the "no' side, and if the "no' side gets caught cheating, it's over. No illegal moves. I mean it."

"Kidney punch, then?"

"It's still illegal," William fumed. "Fuck, Ralf. Look at Dad. He may be eight feet long but he hasn't got a belt. No taller than three-foot five. The first thing the speaker's gonna look for is a punch below the belt."

"He's a fucking politician. He should be used to attacks below the belt."

"Don't try to be funny, mate. It doesn't suit you."

"Okay, okay," Ralf huffed. He sized up the beast and peered at his wristwatch, "You're right. No illegal moves."

"Good."

"We'd better go if we're gonna make the weigh-in."

"Yeah, let's get out of here," William jogged to the car and opened the back door for his father, "You all right getting in?"

The lobster perched its claws on the back of the front passenger seat to enable a successful climb-in.

"Ralf, let's go."

Chapter 6

Lobster Politics (Part Two)

THE VOTE

(Midnight, Hollowpoint Inc.)

Hollowpoint Inc is the biggest unit in *Chrome Valley*'s industrial estate. An ugly, gray affair, its aesthetic wasn't helped by the murky night sky on this cold night.

Hundreds of expensive cars had been parked out front. Tonight was a big night in politics. Either Proposition 118 would pass, or it wouldn't. It all depended on who had the most energy and threw the most vicious punch.

Ralf and William ushered their father, the lobster, through the reception area. The attendees gasped and stood back to allow them through.

An assortment of backbenchers and cabinet members of parliament. The only one who wasn't present was the Prime Minster.

Algernon moved through the crowd and joined the brothers as they headed toward the door, "I say, chaps. How is Humphrey tonight?"

"Dad's fine. How's Mr. Hester?"

"About beat the daylights out of your father, by all accounts."

"We'll see about that, Algernon," William pushed the door open, "Can you keep the crowds back, please?"

"Certainly," Algernon turned around and held out his hands at the crowd, "Some privacy for Mr. Ingham, please."

The brothers marched the covered lobster into the changing room. Ralf took off the mutant's gown and threw it over his right shoulder.

A giant weighing scale sat in the corner of the room with Seth standing on it. The speaker of the house measured the result on his iPad.

"Okay, that's one-hundred and sixty-two pounds. Middleweight, ready."

The speaker pressed the digital readout on Seth's temple, "Brain damage reads at 1.18. Excellent. He's now evenly matched with his opponent, who's a lobster. Please step off the scales."

Seth stepped off the weighing scales and turned looked over at the lobster and its two sons.

Max Dark appeared from the shower room in high spirits, "Ah, you made it. We thought you might not turn up."

William walked his father toward the scales, "We're ready for you, dickhead."

"Now, now," Max giggled. "No need to be nasty."

Seth looked different, today. He was beaten so badly the night before that his jaw needed stapling back in place. Two metal bolts held his face in place. His right eyeball was missing.

"Should be an easy victory for you, then. See, my guy is missing an eye."

Brian and Leo emerged from the toilet and joined Max.

"Rest assured, gentlemen. Mr. Hester, here, is no slouch," Max beamed. "We've pumped so many volts through the spastic's cranium it's a wonder his head hasn't exploded."

"Can we have Mr. Ingham in for the weigh-in now, please?" The speaker stepped aside to allow the lobster onto the scale.

It crawled onto the surface. The bar tilted to the right, enabling the black meter to slide along.

"Well, I hope your guy can withstand a vicious strike," Ralf threatened Max.

"Oh yeah? Been training him hard, have you?"

"Fuck, yes."

Max chuckled at the eight-foot monstrosity, "That useless, red blancmange doesn't have the agility or movement that Mr. Hester has. Am I right, guys?"

"Nah, man," Brian giggled. "Seth's gon' fuck your boy up, good."

"Order, gentlemen," the speaker interrupted and addressed William and Ralf, "Okay, your fighter is one-hundred and sixty-five pounds. I can confirm the appropriate weight."

"Good." Max giggled and bopped Brian on the arm, "We gotta go, may the best man win."

"Or non-man, in our case," Ralf spat, sarcastically.

"Yeah, right," Max turned to Brian and Leo, "I need a word with you pair of homosexuals. Outside."

Max threw a blue gown around Seth's back and walked him - and Brian and Leo - out of the room.

A few minutes later, Max and Brian reached a giant truck in the car park.

The engine was still running.

"Brian, when the fight's over, I need you to do something for me."

"What's that?"

"I want you to get in this truck."

Hollowpoint Arena.

The politicians made their way into the giant room. In the middle stood a full-size boxing arena. Three ropes surrounded squared circle elevated six feet off the ground. Four Perspex walls lined against the ropes.

The attending crowd split into two factions.

"The blues' - dressed in dark blue, the proponents of Proposition 118, known as the "Ayes', took the west and south walls.

"The reds' - all decked in bright red attire, the opposition to the bill, known as the "Nos', filled the north and east sides.

Those for and against were equally represented. An even fifty-fifty split.

Including their professionalism.

Their enthusiasm.

Their decorum.

Loud rock music played through the speakers as the two fighters made their way to the ring.

The crowd whooped and cheered as they made their way through to the ring.

The see-through glass walls slid down into the ring itself. It enabled Seth and the lobster to climb through the ropes at the opposing corners.

The blue corner for Seth.

The red for the lobster.

William and Ralf wiped their father down. It carried the gown on its back.

The speaker of the house entered the ring as the music ground to a halt.

He lifted the microphone to his mouth.

"My Lords, Ladies, Gentlemen, and various attending creatures. Welcome to tonight's vote for Proposition 118."

The attendees clapped and murmured amongst themselves.

"Tonight's vote is a very special one. A historic date for democracy. For tonight, we decide, whether to enact one of the more contentious bills ever put before us."

The crowd piped up as the speaker held his hand out toward Seth.

"In the blue corner, hailing from Chrome Valley, and with an unopposed majority of over twelve thousand votes. I give you Seth "*The Molester'* Hester, right honorable MP for *Chrome Valley West.*"

Seth punched the air and tried to roar, but swallowed back the urge. If he had done so, his mouth might have fallen off.

Even so, the blue crowd went wild for him.

"Yeah, my man," Max screamed. "You fuck 'em right up the asshole."

"Order, order," the speaker quietened down the crowd as a gorgeous female MP dressed in a pink bikini entered the ring with a placard. She joined the speaker and showed off her curves and beautiful smile.

"In the red corner. Hailing from the northwest London, the mayor of Chrome Valley for the 'Nos', Mr. Humphrey *"Homarus No"* Ingham."

The red crowd jumped up and rooted for their fighter.

"Gentlemen, ladies, crustaceans," the speaker sucked in a huge amount of air, "Let's ha-get a-ready to-a *vote.*"

Max jumped up and down, enthralled at the prospect of winning, "Let's get this fucking bill *passed*, my niggers."

William and Ralf looked over at him and scowled, "We can't lose this vote, man."

"He *won't* win," Ralf whispered to his brother and pointed at the dazed Seth, "Look at him. He doesn't belong at a boxing match. He looks like a fucking train has hit him."

The speaker ran into the middle of the squared circle and held out his arms.

Seth stumbled from the blue corner toward the middle of the ring.

William turned to his brother, "That's it, we're on. Good luck, Dad."

The lobster slid off the chair and landed all eight of its feet on the canvas. It scuttled forward, appearing to have grown since the weigh-in.

The two opponents sized each other up. Seth's stapled face had an issue remaining on its neck. His eyes were a sparkling silver color.

The lobster batted its claws together, ready for the fight.

"Okay, guys," the speaker opened. "I want a nice, clean fight. No fouls, no fuck-ups. No racist shit, filibustering, or wanking each other off. Okay."

The lobster scowled and bent its antennae back. It squinted at the reanimated politician in front of him.

"Now, touch gloves."

Seth held up his right glove and spoke like Stephen Hawking, "Fuck you."

The lobster patted it with his gloved claw and moved back. A bikini-clad female MP with blond hair and red-rimmed glasses climbed into the ring. She held up a sign that read: *Round One.*

DING! DING!

"Go."

The crowd went wild as the first round sprang to life. Seth walked around and spat to the floor, "Come on, big boy."

He threw a couple of test punches and tried to intimidate the beast. It didn't flinch and kept circling around.

"Seth, Seth, Seth," chanted the crowd on the west side. They threw their blue banners up and fist-bumped the air.

The lobster launched forward and raised its left claw.

WHOOM!

A vicious uppercut, and a near-miss. Seth ducked, rolled his shoulders and bounced to his right, "C'mon, you fucker."

He stepped forward and smacked the lobster in the side of the face.

"Oooooh," The crowd gasped as the lobster reeled from its blow.

William gripped the top rope, "Go on, Dad. Fuck his retarded shit up," he roared and pretended to throw a couple of punches himself.

The speaker waved his hands to encourage the opponents to re-engage.

The lobster wasted no time and launched into the air.

THWACK!

Its right claw connected with Seth's abdomen. "Ooof," He staggered backward and almost lost his foot.

"Yes. Get him," Ralf screamed and threw his arm around William's shoulder, "Go on."

Seth scrambled to his feet and went for an uppercut.

He missed. The lobster delivered a dirty one-two punch to Seth's left kidney, spinning him around one hundred and eighty degrees.

DING! DING!

Saved by the bell. Round one was over.

William ducked through the ropes and kicked the chair out from the corner. The lobster moved back and fell stomach-first to the chair.

The crowd simmered down and watched the brief respite from the side-lines.

Ralf squirted some bottled water over his father's shelled face, "Nice one, Dad. You had him. He was nearly out for the count."

William noticed a cut on his father's face, "Shit. We gotta get you patched up, wait a second," he reached into his bag and took out a plaster.

In the blue corner, Seth was being attended to by Max, "You out of breath, you fucking retard? Are you?"

He slapped him across the face. Seth reeled and spun his head back to Max, who greeted his return with his sparkling white teeth.

"Listen to me, you fool. Next round, you fucking go for the antennas, you hear me?"

Seth nodded and placed his hands around his neck.

CRUNK.

He re-lodged his broken neck back onto his shoulders, "Sleerrgsshh."

"What's that, fuck face?"

"Gllressshh."

"I can't understand you," Max mopped Seth's brow. He breathed onto a staple and wiped it clean with his sleeve, "You want this fucking bill passed, don't you?"

Seth nodded. The force of his affirmation caused his head to slip off his shoulders. Max pushed his forehead back in place in the nick of time.

DING! DING!

"That's it, my learning-difficulties-superhero," Max roared. "Get out there and. Remember," he pointed at his forehead.

The female MP held up a card reading: *Round Two.*

"Go get 'em, my window-licking friend." Max clapped as Seth staggered like a zombie into the middle of the squared circle.

"Go, Dad," William roared after the lobster as it made its way to the middle of the ring.

The crowd piped up once again. The chants of "Seth! Seth! Seth!" were near-deafening.

"Man, they really want this fucking law passed," Ralf observed the crowd behind him. The attendees to the right, dressed mainly in red attire, weren't nearly as lively as their opposition.

"The opposition ain't very lively, are they?" William remarked.

THWACK!

Seth smashed the underside of the lobster's face. It all happened in slow motion. The complicated structure of the beast resembled a giant Jenga tower. It toppled over its own flippers and landing on its back.

"No. No," Ralf shouted. The crowd cheered and hollered as the lobster lay on its back, kicking its feet. It sounded as if it was squealing for help.

"Order. Motherfucking *order.*"

Apoplectic, the speaker of the house grabbed both its claws and yanked the lobster back to its feet, "No more of that."

"Blaa-aa-aarrrggh,." was all Seth had to say as the speaker of the house resumed the match.

"Fuck that giant, red dildo up, you senseless retard," Max roared with his hands cupped around his mouth.

Seth lifted his right hand in the air, ready to strike. The lobster saw this move as an opportunity, though. If he could sneak in a sucker punch into Seth's side, it could cause quite a bit of damage.

Seth's left hand guarded his face. He beckoned the monster over, "Meere."

The lobster leaped forward and jumped into the air. Its right claw wound up and punched straight into its opponent's side.

Seth knew this was about to happen, and so stepped to his right. The lobster's strike missed, sending him racing toward the blue corner.

It squealed as its claw and head became entangled in the ropes.

"Sweeeeeee—"

Seth raced over and socked the lobster in its back, causing its head to tilt back.

Max squinted at Seth, "Do it. *Do it.*"

Seth grabbed both antennae in his hands, "Grrrrrr!" he groaned and yanked them back with all his might.

"Order. Order," the speaker yelled and tried to get between the fighters, "Order."

Seth leaned his entire body weight back. The right antenna snapped off, shooting blood out of the cavity. The lobster roared in a high pitch tone in sheer agony.

"Yes. Fuck that big, red bastard up," Max jumped up and down on the spot, giddy with excitement.

"Get off him," the speaker of the house screamed and wrapped his arms around Seth from behind. He pulled the man off the beast.

RRIIPPPP!!

The left antenna tore from the lobster's head as Seth kept his grip.

The lobster fell to its legs. Its flippers vibrated as it rolled onto its side.

DING! DING!

The speaker grabbed Seth's shoulders before it could go back to its corner to rest.

"You conduct a foul like that again, my friend, and it is over. You understand me?"

Seth walked away from the speaker and headed for his chair in the blue corner.

The lobster wandered around in a daze back to the red corner. The blood had stopped squirting from the cavity, and it looked as if the beast was in pain.

The lobster slumped onto the stool. William jumped through the ropes and analyzed his father's crustacean face, "Shit, he's lost his antennae."

Click. Click. Click.

He snapped his fingers three times to see if the lobster was responsive, "Shit, Ralf, man."

"What, what?"

"I don't think he can see," William panted as Ralf shone a torch into his father's beastly eyes.

"No, no, looks all okay here," Ralf traced his father's pupil movements with his forefinger, "He's responding."

"Dad, listen," William blurted into his father's face, "Round three. We *need* that motherfucker on the ground."

"No," Ralf applied a wet cloth to the lobster's sweaty face. He scooped some of the clear blood away from its face, "No foul play. Not yet, anyway."

"Bro, he's one punch away from—"

"—Ah, shit," Ralf finally settled on his father's red face, "He can't hear us."

"What do you mean?"

Ralf turned over his shoulder. Max was holding on to both antennae and waving them around like swords, giggling with Seth. To his right, the female MP came back in, ready to announce the third round.

Ralf turned around and looked at his father. He snapped his fingers to the right of his head, then the left, "Dad, can you hear me--"

DING! DING!

Round three.

The lobster jumped up from the stool and scurried toward the center of the ring.

Ralf watched wide-eyed and nudged his brother in the ribs, "He's deaf."

"What?"

"I said he's *deaf*," Ralf repeated. "He can't hear anything. Look at the way he's moving."

The lobster swayed from left to right and kept its guard up. Seth moved forward and sidestepped to the right, keeping light on his feet.

The crowd began chanting once again. It was clear to anyone watching that Seth just needed one more strike.

"Shit, if he lays a blow, Dad's fucked. And then we're all fucked," Ralf closed his eyes and expected the worst.

The speaker of the house jumped back and held out his hands, "Order. I mean it! Any illegal moves and you're fucking disqualified."

Seth smiled and held his head between both gloves. Max gripped the rope and yelled above the chanting crowd, "Yeah. Fuckin' finish the bastard off."

Seth turned to Max and smiled. He scowled as he saw two men approach his coach. One with a hood, the other with a red balaclava.

"Hey, we nearly missed it."

Seth's face fell. The two men who had turned him into the retarded fighting machine had come to gloat and assist Max.

SMACK!

Everything went dark for Seth. A piercing sensation flew through his brain as if he'd head-butted a lump concrete.

The crowd's hollering echoed and slowed down. An ungodly ringing noise flew around the chasm of darkness.

"One. Two. Three," the speaker's voice flew around the emptiness.

"Waaaakkkeee uuu-uupp," Max's voice bounded around shortly after.

A blast of white light flooded Seth's field of vision. The image bleached out.

The speaker of the house was counting with his fingers over his face. He'd received a violent right hook to the side of the head and was out for the count.

"Get up, you useless flap of filleted foreskin," Max screamed and yanked the rope rope.

"Four. Five."

Seth jiggled around. The back of his head hit the canvas and rolled to its side.

The rest of his body climbed to its feet and prepared for battle.

Seth's head watched on from the floor as his headless body threw a series of punches at the lobster.

"Hey, this is illegal," William screamed to the speaker.

"Order," was the response from the speaker, who allowed the match to continue.

"He hasn't got a head."

"And your father can't hear, so I'd say they're evenly matched," The speaker yelled as the fight resumed.

Max looked down at Seth's severed head, "You're useless, you know that? Like a retard and a turd crossed together. A *returd*."

BOP!

Max kicked Seth's head. It rolled across the canvas and slid under the bottom rope, crashing nose-first to the floor.

The lobster threw a combination of punches. Double jab with the left, which caused Seth to hop back. The beast moved to the side, knowing that Seth couldn't see him. It allowed for a left hook to the small of the back and a violent uppercut between the shoulder blades.

The last attack lifted Seth's headless body five feet into the air.

"Yes," William screamed and held up his fist.

DING! DING!

Max crept through the middle rope and ran over to the speaker of the house, "Mate, this is fucked up."

"Order," the speaker shouted into his face, "Mr. Dark. You will take your fighter back to your corner for respite."

Max shoved the speaker in a fit of fury, "Listen, *gay-face*. My fighter has lost his fucking head."

"His *mind*, more like," the speaker spat with a sarcastic undercurrent.

Max lost his mind and stomped to the ground, "How can he fight if he can't see?"

"Not my problem, pal. I suggest you regroup and change tactic."

The speaker walked off to the far ropes.

"Fucking imbecile," Max clocked Brian and Leo drag Seth's body back to the blue corner. They lifted the body under its arms and plonked it on the stool.

Max crouched in front of Seth and addressed his severed neck.

"Now, Seth. Listen to me, I—" Max blinked at the where his fighter's face *should* have been, "No, no, this is no use. I can't give a pep talk to someone without a head. Brian, where's his head?"

"Here," Brian clutched Seth's head by the hair and lifted it in front of Max's face.

"Okay, good. Seth? Can you hear me?"

Seth tried to move his lips, but his vocal cords hung through the neck hole and were of little use. Brian placed the head onto the severed neck. Leo moved in and held a staple gun to the connective tissue.

SNAP! SNAP!

"Earth to retard, hello?" Max moved his head to the side as Leo stapled Seth's head back to his neck, "Okay, blink once for yes, twice for no. Understand?"

Blink.

"Good. Look, you just need to put the big, red mound of cunt on the floor, once. Get him on his back. It'll be impossible for him to get back up. Understand?"

Blink.

KA-CHUNT, KA-CHUNT.

Leo applied the metal staples and pocketed the staple gun, "All done, Mr. Dark, sir."

"Nice one, Leo," Max grinned and turned to his fighter, "Seth, if you fuck this up, we're all trapped in this junkie's fucking head, possibly forever. We *need* this bill passed. Do you understand what I'm saying?"

Blink.

"Kidney punch the fucker this round. Brian will keep your face trained, so you'll have to do your best—"

DING! DING!

Round four.

The red corner.

Humphrey the lobster was out of breath. A quick sip of squirted water from Ralf's bottle did the trick.

William leaned into his Dad's scary lobster face, "Dad, this is it. Rabbit punch him in the testicles. But let him throw the first punch so it's not too obvious."

The lobster blinked all six of its eyes and wagged its tongue in approval. He was hungry for murder.

Ralf patted his brother on the back, "Will, bro. He can't hear you."

"Oh," William held two fingers up on each hand above his head. He lifted his top lip and mimicked a rabbit.

The lobster nodded its head and hopped to its eight feet.

"Remember, Dad. Let him throw the first punch."

"Fight. Fight. Fight," screamed the crowd. The east side of the room piped up their chants.

Blues versus the reds, "Ayes" versus the "Nos."

"C'mon, you mental motherfucker,!" Max screamed at Seth and threw his fists into the air. "Proposition 118."

The blue crowd cheered what Max had screamed over and over again.

Seth skipped around the canvas and held up his fists. The lobster clunked around the ring, keeping his guard up.

The silence inside the lobster's head was almost deafening. It could see the chanting crowd and the ringside support. The lack of any audio stimulation forced all its attention on its opponent.

A stapled enemy, begging for his block to be knocked off.

"Go on, Dad," William roared from the ropes. "Fuck him up."

The lobster heaved forward and swiped at Seth, but missed. Its opponent skipped to the far corner and beckoned the beast toward him.

The lobster turned around and made for its enemy.

SWIPE-SMACK!

A violent right hook, straight in Seth's side. The crowd cheered and hollered.

A follow-up from the left claw, then the right and a vicious uppercut sent Seth flouncing backward.

"Noooo," Max screamed and slapped Brian's face, "*Motherfucker.*"

"Hey, man," Brian yelled. "Don't hit me."

Max watched as Seth climbed to his feet and made a play for the lobster.

"Yes. Do it. Right in the flippers."

SWIPE!

Seth threw a punch and missed. The lobster preyed on his opponent's error and slammed him in the ribs.

"Offgghh," Seth buckled slightly and vomited to the floor.

The lobster pushed forward and issued a disorienting blow between Seth's shoulder blades, sending him forward against the ropes.

As he gripped the top rope, he tried to turn around. It was futile.

There, presented in all its glory, was the small of Seth's back. The lobster jumped back two feet and raised its right claw.

"No. *No*," Max tried to catch the speaker's attention, "Illegal move, man. Come on."

The speaker turned around to Max and held his forefinger over his lips, "Order. Shhh."

The lobster pulled its claw back and then—

SCHTAAAA-AAAAAAMMMMM!!!

The sound of the connecting punch rattled through the auditorium like a thunderclap.

Seth's prolonged death-squeal rattled around the walls.

"Oh m-my God," William stammered and held his startled brother's hand, "He's done it."

The lobster's right rabbit punch dug so far into Seth's kidneys, they burst out through his abdomen.

The crowd gasped in frenzy at the sight.

The lobster flung its gloved claws out and stepped back. Seth's body toppled backward and crashed to the canvas like a stack of cards.

"Illegal *fatherfucking* move," Max screamed. "That's a fucking foul."

Seth's back smashed against the canvas. The speaker of the house raced over and began to count.

"One. Two. Three."

"No," Max screamed and immediately whispered to Brian, "Get the thing, now. Do it."

"Okay, okay."

"Four. Five. Six."

Max knew it was over. If Seth didn't wake up very soon all his plans were over. He shot William and Ralf a look of pure, concentrated evil.

"I'll get you, you mayonnaise-based cunts. Just wait and see."

They each held their middle finger back up at Max, "Fuck you."

"Eight, nine, and that's a ten."

DING! DING!

"I don't fucking believe this," Max closed his eyes and folded his arms. He nodded at the speaker as he addressed the cheering crowd.

"My Lords, Ladies, Gentlemen, Anthropoids, and other assorted non-binary genders. We have a decision on Proposition 118."

The red crowd cheered at the top of their lungs as the speaker waved the lobster to walk up to him.

"Go get 'em, Dad," William chuckled.

Max took out a walkie-talkie from his pocket, "Okay, Brian. Bring the vehicle in. Now."

"Yes, Mr. Dark, sir," Brian's voice confirmed from the other end of the frequency.

The beast approached the speaker. He grabbed its right claw and addressed the crowd.

"In four rounds, and due to a knockout, the Ayes in blue have ten hits to the Nos in red's fifteen."

The reds cheered even louder.

"Therefore," the speaker continued, "For Proposition 118, the Nos have it! The middleweight champion of the world, the mayor of *Chrome Valley*, Mr. Humphrey Ingham."

"Woohoooo," the crowd screamed with jubilation.

The blue corner was less than happy.

Max climbed through the rope and offered the lobster his congratulations. He took the microphone from the speaker of the house and waved the crowd to quieten down.

"Every*fucker*. Can I have your attention please?"

The crowd's frenzy died down. Max smiled and held out his hand at the lobster who took his gold middleweight trophy from the female MP.

"I'd just like to take a moment to congratulate Mr. Humphrey Ingham on his win for the vote tonight. A most *motherfucking* auspicious moment in his career."

A polite round of applause and approval filtered around the room. Max pointed to the south wall of the arena.

"People thought I might have been a bad sport about losing. I can assure you that this is *not* the case."

William and Ralf ran into the ring and hugged their father, the lobster.

"As you all know, Proposition 118 was a bill designed to free us from our plight. The disabling of our deity's senses. To wake him up from his perceived, heroin-induced purgatory. Sadly, the vote is in. You have voted *not* to enact this bill. Fifty-two points to forty-eight, like the fucking idiots you are."

The crowd gave a round of applause. Many of the blue attendees began to boo and get aggressive.

"Humphrey has done well to represent the will of the people, of *Chrome Valley* and, indeed, the country at large."

A rumbling noise grew louder and louder from the south wall of the arena. Max chuckled to himself and continued his speech.

"But this religious nonsense doesn't recognize international law. You have made a fucking *massive mistake.* It affects everyone on the planet, within our sphere of existence," Max turned to the crowd behind him and made sure he addressed each audience member, "So, when a genius such as me finally brings the truth to you all, I expected you to embrace it with open arms and an open mind. And, in some cases, open legs, too."

The arena's southern wall began to rumble and crumble apart.

Max's mood flipped from gracious to livid, "But *noo-oo-ooo.* You motherfuckers want to remain in your little bubble, don't you? You're quite happy to be trapped in your pathetic, false existence. You, you cretinous little urchins, don't care that you don't exist. That you're enslaved. You're all happy with your distractions, aren't you? The fact that you're all figments of a heroin junkie's imagination is too stupid to be believed, right?"

The crowd blinked back at Max. It wasn't *their* fault that they didn't believe his erratic ramblings of a divine nature.

"You sicken me, you deluded fucks. Well lemme tell you something, right now. Each and every one of you cunts will rue the day when you realize I was right all along. Now, I have to devise another plan to free us all. I'd like to thank this giant, fucked-up abomination for successfully curtailing the one and only fucking chance we had to escape—"

BLAAAMMM!

The south wall broke apart. A giant set of headlamps flooded the arena as the cold wind blew through.

The truck beeped as it backed up and crushed the crowd below its wheels.

"I did wonder, though," Max finished. "What Humphrey Ingham would have thought of *this*?"

The truck backed up toward the ring and slammed against the ropes.

BEEP. BEEP. BEEP.

The twenty-foot crate on the back lifted up, pouring its contents into the boxing ring. A massive ghost of steam rose into the air as the crowd watched in terror.

"Ha-ha."

Max dropped the microphone and climbed through the ropes. He turned to Brian and Leo and brandished a Glock 17.

"Thanks, boys," Max smiled and flicked the safety catch back.

"What are you doing?"

"Tying up loose ends," Max aimed the gun at Brian's head, "Thanks for your help, by the way."

BANG!

Brian's head exploded, propelling the contents of his skull against Leo's screaming face.

Leo cried and wiped his friend's gray matter from his eyes, "What did you do that for?"

"For the will of the people," Max grabbed his arm and pulled him away from the ring, "The cunt threatened to kill me, don't you remember? C'mon, let's let this fucker cook alone."

As they ran off, four giant glass partitions slide up on each side of the ring, hitting the top rope.

It had created a boxing ring-sized Perspex box. The lobster was still inside and struggled to climb the walls.

"Oh fuck. *Fuck*," William screamed as he stepped over Brian's headless corpse. It's boiling water."

Ralf wasted no time. He grabbed his father around the thorax and slung his arm under its left pereiopod, "Quick, let's get out of here."

The ring filled up with boiling water at a ferocious rate. The crowd ran out through the crater in the south wall screaming for their lives.

"Fuck, my feet," Ralf hopped around, trying not to step in the knee-deep scalding hot water.

SPLASH!

"Dad," William sloshed through the scorching red water. "Fuck, my legs. Help."

Ralf climbed onto the top buckle and reached down for his brother. William slipped to his knees, "Nooo, help. My flesh is burning."

"Will, man, take my hand."

William threw his palm out.

SMACK!

Ralf caught him and lifted his brother from the swimming pool of boiling water. William's clothes melted off his legs and waist, infusing with his bubbling, red raw skin.

"Gaaaaahhh," he screamed as he pushed himself over the top buckle and onto the floor. Ralf jumped down and helped him to his feet.

"You okay?"

"*No, I'm not fucking okay*. I'm pretty far from fucking okay, okay?" William cried and looked at his thighs, "Aww, it hurts so bad."

"C'mon, let's get out of here," Ralf yanked William with him around the side of the ring.

"Wait," William screamed in pain, "Dad."

"What about him?"

"Where is he?" William asked.

"I dunno. Didn't he make it out?"

BOMPH. BOMPH.

Ralf and William turned to the ring. Their Dad, the lobster, hadn't made it out of the ring of boiling water. It bopped its claws against the Perspex glass and stared its sons in the face.

"Oh, nooooooo," William threw Ralf's hand away and made for the ropes. "Dad?"

"William, no," Ralf yelled after his brother. "Don't, it's over."

"No, I have to save him."

Ralf grabbed William's waist and brought him down to the ground. He tried not to cry, "No, it's over. Look at him."

They turned to see the lobster cooking alive in the ex-boxing ring.

"Dad," William cried, tracing his finger tip along the glass. The lobster ran its claw along with it.

"I'm s-so sorry."

The lobster tilted its head. Then, a burst of bubbles, followed by a death squeal, erupted from its face.

The shell softened. Much of it drifted away from his claw. The pink flesh bubbled away in the boiling water.

Its legs drifted away, leaving behind spindly little grey sticks. The head detached from the body and wandered towards the ropes.

Humphrey Ingham was no more. A thoroughly cooked and disintegrated lobster that would never live to tell the tale.

He did, however, leave an indelible mark on society. He'd successfully killed Proposition 118. There'd be no disabling of the senses for the citizens of *Chrome Valley*, or the country at large.

Ralf and William exited the arena. They knew they'd have to explain all this to their mother. Neither had answers for the inevitable questions that would follow, though.

Why did it happen?

How did they keep it a secret from her?

Who was Max Dark?

What was the purpose of Proposition 118?

Why was everyone told that they *weren't real?*

Chapter 7

Mace Kevlar: 500,000 Volts

Mace Kevlar stood at the wash basin and stared at himself in the mirror. He was a whopping 6'6" and weighing no more than one hundred and ten pounds. The stick-thin and cadaverous man in the mirror stared back at him.

He was way down the pecking order of potential mates if you compared his stature and pulchritude to that of his sixth form classmates. Way, way down.

In both the Biblical and platonic sense.

Chrome Junction Academy had gone through something of a renaissance. It experienced its first ever terrorist attack before the summer.

In the cold Autumn nights, Mace knew that his peers would be jollying it up at house parties. He'd never get an invite.

Mace wasn't even a good student. He'd skipped a lot of classes during the year. His prospects of completing his course were as slim as he was.

A splash of water to the face might help? He ran the tap and cupped his hands and threw the contents to his forehead.

Blink. Blink.

Ugh, that soapy, lime-scaled water wasn't doing his eyeballs any good. He rubbed a knuckle over his right eyelid and tried to open it.

Yep, the same ugly motherfucker who always made an

appearance in the mirror was staring right back at him.

Mace's black jacket sleeve rolled back down his arm, covering the scars on his wrist. Always dressed in black, he was technically a goth.

He had jet-black hair, slicked with a tonne of grease. His black clothes perfected the miserably look. If Marilyn Manson and Charles Atlas had a kid, then Mace was the result.

Still, it was time to make his way home and confine himself to an evening of solitude. Away from his family.

***

Mace walked toward the car park. He looked up at the sky and saw that rain was imminent. The clouds were piling together and forming an ugly-looking array of grey. It was a twenty-five-minute walk back to *Three Springs*, where he lived with his mother. It was a pleasant enough journey. Away from the shops and the park.

If it rained, though, then he'd need to take the less favorable shortcut past *Waddling Gate* cemetery. A quick check on his smart phone suggested that rain was due two hours ago. It was going to piss down.

So, the cemetery path was the one he took.

"Hey, Mace," a young girl hollered from the other side of the road. He looked over as she joined him.

"Oh. Hey, Mesi."

She joined him as he continued past the mini roundabout, "Mind if I walk with you?"

"Yeah, that's fine," he said, noticing that she was fiddling with her necklace. A small gold-plated syringe with a tiny fetus in it.

"I didn't know you were religious?"

"Yes. We all are in my family," she held the pendant to her lips and kissed it, "Today is my birthday. I carry Ferrari everywhere I go for protection."

"Happy birthday."

Mace's phone beeped as he was about to slip it into his pocket.

"Oh, hey," Mesi said. "Did you hear about all these clown sightings happening around here?"

"Yeah," Mace didn't give much of a shit about the conversation, "It's all made up. I've never seen one."

He swiped the screen on his phone and read the instant message.

I can see you, fuckhead. You're dead.

"Ugh," Mace stopped in his tracks.

Mesi turned around and squinted at him, "What's up?"

"Nothing, uh," Mace looked up from his phone. The trees and surrounding foliage looked intimidating, "Look, it's probably better that you go on ahead, Mesi."

She giggled and shot him a look of *"oh, really?"*

"You don't want to be seen with me, isn't it?"

Mesi had reason to believe that Mace didn't want to be associated with her. She was a pudgy African girl. In this day and age, it shouldn't have mattered, but *Chrome Valley* had an issue with racism for decades.

Mace knew this. Mesi knew it, too.

What she didn't know was that Mace couldn't have cared less about her skin color. It was her safety he had in mind, given the nature of the text message he'd received.

"*Is it 'coz I is black*?" she mocked in an attempt to suppress her joviality.

"God, no," Mace stepped forward and held out his arms. "No. It's just that—"

"—What?"

Mace slipped the phone into his pocket and paced along the road, "Ah, fuck it. Who cares. Let's go."

Ten minutes later, Mace and Mesi walked along the busy main road. The cars taking the children home had piled up at the lights. Walking was a fantastic idea.

That is, until the first few spots of rain hit their faces.

"Ugh, shit," Mace huffed. "We're gonna get soaked."

"Oh, I don't mind the rain," Mesi smiled at him and took his hand. "I like being wet."

Mace attempted his first ever joke as they approached the convenience store, "You do realize that sounded wrong, don't you?"

"Haha," Mesi nudged his arm, "Oi, you. Naughty."

A young girl ran out of the store and almost hit Mace as she ran off down the pavement.

"What the hell?"

Another young girl bolted out of the store and joined her friend. They cackled like witches as they ran off around the corner.

"Hey, come back," the shopkeeper ran out onto the pavement, "Thief, stop."

"Did they steal something?" Mace asked.

The shopkeeper held out his arms and shook his head. He was livid, "These God damn school children. Two young white girls stole a shelf-full of sweets just now."

Mesi stepped forward and peered around the corner. She couldn't see the girls, "You want to call the police?"

"Nah. What is the use, anyway?" the shopkeeper huffed and made his way back into the store, "They never catch them. Not enough police around, anymore."

A small rumbling sound of thunder fired off in the sky. Mace looked up and held his palm above his eyes, "Well, if we're gonna get wet, we may as well get soaked together."

He slowed his speed down as they turned a corner toward the cemetery.

"So, what you got planned tonight?" Mesi asked.

"Dry off. Maybe catch up on some work," Mace said. "I dunno, maybe I'll kill myself. Might be fun."

"Don't joke about things like that," Mesi said. "It's not funny."

Mace tried his luck, "Or, you could come back to my place?"

"Oh no, not tonight. It's my birthday, today. Mel and I are going to a club."

"Ah! Happy birthday," Mace noticed two white girls at the far end of the road by the gate to the park.

"Thanks."

"Hey, can you see that?"

Mesi squinted and looked to where Mace was pointing, "Oh, yes."

Man dressed in bright colors carried two unconscious teenage girls into the back of a van.

"Is that *a clown*?" Mesi asked out loud.

Mace reached into his pocket and took out his phone, "I think so."

"Shouldn't we stop him?"

Mace hit 999 on his phone and pressed it against his ear, "No, I'll call the police—"

The phone flew out of his palm. Someone had snatched it from him. Mace turned around to see three youths threatening him.

Flex, the tallest of the three bullies, roared at Mace's face, "Hey, *faggot*."

Mesi jumped in and pushed Flex backward, "Hey, give him his phone back."

"Fuck you, bitch!" Flex spat from under his hood to the amusement of his two friends, "Yo, Howie, man. Check this nigga bitch out."

Howie, Flex's friend punched his fists together and licked his lips. He looked Mesi up and down, "Fuck yeah, bro. 'Low that fat ass. You want *sum fuck*, girlie-girl?"

"No, I do *not*."

The third lad in the group stepped forward and took the phone from Flex's hand, "Let's see what we got here."

"Peeby, man. Check out his album."

"Give me my phone back," Mace yelled and went for his phone.

Flex shoved him back into Mesi. They almost fell over in the rain, "Fuck off, vampire."

Peeby chuckled as he scrolled through the phone, "Fuck, man. Flex, check it out."

He showed his friends the screen. Several images of Mace kissing his arm flipped by.

"You kissing your fucking hand, man?" Flex chuckled. "That's sick, blud."

"Hey, stop it," Mesi stepped forward and went for the phone.

THUMP.

Flex punched her in the face and grabbed the back of her hair. Mace was outnumbered. He wasn't a fighter. All he could do was stand and watch.

"Yo, Peeby, man," Flex wrenched Mesi around by her hair, "You wanna take this little birthday coon behind a gravestone and learn it some cock?"

"Nar, man," Peeby looked up from the phone and shove the device into Howie's chest, "Yo, goth boy. Look at me."

He stepped up to Mace and tilted his head.

"The fuck you looking at, Marilyn fucking Manson?"

"N-Nothing, I p-promise."

Peeby shoved Mace back and rolled his shoulders. He noticed his jet black hair and looked over at Flex and Howie, "Let the nigger go, man. No dick today."

Flex kicked Mesi's in the back and revealed his blade to her, "You ain't peeped us, yeah?"

"How d-did you know it was my b-birthday—"

"—Fuckin' shut up, you little bitch," Flex roared into her face.

She stared as best as she could through the tiny gap in Flex's hood. Something about this boy felt a little too familiar.

"Now, ghost."

Mesi burst out crying and ran off down the road. All three hoodlums turned to Mace.

He was on the verge of crying himself, "Please, g-give me my phone back."

"Aww," Flex giggled and released the phone from his palm. It splashed into a puddle that had formed from the beating rain, "The little goth faggot wants his phone back."

SMASH!

Howie stomped onto the screen. The glass shattered in all directions like a spider's web.

"No."

"Hey," Peeby screamed into mace's phone, "You fucking gay ass-fucker. You should be more careful with your shit."

He grabbed the back of Mace's hair and yanked his head back.

RRIIPPPPP!

Mace's wig came off in Peeby's hand. The jet black hair was a wig. Quite a revelation. A pang of consternation for Mace, and a wealth of amusement for his attackers.

"Oh, man. *Fuck,*" Peeby's gasped turned to a roar of hilarity, "The *fuck*, man? You got cancer or some shit? Chemo-boy?"

"Please, give me it back," Mace begged.

SCCCHHH-POWWWWWW!

A bolt of lightning hit the small church in the cemetery. A few screams from a hundred feet away echoed through the cemetery.

"Charlie fuckin' *wept*," Flex yelped. "Man, let's do him quick and fuck off."

Peeby turned to Mace and wiped the rain from his bald head, "Nuthin' personal, innit? But me and the boys gotta fuck your chemo ass up."

Mace squealed in terror as Flex took the first hit.

THUWMP

Right across the face, sending Mace onto the ground. Peeby and Howie each took turns kicking Mace in the ribs and abdomen.

"You fuckin' goth fag."

"Fuck, 'low it, man," Flex snorted some phlegm and spat it at Mace's face, "Leave chemotherapy wig boy alone, innit. We'll get him proper after class tomorrow."

Peeby stepped back and pointed at Mace, "You're lucky it's raining, innit?"

"C'mon man, let's ghost." Howie yelled and jogged up the road. The others chuckled to themselves and followed him.

Mace coughed up some blood and climbed to his knees. He winced in pain and hugged himself.

His phone lay in the puddle, cracked to within an inch of its life. He crawled forward and clutched it in his palm.

Mace's thumb staggered as it swiped across the screen to the keypad feature.

"999" displayed on the phone, urging to be pressed. He pressed his thumb against the green button.

SCHWWIIPPP-SCHTAAA-AA-AAAMMM!

A bolt of lightning hit Mace in the hand. His scalp sizzled and burned as his entire body convulsed and writhed around in the rain.

"Gaaaaaah!"

The phone hit the floor.

All that remained of Mace was a pair of smoking trainers.

***

"*Man.* That lightning bolt really kicked your ass, didn't it?"

Mace opened his eyes. A burst of white light entered his field of vision. The pain that shot through his brain was intense.

"Whoa. Easy there, my friend."

Mace closed his eyes again. He wanted to stop the pulsing headache that the light in the room was causing, "Where a-am I?"

"Open your eyes," the man instructed. "But slowly this time. Let your retinas adjust to the light."

"Okay."

The two slits moved apart. The light was bright, but not unmanageable. A couple of blinks set him right.

He found himself sitting on a chair in a room of pure white. Standing in front of him was a man in a suit. He had silver hair and carried a cane.

"Hello, Mace."

"Who are you?"

"You're gonna love this," the man held out his arms and took a bow, "I'm the devil."

"The d-devil?"

"Nah, I'm just fucking with you. But I am the nearest thing in this awful nightmare. Allow me to introduce myself. My name is Max Dark."

"Max Dark?" Mace blinked a couple of times. He was very, very confused.

"At your service," Max took a bow.

"Am I dead?"

"Hold on. No. You're at *my* service. And no, you're not technically dead," Max corrected himself, "For that, you would have needed to be alive in the first place. It's all rather complicated, to be honest. Thank God this isn't a work of fiction or else it would have been damn-near impossible to explain."

"What?"

"Yeah, you're a figment of some drug addict's imagination. I know this is a bit difficult to swallow, but if it helps, you're not even *that*, anymore."

"Wait, stop—"

"—Yes?"

"Am I dead?"

"Yes, okay. If it helps. You're *dead*," Max exhaled and looked at his watch. "Very dead indeed. And I know how it happened, too."

A giant screen snapped to life on the white infinity wall behind Max. It showed the cemetery from several miles in the sky.

He pointed his cane at the bottom of the picture. The white gated entrance to *Waddling Gate Cemetery*, "This is where you were killed."

"I was hit by lightning? I remember my hand got—"

"—Yeah, who cares. That's not important. Have a look at this."

Max drew an outline of a man all around the cemetery location, "I have a little problem I'd like you to sort out for me."

"What?"

"See this shape, here?"

As the edge of the cane traced around the image, it drew the outline of a man's body.

"What are you doing?" Mace asked.

"A bunch of money-grubbing chancers had a stun gun fight at the cemetery a few minutes ago. They've woken up a sleeping giant. Morton Mulberry. Do you know him?"

"No?"

"Ah well, it doesn't matter," Max continued. "The thing is, this *beast* of a man is about to rise up from the ground. It'll obliterate everything we know. We're all going to die. I need you to help me wake him up."

"Why?"

"Because it's the manifestation of our Lord and savior, Charlie Ferrari. He's about to wake up, and if he does, we'll all be free. We need to, uh, encourage him a bit more. I think a healthy zap to the nuts might do the trick.."

"How am I meant to do that?"

"The electricity is waking him up, but it's not quite enough. I want you to drag the three thugs who attacked you to the cemetery and offer them as a sacrifice."

"Fuck that bull shit. I don't believe in God. You're a nut case," Mace stood up and kicked the chair across the room.

"Ugh. *Another* atheist?" Max watched as the chair rolled over and hit the wall, "Nice shot, by the way. A helluva kick you got, there."

"You *really* expect me to believe Charlie Ferrari is coming back. A second coming?"

"Er, yes?"

"You must think I'm mad. Fuck you," Mace turned around and headed for the door.

"Don't take my word for it, Mace," Max yelled after him. "Your death was an unexpected gift. You can help me. You can help wake him out of his coma."

Mace reached a door in the wall. He grasped the handle and yanked down, "You're insane in the brain, you prick."

"Mace, come back. Don't walk through that door, it's—"

"Fuck off," he ignored Max, pulled open the door and walked through it.

***

Unfortunately for Mace there was no ground on the other side of the door.

Just an endless pit of black.

He screamed as he plummeted through the dark tunnel. The rush of air ruffled through his clothes and face.

Streaks of fiber-optic lines whizzed around him. Some were blue, others were bright yellow.

The sides of his falling body sparked like metal grinding against a concrete floor.

Several screens popped up all around him as he continued to hurtle down.

The first showed Howie in his bedroom, looking at something on his laptop.

The second showed Peeby urinating against a brick wall.

The third displayed Flex at home, watching television with his father.

The three screens grew larger and larger. Mace bent his body and dived toward the first screen.

THWOPPPP!

A Mace-shaped hole burned through the image of Howie on his laptop.

Howie sat naked on his bed watching a video on his laptop. He reached down and played with himself.

THUD! THUD!

"Howie, come down to dinner, now," came an angry male voice boomed from outside his bedroom door.

"In a minute," Howie screamed and returned to his video, "Man's gotta unload, you know."

The video displayed two white men making love to a black woman. She guzzled down the man standing at the end of the bed as she *entertained* the other between her legs.

"Yeah, that's it," Howie panted as he played with himself, "You're gonna get it."

As the woman released one of the men from her mouth, she moaned, getting pounded from behind.

"Ohhh, yeah baby," she screamed at the man standing in front of her.

Howie got into the action, "Ohh yeah, *yeah, baby."*

"That's right Howie," she turned to the screen and addressed him point blank, "You wanna meet a friend of mine?"

Howie squinted in confusion, "Eh?"

The black woman looked up at the nude man standing in front of her. The camera tilted up to reveal it was Mace, looking directly into the screen.

"What the fuck?"

"Hello, Howie," Mace reached for the screen.

"Fuck," Howie scrambled along the bed and dropped the laptop, "Mace?"

Mace's hand pushed through the screen and unclasped its fingers.

"Get away from me, man," Howie screamed for dear life.

THUD! THUD!"

"Howie, come down for your dinner," screamed the

voice from behind the door.

The arm extended longer and longer from the screen. Pangs of electricity shot around the limb. It grabbed Howie's neck.

Howie touched the arm.

SCHPAAANNGG!

Electric sparks bounced his hand away in severe pain, "Gaaooowww."

SCHWOOOMPH!

The arm snapped back into the laptop, taking Howie with it. His head and body crashed through the screen, breaking the plastic edges.

His bare feet slipped through the screen.

Howie tumbled onto the bed beside the black woman. She ran a finger down the side of his face.

"Mmm, Mace, sweetie," she chuckled at the terrified boy. "You never told me you had such a cute friend."

"He's no fucking friend of mine. Have fun with him."

"What are you d-doing?" Howie screamed as the black woman held his hands down and allowed the two men to manhandle him.

"Get on your hands and knees, sweetie," the woman said. "You're going to take my place."

"No. No."

The men pushed him onto all fours. One of them grabbed his head and forced his penis into Howie's throat. The other took a more violent approach to hole between his buttocks.

"Gluumpphphhhhhh," Blood shot out through Howie's nostrils as he gagged on the porn star's member.

"Yeah, yeah," the man screamed, thrusting deep into the poor boy's face.

The man at the other end jumped onto the bed and squatted over Howie. He pounded away between his legs.

"Sweetie," the woman said to Mace. "We got him, now. Go kill the others."

"Yeah, yeah," Mace turned around to see a fifteen-inch rectangle in the air. He gripped the edge and and hoisted himself through.

Peeby zipped up his jeans and continued to walk along the road. The rain had let up as he made his journey home.

The cemetery was a hundred feet away in the distance. Lost in his own world, he walked and listened to the music playing on his phone. He walked along to the tune of an aggressive hip hop track.

Man's gotta feel, yo,
Finna dem bitches,
Tie "em up head to toe,
Gotta know who da boss, doe.

Peeby walked alongside the white fence that separated the cemetery plot from the main road. In the distance, he could see what looked like bodies littered around the mud and grass.

One of them sunk into the ground, covered by the mud and grass.

"The fuck?" Peeby removed his earphones and squinted at the vanishing body.

The ground came alive. The gravestones warbled left and right as the middle of the plot took a deep breath and then exhaled.

Peeby shivered and chose to ignore what was going on. He continued down the path and reinserted the earphones back into his ears. The singer's voice, this time, seemed even angrier than it was before.

My man's gon' fucked up,
I'mma finna this lousy-ass snitch,
Coz he played me and my girl,
His name's Pee-by, the skinny little bitch.

It took a few seconds for Peeby to realize something was *desperately* wrong with his music. A shot whizzed by as he stopped in his tracks once again.

"Huh?"

He took out his phone and looked at the screen. The app icons were normal, but the music ground down to a halt.

A few seconds later, the track ground to a complete halt. Peeby knocked the phone on the side of his hand, hoping a little light violence might perk it up.

It didn't.

Peeby held the screen to his face and noticed that a new app had appeared: "InstaBate."

A text bubble appeared over the icon, "Press this."

So he did. His thumb landed on the icon and opened up a picture of Mace.

His head was bald, covered with black, smoking scars.

"What the fuck is going on?"

The photo of Mace sprang to life, "Hello, Peeby."

"Charlie Ferrari," Peeby let go of the phone. He scrambled to stop it from hitting the floor and caught it between his knees. He reached down and pulled the screen back to his face.

"Don't take the Lord's name in vain, Peeby," Mace giggled from inside the screen, "It doesn't suit you."

"You fuckin' prick. Mace?"

"Yes," Mace smiled. "Listen, we don't have much time."

"What are you doing in my fuckin' phone?"

"I'd take your earphones out if I were you. *Mate.*"

"What?" Peeby could hardly believe what he was seeing or hearing, "Allow me, man. This some kind of joke?"

"I promise you it isn't."

"Man, fuck you," Peeby lowered the phone and began to jog along the road. Spooked, he didn't want to return to the screen.

Mace changed his tune and spoke to him through the

speakers.

"No, don't walk away," Mace's voice came through the earphones.

"Nar, man. I ain't listening to you," Peeby muttered, "I must be asleep or something."

"Don't walk away from the cemetery, you fucking prick," Mace roared through the earphones. Peeby picked up the pace of his jog. If he could cross the road, he'd at least be in the company of some pedestrians.

"Nar, nar, this is sick—"

"—Okay. Don't say I didn't warn you."

Peeby's jog ground to a halt. He didn't want to stop, but something compelled him to.

His eyes widened. Then, his arms stretched out, quite against his will.

"Hey. What the *fuck*?"

SCHLLAAAAAAAPPPPPP-ZZZZZ!

A million blue sparks flew out of Peeby's head, making his body convulse where he stood.

The music stopped playing.

His mobile phone slipped out of his right hand and smashed against the concrete pavement.

Peeby blinked a few times and looked down to his shoes. He lifted the sole and inspected it.

"Hmmm," Peeby said, this time with a slight Mace inflection, "Nice sneakers."

Peeby turned around and looked at the cemetery, "Okay, now for some fun."

Mace walked Peeby's body back along the white fence. He rubbed his eyes and looked at the gravestones. The wet ground shifted once again.

"Let's see if this wakes the bastard up," Peeby muttered under his breath.

He climbed over the white fence and approached the metal railings next to the *"Danger! Electrified Fence!"* sign.

His hands reached through his zipper and pulled out his penis. "Goodnight, fuckhead," Peeby said to himself.

A spray of urine shot out of his penis and splashed against the fence.

ZWIP-ZWIPP-PP-ZWIPP…

Blue sparks flew off the metal railing as the globules of urine splashed against it.

"Come on," Peeby muttered under his breath.

He managed to get a powerful stream going. The volts ran from the fence and climb up the stream.

SPPPAARRRRRKKK!

The current traveled up Peeby's penis and fried it into a slab of black, smoking meat.

"Whoooaaa, what a rush," Peeby chuckled as his hands caught fire.

His head burst into flames. Underneath his clothing, his entire body cooked. Hundreds of thousands of volts pummeled their way through him.

WHVOOOOM!

Peeby's body caught fire as he laughed insanely into the night air, "F-f-f-f-f-fuuu—"

He arched his inferno of a body back as the volts ran through the grass of the cemetery.

Peeby released the grip on his penis and staggered back onto the floor. His corpse roasted as the ground of the cemetery rumbled violently. An ocean of blue light shot out from the body, via the metal railings, and streaked through every blade of grass.

SMASH! SMASH! SMASH!

One by one, each gravestone exploded. Fragments of marble and granite flew into the air as the electricity invigorated the ground. The action encouraged whatever lay beneath to come to life.

If you had a bird's eye view of the cemetery you'd see the outline of a huge one hundred foot head rise up from the ground.

Underneath that, an almost clear acre of a torso and abdomen, followed by a pair of arms and legs.

It looked like the grass was coming alive.

A rapturous thunderbolt zipped down from the clouds and hit the growing beast in the heart. A thick jet of blood flew into the air from the embossed ground.

Something in the ground had woken up.

***

Flex fiddled with his phone in the front room, ignoring the television. His jacket lay across the back of the chair. Several helium balloons of all shapes and sizes said "Happy Eighteenth Birthday!"

"In local news," the news anchor announced, "Radio show host Sebastian Sibald, host of Virile FM's *Suicide Hour*, was found dead in his studio this morning. Police are ruling Sibald's death as a *suicide*."

His father, a giant of a man named Jelani, walked into the front room and turned off the TV set with the remote control, "Look at you. Sitting around doing nothing."

"Allow me, man, Dad," Flex said into his phone, "Man's just chillin', innit?"

Jelani grabbed him by the shoulder and hoisted him to his feet, "Don't you talk that gangster shit to me."

"Sorry, Dad," Flex looked terrified as his Dad towered over him, "Just busy, that's all."

The front door burst open. Mesi ran into the hallway looking rather disturbed. She closed the door and hung her jacket up on the coat stand.

"Mesi," her father asked. "Is that you home, now?"

"Yes, Dad," Mesi raced into the front room. She looked like she'd seen a ghost. "I tried to call you, but you didn't answer."

"Where have you been?" Jelani asked as Flex returned to his phone.

"I went to Mel's house. Me and another kid from school were attacked on our way home."

"Who did it?" Flex asked, knowing he was one of the three perpetrators.

"I don't know. They let me go so I ran off. But they beat up my friend."

Jelani looked her up and down, relieved that she wasn't in any physical harm, "Did you call the police?

"No," she quipped. "but I wanted to wait a few hours till I came back."

"Good. No police," Jelani said. "You okay?"

"Yes, I'm fine. I think Mace managed to run off, too."

Jelani smiled and gave her a hug, "Happy birthday, my sweetie."

She hugged him back, "Thanks. I gotta get ready, Mel's picking me up soon and we're going out."

"Okay," Jelani said, turning to his son. He was fiddling with his phone once again, "*Phillip Orji*?"

"Yes, father?" Flex said.

"You don't say happy birthday to your sister?"

"I will, I will—"

Jelani shook his head in disapproval and joined his daughter in her bedroom.

P-TCHING! A *Headbook* message appeared on Flex's phone. He hit the icon on the screen.

Then, his face fell.

I can see you, fuckhead. You're dead.

Flex blinked a few times and re-read the message. The same threat, from a person named Mace Kevlar.

"The fuck?"

Flex typed a response.

Flex: How u find me?
Mace: I know what you did.
Flex: How u find me?
Mace: Fuck you.
Flex: Nuff shit, man. Fuck you, too.
Mace: I'm going to close the front room door.
Flex: Yeah? Bullshit.

Mace: I'm going to kill you.

Flex scowled at his phone and looked at the door. Nothing happened.

He breathed a sigh of relief and smiled, "Yeah. I thought so."

WHUMP!

The door slammed shut. Flex jumped back in fright. Then, the television came to life. Footage of firefighters trying to fight a tower fire on the screen.

"—when more than eighty people perished in Freeway One. The fire is thought to have been caused by faulty electrical equipment."

The anchor appeared on the screen and smiled at Flex, "Hey, man."

"Wh-what?" Flex looked over his shoulder and back at the news anchor, "Who, me?"

"Yes, *you*," The anchor grabbed the back of his hair and tore his face away from his head.

Covered in blood and skull, the man wiped his face with his hand. The smears of blood scooped up into the sides of his palm, revealing the man to be Mace.

"What?" Flex took a step forward towards the television.

"That's right," Mace said from behind the news desk, "Come closer."

Cautious, Flex put one foot in front of the other, "B-But…"

"Keep walking, *gangsta*," Mace beckoned him toward the screen, "Okay, stop. Give me your phone."

Flex stopped a few inches away from the TV. He gripped the phone in his right hand, "No."

"Yes."

"No—"

The ceiling light bulb burst apart and caused an almighty racket. Flex jumped back, feeling very threatened, "Okay, man. *Okay*."

"Good. Throw it here."

Flex tossed the phone at the screen. Blue sparks erupted around the device as it traveled through the screen.

Mace caught it and chuckled. He examined the screen, "Very nice, my friend."

He plugged the phone into the laptop on the news desk.

"What are you d-doing?" Flex asked.

"I told you I was gonna kill you."

"Fuck this *shit*," Flex ran to the front room door. He rattled the handle, but it wouldn't open.

Strange, because it had no lock.

THUD! THUD! He slammed his fists against the door as Mace laughed from inside the TV.

"Dad. Mesi," he screamed for dear life, "Help me."

His incessant screaming and slamming caused his elbow to knock the Charlie Ferrari statue off the cupboard.

"Oh, *no*," Mace screamed. "Now look what you've done."

Flex stepped away from the door. Rescue wasn't coming. He wasn't getting out alive.

Charlie's porcelain face had broken down the middle. Its right eye wandered up and over at Flex. Red blood trickled onto the carpet from the chasm in its cheek.

"Oh sh-shit, man."

"Oh, *Fleeee-eee-eee-cks*?" Mace said from the other side of the room.

Flex turned around to see Mace throw his right leg through the TV screen and walk into the room. His body had become a confusing array of white noise and transparency. A low-pitch hum completed the terrifying presence.

Mace set the laptop on the coffee table and turned it to Flex, "See this? This is you, isn't it?"

Flex ignored the question. Resigned to the fact that he was in the presence of a deity, he held his hand out. The desire to touch this bizarre electronic creature was overwhelming. As if he was the hand of God.

"I b-believe," Flex recited to himself. "I believe. I believe—"

"—Better believe this shit," Mace giggled and pointed to the screen, "Come here."

Flex nodded solemnly and obediently followed Mace's instructions.

"I believe in you, master."

As he neared the white-noise shaped Mace, he made the mistake of touching his shoulder.

ZAAAPPPP! SPISSSHHH!!

Flex's arm flew back, shocked by the connection, "Yargh."

"Don't touch," Mace screamed. He pointed at the USB port in the side of the laptop, "Now, get in there, you cunt."

"Wh-what?!"

"Do it."

Flex looked at the twelve-millimeter hole. Far too tiny to get through, "I can't get in there."

"Let's try, shall we?" Mace roared. "I can't fuck around all day, have a flight to catch."

Mace grabbed Flex by the arm. Violent orange sparks and white lightning smothered the room as he made contact.

Flex screamed his last as the prolonged contact between him and Mace blew the television set apart. The pictures on the walls burst open.

The longer Mace clutched Flex's arm, the more his body burned. The connection between the two was aggressive and fatal.

Flex tried to escape. The flesh on his legs cooked away through the skin, melting into his jeans.

"Gaaaahhhhhh."

His right knee hit the floor, smashing the knee bone. His entire body continued to fry as his other knee shattered upon the carpeted ground.

The fibers of the rug under the coffee table caught fire as the windows blew out.

"Fuck you," Mace yelled into Flex's fireball of a head.

SPARK! BOOM! SMASH!

Flex's jaw melted from his head. Mace blew the thunderous sparks along the top of his victim's head, scorching his hair.

Flex's right arm came off in Mace's hand. The rest of his flaming body hit the floor, dead.

Despite the front room being completely ablaze, no one had rushed to Flex's rescue.

Mace snapped the fingers on the severed right arm. He tore them away and shoved them into the glowing USB socket.

He bent the elbow back and snapped it apart like a chicken wing. A mighty push on Mace's behalf got the ash-like arm inside the socket.

Mace took a step back and took a running jump for the USB port.

He launched into the air. The white noise that formed his body swirled into a corkscrew and twisted itself through the port.

SPATCH! SPARK!

The laptop began to vibrate. A huge sucking noise emitted from the USB port.

Flex's headless corpse shot straight toward the port. The bones in his body crunched and snapped as it folded over itself.

CRUNCH! SNAP!

The laptop munched away at the torso and swallowed it through the opening

Mace's face appeared on the laptop screen. He extended his arm through the glass and grabbed Flex's upper palate and brought it in with him.

The front room burned, melting the couch, the television and the furniture.

The laptop set ablaze. The screen cracked and spat out black dust. The keys turned to mush and slid down the fiery coffee table.

***

Darkness.

"Where am I?" Flex's was terrified.

"You're *mine*, now," Mace said as the light snapped on.

A white, endless infinity room. Mace sat on a chair with the laptop on his thighs.

He typed away on the keys.

Flex's voice came from the laptop speakers, "Wh-what are you d-doing?"

"I'm programming a flight, if you *must* know. Not that it's any of your business."

"What?"

"But first I'm going to take care of you."

Flex's profile picture on his Headbook page looked around from inside the screen.

"You spend all your time on social networking, right?"

"What the fuck?" Flex grabbed the box that surrounding his facial profile picture. "Let me out."

"Ah, na, na," Mace giggled. "I promised I'd kill you. So, let's have some fun."

Mace hit a button on the keyword. An email browser appeared alongside Flex stuck on his Headbook page. He looked to his right and gasped, "Wh-what are you g-gonna do?"

Mace sniggered and composed a new email. He typed on the keyboard.

Flex watched the words appear on the screen next to him.

Subject: *It was me.*
Body text: *Dear Mesi.*
Earlier today, Howie, Peeby and I attacked you and Mace on

your way home. You didn't know it was me. I hope you'll forgive me. Happy birthday. Love, Mace x.

"What the fuck, man?" Flex climbed out of his profile picture box, ready to jump over to the email window.

"No, don't do that."

"Why not?" Flex asked, terrified.

"Because you'll soak up into the algorithm. You'll become an endless string of ones and zeros. With an emphasis on *zero*."

Desperate, Flex closed his eyes and jumped, "You can't send that email, man."

He landed in the first status update box, trapped in its four walls, "Shit, *shit*."

"Stay where you are," Mace chuckled. "This is the part where you die."

"What?"

Mace hit the paper clip attachment button on the email message. He selected a file named *flex.nfg* and hit the *"attach"* button.

"Wh-what are you doing?"

"What does it look like?"

The attachment bar loaded from left to right. Flex's body flattened into a 2D image and began to disappear.

"You'll go straight to Mesi's junk folder. Rather fitting, right?"

"No, no," Flex tried to barge his way out of the status updated box. It was a prison. There was no escape, now.

Mace roared with laughter at Flex's suffering. He vaporised as quick as the attachment took to load.

"If she reads the email, the truth will be out. She'll *delete* you," Mace explained. "But if she doesn't see it, well, in thirty days, you're dead."

"Noooooo," Flex's body attachment loaded into the email, "See ya, *Flex*."

Mace hit the send button, sealing his victim's fate once and for all.

Chapter 8

Max Dark's Infinite Cerebellum Spectacular!

The 767 aircraft taxied from the main terminal to the runway.

Today, the aircraft was nearly at full capacity with over one hundred souls on board.

The cabin crew made their journey down the aisles. They assisted the passengers with their bags and checked their seat belts.

Toward the front of economy class, a five-year-old girl named Pippa fiddled with her strap in her left hand. She tried to balance her doll in her right arm.

"Here, poppet," her mother said from the aisle seat, "Let me hold Babydoll for you."

"Okay, mommy," Pippa passed the doll and managed fastened her safety belt, "I did it."

"Good girl."

Mom didn't look very happy. She eyed the doll in her daughter's hands. Its wonky right eye lilted left and right. A creepy lump of plastic.

What little Pippa didn't know was that her mother was a nervous flier. She'd not taken many flights in her life. The Valium she'd taken before boarding hadn't kicked in yet.

Pippa, on the other hand, was giddy with excitement on her first ever flight.

She marveled at the slow-moving runway, "Mommy, look. We're going to take off."

"Yes, yes. I know," Mom gripped the armrest and closed her eyes.

"Is everything okay, madam?"

A pretty airline steward smiled back at her. Mom opened her eyes and clocked the name badge: *"Rhonda."*

"I'll be okay, thanks."

"I could get you a cup of water if you'd like?"

"No, no," Mom tried to smile. "I'm sure I'll be okay."

"Well, just hit the passenger light and I'll be right over," Rhonda threw her a friendly wink and looked at Pippa, "Hello, you."

"Hi," Pippa beamed.

"Your first time flying high in the sky in a big plane?"

"Yes."

"Gosh, how exciting," Rhonda giggled. "What's your name, sweetie?"

"Pippa."

"Well, Pippa, maybe when we're in the sky I can take you to meet the pilots?"

"Really? Wow."

"Sure," Rhonda closed the luggage compartment above their heads, "You just look after your mom, here, okay?"

"Okay," Pippa jumped for joy in her seat and returned to the view on the other side of the window.

Mom looked up at Rhonda, "Thanks so much, you've really made her day."

"Not at all."

Pippa's mother felt a lot better, now. The pills started to kick in. As Rhonda moved away, she caught sight of a man with silver hair sitting in the middle bank of seats.

He didn't see her. The man was busying himself with a bag resting between his knees.

Something didn't seem right.

"Ladies and gentlemen, this is your captain speaking. On behalf of our flight crew, I'd like to wish you all a pleasant journey and thank you for flying *Uterox Airways*. The time is seven forty-five, and we'll be taking off in a few moments. Just a reminder that you should keep your belts fastened at all times."

The silver-haired man zipped up his bag and reached into his pocket. He looked over his shoulder at another man in a suit two rows behind him. They nodded at each other and turned to the front.

Mom's nerves were not helped by the visual display of the runway on the screens above their heads. The white lines moved down, over and over again, suggesting that the plane was moving.

Pippa looked down at her mother's sweating hands gripping the armrests, "Mommy? Are you okay?"

"Yes, poppet," she gulped. "Just leave mommy alone for a bit. Look out of the window, okay?"

The pilot finished his announcement, "We should be taking off in the next minute or so. Our journey time to Fallopia today will be eleven hours and ten minutes. Cabin crew, prepare for take-off, please. Thank you."

Mom opened her eyes and watched Rhonda and her crew take their seats, facing the passengers. She folded a chair down from the wall compartment and sat into it.

The aircraft's engines kicked up several notches. The cabin vibrated. It felt as if the whole thing was going to collapse.

PING. The seat belt signs lit up.

Mom felt that this was the end. The plane began its take-off.

She started muttering to herself. Pippa couldn't make out what she was doing. It sounded like she was praying.

"Mommy, what are you saying?"

She ignored her daughter, closed her eyes and continued to mutter. Her hands gripped the armrests.

Eventually, the plane lifted into the air.

Mom pressed the back of her head against the seat as

the ascent took place.

She felt her stomach tighten as the plane made its ascent into the clouds.

Of course, Pippa found the view fascinating. The ground sunk lower and lower from the window.

The terminal disappeared. The houses and buildings became smaller and smaller.

Soon, white fluffy stuff smeared over the view. The clouds ran under the violent engines.

"Wow."

Her doll rolled around and hit the floor underneath Pippa's feet. She didn't notice, though.

Before long the plane was among the clouds. A smooth take off by all accounts.

PING! The seatbelt signs dimmed. Rhonda unclipped herself from the crew seat. She made her way to the staff area behind the toilets.

"Mommy, we're in the sky," Pippa clapped her hands with excitement. "Look at all the pretty clouds. They look like lines of heroin."

"Huh? Did you just say heroin?" Mom opened her eyes to a confused-looking daughter.

"Sugar, mommy. I said sugar. Are you feeling okay?"

Mom opened her eyes and took a deep, deep breath, "Whew."

"What is *heroin*?

"Forget it, poppet. I must have drifted off."

"Your hands are all wet, mommy."

Mom wiped her palms on her shirt, "I know, poppet."

"Why are they wet?"

"I don't know. I'm feeling a bit hot."

Mom looked to her right and saw the silver-haired man cradling a baby in his arms. He wrapped a cloth around it and shot Mom a look.

Embarrassed, she turned to face the front. Rhonda pushed a trolley with drinks down her side of the aisle.

"Would you like a mineral water?" she asked.

"Oh," Mom scrambled to arrange her thoughts. She'd survived certain death in her own silly little mind, "Not for me, thanks."

"How about you, Pippa, sweetie?" Rhonda asked. "Would you like a drink?"

"Yes," Pippa said. "Can I have orange juice."

"You got it," Rhonda opened up a can and passed it to her, "There you go,"

Pippa took her drink, "Thanks"

Rhonda moved up the aisle with the trolley, clearing the view of the man with the baby. It was Max Dark, although she had no clue who he was.

The baby started to shuffle and complain. He whispered something to it and bounced it around in his arms.

Mom found his behavior strange. Max wasn't with anyone else. There was no one sitting in any of the three seats either side of him. No sign of a mother. She felt somewhat prejudiced that the sight of a man carrying a newborn baby on a plane was odd.

These days, though, surely it wasn't *that* weird?

Max stood up and strapped a baby carrier around his waist.

Clip, clip.

He slipped the baby feet-first into the front and leaned back in his chair.

"Excuse me?" Mom asked.

Max shot her a look of disdain, put-out by the intrusion. He adjusted the silver name badge on his lapel, "Yes?"

"Why are you doing that?"

"Oh, this?" He pointed to his baby strapped to his front, "Ah, it's just for security."

"Shouldn't you have a special seat or something for her?"

"*Him* actually," Max turned the baby's face in her

direction. A small sliver of fine, green hair crept over its scalp, "Shh. He's sleeping."

"Oh, I'm sorry," Mom smiled. "What's his name?"

"Full of questions, aren't you? Are you usually this nosy?"

"I'm sorry, it's none of my business—"

"—Charlie," Max beamed. "His name is Charlie."

"Aww, that's such a sweet name," Mom thought for a moment. "Like the son of God?"

"Something like that," The man ignored her and nodded over to the man two rows behind him, "Okay, that's a *go*."

"Eh?" Mom said.

Max took out a DC9 semi-automatic gun. He rested it on his lap.

Mom squeezed the armrests and widened her eyes, "*Charlie Ferrari.* Umm, umm," She didn't know what to do. Or how to react.

Max held his forefinger over his mouth, encouraging her to keep quiet. "Shhh!" He palmed a fresh magazine into the gun.

"Okay, *now*."

He jumped to his feet and aimed his gun at the luggage compartment.

BANG!

Everyone screamed and looked over at him. His friend, two rows back, carried exactly the same gun. He held it at the other passengers as he made his way into the aisle.

"Ladies and gentlemen, can we have your attention, please? Could anyone who wishes *not* to be shot raise both arms."

All the passengers held up their arms. No one wanted to die. Rhonda pushed the trolley away and held out her hands.

"Please, sir—"

"—Shut up." He swung his gun at her face. The baby kicked its legs and began to cry against his chest, "Come here."

Rhonda made her way back down the aisle as calmly as she could. Two stewards peered from behind the staff area.

They were caught by the man's colleague, "You two, out here. Now."

The two stewards did as instructed. They moved quickly toward the second gunman.

"My name is Max Dark and this flight is changing its destination," Max looked at Rhonda and pulled the front panel of the baby harness down. The baby had a small, green sliver of hair over its scalp.

"You see this baby?"

Rhonda nodded.

"We need to protect him. Take me to the flight deck, now," Max turned to the passengers and smiled. "My colleague here, Gideon, will be looking after you all."

The second gunman waved at himself and clutched his gun with both hands.

"Just to prove to you all that we mean business, Gideon will now demonstrate what will happen if you *fuck* around. Gideon?"

"You," he barked at the male steward, "Come over here to me."

The passengers gasped and watched the male steward run over to the gunman.

"What's your name?"

"Z-Zack."

"Don't look at me," Gideon said. "Turn around and face them."

"Okay, okay."

Zack turned around to face the passengers, "What d-do you want me to d-do?" He looked at his colleague in despair.

The second steward took out a machine gun from the overhead compartment.

He took aim at the rest of the passengers, "Sorry Zack.

Just do as he says."

Gideon leaned in behind Zack's ear and whispered, "Tell them *this* is what will happen if anyone tries to be the hero. Say it."

"This is what will happen if anyone tries to be the hero—"

BLAMM!

Zack's forehead burst open. His head splattered the middle section of passengers-cum-hostages in brain, blood, and skull.

Everyone screamed for dear life. Gideon and Max found the whole scene hilarious.

"Ewwww," Max giggled and held his hand over his mouth, "That was disgusting."

Little Pippa held her hands over her eyes and screamed at the top of her lungs. It caught Max's attention.

"Oh for fuck's sake," he screamed and swung his gun at her, "Shut the fuck up."

"P-Please," Mom shouted and held out her hands, "D-Don't shoot."

Max calmed down and glanced at Rhonda, "Take me to the flight deck."

Rhonda swallowed hard and walked forward. Max slotted himself in behind her and kept the gun pointed at her neck.

He kicked Rhonda forward, toward the flight deck door, "Play it calm. Do what you usually do and get us in."

The baby strapped to Max's front began to cry, "Hush, now, Charlie. It'll all be over, soon."

KNOCK. KNOCK.

Rhonda knocked on the flight deck door. It unbolted and swung inward. The first officer had opened it.

"Ah, hi. Rhonda, right?"

She nodded and bit her bottom lip. He could sense something wasn't right.

"What is it?"

"Umm," she said. "There's someone here to see you."

"What? Who?"

"Me," Max pushed her out of the way and barged into the cockpit.

The pilot turned around and gasped, "What the fuck?"

"Gentlemen," Max slammed the door shut behind him, "We need to change course."

"We c-can't do that,"

Max aimed the gun at the first officer, "You wanna bet your life on it, *fuckstick*?"

"No, please, don't kill me—"

BLAM!

Max shot the first officer in the chest, killing him. The body smashed against the virtual horizon screen. The corpse lilted down over the controls.

"My gun begs to fucking differ," Max shouted and aimed the gun at the pilot. "You. Turn this plane around. Now."

"Where? Where to?"

"Plot a course for oh one-four and oh one-five."

"You want us to go *back*?"

"Oh. Um, yes, please," Max took the handset from the cockpit wall. He held down the button, "Ladies and gentlemen, it's me again. One of the pilots has been taken *dead*. I'm afraid we're having to turn back. There's no need to be alarmed."

All the passengers in the main cabin freaked out. They kept their hands held above their heads, hoping not to get shot.

Pippa was crying her little eyes out from her seat. Mom's nerves threatened to get the better of her.

"You're going to hear a little bang," Max's voice came through the speaker system. "Please don't be alarmed. It's just the two engines exploding."

"What?" a passenger screamed from five rows behind Pippa and her mother. He stood up and lost his shit, "We're all going to die."

The steward with the gun swung around and put his finger on the trigger, "You *will* die if you don't sit the fuck down."

"No, no," the man climbed over his neighboring passengers, "We have to do something."

THRAA-AA-TAT-TATTT!

The steward opened fire on the man and his nearby passengers, killing them instantly. Their bodies jiggled in their seats, spraying blood up the compartment walls and window.

The man's corpse fell over his dead neighbor's lap.

Everyone roared in terror.

"Shut up," Gideon screamed as he made his way down the aisle, "I swear to almighty Charlie Ferrari himself I'll kill every last fucking one of you."

"Yo, Gideon," the armed steward said. "Get the chutes."

"Where the fuck do you think I'm going, you fool?" Gideon roared as he reached the staff compartment area. He flicked the curtain away and yanked a trolley into the aisle.

"Mommy, what are the men doing?"

"I d-don't know, sweetie," Mom hushed, trying to keep her heart from exploding.

Gideon's trolley drifted to the left as the plane banked and turned around on itself.

"Right, everyone stand the fuck up."

None of the passengers wanted to be the first. All sets of crying eyes blinked and waited for someone to brave the order.

"I said stand *up*," Gideon fired a round of bullets into the overhead compartment.

Pippa was the first to stand, "I'm standing, mister."

"Good girl," Gideon kicked the trolley against the side of her mother's seat. Several medium-sized bundles of cloth fell from the trolley and onto the aisle floor.

Everyone else rose to their feet with great caution.

"Everyone get the fuck up. Now," Gideon turned to the steward with the gun, "Make sure everyone's strapped. We don't have much time."

The steward swung his gun around to the hoard of crying hostages, "Okay, *fuckheads*. Everyone up. Let's go."

The speaker system sprang to life, "Guys, this is your new pilot, Max Dark, speaking. Prepare for engine fire. Three and four."

"Okay everyone," Gideon screamed as he took one of the bundles of cloth into his hand, "Grab hold of something, now."

PING. The safety belt signs lit up once again.

"Engine fire in three, two," Max's voice advised.

KRA-BOOOOMMMMMM

The aircraft shook violently as the two engines either side of the plane erupted into a ball of fire.

The passengers screamed in horror as the cabin jiggled from left to right. Some of the passengers tumbled onto the seats in front of them.

"Holy shit."

"Right, everyone shut up."

Pippa looked through her window. One of the engines was ablaze, rupturing and losing its casing, "Mommy, mommy. *Look*."

Mom looked out of the window and gasped in shock, "Oh, God."

Gideon kicked the trolley into the middle of the aisle, "Everyone, take a parachute."

"A parachute?" one of the female passengers screamed, "Why do we need a parachute?"

"What's your name?" Gideon asked.

"Karen."

"Because, *Karen*, the plane is about to fucking nosedive and crash."

Sandra took one of the bundles and opened it out. A body harness connected to a sack unfurled in front of her. She threw it over her shoulders and clipped it around her waist.

"Everyone, look at Karen, here," Gideon yelled. "You put on these chutes. When you're out, the cord at the front will open it. You'll be perfectly safe."

The passengers wouldn't stop screaming. Half of them had heard the instruction. Some of them flat-out fainted, thinking they'd die.

"Pass them around, quick," Gideon ordered Sandra.

She took a bundle of parachutes into her arms and began tossing them at random passengers.

One of them, a small boy, caught it and opened it up. He seemed to be enjoying the whole thing. His father was out of his mind with worry.

"Quick, put it on."

The armed steward reached the plane door and lifted the handle, "Cabin pressure drop."

Gideon kept his gun aimed at the passengers. They fumbled around to strap the parachutes to their bodies.

"Okay, everyone, we gotta be quick. We're about to lose pressure, we grab an oxygen mask when they fall."

"Here we go, team," Max's voice came through the speaker system, "Oxygen masks are now being deployed."

BANG!

Scores of dead babies dropped from the overhead compartments. The tiny corpses swung back and forth by their umbilical cords. They weren't oxygen masks at all.

"Everyone take a mask, now," Gideon ordered. "Strap it around your face."

Pippa reached up and took one of the dead babies in her hands, "Mommy, these aren't masks."

"Oh shit," Mom jumped back and clipped her parachute around her waist, "Put it in your mouth, poppet."

"What?"

"Watch mommy," Pippa grabbed her dangling stillborn baby and opened her mouth. The head and shoulders flew in. She clamped her lips around its waist and began to chew.

Pippa attempted to do the same as her mother. She opened her mouth and inserted the dead baby between her lips.

As did the other passengers behind them.

Sandra pushed the tiny feet of her stillborn into her mouth. She bit down and breathed in.

"That's it, good," Gideon yelled over the loud rumbling of the plane.

"Ladies and gentlemen," Max's voice blew through the speakers, "Please make your way to the main cabin door. Upon exiting the aircraft please head toward the purple flare for touchdown."

The passengers shuffled in single file down the aisle, toward the cabin door.

The armed steward kicked the door open.

SCHWWOOOOOOOOOOOOOOO.

The oxygen and air blasted out through the door. All the passenger held onto each other as the steward stood back and ushered them out.

"Let's go. Head for the purple flare down below and pull the cord."

The first passenger let the handle go.

SCHWWOOOPPP!

His body flew into the night sky. The passenger behind him looked down and watched the man fall downward.

"Charlie Ferrari."

"Don't blaspheme," the steward said to the second passenger, "Just jump."

The steward pushed the man through the cabin door.

He tumbled down through the air at a terrific speed. A purple fireball lay several thousand feet below him.

The passenger shifted his body and straightened his arms and legs out. His hands pressed to his side as he plummeted head-first toward the flare.

The passenger several hundred feet ahead of him

exploded into a human ball of fire. He'd just yanked on his cord.

"Oh, *fuuuck*."

The man looked down to his chest and tried to raise his arm and grab his own cord.

He clutched the end between his fingers and yanked it.

WHVOOOOOM!

The passenger burst into flames, killed in an instant. His fireball of a body rocketed toward the purple flare.

SCHWOOOOOOOP!

His blazing body left a streak of orange through the air and crashed into the ground. The impact smashed a nearby gravestone to pieces.

BLAAMMMMM!

His body punctured the grass.

SCHWOOOP! SCHWOOOOP!

Two more human fireballs followed the first passenger. Upon explosion, the corpses had yanked their cords thinking they were parachutes.

They weren't. They were detonators designed to turn the passenger into a blazing ball of fire and hit their intended target.

"My God. They're not parachutes, they're *bombs*," screamed the next man in line to jump. There were several dozen passengers behind him freaking out.

"Shut up," screamed the armed steward.

"Go, go," Gideon kicked the passengers forward. One of them spotted the streaks of fire and knew something was amiss.

"They're all dying. The parachutes are exploding."

"I don't give a shit," Gideon kicked the man in the small of his back, "Get moving."

"Mommy," Pippa shuffled forward with the *"parachute"* across her back. "It's not safe. I don't want to jump."

"Poppet, we have to," Mom said. "Or the bad men will shoot us."

"C'mon, let's go."

SCHWOOOP! SCHWOOOOP!

Two more passengers got sucked out of the cabin door, toward their fiery doom.

The armed steward pushed five more passengers out of the cabin door, "Let's go, fuckheads. *Come on.*"

The five passengers rocketed through the night sky, headed toward the purple flare. Dozens of orange streaks from the preceding jumpers scorched toward the ground target.

The sight was quite beautiful. Long, fire-streaks headed toward the purple haze.

One of the five passengers tugged on his parachute cord.

KRA-BLAAAAMMMMMM

His body burst into flames and rocketed down to the purple flare.

The cemetery ground came to life. The grass and mud had formed arms and a torso. The shape of a man's head lifted through the headstones.

The figure was over an acre tall.

A purple mist hung over its chest and head as it rose into the air.

A slit formed in the ground opened up and released a deathly cry, "Gwaarrrr."

SCHWAAA-BLAAMMMM!

A fireball hit its chest, puncturing it deep and causing it to bleed. The giant's body seeped up through the ground in extreme agony. The headstones toppled over and shattered on the ground.

The left arm rose slowly into the air. The monster seeping through the ground was enormous.

SCHWAA-SCHTOOMMPP!

Three more fireballs hit the beast like a bullet from a gun. The beast's grassy face turned to its side and screamed in agony. Scores of passenger fireballs exploded and punctured through its chest and head.

There were at least a hundred more to come.

The beast pushed itself up by its elbows and cried in pain as the balls of fire continued to plummet into its chest.

Max strapped baby Charlie to his chest and made his way to the coach cabin.

He observed the rest of the passengers jumping out of the plane to their certain death.

"Well done, my friend," Max screamed over the noise created by the drop in pressure. "It's working."

"Good," Gideon said. "Buckle up, we're next."

SCHWOOOP! SCHWWOOOOOP! SCHWIIP!

Three more passengers launched themselves out of the cabin door. There were ten of them left to jump.

Two of them were Pippa and her mom, at the end of the line. Max noticed Pippa crying and losing her mind.

"Hey, you," Max roared as he ran past the seats. He arrived at Pippa and held her shoulders, "Little girl."

Pippa looked up at him, traumatized, "I don't want to fly anymore."

"You're going to be okay."

The line shuffled forward as more passengers jumped out of the plane door.

"Am I?" Pippa believed his lie and began to calm down. Her mother had resigned herself to the fact that they had to jump to survive.

"Yes, look. This isn't real," Max showed Pippa baby Charlie fast asleep against his chest. "See?"

"Oh," Pippa reached out and touched the baby's face, "We're not real?"

"No, sweetie," Max explained. "We're doing a good thing. We're all going to be better once we jump out of the plane."

"We're all trapped inside his head. But we're going to wake him up and be free."

"Okay." Pippa looked up at her mother and gripped

her hand.

Mom looked at her daughter and smiled, "It's okay, poppet. Let's go."

They moved forward. The last two to jump. Gideon nodded at them.

"Here we go," Mom moved her daughter in front of her body, "Let's do it."

"Charlie bless you," Gideon shouted over the noise.

Pippa and her mum jumped through the door.

Mother and daughter rocketed through the night sky, toward the purple light. They squeezed each other's hand.

"Mommmmmyyyyy," Pippa squealed, squinting her eyes. The rush of air was almost blinding.

"Poppet," Mum shouted and grabbed her own cord, "Pull the cord when I say. We're following the orange flames."

"Okay."

Pippa reached over to her chest with her free hand and gripped it in her little fingers.

The purple haze and orange scorch marks whizzed toward them.

KRAAA-BA-BOOOOOOOM!

Mom shifted her body around and kicked back. Looking down the length of her body, she saw the entire plane catch fire. It nose-dived a thousand feet above them.

"Okay, poppet, *now*."

"Okay, mommy."

Mom yanked down on her cord.

WHVOOOOM!

Her body exploded into a ball of fire. Her hand flew away from Pippa's as she reached down for her cord.

Pippa yanked down on it.

WHVOOOOM!

She, too, exploded into a raging inferno. The explosion killed her instantly.

The plane dived down after them.

The two fiery corpses created a streak of fire in the air as they plummeted toward the cemetery

SCHWUMP!

Mom's fiery carcass shot into the beast's chest, punching its entire body back to the floor.

"GWAAARRRRRRR!"

Pippa's body burned as it headed straight for the beast's heart.

SCHWOOOOOOOM-SCHPLATTTTT!

A direct hit into the middle of the ghastly beast. Its heart exploded and coughed up a tonne of blood into the air.

Max, Gideon and the armed steward made their way to the flight deck. The pilot had a bullet in his brain. His body slumped over the controls.

Max kicked the pilot's body to one side and took a hold of the controls.

He throttled the plane downward, following the orange streaks in the sky.

"Okay, gentlemen. Moment of truth."

NYAAOOOOWWWWWWW!

The blazing lump of metal took aim at the beast's forehead. Max and Gideon held the sides of the flight deck as it rocketed toward the beast.

The angle of the plane got the better of the armed steward. Caught unaware, his body flew backward, sucked out through the cabin door and into the night sky.

Max turned to the screen and laughed. Baby Charlie kicked his feet and wailed.

"Hush, Charlie," Max whispered. "You'll know it when you feel it. It'll feel like a million red-hot irons puncturing your body, and a final blow to the brain."

Baby Charlie screamed for sheer murder.

NYARRRR-CRAAASSSHHHHH!

The fiery plane slammed into the beast's forehead like a bullet.

***

Charlie's body flinched. The force of the movement sent his lifeless arms inches into the air.

Dr. Mulberry and Dr. Thatch hadn't noticed. They'd removed the five-inch tumor from the back of his head and placed it into the metal tray.

The electrics in the operating room dimmed for a few seconds.

"What was that?" Dr. Mulberry looked up and over at the brain screen on the wall.

"I don't know. Maybe a short circuit, somewhere?"

"Hmmm," Mulberry turned to Charlie's body, "Let's get Mr. Ferrari sewn up and—"

"—Gaaahhh," Charlie screamed. His body convulsed.

He was waking up - *for real.*

BUWP… BWUP…

His head moved between the clamps. Charlie was in severe pain. Half of the back of his brain was still exposed. The large flap of skin rattled around over his head.

"My God," Mulberry dropped the tumor onto the tray and raced back over to his patient, "He's awake."

"Gaaaaaahhhh."

Charlie raised his hands and gripped the clamps either side of his head.

"No, d-don't do that—"

It was too late. Charlie wrenched his head from between the metal screws.

The sides of his head stayed put as he raised his head into the air. The action tore all the skin off the back of his head. He closed his eyes and pushed himself up onto his knees.

BZZZZ. BZZZZ.

The fluorescent lighting zipped out and sparked. The whirring and beeps from the machines fired on all four cylinders.

SNAP.

The room fell into utter darkness. Mulberry and Thatch could hear Charlie's turmoil. The bed shifted around - the metal squeaks were unmistakable.

"Get the emergency lighting on," Mulberry screamed in the hope that Thatch could do something.

He couldn't.

"This *is* the emergency lighting."

"Ugh, ugh, ugh," Charlie panted and slapped the bed around his legs, "What's h-happening to m-me? Where a-am I?"

"Mr. Ferrari, can you hear me?"

Charlie took a deep breath, afraid for his life. He'd been out of action for a week. He had no clue where he was in the darkness, "Who's that?"

"It's Dr. Mulberry, sir," he cautioned. "Please, do not move."

"Why not--"

CLANG!

"Oowwwww," Charlie screamed. A pitter-patter of garbled footsteps raced around the room. Charlie had managed to land his bare feet onto the cold ground.

Pat, pat, pat.

"Where am I? Stay away from me."

"Sir," Thatch stepped forward and held his hands out in case he walked into something, "I know this is strange, but you're halfway through a craniotomy. It's not safe. You must remain exactly where you are, otherwise, you'll hurt—"

"—Bullshit," Charlie grabbed something cold in his hands. A small syringe. He didn't know what it was, though, "You've kidnapped me. Complex, man, is this some kinda fucked-up joke?"

"No, sir," Mulberry screamed. "It's not safe. Please, stay where you are and let us help you."

"I don't fucking believe this. Where the fuck is the emergency lighting?" Thatch cried. Even the corridor lights had gone out. The entire hospital was without power.

Mulberry and Thatch needed Charlie to remain perfectly still until they found him.

"S-Stay away from me," Charlie's voice pierced through the sheer blackness of the room, "I've got a syringe. I'll fucking use it."

"Yeah," Mulberry quipped, "That's *precisely* how you got into this predicament in the first place."

"Stay back," Charlie panted.

Scooch, scooch.

The soles of his bare feet slid across the smooth floor's surface, "This is some kind of sick fucking joke—"

Charlie stopped speaking. He felt around his face. Something wasn't right.

He was expecting to feel coarse skin - soft fibers, or a wrinkle. The substance French kissing his fingertips felt wet and smudgy. It stung every time he prodded around.

"What's h-happening to me."

He felt a hand grab his shoulder through the hospital gown, "Sir, I've found you."

BWAAZZZZZZZZZZ!

The lights snapped on like a direct thunderbolt from the heavens.

Thatch looked at Charlie and gasped. Mulberry rubbed his eyes and took a look at his patient.

CLANG.

He dropped the metal tray to the floor in horror.

Charlie stood before them. Half of the front of his face hung down the right side, "What is it?"

"Oh, Mr. Ferrari, sir," Thatch gulped. "You're very sick."

"No!" Charlie pushed Thatch away and held the syringe to his face, "Don't come near me or you'll get a fucking vein full of air. Instant death."

"Sir, please—" Mulberry tried.

"—Nooo," Charlie turned around and made for the

theater door. As he did, the gaping hole in the back of his head shone into view. His exposed brain slipped through the rectangular hole.

"Oh, shit," Mulberry yelled. "Your head."

"What is it now?" Charlie spun around. The angry movement caused his cerebellum to dangle from the rectangular chasm.

"Mr. Ferrari, your brain is hanging out," Mulberry reached behind his own head to play out what he meant, "Look."

"What?" Charlie's fingers reached the back of his neck and pressed around, "My b-brain?"

"It's the cerebellum, sir," Thatch stepped back, "The part of the brain that deals with the senses, it's vital that—"

Thatch's lips kept moving, but everything went silent. He continued to explain what was happening. He had no idea that Charlie had lost his sense of hearing.

The squelchy part of his own cerebellum flopped between his fingers like jelly. Charlie yanked down on it.

Every time he pulled down, the cerebellum fought to bungee back up into his head.

Taking his vision with it.

A flop of his own cranium fell into his hand. He moved it in front of his face and yelled.

Charlie mouthed in terror, "What did you do to me?" He stopped screaming, wondering why he couldn't hear himself talk.

Mulberry held out his hand and begged Charlie to stop fighting them, "Sir, please," he mouthed. "Come back to the bed."

He pointed at the trolley and the screen hanging just above it.

"Stay the fuck away from me," Charlie flung the remnants of his own brain to the floor and held up the syringe.

SQUEEEEEEEEEEEEEEE.

A deathly piercing sound shot through Charlie's head. It underscored the perfect silence he was experiencing.

As he stepped back toward the door, he couldn't hear his footsteps. He couldn't hear a *damn thing.*

"No, no," Charlie yelled. He noticed a small, red spot forming on Mulberry's forehead.

"Sir, please come here. It's not safe," Mulberry mouthed at his deaf patient, "Please—!"

The red spot grew out across Mulberry's forehead. At first, it looked like an Indian bindi. A few seconds later, it bled. The red liquid streaked out across his forehead, cutting through the skin and bone.

"No," Charlie screamed and pointed at Mulberry's head. "Your face, man. Look at your face."

Mulberry stopped. He had heard Charlie's question. He felt across his forehead and pressed into the hole.

As he did, the top of his skull slid off to the side and hit the floor.

Mulberry turned to Charlie, "Mr. Ferrari?"

Charlie didn't respond. He watched Mulberry feel around his exposed skull. His eyes turned up in their sockets.

Thatch burst into flames.

"What the *fuck*?!" Charlie gasped.

"Arrggghhhhh," Thatch spun around on the spot and threw his hands before. He crashed onto the trolley and rolled around on top, trying to put himself out.

Charlie closed his eyes hard, which rendered two of his senses utterly useless.

He couldn't hear the commotion but could certainly *feel* the strength of the heat from the burning man on the bed.

Inside the darkness of his eyelids, all he could see were orange streaks of fire.

They all led to a purple mist way, way into the distance. The sound of a jet engine - or, more precisely - the *feeling* of the sound of a jet engine.

The intensity of the sensation was enough for Charlie

to open his eyes. It felt like hell.

The operating theater had caught fire.

He needed to leave.

SLAM!!

The door hit the wall as Charlie burst into the corridor. He was unaware that every small movement caused his brain to try to escape through the cavity in the back of his head.

As he ran, he tripped over his own feet and crashed into an empty trolley at the side of the corridor.

He scrambled up to his feet and pushed the trolley away. He turned a corner…

… And ran right into Rhonda, his sister. Her response was that of someone who'd seen a ghost.

"Charlie."

"Whaaaa," Charlie skidded to a halt and landed on his knees.

"Rhonda."

"Daddy," Johnny stepped out from behind his auntie, "How are you feeling?"

"Johnny," Charlie screamed and held out his bloodied hands, "Come here."

The boy looked down at his fluffy black and white toy cat and shook his head, "No."

"No?"

Rhonda looked over her brother's shoulder to see the corridor was ablaze. Thatch's body had caused quite the inferno within the building.

There seemed to be no one else around. No doctors, nurses, orderlies - even other patients and their visitors.

Nothing.

"Charlie," Rhonda lifted him to his feet. The sound of the environs slowly crept back in through his ears. He made out his sister's voice, "The building is on fire."

"I know," he screamed. "We need to get out of here. Now."

He grabbed her hand. She grabbed her nephew's hand. All three ran down the corridor toward a set of double doors marked *Theater 118*.

"We'll go through here," Charlie yelled as they ran, "There ain't no other doors to go through."

Charlie pulled Rhonda with him. They ran faster, hoping to escape the fireball.

But the more they ran, the slower the double doors seemed to come, "Run. Run."

Johnny's little feet couldn't keep up.

Rhonda turned around and picked him up. She cradled him in her arms and ran behind Charlie.

"Nearly there!" he panted, picking up the pace. Rhonda noticed more clumps of his brain slipping through the cavity in the back of his head.

A lump of brain fell into Rhonda's path. The jellied piece of his cranium beneath her shoe as she ran.

"I'm okay."

They reached the double doors of theater 118. Charlie gripped the handle and yanked down.

"That's it. We're nearly out."

Charlie ran into Theater 118. Rhonda followed, carrying Johnny in her arms. He skidded to a halt and held her back.

His eyes grew. He hadn't expected to see what he was seeing.

A gargantuan theater in the traditional, non-medical sense. The size of a football pitch. A vast auditorium with a one-hundred foot stage.

Five hundred rows of audience members chattered amongst themselves. They waited for a show to start.

Charlie blinked and looked back at Rhonda, "No, no, this isn't right."

"What's this?" she whispered to him as the sound of tuning instruments came through the surround speakers.

"No," Charlie fell anxious. He yanked down on the

door handle, hoping to get out. It wouldn't move, "No, no, no."

Charlie, Rhonda, and the now-sleeping Johnny found themselves trapped inside.

"We can't get out," Rhonda whispered as the house lights died down.

Charlie rattled the door handle once again, "Fuck. We n-need to get out of here—"

"Laaaaayyydiiieees a-haaand gentlemennn. Welcome," announced an excited male voice through the speaker system.

The audience piped down and sat in their seats, giddy with anticipation. None of them could be made out due to the shadows cast from the main stage lights.

Loud anthem music began to play, causing the excitement in the room to reach tipping point.

"—to Max Dark's *Infinite Cerebellum Spectacular*!"

BAAAAANNNNGGGG!

A cloud of confetti exploded from the rigging above the audience to a chorus of angelic rock music.

"What the *fuck*?" Charlie's jaw dropped. Rhonda couldn't believe her eyes.

"Please welcome your host for this evening, the one, the only, the indomitable - Mister Max Dark."

The audience rose to their feet and whooped and hollered. A huge light show illuminated a fifty-foot effigy in the middle of the stage.

A giant upturned syringe with glistening, purple solution drifting around inside it.

A second theater light shone across the contents of the barrel. A fetus slept inside it, bent over itself.

The audience clapped as Max Dark walked down the left-side curved stairs.

He reached the main stage and threw out his hands. A microphone fired up through his sleeve and into his hands.

Twenty-five children walked onto the stage dressed in cream-colored bikinis. White feathered headdresses and crystal earrings adorned their heads. They formed a long row behind Max.

He put the microphone in front of his face and began to speak. The music softened under his voice.

"Ladies and gentlemen, we are here today, to praise our Lord and saviour, Charlie Ferrari. Can I get an amen?"

"Amen," the crowd roared in unison.

The enthusiasm from the audience forced Max into the moment. He hopped to the left side of the stage and spoke to the five-hundred-odd audience members. "I know you, like I, love the lord himself. Charlie Ferrari. I need another motherfucking amen."

"*Motherfucking Amen*, brother," they hollered back at him and cheered.

"And how about the right side? Can I get some love for the lord over here?" Max ran to the right side of the stage.

"Amen, amen," they yelled back at him.

Max walked to the middle of the stage to an adoring crowd. The backing dancers formed a row and kicked their legs out.

Max took the microphone and launched into a song and dance.

Our son, the gifted child,
Hark! The cherubim chime.
Our savior, he overdosed for your sins,
And his and hers and mine!

The audience clapped and sang along with Max, getting into the spirit of the song.

Max held out his hands and mimed applause for the backing dancers. They stepped forward and strutted their stuff as he continued to sing.

KA-BOOOM!

A lightning-bolt hit the stage and shattered the barrel of the syringe. The purple contents fountained out of the cracked enclosure and flooded the stage.

A remarkable effect.

The audience loved every single second of the proceedings. The fetus fell into Max's hands.

Blessed child, he lies comatose,
From that fatal opiate overdose.
Bless the baby Charlie Ferrari,
All powder angels, hear our cry!

The lines of child dancers broke away in two, making room for Max to lay the fetus on a prop hospital bed.

"O Lord," Max's voice thundered around the auditorium, "The son of all that is holy and mighty, our savior, Charlie Ferrari. He ODs for our sins, so that we may learn from his mistakes. Amen, Ferrari, Amen."

"Amen," shouted the crowd. They took the ceremony very seriously.

Charlie looked at Rhonda. He didn't know what to say. Fortunately for the pair of them, and Johnny, they were in the shadows at the back of the auditorium.

No one knew they were there.

Max laid the fetus onto the trolley and bowed his head. The lights dipped and formed a spotlight on the new effigy.

He held out his arms and spoke into the microphone.

"It is our belief, Charlie Ferrari, that someday you shall return to us. We, your humble servants, observe your teachings and try to do right each and every day of our lives."

Max stroked the side of the fetus's face as if it were his own child. As he ran his palm over the baby's head, a green Mohawk bristled out through his fingers.

"All hail our lord and savior, Charlie Ferrari!" Max ordered through the microphone.

"For he is the father, the son and the holy spirit," the audience recited in reverence.

"And through the virgin Rhonda, we do thank her for

giving birth to the greatest teacher, he of the wise."

The audience finished the prayer, "Blessed be to you, Rhonda Ferrari."

The child dancers fell to their knees and pressed their palms together.

"I know you can hear me, Charlie," Max's utterance crept softly through the speakers, "Please, for our sake. Let your presence be known."

Charlie took a deep breath and reached behind his head. A clump of his brain fell into his hand, "Rhonda, I'm awake."

"No, Charlie," she begged. "Please, let's just get out of here. These guys are nuts."

He took her chin in his palm, "No, sister. Look at me."

She did so. A tear rolled down her cheek. The silence from the four thousand-strong crowd was almost unbearable.

"Charlie," Rhonda stammered through her crying, "It's *not real*, sweetie."

Charlie looked down at the sleeping Johnny in her arms

"You're still asleep. You're still in the coma."

"No. I'm not," A smile streaked across his face. He turned to the audience to see that a line had formed in the middle of the auditorium.

Each attendee approached Max. He rolled up their sleeve and slid the syringe from his needle into their arm and pressed down on the plunger.

"Body of Ferrari."

"Thank you, Mr. Dark," the audience member clutched her arm and returned to her seat.

A man wearing a Hazmat suit replaced her. Max smiled at him and rolled up his sleeve. He slid the needle in and injected the solution into the man's vein.

"Body of Ferrari."

"Thank you, Mr. Dark."

He moved off and another took his place. The epic music piped back up as every attendee received the sacrament.

Charlie looked to Rhonda, "I'm going to announce myself. It'll all be over, I swear."

"You swear?" Rhonda sniffed, "Swear to *whom*?"

Charlie thought over his response for a second. He touched Johnny's face and looked at his sister in earnest.

"Myself."

The last audience member took her seat. Max returned to the middle of the stage, just in time for an angelic music track to kick in.

He clutched his silver name badge.

"Over the course of our lifetime, ladies and gentlemen, boys and girls, we've experienced some true horror. Things we cannot explain. The mysteries of our existence. Why we all transform into one another. The ignominy of self-sacrifice and loss. We do not know why our world operates the way it does, but we are all agreed on the one thing that we hold true to our hearts. Faith."

The audience agreed and nodded their head, "Amen, brother Dark," shouted one of them.

"Thank you, madam," Max continued. "Through our reverence of the lord Charlie Ferrari, we recognize his importance in our life. That if we *believe* we can be good people, then it shall be. His teachings make us what we are. We continue to believe in his sacrifice. Overdosing on opiates for our wrongdoing, so that we may live a complete life."

The audience tapped their head with their right hand, and then their left upturned wrist.

"Amen," Max copied them. Forehead with the fingers on his right hand, down to his left wrist, "Brothers and sisters."

"Amen," the crowd responded.

Max looked to the spotlight a hundred feet up in the air, "Charlie Ferrari, O Lord, if you can hear us. Please know that *we* await your arrival."

"I am here!" Charlie bellowed from the back of the theater. He sprinted down the middle section of the auditorium to thousands of amazed faces.

Rhonda carried sleeping Johnny in her arms.

"My word," Max felt exhilarated. "It is *He*."

Charlie traveled down the gangway that led to the stage. He passed several recognizable faces.

A clown with red hair…

A brown-skinned woman with a charred face…

A black and white cat purring in the arms of a blow-up doll…

A pregnant woman with a dead baby in her arms…

Two men, a lobster, and a giant cobra…

The crowd fell to their knees as he walked past them, causing a Mexican wave of utter admiration.

"Please, do not bow," Charlie said as he reached the stage.

"I never thought I'd see the day," Max marveled as the man he'd been waiting for his entire life stepped onto the stage.

"I am Charlie Ferrari," he offered Max his hand. "I don't know what's going on."

Max fell to his knees, shortly before the microphone hit the stage.

Feedback shot through the speaker system. The audience winced and plugged their fingers into their ears.

"I am not worthy, Lord."

Charlie looked down at the patronizing Max, "Shut up and get on your feet."

"Yes, my Lord," Max smiled and gave Charlie a tight hug, "I thought you'd never show."

Embarrassed, Charlie hugged Max Dark back, "It's over."

Max choked up and wiped a tear from his eyes. He turned to the audience and could barely contain his excitement. "It's *motherfucking* Charlie fucking Ferrari, everyone. Or should I say *sisterfucking*? The second coming."

The audience clapped like mad and hollered at the top of their lungs.

"He's back."

Charlie enjoyed the adulation from both Max and his crowd. Four thousand followers all applauding him. The one true person they held dearest in their lives.

Max Dark, a host who had made a fortune from being the middleman between Charlie and his flock.

To them, Charlie Ferrari was a God. He had returned to them.

Max offered Charlie the microphone, "What do you have to say to everyone, Charlie Ferrari, my Lord?"

Charlie took the microphone, "Thank you, Max. I realize after all this time that I have created an imperfect world for you all. The only advice I have is not for all of you. Just for me."

"And what's that, Charlie?"

"*Wake up.*"

Charlie passed the microphone back to Max to a cheering crowd.

"That's great," Max produced a black book. He flipped through the pages and arrived in the middle. The name of the book took place on the front in gold lettering.

Pure Dark: The New Testament.

Max read from the book, "For I shall live on. Through the turmoil and trials and tribulations of my existence I will be reborn again."

Charlie observed Max closing the book, "I see you have brought your wife with you."

Dr. Long wheeled a chair with stirrups onto the stage and placed it in the second spotlight.

Max walked over to Rhonda and gave her a hug.

"Charlie, what is he doing?"

Charlie bowed his head, "It is time, sister."

Max walked over to Dr. Long and held out his hands. She lifted off the top sheet of the chair and produced a newborn baby.

Max took the crying child and stepped back, "Rhonda, the virgin birth. Please, take your seat."

"No. No."

Charlie closed his eyes and nodded, "Please, sister."

"What? No. You can't do this."

The crowd became antsy and started to jeer, "Do it, do it, do it."

Two men in white coats approached her from behind and manhandled her over to the chair. She kicked her feet in protest, "Charlie, no."

Max chuckled to himself as he unwrapped the blanket from the newborn's body.

The men pushed her into the chair. They each took one of Rhonda's legs and strapped it into the stirrups.

"Shhh, Mrs. Ferrari," Dr. Long flicked her red hair over her shoulder and pressed her end of her stethoscope against the woman's chest.

BADDUM-BADDUM-BADDUM.

Rhonda's heart rate raced through the roof. The crowd was in shock.

"She seems fine to me," Dr. Long said to Max. "Please, Mr. Dark, the savior?"

"With great expediency, Dr. Long." Max passed her the baby. Rhonda looked down the length of her body.

RIP, TEAR!

The men ripped off her trousers and pulled apart her blouse.

Max pushed the stirrups right back, exposing Rhonda's genitals to the crowd.

"And now, re-birth."

The audience chanted in anger, "Re-birth. Re-birth."

"Charlie," Rhonda screamed. "Help me. Please, help me."

He looked down at his wrists. Two bloodied holes

apart on them. He looked up to his sister, "It is time for me to go, Rhonda. My beautiful baby sister."

"No, no." Rhonda screamed, "Charlie, no. Help me."

He didn't help.

Instead, he reached the back of his head and stepped back into the darkness, out of the spotlight.

Max placed one knee on the chair and held the baby to Rhonda's vagina. The newborn in his arms kicked and cried for its life.

Max looked up at the men and nodded.

They snapped on a pair of gloves and pulled her vagina apart.

"Hush now, Charlie," Max whispered. "You're going home."

The baby wailed for dear life as Max slipped his hand under its head.

He carefully inserted the baby's head into Rhonda's uterus. The bulbous, fleshy object slunk between the lips of her vagina with incredible ease. The action caused the muffled cries to dampen.

"You're safe now, Charlie," Max whispered.

Dr. Long stood behind Rhonda, wiping her brow with a wet cloth. She leaned down and whispered into her ear.

"It's okay, sweetie," she said. "Just breathe."

Rhonda panted hard and fast as the baby's neck and torso slipped inside her. The lips of her vagina fought against the pressure applied by the two men.

Faceless, featureless men.

"Nearly there, sweetie," Dr. Long hushed. "Keep breathing."

Max grabbed the newborn baby's legs and pressed his thumbs under its behind. The majority of its body slid inside Rhonda, leaving just the legs hanging out.

A rush of blood and jelly spat out around the body of the baby. It kicked its last as Max grabbed its ankles and pushed its feet in.

Rhonda's heart beat so fast. The entire rebirth was too

much. Her head wilted. She passed out into Dr. Long's arms.

"Aww, congratulations, Mrs. Ferrari! Max wiped his hands. "It *was* a boy."

The two men released Rhonda's vagina. It closed back up, having swallowed the baby back into her uterus.

"Ladies and gentlemen," Max screamed into the microphone, "The second coming."

The audience stood to their feet with elation, "Woo-hoo."

Dr. Long jumped up and down on the spot, barely able to contain her excitement, "Yay."

As for Rhonda, the overwhelming congratulations dulled across her mind. She was unconscious. She'd taken her brother back inside.

It was just a matter of time before the fetus stopped kicking, reduced in size and became an embryo.

Soon thereafter it would become nothing at all.

Like it never happened.

***

Rhonda's chest heaved, up and down. Her breathing slowed down to normal. She was at peace.

Except for the prolonged squeal. The voice of a small boy screaming for his life.

She opened her eyes. The light from the fluorescent bulb on the ceiling blinded her at first. She held her hand over her face and looked down at her stomach and feet.

There was nothing in her belly.

"What the hell?"

She shook her head and double-took. Her feet hit the ground. She had clothes on, at least.

Rhonda lifted herself onto the floor. She wasn't in a theater but in the hospital waiting room, sitting in a chair.

The squealing continued. Whoever the child was that was making the noise was very upset.

She looked at the corner of the room. Johnny clutched the cat in his arms, crying.

"Johnny."

He kept squealing. She raced over to him and shook him by the shoulders, "It's okay, it's not quiet. It's me, your auntie Rhonda."

Johnny stopped screaming. The silence dissipated.

"I must be going out of my mind," she whispered to herself.

"You fell asleep."

"I know, sweetheart," Rhonda stretched out her arms and yawned, overwhelmed by the nightmare she'd had.

Or *supposedly* had. It all felt *so* damn real.

She patted herself down, checking that she wasn't injured.

Dr. Long walked into the hospital waiting room. Rhonda stood up and smiled at Dr. Long.

"Oh, this must be Johnny?"

Rhonda tried to not break out in tears, "Yes, that's right."

Dr. Long crouched in front of him, "Hey, Johnny."

He didn't say anything. Instead, he stroked the fur of his black and white toy cat.

"You're here to see your Daddy?"

Johnny pressed the paw of the toy to its face and pretended to shoot a claw at her.

"Ptchoo."

Dr. Long scowled at Johnny. She had no idea who this weird kid actually was.

He pointed to her stethoscope.

"Oh, this?" She picked the end up and removed the ear tips from around her neck. She pushed them into his ears, "It's for your heart. Say something."

Two minutes later Dr. Long and Rhonda walked into the corridor, leaving Johnny to play with his toy.

"He's just through here. Follow me."

"Thank you."

As they walked, Dr. Mulberry approached them from the other end of the corridor.

"Ah, hello. Dr. Long."

"Dr. Mulberry," she smiled back.

"How was the funeral?"

"Oh, you know," she said, "About as good as expected."

"Your father was a good man, Jennifer. I worked with him for fifteen years. One of the best surgeons we ever had."

"Thanks, that means a lot."

"If you ever need to chat, I'm always here for you."

"I know. Thanks, Dr. Mulberry."

"Please, call me Morton," Dr. Mulberry smiled at her and continued down the corridor.

Rhonda turned to Dr. Long. She felt sorry for her, "I'm sorry to hear your father passed away."

"Whatever," she sniffed. "It's personal. I'm trying to keep myself busy. Let's go and see Charlie."

"Okay."

They continued to the last room in the ward. Dr. Long stopped by the window and pressed her fingers against the pane, "He's done so well. Got through the surgery without a hitch."

"Oh, thank God."

"Yes, you have Dr. Mulberry to thank for that," Dr. Long opened the door and ushered Rhonda in, "A five-inch tumor, as well. Pretty impressive. Isn't that right, Charlie?"

Dr. Long adjusted the sheet over Charlie's sleeping body. Still attached to the life support machine. The breathing apparatus still attached to his face.

He looked at peace.

"My God. His hair," Rhonda held her mouth in half-shock. "He l-looks so *different*."

"Yes. They had to shave it, of course. Before the surgery."

"Yes, of course."

Rhonda moved forward and reached out to touch her brother's face, "You look so frail, Charlie."

Dr. Long grinned and moved out of the room, "I'll leave you two to it."

"Yes, thank you."

She closed the door behind her as Rhonda took her seat next to him.

BEEP. BEEP. BEEP.

The only sound was of Charlie's support machine representing his heart beat.

Rhonda chewed back her tears. She looked at the snow globe on the corner of the desk. A little crucifix lay inside, covered in swirling snow.

"I c-can't k-keep doing this, you know."

Charlie didn't move.

"I have a life, Charlie. I keep coming to see you, but you never wake up. I'm looking after Johnny. He's wondering where you are."

BEEP-BEEP. BEEP-BEEP. His heart rate picked up.

"I keep having these nightmares, Charlie. I don't know why and I d-don't know where they're coming from."

Rhonda burst out crying. She sobbed into the sleeve on her arm.

"What you did to me years ago keeps coming back to haunt me. I thought I was over it. Years and years I spent blocking it from my mind, but it's come back. It's come back so strong, you know."

Charlie's cheeks and eyelids started to flutter. Rhonda didn't notice. She was too busy crying.

She thumped him on the chest.

"How could you do that to me, Charlie?! You ruined my life, our family's life, our reputation. You no-good, useless fucking junkie."

His eyeballs moved within his closed eyelids. The beeps

from the machine remained constant.

"I can't do this anymore."

Charlie opened his eyes. He blinked a couple of times. Rhonda noticed and fell back off her chair.

"Jesus Christ."

Rhonda picked herself up from the floor and stood up straight. Waved her hand in front of his face, trying to get his attention.

"Charlie?"

He remained perfectly still in the bed and stared at the ceiling, "I'm sorry, Rhonda."

"Oh my God," she squealed and took a step back.

Charlie closed his eyes and returned to unconsciousness.

Rhonda swallowed hard and took a moment to digest what had happened.

She looked at the life support machine. His heart had returned to normal.

"Nurse," Rhonda turned around and screamed. She ran out of the room and shouted after Dr. Long down the corridor, "Nurse, he's waking up. Charlie's waking up."

SLAM!

Rhonda pushed the door shut and ran off the down the corridor. The force of the closing door caused the room to rattle. The snow globe to slipped off the edge of the desk.

It smashed against the floor and shattered into exactly one hundred and eighteen pieces.

Acknowledgements

For K

Also to:

My immediate family
The CVB Gang Members / ARC Street Team
Jo Huber, Goddess of all PAs
The members and admins of 20BooksTo50K
Adele Embrey and Peri Dwyer Worrell
My two younger brothers for developing *Spunx*
My stalker, Jennifer long.
For those with a terribly warped imagination.
Is it working?

Also, check out ***Versus,***
Convenience *and the* ***In Their Shoes*** *series…*

About the author

Andrew Mackay is an author, screenwriter and film critic. A former teacher, Andrew writes in multiple genres: satire, crime, horror, romantic thrillers and sci-fi.

His passions include daydreaming, storytelling, smoking, caffeine, and writing about himself in the third person.

A word from the author

I hope you enjoyed this book. Please check out my other books at Amazon and remember to follow me there.

If you enjoyed the book, please leave a review online at Amazon US, UK and Goodreads. Reviews are integral for authors and I would dearly appreciate it.

I love to engage directly with my readers. Please get in touch with me - I look forward to hearing from you. ***Happy reading!***

Email: *andrew@chromevalleybooks.com*

NOTE: If you purchased this title at Amazon, then you can download the e-book version for **FREE** with Kindle Matchbook. The last pages of the e-book version contains exclusive author notes and behind-the-scenes material for each title. It's a real treat for fans, so *download it now*! ☺